WHIRLPOOL

Douglas Scott

THE SHERIDAN
BOOK COMPANY

This edition published in 1993 by
The Sheridan Book Company

First published in Great Britain by
Century 1988
Random House, 20 Vauxhall Bridge Road, London SW1V 2SA
Arrow edition 1990

Printed and bound in Great Britain by
Cox & Wyman Ltd, Reading, Berkshire

ISBN 1-85501-438-6

Contents

PART THREE – ANOTHER MOUNTAIN, ANOTHER RIVER

Prologue

The man standing amongst a uniformed group of French police near the landing stage on the Old Pier looked out of place in his light grey suit and rather shabby felt hat. He was some distance away from the official welcoming party, staring sourly up at the belfried tower of the church of Notre Dame and considering its usefulness for a sniper but deciding that the range was far too great. His attention had been drawn to the belfry by the glint of October sunshine on metal. A polished rifle barrel had not, however, deflected the sun's rays. The gleam had come from above the belfry, from the sunlight striking the gilded statue of the Virgin on top of the tower.

Not only did the man in the grey suit look out of place amid the dark uniforms of the police posse, he felt alien to the entire scene: the Old Pier, the maritime setting of bustling Marseille and the air of carnival that prevailed. The buildings of the port were bedecked with flags. Crowds of sightseers thronged the approaches to the quay and lined the route that the royal cavalcade was to take.

Crowds made the man in grey uneasy. By his reckoning, any gathering of more than ten people constituted a mob. And mobs were dangerous; their moods unpredictable. The happy babble of excited anticipation, together with a family-occasion atmosphere in the well-behaved throngs near the dock did nothing to dispel the man's unease. The more good-humoured and welcoming the crowd, the better it afforded concealment for troublemakers.

7

The gendarmes near the landing stage were all smiling and relaxed, as if infected by the general mood of fête. Only the man in grey did not smile. He had been unimpressed by the French security arrangements and by assurances that the ties of friendship uniting the peoples of France and Serbia would ensure for the King of Jugoslavia a welcome of unparalleled warmth, free from incident.

The man in grey set no store by these assurances. He trusted the people of France even less than he trusted the citizens of his native Belgrade – and heaven knew he put little trust in *them*. The French authorities were naive beyond words if they believed even half the platitudinous generalities they mouthed about the friendship of peoples.

Ten years in the Jugoslav political police had drained the man in grey of whatever faith he had had in his fellow men. He was without illusion about man's capacity for treachery. He was not discriminatory in withholding his trust. He afforded it to none, making no exceptions. He would not have trusted his own brother.

It tells much about the man and the shadowy nature of his profession that very few, outside a close circle of associates and family, knew his real name. He was known simply as Luk. It was derived from the first two letters of his Christian name and the initial of his surname. He had adopted it as a kind of *nom de guerre* during a secret operation against anarchists – and it had stuck with him ever since, usurping his given names.

As his career blossomed and his reputation grew, so the name had become feared in that twilight Balkan demi-world where the secret apparatus of state grappled with the forces of revolution and political conspiracy. Friends and enemies alike came to have a healthy respect for the anti-terrorist officer who was known only as Luk; and the legend attaching to the name grew as he waged war on the King's enemies with implacable zeal.

It was whispered in Belgrade that Luk had played a leading part in the murder of the Communist leader, Bracanovic – a bullet in the back of the head and the body dumped in a ditch – and that the crime had hastened his promotion. Certainly, Luk's star had been in the ascendant since that officially unexplained event. At any rate, the name now inspired calumny and loathing among the agitators and political subversives who conspired in secret against Belgrade's royal dictatorship. They reviled the name Luk, and promised themselves a celebration on the day that Luk was chopped in little pieces – a fate they deemed appropriate for a man whose name meant onion in Serbo-Croat.

Luk smiled to himself when he was the butt of 'onion' jokes – one left-wing magazine had taken to caricaturing the state police by portraying them with onionlike heads – because Luk believed that he would be the one to have the last laugh. It had, after all, been his own private joke since the day he had styled himself Luk. The onion had seemed an appropriate symbol to adopt: a tough outer skin concealing layer after layer of unrevealed persona and the whole characterised by a taste that was sharp to the tongue and lingered long.

Luk knew that it was a signal of the esteem in which he was held that he had been assigned to liaise with the French on the security aspects of King Alexander's state visit to France. But he had not welcomed the task. France was a haven for revolutionaries and scoundrels of every political colour and, after preliminary discussions with the French, Luk had vigorously urged his Belgrade superiors to do all they could to have the visit cancelled. The King would be in mortal danger if he set foot on French soil; Luk himself had a list of nearly two hundred Jugoslav anti-royalists known to be living in France, but the French had refused to arrest a single one of these potential assassins as a precaution. He was appalled by what he interpreted as French indifference to his fears for his monarch.

It was a bitter disappointment to Luk, as he waited on the Old Pier at Marseille, that all his warnings and the urging of his superiors had come to nought. The King himself had made the decision that the state visit would proceed as planned. At no time since the Great War and the subsequent unification of the South Slavs under the Karadjordjevic dynasty had Jugoslavia been more in need of the support and friendship of France than in this fifth successive year of global depression, 1934 – and Alexander was not to be deterred from his royal obligations by threats upon his personal safety.

Luk fished in a waistcoat pocket for his turnip watch. The hands showed five minutes to four. Heavy with foreboding, he returned the watch to his pocket and stared out towards the cruiser *Dubrovnik*. A motor launch had detached from the ship's side and was heading for the Old Pier with a white feather of foam at its bow. The King was going to be right on schedule and step ashore in France at precisely four p.m.

A spirited cheer went up from the crowds on the shore as a military band struck up the Jugoslav national anthem and King Alexander stepped without assistance on to the landing stage. A top-hatted figure moved out from the official welcoming party to greet the slightly stooped royal visitor. The two men embraced warmly.

Luk fidgeted uneasily as the King and the Foreign Minister of France, Monsieur Barthou, showed no haste to proceed to their waiting car. The pair remained on the landing stage at the end of the picturesque pier of the old port, conversing like long-lost friends. They talked for fully five minutes, while the band played on and the crowds cheered themselves hoarse.

At last, King and Foreign Minister moved towards the car, arm-in-arm. This open token of friendship moved the crowd to cheer louder than ever and the King, clearly delighted by the warmth of his reception, waved his hand and raised his hat in salute to the people.

Luk, eyes scanning the smiling spectators as the gendarmes around him closed in to form a protective cordon behind the royal party, snorted with impatience at the leisurely pace of the proceedings. Now, the King was shaking hands and chatting with General Georges, a member of the French Supreme War Council. Now, the King was getting into the royal car, followed by the General and a beaming Monsieur Barthou.

Luk had been assigned a place in the police car immediately behind the royal vehicle. He angrily dismissed an invitation to sit with a senior police officer in the back, insisting that he would ride on the running board. The French officer shrugged expressively and took his seat, scowling. Luk ignored him, keeping his eyes on the car ahead. He hooked his arm through the open rear window and around the door pillar, and took up his perch on the running board.

Ahead of the royal car, the cavalry escort moved forward at a command from an officer who had wheeled his mount to a flanking position close to the shining limousine. The big motor purred forward at walking pace, followed closely by Luk's car. Luk fumed at the open window of the car he was riding, demanding his French counterparts do something about the snail's pace, which was a folly beyond belief. But, of course, there was nothing they could do. And the looks they cast in the direction of the constantly griping Jugoslav suggested that they found the officer from Belgrade more than a little tiresome.

The cavalcade had moved less than two hundred metres and was entering the Place de La Bourse when a succession of events occurred which took even the alert Luk by surprise, registering before his eyes like a nightmare, occupying only seconds. Even though he was instantly alive to the danger and reacted positively and with speed, his reflexes were still not quick enough to influence the incidents already in train.

He spotted the fat man in the instant that he thrust himself through the front rank of the cheering crowd. The intense look on the man's face was enough to trigger instant alarm in Luk's brain. This was no happy sightseer intent on gaining a better vantage point, but a man charged to the limit of his courage and committed, mind and body, to desperate enterprise. The nature of that enterprise was not hard to guess. Luk had dropped from the car on which he was riding and was running before the fat man had taken three swift paces towards the royal limousine. But Luk's path was barred by the steed of the cavalry commander. The animal pranced and reared as the fat man dashed in front of it and leapt on to the running board of the King's car. As Luk fought to find a way round the gleaming haunches and kicking hooves of the backing horse, six shots rang out in sharp succession.

The crowd was stunned to sudden silence by the spectacle and sound of the fat man firing through the open window of the royal car The liveried chauffeur at the wheel of the limousine was the first to react. Stopping the car, he whirled in his seat and lunged at the fat man with his hands, seizing him round the neck. His reaction was fractionally faster than the cavalry officer whose mount had reared in fright as the fat man raced across its path. The officer, sabre held high, fought to control his skittish horse and urged it at the assassin. The sabre came down, slicing at the neck and shoulders of the King's assailant.

The blow and the pressing horse dislodged the fat man and sent him sprawling in the roadway. A scream rose from the valiant chauffeur as the assassin was ejected from his grasp and he was left to stare in horror at the bloody wounds the sabre had inflicted on his hands.

The fat man – blood pouring from his neck and shoulder – was far from finished. Rolling on the ground, he contrived to fire bullets in all directions from the gun

12

in his hand. A gendarme fell, blood streaming from his head. A woman in the front rank of the crowd slumped back into the arms of those behind, a bullet through her heart. The crowd – only moments before in happy holiday mood – was now frenzied with outrage. They could not run from the assassin's wildy directed bullets, so they fell on him, tearing at him with their bare hands and lashing at him with their feet. Even as the killer's gun, its magazine empty, was kicked into the roadway, the cavalry escort rode into the crowd and unceremoniously forced a clearing in the sea of heaving bodies. Police, with batons employed indiscriminately, augmented the clearing operation until the King's car was isolated within a ring of trooper and horse and gendarme.

Luk, closely followed by a security officer who had pooh-poohed the Jugoslav's anxieties as alarmist, was the first to reach the King's car. Alexander Karadjordjevic was unconscious, blood streaming from a wound in his chest and trickling from the side of his mouth. Monsieur Barthou, the French Foreign Minster, had been hit in the stomach and was bleeding profusely. General Georges was conscious, but he, too, looked critically wounded.

Luk help to carry the King to the Prefecture, which was close by. They laid him in the Prefect's room on a couch covered in green silk. An appeal to the crowd congregating outside brought a doctor. He was ushered through the throng of silent white-faced dignitaries.

The doctor felt the monarch's pulse and detected a flicker of life. He made a quick examination of the King's wounds. There were two. One bullet had opened a gaping hole in the chest, close to the heart. A second had pierced the abdomen. The doctor worked quickly, extracting a hypodermic syringe from his bag and injecting adrenalin to the heart. Luk watched the struggle to save the King's life, tears watering his eyes.

What would happen to his country if this man who held it together died? Alexander's son and heir was a schoolboy in faraway England, too young to shoulder the massive responsibility of ruling Jugoslavia.

Emotion hung in the hushed room, filling the air. To inhale was to drink it into the lungs. France's Minister of Marine, Monsieur Pietri, was staring at the figure on the couch, with tears coursing down his cheeks. The wife of one official suddenly started to sob. The doctor, who had been bent over the King, rose and faced the assembly with a face like stone.

'*C'est fini*,' he announced. '*Le roi est mort.*'

Luk did not move. All he could feel now was anger, a surging lust for revenge. No one spoke.

A woman moved forward towards the couch. It was Madame Jouhanneau, the wife of the Prefect. She stooped over the dead King and closed the staring eyes. She tidied the open shirt front and rearranged the red ribbon of the Legion of Honour – it was stained a deeper hue with Karadjordjevic blood.

Luk took his turnip watch from his waistcoat pocket and noted the time. It was twelve minutes to five. The King had survived less than hour on French soil; the fatal shots had been fired approximately ten minutes after he stepped on to the landing stage. Luk had warned that it would happen – but never in his wildest imaginings had he believed that his prophecy would be fulfilled with such mind-numbing rapidity.

The Chief Inspector was a tall thin-faced individual with a vinegary disposition. He showed Luk into the narrow police cell where the assassin's body had been unceremoniously dumped. They had not bothered to cover the corpse with a blanket.

Luk wrinkled his nose with distaste as he examined the remains of the fat man. The face and head were badly mutilated. Beyond recognition. The grotesque sprawl of

14

the body and the way the limbs were twisted like a rag doll's told the story of the man's death. He had almost been pulled apart by the avenging crowd, kicked, stamped on and trampled underfoot like a cockroach.

'Any papers of identity?' Luk asked.

'A passport. He's one of yours, not ours,' the Chief Inspector replied. It seemed to please the police officer that the assassin was Jugoslav and not French.

'I'd like to see the passport,' Luk said.

The Chief Inspector led the way from the cell to an outer office. At his order, a gendarme brought a mesh tray containing the assassin's possessions. The passport, issued in Zagreb and franked there on 30 May 1934, identified the fat man as Petrus Kelemen, businessman. It gave Zagreb, Croatia, as the place of his birth, in 1899, and it showed that he had entered France on 28 September 1934 – just eleven days ago.

'The passport should make things easy for you,' the Chief Inspector said.

Luk flung the Frenchman a look that was icily contemptuous.

'A forgery,' he said flatly. He did not *know* that the passport was a forgery – it looked genuine – but he was prepared to bet his last dinar that whoever the fat man was, he was not Petrus Kelemen. He had never heard of any Petrus Kelemen, and that meant that Petrus Kelemen – if he existed – did not have a record, and that did not make sense to Luk. The fat man had been a pro – a hired bravo – and it was Luk's bet that the fat man would prove to have a record a mile long.

If Luk had had the slightest doubt about the fat man being a professional killer, it would instantly have vanished when the murder weapon was produced for his examination. The automatic pistol placed in front of him was a fearsome weapon: the nearest thing there was to a hand machine-gun. It could be fitted with belts of ten or twenty 7.63 mm cartridges and, in the hands of an

15

expert, was capable of achieving a firepower of 280 rounds per minute. The assassin had been equipped with two such pistols. From one – the murder weapon – the fat man had expended a full belt of ten shots. The other gun, although fully loaded, had not been fired. Thanks to the fury of the crowd, the fat man had not been given time to pull it from his jacket pocket.

As Luk examined the formidable armoury, the Chief Inspector was called to the telephone. He returned, grim-faced.

'Your country is not the only one to suffer tragic loss at the hands of that maniac,' he said to Luk. 'In addition to a fine police officer and an innocent woman who was no harm to anyone, France has now lost one of her finest statesmen. Foreign Minister Barthou died in hospital a few minutes ago.'

The police officer's tone was almost accusatory, as if Luk was somehow personally responsible. The Jugoslav bristled, drawing himself erect.

'France will find a foreign minister a lot more easily than Jugoslavia will find someone to fill the King's shoes. This has been a disaster for us – and one that wouldn't have happened but for French incompetence.'

It was the Chief Inspector's turn to bristle.

'You'll find a new king, monsieur,' he snapped. 'You always do. They're ten a penny in that tribal Balkan backwater you come from.'

'I find your words and tone offensive, sir,' Luk growled, eyeing the officer like a fighting cock ready for battle. The French officer did not back down. He had never liked Slavs, nor ever been able to understand their perpetual internecine feuding with one another. It had been a Slav whose murderous shots, only two decades ago, had turned the whole of Europe into a battlefield, and now they had brought their homicidal madness to the very streets of Marseille. To *his* city! They would not be content until they had started a second world war and dragged down every other civilised country into the whirlpool of their own irreconcilable hatreds.

'I did not invite you or your King to Marseille,' the Chief Inspector said, 'nor the anarchy that you brought with you. Forgive me if my plain speech is lacking in diplomatic niceties, monsieur.'

'It is not in my nature to forgive,' Luk said. 'Nor to forget.' He shrugged. 'It is a national characteristic of the Serbs. Some say it is a failing.'

Later, when Luk was making a full report of the assassination and analysing the French security arrangements – and knowing that the details were to be made available to the French Government for internal inquiry – he particularised what he saw as grave incompetence in the Marseille police, naming officers.

The Chief Inspector was one of the three officers who were summarily sacked from their posts. The dismissals were reported in the Belgrade newspapers.

Luk was back in Belgrade by then, where Prince Paul – the late King's first cousin – had become Regent and was ruling with dictatorial powers. Luk allowed himself a smile of satisfaction when he read the news item about the Marseille sackings. The French, it seemed, always had to find scapegoats. It was ironic that he, Luk, had never been so secure in his own job as in the aftermath of Alexander's assassination – an event contrived by Croatian nationalists and Italian money – and he had never been busier. Enemies of the Jugoslav state abounded and had to be suppressed. The new Regency Government had a knack of making few friends and many enemies.

PART ONE
BELGRADE

1

Belgrade

Jamie Kyle was prepared to concede that Belgrade was *interesting*. But beautiful it was not. For as long as he could remember, Jamie's mother had been telling him that Belgrade was beautiful – but she did tend to misuse that particular adjective, because whatsoever Jelena Kyle loved dearly was beautiful in her eyes.

She even thought Jamie was beautiful, and told him so frequently. The notion, of course, was absurd. He squirmed with embarrassment when his mother called him her 'beautiful baby'. Dammit, he was seventeen – a man!

Because she was his mother, Jamie had to forgive Jelena Kyle some extravagance in her choice of terms of endearment. Likewise, because she was his mother and Serbian-born, she had to be forgiven a proneness to overstate Belgrade's claim to beauty.

Some might have said the city was downright ugly, but Jamie was not prepared to be that uncharitable. Belgrade was more like a middle-aged woman whose eyes still sparkle and whose figure is still good. The place had a maturity, and a charm that was not cosmetic nor all on the surface. The charm was exerted subtly with closer acquaintance, and grew as unsuspected qualities were discovered.

The sparkle in Belgrade's eyes was its people. Like Jamie's mother – who was one of them – they were vivacious and friendly, proud almost to the point of arrogance but outgoing and kind, especially to the stranger in their midst. During his first six months

21

among them, Jamie spent the long hot summer days getting to know Belgrade and his mother's people.

He took tram rides here, there and everywhere but, most of the time, he walked: from the bridge over the Sava, near the railway station, to the banks of the brown Danube on the far side of the city; from the unremarkable fountain in the Terazije, the town centre, to the Kalemegdan, the ancient citadel fortress that dominated the confluence of the Sava and the Danube.

The old moated citadel fascinated Jamie. It had the reek of history, although the fortifications were modern by Belgrade standards. They were the work of the most recent foreign occupants, the Austrians. The Scots half of Jamie wondered at the knowledge that the site had first been fortified by the Celts at the dawn of European history – long before their tribes penetrated his father's homeland, Scotland. It provided a mystic link, joining his mother's Balkan heritage with that of his Caledonian forebears. He was the child of both, which may have been one.

The Celts who had dwelt at the meeting place of the Danube and the Sava were followed by the Romans, who had built a city there. After the Romans came the Huns, the Goths and the Avars, before the Slavs finally settled and called the citadel their own. Around it, the Kingdom of Serbia had arisen and spread and had, somehow, survived four centuries of Turkish possession. Beograd – to give it its true name, meaning White City – had been destroyed twenty or more times by one marauding power or another and yet – phoenix-like – it had risen again from the ashes.

The saddest thing to Jamie's eyes in that summer of 1934 was the poverty that haunted Belgrade. It did not flaunt itself – perhaps because summer does not reveal the worst aspects of poverty – but it was there. It was to be seen in the hungry eyes of the children who ran barefoot in the streets. It was in the gaunt faces of the

22

men, young and old, who streamed in from the country with their meagre belongings in brown paper bundles, looking for work that was not there.

Jamie saw the poverty as a regrettable fact of life rather than as a condition that could be cured. It was a curse that afflicted the world, like the diphtheria that had taken the life of a ten-year-old classmate at the village school he had attended, back in Scotland. At the time, Jamie's doctor father had tried to console him.

'There's no cure for the disease, Jamie. God grant that there was and I could have saved your young friend – but it was a battle I could not win. It was the will of God that he was taken from us, and if it perplexes you that this must be so, it perplexes you no more than it does me.'

Although Belgrade's poverty was not hidden from sight, it was veiled by a strange abandon in the city's social life. The gaiety and laughter that rang through the night haunts might have lulled the visitor into believing that things were, perhaps, not quite so bad after all. The cafés and bars did a roaring trade – wine was cheap – but the carousing had a desperate quality to it, as if the citizens were hellbent on showing defiance to the grim economic realities.

The hedonism was not confined to any one social group. The very rich drank and danced the nights away at elegant soirées, as if suddenly aware that today's wealth might disappear tomorrow and they might as well enjoy it. The Wall Street crash of '29 had reverberated round the world and it was still ringing in their ears. The bourgeoisie, equally beset by the uncertainties of the times, hid their fears in the frantic pursuit of pleasure. The poor – who scraped for work and bread – drank intemperately to anaesthetise the misery of their existence.

One institution which was a microcosm of Jugoslavia and all its strengths and weaknesses was the University of Belgrade. It was also fairly representative of the country's social mix – although it must be admitted that the sons and daughters of the bourgeoisie claimed the lion's share of the places. The University was, nevertheless, the only place in Belgrade where all the elements of Jugoslavia's heterogeneous society met as a single body and reflected the fears and aspirations of the people as a whole. It retained some independence in a land where parliamentary government had been suspended indefinitely and the only forum for popular dissent had been removed. And it was into this concrescence of Serbs, Croats, Slovenes and Montenegrins that Jamie was admitted in the autumn of 1934.

His decision to enrol for an Arts course that incorporated the study of literature and languages (Russian and German), was a fateful one – it settled for good the question of returning to Scotland.

For as long as he could remember, it had been tacitly understood at home and at the eminent fee-paying Secondary Academy in Crieff, where he had shone scholastically, that Jamie would follow in his father's footsteps as a doctor. That would have meant a sixth year back at his old school – as a boarder rather than a day pupil – and then on to Edinburgh University to study medicine. Jamie had never opposed these hopes for him, fostered by parents and teachers alike, but in his heart of hearts he had not shared them.

Much as he had admired his father, Jamie felt no strong vocational pull to a career in medicine. Indeed, the thought of trying to emulate his father as a doctor scared him. The more he had witnessed the immense dedication which his father brought to the demands of his scattered Highland practice, the more Jamie had become convinced of his own unsuitability.

Dr Hamish Kyle had been of a rare mould: a man who gave not a fig for material possessions or personal enrichment. His life had been one of unremitting service to mankind, without counting the cost to himself. Even home and family had come second to his chosen mission: to minister to the sick, wherever and whenever he was needed. There had been times when Jamie, not understanding what drove his father, resented the care he lavished on others. Jamie and his mother, it seemed, only got a small part of him. At other times, Jamie had seen the effort it cost his father to drag himself out, dog-tired, to face yet another errand of mercy and had wondered at his capacity to make light of it. As a result, Jamie had come to believe that doctoring required qualities of saintliness and self-denial that he had not inherited.

Dr Hamish Kyle had worked himself to death, literally. On a January day in 1933, he had struggled on foot through waist-high snowdrifts to reach the lonely cottage of a glen shepherd whose wife was in labour. On his return home from a successful delivery, Hamish Kyle had complained of feeling tired, plumped himself down in his favourite fireside chair, and died. It was somehow typical of him that, at the age of forty-eight, he had died as he had lived – with a total absence of fuss.

Jamie's loss was shared by the entire community. On the day Hamish Kyle was laid to rest, the tiny village church could not contain the mourners who came from near and far and in every conceivable kind of transport to pay their respects. They came from all over Strathearn and from the off-lying glens: gentlemen landowners in morning coats and striped trousers; ploughmen, looking uncomfortable in starched collars and black Sunday serge; ex-servicemen in bowler hats and wearing medals on their coats; cloaked nurses from the cottage hospital; shepherds and gamekeepers in heavy tweeds and black ties; ruddy-countenanced farmers of grave demeanour, flanked by sturdy women with sorrowing faces.

The Crieff paper gave over most of its lead page to Hamish Kyle's obituary. It told of his war service with the Royal Army Medical Corps in Serbia and how he had met and married his bride, Jelena, while attached to the Serbian Army. It told how the doctor and his young wife had taken part in the Great Retreat into Albania and had eventually reached Corfu, where Jamie was born. It spoke of Hamish Kyle's heroic fight against the cholera epidemic that had ravaged the Serbian refugees and how he had contracted the disease himself. His suffering from that and the effects of the harrowing march through the mountains of Serbia had taken their toll of his health and had undoubtedly contributed to his early death at the age of forty-eight.

Jamie, with a child's perception of these things, had attributed moments of brooding unhappiness in his mother to his father's total absorption in his work. More than anyone, he had been aware of the long hours of loneliness endured by his mother because of his father's absences at all hours of the day and night. Quite wrongly, he had construed a growing bitterness towards his father in her moody irritability on those occasions.

In fact, Jelena Kyle's devotion to her husband had never wavered. She would have endured all the torments of purgatory for the man she loved. She understood her husband's compulsion to serve, had known it from the day he first came into her life, and she had not sought to change him. She had wedded Hamish Kyle's purpose in life as willingly as she had wed the man. She was his support and inspiration, always there, never failing him. That was why she had willingly followed him to the beautiful but alien land that was Scotland and had uncomplainingly accepted all the sacrifices that this transplantation entailed.

The death of Hamish Kyle had left her desolate. And it was only in its aftermath that Jamie came to appreciate the real reason for the unhappiness that he had glimpsed in his mother. It had stemmed not from marital discord but from lingering homesickness: a longing to see her native Serbia and those loved ones whom she had left behind. Jelena Kyle, long resigned to never seeing either again, would not have admitted her homesickness to a living soul while her husband was alive and needed her. When she no longer had him, it was easier to acknowledge that private longings existed – and to consider the possibility of their fulfilment.

The only obstacle was Jamie, now at a critical stage in his schooling at the academy in Crieff. His eagerness to see Jugoslavia was so great that he would have dropped everything there and then for the adventure of travelling across half Europe. But Jelena had to quell her own eagerness by insisting that Jamie's education came first. It would be time enough to think about a move to Belgrade when he had matriculated from school or, at least, finished the exams.

Jamie's enthusiasm to see her homeland should not have come as quite the surprise it did to Jelena Kyle. From his infancy, she had regaled Jamie with tales of Serbia, teaching him her native tongue and making sure that he was as fluent in Serbo-Croat as he was in English. He soon outdistanced his father's limited knowledge of the language, and he had grown up as familiar with Cyrillic script as with Roman lettering. Indeed, the ease with which he became bilingual may have been an early signal of the aptitude he was to show for languages at school, where he regularly topped his class in Latin and French.

When, in May 1934, the widowed Jelena and her son eventually departed for Belgrade, all of Jamie's future was a question mark. The house in Perthshire had been sold off but no decision had been made about Jamie's possible return for a further year at his Crieff school before trying for a place at Edinburgh University as a medical student. Jelena Kyle's future was equally in the melting pot. On the death of her husband, her brother

Milan had written to her, entreating her to come to Belgrade and make her home permanently with him. Jamie was guaranteed no less a welcome than his mother. Milan knew that a career in medicine had been talked about for Jamie but there were opportunities in Belgrade, too, for a bright young lad.

Milan had reminded his sister that his printing business was thriving, in spite of the Depression, and that – as a bachelor – he had no male heir to keep it going as a family concern. If Jamie chose it, he had a splendid career in printing ahead of him.

Wisely, Jamie's uncle did not press for immediate decisions from Jelena. The important thing – he had assured her – is that you come home to us. Look on it as a long, indefinite holiday. You know that both you and Jamie will be welcome for as long as you want to stay. Decisions can wait. My home is your home.

So it was that the summer started as a holiday, with decision-making temporarily in abeyance. It was a happy time, so much so that when the time came for decisions to be made, there was no chagrin or dispute. Everyone was happy at the outcome. Jelena Kyle wanted to stay in Belgrade and she was pleased that Jamie wanted to do so, too. Perhaps happiest of all was Jamie's uncle Milan.

The return of his beloved little sister brought a joyous new dimension into the life of Milan Alexandrovic, renewing a bond of devotion that had been forged in childhood. From the moment that the baby Jelena gurgled happily from her cradle at her five-year-old brother, Milan became her worshipping protector. Their closeness – in a family which included three girls older than Milan – had become a by-word. When their soldier father was killed, fighting the Turks in the war of 1912, Milan's jealous guardianship over his little Jelena took on a new intensity.

Then came bitter separation. The 1914 war not only

scattered the Alexandrovic family, it all but wiped it out. Milan went off to fight for Serbia, and that was the last his mother and sisters heard of him before they, too, were caught up in the battle for their homeland. They heard later that Milan had died in the defence of Belgrade. But Milan had not died. Thrice wounded, he had survived the confusion of the Great Retreat and was in good enough shape to be among those shipped to the Salonika front to continue the fight. He finished the war in the vanguard of the victorious armies thrusting north through Macedonia.

It was not until 1919 that Milan discovered that his beloved Jelena had not perished, as their mother and sisters had. With the help of the Red Cross, he found that she was living in Scotland and had acquired a husband and baby son since he last saw her. The discovery did not lead to a reunion between the brother and sister who had each given the other up for dead. But it led to a joyful exchange of letters: letters that were read and re-read and stained with tears of happiness, fore-runners of the letters which were to pass between the pair for the next fourteen years.

The practicalities of the times were such that the distance between Jugoslavia and Scotland could have been inter-planetary, and brother and sister resigned themselves to living out their lives apart, with the fortnightly letters the only consolation.

Hamish Kyle's death had changed all that. Jelena may suddenly have found herself rudderless – her husband's needs had dictated the course of her life – but widowhood brought a kind of freedom which she had not hitherto contemplated. All her old longings to see Serbia, her brother, and those cousins of hers who were still alive, bubbled back as she came to terms with her grief. What before had seemed an impossible dream swam temptingly into reach. Hamish Kyle had not only left her the opportunity but the means.

The prudence with which Hamish Kyle had provided for his surviving wife and son – as if he had long anticipated his early death – came as a surprise to Jelena. Throughout his life, he had displayed a total indifference to money – in a way that had exasperated Jelena at times – but, quite unknown to her, he had taken scrupulous care to make sure that she and Jamie would not face a penniless future without him.

The discovery of his providence was a revelation. He had been the world's worst book-keeper, as Jelena discovered each time she was enroled to assist in the surgery's haphazard accounting.

She knew that half the bills, which she helped him to send out to patients, were never paid. But it never troubled him. Some bills were never sent out. He would consign one to the waste-paper basket with the comment that old so-and-so had been laid off work and that he had worries enough. Other bills would follow the first.

'That woman's having a hard enough time trying to feed her five bairns,' he would say. Or: 'Fraser's lost his entire potato crop. Forget that one.'

Jelena, who thought he was a soft mark at times, made no headway on those occasions when she urged him to be a bit more businesslike.

'I'm a doctor, not a debt-collector,' he would say shortly and there would be no more argument. Often, however, there would be a sequel. The Scots country folk did not welsh voluntarily on their doctor's bills and Hamish Kyle's good turns were seldom forgotten.

Gifts turned up unexpectedly at the surgery, often months and sometimes years after some act of kindness. A half-hundredweight bag of potatoes would be left on the doorstep with a note of thanks, or it would be a salmon or half a dozen trout rolled in rhubarb leaves, or a shoulder of lamb, or a basket of eggs.

Hamish Kyle had valued these unsolicited gifts much more than the three half-crowns pressed self-consciously into his hand by a patient, the standard reward for a house call. His indiffence to money notwithstanding, a great number of half-crowns must have gone every week towards maintenance of the hefty insurance premiums to which he was committed. Their settlement, after his death, was to leave Jelena Kyle in circumstances of far greater financial security than her doctor husband had enjoyed in his lifetime.

Without being privy to the pounds, shillings and pence of his mother's resources, Jamie worried privately about being a greater drain on them than he actually was. Much as he enjoyed his exploration of Belgrade and the idle nature of his first Balkan summer, he suffered pangs of guilt over his total dependence on his mother and his Uncle Milan. It bothered him that, at an age when most of his generation were looking for work, he was making no contribution to the family budget.

So, towards the end of summer – with the decision made that he would go to Belgrade University, instead of returning to Scotland – he sought ways and means of earning money and ridding himself of the feeling that his existence was parasitical. First, he wanted to make himself feel useful to his Uncle Milan who had welcomed his sister's son as his own and whose affectionate regard for Jamie had grown from the day of their first meeting – an occasion of unforgettable emotional warmth and happy tears amid the steam and clamour of Belgrade's main railway station. Jamie offered his services to his uncle as handyman around the house or odd-jobber at the printing works.

'But why?' Uncle Milan had asked. 'There is still so much for you to see and do while the weather is fine – that excursion on the Danube you wanted to take.'

'I want to make myself useful to you,' Jamie had tried to explain, 'I'll do heavy work . . . . anything. I eat your food and sleep under your roof but I don't do anything in return. I don't want paying. I just want to feel that I'm doing something to earn my keep. You are so good to us.'

'Just having you here is enough. I do not expect you to work for bringing pleasure into my life.' Uncle Milan had sounded a little offended. Nevertheless, he had recognised commendable motives in Jamie's offer and conceded that there were occasions when additional manpower at the printing works could be a godsend. He insisted, however, that Jamie be paid the going rate for the labouring and delivery chores which, thereafter, he contrived to push Jamie's way.

Milan Alexandrovic was also helpful in getting a second enterprise started. Jamie had the bright idea of advertising his services as a teacher of colloquial English, charging the most modest rates. His uncle thought this a most splendid initiative and offered him use of a small office as a classroom. This would be available on Sundays, the only day that the printing works closed. All Jamie had to do was find some pupils.

Consequently, Jamie placed a notice in the press announcing the commencement of an English conversation class for beginners on the first Sunday in September. Half an hour before the appointed time on that Sunday, he was pacing about nervously in front of the main door to his uncle's works, wondering if any prospective pupils would turn up.

One did.

She was quite the most captivating creature Jamie had seen in his life. He first caught sight of her at a distance: a petite figure in a pale blue skirt and lemon-coloured blouse, moving slowly along the street as if searching for an address. She had a blue and yellow polka-dot kerchief in a careless knot at her throat. Her shoulder-length hair was as black as a raven's wing and seemed to float languidly with every movement of her body.

Jamie stared in mesmerised fascination as she approached, halted uncertainly and stared at him with an inquiring expression.

'Do you know if it is here that they hold the English class?' she asked in a low husky voice. Mischievous lights danced in her dark eyes, as if the idea of holding English classes in what appeared to be a small factory was both novel and amusing. Jamie did not reply immediately. The eyes in that perfect oval face enchanted him, robbing him of speech. He looked down embarrassedly and found himself staring with no less fascination at ripe young breasts thrusting against the fabric of the yellow blouse. As he stared, and realised he was staring, he felt a rise of blood flushing his face.

'Yes,' he stammered, in belated reply to the girl's question. 'This is the place.'

She brightened.

'You, too, are a pupil?'

'No.'

'You are the professor's son?'

Jamie's eyes widened.

'Professor?'

'The teacher of English. You are his son?'

Jamie, strangely tongue-tied, managed to explain that he was the teacher of English. Disbelief registered briefly on the girl's face, then delight.

'I expected some old fuddy-duddy,' she confessed. She looked around. 'Where are all the others? Are they inside?'

'There are no others,' Jamie said. 'You're the only one. I was beginning to think there wasn't going to be anybody. . . . Does it make a difference to you, being the only one?'

She smiled in a way that made Jamie's heart turn over.

'Why should it? It's not what I expected . . . but I don't mind.'

Her name was Mara Richtman, and she was so open and friendly that Jamie had great difficulty concentrating on the job of teaching her English. He could easily have spent the day in shy conversation with this delectable stranger, finding out all there was to know about her. The discovery that she, too, would be starting at the University of Belgrade the following month, and that their courses had subjects in common, made him positively voluble; and the pair of them prattled on as if the English lesson was the last thing on their minds.

When Jamie did eventually get round to initiating Mara in conversational English, attempts at solemnity were short-lived. Mara had an impish sense of humour and kept undermining Jamie's efforts to maintain an earnest front. He soon stopped trying. He abandoned his carefully prepared notes and his plan to work his way through the conjunctions of essential basic verbs and improvised to suit the mood of the occasion. Thus, they progressed with much hilarity from the childish enumeration of fingers, with 'This little piggie went to market' to the marginally less puerile recitation of 'One, two, three, four, five, once I caught a fish alive . . . Six, seven, eight, nine, ten, then I put it back again.'

So quickly did the time pass and so much did Jamie enjoy himself that he recklessly waived any fee insisting that the first lesson was introductory and there was no charge. Mara promised that she would return the following Sunday and, as far as Jamie was concerned, she could have offered no greater reward. He walked on air for a week, willing the hours and minutes to pass until he could once more be in the company of this enchanting girl.

The second lesson, however, was not the cosy two-some that Jamie had so joyously anticipated for seven long days. Mara arrived with a young man in tow, happily announcing that she had recruited another pupil for the class. Jamie found himself staring into the friendly eyes of Stefan Markovic and trying not to look too crestfallen at the realisation that he was not going to get Mara to himself after all.

'Stefan's a writer and he's going to be very famous one day,' Mara told Jamie, and her obvious admiration for her companion caused Jamie's heart to sink. He tried not to show his dismay and exhibited delight that, through Mara's thoughtfulness, his class – and his income – would be doubled. A new pupil stood before him, but Jamie could see only a rival.

'Don't pay too much attention to what Mara says,' Stefan was quick to advise Jamie. 'She has a kind heart but she exaggerates everything. I'm a student at the University and I do a little writing, which helps me to pay the rent . . . but I have a long way to go to catch up Tolstoy.'

'Don't you believe it,' Mara chimed in. 'Stefan's a genius. Everybody says so.'

'See what I mean?' said Stefan, with a broad grin at Jamie. 'She just can't keep a sense of proportion. You should hear what she's been saying about you.'

'About me?'

'The greatest teacher since Plato. Didn't you know the impression you made? She's been raving on about you all week. That's why I'm here.'

'I hope you won't be too disappointed,' Jamie said. 'I don't have any real qualifications to teach.'

'Mara says you're a genius – and, in your case, I believe it,' Stefan said, with a grin. 'Anyone who can teach her to count up to ten, in English, is a miracle-worker. She couldn't count up to five before – in any language!'

'Oh, you beast!' Mara shrieked at him in mock outrage, and pummelled him about the shoulders with her fists. Stefan endured the assault good-naturedly while Jamie watched with amusement. Mara clearly took no offence at Stefan's banter, which was devoid of malice and obviously part and parcel of a happy relationship. There was something very charismatic about Stefan, and Jamie – who had been ready to resent him for existing – found himself drawn to his rival.

Indeed, the better they became acquainted, the more impossible Jamie found it to harbour other than the friendliest feelings towards Stefan. He had a warm, outgoing personality that invited friendship, and yet there was a lot more to him than that. He was humorous and modest and had a gentleness of nature that cloaked an undefinable vulnerability. Jamie would not have identified it as such, but there was a basic goodness in Stefan, which he sensed and to which he had to respond.

It quickly became apparent that Stefan's desire to learn English had not been born of a whimsical need to indulge Mara. He was genuinely eager, and Jamie could not have asked for a more attentive or a more apt pupil. Stefan was possessed of an almost insatiable hunger to *learn* – not just English but anything that would add to his knowledge and understanding of the wider world. He questioned Jamie endlessly about what it was like to grow up in Scotland: the social conditions, the system of education, the politics, the economic climate, the industries, the cultural pursuits. One Sunday a week, learning English with Jamie, was not nearly enough to keep Stefan satisfied – with the result that the Sunday class spilled over into the other days of the week and became Jamie's social life.

Stefan was anxious to introduce the Professor – as he nicknamed Jamie – to his and Mara's friends and, although the Sunday class was maintained through September, the extra-mural activities of Jamie and his two pupils soon took over in importance. A nondescript café, called the Dancing Bear, was their principal rendezvous, and Jamie found himself swept into a new and exciting world that he had not known existed.

The patrons of the Dancing Bear were a Bohemian lot: would-be artists and writers who talked a lot about Paris; students, like Stefan, who had already spent one or two years at the University; well-heeled young

36

socialites who liked the hoi-polloi gaiety of the rather seedy establishment. They talked, they drank, they talked, they sang, they talked, they danced, they talked. Always they talked. The arguments flowed back and forth in torrents as the world was set aright fifty times a night – and Jamie loved it. The talk was as heady as the cheap wine he sipped. He drank sparingly, taking his cue from Stefan. Whether Stefan drank carefully because he liked to retain control of his senses or because he could not afford to squander too much money on wine, Jamie did not know – but Stefan was the natural leader and the one he admired most, so Jamie imitated him.

Subconsciously, in modelling his own behaviour on Stefan's, Jamie might have been trying to win favour with Mara. She was fond of Jamie but she *adored* Stefan – and Jamie would dearly have loved to have been the object of the same slavish devotion.

This did not lessen Jamie's regard for Stefan. Indeed, so much did he admire Stefan on his own account that he understood only too well why Mara was so smitten. He was as much under the spell of Stefan's charismatic personality as Mara was.

It was, therefore, a triangle without conflict. Jamie adored Mara, Mara adored Stefan; and Stefan accepted both as his dearest friends, never exploiting Mara's adulation for him at Jamie's expense nor exhibiting a possessiveness that might have created discord. Jamie did not feel the need to compete against Stefan for Mara's affections. Although Mara did not lavish him the blind kind of adoration that she reserved for Stefan, he still found much favour in her eyes and that was promise enough of heaven for Jamie.

Mara and Stefan were often joined by their older brothers during their evenings at the Dancing Bear. They invariably arrived with their girl friends of the moment. Both young men were officer cadets at the Military Academy and cut a dash in their uniforms.

Petar, Mara's brother, was as blond as she was dark, and handsome with it. He tended to argue a lot with Stefan when the talk was of politics, but he was a courteous debater and had a chivalrous way with him. Jamie liked him. Marko, Stefan's brother, was a big man: broad-shouldered and thick-set, in contrast to Stefan's pale good looks and almost delicate physique. Wine, women and song seemed to be Marko's chief interests in life and he quickly became bored if the talk became too cerebral. He was clearly fond of Stefan but he became embarrassed and unhappy when his younger brother argued politics. Stefan's views were a great deal too radical for Marko's peace of mind. It was Marko's opinion that Stefan's tongue would get him into trouble one day, but Stefan just smiled at the brotherly warnings that came his way.

Jamie was bewildered by much of the political talk – he was not familiar enough with the names that peppered the discussions – but he was fascinated by Stefan's polemical skill and eloquence. He was a most persuasive debater. Stefan's chief ally, of course, was Mara. Her interest in politics was a surprise to Jamie – he had always believed politics to be a male preserve – and her vehemence was an eye-opener. Even to Jamie, however, it seemed that Mara's spirited support of Stefan's views owed more to loyalty to her adored Stefan than to a deep understanding of the topics he argued so capably.

It was on an evening in late September that Jamie was given his first insight into a more sinister aspect of Belgrade life than he had hitherto encountered. The usual group had gathered in the cellar bar of the Dancing Bear and were occupying their favourite corner, a recess with a long table and bench seating for more than a dozen. The air was thick with tobacco smoke and a noisy chatter rose from the fifty or more patrons crowded into the badly ventilated basement premises.

Suddenly, the buzz of conversations stopped and eyes were directed upward to the top of the stairs, where two men had appeared. They did not descend but stood, looking down from the rail of the pulpit-like gallery, their eyes searching the throng below. They seemed to enjoy the effect of their presence, which could not have been more pronounced if they had been undertakers interrupting a wedding feast.

Jamie's group had fallen as silent as the next. They watched as the younger of the two men came down the stairs. The other – a dumpy individual of about forty – remained like a guard at the top of the stairs, blocking them. The younger man came towards Jamie and his friends. He did not hurry. His approach was deliberate, swaggering. He displayed a smiling arrogance that was calculated, provocative. He wore a flashy suit of cheap material. It was badly cut and seemed two sizes too big for his angular body but he seemed unaware of his faintly ridiculous attire. It was completed – in spite of the unseasonal mildness of the evening – by kid leather gloves encasing his hands and a snap-brimmed black hat pushed to the back of his head. To Jamie, he looked like something out of second-feature gangster movie and, indeed, his first thought was that the newcomer must be the Belgrade equivalent of a cheap Chicago hood.

In character assessment, he was not too far off the mark. The man stopped, facing Stefan, and stared at him.

'I know your face,' he said. 'The riots in Ratarska Street . . . the student mob. You're one of the trouble-makers from the University.'

Stefan stared back, his expression impassive. He did not reply.

'Do you deny it?' the man persisted. 'I'm very good at remembering faces. Especially lily-skinned Bolshie faces – like yours!'

Still Stefan said nothing. He was saved the necessity by Mara's brother, Petar, who got to his feet and leaned across the table, partially screening Stefan from his accuser in the process. When he spoke his tone was excessively polite.

'Can we help you? Or are you just doing the social rounds?'

The man turned his full attention to Petar and looked him up and down, as if with approval.

'Ha!' he exclaimed. 'A military gentleman! A fellow like myself, in the service of the King!' He beamed. 'Almost a colleague, would you say?'

'I would not say,' Petar declared firmly.

The man's thin bony face darkened with anger.

'Don't give me your lip, sonny. You're in bad company and that can be big trouble for you.'

'The question of bad company can easily be put right,' Petar replied icily. 'You could leave.'

The retort fuelled the other's fury. His face twitched with rage. For an instant, it seemed that he was about to lash out at Petar with his fists – but something in Petar's unflinching stance made him hesitate. Perhaps it was plain cowardice that inspired the man's caution, perhaps fear that the young soldier defying him so calmly was the son of an important family – but he backed down before Petar's resolute stare. His retreat was not without bluster.

'I'll remember this,' he promised, threateningly. 'You lot can thank your lucky stars it's somebody else I'm looking for tonight. You can count yourselves lucky I got other business. Any other time. . . .' He did not complete the threat of what might happen any other time. He paused and allowed his eyes to speak for him. They went over every member of the group, as if recording the faces for future reference. 'I'll remember you,' he said to Stefan, with menace. 'And you,' he said, staring long at Jamie.

Then he left them.

He made a circuit of the cellar, looking at faces but not lingering at any other table. Then he took the stairs two at a time and rejoined the older man, who had not moved from his position at the top. They conversed briefly, before hurrying out. Their departure triggered an explosion of chatter as the customers in the cellar all began talking at once.

'Who were they?' Jamie burst out, bewildered by the episode. He seemed to be the only person in the cellar who had no idea of the visitors' identity.

'Two of Luk's gorillas,' Stefan informed him briefly.

'Who is Luk?'

Jamie's ignorance suddenly became the concern of all the others. He found himself being educated from several directions simultaneously.

'Luk's the head of the secret police.'

'He's the King's hatchet man.'

'He's a political cop. He goes round beating the daylights out of anybody who criticises the dictatorship.'

Jamie turned to Stefan.

'The one who accused you . . . he was a policeman?'

'Of sorts,' Stefan replied. 'More a licensed thug.'

'He seemed to know you, Stefan. Did you really take part in a riot?'

'A couple of demonstrations I was on did get a bit out of hand – but I don't remember seeing that goon before in my life. You stood up to him well, Petar,' he said, with a grateful look towards Mara's brother. 'You really gave him a flea in his ear.'

'I don't like bully-boys,' Petar said, with a shrug.

'He's part of the system that you're pledged to defend, Petar . . .'

'I've told you before that the system is a long way from being perfect. I want to see it reformed as much as you do. If I had the power, I would abolish the secret police tomorrow.'

'But if you abolished the secret police, the monarchy would collapse. They're the only thing that's propping it up.'

Petar sighed.

'And that would please you, Stefan, wouldn't it, if the monarchy collapsed? You'd clap your hands if somebody came along and slaughtered the King and all the royal family, and some factory worker from Slavonski Brod or Kragujevac set himself up in the palace and declared a soviet republic.'

Stefan laughed.

'In some respects, that wouldn't be setting a precedent, Petar. I seem to recall that our dear King's family came to power only thirty years ago by butchering our other great Serbian dynasty. I, personally, would not harm a hair of the King's head, but I admit I would not be too upset if history repeated itself – especially if the end result was a regime that put power into the hands of the people.'

It was Petar's turn to be amused. He smiled, albeit a little sadly.

'You're a dreamer, Stefan. You think that, by exchanging one regime for another, all our troubles would be over. Unfortunately, the world isn't like that. You'd probably just be exchanging one imperfect system for another that's a hundred times worse.'

'I'm willing to take a chance on it,' said Stefan. 'Maybe we should have a Croatian king for a change, instead of a Serb. Would that please you, Petar? Maybe, you Croats would make a better job of things and give freedom and justice back to the people. You're the ones who are doing all the shouting about independence from Serbian rule. Would you do a better job, Petar?'

Petar grinned.

'Mara would,' he said. 'She's the separatist in the family. Me, I'm just a soldier who's still serving his apprenticeship, not a politician. And I'm for peaceful evolution, not revolution!' He turned to Jamie. 'What about you, Jamie? What is the British point of view? Whose side are you on?'

Jamie thought for a moment.

'I think I agree with both of you,' he said. Everybody laughed uproariously.

The memory of the secret policeman threatening to remember his face stayed with Jamie like a bitter taste in the mouth. The incident caused tiny flutterings of fear and anger to ruffle his peace of mind whenever he thought about it: fear, that innocence of any wrongdoing would be no safeguard against the ruffian's vengeful nature; anger, at the injustice of having been singled out by the agent without any provocation.

'Don't let it worry you,' Stefan had consoled him later. 'The guy only picked on you because you look so inoffensive.'

But the incident did worry Jamie, in a nagging way. He had been falling in love with Belgrade and his new way of life, and the unexpected encounter had soured his growing enthusiasm. Doubts rose where none had existed before. For the first time he began to wonder what kind of land this really was that entrusted power to swaggering bullies in flashy civilian suits.

Only Stefan, among Jamie's new-found friends, seemed to sense his misgivings. And it was Stefan alone who tried to make Jamie take a more realistic view of his mother's homeland.

'You're a romantic,' he told Jamie. 'You'll really have to learn to take us as we are and not how you want us to be.'

It was the day before the University was due to resume after the summer vacation, a day of low cloud and intermittent drizzle that drifted in over the Sava on the northeasterly breeze. The pair were walking by the river, below the high bluffs of the Kalemegdan.

'What's wrong with being a romantic?' Jamie protested amiably.

'They get hurt, Jamie,' Stefan said. 'They get hurt. Disillusion is twice as cruel to a romantic. A realist looks at a wart on a woman's face and calls it a wart. A romantic, if he acknowledges the wart's existence, pretends it's a beauty spot. It hurts when he has to admit the truth, which he should have admitted in the first place, that the wart is a wart and ugly – and it probably won't go away by wishing it wasn't there.'

'What are you trying to tell me, Stefan? That one day I'll wake up hating you and Mara and Petar and Belgrade . . .? Because I can't accept you as you really are?'

Stefan laughed softly.

'I hope that never happens, Jamie. I know you like it here and I hope you always will. All I was trying to do was warn you against yourself. Because I like you so much. Because I feel I could trust you with my life and you'd never betray me. But I don't want you to have illusions about me . . . about Belgrade . . . about the people who live here.'

'You think I do?' asked Jamie.

'I think you look at the world through rose-tinted spectacles. Belgrade isn't the quaint little paradise you seem to think it is. You see the smiles on people's faces, you hear their laughter, and your heart sings and you are happy, too – but this is not a happy country, Jamie. It's torn and bleeding from self-inflicted wounds. Most of the people are desperately poor and lack the basic necessities of life. More than half of them will never get the chance – as you and I have – of learning to read and write. All the power and all the wealth is concentrated in the hands of a very few, who are determined to hang on to what they've got, even if it means condemning generations of their fellow human beings to misery. We are ruled by a regime which allows us no voice and which will savagely suppress anyone who dares to speak out against it or anything that seems to threaten it. Our land, Jamie, is a melting pot of three religions which have only one thing in common: intolerance, and of half a dozen tribal nationalities who can agree on nothing. This land that you like so much, Jamie, is a land without freedom, a land without justice – and I despair for it! Love it as I love it, Jamie, but have no illusions about it. All it can offer you is agony.'

Jamie would have had to have been made from stone not to be affected by the heart-baring passion of Stefan's speech. He spoke from burning conviction and with a sincerity that revealed the inner man in such a way that Jamie felt both awed and privileged to receive his confidence.

'You really feel strongly about things, don't you?' Jamie said, and was aware that he sounded banal.

'I care,' said Stefan, 'if that's what you mean. I care deeply.'

Jamie grinned.

'Being a realist seems to have problems, too. You seem to be carrying around more than your fair share of that agony you talked about.'

'If only there was a ray of hope,' Stefan murmured, almost to himself.

'There's always hope,' Jamie declared, his optimism reasserting itself. He pointed out that Stefan's friends all got on well enough together in spite of a wide assortment of ethnic origins and religions. Take Mara and her brother: they were from Croatia, came from a Catholic family and spoke German in the home. Stefan himself was a Serb from an Eastern Orthodox background. Jusuf, the student from Bosnia who often joined them at the Dancing Bear, was Muslim. Then there were the two Montenegrin boys who were part of the crowd; one was a Muslim and the other was an out-and-out atheist who thought Stalin was the light of the world. Surely – Jamie pointed out – if so many young people could get together, if only to talk and argue, then there was hope for Jugoslavia. They were the country's future.

'Maybe I do feel things too strongly,' Stefan conceded. He smiled at Jamie, liking him for his optimism and reasonableness. There was a sadness in his voice, however, as he reflected on Jamie's grounds for hope.

'I sometimes fear, Jamie, that being young is the only thing we all have in common. We're young and we like to think of ourselves as civilised, principled and rational. Right now, all of us are in our own ways rebelling against the restraints and prejudices we grew up with. We are kicking against all the ills that weren't of our own making, the wrongs we've inherited which face our generation. . . . But what will happen when we're all part of the real world and the real battle lines are drawn up . . . when we have to stand or fall by the choices we make individually? How many of us will have the strength or guts to make a complete break with the past? How many of us will go scurrying back to the barricades that our fathers and grandfathers built, because only there will we feel safe from the future?'

There were times when Stefan's intellectual ranging left Jamie floundering in his wake and he felt obliged to return the conversation to a more mundane level. This was one such occasion. He did not share his friend's compulsion to be so gloomy about the future.

'What do you say we let tomorrow take care of itself, Stefan?' Jamie entreated brightly. 'Things are never as bad as they seem. Do you know what my father used to say to patients who worried too much about things that might never happen? Cheer up, he used to tell them, we never died of winter yet.'

Stefan looked at him, puzzled.

'It does not get cold in Scotland in winter?'

Jamie laughed.

'It gets very cold. But that isn't what my father meant.

It was his way of saying that while there's life, there's hope . . . that other winters had been survived and that the present one was nothing to worry about. Summer would come just the same – and better times.'

Stefan glanced sideways at Jamie.

'Your father, he was like you, eh? An optimist?' he said. But Jamie had gone suddenly thoughtful.

'Yes. Yes, I suppose he was,' Jamie answered absently.

'Is something wrong?'

'It was just a thought. Something that never occurred to me before. About my father. It seems ironic now, him always saying about never dying from winter . . . because it was winter that killed him in the end. He went out in the snow, to a patient. He shouldn't have gone. He might have been alive today if he hadn't gone. . . .'

Jamie had stopped walking, lost for a moment in private thoughts. Stefan halted, a pace ahead, and stared at him, feeling and sharing his friend's sudden sadness. When he spoke, it was no more than a whisper; but Jamie was always to remember the words, offered in comfort but in that tense, prophetic way of Stefan's, as if his eyes could see into the dense mists of the future.

'It was your father's choice, Jamie, to go into the snow. He had to go, no matter what. He was committed to his path. You will do it, too, Jamie, when the time comes and you commit yourself to the way you must go. You will see your path as clearly as I see mine . . . a path that leaves no choice because our feet are already on it. We shall both go out in the snow.'

2

Commitments

One of Milan Alexandrovic's greatest joys was to witness and encourage his nephew's enthusiasm for the culinary delights prepared by the household's venerable cook-housekeeper, Lucija. The old woman had been in Milan's service for years and was a law unto herself. She had resented the arrival of Milan's sister until Jelena Kyle had made it plain that she had no wish to interfere with the old woman's absolute rule of the kitchen. For all that, the relationship between the two women was one of uneasy coexistence. Jelena had no cause to complain of the quality of old Lucija's cooking, which was superb, but she did have reservations about the quantities of food set before the family, which she deemed excessive. Lucija, on the other hand, was impatient with the way that Jelena picked at her excellent fare like a finicky sparrow.

The outcome was that Jelena took to retreating early from the dinner table, rather than witness the spectacle of Jamie attacking a second helping of dessert while his uncle applauded and old Lucija looked on indulgently. With the excuse that she would drink her coffee in the next room and catch her favourite programme on the radio, Jelena sought to avoid the impression that her withdrawal was an outright admission of defeat.

By the time Jamie's university term had begun and there was a wintry bite in the winds that blew down from the plains of the Vojvodina, Jelena Kyle's early departures from the dinner table had become a habit more than a mark of disapproval and, if the truth be told, both

Jamie and his uncle would have been sorry if it had been otherwise. It became their habit to linger over cups of thick Turkish coffee and talk, getting to know each other and making up for all those years of separate existence a continent apart.

Milan Alexandrovic represented a life experience and set of values that were quite different from those Jamie encountered with Stefan, Mara and their young student friends.

Jamie had no doubt that to Stefan, for instance, Uncle Milan would appear conservative and reactionary – a traditionalist riddled with prejudices. But when Milan related to Jamie the experiences that had left him with a hatred of the Turks (as Milan termed all sons of Islam), his aversion to Muslims seemed thoroughly justified. Milan's devotion to private enterprise was another thing of which Stefan might not have altogether approved. Milan was a self-made man who had started with nothing but one pair of hands and the will to work, and he despised those radicals who fomented labour unrest and paralysed the industries on which their members depended for a livelihood. He did not dispute the fact that many employers exploited a surplus of labour in the market-place but the answer, he believed, was not to drive the creators of wealth out of business. They had to be enlightened, not destroyed. Milan considered himself to be an enlightened employer. He paid a fair day's pay for a fair day's work. And woe betide the outsider who tried to to tell him what he could or could not afford to put in his workers' wage packets.

Milan Alexandrovic lived well but not ostentatiously . His house was a large one for a bachelor's residence but far from grand for a man of his means. It was a roomy single-storey building, a thirty-minute tram ride to the south-east of the city. The house itself was L-shaped, forming two sides of a rectangle that was completed by a high wall enclosing a pleasant garden. An arched door from the dining room led to the garden, and it was Milan's pleasure, during the summer evenings after dinner, to fill his pipe and stroll in the shady garden amid the dwarf cypresses and sweeping wall-trained grandeur of purple-leafed plum and Japanese cherry. Very occasionally, Jamie joined his uncle on this ritual perambulation of the garden's paved walks and shady corners – and he did so at his uncle's invitation one October evening when Lucija had served *palacinke* for dessert and Jamie had been regaling his uncle with an account of his first week at University.

'Is it true that there is much feeling against the King at the University?' Milan asked Jamie, as he stoked his pipe.

Jamie shrugged.

'Yes and no. Those who are for the King don't shout about it. And those who are against him look over their shoulders to see who is listening before they say anything. Even then, they are very guarded in their criticism.'

'What kind of things do they say, Jamie?'

'They say the King is the dupe of some army general or other, who is the real boss. Nobody has a good word for the dictatorship. They say that Jugoslavia will never be able to call itself a free country until there is a return to democracy.'

'And is that what you think, Jamie?' Milan asked.

'I don't know what to think,' Jamie confessed. 'I don't know enough about it. The more I hear, the more confused I become.'

'Don't you let anyone run down the King,' Milan advised. 'He is a good man and has an almost impossible job. It wasn't his fault that the politicians made a mess of things. We would still have parliamentary government and free elections if the politicians had done the job they were elected to do. Instead they made the Parliament a battleground. It was a disgrace.'

'I didn't know it was that bad.'

'Good heavens, Jamie, a Member of Parliament was shot dead on the floor of the house! The King had to act. That's why he imposed dictatorship. We would have had bloody anarchy if he hadn't.'

'But haven't things gone too far the other way?' Jamie asked, mindful of all the things he had heard from Stefan and Mara and the others. 'There's a boy at the University whose father was sent to jail because he protested about prisoners being tortured for their political beliefs.'

'The man was probably a Communist,' said Milan.

'He wasn't,' Jamie declared. 'According to my friend Stefan, he was one of the most respected men in the country – a Serbian. I think he said he was a Christian Socialist or Democratic Socialist . . . something like that. Anyway, he'd been a Member of Parliament when there was a Parliament . . .'

'He must have broken the law. He wouldn't be sent to jail for nothing.'

'They say his only crime was saying in public what everybody else is saying in private.'

Jamie's uncle pondered this unhappily.

'There are things that happen that make me uneasy,' he admitted. 'Injustices. . . . But it is a difficult time, Jamie.'

Jamie had never mentioned to his uncle or mother the story of his brush with the secret police. Now he told his uncle. The older man was plainly worried by the revelation.

'Perhaps you should say nothing about this to your mother,' he counselled cautiously. 'She worries enough about what you get up to with your young friends. And Jamie, you must promise me, for heaven's sake, don't get into any arguments with these government cops. These fellows don't play games.'

'I've got no intention of getting into arguments with

them,' Jamie said, with some feeling. 'But what if they pick on me? From what I hear – and I believe it – they're just a bunch of thugs.'

'They won't touch you, Jamie, unless you give them some excuse. Just don't give them any excuse.'

'Does that mean you approve of them, Uncle Milan?' Jamie could not keep disappointment at his uncle from his tone of voice and from his questioning eyes.

The older man was perplexed.

'It's got nothing to do with me approving of them or disapproving,' he said, a trifle edgily. 'I don't particularly like their methods but that is by the way . . . I wouldn't thank you for the job they have to do. They've got their work cut out, dealing with murderers and terrorists, and you can't afford to be namby-pamby with them. You've got to meet violence with violence.'

'You *do* approve of them!' Jamie exclaimed in shocked tones, and the accusation seemed to cause his uncle physical pain.

'No, Jamie, no.' Sorrow, rather than anger, filled the older man's eyes. 'Whether I like it or not, they *exist*. That's all I'm saying. I don't approve of them any more than I approve of bomb-throwers and assassins – but they exist, too. And as long as you have one, you'll have the other.'

'But I'm not a murderer!' Jamie protested. 'My friends aren't murderers!'

Milan Alexandrovic sighed.

'I know they're not, Jamie. But how can I make you see?' He groped for words, anxious to heal the breach that suddenly seemed to have arisen between him and this boy, whom he loved like a son. 'You are young, Jamie. And your friends are young. And the young are impetuous. They see things simply, although nothing on this earth is ever quite as simple as it appears. Take my word for it, because no one was more impetuous as a young man than I was. Right was right and wrong was wrong and there was nothing in between. But I am older now and my judgements are greyer. Nowadays, what is right is a long way from being wholly perfect, and what is wrong is never wholly imperfect. Take this country, Jamie. It's a long way from being the ideal place we thought we could make it after the war – but it's a lot better than the place it was, even with political police and anarchists who blow up passenger trains and kill innocent people.' Milan Alexandrovic paused, realising that he was straying from the point he was trying to make. 'What am I trying to say?' he asked with a rueful smile. 'Am I asking you not to be impetuous, Jamie? Not to be young? Not to make mistakes? Or not to judge me too harshly because I have neither the will nor the power to change the things that you would like to change? No, I am asking none of these things. All I am asking is that you take care. Do not seek out trouble – because it is easily found. Let trouble find you, if it must. But don't go looking for it. Don't get involved with the political hotheads at the University. You concentrate on your work and, if you want to take your mind off that, find yourself a nice little Serbian girl. . . . But don't tell your mother I told you.'

Jamie laughed. That last bit of advice was somehow typical of Uncle Milan, offered as seriously as all that had gone before. It made whole again any breach in the almost conspiratorial bond between uncle and nephew, overriding the dismay Jamie felt at Uncle Milan's seeming acceptance of institutions like the secret police as a necessary evil. Uncle Milan was tolerant enough to make allowance for the impetuous nature of youth, and it behoved Jamie to be equally tolerant of his uncle's conservative attitudes in return. What had shone through the older man's rather uncertain homily was his deep concern for Jamie and, recognising this, Jamie could only respond with understanding and affection.

'You have my solemn promise that I won't let myself

be led astray,' he assured his uncle with a broad smile. Then he added: 'Unless it's by one of those wonderful Serbian girls you recommend!'

Milan bellowed with laughter, happy that the easy rapport that had existed between them was unimpaired. He put an arm round Jamie's shoulder as they continued their stroll round the garden.

'You gladden my heart,' he told Jamie, with a gush of warmth. 'That's why I subject you to my well-meaning lectures. You must find me a boring old antique most of the time. I suppose I've done well enough in a business sense, but I've made so many mistakes in the private running of my life that I scarcely qualify to be anyone's philosopher and guide.'

'I don't find what you say boring,' Jamie quickly asserted.

'It's kind of you to say so, Jamie, but I know I've never profited as much as I should have done from the lessons life has taught me. Some devil in me has prompted me to make the same mistakes over and over again, instead of changing my ideas. There's a stubborn streak in us Serbs, a kind of pride that is our most precious virtue and our worst fault at the same time. Take the way I feel about the Turks. . . . '

'You don't like them,' Jamie said, with a smile at his own understatement.

Unlce Milan acknowledged it with an answering smile.

'I hate them with my blood,' he affirmed. 'And with the blood of my father and my father's father and with the blood of his father's father before him. The Church teaches us to forgive our enemies, but five hundred years of hating cannot be changed into love and forgiveness overnight. Perhaps it will take another five hundred years to reconcile the Cross with the Crescent . . . perhaps a thousand . . . maybe a million. . . .'

'Perhaps never,' said Jamie, awed by the bleakness of the thought.

'My blood says never,' Milan agreed. 'And yet my heart questions such hopelessness for humanity. It illustrates, Jamie, what a mass of contradictions we humans are. Take me – the way I hate the Turk. Nothing will change me. I will hate the Turk till the day I die, and I may curse him with my last breath. But look at this house of mine and this garden, which I love – and damn me for my inconsistency.'

Jamie did not get the point his uncle was making. Milan was quick to elaborate.

'The Turk has given me this garden. Its whole concept of peace and shade is Turkish.' He made a sweeping gesture with his hand. 'I can embrace all this. The architecture of my house is Turkish.' He thrust his glowing pipe in front of Jamie, so that its pungent vapours tickled at his nostrils. 'Even the tobacco that I smoke is Turkish. How is it, Jamie, that I can cherish and embrace so much that the Turk has given me but would sooner die than kiss the cheek of the man who bows on his mat to Mecca?'

There may have been an answer to Milan Alexandrovic's question, but Jamie could not think of it.

Some miles away across the city, a different question was left unanswered by another young man. Bradislav Mannion – Brad to his friends – hestitated to tell the truth to the middle-aged consular officer who had put the question to him. The two men were sitting on opposite sides of a table in a small office in the US Embassy, a room that was spartanly furnished and used only for interviews where a degree of privacy was required.

'I'll ask the question again, Mr Mannion,' the consular officer said. 'You have stated that the object of your visit to Belgrade was to find a man whose name you do not know but who is known as "the Chauffeur". What do you intend to do if you find him?'

Mannion smiled.

'I shall probably kill him,' Mannion said.

'Very droll, Mr Mannion. And what will you plead when you are arraigned before a Jugoslav court for murder? Insanity?'

'How about justifiable homicide?' Mannion suggested. 'Or maybe self-defence? The rumour is that this guy has boasted that he will put so many bullets in me that I'll look like dogmeat . . . like my grandfather and my cousin and my cousin's husband and their four-year-old daughter.'

The official stared hard at Mannion.

'You really do intend to take the law into your own hands?' he said. It was a statement edged with disbelief.

'You asked me what I would do if I found the man I'm looking for. I outlined a probability,' Mannion said. 'I was being realistic. My intention is to bring this man to justice, one way or the other. It would be unrealistic to imagine he will come quietly, so I am anticipating that it may be the other.'

'You're crazy,' said the official.

Mannion smiled.

'So I've been told. More than once.'

'You are also placing this embassy and the US Government in an invidious position – one that they have no intention of tolerating.'

'I'm not asking for your blessing,' Mannion replied. 'And I don't need your protection. I can look after myself.'

'They may write these words on your tombstone, Mr Mannion,' the official said, with an icy glare. 'What you do not seem to appreciate is that, whereas you may feel no responsibility towards the United States, the United States is obliged to exercise responsibility for you, as one of her citizens.'

'I absolve them of that responsibility. The State Department guy I saw in Washington made it quite clear that you people have no jurisdiction in crimes committed by non-US citizens against non-US citizens outside of the United States. So you don't need to bother your goddamned ass about me.'

The official kept calm, with visible effort.

'Kindly moderate your language, Mr Mannion. Unfortunately, we cannot absolve ourselves of responsibility with quite the ease that you dispose of yours. We have a duty to you and we intend to exercise it whether you like it or not. Where are you staying in Belgrade?'

'At the Hotel Moscow.'

'That's as good as anywhere,' the official said, scribbling down the information. 'It will only be for tonight.'

'What do you mean, just for tonight?' Mannion demanded, angry.

'Because you'll be leaving Jugoslavia tomorrow, Mr Mannion. And just to show how generous, we'll supply you with a first-class rail ticket. Have you any particular preference? Shall we say Vienna? Or Milan? Just you name it. The tickets will be delivered to you at the Hotel Moscow before nine o'clock tomorrow morning.'

'You can't run me out of the country,' Mannion protested.

'Oh, but we can, Mr Mannion,' the official retorted smugly. 'And we will! You see, your presence here is a great embarrassment to us, Mr Mannion, and an embarrassment to the Royal Jugoslav Government, with whom we happen to be on the friendliest of terms. If you are not out of the country within twenty-four hours, Mr Mannion, we shall withdraw the privileges you enjoy as an American citizen and shall arrange for your removal by the Jugoslav authorities. In which case, you will certainly not be leaving first-class.'

The official clasped his hands in front of him and stared at Mannion with a look on his face that said the interview was over. Mannion felt an urge to punch the smug face. He resisted it.

'I'm not going,' he said bluntly. 'When I start out to do a job, I finish it.'

'You're adopting a very foolish attitude, Mr Mannion. The Jugoslav police have been searching for your grandfather's killer for nearly a year. What makes you think that you will succeed where they have failed?'

'Because the Jugoslav police couldn't give a god-damn. They say the motive was robbery and not a goddamn thing was stolen. They say nobody saw the killer, but I know that three witnesses saw the guy hanging round the railroad station and gave the police descriptions. I also know that the descriptions tallied with a hoodlum who is wanted for more than forty murders already.'

'This man you call "the Chauffeur"?' the official prompted, with the air of one who is exercising extreme patience.

'He has used dozens of aliases, but that's how he advertises himself for hire – as "the Chauffeur". Only, it's his gun that's for hire. He ain't no driver in a fancy hat.'

'You seem to know a great deal for someone who hadn't set foot in Jugoslavia until yesterday.'

'I have my sources,' Mannion said quietly.

'Oh, yes, that expatriate Serbo-Croat society in New York. What do they call themselves – the Sons of Freedom? Mostly construction workers, I'm told. Your father was a founder member, I believe? What was his name before it became Mannion?'

'It happened to be Djurkovic. And yeah, he was a construction worker – until an accident put him in a wheelchair. I was in the construction business myself. There something wrong with that?'

'You should have stayed in the construction business, Mr Mannion. I suppose it was the Sons of Freedom who put up the money for this crazy one-man crusade of yours?'

'They helped with the boat fare. That's all. I've staked every last dollar I've got in coming here, mister.'

The official sighed.

'It's a pity that rag the New York *Daily News* ran that stupid story on you, Mr Mannion.'

'That wasn't my doing.'

'Nevertheless, it has proved rather an embarrassment to us. The Royal Jugoslav Government have made it clear that they do not welcome the interference of foreigners in their domestic affairs, especially when there are political undertones.'

'Oh,' said Mannion, brightening, 'then they're admitting it *is* political?'

'No, they are satisfied that the murder of your relatives was the work of a thief with psychopathic tendencies. The political element is supplied by your grandfather's reputation. He tended to be rather outspoken, although no one seems to be very sure what school of political thought he represented. He hit out at everything – the Government, the Separatists, the Muslims, the Catholic Church, the Orthodox Church . . . you name it, he was against it.'

Mannion got to his feet.

'And that puts it in a nutshell, don't it?' he demanded. 'That's why nobody gives a goddamn who gunned him down or why! Well, this is one guy who does give a goddamn and aims to do something about it! And to hell with you, the US Government and the Royal Jugoslav Government! So, mister, you just keep your rail tickets and tell your Jugoslav friends not to bother'n come looking for me, because I got business to take care of! Family business!'

Mannion turned on his heel and walked out of the room. He ignored the angry official's shout to come back and stop acting like a fool. He continued to ignore the man, who followed him into the corridor as he strode towards the hallway and main entrance. Warnings that he was heading for trouble and that he would be sorry followed Mannion all the way. No one tried to stop him leaving the building.

It was a cool evening and Mannion had no coat. He turned up his jacket collar against the chill and walked briskly. The Terazije had all but been deserted by the evening promenaders when he got there. Reaching the Hotel Moscow, he pushed past a trickle of customers heading for the Cellar Bar. A clerk with a magnificent Serbian moustache was on duty at the hotel desk. Mannion approached him and asked for his room key.

'Can you tell me if there are any trains to Subotica tonight?' he enquired, as his key was placed on the desk before him. The man consulted a railway timetable, which he fished from a drawer. Yes, there was a train to Subotica. One left in just over an hour's time. Was the gentleman checking out?

Yes, Mannion was checking out. He paid his bill and arranged for a porter to call at his room in fifteen minutes. There was one heavy suitcase, which he wanted carried to the railway station.

Upstairs in his room, Mannion packed some shirts and toiletries into a small attaché case, transferring them from a heavy suitcase. From deep in the suitcase, he took a towel-wrapped bundle and unrolled it on his bed, revealing a small oilskin package. He opened it and removed a small Frommer automatic that snuggled there. He pocketed the weapon and slipped two packets of cartridges into another pocket. By the time the porter called to collect the suitcase, it was repacked, locked and waiting for him, and Mannion was ready to leave.

He walked to the railway station, with the porter a few paces behind, hefting the big suitcase on his shoulder. At the station, Mannion paid off the porter and then deposited the suitcase at the left-luggage office. Then, carrying the small attaché case and with his coat slung over an arm, he made his way to the ticket counter and purchased a ticket to Zagreb.

The train to Zagreb pulled out twenty minutes before the train for Subotica was due to leave. Mannion was on it.

It was soon after Jamie had made his promise to his Uncle Milan that he would not get involved with 'political hotheads' that he noticed a subtle but discernible change in Stefan. Jamie classed neither Stefan nor Mara as 'hotheads', despite their passionate interest in political matters, so he did not for a moment consider that his continued association with his two closest friends ran counter to the assurance he had given his uncle. Nor did he give the new strangeness in Stefan's behaviour a political connotation. Had Jamie but known it, however, Stefan had made a decision of political commitment that was to affect not only the course of his own life but also to have a profound influence on the lives of all around him.

What Jamie noticed about Stefan was a secretiveness in his manner. He became more withdrawn, as if carrying some private burden that he would not or could not discuss with his friends. There was, too, his odd reaction when a leading magazine accepted and published one of his short stories, acclaiming the literary talent of the young author.

Mara went into ecstasies over Stefan's success and Jamie was quick to add his congratulations, but Stefan rejected her adulatory joy with such untypical anger and cruelty that relations between them cooled noticeably. Mara carried her hurt like a sad-eyed puppy that had been unjustly whipped. Stefan, while rejecting Jamie's congratulations, did so less brutally. Stefan's misery at his success bewildered Jamie.

'What's got into you, Stefan?' Jamie asked, perplexed. 'You should be over the moon at being hailed as the literary find of the generation. Instead, you're acting like a bear with a sore head. Aren't you *pleased*?'

'Pleased? Pleased!' Stefan echoed, like a man in torment. 'To realise that I am a prostitute. Because that is what I am! I have sold myself and everything I believe for a few pieces of silver. I am ashamed!'

'But why, Stefan? Why should you be ashamed? Everybody on the campus is talking about your story and how good it is. You're famous.'

'Famous?' Stefan dismissed the notion with contempt. 'I should feel pride at being a *famous* prostitute? I did it for money, Jamie. I despise that magazine and all it stands for. It is the antithesis of all I believe. Oh, it's good for my ego, for the writer in me, to know that my talent has commercial value. But I know now that I would rather bury my talent in the ground than sell it like a whore to editors who masquerade as creative thinkers and lovers of truth and who, in reality, are only the toadying mouthpieces of the ruling class. I have corrupted myself, Jamie, by selling myself to those morally bankrupt jackals who applaud and perpetuate all that's rotten and stinks in our unjust society. But never again, Jamie! Never again! I will give up writing. . . .'

Jamie was aghast.

'But your writing is the most important thing in your life. It's what you live for!'

'*Was* the most important thing,' Stefan corrected him. 'I have rearranged my priorities. I have decided that more important than what I might want to live for is what I would die for.'

Jamie felt a prickle of fear for his friend. He was so intense. A fire burned in his eyes with a radiance that contrasted sharply with the dark sockets and emphasised the drawn pallor of his face, giving him a fevered look. Stefan was consumptive, Jamie knew, but this fever was not organic to the body. It had other origins. Stefan's fever was of the soul. Jamie was silent, afraid to ask Stefan the nature of the cause that took precedence over the literary ambitions to which he had previously been wholly dedicated. The answer, he feared, would betray a monumental folly; a folly from which Stefan would not be dissuaded; a folly that had the smell of disaster.

'Don't ask me any questions,' Stefan told him, as if sensing the fear his startling revelation had provoked. 'I've only known you a short time, but you are as dear a friend as I possess and I don't want you to suffer for what my conscience forces me to do. I hope we can always be friends, no matter what.'

'You know we will.' The words came almost as a cry from Jamie, who found the portentous seriousness of Stefan deeply disturbing. It was as if all the laughter and joy of life had gone out of his friend, and it seemed wrong to Jamie that this should be so. They were young and should be exuberant, instead of facing each other as if it was their last day on earth. 'What is it you've done, Stefan?' Jamie cried out in an emotion-charged voice. 'What is it you've done?'

'I've made a choice, Jamie. That's all.' Stefan's voice was quiet, devoid of emotion. 'I've been looking at myself and I didn't like what I saw. I saw a weak-minded fellow with pretensions about being a great writer . . . one who was being seduced by the flattery of false fame and easy money. All he had to do was to conform, to lock away all his ideals in a closet where they could be conveniently forgotten. That was the easy path, Jamie. That was the way I was tempted to go. It was so much more comfortable than the other path – the path that offered only torment and suffering for remaining faithful to the truths that are holy to me. I had to choose my path, Jamie, and the choice I've made is not for the comfortable option – because to go that way, I could never have kept my self-respect. I can't leave it to others to fight for the kind of world I want to see, Jamie. I've got to take up arms with them. I've got to be part of the struggle . . . of the revolution that must come.'

That was the closest Stefan came to revealing the precise nature of the irrevocable course to which he had committed himself or his reasons for doing so. He did not say that the decision he had made – one he saw as a personal crossing of the Rubicon in its fatefulness – was to join the Communist Party. To Stefan, it was an act of similar significance to embracing a faith that would hold him fast for life and taking holy vows. It was certainly an act of great significance in the Jugoslavia of 1934.

Of all the forces at work for change in that trouble-torn country at the time, the Communists had appealed to Stefan's idealistic imagination more than any other, for two compelling reasons. They were the most consistent in their opposition to injustice and they were the most brutally persecuted. Their refusal to change or dilute their political beliefs and readiness to martyr themselves appealed to all that was noble and heroic in Stefan's Serbian blood, and all his Slav compassion was aroused by the suffering they endured. He could not comprehend the Christianity of the Orthodox priesthood who acquiesced, even actively engaged, in the persecution of this humble minority who spoke up for the poor and oppressed. It was as if the Pharisees had taken over the movement that had originally exposed their corruption and hypocrisy.

To Stefan, the Communist movement had appeared to have much more in common with the early Christian brotherhood than the Apostles' successors, who paraded in vestments of gold and paid lip service to the creed to 'love thy neighbour as thyself'. Indeed, there were other similarities between the first disciples of Christ and the Jugoslavs who preached twentieth-century revolution. One did not *join* the Jugoslav Communist brotherhood, an organisation that enjoyed no status in law; the brothers were 'called' and admitted only if they were found worthy. And the call to serve offered only rewards of pain, persecution and death. The faithful were not even given the lure of paradise in the call to serve; not one that they would see at any rate. Their sacrifice today, however, might lead to an earthly paradise into which the children of their children's children could be born. This was the glory that they held before them: that, with their blood today they could buy paradise for the unborn. For sustenance, they looked to the east and the glorious sunrise that had ushered in the day of a new society in Russia. Serbians had long memories of Russia's help and succour in times past, and the bond remained mystic despite that country's not infrequent abandonment of their Balkan brothers when self-interest dictated. Past betrayals could be laid at the door of the Czars, however, not the people. In Russia now the proletariat reigned and were building the foundations of a new freedom that would sweep the world.

Jugoslavia's infant Communist Party – which had provided fifty deputies to the post-war Parliament of the newly unified country – had all but been destroyed in the upheavals that followed the end of parliamentary rule. Its leaders had been killed, imprisoned, or harried into exile, and it had virtually ceased to exist as an organised political force. By 1934, the Party was beginning to reorganise with the establishment of clandestine cells. Ostensibly, these cells took their orders from a caucus of leaders in exile in Paris, who transmitted their wishes by means of Moscow-trained Jugoslavs smuggled into the homeland. Communication between the various groups of activists was poor, however, and bedevilled by factional rivalries and the political police, who had the aid of an army of paid informers.

It was into this web of intrigue and clandestine war that Stefan Markovic threw himself with his eyes wide open. It was a world where the identities of its inhabitants were hidden by false names and forged papers, where meetings were conspiratorial and cloaked in secrecy, where communications were whispered from behind the hand and furtiveness was a way of life.

It was a measure of Stefan's trust of Jamie and Mara that he had been prepared to confide the little he did, for to confide anything at all was dangerous. It only needed a careless word, spoken in all innocence, to betray the confidence.

Mara was more hurt than Jamie by the change that came over Stefan, by his furtiveness, his reluctance to embroil her in his dangerous activities. So noble in mind did Stefan appear to her that she would have embraced any cause he had chosen with equal fervour. But Stefan did not give her the chance. And the pain of being shut out was almost more than she could bear. She did not appreciate that if her 'political enlightenment' had been born of her own intellect and not of blind devotion to him, Stefan would have had no inhibitions about sharing his mission with her.

A consequence was that Mara turned more to Jamie for the companionship and closeness that Stefan had previously provided. Jamie was only too happy to give her all the consolation she needed. Stefan, because his cause demanded more of his time, saw less of them than in the past – with the result that Jamie found himself, more and more often, exclusively in Mara's company of the sorrowing girl.

He felt elated when they walked through the botanical gardens and she took his arm in hers and their thighs brushed as they walked. He floated on a cloud after she had proffered her lips for a goodnight kiss. That first kiss was rather chaste in its brevity. But the second, two nights later, was limb-shaking in its passion and sent Jamie home in a state of euphoria.

Next day, in the Russian class, they sat together and exchanged scribbled notes in which each tried to outdo the other in composing outrageous nicknames for the Professor of Russian. He was a fierce-looking man with a terrifying manner, and they tried to improve on the label of 'Ivan the Terrible' given to him by the students.

After class, Mara asked Jamie if he would like to keep her company at an imminent meeting of one of the Croatian societies she had joined. It sounded deadly dull to Jamie – a guest speaker, followed by chat and coffee – but he had no hesitation in agreeing to go. The prospect of walking Mara back to her lodgings afterwards filled him with anticipation. He thought of nothing else that evening as the tram carrying him home from University rattled through the streets that were wet with autumn rain.

He was only vaguely aware of something unusual in the evening stir beyond the rain-streaked glass through which he stared – a lot of police about and, in King Milan Street, dozens of soldiers were milling about in the vicinity of the Royal Palace. It was a passenger boarding the tram who startled the homeward-bound commuters and provoked a hubbub of excited talk by tersely announcing the reason for the commotion.

'It's because of the King,' he shouted at the sea of faces. 'There's just been an announcement on the radio! He's been shot! It happened just after he landed in France.'

'Is he dead?' someone asked in a shocked voice.

'I don't know,' the bearer of the tidings confessed. 'They said only that he is gravely wounded and that the country must be ready to expect the worst.'

Mannion heard the news of the King's assassination in Zagreb. He had been in the city a week, staying at the home of a contact whose name he had been given in New York. The only occasion he had ventured out during daylight had been to purchase nondescript clothes and a pair of worker's boots at the market. He had crammed his American-made suit and smart city shoes into another purchase, a rude canvas carrier bag, and he intended to leave them there indefinitely. If the police were looking for him, the clothes were a giveaway.

It was from the Zagreb contact that the Sons of Freedom in New York had received the information that the gunman who had killed Mannion's grandfather and the other three occupants of his car was the man known as 'the Chauffeur'. The contact's name was Kosta, and he had been less than overjoyed when Mannion arrived at his house in the middle of the night, seeking his help. Kosta nevertheless offered the hospitality of his tiny three-roomed home in the Kaptol to the stranger and tried to conceal his dismay at the news that his guest might be the object of a police hunt. It was Kosta's idea that Mannion got rid of his conspicuous American clothes and laid low during daylight.

'Now you are here, you had better stay,' Kosta told Mannion, 'but it would be safer for both of us if we keep it secret that you are in my house, and if we are never seen together outside.'

It became plain to Mannion that Kosta was afraid of more than discovery by the police. He seemed regretful now that he had passed information on to New York, where his three brothers lived. It had never crossed his imagination that a relative of poor old Djurkovic would come hot-footing it from America thirsting for revenge – at least, not in a way that involved him. He had heard, of course, about the story concerning Mannion in the New York newspaper but he had not taken it seriously. Very few had – especially the man called 'the Chauffeur' and the crowd he ran about with. They thought it was a great joke.

'You know these people?' Mannion inquired.

The question made Kosta uncomfortable.

'I hear a lot,' he hedged. 'In the bar where I work. But it can be unhealthy to talk too much.'

'You told your brothers in New York about "the Chauffeur".'

68

'I tell them everything I hear. Much of it is gossip and doesn't mean anything. And my brothers are far enough away for it not to matter.'

'But it mattered to me, Mr Kosta. Enough to bring me five thousand miles.'

'Why, Mr Mannion? Why?'

'Because the man who killed my grandfather and my cousin and her little daughter is walking around free, and nobody seems to be doing a goddamned thing about it! That's why, Mr Kosta!'

'And what do you hope to achieve?'

'I want to see this killer brought to justice – and the people who were behind him.'

Kosta stared at Mannion in disbelief. He said, pityingly: 'You are naive. You just don't know what you're up against, do you?'

'You tell me.'

'Do you know why your grandfather was killed, Mr Mannion?'

'The police say the motive was robbery . . . that he was the victim of a madman. I don't believe that.'

'Only a fool would,' Kosta agreed. 'Your grandfather died because he disapproved of violence and he was opposed to Croatia's separation from Serbia. He had a lot of influence with supporters of what was the old Croatian Peasant Party. And he had no time for the Pavelic Nationalists with their strong-arm methods and their Fascist money. He never missed a chance to call Pavelic all the names under the sun and heap ridicule on his Italian and Hungarian paymasters. "Mussolini's performing hyena" was what he called Pavelic. It was asking for trouble – as good as signing his own death warrant. "The Chauffeur" was paid to silence your grandfather, Mr Mannion. And everyone knows who paid to have it done.'

'This . . . this Pavelic?'

Kosta had shrugged expressively.

'Perhaps not Pavelic personally. But you can bet your last dinar that his Nationalist Revolutionaries were behind it. The trouble is that they hardly ever do their own dirty work. They hire foreigners, bravos from Italy and Bulgaria who take their money and run.'

'You think that "the Chauffeur" was a foreigner?' Kosta had laughed.

'Think? It's a certainty. From what I hear, he learned his trade as a hit-man with the VMRO – and that's another nasty bunch you don't want to tangle with.'

'Who are they?'

'They're the mob who want to make Macedonia part of Bulgaria.'

Mannion was disappointed.

'That means that he's probably gone back to wherever he came from . . . that he's not even in this country?'

'Not if all I hear is correct. The word is that Pavelic and his chums sent for him not very long ago. And, only a couple of weeks ago, a friend of mine was talking about three foreigners drinking in a bar where a lot of Pavelic's bully-boys hang out. My friend reckoned that one of them – a fat guy with a Bulgarian accent – was the famous Chauffeur.'

This news excited Mannion. He had not held out much hope of picking up the long-cold trail of his quarry in Zagreb. The discovery that the Chauffeur had possibly been in the city during the past month was a stroke of luck of extraordinary proportions: like striking gold. There were times, too, during the following week, when he felt that the seam he had struck was a rich one indeed. But the promising nuggets he succeeded in digging up turned out to be no more than that. The seam petered out.

Kosta, in spite of an anxiety not to become involved too deeply with Mannion and his quest, was extremely helpful. He told Mannion where he would find the informants who might be useful and how much money would be required to make them talk. All Kosta asked in return was Mannion's absolute discretion about his own role.

'You can take on the entire Croatian Revolutionary movement if you like,' he warned Mannion, 'but keep me out of it. I know when I'm outnumbered, and I want to go on living here. I don't want my body to be fished out of the Sava in half a dozen different places.'

So it was that when Kosta – a widower and a rather lonely man – went out to work at his barkeeper's job in the evenings, Mannion ventured out into the narrow streets of the Kaptol to do his rounds of those haunts where information could be traded if the money was right.

In spite of his market-bought garb, Mannion felt as conspicuous as a daffodil in a pot on these sorties – but it was not his clothes that drew second looks and polite inquiries. It was the way he spoke that identified him, if not as a foreigner, as a stranger from some far-flung corner of the kingdom. He learned to turn this to his advantage, admitting that he was not from these parts and saying that he was looking for three Bulgarian compatriots who, he had heard, had been living in the town.

The nuggets came slowly and he lost count of how many circuits of the high town and the low town he had made in extracting them. At the end of a week, he knew that he had found all he was going to find in Zagreb and that it was time to leave. Kosta endorsed this last conclusion. In the bar where he worked, a policeman had come in and asked Kosta if he had seen anything of an *American* who looked like a peasant, spoke with a Bulgarian accent, and was doling out dinars to half the riff-raff in town.

'So much for me pretending to be something I'm not!' Mannion lamented, a great deal more shaken than he cared to admit.

71

'I know this cop,' Kosta told him. 'He's as crooked as the road to Podplat. I don't think he was asking about you because the cops in Belgrade have put your name on the wire. What he's interested in are those dinars you've been handing out. He's sore at being missed out.'

'I still don't like it,' Mannion said. 'I think it's time I was getting back to Belgrade.'

Kosta agreed, and adamantly refused to take any money for the week Mannion had spent in his home. He was deeply hurt by Mannion's offer to compensate him and earnestly expressed the hope that his brothers in New York never got to hear of the offer. They would be equally ashamed that it had been made. He shrugged indifferently when Mannion asked him at least to accept his leather attaché case as a memento. The expensive quality of the case did not match Mannion's peasant clothes. He crammed everything he had into the canvas carrier.

He sauntered into the railway station in the lower end of the town an hour after dark, and almost lost his nerve when he saw the number of gendarmes mixing with the crowds and taking a suspicious interest in all the travellers. It was then that he learned from a voluble passer-by of King Alexander's assassination in Marseille. He joined the queue for tickets, filing past the little serving window of the booking office. Two gendarmes were eyeing everyone who approached the window. Mannion steeled himself to ignore them. He bought a second-class ticket to Belgrade.

When he left the head of the queue, one of the gendarmes tapped him on the shoulder.

'Where are you going?' he demanded.

'Belgrade,' Mannion answered, looking cowed. It was not pretence. He felt intimidated.

'Why are you going there?' the gendarme demanded.

'To look for work,' Mannion said. His heart was hammering. He was thinking that, of all the policemen in Zagreb, was this the nosey one who had been quizzing Kosta? He was never to find out because at that moment a commotion broke out at a ticket-barrier some thirty metres away. Two gendarmes were struggling with a big man, who was showing no intention of coming quietly. The two gendarmes who had stopped Mannion went racing to their colleagues' assistance.

The big man had a gun in his right hand, which was forced high above his head by one of the policemen who had seized him. The second gendarme had drawn his baton and was raining blows on the big man's head and face. The gun went flying from his hand, to be retrieved by Mannion's recent interrogator. The gunman was quickly overpowered. He went down, and the gendarmes made sure he stayed down. They continued to beat him mercilessly. More gendarmes arrived. The last Mannion saw of the gunman, he was being dragged away by the arms, feet trailing. His face was a mask of blood.

Mannion found a shadowy corner and sat there on his bag, willing the minutes to pass until the train was due. It was one of the longest hours of his life. It was not until he was seated, jammed in the corner of a crowded compartment, that he felt his tension begin to drain. A sigh of relief escaped him as the train began to move.

Wedged into a corner as he was, he closed his eyes and ears to the jabber of the other passengers and reflected on the results of a nerve-sapping week in Zagreb. What had it produced? More bad luck than good, perhaps. He knew now that his quarry, the infamous Chauffeur, had almost certainly been in Zagreb during the month of September. To some, he was known by the name Vlada, and nothing else. Mannion had discovered, however, that the same man had been using the name Petrus Kelemen. Furthermore, Mannion knew what Kelemen, or Vlada, looked like. He was black-haired, swarthy complexion, with a dark moustache. He was of medium height, but fat and bulky, weighing ninety kilos or more. He dressed well, if untidily: usually a dark suit and dark tie.

That was the extent of Mannion's good luck in his search for his grandfather's killer. The bad luck was the certainty that the Chauffeur had left Zagreb a week or more before Mannion arrived. He had left in the company of the two 'foreigners' with whom he had arrived. They had left by car, but to what destination was anybody's guess.

Mannion had just one lead. He knew the name of the car's owner: a Mr Vladimir Graz, who lived in Belgrade, where he was in the motor trade. Apparently he operated an agency for foreign cars. And he had been at the wheel of the car in which the Chauffeur and his cronies left Zagreb.

Belgrade had taken on the trappings of a city in mourning. The shock of the King's assassination and its manner had affected even people who were far from royalist in their sympathies. There was scarcely a household into which the national sense of horror had not reached. Wherever sympathies lay, the general consensus was that the tragedy did not bode well for Jugoslavia. Things would only get worse, not better. No good would come of it.

These were the sentiments that prevailed in the house of Milan Alexandrovic, and Jamie shared the gloom that seized his uncle and his mother. At the University, where anti-monarchist views were not uncommon, even the most vocal opponents of the monarchy were outraged by the assassination of Alexander and condemned it. Assassination was not the civilised route to political reform.

Jamie wondered if the declaration of national mourning would mean the cancellation of the Croatian Society evening to which Mara had invited him. Privately, he hoped that the meeting would be called off and they might go to the cinema instead, but Mara dashed these hopes. There was to be no cancellation, although the venue had been changed from the University precincts to a small meeting hall used by Catholic groups.

Less than thirty people turned up and, surveying the gathering, Jamie feared his suspicions that the formal part of the evening would be a bore were about to be confirmed. A talk by the guest was first on the agenda.

His name was Vladimir Graz.

3

The Meeting

The train journey from Zagreb to Belgrade took most of the night. There were interminable stops and long delays, for which no explanation was offered. Not sure what awaited him in Belgrade, Mannion endured the tedium and the discomfort without the relief of sleep. Others in the crowded compartment managed to snore contentedly throughout the stop-start journey, undisturbed by shrieking discharges of steam and the jarring violence of carriages colliding buffer to buffer.

There was a big police presence at the rail depot in Belgrade but Mannion shuffled through it, bag on shoulder, ignoring the importuning porters who vied for business. One porter was more persistent than the rest and followed Mannion out beyond the station precincts, offering his services at a pitiably reducing tariff.

'Do you know where I can find rooms?' Mannion was finally disposed to ask him. The man, scenting that his persistence was about to pay off, assured Mannion that there was nothing in Belgrade that he could not find for him. The outcome was that he led Mannion to a modest rooming house on Balkanska Street – where there were many such establishments – and acted as intermediary in negotiating the price of his lodgings. Mannion tipped him handsomely and won a friend for life. His gratitude moved Mannion to offer him further work, if he returned to the address later in the day.

The porter returned at noon and Mannion decided to trust him with the task of retrieving the luggage he had left at the station. The man was back within the hour, carrying Mannion's heavy bag, and was suitably over-joyed with Mannion's reward for his honesty. Still eager to be of service, he jumped at the opportunity to do some snooping on a Mr Vladimir Graz for Mannion – especially when the sum of money to be earned was mentioned. He did not seem to care that all Mannion had to go on was that Graz was a dealer in foreign cars, somewhere in Belgrade: he was confident of tracking him down. He went off with Mannion's exhortation about the necessity of discretion ringing in his ears. The conspiratorial nature of the assignment seemed to delight the porter, who showed no curiosity in Mannion's motives.

Mannion used the afternoon to shop for more clothes, purchasing a suit that was less outlandish than his Zagreb outfit. He wanted to be able to mingle with the city crowds without proclaiming an identifiable social status or announcing himself as 'foreign'. In the evening, he ate at a seedy café not far from his digs and then returned there to await the porter. But the man failed to show up that night.

It was late the following afternoon – when Mannion had all but convinced himself that he would not see the porter again – that he reappeared in Balkanska Street to confound all Mannion's doubts about him. The porter had had no difficulty in locating the business premises of Vladimir Graz – an office and yard near the Sava docks, where imported German cars were on sale to the status-conscious among Belgrade's *nouveaux-riches*.

Mr Graz himself, it appeared, was *nouveau-riche* and had a somewhat mysterious background. Nobody knew where his money had come from, although rumour had it that he was the front man for foreign interests other than the automobile company he represented. Some said his backers were Austrian. Others said that they were German and Hungarian. All agreed, however, that for a poor boy from a village near Zagreb, he had done very well for himself. He had an elegant city apartment and another home in Zagreb, where his wife and family preferred to stay.

Mannion was astonished by the amount of information that the porter had been able to unearth in so short a time and was curious to know just how he had achieved it.

'It was easy,' the porter said, and confessed that there were few secrets in Belgrade to which the portering fraternity did not have access. They had to keep in with hotel clerks, janitors, concierges, landladies and so on in order to get work, and heard all that was going on from them. It paid, of course, to turn a blind eye to a lot, but, if the price were right, information could be discreetly obtained by tapping the network.

The porter's chief informant had been the janitor of the apartment building where Graz lived. For a few dinars, he had been very loquacious on the subject of Mr Graz. And, for a few dinars more, he was prepared to be even more talkative. He was ready to provide the name and address of Graz's mistress and tell on which nights she visited him. The janitor had hinted, too, at questionable goings-on when Graz entertained businessmen from out of town: drinking parties, to which young women of doubtful virtue were invited.

The porter – who had somehow formed the impression that Mannion was seeking revenge on Graz because of a wrong done to a woman in his family – was disappointed that Mannion was more interested in Graz's male acquaintances than female ones. He was nonplussed when Mannion asked him if Graz was known to have any political associations.

'All I know is that the janitor is convinced that Graz fought for the Austrians during the war, and depises him for it. But the janitor is a Serb and he depises all Croats. He is an old Salonika soldier himself.'

Mannion allayed the porter's disappointment at not

being commissioned for more detective work by paying him off with a bonus on top of the promised reward. He was impatient to see the mysterious Graz for himself, preferably face to face.

His mind made up – but without any clear plan of action in mind – Mannion felt a quickening of the blood when he left the rooms in Balkanska Street to find the apartment building where Graz lived. The porter had said it was only twenty minutes' walk away and had given him directions. Mannion chose to walk, invigorated by the sharp evening air on his cheeks. The gun in his raincoat pocket bumped gently against his thigh as he walked. It afforded a kind of comfort.

From the porter's description, the building where Graz lived had sounded luxurious. To Mannion's eyes, it was a long way short of Fifth Avenue standard. The entry was guarded by a tiny windowed office, where the janitor sat surveying the gaslit hallway. There was an elevator in the centre of the stairwell: a venerable contraption enclosed by a wrought-iron grille from which the gilt paint was peeling to reveal dark metal below.

Mannion decided on a bold approach to the janitor.

'Can you tell me if Mr Graz is at home?' he asked.

'You're too early for Mr Graz,' the janitor informed him. 'He won't be in for another twenty minutes. You have business with him?'

'In a manner of speaking, yes,' Mannion said.

A knowing look crossed the janitor's face.

'You're the one who's so interested in him and his lady friends. You've come yourself this time, have you? Well, watch yourself with him, that's all I can say. He's a slippery one.'

'You don't seem to like him much,' Mannion said.

'I don't – and he knows it. He's not the same class as the other tenants – a jumped-up nobody, he is.' A frown of worry wrinkled the garrulous janitor's brow. 'You're not a friend of his, are you?'

'No,' Mannion said, and the janitor seemed relieved. 'I want to meet him, but I don't think he'll be very pleased to see me. Is there somewhere I can wait?'

'There's a café across the street. By the time you drink a coffee, he should be here.'

Mannion retired to the café, stopping only to buy a newspaper from a vendor. The table nearest the window was empty and he sat there, watching the front door of the apartment building across the top of the newspaper. He had no intention of reading the newspaper, which was full of King Alexander's assassination. But a sub-heading on the front page leapt out at him – or, at least, two words registered like a blow between the eyes.

'ASSASSIN NAMED BY FRENCH AS PETRUS KELEMEN' the heading shouted. *Petrus Kelemen*! Mannion could not believe his eyes. The Chauffeur! Mannion read how Kelemen had been lynched by the French crowd in the turmoil following the attack on the King's car.

Conflicting emotions raged in Mannion. He was glad that Kelemen was dead but, at the same time, he felt cheated. His mission of justice had been robbed of its prime purpose. It was awesome, too, to know that the forces that had destroyed a reigning monarch were also responsible for the cold-blooded massacre of his grandfather and other relatives. It was almost too much to take in. He read and re-read the news items about the King's murder so avidly that he forgot the purpose that had brought him to the café. While he was engrossed, Vladimir Graz – unaware even of Mannion's existence – entered the door opposite and rode the rickety elevator to his apartment on the fourth floor.

The elevator was operated by a big brass handle which protruded from a wheel-like casing the size of a dinner plate. The casing edge had been embossed with Latin numerals to indicate the floors. Mannion rotated the lever to 'IV'. Somewhere overhead, the winding machinery started with a whirring and clanking that reminded Mannion of a steeple clock about to strike the hour. The cage was jerked up a few inches, and then with a creaking of cables and gears, began to ascend at an excruciatingly slow pace. Mannion looked out from the grilled cage as the lift crawled upwards. The stairwell was lit by the same kind of fluttering gas lamps as the main hallway. The lamps threw dancing shadows, whose movements seemed to leap in tune with the fluttering of Mannion's nerves.

Gone, for the moment, were the uncertainties and doubts that had gripped him in the café. He was ready to confront Graz now. The death of the Chauffeur in Marseille had not, he decided, written *finis* to his quest for justice. That would end only when all the men behind his grandfather's murder had been made to account for the crime. His task had barely begun. Back there in the café, his resolve had weakened. For a moment, he had allowed himself to think that the Chauffeur's death had let him off the hook, that it had somehow released him from the solemn vow he had made to his father. Only his own death could release him from that pledge of honour: that he would forfeit his title of son if he did not avenge the spilling of Djurkovic blood with the blood of those responsible.

The mantle of avenger should, by rights, have fallen on the shoulders of Mannion's father. And, even in his crippled state, he had been prepared to accept it. Only with reluctance had he surrendered the task, which he saw as a sacred duty, and allowed it to pass – because of his infirmity – to his eldest son. Mannion, despite mixed feelings about the pursuit of tribal feuds as a sacrosanct obligation in the twentieth century, had willingly enough accepted the role that family honour had placed on him. But he had lived uneasily with the knowledge of what he was about. The educated American in him clung to the belief that his vow could be implemented within the law and that, in carrying it out, he would merely be assisting the judicial process. The Slav in him never quite believed this but recognised, in his father's and the tribe's expectations of him, that judicial law was incidental. He was expected to exact bloody vengeance, and the only law obtaining was the primitive dictat that demanded an eye for eye. Mannion had thus walked a tight-rope: hoping against hope that he could remain within the law but knowing in his heart, when it came to the crunch, that luxury would be denied him.

As the lift trundled slowly upwards, Mannion's blood tingled with the knowledge that the crunch point was perhaps only seconds away.

The cage had reached the third floor when Mannion heard the slam of a door somewhere above. The sound was followed by the rapid beat of footsteps clacking on the stair. A man came into view on the stairs, going down. He wore a brown leather coat and a broad-brimmed brown hat. His receding footsteps echoed up the stairwell as the elevator inched to a halt at the fourth floor.

Mannion jerked the concertina-like gate open and ran swiftly along the corridor to the right. The janitor had said that the apartment number was 44 and that Graz had gone up half an hour ago. Mannion mentally cursed himself for having missed his quarry's arrival and not even getting a glimpse of him. If the janitor had not come to the front door and signalled across the street to him, he might have been sitting in the café yet! Mannion was galvanised by the fear that the man he had seen on the stairs was Graz, going out.

He hammered loudly on the door of number forty-four but there was no sound from within. Mannion did not wait. He raced for the stairs and went hurtling down, handing himself off the walls as he rounded the landings. The janitor stared out of his window at the commotion as Mannion skidded into view in the hallway.

'He just went out, this minute,' the janitor announced, anticipating Mannion's question. Mannion scarcely broke his stride. Out on the street, he looked both ways and sighed with relief when he saw the man in the leather coat and brown hat. He was no more than fifty metres away, to the right. He had stopped under a street lamp and was lighting a cigarette. Then he moved off.

Mannion ran a few paces to shorten the distance between himself and Graz. Then he slowed, keeping the other man in sight. He debated with himself whether or not he should overtake Graz and beard him there and then, in the street, but there were too many people about. A scene in public could be awkward. Graz was walking at a steady pace, without hurrying. Mannion followed. He would pick his moment.

Jamie had decided that he was not very impressed with Mr Vladimir Graz. The speaker had an accent that made many of his remarks unintelligible. And he had an annoying habit of lauding a particular point of view and then seeming to do his best to contradict it. It was very difficult to grasp what it was that Graz was advocating. Was he supporting what he purported to oppose? Or was it the other way round?

His address had been titled 'Whither Croatia?' and had been well received by some in the small audience, while making others – including Mara – decidedly restive. Graz had started off on the wrong foot as far as Mara was concerned, much too unctuously flattering the chairman of the meeting and paying an excessively glowing tribute to this small Church-oriented University group, who were dedicated to the preservation of Croatia's cultural heritage.

Graz went on to express regret at the shadow that had passed over the nation with the death of the King. None lamented his passing more than he, but – and there were a lot of buts – it was possible to understand the anger and frustration that arose in some Croatians when their aspirations were denied and their sense of national identity was threatened by alien ideas imposed from above. It was all too easy, too, to comprehend the rebelliousness of Croatians who reacted violently against punitive taxes which seemed reserved for them and them alone and from which they derived no benefit in return. Most Croatians – and Graz included himself in the number – were the most devoted and loyal subjects of the late King, but even they had seen their loyalty strained to breaking point at times because the voice of Croatians was never heard in Belgrade. The only voices the King heard were Serbian voices, because the throne was surrounded by Serbians. The only sermons he heard were the sermons of Orthodoxy. How easy it was for discontented Croatians to see the King, not as the inspiration he sought to be, but as the symbol of a faith that was inimical to their own and bent on smothering it.

Graz condemned violence as a means of achieving autonomy for Croatia – as he was sure all members of the society which he was addressing condemned violence – but he also recognised that radical change was seldom achieved without it. They must ensure that the changes that must come as a result of the King's assassination were the changes that all Croatians wanted: a Croatia that was free and independent, a Croatia that was governed by Croatians for Croatians. The occasion of the King's death must not be used to start a campaign of hate against Italy, with whom Croatia shared her Catholic faith, against Austria, to whom Croatia owed so much of its culture; nor against Hungary, who had so long championed Croatian aspirations.

There was much more, along the same lines. Graz came over as the most moderate of moderates, with a strange sympathy for all that was immoderate.

Throughout his discourse, Mara had reacted more to

the style of the man than what he was actually saying, causing Jamie to smile because it was typical of her. She didn't like his shifty eyes, nor the way he was dressed. His fingers were heavily ringed, like those of a gypsy woman – a sign of vanity, Mara said. The diamond that flashed in his tiepin was disgustingly ostentatious, especially when half the children in the land could not get enough to eat because their fathers had no work.

Graz, of course, had initially roused Mara's scorn by the way he buttered up the chairman and the audience. From that point on, she had been ready to doubt the sincerity of anything the speaker said.

'He has the heart of a fox and the mind of a chicken', had been one of her pithier whispered comments to Jamie, while Graz was speaking. And she had waited in vain to hear some comment on the widespread poverty and appalling social conditions – matters of deep concern to her. Graz's failure even to touch on the subject seemed an unforgivable omission to Mara.

Jamie reacted much less emotionally. The truth of the matter was that the talk bored him stiff. He found the audience more interesting than the speaker. Most were students, but there was a sprinkling of older people. There was a priest, whose bushy eyebrows shot up in surprise with some regularity at what was being said. Then there were the two men who had arrived with Graz. They were an odd pair: big men – bruisers by the look of them – who spoke to no one, not even to each other. They sat, unsmiling, uninterested. Were they bodyguards, ready to come to the speaker's rescue if the audience turned hostile? They looked so out of place that it amused Jamie to speculate on the purpose of their presence. He wondered if Graz needed protection from people overcome by boredom.

Another member of the audience intrigued Jamie: a tall man in his mid-twenties. He had slipped in late, after everyone else was seated, and had taken a seat in the empty row of chairs behind him and Mara. Now *there* was someone who did not seem to be the slightest bit bored by Graz. He hung on every word, staring at the speaker in an intense way. His eyes never left Graz for an instant. This stranger, too, seemed out of place at the gathering – although Jamie could not put his finger on a reason for thinking so. It was not his clothes, nor his features – he had handsome looks – but there was something about him that was *different*.

When Graz had finished speaking, the chairman – a gangly senior student from the Law School whose stiff wing-collar was so well starched that its edge drew flecks of blood from his throat when he moved his head – stood up to thank Graz and ask if the audience had any questions for the speaker. He clearly expected none, because he was quite taken aback when the lone man behind Jamie and Mara stood up.

'I have a question for Mr Vladimir Graz,' he said. There was a tremor of emotion in his strangely accented voice. Graz, who had sat down at the table facing the audience, looked even more startled than the chairman. People turned to stare at the stranger, wondering who he was. The chairman was wondering the same thing.

'I'm sorry, sir,' he blurted out, 'but I don't think I know you. Are you a new member of our society?'

Mannion did not know what impulse had taken him to his feet. Perhaps it was the anger that had gripped him as he listened to Graz's speech. Several times, he had had to control the desire to interrupt, to shout, 'Liar! Murderer!' At the end, he had been unable to contain himself. There were a lot of questions he wanted to hurl at Graz, and here and now, in public, seemed as good a place as any. Everyone was staring at him, waiting. . . .

'I am the grandson of Pavle Djurkovic,' Mannion announced, answering the chairman's question indirectly. His voice was calm, although his blood was racing. 'His name was not unknown in Croatia . . .

prominent enough for Mr Graz to have heard of him.'

'What is your question?' the chairman asked.

Mannion seemed to deliberate before replying.

'In view of Mr Graz's sorrow at the death of King Alexander,' he began carefully, 'and, in view of Mr Graz's close acquaintance with Petrus Kelemen, the King's assassin and the man who murdered my grandfather and my cousin and my cousin's husband and their four-year-old child, would Mr Graz care to –'

That was as far as Mannion got before his words were drowned in uproar. Some students in the front row who had been most receptive to Graz's speech were on their feet, protesting noisily at the unexpected allegations against their guest. Graz himself had risen, shouting: 'This is an outrage!' He had gone pasty-faced with shock at the mention of Petrus Kelemen. Others in the audience, and Mara was the loudest among them, were shouting for the stranger to be given a chance to say what he had to say. The chairman appealed in vain for order as noisy arguments flared up all over the place.

Jamie, thoroughly bemused by the sudden excitement but right behind Mara in her support of the stranger, saw the signal that passed between Graz and the bruisers whom he had tagged as his bodyguards. The two men went thrusting towards the back of the audience and Mannion. Chairs went over and pandemonium reigned as arguments gave way to fist-fights.

Mannion saw Graz pulling on his leather coat and making for a rear door. He knocked over chairs as he tried to take the shortest route to cut Graz off; but it was one of the big men who cut off Mannion, falling on him like a Sumo wrestler and pinning his arms. Then the second bruiser joined in.

Mara, outraged, went kicking and screaming to Mannion's rescue. One of the bruisers had pushed her roughly away before Jamie, his blood up at the sight of

Mara going sprawling, threw himself into the fray. He succeeded in making one of the men release his hold on Mannion. The success merely freed the snarling giant to devote his full attention to Jamie, and he did so brutally.

Pain exploded in Jamie's head as a huge fist suddenly materialised before his eyes like a rushing comet and blotted out the light. The blow lifted him clean off his feet and he went hurtling backwards, ploughing through three rows of chairs before he came to rest. He tried to move but his arms and legs were like jelly appendages, incapable of control. To his open eyes, the world was a spinning disc viewed through a red mist.

When he could focus his eyes, it was to find Mara bending over him. There was a trickle of blood at her lips where one of the men had hit her. Jamie's anger flared anew. He hauled himself groggily to his feet.

'I'm all right,' he insisted sharply, in response to Mara's anxious questions.

'Oh, Jamie, they'll kill that poor man,' Mara cried. 'We've got to do something! They've dragged him out the back way!'

Private battles were still being waged in several parts of the hall, with only the priest and the gangly young chairman making any attempt to restore peace. In obedience to Mara's entreaties, Jamie propelled himself unsteadily towards an open door at the end of the hall. The door led into a small kitchen and out through another door to the grounds of the adjacent church. A pile of rough timber logs, neatly stacked and waiting to be cut up for firewood, stood by the door. Jamie heard groans and angry monosyllabic shouts from near at hand, in the dark parkland area behind the church. Arming himself with a stout piece of wood from the pile, Jamie made towards the sounds, with Mara at his heels.

Mannion was still putting up a fight, although he could hardly stand. When he was dragged from the hall, resistance had all but been beaten out of him and he had no doubt that the only objective of his hefty captors in hauling him outside was to finish him off. But the brutes were in no hurry. Mannion was thrown on wet grass and given time to collect his scattered senses and drink the air into his gasping lungs. He spat blood from his mouth, unsure if it came from a broken tooth or if he had bitten his tongue. His face and jaws were a welter of pain.

They had thrown him face down, but now Mannion struggled to his knees and then tried to stand. A shadow nearby moved – and a fist struck Mannion in the ribs, sending him down again. The blow was followed by a second as he lay on the ground. A boot thudded into him.

'Who are you? Who sent you? Who told you to say those things about Mr Graz?'

Mannion heard the questions but did not answer. He tried again to get on his feet, his eyes on the dark shape that had hit and kicked him. The attack came from another side this time. The second man kneed him in the hip and sent him sprawling.

'Finish him,' Mannion heard him say. 'We're just wasting time.'

But his companion ignored him. He snarled some more questions at Mannion and booted him again, to encourage response. Mannion did not try to rise immediately. He lay, groaning, pretending to be utterly beaten. He willed strength into his body. Next time he moved, it would have to be quickly.

The two men debated his fate argumentatively. One was insisting that Graz would not thank them for keeping Mannion alive. The other was for making him talk . . . first. Mannion tensed himself, preparing to move.

The speed with which Mannion acted took both men by surprise. He made a sudden roll and then shot to his feet, knowing that his life depended on evading another of those clubbing blows. The man nearest to him swung at him, but he dodged the looping arm and charged. His shoulder hit his would-be attacker in the chest and his momentum sent the man reeling backwards.

Mannion stumbled over the man, kneeing him in the face as he tried to wind his waving arms round Mannion's legs. Mannion was breaking free when he heard a warning, shouted by a girl. It was Mara – but her screamed warning was unnecessary. Mannion caught a blurred sight of Jamie launching himself into the attack. There was a sickening crack and a scream as Jamie swung his timber club like a claymore and its whirling arc was arrested by fierce contact with the face of the second bruiser. It struck him at an angle, across nose and forehead. The man fell to his knees, hands clutched across his face, howling pitifully.

The man Mannion had charged to the ground was already struggling to his feet, but Jamie was alive to that danger and had changed the direction of his attack. He had delivered the first blow with a right-handed sweep; now he swung left to right and down, and caught the second man a crippling thwack across the knees. The man fell, and Jamie helped him on his way to earth with a two-handed chop across the head and shoulders.

'Get him out of here!' Jamie yelled at Mara, meaning Mannion. 'I'll catch you up. Hurry!' he screamed, as the pair hestitated. To his relief, they did as he had bidden them and ran off through the trees.

Only one of Graz's hoods had any appetite left for fight. The man who had taken a blow across the knees was in slightly better shape than his broken-nosed friend. Hobbling, but grunting with anger, he came warily towards Jamie. He had a knife in his hand. He feinted with the knife hand but Jamie held his ground, waiting, his timber club held ready, like a baseball bat. When the man lunged a second time, Jamie took a step towards him and swung with all his strength. The hood raised his left arm in an attempt to ward off the attack and his wrist took the full impact. There was a crack like a rifle shot. The blow swept the raised arm aside and continued with undiminished force to strike the knife out of the man's other hand. It went sailing into shrubbery several metres away.

The knife's owner had had enough. He was weeping with pain, his wrist almost certainly broken. He backed away from Jamie, nursing his injured arm close to his body and whimpering his distress.

Jamie felt elated. He had won. He threw away his weapon and went hurrying back towards the church building. As he skirted it, he became aware of intense activity in the adjacent street. From behind a tree, he peered at the scene in the vicinity of the hall. There were uniformed gendarmes everwhere and, outside the hall, a dozen or more people were being herded into a large Black Maria.

Suddenly, from out of the darkness away to his right, came a shout and the sound of three shots. These were followed by a girl's scream and then by two more shots. For a moment, Jamie stood transfixed with fear and then he was running towards the sound of the shots. The scream had been Mara's. Of that he had no doubt, and he dreaded to think what could possibly have happened to her. His mind rioted with terror for her safety as he ran headlong, trampling the withering plants of a flowerbed before his feet found the soft flattened earth of a broad pathway. Light from the windows of a tall building overlooking the park was diffused by foliage, and it was towards this speckled brightness that Jamie ran. He almost fell over the body of the softly groaning man kneeling on the path. The man was holding a shoulder with his one good arm. The other hung limp as he rocked gently on his knees and moaned with pain. There was no sign of another person. Here, the path was fitfully lit by a lamp above an open gate leading to a narrow street beyond: no more than a lane, a thoroughfare hidden by a stone wall. The path was empty.

Jamie stooped over the injured man, who was barely conscious. He was reluctant to go dashing by, when help was so obviously needed. And there was no sign of Mara. He called her name, softly. Then again, more loudly. There was no answering sound.

He bent again over the man.

'Can you stand up?' he asked. 'Look, put your good arm round my neck and I'll get you over to that bench. It'll be more comfortable. It's muddy here.'

The man's head lolled as Jamie lifted him and supported him towards a wooden park seat. He cried out at the hurt caused by movement but he seemed easier when he had the support of the bench. As they manoeuvred towards the bench, Jamie's foot knocked against an object lying in the mud. From its shape, it looked like a handgun. The fact registered in his mind with shock. The injured man was a slippery burden. He was wearing a leather coat that slid as Jamie tried to hold him firmly.

On the seat, he turned the man round and tried to support his head. Light from above the gate lit his features. Recognition jolted Jamie with fresh shock. The eyes in the lolling face opened wide and stared at Jamie through pain. They widened, too, in recognition. The man was the police agent from the encounter in the cellar bar: the one who had sported flashy clothes and promised never to forget Jamie's face.

Jamie got little time to reflect on the discovery. He heard running feet coming towards him and turned to face two angry-looking gendarmes with truncheons in hand.

92

4

Mannion's Choice

Mara supported the stranger as they tried to run. Each breath he drew was a wheezing gasp in her ears. He begged her repeatedly to leave him and save herself. He had brought her only trouble and she could expect a great deal more if she was found with him. Mara ignored his pleas. She would not abandon him now. She could not, for all that she was sick with worry over what might be happening to Jamie, battling it out alone with those two toughs. Jamie will be all right, she told herself over and over in her mind. He had really sorted out those clowns. It was the first time she had ever seen Jamie with his temper up, and the change in him had been almost frightening. Normally, he was so mild and self-effacing that she had thought him incapable of anger, far less violence. But the way he had laid into those two thugs – whirling that heavy timber like a battle-axe – had been a revelation, showing a side of Jamie that she had not suspected to exist. And it had not been because the two men had hurt Jamie – which they had – but because they had hurt *her*. That was what had brought out the fighting madness in him. It awed her to know: that she could inspire such tigerish passion.

The stranger was in a bad way, having taken that merciless beating and, on top of that, the bullet wound. Blood was running down his leg from his calf, where the bullet had gouged a track through the flesh, and the lower part of his trouser-leg was saturated. It was crippling him now as he tried to run.

He had first entreated her to leave him and save

herself in the lane behind the park, but she had stubbornly refused to do so, in spite of her fears for Jamie. There was little she could do for Jamie but pray that he would make himself scarce as soon as he realised that there were police all over the place.

It had been a shock to both Mara and Mannion to see the swarms of gendarmes in the street beside the hall – and they were running in everybody. How they had arrived at the fracas so quickly, and in such numbers, was a mystery – but there had been no argument between Mara and Mannion over what they should do about it. The decision to escape across the park had been mutual, and reached without debate.

They had almost reached the gate into the lane when they had heard pursuing footsteps and been challenged to stop by a man who was certainly not a gendarme. Their pursuer had not waited for them to halt but had fired three shots, one of which had hit Mannion in the leg, bringing him down. Mara had screamed, terrified at the sight of Mannion falling and by the fact that two bullets had narrowly missed her. They had gouged lumps of stone from the pillar of the nearby gate and must have missed her head by centimetres.

Mannion's reaction to being hit had come as a total surprise to her, augmenting her initial shock. Sprawling on the ground, he had screamed the one word 'Graz!' – and fired two shots from the gun that had appeared in his hand. Mara had seen the leather-coated figure suddenly stop in his tracks as he ran towards them. Then he had fallen.

'Run!' Mannion had shouted to her – but she had not run.

By the time they were two streets away from the park, Mannion had stopped telling her to leave him and save herself. She had wormed from him the information that he had a room in Balkanska Street and she had promised that she would get him there. In an unlit alley, Mara made him rest and took the opportunity to strap his bloodied leg as best she could. She removed and tore up an underskirt to use as a bandage, but the darkness prohibited more than the roughest of first aid.

Mara sought the quietest streets as she guided Mannion, but the occasional passers-by they encountered regarded them oddly before hurrying on, wondering perhaps at the sight of a girl helping a drunken friend homeward. By the time they reached Balkanska Street, it was raining heavily and the downpour had emptied the streets.

The pair evaded the usually watchful eyes of Mannion's landlady and reached the sanctuary of his room. While he sagged in the single horsehair armchair, Mara filled the big china washbowl with water from its matching jug.

'You should be in hospital,' she adjured Mannion, as she began the task of tending his hurts. He shook his head, but made no protest when she pulled off his trousers and gave first attention to the ugly bullet gash, which had exposed the calf muscle. Then she gently bathed his face, wiping blood from his swollen purpled lips and the swellings under both eyes.

'Who are you? Have you any friends who can help?' Mara asked.

He told her his name. It hurt him to speak. The effort even of breathing was an agony, and he wondered if the kicking he had taken had broken any ribs. Mara hushed him to silence; her questions could wait. She manoeuvred him towards the bed, where she eased him out of his jacket and shirt. The operation made him sweat with pain. He sank back on the pillow, wanting only to close his eyes and surrender consciousness of his body. But he fought the clamour of his body to submit to the pain that racked him. He had to thank his unknown angel of mercy for all she had risked for him.

Raising himself on an elbow, he sought to find the

words. Again, she hushed him, seeing the agony of his effort.

'Try to sleep,' she urged him. 'I must go now – but I'll come back in the morning.'

He needed no urging to sleep. He welcomed the black oblivion that offered refuge, fighting it no longer.

Jamie found out the hard way that Belgrade's gendarmes were not in the habit of asking questions as a prelude to making an arrest. They arrested everyone in sight as a matter of priority and left it to their superiors to investigate such niceties as whether the arrested parties were innocent or guilty of any crime. Jamie made no attempt to escape the onrushing police but he was rash enough to try to explain that he was not the cause of the injured man's wound and had only gone to his assistance. For this information he was rewarded by an unceremonious belabouring about the arms and shoulders by the truncheon-wielding gendarmes. His protests were interpreted as resistance, earning more painful whacks and the indignity of handcuffs being snapped on his wrists.

It was no consolation to Jamie to realise that the same rough treatment might have been handed out to the wounded man had he not screamed out that he was a plain-clothes colleague. They advised him to stay where he was until they had got Jamie in the van, when they would summon an ambulance.

'Is this the one who was doing the shooting?' one of Jamie's captors asked the wounded agent.

'I don't know,' the agent snarled. 'There was more than one of them trying to get away. If you clodhoppers had been half awake, we could have got the whole gang. . . .' He broke off, obviously in pain and in danger of keeling right over. 'For God's sake, get somebody to see to me. Can't you see I'm bleeding like a stuck pig? I'll die if I don't get help.'

'No need to make such a song about it,' the gendarme advised him insensitively. 'Clodhoppers, are we? Well, we've got work to do, the same as you. You'll just have to bleed a little longer. We said we'd get help, didn't we?'

It was abundantly clear that the two uniformed men did not give a fig whether their colleague from the political arm lived or died – an indication of the lack of amity between their respective forces – and the agent was left where he was while Jamie was frogmarched back across the park. Outside the hall, Jamie was bundled roughly into the back of a black police van. It already contained half a dozen prisoners, mainly students who had participated in the rumpus in the hall. Most were nursing bruises and cuts, which might have come from their brawling or from the police truncheons. All, however, were subdued and feeling very sorry for themselves. Five minutes after Jamie had joined them, the van moved off. Its destination was the Central Police Headquarters.

Jamie was arraigned before a desk officer who had difficulty with the name Kyle. He seemed to think that Jamie had invented the surname and was being obstructive. The man also assumed that Jamie came from Croatia, and he became quite bad-tempered when Jamie assured him otherwise. The more Jamie tried to explain his true origins and his unusual accent, the more hostile and suspicious the officer became.

When, eventually, Jamie was hustled off to be in-carcerated in a subterranean cell, as a consequence of the desk officer's displeasure he was kicked and pummelled all the way down the stairs by his escorts. The cell was primitive: stone walls, stone floor, and the only light admitted by a tiny window in the stonework above the door. It had the smell of a neglected public urinal. Jamie stumbled into the interior and made the discovery that the cell was already occupied. Four other prisoners were already in residence. They were lying on the floor, on the wooden boards that served as beds.

The dull clanging sound of the heavy door closing behind him echoed in Jamie's ears. It was followed by the clicking fall of metal tumblers as the key was turned in the heavy lock. In spite of the presence of the four unfortunates already in occupancy, Jamie had never felt more alone in the whole of his life. Nor had he ever felt more afraid.

Milan was in a deep sleep when the telephone wakened him. He hurried to answer it, wondering what was so urgent that he should be roused at one o'clock in the morning. His surprise was tinged with displeasure when he discovered that the caller was a girl and that she wanted to speak to Jamie. He padded on bare feet along to Jamie's room to fetch him, with every intention of reminding his nephew that calls from his admirers should be confined to more social hours. It came as a shock to Milan to find that Jamie's room was empty and that his bed was undisturbed. His sudden worry for the boy became alarm when he informed the early-morning caller of this fact and the news was greeted with a fear-ridden cry from the other end of the line. Milan demanded to know the cause of it.

He listened with growing horror as Mara gave him a tearful account of the uproar at the meeting to which she had taken his nephew. Her account was short of detail, inasmuch as she did not mention her involvement with the gun-carrying stranger and their escape. She concentrated on Jamie's attempt to rescue a gate-crasher at the Croatian meeting from a murderous assault by two toughs, and told how he had seemed in command of the situation when she last saw him. But the police had appeared on the scene and there had been shooting. . . .

Milan's fierce interruption at this stage did not help Mara to supply a more coherent picture of what had happened. She had to assure Milan several times that

Jamie had not been involved in the shooting and had been nowhere near it. In response to Milan's anxious questions, she sobbed out her belief that one of two things must have happened to Jamie. Either the two toughs had somehow turned the tables on him and he was hurt, or the police must have arrested him, because they were arresting everybody they could lay their hands on. She was distraught.

Having ascertained from the girl where he could find her, Milan advised her to leave everything in his hands and to try to get some rest. He rang off. There was to be little rest for him that night.

The Assistant Deputy Minister lived in a house that looked south towards the well-kept parks that bounded one side of King Alexander Street. He was standing at a first-floor window, contemplating the view, when Milan was shown into his presence. The two men stared at each other solemnly for a moment and then smiles lit their faces. They advanced, meeting at the centre of the elegant Persian carpet to embrace in a warm hug. Their comradeship went back a long way: to the war, where it had been forged. Milan stood back, surveying his friend's formal attire of black tailed jacket and striped trousers.

'Are you going to a wedding, Georgie?' he asked, using the familiar style of address that was as old as their friendship.

The Assistant Deputy Minister laughed.

'This is the only uniform I wear, these days,' he said. 'It impresses people – especially when I have to visit Police Headquarters at six o'clock in the morning.' He frowned. 'I hope you appreciate it, Milan, that you are the only person alive who could have persuaded me to get up at such an hour and go throwing my weight around as a favour for old times' sake.'

'I'm grateful to you Georgie,' Milan assured him.

'I've been frantic with worry about the boy. And his mother's up to ninety-nine. Are the police going to let the boy go?'

Worry furrowed the Assistant Deputy Minister's brow.

'It's not just as straightforward as you seem to think, Milan. There are complications . . . . The secret police are involved and one of their officers has been shot and wounded.'

'But you must have some influence on them, Georgie.'

The Assistant Deputy Minister shook his head.

'They're not answerable to the Interior Ministry. They're not answerable to anybody, really. Officially, they're part of the Civic Administration – but that's camouflage. They pay no more attention to the city than they do to us. They know they've got the backing of the old guard at the Palace, and that makes them untouchable as far as the rest of us ordinary mortals are concerned.'

The Assistant Deputy Minister went on to tell Milan all that had transpired since his old friend had telephoned him in the early hours and sought his intervention on Jamie's behalf. He had gone personally to Police Headquarters, where a senior officer had told him that Jamie was one of several detainees – mostly Croatian – facing charges of riotous behaviour. There was a chance, however, that Jamie might face a more serious charge: that of wounding with intent to kill. The victim of this alleged attack was an agent of the special police who had been engaged on a special operation against Croatian conspirators suspected of involvement in King Alexander's assassination. Both the civil police and the secret police had a part in this special operation, which was to have culminated with a raid on a meeting of a student Croatian society.

Some confusion had been caused by a last-minute switch of venue for the meeting, which was to be addressed by the prime suspect – a Croatian called Vladimir Graz. It had been the secret policeman – the one who later stopped a bullet – who had discovered the new location of the meeting and summoned the raiding force. Unfortunately, minutes before the police raiders arrived, the meeting had broken up in disorder – with the result that Graz had escaped.

The secret police were furious over the fact that Graz had got clean away and that one of their agents had been shot. They accused the gendarmes of bungling their part in the operation and they were shouting for blood. The gendarmes, incensed by the accusation, were loudly denying imcompetence and casting around in all directions to show how efficient they were. They were boasting that they had arrested a foreigner – Jamie – and that the wounded agent owed his life to their timely action. The foreigner had been overpowered in the act of 'finishing off' the wounded agent.

Milan listened to this chronicle with disbelief and mounting dismay. He was prepared to wager his life that Jamie had never handled a gun, far less possessed one. Had the gendarmes given the Assistant Deputy Minister any indication of what kind of weapon Jamie was supposed to have used, or where he might have got it?

His friend shrugged.

'They say a gun was found, but it was the agent's. They are searching for a second weapon in the park where it happened. Your nephew put up a struggle, apparently, and the police think he may have thrown his gun away or dropped it.'

The Assistant Deputy Minister put an arm round Milan's shoulder.

'My advice to you, old friend, is that you find the best lawyer in Belgrade and get him on to your nephew's case right away. The boy is in a lot of trouble.'

Milan promised that he would. He thanked his old comrade-in-arms for the inconvenience he had caused him. Then he took his leave, declining his friend's invitation to stay for a bite of breakfast or at least a cup of coffee. Milan would have given an arm for the latter but he grudged the minutes it would have cost when there was so much to do. It was now 8.15 a.m. and a long talk with Jamie's girl friend, Mara, was overdue. This time, Milan hoped, the girl would make a lot more sense than she had when she telephoned in the early hours of the morning.

When he left the Assistant Deputy Minister's house, he walked the short distance to King Milan Street, where he stepped aboard a northbound tram.

The woman who had rented Mannion a room looked at the two strangers on her doorstep with dour-faced suspicion. The man was well-dressed and about her own age – in his fifties, she guessed – and the girl was a pretty little thing, but red-eyed, as if she had been weeping. Were the pair father and daughter?

'What makes you think the person you want to see lives here?' the woman asked. 'What did you say the name was?'

'Mannion,' said Mara.

The woman shook her head.

'There's no one here of that name. Sounds foreign to me.'

'His room is the ground floor back,' Mara said desperately, 'He was. . . . He had an accident last night. . . . I came here with him – to make sure that he was all right.'

'He may have given you a different name from Mannion,' Milan volunteered, from over Mara's shoulder.

'Is he in trouble with the police?' the woman asked, alarmed. 'What do you want with him?'

'We've got to talk with him,' Milan said. 'He was hurt. He may need a doctor. Please, let us in.'

The woman was suddenly aware that the doorstep confrontation was attracting the curious stares of passers-by. Four youths had stopped and were taking a frank interest in the proceedings.

'Haven't you got anything better to do?' she shouted at them, and allowed the girl and man to push past her into the stone-floored passage beyond. Mara made straight for a room at the end of the passage.

'That is Mr Djurkovic's room,' the landlady said. 'I'm sure you must be making a mistake.'

Mara knocked and, without waiting for a reply, tried the door. It was unlocked. Mannion looked up from the bed as she poked her head round the door and said: 'It's me. And there's somebody with me. . . .'

Milan followed her into the room and the landlady would have gone in, too, but he barred her entry by partially closing the door and staring at her through the remaining gap.

'Thank you,' he said. 'We'll see that everything's all right now.' She retreated into the passage but her face showed her displeasure at being excluded.

Until Milan turned and faced the young man on the bed he had no idea of what kind of reception to expect. Mara had assured him that Mannion would make no trouble – but Milan had not told Mara that if it came to a choice between Jamie and this stranger, he would have no hesitation in handing the stranger over to the mercies of the police. He was under no illusions about the risk he was taking in accompanying Mara to Balkanska Street. If the young man had shown no compunction in swapping fire with the secret police, he was unlikely to think twice about shooting him.

A glance at Mannion, however, was sufficient to suggest that he was going to pose no threat to anyone. He could barely raise his head to see who his visitors were, and it was debatable if he could see anything from the slits of eyes from which he stared. The area around both eyes was puffed up and discoloured. His face in general had been made grotesque by the beating he had taken – as if he had survived a thirty-round hammering by a merciless bare-knuckle pugilist.

'The sooner we get you to hospital, the better,' Milan opined, appalled by Mannion's injuries and enfeebled state. He was so weak that he was unable to prop himself up on an elbow and speech was an effort. Milan turned to Mara. 'We must get a doctor, at least. Ask that woman to fetch one . . . there must be one nearby.' He saw Mara's uncertainty and, taking a roll of banknotes from his pocket, he peeled off a couple and handed them to the girl. 'She may have to pay in advance. I know how things work around here. Half is for her and half is for the doctor. Tell her it's urgent.'

When she had gone, Milan sat on the edge of the bed.

'Do you still have the gun?' he asked Mannion.

'In my coat,' came the reply. Mannion tried to indicate the whereabouts of the coat with a turn of his head, but it amounted to no more than a movement of the eyes. 'Are you police?' he asked Milan.

The older man shook his head.

'No. I'm the uncle of the boy who tried to save you last night. He's in a lot of trouble because of you.'

'The kid who was with that girl?'

'Yes. The police have him. They're going to charge him with attempted murder.'

'Because of what he did to those two gorillas? The ones who were kicking the hell out of me?'

'No. You shot a man. That's what they're trying to pin on my nephew. They think he did it.'

'They think your nephew shot Graz?'

'It wasn't Graz who was shot. The police are still looking for Graz. The man you shot was a secret policeman. Didn't you know that?'

Mannion did not know. The shock of learning that it was not Vladimir Graz who had opened fire on him and the girl was almost more than his pain-blinded mind could take in. He had spent a night of agony and despair, made endurable only by the belief that he had put a bullet in one of the architects of his grandfather's murder. And now that meagre consolation was taken away from him. The failure to accomplish anything in coming to Jugoslavia was not just partial, as he had resigned himself to believing; it was absolute.

As she returned to the room, Mara heard his groaning cry of despair. In his misery, he reverted to English.

'Oh, Jesus, Jesus!' he cried out. 'I've fouled it up! I've really screwed it up!'

'The woman is bringing a doctor,' Mara informed Milan in a stage whisper, but she was glancing anxiously at the bed. 'What is wrong with him?'

Milan shrugged.

'I told him about the agent. He seems as distressed as you were when I told you. You did not tell me he was a foreigner.'

'Because he talks differently?' The girl shrugged. 'Is it important? What are we doing to do? What are *you* going to do?'

'That,' said Milan, 'depends entirely on this young man here and what it was that prompted him to accuse Graz in public the way he did. From what I've been told, he would have been doing the hangman a favour if he'd shot Graz. One thing is sure – I'm not going to let Jamie take the blame for something he didn't do!'

Although there was no doubt in Milan's mind that the mysterious stranger was the root cause of Jamie's predicament, he found it impossible not to feel a certain sympathy for him. He had already suffered considerable punishment for the chapter of unfortunate events which he had so recklessly set in train. The shooting of the agent seemed, at best, to have been an act of self-defence. At worst, it was a case of mistaken identity. He was culpable, but with extenuating circumstances. A good lawyer could present a reasonable defence on the little Milan already knew.

Mannion, lying helpless on the bed, was staring hopelessly at Milan, overcome by the knowledge of his own impotence to help himself and by his sense of failure. He knew that he was completely at the mercy of the stocky grey-haired man who had declared so firmly that he was not going to let his nephew take the blame for something he had not done. Well, that wasn't Brad Mannion's way either. No innocent guy – especially one who had risked his neck for him – was going to take the rap because Brad Mannion had screwed things up.

Mannion tried to struggle up on an elbow once more. This time, he succeeded – although the pain that gripped his chest was almost unbearable, causing him almost to faint as he struggled for breath. His action brought Milan to the bedside, but he resisted the older man's concerned plea to lie back.

'You must send for the police,' he told Milan, with every word needing an intake of breath and every intake of breath causing a fresh stab of pain. 'I'll . . . tell . . . them . . . the . . . kid . . . didn't . . . shoot . . . the . . . cop. . . . It . . . was . . . me.' He had to rest briefly. Then he went on, 'They'll . . . have . . . to . . . let . . . the kid . . . go.'

Only then, when he had spent himself with the effort of saying what he had to say, did he allow Milan to lower him gently back on the pillow.

'Don't try to talk,' Milan said, almost whispering the words. 'There will be time for talk, and there will be time to bring in the police. But the time is not just yet.'

Mara had been watching, moved by the injured stranger's determination to be heard and by his anxiety to clear Jamie, regardless of the consequences to himself. She could sense, too – in Milan's gentleness with him – that Jamie's uncle was equally stirred to compassion. Milan turned to her now, his expression reflective and sad.

'There are things I want you to do, Mara,' he said, still deep in thought. Then he regarded her with eyes wide and a grimace that was midway between a smile and a frown. 'You know, it's been puzzling me what instinct it was that made you and Jamie feel you had to support someone who was a total stranger to you both. . . . Now, I think I know. Look at him. . . . He is beaten, defenceless, alone – like a wolf that has been snared by the leg and deserted by the pack – but he does not beg for himself. His one care is for the foolish cub who tried to keep his enemies at bay.' Milan smiled. 'We can't abandon him now, can we?'

What Milan wanted Mara to do was to proceed as fast as her legs would carry her to the offices of the brothers Simovic, who handled all Milan's legal affairs. The elder brother – who lectured in Law at the University – had only a minor interest in the practice, and it was Draga, the younger, whom Mara had to seek out and bring to the address in Balkanska Street.

'Tell him that it is his old friend Milan Alexandrovic who needs him and that it's a matter of the greatest urgency,' Milan said. 'He will tell you that it is impossible to come, that he has appointments and that he is snowed under with work – but you must not take no for an answer. Tell him that if he has something more important to do, it is something that he must value a great deal more than our friendship.'

Mara left, a little stunned by the nature of the errand with which she had been entrusted but buoyed, too, by the way Milan had taken command of the situation and seemed bent on positive action.

Minutes after Mara's departure, the landlady appeared at the door of Mannion's room with a doctor. To Milan's surprise, he was a dark-skinned man, with the name of Suleiman – a 'Turk' – but Milan kept his prejudice in check. He was prepared to concede in his own mind, if not to the world at large, that – like his

107

tobacco, his garden, his house and his favourite coffee – medical treatment of the 'Turk' variety was likely to be of high quality.

Dr Suleiman certainly set about his work in a thorough and confident manner. First he examined Mannion from head to toe, probing here, probing there, asking the occasional question and testing reaction for severity of pain. Then, methodically, he set about the task of cleaning and, where possible, dressing the many abrasions. With immense care, he encased Mannion's chest in broad firm bandaging, propping his patient up and advising him to remain sitting upright rather than lying flat. The binding seemed to help Mannion's breathing and make movement less painful.

Next, the doctor bent his shiny bald head over the calf wound, which was surrounded by inflamed flesh and beginning to show signs of infection. He cleaned it a second time and re-dressed it. After half an hour's work, he seemed satisfied with his labours.

'That is as much as I can do,' he said, regarding Milan solemnly. 'The rib injuries are the most serious. There is a danger of the lung being pierced when fracturing occurs. However, I do not think any ribs are broken. Three are cracked, perhaps they have not fractured. One would need an X-ray photograph to gauge the precise extent of the damage. . . .'

'Perhaps later,' Milan said. 'We did not think it wise to move him before getting expert advice.'

Dr Suleiman gave a gracious little bow of the head.

'Any movement must be attended by great care. There is the matter of the leg wound – it appears to have been caused by a bullet.'

'Does it?' said Milan blandly.

'I have seen many bullet wounds,' Dr Suleiman said. 'This one is no more than a nasty graze but, nevertheless, it should still be reported to the correct authorities – as should the other injuries. The patient seems to have been the victim of a savage beating.'

Milan smiled.

'You have my assurance, doctor, that the authorities will be fully acquainted with all the circumstances. The first consideration was to have the injuries attended. We are most indebted to you for your prompt help.'

A faint smile crossed Dr Suleiman's dark face.

'Your indebtedness, sir, amounts to no more than a few dinars to meet the cost of those bandages and medicaments which I have used.' He named the exact sum and bowed his thanks when Milan fished in his pocket for his money and doled out the requisite amount.

When the doctor had gone, Mannion, insisting that he was fit enough, wanted to get dressed. Milan made no objection and helped with the operation when it became obvious that Mannion could not undertake the task unaided. He commented appreciatively on the quality of the smart grey suit which Mannion wanted to wear.

'This must have cost a lot of money,' he said.

'It did,' Mannion agreed. 'Maybe it'll make a good impression. If I'm going to give myself up to the police, I want to look my best.'

'It's what you want to do?' Milan asked. 'Give yourself up?' He was eyeing Mannion sharply, watching his reaction, ready to doubt him. Mannion detected that doubt.

'No need to get nervous,' he said, and there was a hint of reproach in the advice. 'I'm not going to run out on that kid. But, if it's OK with you, I'd like to do things my way. When I turn myself in, I want to do it under my own steam. That way, they'll maybe go a bit easier on me.'

'I've sent for my lawyer. Let him advise you. If you want to surrender yourself to the police – under your own steam, as you say – that's fine. But let him accompany you . . . let him speak for you. And don't worry about paying him. I'll take care of that.'

'Why should you do that for me?'

'I'm not doing if for you. I'm doing it for Jamie, that headstrong young nephew of mine.'

'I got some money. I'm not broke.'

'Enough to get a good lawyer?'

'Maybe not.'

'Then we'll say no more about it,' Milan said firmly. 'Draga Simovic will represent you. You must tell him everything. I just hope to God he can make some sense of what has happened, because I'm damned if I can. What possessed you to go to that meeting last night with a gun? That on its own is against the law. People have been hanged for less.'

While they waited for Mara to return with Simovic, Mannion told Milan why he had come to Jugoslavia and why his interest had centred on Vladimir Graz. Milan listened to the account with dismay and incredulity, concluding that the young American's naivety had been exceeded only by his stupidity.

'This is not the Wild West,' he saw fit to protest, convinced that Mannion must have embarked on his mission of family honour with a head stuffed with too many notions gained from viewing Tom Mix movies. 'Did you honestly think you could come here and take on a couple of thousand Croatian revolutionaries like a Texan sheriff rounding up a gang of cattle rustlers?'

'I didn't know what I was taking on,' Mannion confessed honestly. 'And all I know for sure is that I made the most God Almighty mess of it. OK, so I don't win any prizes for being the brightest guy in town.'

'What possessed you to go into that hall *after* you'd seen Graz meet up with those two bravos? You must have known it was asking for trouble.'

'I got tired hanging around, waiting for him to come out. I wanted to know what was going on in there, so I just walked in. . . . Nobody stopped me.'

Milan shook his head at the admission of such folly.

'That was bad enough,' he said, 'but standing up and

shouting about him having something to do with the King's assassination was downright crazy. What made you do such a thing?'

'It was the lies he was telling , the way he was going on about peace and understanding and the civilised path to change. I just got mad. I stood up without thinking. . . . I wasn't the only one who knew he was phoney – but nobody spoke up, and I just had to do something!'

Milan nodded sadly.

'With the most unfortunate results. If you'd only kept your silence, it would have been Graz who was in a police cell and not Jamie, you would have been feeling a good deal better than you are, and everyone would have been a damned sight happier!'

The one aspect of the case that gave Milan grounds for optimism was the fact that Mannion was an American. The citizen of a foreign power could sometimes get away with things that the native could not. Milan sought to cheer the younger man by voicing this hope.

'The authorities here will think twice of being too hard on you if they know you have the support of the American Government,' he said brightly. 'They will be nervous, too, if your family and friends make their voices heard –'

'My family and friends will not lift a finger,' Mannion interrupted. 'They may grieve over the mess I've made of things, but they will say nothing, do nothing, unless I ask release from my obligation of honour. That is something I will not do. It is the ultimate shame – even worse than the admission of failure.'

'You can't go on with this folly,' Milan protested.

'I can't go back,' Mannion said.

Jamie walked out into late afternoon sunlight, flanked by his uncle and Draga Simovic. The lawyer's car, a long-nosed black Citroën, was parked a short distance away along the street. The trio went towards it.

111

'You've really been in the wars,' Milan said. 'Your mother's going to have a fit when she sees you.'

'I don't think I'll ever feel clean again,' Jamie said, his voice bitter. 'The stink of that place will be with me for months.' He glanced back at the police buildings and gave an involuntary shudder. 'I'd no idea that places like that existed. I was really frightened in there, Uncle Milan.'

Milan put an arm round his shoulder.

'Learn well from the experience, Jamie. Take good care that there's never a second occasion. We had to pull a few strings to get you out.' He squeezed Jamie's shoulder affectionately and was surprised when the boy winced.

'Those cops were a bit free with their truncheons,' Jamie explained. 'You touched a tender spot.' He saw anger flash in his uncle's eyes at the revelation.

'Do you hear that, Draga?' Milan asked in an outraged voice, turning to the lawyer. 'They beat the boy!'

'That's their way, Milan. It's what comes from recruiting the police force from the back of beyond. A lot of them would have difficulty writing their own names. Thick as granite, most of them. . . . They use their truncheons instead of brains, because they've got no brains!'

'I've a mind to go back and raise hell with them!' Milan declared, far from mollified.

'It wouldn't do any good,' said the lawyer. 'Besides, you've done enough for one day.'

'Mr Simovic is right, Uncle.' Jamie was quick to support the lawyer. He was anxious to get as far away from Police Headquarters as it was possible to be; to wash the stink of the place from his body, to lie between clean sheets, to luxuriate in a commodity that had never been more precious to him than it was now – freedom.

'Yes, it has been a long day,' Milan conceded, sensing

just how great a shock the night in custody had been to his nephew. 'Will you drive us home, Draga – and stay to dinner, of course? Lucija will have fattened the calf for the return of the prodigal son.'

If the lawyer needed any persuasion, the inducement of Lucija's cooking was enough. When the three were in the car, Milan brought Jamie up to date with the day's events – in particular, the part Mannion had played in helping to effect Jamie's freedom. Although weak and hobbling like an old man, he had insisted on walking into Police Headquarters and asking to see the Chief of Police. That gentleman had been considerably impressed by the American's bearing and his statement that he was surrrendering himself to the authorities to prevent a miscarriage of justice. A student was being held for a crime of which he was entirely innocent: a shooting for which he, Mannion, was prepared to offer a full explanation. He had then handed over the gun from which two shots had been fired.

The Chief of Police, to whom the situation was entirely novel in his experience, had reacted with commendable sympathy to Mannion. He had been impressed, too, when he discovered that Draga Simovic had been engaged to represent the American and that a respected businessman, Milan Alexandrovic – who had friends at the Interior Ministry – was prepared to act as guarantor. Jamie's immediate release had been ordered. Mannion, after surrender of his passport, had been driven to hospital in a police car. There, he had been placed under police guard – not because it was feared he would try to escape but to forestall possible attempts on his life by Croatian revolutionaries.

Milan was optimistic that when a full investigation, ordered by the Chief of Police, had been made, the American would face nothing worse than deportation. Simovic was more cautious. He had been surprised by the lenient attitude shown by the civil police, who were still hopping mad that Graz was at large. They were going to be unhappier still when they discovered that a foreigner who had somehow got on to Graz's trail ahead of them and had by his interference facilitated Graz's escape was also responsible for shooting their agent.

Simovic's fears, however, were not allowed to interfere with the joyous welcome home that Jamie received from his mother and Lucija. A bonus for Jamie was finding Mara already at the house; Milan had sent her ahead to give news of his hopes for Jamie's release. All three women shed tears of relief at Jamie's deliverance, but it was Mara's which moved him most. Her moist eyes shone with feeling for him in a way that made his heart soar. He wanted to take her in his arms there and then, but the presence of the others inhibited him and seemed to inhibit her, too. They clasped hands in greeting and she lightly kissed his brow before drawing back shyly, lowering her eyes to veil the longing that he alone had been allowed to glimpse in all its burning intensity. The intimacy stayed with him like a promise as he soaked in a hot bath and scrubbed the stink of prison from his skin. It was renewed in stolen glances over the dinner table, which groaned with the platters of food set before them by Lucija. The old housekeeper had prepared enough food for a company twice their number, and Milan was in his element as host, dispensing wines as if it were a wedding feast.

After the meal was over – with Milan and the lawyer reminiscing about the war and Jelena and Lucija washing dishes in the kitchen – Jamie and Mara slipped out to the cool of the garden. There they strolled in silence, hands joined, and then, as if each had counted the seconds to this moment, they clung in shivering embrace. No words were spoken. None were needed. Their need was for each other and the blessed reassurance that only their bodies could provide. The nightmare of the last twenty-four hours was over and the proof was in their clasped closeness.

It was Mara who broke the silence.

'Oh, Jamie, Jamie, I am so happy. I want to hold you forever. I need you so much.'

He brushed a strand of hair from her forehead. The heel of his hand touched softly against her cheek. He felt the wetness of tears.

'You're crying, Mara.'

'Because I'm happy. Because I've wanted you to hold me. Because I feel the way I do. Kiss me, Jamie.'

He pressed his lips down on to hers and their tongues sought each other's. He was aware of pain in his upper lip – it was bruised and still a little swollen from the punch that had floored him the night before – but the sweetness of her mouth was the more compelling sensation. The thrust of her soft body against his thighs stirred a glorious fire in his blood, intoxicating his senses.

'I love you, Mara,' he murmured, as they drew back for breath. 'I've loved you from the moment I first saw you.'

'I was the blind one, Jamie. I thought that what I felt for Stefan was love . . . but it does not compare with what I feel for you now. I want only to be yours and to hear you tell me over and over again that you love me as much as I love you.'

'I love you, Mara. I love you. I always will. I'll love you to the end of time.'

Their lips met again and a dizzy rapture filled Jamie as he pulled her closer. His hand slid down her back and spread over her slim buttocks as he raised and drew her hard against him. He could feel the pulsing heat of her loins against the throbbing urgency of his own. She was cradled thus in his arms, her eager tongue probing hungrily for his, when a voice from across the garden intruded into their magical wonder.

It was Milan. Draga Simovic was leaving and wanted to know if Mara would like a lift back to town. With reluctance, Jamie and Mara descended from their private plateau and their goodnights, a few minutes later, were decorous and restrained after the passion of the garden. But the signals that passed between them – a squeeze of the hands, an exchange of looks with eloquent eyes – communicated a significance of mutual discovery and knowledge that stoked the fires of inner joy. It was the acknowledgement that their relationship, happy and close as it had been, had taken a giant leap forward into an unknown of inestimable pleasure – and it would never be quite the same again.

Indeed, as autumn progressed into winter and winter eased towards spring, Jamie's and Mara's love grew and blossomed from its first declaration. They became as inseparable as their respective studies at the University allowed them to be. Marriage was not discussed, but neither doubted that it was towards this cementing of their commitment to one another that they were heading. All their hopes and desires of conventional union hinged for the moment on a natural progression. First came the need to achieve the qualifications and employment that were the prerequisite of setting up home together and facing the future as man and wife. So they both worked hard at University, and allowed their loving attachment to follow a conventional path. Their lovemaking grew torrid at times but, by mutual consent, never went all the way to final consummation; each took it in turn to exercise strength to deny the fulfilment for which both their bodies hungered. When it was Jamie whose passions were the more recklessly enflamed, it was Mara who persuaded restraint. When Mara weakened and offered herself in glad surrender, it was Jamie who drew back.

Brad Mannion, meantime, was released from hospital and enjoyed a brief spell of paroled freedom. Both Jamie and Mara got to know him quite well during this period, having become implicated in his ill-fated 'mission of honour' and being sympathetic to his plight. 'Our crazy American' was how Jamie and Mara thought of him. He was the catalyst whose appearance in their lives had caused the crystallisation of their relationship, their recognition of it as love – and so they adopted Mannion and Mannion's problems as their own. The more they saw of Mannion, the more they liked him. And their affection for the American was reciprocated with interest. To Mannion, they were both special – his friends from nowhere: Jamie, who had come to his rescue like a Comanche on the warpath, and Mara, his angel of mercy.

How short of friends Mannion was became apparent when Simovic, who sought the support of the US Embassy in securing his release from charges, came against a brick wall of non-cooperation. The American Government's representatives made it clear that, in declining to accept their mandatory instructions to leave Jugoslavia, Mannion had cut himself off from any expectation of help. If he chose to behave like a gangster, he could suffer the consequences. The US Government was certainly not going to interfere now in the internal affairs of a friendly sovereign state, especially not in this case, with its political undertones and implications.

It may have been the US Embassy's haste to distance itself from Mannion that caused the Belgrade civil police authorities to take a sterner view of the American's 'crime' – or it may have been internal friction between the civil and secret police that caused a hardening of attitude – but what had, initially, seemed official sympathy to Mannion underwent a drastic change.

The first signs were apparent in the length of time the Public Attorney's office was taking in formulating the charge or charges to be brought against Mannion. Simovic, pursuing the matter, found himself repeatedly stalled by prevaricating bureaucrats who were obviously playing for time and would not be pinned down. Then there was argument as to whether proceedings against the American came within the responsibility of the Central Criminal Court or should be put in the hands of those examining magistrates who were specially commissioned to consider 'offences against the state'.

Simovic fought tooth and nail to prevent Mannion being arraigned for offences against the state because the special courts convened to hear such cases – usually spying, sabotage, subversion and crimes of a political nature – enjoyed a latitude that other courts did not. The most meagre evidence produced by police witnesses for the prosecution was usually enough to secure a conviction, no matter how valid the defence case.

Defeat for Simovic in this initial battle was signalled when Mannion's brief spell of paroled freedom came to an abrupt end. On his release from hospital, he had returned to his former lodgings in Balkanska Street and it was there, in the early hours of a November morning, that he was arrested by the secret police. He was removed to a small island prison in the Sava River, where political detainees were held to await trial.

Apart from Simovic, he was permitted no visitors. Jamie and Mara, shocked by what had happened to their friend, tried to keep his spirits up by sending him gifts of food and reading material; but this was their only contact.

It was not until mid-March of 1935 that Mannion's trial took place. It was held in camera, with press and public forbidden access. Only the verdict and sentence were published. Not a word of Simovic's eloquent defence was ever reported.

All that the world was told was that Bradislav Mannion or Djurkovic had been found guilty of offences against the state, which included: possession of a loaded weapon in a public place, the reckless discharge of firearms when challenged by an agent of the state, the attempted murder of that agent, and activities prejudicial to the interests of the state.

He was sentenced to serve seven years in a penitentiary.

Simovic came out to Milan's house to break the news personally to his friend and Jamie. They were stunned.

'But it is monstrous!' Milan declared. 'At no time did that young man do anything or say anything that was injurious to the state. All he did was pursue the state's enemies – the cut-throats who murdered our King! And this is how the state rewards him! That isn't justice, Draga! It's madness!'

Simovic did not disagree. He was weary with disillusion.

'Young Mannion was punished because Graz got away, not for what he did,' the lawyer said. 'That was the unforgivable thing as far as the secret police were concerned. Graz got away. If Mannion had killed Graz, they would have made him a public hero. Instead, Graz is living it up in Italy and thumbing his nose at us, and neither the secret police nor anybody else can do a damned thing about it! And Mannion's the one who's being made to pay.'

'I thought that his people in America could have brought more pressure to bear than they did,' Milan said bitterly. 'But they were no help at all.'

'They're in trouble with their own government,' Simovic said. 'The people who put Mannion up to this crazy stunt of avenging his grandfather have the FBI on their necks. They are being blamed for labour troubles and a lot of the anarchy that's been taking place. They were never going to be much help to the boy.'

'How did he take it?' Milan asked. 'The sentence, I mean?'

'With a brave face. It was a shock, of course; much worse than we ever expected. But he took it a lot more calmly that I did. I just could not believe my ears when the sentence was pronounced. It was the worst moment of my life, Milan.'

'Where will he be imprisoned?'

'I don't know. That's another damnable thing about those political courts. They not only keep the proceedings secret, they never say where the prisoners are sent. Not immediately, at any rate. I suppose we shall find out eventually.'

'Will Mara and I be allowed to visit him?' It was Jamie who spoke. He had listened to all that had been said, his face still white with shock. Prison, to him, was synonymous with the stinking cell he had endured for a night and a day, and the thought of Mannion having to endure more than two and a half thousand nights and days in like conditions was a horror beyond words.

'I don't know,' the lawyer confessed. 'He will be moved from the Ada Ciganlija, where he is now, but to which prison, I can't say. It could be the Lepoglava or the prison at Sremska Mitrovica. We shall just have to wait and see.'

Next day, Jamie was leaving the University – having spent most of the day preoccupied with Mannion's fate – when a voice hailed him, asking him what the hurry was. He turned to face the insolent-eyed smile of the police agent with the taste for flashy clothes. He seemed to have recovered well from his shoulder wound.

'Got a date with your Croatian floozy? Is that your hurry?' The taunting smile never left his face as he spoke. Jamie did not allow his anger to show.

'I'm on my way home, if it's of any interest to you,' he said.

'Everything you do is of interest to me,' the other said. 'Now that your Yankee friend has been put away, I intend to keep an eye on you. I know who you are now, where you live, who your friends are. We could be friends, too, if you wanted it.'

'I doubt that very much,' Jamie said.

'Do you? That is unwise. We could still run you in for what happened that night, you know. We've got more muscle than your uncle's friends. We could lift you at any time at all.'

'What do you want of me?' Jamie asked.

'I said we could be friends.' The agent continued to smile in that provoking way. 'After all, I've done you a good turn. I thought you would be grateful.'

Jamie showed his surprise.

'You've done me a good turn?'

'Sure. I've kept the heat off you. And your girl friend. Haven't you wondered why you got away with things so easily? We wanted to nail your crazy friend the Yank, but we could have had you, too. And the girl. I said you were harmless. That's why you haven't had a bad time.'

Jamie's mind was working overtime. He began to see a reason behind the agent's desire for friendship.

'You believe you've done me a good turn, and you want me to do something for you? Is that it?' he asked.

'We could be useful to each other,' the agent said.

'Could we?'

'Of course. You're a bright fellow, from what I hear. I bet there's not much that the students get up to that you don't know about. I bet you know who the real troublemakers are, and where they hang out. It would be in your interests to pass on what you hear. . . .'

Jamie was flabbergasted.

'You want me to spy for you!'

'Don't shout, for God's sake,' the agent hissed at him, looking round anxiously to see if Jamie's raised voice had been heard. 'Let's walk, shall we? We'll find somewhere to talk that isn't quite so public.'

'You can go to hell!' Jamie told him, and pushed away the hand the agent had placed on his sleeve to draw him along the street. But the agent was not going to be pushed off. He renewed his grip as Jamie tried to walk away. Low-voiced, the man tried to persuade Jamie not to be so hasty. He became more threatening when, for a second time, Jamie told him to go to hell. He gave up when Jamie broke away and joined a group of students hurrying towards a tram. But his final threat rang in Jamie's ears.

'You're the one who's going to find out all about hell!' he promised.

5

Ordeal

The land was awakening after the grip of winter. From the train chugging south, the budding splendour of spring was everywhere to be seen in the fertile farmlands and the fresh greenery of valley and hill. Mara, seated at a window, gave Jamie a running commentary as she recognised familiar landmarks and pointed them out. She was excited – and a little nervous, Jamie suspected – at the prospect of introducing him to her parents. The previous Easter, it had been Stefan whom she had taken home – and, from all accounts, it had been something of a disaster. Stefan and Mara's father had not hit it off. It had been disadvantage enough that Stefan was a Serb and not a Roman Catholic, but he had compounded these twin handicaps by airing views that had not endeared him to the head of the household.

After they had changed trains at Zagreb, Mara tried to prepare Jamie for the meeting with her mother and father. They would make him very welcome, she insisted, but he would have to make allowances for them. They were old-fashioned and, it had to be said, could be very rigid and intolerant in their attitudes. Jamie would get on fine with them, she told him, if he just acted his usual charming self with her mother and did not – as Stefan had done – try to argue politics or religion with her father. Mara said just enough to make Jamie a great deal more apprehensive about spending Easter in Karlovac than he had been when he accepted her eager invitation.

Accompanying the pair was Mara's brother, Petar,

who had two weeks' Easter leave. He was much amused by Mara's attempts to brief Jamie on parental foibles. He teasingly hinted that her warnings were only a shadow of the truth and that she was deliberately playing down how fearsome their parents really were. She was obviously scared that Jamie would take fright and take the first train back.

'What you have to appreciate,' a twinkling-eyed Petar told Jamie, 'is that our revered parents believe that Belgrade is a sink of iniquity – a kind of Sodom-and-Gomorrah-on-Danube. They have never forgiven Mara for choosing to go to the University there when she could have gone to Zagreb, or even Vienna. In their eyes, she is already a fallen woman and they are ready to be appalled by any boy she brings home with her.' Seeing the look on Jamie's face, he offered a crumb of consolation. 'But they'll like you, Jamie. You have an honest face and you don't look too depraved.'

Nothing that Mara or Petar had told him about their home or their parents did, in the event, prepare Jamie for what he found in Karlovac.

At the railway station in Karlovac, a horse and trap were waiting to convey the young trio to the Richtman home. The mode of transport was the first of many delightful surprises in store for Jamie. As a small boy in Scotland, he had often ridden in the pony and trap, which his father had used to make his rounds. Their replacement with a sturdy Morris saloon had been a sad day in Jamie's life, in spite of the excitement of motor travel.

The Richtman home was a second surprise: a handsome villa, with a single turret that gave it the look of a château. It stood amid twenty acres of wood and pasture, edged by the River Kupa, and was an enchanting place. Their surname of Richtman had suggested Germanic antecedents, as did the fact that German – or a form of it – came as readily to their lips as English to

Jamie's. The discovery, therefore, of a rich history to the Richtman family tree – and a tradition of aristocratic pretensions – was a considerable surprise to Jamie. So, too, was the comfortable elegance of their home and the almost feudal splendour in which the Richtmans lived. The Great War had not robbed them of the land and social position that had been won in the heyday of the Austrian Empire. They had somehow survived, and the family clung still to a culture and life style that owed more to Habsburg Vienna than Karadjordjevic Belgrade.

Walking in the grounds with Mara, later, Jamie had wondered why she could bear to leave such a place and exchange its tranquillity for the noise and bustle of the city.

'Because it's an anachronism,' she tried to explain. 'I love it here. I really do. But it doesn't belong in this century. Neither does my family. Mama and Papa live in the past. They want to keep everything as it was a hundred years ago, when land meant power and power was a licence to grow rich on the suffering of others. They don't seem to realise that the world is changing and they'll have to change with it.'

'You sound like Stefan,' Jamie said.

'Stefan hated it here,' she said, and then modified it. 'Not the place, but the way we lived. Us in our grand house and, down the road a little, somebody like Jovan the herder, living with his wife and ten children in a two-roomed shack with no water and no sanitation.'

Mara's father was a tall man, white-haired, who carried himself in a stiff unbending manner. He rarely smiled. Jamie never felt comfortable in his presence. Mrs Richtman was a warm bubbly woman, rather plump, but she seemed to walk in awe of her husband, scarcely opening her mouth in his presence unless he invited her to endorse something he had said.

The father's austere personality so dominated the

household that Jamie began to understand why both Mara and Petar had fled the nest at the first opportunity. They must have felt oppressed and stifled by that dour autocratic presence. It said much for both Mara and Petar that they had grown up as lively and independent-minded as they were.

The moment came, as Mara had feared it might, when her father demanded a talk with Jamie. One of the servants informed Jamie that the master was waiting to see him in the library. Jamie entered the room in trepidation. He felt like a small boy who had been summoned to the headmaster's study to account for some unspecified misdemeanour.

Richtman did not beat about the bush.

'Are you another Marxist atheist?' he asked without preamble.

Jamie was too surprised to form a coherent answer.

'The last fellow was a writer – a godless cretin. She must have told you about him,' Richtman said impatiently. 'I want to know if you're another of the same?'

'I don't think so,' said Jamie. 'Why do you ask, sir?'

'Because Mara's my daughter,' Richtman said sternly. 'And she doesn't have much sense when it comes to picking friends. The last fellow filled her head with a lot of idiotic ideas about world revolution and free love and God knows what else. Are you peddling the same kind of rubbish?'

'I'm not peddling anything,' Jamie said defensively.

'You're not thinking of marrying her, are you?'

'We're too young –' Jamie began. Richtman did not let him finish.

'And you're not one of us!' he reminded the younger man forcibly. 'When Mara gets married, it will be to one of her own kind. You'd do well to remember that.'

Jamie said nothing. He was determined to keep his temper. His silence seemed to please Richtman, who misinterpreted it.

'Well, we seem to understand each other,' he said, with an air of satisfaction. 'I believe in plain speaking. I hope you understand why it was necessary.'

'I'm not sure that I do,' said Jamie politely.

Richtman stared hard at him, suspecting insolence.

'Mara has always been a difficult child. She thinks because she if far away in Belgrade most of the time that she can do as she pleases. It gives her a perverse delight to try to shock us by coming back to Karlovac every so often and letting us see the kind of friends she has. The more unsuitable, the better.' Richtman made a deprecatory flourish of his hands. 'I say that to you without ill feeling. You may be a decent enough boy, but you probably know well enough without me telling you that Mara's not for you. She's just using you to try to upset her mother and me.'

Jamie flushed.

'I don't think Mara's like that,' he said softly.

'She has always been like that,' Richtman said smugly. 'I know my daughter. It's my own fault, of course. I've always indulged her too much. But we're not so easily shocked as she seems to think. Let her play her little games. It does no harm so long as no one takes them seriously. Especially you. That's why this little talk was necessary. I'm sure you understand.'

Jamie made no attempt to argue with the older man. It would have been a futile exercise. He doubted if there was anything he could say that would have pierced the layers of monstrous insensitivity that shut Richtman off from the rest of the human race. The man's mind worked at a level that did not permit two-way communication – like a radio that was pre-tuned to transmit on a single waveband and could not be adjusted to receive incoming signals.

What was incomprehensible to Jamie was how a girl as sweet and considerate as Mara could be the progeny of such an insufferable boor. His pride was sufficiently hurt by the interview to make him want to return at once to Belgrade. Only Mara's tears stopped him from doing so.

She was mortified when Jamie told her what her father had said.

'I hate him!' she cried with passion. 'He has no feelings – for my mother, for me, for Petar, for anyone. I have never known him to do an act of kindness, to say a kind word, even. He makes me ashamed . . . so ashamed.'

Jamie was affected by her distress. He gave no credence to her father's claim that Mara had used him to upset her parents. It was simply further illustration, if any were needed, of how small Richtman's understanding of his daughter was.

'Please don't go back to Belgrade,' Mara pleaded with Jamie. 'It would be giving in to him. And I don't want you to go. None of us do. Mama likes you – and Petar would never forgive you if you gave Papa the satisfaction of frightening you off. If it weren't for Mama, I don't think he would ever come back here at all. Please stay, for my sake – for all our sakes.'

Jamie stayed. And happily for all concerned, Mara's father suddenly took off for Maribor on business that would keep him there indefinitely. He showed little concern that his son and daughter would probably be gone before he returned. His departure signalled a change of atmosphere in the stately villa, where his presence had engendered gloom and strain. It was as if all the curtains had been opened and the windows thrown wide to admit the sunlight and warm hope of spring.

If their holiday had started badly, it soon took on an idyllic quality for Mara and Jamie. The pleasant valley seemed to have been fashioned for young lovers, and it took on the qualities of another Eden as they explored its sunlit tracks and grassy woodlands on horseback. All heaven seemed to smile on them as they picnicked happily by the banks of the Kupa and waved to the crews of wheat-laden motor barges heading upstream for the docks at Karlovac.

The clouds of the gathering storm were nowhere to be seen.

An early-morning mist hung over Belgrade. It would disperse when the April sun got up but at this hour – it was a little after four a.m. – it clung low over the city and wreathed the bluffs of the Kalemegdan. Luk sat in the back of the small black car, directing the driver as the vehicle cut diagonally across the city, turning left and right alternately at the junctions. The streets were deserted and the mist had made the tramlines greasy, so that the tracks tended to trap the solitary car's tyres and make the vehicle slip as the driver cornered.

Luk ordered the driver to slow down in Dusinova Street.

'Turn left along here,' he told him. 'And let Banjo get out. I'll stay in the car.' The man referred to as Banjo got out when the car stopped. He had been sitting beside the driver and, when he got out, he kept the door open and waited for Luk's instructions.

'You know the house,' Luk said. 'Keep out of sight and watch it. We'll turn the car round and sit here. Get back here quickly if our man leaves the house.'

'Right, chief,' the man called Banjo acknowledged. 'If my tip-off is right, he's an early bird. We shouldn't have long to wait.' He slammed the passenger door shut and, turning up his collar against the early-morning chill, he walked briskly back towards Dusinova Street.

Luk sat back in the car and lit a cigarette. He hoped Banjo's tip-off had been a good one, for the young officer's sake. The department had been after Banjo's 'early bird' for some weeks now, and someone was going to get the rough edge of Luk's tongue if this turned out to be a false alarm. Luk was aware that the young officer tried to ape him, that he had aspirations of being a second 'Luk, the Legend'.

He even prized his nickname, 'Banjo', preferring the jokey appellation to his given names, in the hope that legend would stick to it, as it had to Luk's. Luk should have been flattered, he supposed, at being the younger man's model. But he was not. He had reservations about Banjo. For a start , he was not the brightest of specimens. He lacked intelligence and subtlety. He favoured the crude approach because he was incapable of any other. But maybe he would learn. Everybody had to learn. The trouble with Banjo was that he took longer to learn than most. Stopping that bullet in the shoulder should have taught him something, but there was not much evidence that it had. He was still fond of clothes that made him look like a brothel-keeper's tout. Sooner or later, he would find out that it paid in the service to cultivate the art of being inconspicuous, that anonymity was an asset.

Luk had smoked a second cigarette and was contemplating a third when the agent, Banjo, came hurrying towards the car.

'He has just left the house,' he told Luk through the open window. 'I'm sure it's our man.'

'Is he carrying anything?' Luk asked.

'A bag – like a worker's tool bag.'

'That's promising,' Luk said. 'It could be the goods. Well, this time, he doesn't deliver. Get in. We'll pick him up.'

The car crawled the short distance to Dusinova Street and, on Banjo's direction, turned right. A hundred metres away, a lone figure was trudging along the street. The car quickly overtook him and drew up. Luk and Banjo were out of the car before it had stopped, and they confronted the solitary walker before he realised what was happening. He stood poised for a moment, as if considering the possibility of making a bolt for it. But the gun in Banjo's hand was sufficient deterrent. He dropped the tool bag and raised his arms in response to the agent's crisp command.

'What is you name?' Luk asked, as Banjo frisked the detained man for a weapon.

'Markovic . . . Stefan Markovic.'

'What is in your bag?'

'Nothing.'

Luk stooped and opened the bag. It was crammed with leaflets. He stared up at Stefan and shook his head sadly.

'The usual stuff, is it? Workers of the world unite, you have nought to lose but your chains?'

Stefan said nothing.

'Unite him with his chains,' Luk said, with a nod to Banjo. The agent handcuffed Stefan and bundled him towards the car. He punched Stefan in the kidneys as he pushed him into the back seat.

'Save the rough stuff,' Luk commanded the agent. 'You get the bag.' He climbed into the back of the car beside Stefan, while the agent retrieved the bag containing the leaflets. The driver looked back over his shoulder at Luk and the prisoner.

'Where to, chief?'

'Glavnjaca.' He smiled grimly at Stefan, aware that his prisoner had stiffened involuntarily at mention of the prison. 'Been there before?'

'No,' Stefan said tersely.

'Smelly place,' said Luk. 'But they say you get used to it.'

At the Belgrade Central Prison, Stefan was escorted downstairs to the cellar block. Luk accompanied him.

'You're getting number six all to yourself,' he told Stefan. 'You're lucky. It's not usually empty.' He entered the roomy cell with Stefan, who stared at him defiantly as his handcuffs were removed.

'I'm going to give you a little time to think about

131

things,' Luk said. 'While I'm having breakfast, you can put the time to good use. You can think about the mess you're in and how hopeless things are for you . . . how hard the system is on poor deluded mugs like yourself, who've been caught bang to rights. My guess is that you could get anything from five to ten years just for that bundle of seditious claptrap you were carrying. Now, if you've got any sense at all, you'll cooperate with us. You'll tell us everything we want to know. That way, you can save us and yourself a lot of grief.'

'I'll tell you nothing,' Stefan said fiercely. The outburst caused Luk to stare at him sorrowfully. He had seen bravado before. He was no stranger to defiance, to brave words. Once, they had angered him. Now, they saddened him.

'Think over what I have said to you,' he advised Stefan. 'You're young, and I know how strong the temptation is to play the martyr. But our cemeteries are full of martyrs and our prisons are full to overflowing with others who would like to be. It's a damnable waste, sonny. Don't add to it.'

He turned and walked out. Stefan was left undisturbed for fully two hours: time to make himself fully acquainted with every corner of the cell and to prepare for the interrogation which he knew would come in due course. He thought the moment had come when he heard the key turning in the lock and the cell door was flung open. But it was not Luk who stood there, framed in the light. A terrified youth cowered in the grip of a figure Stefan recognised as the younger of the agents who had arrested him; Stefan also recognised him from an encounter in the Dancing Bear, and knew he had been involved in the shooting incident with Mara, Jamie and the American. The older of the agents had addressed him oddly. Banjo, he had called him. A funny name for such a thug.

He betrayed thuggish qualities now. He threw the

quivering youth into the cell, sending him sprawling on the cement floor. Then he followed up by lashing out at him with his feet, kicking him twice in the body.

He muttered an obscenity and, with a harsh laugh of satisfaction, straightened his clothes and strode out of the cell. The heavy door clanged shut. Stefan was already bent over the youth, trying to comfort him and find out how badly he was hurt. The boy had taken several knocks before the kicks Stefan witnessed, and he was weeping uncontrollably. The weeping had given way to sobs and Stefan was mopping blood from the boy's face when, in the abysmal light, Stefan recognised him. He was the engineering apprentice who roomed next to him in Dusinova Street and with whom he shared a small kitchen.

'Petko!' Stefan cried. 'It's you! Why have they done this to you? Why have they run you in?'

The youth's sobbing halted as he stared up at Stefan, realising the identity of his cellmate.

'It's because of you, damn you!' he cried accusingly at Stefan. 'I have done nothing! I'm not a Communist! I don't even know any Communists! I didn't believe them when they said you were! You've got to tell them I'm innocent!'

'I'll tell them, I'll tell them,' Stefan soothed. 'But you haven't told me why you've been arrested. You must have done something.'

'I've done nothing!' the youth protested, shrill with the injustice of what had happened to him. 'They were searching your room. That goon who brought me here and another one. I only looked in to see what the commotion was. I didn't know who they were and what they were doing in your room. They just grabbed me and started hitting me and shouting at me. I tried to tell them that I scarcely knew you, that I hardly ever saw you . . . but they said I was lying and that I was in cahoots with you. I don't know anything about any illegal leaflets.

133

You've got to tell them, Stefan! You're the only one who can save me!'

'I'll tell them, Petko,' Stefan assured the frightened youth. 'They're fools. They've made a mistake. You have my promise that I'll swear to your innocence.'

'What if they don't believe *you*?'

The same thought had occurred to Stefan and it worried him. But he tried not to transmit that worry to the distressed Petko. He just had to hope that the secret police would realise that the boy was about as politically dangerous as a bag of cement. If he'd ever heard about Karl Marx, which was doubtful, he was probably not familiar enough with his doctrines to know the difference between them and those of Thomas Aquinas.

Stefan's frame of mind was made no easier when, after ten hours in Petko's company, the cell door was again opened and it was the youth who was removed. He was bundled away in a state of abject terror. He was not returned.

Towards midnight, the cell door was again opened. Stefan was ordered to accompany the two gendarmes who waited in the corridor. He was manacled between them and led towards the stairs. He knew then that the time for his own interrogation had come.

Jamie noticed the small black van parked on the muddy verge near his uncle's house, but thought nothing of it. As he usually did, he entered by the side gate that led through the high wall into the Turkish garden. The family so seldom used the front door that it remained almost permanently locked. The pleasant aroma of chicken roasting tickled at his nostrils before he reached the kitchen, where Lucija was chopping up vegetables on her worktable.

Jamie put down his suitcase and went to give her a hug, and was surprised when the old woman burst into tears as he wrapped his arms around her.

'What's the matter, Lucija? Have you missed me that much?' he teased her, with warm concern. 'I've only been gone ten days.'

But it was not Jamie's absence in Karlovac and the joy of having him back that had sparked Lucija's display of emotion. It was fear for him and dread of what he had come home to.

'The police are here,' she told him, sobbing the words out. 'They have been questioning your mother. But it is you they want! I wanted to telephone for your uncle, but they have forbidden me to leave the kitchen. Oh, if only he were here! I am afraid for you, Jamie. They will take you away again!'

'But I'm not in any trouble,' he assured the old woman. 'It must be a mistake. Come on, we'll go and see what they want.'

Jelena Kyle and the two uniformed gendarmes were in what she called the terrace room, which had access to the garden. She was in total control of herself and the situation, having persuaded the two men to accept cake and red wine – so that the 'mistake' of the arrest order for Jamie could be discussed in a calm and civilised manner. She had explained that Jamie was due home from a holiday in Karlovac and that all the uncertainty would be cleared up as soon as he arrived.

The rough-hewn gendarmes, disarmed by the forceful personality of this elegant and charming woman, were sitting meekly on the edge of cane chairs listening to her holding forth on the subject of mistaken identity. Her son could not possibly have committed any offence in Belgrade – now, could he? – and be somewhere in the wilds of Croatia at the same time. The argument was not one that the gendarmes made any attempt to answer. They had no idea what it was that her son was supposed to have done. Their orders were simply that they had to bring him in – and Jamie's arrival did nothing to weaken their insistence on that point. Perhaps out of respect for their erstwhile hostess, they were apologetic having to handcuff Jamie in her presence. Once they had secured their prisoner, their anxiety to leave the house was great. In any other circumstances, Jamie might have found their relief to escape from his mother amusing.

'Where are you taking him?' Jelena demanded, as Jamie was ushered towards the black car which he had seen outside.

'To Headquarters, *Gospoda*,' one of the policemen replied.

'My brother will have a lawyer there as soon as you are!' was her parting shot.

While the police car was still manoeuvring out into the road, she was ringing Milan's number. He, in turn, lost no time in getting hold of Draga Simovic. Nor did the lawyer delay in presenting himself at Police Headquarters. He arrived there just ten minutes after Jamie had been charged with sedition and conspiracy and taken up in the elevator to a room on the third floor.

A uniformed officer informed Simovic that he was not being permitted access to the prisoner. No one was being allowed to see him. The lawyer demanded to know why.

'It has nothing to do with me,' the officer retorted angrily. 'It is the express orders of Chief Luk. If you don't like it, take it up with him!'

There was a table at one end of the longish rectangular room. Jamie recognised the man sitting there, head bent over papers, even before the man turned to inspect his arrival. There was gloating triumph in Banjo's gaze as he surveyed Jamie.

'So they finally found you, comrade?' he inquired, with a leer. 'I was beginning to think that you'd skipped it. You didn't put up a fight, did you? No, you couldn't have . . . you would have been carried in if you had.'

Jamie's heart was in his boots. Even when those ridiculous charges were read out to him, he had been sure that he was the victim of a crazy mistake – but now he was far from sure. Now, it dawned that he could be the victim of something else, and it was staring him in the face – malice.

'I didn't have you figured for a comrade, comrade,' Banjo was saying. 'I thought you were much too swank for that. Just shows you never can tell.' Jamie did not respond to his taunting – not that he was given the opportunity. Banjo seemed to like the sound of his own voice and was happy to keep up a sarcastic monologue about poor little rich boys who dabbled in revolutionary politics. It was interrupted by the arrival of a stocky older man in a rumpled grey suit. The newcomer had a craggy, worn kind of face that somehow went with the suit, but there was a brightness in the eyes that stared at Jamie from below heavy lids.

'So, this is the other Red,' he said, scarcely glancing at Banjo as the agent hurriedly surrendered his seat at the table. Luk continued to stare at Jamie as he sat down, commenting: 'They're recruiting them young these days. How old are you, boy?'

'Eighteen,' Jamie said. 'And I'm not a Red. Somebody's making a big mistake.'

'Oh?' Luk arched his heavy eyebrows. 'Well, you've nothing to worry about. Do you know who I am?'

'No, sir.'

The man in the grey suit smiled.

'That's refreshing,' he said. 'The name is Luk. And you could say that mistakes are my business. I deal in them. Usually, they lead me to people who break the law. Have you broken the law, boy?'

'No, sir.'

Luk smiled again.

'No hesitation there. Good! I like straight answers. And you're polite, too. I like that. I like a youngster who has the manners to address his elders in a respectful fashion. But, to get back to the law. . . . Do you know that the Communist Party is an illegal organisation?'

'Yes.'

'Are you Communist?'

'No, sir.'

Luk sighed. He riffled idly through papers on the desk in front of him.

'We have information to the contrary. We have information to suggest that you are a Communist or – and it amounts to the same thing – you are the active associate of known Communists and revolutionaries who are inciting the overthrow of this country's legal government.'

'Then your information is wrong,' said Jamie. He threw a worried glance in Banjo's direction. 'Did it come from him? Is it because of his lies that I've been brought here?'

The suggestion seemed to startle Luk. He stared wide-eyed at the agent for a moment and then back at Jamie. He smiled.

'Of course, you two are old friends. Or should I say acquaintances?' He beamed. 'Banjo does let his enthusiasm carry him away at times – but you are quite mistaken if you think that it is he who betrayed you. No, my boy, we have a sworn statement from a witness whose word I have no reason to doubt. And, of course, we have other evidence that is equally damning.'

Jamie felt a prickle of fear at Luk's calm authoritative statement. *What witness? What other evidence?*

'You don't look so sure of yourself,' Luk observed mildly. 'Is it because you honestly didn't know what you were letting yourself in for when you got yourself inolved, boy? Did your so-called friends mislead you?' Luk sighed. 'Friends desert you when the heat's on, sonny. It's a pity you have to learn it the hard way.'

Jamie stared at him, saying nothing. His eyes met the firm unblinking gaze of his interrogator.

'You are a friend of Stefan Markovic?'

'Yes, sir.' Jamie barely whispered the words.

'He rents a room at number forty-three, Dusinova Street. Have you visited him there?'

'Two or three times, yes.'

'And you helped him in the printing and distribution of anti-Government leaflets?'

'No!' Jamie cried.

Luk ignored the denial. He continued to speak in the same flat voice.

'You helped him to obtain paper and printing materials. You obtained these from your uncle's works, probably. . . . You may even have printed the stuff for Markovic on the hand press there. We're checking up on that. We've already established how you made contact with Markovic in the first place. Not the most original of ideas – advertising an English class in the newspaper.' Luk glowered at Jamie. 'Is the Croatian girl one of your cell? Or did you and Markovic use her as cover?'

'None of this is true!' Jamie cried.

'You deny it?' Luk asked, his expression pitying. 'Don't you realise that denying it isn't going to help you? Your denials aren't going to make the proof of your guilt disappear. They are only going to make things go harder for you. So, why don't you do the sensible thing and tell us everything you know? I can afford to take a generous view if you make a complete confession. I don't want to see your entire life ruined because of a crazy impulse that made you think that revolution would make this a better world. I know what it is to be young and idealistic . . . I can forgive the folly of being young and wanting to change the world. But I can't forgive it if you persist in your folly. I can't be generous if you reject the one lifeline I am able to throw you. Help me and I will help you. Tell me everything. Give me names. . . .'

'I can't tell you anything!' Jamie's voice was shrill with despair. 'I haven't done anything.'

His assertion seemed to pain Luk. The latter took a sheet of paper from the desk in front of him: a page of writing paper that Jamie recognised, with surprise.

'Let me read something to you, Luk said. 'I quote: "*Mara has told me all about your difficulties last year with her father. It is a comfort to know that I have made no better an impression than you. Yesterday, I was summoned to His Excellency's presence and made to feel like a worm that has just crawled out of the ground. His first words to me were to demand if I was another Marxist atheist. Which shows how perceptive he is! He clearly had us twigged for two of a kind. I was flattered, of course, to be classed in the same bracket as someone of your towering intellect, even if one of the terms used – godless cretin – was less than flattering!"'*

Luk put the sheet of notepaper down and stared hard at Jamie, who was wondering how his letter to Stefan from Karlovac came to be in his interrogator's hands, only a week after it had been written.

'Well?' Luk's eyes bored into Jamie like gimlets. 'Do you deny that these are your words?'

'No, but how . . .?'

'How are we in possession of the letter you wrote to Stefan Markovic?' Luk smiled. 'It was found in his room, along with a lot of that young man's own writings – a lot of which was seditious. What wasn't seditious was like your letter to him – very indiscreet.'

'What I wrote in that letter – it meant nothing. It was a joke.' Even to his own ears, Jamie's stammered explanation sounded feeble. Luk snorted his derision.

'Joke! It amuses you to describe yourself as a Marxist atheist? You don't throw up your hands in horror. You do not protest and cry that it is untrue. No! No, you comment on the perception of the man who calls you this and accept it as a compliment because it classifies you as a firebrand revolutionary like the friend whose intellect you admire so much!'

Luk got up from behind the table, with the air of one whose patience has snapped.

'I have wasted enough time with this stupid boy,' he said to Banjo. 'Give him some more time in the cells to think about what I've said to him. I shall be back from Zemun at about nine tonight. He has until then to come to his senses and make a full confession.' With a final angry look in Jamie's direction, he left the room.

'You heard what the boss said,' Banjo threatened, prodding Jamie with a stubby finger. 'You've got until nine o'clock to change that tune you've been whistling. Know what'll happen after that if you don't spill the whole works? It'll be me who asks the questions.' His eyes glittered. 'That's something to look forward to. Just you, me and one of the others to hold you down and see you don't yell too loud.'

Jamie had no way of knowing the time, but it was exactly nine in the evening when he was brought for a second time to the room on the third floor. There was no sign of Luk. It was as the agent called Banjo had promised – just him, Jamie and a strapping gendarme. The latter's first act in Jamie's sight was to take off his uniform tunic and roll up the sleeves of the collarless shirt beneath.

In expectation of the nine o'clock deadline, Jamie's mind had been gripped in turn by fear and bewilderment. Now, in this room, fear had gained the ascendant and he was tense with the effort of trying to conceal the stark terror that consumed him. He stared wide-eyed at the implements scattered on the table at which Luk had previously sat: a strange whiplike instrument with a short handle, a length of thin rope, a stave like a broomhandle, a towel, a piece of spongy leather with a strap attached. He dreaded to think what they signified.

'We're ready for you,' Banjo greeted Jamie. 'The chief's sorry he couldn't make it. He's been detained. It'll be nearly midnight before he gets here. I said we'd have a full confession from you by then.'

'I can't confess to things I haven't done,' Jamie said, trying to keep his voice from shaking. 'I'm still not sure what it is I'm supposed to have done.'

'You know all right,' Banjo snapped. 'We caught Markovic with the leaflets and we know you were with him in his little games, up to the neck. But we want to hear it all from you. We want your party contacts – their names, how you meet them, where you get your funds, who gives the orders, how many of you deliver the leaflets. . . .'

'I don't know what you're talking about,' Jamie said.

Banjo slapped his face. Jamie staggered under the blow. The sudden pain and shock of it filled him with anger. He forgot his fear and vulnerability and stared defiantly at the agent.

'I've got nothing to tell you, damn you!'

Banjo nodded at the gendarme. Jamie felt himself gripped from behind and forced down into a sitting position on the floor. He was ordered to remain there. The gendarme took the stave from the table and thrust it behind Jamie's knees, jamming it in the crook formed by his bent limbs. Then he tied Jamie by the wrists, so that they were secured under the stave and fastened to his own legs below knee level. He was thus rendered helpless in a kind of immobile foetus position.

The gendarme rocked him back and forward and then pushed him, so that he fell forward, head tumbling, and rolled on to his back, with his feet in the air.

Banjo's grinning face loomed into view above him. The gendarme had not finished his work. He pulled off Jamie's shoes and socks and trussed his ankles together with cord. Then the man bent over him and told Jamie to open his mouth. The spongy leather which Jamie had seen on the table was thrust into his mouth between his teeth and he was told to bite on it. The strap attached to it was fastened behind his neck.

'Get the cloth,' Banjo told the gendarme. Jamie heard but he did not see the man take the towel from the table and rinse it it a bucket of water that stood in a corner of the room. He placed the wet cloth over the upturned soles of Jamie's feet. Banjo's head and shoulders re-appeared. He was wielding the whiplike implement, holding it by the short handle.

'Know what this is, comrade?' he leered. 'It's a pizzle. We get the prisoners to make them.' Jamie's eyes widened as his tormentor dangled the implement within inches of his nose. 'Ever been this close to a bull's penis before?' Banjo taunted. 'That's what this was before it was stretched and dried. Something to think about, isn't it – how many cows it serviced in its day?'

Jamie heard the thwack as Banjo brought the pizzle down hard on the seat of a nearby chair. His body jerked involuntarily at the shock of the sound.

'Are you going to talk?' Banjo asked, bending low over Jamie. 'All you need to do is nod your head.' Jamie could only stare at him hopelessly. Banjo smiled. 'You asked for it.'

Jamie closed his eyes and waited. He had read somewhere about this form of torture and the Turks' regard for it. Garden architecture, coffee and tobacco were not the only things the Turk had bequeathed to the Jugoslav. It was a shock, nevertheless, to discover in this fashion that anything so medieval as bastinado still existed in the twentieth century.

The first blow, when it came, exceeded all Jamie's expectation of pain. He felt the knifelike cut of the stroke across the soles of his feet and the instantaneous transmission to his brain of lightning-like fire that registered with excruciating shock. He screamed, but the sound was strangled by the gag in his mouth.

The way that Banjo measured the length of time between successive strokes of the pizzle seemed to be calculated to create the maximum psychological cruelty, which made the physical pain all the more difficult to endure. There was an interval between the lingering shock of one blow and the certainty of the next that produced an agony of expectation in the victim's mind, as refined in its torture as the burning bit of the lash. Jamie bit hard into the unsavoury gag as he braced mind and body for each fresh stroke – but each still came with a suddenness that surprised the system, provoking a muscular reaction that made the whole body convulse against its immobilising bonds.

Time ceased to have meaning as the punishment went on. Existence on a conscious level was measured on a pain scale at an extreme register. There were the scream-forcing pinnacles as the lash bit, separated from one another by shallow troughs of lingering pain and outraged senses. The blows fell without number . . . thirty, forty times – Jamie did not keep count. His mind was totally occupied between endurance of the last and anticipation of the next. He did not faint, but slid into an area of consciousness that recognised neither time nor place nor people.

It ended when the sadistic Banjo grew tired of exercising his arm, to no apparent avail. No longer did his victim scream out in agony. Each cut of the pizzle drew no more than a shuddering gasp.

When the gendarme undid Jamie's bonds and propped him up in a straight-backed wooden chair, he had to secure him to it to stop him falling off. Awareness returned to Jamie with a deep sense of humiliation. He felt violated, unmanned, as if his self-respect had been peeled away from him. It shamed him that the whimpering noises he could hear were emanating from his own throat. Tears of shame burned down his cheeks.

And there, taunting him and mocking his tears was his tormentor. Jamie, resistance gone, had not the will to respond to the taunts. He could only endure them. Banjo became more frustrated by the second as a result of Jamie's indifference to his goading. His screamed demands for a confession were met with the same blank indifference. He slapped and pummelled Jamie, but Jamie scarcely felt the blows.

Eventually, Banjo gave up trying to extract a sensible response and retired behind the table to glare at his victim, defeated. It was to this state of stalemate that Luk returned.

The senior officer stared unhappily at the spectacle of Jamie slumped in the chair.

'Untie him,' he ordered the gendarme. To Jamie, he said: 'Can you speak?'

Jamie nodded dumbly.

'Have you confessed?' Luk asked.

Jamie shook his head. Tears blinked unbidden in his eyes.

'I have nothing to confess,' he mumbled.

'It distresses me that it has come to this,' Luk said. 'It takes courage to suffer. You know that it's not over yet?'

'I have nothing to confess,' Jamie repeated.

Luk nodded. His eyes met Jamie's and, for a moment, they were lit by a gleam that might have been sympathy. He said:

'No, you've nothing to confess. That's the tragedy of it. That's the waste. That's the hellish futility of the games we play. Because your confession doesn't matter. Your side will say it was beaten out of you and is worthless. Our side – and, by that, I mean the law and those who are sworn to administer it – will say that it is irrelevant. They don't want admissions of guilt, they want proof of it.' Luk shook his head sadly. 'We can prove your guilt, sonny, and that means you're damned whatever you do. All you can prove is that you're brave. . . . But there are no brave men, sonny – only stupid ones.'

Jamie heard Luk's words but they rolled over him. They were just sounds on the air.

There were to be more brutal interrogation sessions with Banjo, all of which were as unproductive as the first in extracting a 'confession' from Jamie. He was spared further beatings on the soles of his feet but this was scarcely a concession on Banjo's part. He resorted to a variety of crude tortures to hurt and humiliate his prisoner: suspending him upside down and trussed like a chicken, threatening him with castration, knocking him about with fist and boot. There were times when Jamie would have been prepared to confess to any crime, in order to bring an end to his misery. The fact that he did not was due entirely to Banjo's failure to perceive how close he had come to breaking Jamie's spirit. The result was that when Jamie was ready to give up and sought in his distress to indicate his surrender, his intention was misread or ignored and the opportunity missed. The pressure on him was relaxed, and with the relaxation came recovery of Jamie's will. The knowledge of his own innocence sustained him and yet, ironically, it was his tormentors' ignorance of his innocence that fuelled their efforts to break him. The more Jamie resisted intimidation, the more he established his guilt in his captors' eyes. It demonstrated political conviction and fanaticism typical of the Communist hardliners who were their most doughty opponents. Of all the terrorists and conspirators who waged war on the state, the Communists were the most resolute in refusing to compromise their ideals or their comrades. They preferred to suffer and, if necessary, to die. Their code demanded silence before the police. To cooperate, when arrested, meant expulsion from the Party and ignominy.

Silence and non-cooperation formed the basis of Stefan Markovic's behaviour in custody. The reward, from Luk's police, differed little from the treatment meted out to Jamie. He, too, was brought close to breaking by painful beatings and brutal interrogation – but his lips retained, intact, his ideals of the achievement of social justice through revolution. His faith was unshaken and had sustained him through the darkest hours of his ordeal. Jamie had the comfort of no such faith. It was ironic, therefore, that the more Jamie denied adherence to the apostleship of revolution, the more he proclaimed to his accusers a deep attachment to that faith.

It was not until Luk and his lieutenants had decided that Jamie was not going to confess and inform on his and Stefan's fellow activists that Jamie was brought face to face with the witness whose testimony had led to Jamie's arrest. Jamie was not warned of the confrontation in advance. When he was taken from his cell to the familiar room on the third floor, he made his way there with the resigned dread that another interrogation was in prospect.

Both Luk and Banjo were already there, seated at the long table. Jamie, his hands manacled behind his back, was ordered to sit in the solitary straight-backed chair that faced the table. The chair was isolated in the centre of the room, directly below a ceiling light – the prisoner's chair – and Jamie's movement towards it was automatic. When he was seated, the interrogation would begin.

But it did not. Today, the pattern was different. Luk sent Banjo away, having whispered something to him that Jamie could not hear. He regarded Jamie solemnly.

'I watched you walk in here,' he said. 'You were walking on the sides of your shoes. They call that the thief's walk.'

'I have sore feet,' Jamie said. The words sounded defiant.

Luk laughed softly.

'So did the thieves who walked that way. It was a sure sign that the magistrates had let them off with a hundred strokes of the pizzle.' When Jamie did not reply, he added: 'That was a light sentence. The Turks used to chop off hands for petty theft. A cruel people, the Turks.'

Jamie was silent. When it came to cruelty, the Turks weren't the only practitioners he could think of. Luk seemed to read his thoughts.

'You think I'm a cruel bastard, don't you? You blame me for what's happened to you here? You can't forgive it.'

'Is that what you want from me – forgiveness?' Jamie's voice was bitter.

'No, sonny,' Luke said testily. 'What I wanted from you was information – the names of your contacts . . . the names of the people who poisoned your young mind with the false glories of Marxism and Leninism and all the other damned "isms" you worship. I hate the people who've done that to you, boy. But I don't hate you. I'm sorry that you choose to be my enemy, because it's a misguided choice. And because it's my job to destroy you and all the others like you who want to bring anarchy to the streets. Do you think it gives me any pleasure to destroy you? To see you sacrificing yourself and your youth because some jargon-shouting revolutionary socialist has stuffed your mind with ideas you can't fully understand?'

Jamie was shaking from head to toe.

'I can't tell you what I don't know!' he protested shrilly. 'Why won't you listen to *me*? I'm not a revolutionary! I don't know any revolutionaries! It's a mistake! You've got the wrong person!'

His vehemence seemed to take Luk aback. The older man stared at him with the perplexed air of someone pierced by sudden doubt. Then he shook his head – as if to shed the uncertainties from his mind.

'I'll say this for you, boy,' he said. 'You put on a convincing act. You had me going for a minute there. I didn't think the liar was born who could put it over on Luk, but you come close. I was almost believing you. . . .'

'Because I'm telling you the truth!' Jamie's cry was edged with hysteria. It rang with the outrage he felt at the monstrous injustice that had been perpetrated against him. Luk just stared at him: no uncertainty in his expression now – only a grudging admiration for what he took to be Jamie's unflagging obstinacy.

It was at that moment that Banjo chose to return. With him – looking white-faced and nervous – was a young man of about Jamie's age. His face was familiar to Jamie, but he could not place him immediately. Then he remembered. He had seen him before at Stefan's. He roomed at the same house on Dusinova Street.

'Don't be afraid, Petko,' Luk greeted the young man. 'Nobody's going to hurt you. Is there anyone here you recognise?'

Petko forced himself to look at Jamie.

'That's him,' he said.

'The one who brought the paper to Stefan Markovic?' prompted Luk.

'Yes,' Petko replied, his eyes avoiding Jamie's

'Did you know what the paper was going to be used for?'

'No. Not at the time.'

'But you know now,' said Luk. 'And what made you think this one here was a Communist?'

'He and Stefan wanted me to stir up trouble at the factory where I worked. They made fun of me because I worked nights as a dishwasher, just to make ends meet. They said that, instead, I should be organising the workers to go on strike for more money.'

'He's lying!' Jamie shouted. His anger and disbelief were all the greater from knowing that, apart from the briefest courtesies, he and Petko had never engaged in conversation. His attempt to contradict these lies was short-lived, however. Banjo advanced on him as soon as he opened his mouth, and a blow to the solar plexus was accompanied by dire threats of what he could expect if he interrupted a second time. This show of violence had the effect of terrifying Petko into stammering incoherence.

'Pull yourself together, damn you,' Luk growled at the

youth. 'He won't interrupt again, and don't worry about his friends. We'll make sure they won't lay a finger on you. You've nothing to be afraid of.'

Jamie was forced to listen in bewildered silence as, piece by piece, the frightened youth recounted the detail of incidents and conversations that revealed Jamie as the willing partner of Stefan in clandestine political activity. All of it was fantasy, fabricated for no reason Jamie could comprehend by a virtual stranger whom he had never harmed nor given cause to bear ill will. Puzzling Jamie more than anything was the elaborate nature of the untruths, which were prodded from Petko by a patient and painstaking Luk. It was as if the youth, having given utterance to one lie, had to build and enlarge upon it in order to reinforce the imaginative mendacity of the original.

Luk drew the damning testimony from him like a miner chiselling tiny nuggets of rich ore from an unlikely rockface. He cunningly sought to trip the youth into contradicting himself, but he never did. Petko leapt from lie to lie like someone crossing a swift river by boulders brushed by the torrent, sometimes landing awkwardly but gaining confidence when no fatal slip resulted.

When, finally, Luk ordered Banjo to remove the youth, he faced Jamie with an air of satisfaction. Follow that, his expression said.

'Every word was a lie,' Jamie ground out accusingly.

'A court will decide that. And, unfortunately for you, it will be his word they take – not yours.'

'But it was fiction, all of it. You've scared him into making it all up.'

Luk laughed.

'Oh, Banjo put the fear of death in him all right. He's easily frightened, that one. But it was the truth that Banjo frightened out of him. He lied at first, but Banjo only had to wave the pizzle in his face to get him singing like a canary.'

So that was it! Banjo had frightened the life out of Petko, and Petko had simply told him what Banjo had wanted to hear, inventing meetings and conversations that had never taken place – anything that diverted suspicion away from himself. What Petko had done was cowardly and comtemptible, but Jamie knew only too well the kind of fear that had prompted it. He, no less innocent than Petko, had been offered the lifeline of naming names and had been tempted to seize it – to say anything that would free him from the pain and misery of interrogation. Banjo had probably tossed the name of Jamie Kyle to Petko and the boy had seized on it, damning someone who was no more than a slight acquaintance in order to save himself. It would only have needed occasional prompting from Banjo for Petko to fill in the gaps where he himself did not have the wit to invent the scenario.

'It is still only his word against mine,' Jamie flung at Luk defiantly.

'Not quite,' Luk informed him. 'Agent Banjo has been most industrious in the past few days. He questioned more than forty students at the University. At least a dozen of them are prepared to testify to your Communist sympathies and profound admiration for Soviet Russia.'

Jamie could not conceal his shock.

'Then they are liars!' he cried. 'Agent Banjo would not know the truth if it fell on him like a rock! He must have beaten the lies out of them!'

Luk frowned at him, as if his patience was now being sorely tried. He said:

'I will give you one final chance to abandon your senseless protestations of innocence and tell me every-thing about your involvement with the Communist Party.' He waited, but Jamie was silent. 'Have you nothing to say?'

'Nothing that I haven't already said a hundred times.'

'And may regret a hundred times more,' Luk snapped

angrily. 'A hundred thousand times more! There is nothing more I can do to save you now. You know you will go to prison for a very long time?'

A knot seemed to tighten in Jamie's gut as Luk spoke. He sat, hunched and tense, bracing himself.

'At least I'll go with a clear conscience,' he said bravely. And his eyes met Luk's stare, measure for measure. It was Luk who turned away. There was a brightness in the boy's gaze that he abhorred: the shining light of fanaticism. Or so he interpreted it. It had a chilling, blinding quality that could not be extinguished. Fanaticism written on the face of an enemy dismayed Luk – because he lacked the power to destroy it. And because he ascribed innocence to none, Luk could not see it in Jamie's eyes. He did not connect its shining with possession of the truth.

Later that day, Jamie was removed from the Glavnjaca and taken to the Ada Ciganlija prison on the Sava River. There, he was placed in a cell with Stefan and two others. Until the moment of his reunion with Stefan, Jamie had, at the back of his mind, attributed all his troubles to his friend. If it had not been for Stefan's political activities, there would have been no beatings and interrogations to endure, and Jamie was ready to be less than friendly as a result. But such thoughts vanished when he again came face to face with Stefan. The idealistic young writer was barely recognisable from beatings even more brutal than those that Jamie had suffered. The soles of Stefan's feet were like raw meat from repeated flagellation. And yet he still wept tears of real sorrow for the suffering and injustice that Jamie had endured. He had no thought for his own wounds – the accepted price of his ideals – but only for Jamie's. He was heartbroken that Jamie had been made to pay so dearly for his, Stefan's, actions.

In spite of his wretched physical state, Stefan began feverishly to do everything in his power to bring about

Jamie's release. He was granted an interview with the prison governor, at which he swore Jamie's innocence and pleaded for a review – but none was forthcoming. He wrote letters and signed official statements, which were addressed to every authority that might have been able to help – all to no avail. Stefan was told that a full confession of his own activities and the naming of all his Communist Party associates would go a long way to giving credence to the pleas he was making on behalf of his friend, but he drew back from trading one set of comrades for another. He was prepared to suffer death rather than betray his party contacts, even for Jamie's sake – and Jamie's support for his stand was the most adamant. He did not want his freedom purchased with the blood of others, especially when it meant the surrender of all Stefan's ideals.

As the months slipped by, both young men drew strength from each other in their isolation from the lives they had known. They were permitted no visitors, although letters in and out were allowed, albeit heavily censored. Jamie was somewhat comforted by the knowledge that Milan, his mother and Draga Simovic were working relentlessly on the outside to secure his release – even if there were no grounds for believing that they were making any headway. The memory of what had happened to Brad Mannion was still too fresh to encourage optimism.

Indeed, Jamie's hopes were dealt a body blow when he learned in a letter from Milan that his dear friend Draga Simovic had died suddenly of a heart attack. The lawyer had collapsed at the Ministry of the Interior while presenting a petition on Jamie's behalf. The news of the lawyer's death was bad enough, but worse was the revelation that Milan was having great difficulty finding a new legal representative willing to take on Jamie's defence. No one wanted the job.

Jamie's greatest consolation came from Mara's

letters, with their assurances of her love for him and her promises to wait faithfully for him. She lived only for the day when they could be together again. She came every day to stand on the bank of the Sava opposite the prison. And there she would stay until the flutter of a red handkerchief from Jamie's cell window told her that he could see her. The distance was too great for Jamie to see the tears that rolled down her cheeks when he made his signal of recognition. He saw only the wave of her arm and the bright blue of the kerchief she flagged in return.

The days of summer dragged into autumn and, on a chill day in October, Jamie and Stefan were brought across the Sava to the Central Court to stand trial. The public were not admitted, but Jamie got a brief glimpse of Mara, his mother and Milan through the window of the cloistered walk that led from the yard, where the vans unloaded the prisoners, to the court building.

A lawyer known for his devotion to lost causes conducted the defence of both Stefan and Jamie. He was used to defeat, and his low-key plea for greater liberality by Government towards political minorities who had no legitimate means of expressing opinion fell on deaf ears. At no time did he seriously challenge the state evidence brought against Jamie, and he did not even try to refute the case against Stefan. He argued, instead, that the youth of both defendants was a powerful mitigating factor in the crimes of which they stood accused. Neither was a criminal in the accepted sense of the word, but young men of good character whose only fault – if it could be called a fault – was a sincere desire to effect social change and the creation of a more just society.

The three judges on the bench seemed to have heard it all before and wasted little time deliberating before pronouncing verdicts of guilty. The two accused were sentenced to terms of five years' imprisonment in a corrective establishment that would be specified by the appropriate authority.

The small convoy of police vans – there were three in all – bumped along the narrow track that skirted the railway sheds. They pulled up, side by side, in a muddy yard that was lit by an arc light on a pylon. Sleety rain gusted across the yard as some three dozen prisoners were herded from the vans by the police guard. The prisoners were chained by the wrist in pairs. The guards hustled the chained men into a column, four abreast. When the column was in reasonably tidy shape, the order was given to march. Led by two guards carrying lamps, the prisoners followed a rough track that ran parallel to a railway line and was flanked on the other side by rough ground.

The railway line led to a shunting spur, where two cattle trucks sat in dark isolation. The trucks were the prisoners' immediate destination. The column was halted and there was a wait while the doors of the two cattle trucks were slid open. Half the prisoners were allocated to one truck, half to the other.

Jamie, chained to Stefan, was ordered into the rear truck. They hauled themselves aboard together. The interior of the truck had a damp foetid smell. There was straw on the floor. When all the prisoners were aboard, the heavy doors were closed and padlocked from the outside. In their chosen corner, Jamie and Stefan sat in silence. They were cold but here, at least, they had shelter from the swirling wet.

The trucks did not move for half an hour. After the banging and clanging of being coupled to a locomotive, the journey finally began. The first leg was short: no more than a mile. Then there was more shunting and coupling, and the inmates of the draughty trucks realised they were now part of a larger train.

It was a slow-moving train, stopping often for periods of up to half an hour. Daylight was filtering through the barred ventilator panels in the trucks when, after more shunting, the prisoners were aware that the journey through the night was over. The doors were thrown open and they alighted on a spur line, not unlike the one where they had boarded their transport.

Again, they were formed up four abreast and given the order to march. They were at one end of a railway station, where there was access to a muddy road. Ahead, green hills were visible in the early-morning murk. They trudged towards the distant hills.

The prison was in view long before they reached it. The stark buildings were of two distinct styles. One had a baroque tower and resembled a monastery – which it had once been – and the other was all concrete and brick and small symmetrical barred windows. Both buildings were heavily fenced off.

As the column of prisoners passed through the gate, Jamie jerked his chained hand to point at a wisp of blue sky that had suddenly appeared in the cloud above the monastery tower.

'You're a literary man, Stefan,' he said. 'Did you ever read Oscar Wilde?'

'No. Why do you point to the tower?'

'It's the sky I'm pointing to – that little patch of blue. It made me think of something Wilde wrote when he was in Reading Gaol. He said: "I never saw a man who looked/With such a wistful eye/Upon that little tent of blue/Which prisoners call the sky . . . ".'

Stefan looked sideways at his friend.

'I hope the poetry sounds better in English than it does in Serbo-Croat. Was this fellow you mentioned put in prison for writing bad poetry?'

Jamie laughed. The unlikely sound coming from the midst of the prisoners caused a guard to stop in his tracks and demand silence in the ranks. There was to be no talking.

The column was halted in the yard. While they stood there, a work gang of convicts carrying hoes emerged

156

from the brick-and-concrete barracks nearby. As they passed, Jamie recognised one of them. Neither the brimless canvas cap nor the drab prison garb disguised the unmistakable features of Bradislav Mannion. With no guard immediately in view, Jamie risked a low whistle to attract the American's attention.

It took a moment or two for Mannion to recognise Jamie in the new intake. When he did, his surprise was considerable.

'Jamie, what the hell?' He stopped and let the rest of the work gang pass. 'You been railroaded, too?' he called.

'Two of us,' Jamie called back. 'We got five years.' From a corner of his eye he saw a guard hurrying towards them. He made straight for Mannion and demanded to know why he had fallen out of the work gang.

Mannion doffed his cap – it was a rule to do so to all prison staff, Jamie was to discover – and explained that he had only stopped to bid good morning to the new prisoners. The guard was plainly puzzled by the explanation and by Mannion's poker face. He continued to look on with puzzlement as the American turned to face the new intake and make a courtier-like flourish with his cap.

'Good morning, gentlemen,' he called. 'Welcome to the Waldorf-Astoria.'

Then, he was on his way to rejoin his gang, dodging as the guard – now irate – pursued him, lashing out with his stick. A ripple of laughter rose from the ranks of the thoroughly entertained intake. Jamie and Stefan were grinning broadly at each other. A few moments later, they passed into the main prison building.

By then, their grins had faded.

PART TWO
ESCAPE TO WAR

1

On the Run

A spring frost, after rain, had left a skin of ice on the puddles that had gathered in the churned earth around the pigsties. Yesterday the yard had been a squelching quagmire, but this morning the drop in temperature had left a fragile crust on the mud. It crunched underfoot as Jamie opened the first sty and ushered its squealing occupants into the yard. Stefan and Mannion were releasing pigs from neighbouring pigsties. Watching the three men, but without conspicuous concern, the rather corpulent guard – whom they had nicknamed Big-nose – was blowing on his clenched fingers, a fist at a time, to breathe warmth into his podgy hands.

'You, the thin one!' he called out. 'Get the wagon yoked up! Leave the other two to get the muck out.'

The thin one was Stefan. The years in prison had emaciated him, aggravating his tubercular weakness and giving him an almost permanent cough. Jamie, in contrast, had filled out – he had a broader and harder look – and was a tougher, manlier edition of the boy who had walked through the prison gates. Mannion, like Stefan, had lost weight but, unlike Stefan, had not missed it. He was now harder, and sinewy in the right places. What was lost had been surplus.

Stefan, with a nervous look towards the others, went off to do the guard's bidding. The task of yoking the ox to the primitive wheeled farm cart was no new one to him. It was only this spring morning that was different: a morning that had been waited for, plotted for, schemed for, prayed for. Twelve months of intense planning and replanning and furtive communication had gone into preparation for this day. Now, the day was here.

By the time that Stefan had yoked the ox to the cart and led the combination back into the yard, Jamie and Mannion had cleared the sties of much of the ordure and straw that littered their interiors. With shovel and brush, they had worked methodically along the concrete-lined sties, heaping the harvest of pungently odorous manure at the gates. Now it had to be forked on to the cart, and Big-nose retired to smoke a cigarette, upwind of the operation, while the three began the loading.

A second ox-drawn wagon arrived in the yard before the loading was completed. It, too, was attended by three convicts. They brought a load of fresh straw and two large drums of swill from the prison kitchen. The trusty in charge of the pig-feed was a big bruiser of a man who was doing a twenty-year stretch for a string of robberies. He was perched on the side of his cart and his eyes were on Mannion, who temporarily halted his labour. As Mannion looked up, the other man gave a barely perceptible nod of his head.

Big-nose walked towards the newcomers, demanding to know what had kept them – they were late. He shouted across to Mannion to get his load of muck out of the yard.

'You know where to take it,' he yelled. 'I'll catch up when I've done with these layabouts.'

Jamie and Stefan exchanged smiles. The scenario they had anticipated was working out ahead of expectations. Mannion prodded the ox into motion and then led it out of the yard. They left the straggle of buildings where the livestock were housed and followed a muddy track that led slightly uphill, away from the X-shaped spread of the concrete prison block and its baroque-towered neighbour. The track was bounded on one side by a high perimeter fence and, on the other, by a cultivated field

162

where green shoots were showing through the ground.

They had travelled perhaps a quarter of a mile when they heard voices raised from the direction of the yard. The three men grinned at each other. The 'accident' – designed to detain Big-nose where he was – had happened. The scenario had not called for serious injury to befall the corpulent guard but to incapacitate him temporarily. All depended on the long-term prisoner carrying out his part of the bargain. He had willingly accepted the undertaking in order to erase a large tobacco debt to Mannion, and he had been confident of putting Big-nose out of action for half an hour without foul play being suspected. The plan was for the beaky guard's attention to be drawn to some difficulty in unloading a bale of straw from the feed wagon. His investigation of this difficulty was to be rewarded instantly in dramatic fashion. A minor act of cruelty inflicted on the ox between the shafts was to dislodge the bale of straw and a very large convict from the wagon, in such a manner that the unfortunate guard would not know what had hit him.

Although Big-nose's fate of being laid low by a hundredweight bale of straw afforded Jamie and his companions some amusement, it was amusement tinged with anxiety. Things could go wrong. The delaying ploy could misfire. The guard might escape from the falling bale. Or he could be seriously hurt, even killed.

As they forced their own plodding ox faster uphill along the curving track, the three men glanced anxiously behind for sign of Big-nose's emergence from the yard. There was none, and they speculated with nervous laughter on the possibility that a drum of pigswill might have inadvertently fallen on the guard to add to his discomfort.

As they worked their way round the slope, the prison complex was lost from view behind the curve of the land. Ahead, a guard hut and lookout platform abutted the perimeter fence. The guard occupying the platform descended the ladder from his roofed eyrie as they approached and came down the track to meet them. His rifle was slung over one shoulder and he was as tall and reedy as his colleague Big-nose was squat and tubby. He wanted to know where Big-nose was.

'He's still at the piggery,' Mannion said. 'He said he would be up later. Is the truck here?'

'Over in the trees,' the guard said. 'It's a new man. One I've never seen before. Move yourselves. We haven't time to waste.'

He led the way along the track, past the guardpost to a large wire gate in the fence. It was heavily chained and padlocked. The guard undid the padlock with a huge key and ordered Mannion to open the gate. It creaked on its hinges as they pushed the double sections open.

Directed by the guard, the wagon was driven out through the gate towards a copse of trees a short distance away. There, an ancient motor truck was parked. Its driver, a peasant type in an oil-stained overall, jumped down from the square-fronted cab. He was clearly relieved to see the arrivals.

'Get to work,' the guard shouted at the prisoners, and engaged the truck's driver in conversation. Mannion exchanged a look with Jamie. The ritual now taking place, between the guard and driver was one they had witnessed countless times – ever since Big-nose and his friend had decided that the trio's trust could be purchased for two cigarettes apiece. It was a miserly payment for complicity in the two guards' sideline of selling a variety of prison produce through the fence – they saw it as a perk that went with the job – but the profits were never high. Today, it was pig manure for sale and Big-nose and his friend were certainly not going to get rich on that.

While the guard was complaining bitterly to the truck driver at the pittance he was being offered, Mannion was letting down the tailboard of the truck. The back was empty, except for a piece of sacking. Mannion fumbled under the sacking. His fingers closed on the butt of a revolver that was hidden in its folds. It was an antique, prewar by several years. It had no safety catch. A quick check showed that it was loaded. He slipped it under his jacket into the waist-band of his trousers. He sauntered round the truck as Jamie and Stefan began to shovel manure from the wagon into its capacious back.

By going round the truck, Mannion was able to approach the two men from behind the guard's line of vision. The guard suspected nothing wrong until Mannion was only three paces from him. When he did glance over his shoulder, it was to stare into the long barrel of the fearsome-looking pistol that Mannion was brandishing. The shock temporarily robbed him of speech. Recovering it, his attempt to speak was talked down by Mannion's sharp command to throw down his rifle. The driver, although he was privy to the escape plan in some of its details, feigned fear at the development. He was ordered to raise his hands and keep quiet. His part as the prisoners' accomplice was not to be advertised to the guard. The break was to appear spontaneous.

Jamie and Stefan jumped down from the wagon.

'You know what to do,' Mannion said. 'I'll get the truck started.'

Stefan nodded. Picking up the guard's rifle and covering him with it, he motioned in the direction of the gate. Jamie relieved the guard of the keys he was carrying.

'I'll take care of the telephone wires,' he said, and ran ahead of Stefan and the guard towards the post.

Mannion had the truck's motor running by the time they returned. They had tied the guard up and left him locked in his own hut. The big double gates in the fence had been closed, chained and padlocked. There was one chore still to do. Jamie released the patient ox from the shafts of the wagon and gave it a slap on the rump. It ambled off.

There was only room in the truck's cab for Mannion and the driver – who seemed disappointed they had not shot the guard – and so Jamie and Stefan rode in the back. They were soon bowling down the fearfully pitted track that led they knew not where. From here on, the escape plan had been orchestrated by their friends on the outside. They exulted in their freedom and the knowledge that part one had gone without a hitch. They had got through the wire where and precisely when they had said they would. Now, all depended on Mara, and the twelve months of scheming she had put into phase two.

The track gave way to a road of indifferent quality. The only sign of life they encountered was some peasants working in a field. These Croatians stood for a moment, pausing in their labours to watch the truck's passage, before bending again to their work.

The truck had travelled no more than five miles from the prison when the driver indicated a derelict cottage ahead. Beside the roofless stone, a sleek grey roadster with gleaming silver headlamps was parked.

'The girl is waiting for you,' the driver said. As he spoke, a slim figure in red emerged from behind the car and waved. It was Mara.

Jamie had seen her from behind the cab and his heart was racing. This was not how he had anticipated their reunion, clad in prison clothes and reeking of pig manure – but this sight of her, vibrant and prettier than ever, was the one goal he had held before him, the only one that mattered or had any meaning. Now that it was a reality, his surging joy was tempered only by realisation of what the cost might be. She must have run enormous risks in planning his freedom – and what kind of freedom would it be if every gendarme in the land was looking for them?

He dared not think the worst: that they would have their hour of freedom but it would end with endless years in prison, not just for him but for her, too.

He was down from the truck as it was still braking, and she ran to his arms.

'Mara . . . Mara, my love,' he cried softly, as she rained kisses on his lips, his cheeks, his eyes, hugging him. Their tears intermingled as they were lost in their emotion and each other.

Stefan looked on ruefully, almost with envy. There was a more womanly look about Mara than he remembered. She was not a girl any more but a physically desirable woman. She had blossomed considerably from the over-eager adolescent of those calf days in Belgrade.

It was Mannion who broke things up.

'Hey, Angel, how about saving a kiss for the other guys?' he intruded good-naturedly. Mara happily kissed Mannion and Stefan in turn. Only then did she wrinkle her nose and stare at them questioningly.

'Pig manure,' Mannion explained. 'Maybe you should have waited until we all had a bath.'

She laughed.

'Maybe I could get used to it. On the other hand, I've got some scent in my bag. Maybe you should drench each other with it when you get rid of these clothes. I've got trousers, jackets, shirts, socks . . . two suitcases of stuff. It's all in the car. You'd better help yourself to whatever fits.'

The driver of the truck was now eager to be on his way. The others watched as Mara paid him off from a huge bundle of banknotes which she took from her handbag.

'You played your part well,' she said, and the others joined in to voice their agreement and thanks.

'I have been in prison,' he said. 'I was happy to be of help. Now, I must hurry to return the truck to its rightful owner. If he has woken up yet – which I doubt – he will

167

not be feeling very well. Last night, I filled him so full of wine that it was spilling out of his ears.'

'How will you get back to Belgrade?' Mara asked him.

'Don't worry about me,' the man assured her. 'I'll get rid of the truck and be on the noon train from Lepoglava.'

When he had gone, Mara split the bankroll she was carrying between Jamie, Stefan and Mannion. The amounts staggered them.

'We can't take this money,' Stefan protested.

'You can and you will,' Mara replied. 'It comes from the Liberation Fund – yours and Jamie's. I started it the day after you went to prison. Nearly everyone at the University has been contributing to it, and I was given carte blanche in how it was spent. I was told to bribe politicians and judges . . . do anything with it that would get you out of that hellhole.'

Behind the crumbling walls of the broken-down cottage, the three men changed into the clothes which Mara had brought, having first washed as best as they could in pools of icy rainwater. Mannion drooled over the sleek grey car.

'Where did you get this baby?' he asked Mara, stroking his fingers over the polished chrome of the headlamps.

'I borrowed it. It's my father's,' she told him.

Stefan and Jamie arrived from within the cottage in time to hear this.

'Your father's?' Stefan's eyes were wide with amazement. 'Did you tell him why you wanted to borrow it?'

'He doesn't even know I've got it,' Mara said cheerfully. 'He's in Vienna – and likely to be there for a long time. Quite the political big shot now – a special emissary of the Cvetkovic-Macek Government, no less! I doubt if that will endear him to you, Stefan.' Her face clouded. 'Petar's in Austria, too. At a special mountain warfare school run by the German Army. He was one of three officers selected from over a thousand to go on the course.'

'He's training with a Fascist army!' There was heart-felt contempt in Stefan's voice.

Mara shrugged.

'Petar doesn't look at it that way. He's a soldier – and you know as well as I do that he has no time for politics or politicians. He certainly has no time for the Nazis, although he does admire the German Army. He says they have the best professional soldiers in the world. . . . '

She broke off when she saw the strange way Jamie was looking at her.

'The Germans are fighting *my* people,' he said, almost accusingly. 'They've obliterated France, Poland, Denmark, Norway . . . and Petar *admires* them!'

Mara flushed.

'I can't be responsible for Petar, Jamie. You know how he talks. It's how wars are fought that interests him, not *why*. It's the same if he's watching two football teams. All that interests him is the skill, the tactics, the game. Who wins doesn't matter to him half so much as how the game is played. He admires the British, too.'

'I hate to butt in on this little discussion,' Mannion said, 'but it's time we were getting the hell out of here.'

His words had a sobering effect on the others. They had wasted between fifteen and twenty minutes at the rendezvous and they were still much too close to the prison for comfort. Apologising for the discomfort that it was likely to cause, Mara asked Jamie and Stefan to ride in the back of the grey roadster with the canvas rain-cover buttoned down over their heads. It meant dis-posing their bodies between floor and back seat in rather cramped fashion, but they stoically accepted the necessity. The police, should they encounter any on the road, would be looking for three men, so it made sense that two of them stayed out of view. Mannion got the honour of riding in the front with Mara by merit of clothes he had rummaged from Mara's supply. He, more than the others, looked the part of a well-heeled young man, and it was important that Mara's visible companion did not look out of place in the expensive car.

Mara was a good driver, but not even her careful driving and the well-sprung car could protect Jamie and Stefan from a very bumpy ride. The road had been built for four-legged traffic with an ability to step round the potholes and stay out of the ruts, not for motor transport. There was a marginal improvement when they reached the main road south to Zagreb, but even this winding thoroughfare left much to be desired. They met little traffic on it that was not drawn by horses or oxen. Most Croatians, it seemed, preferred to travel by the railway, which ran close to the road and on which could be seen the occasional crowded passenger train.

The fifty-odd kilometre run into Zagreb passed without incident. Mara drove around the Lower Town for some time before she found a deserted lane where Jamie and Stefan could emerge from concealment without attracting attention. Their safe delivery in Zagreb marked the completion of Mara's role in the escape. Here, Stefan had organised succour from his friends in the strong and well-organised network that the Communist Party had established in the Croatian capital. An open-ended system of contact had been devised for the escapers. Each, day, between the hours of two and four, an artist would be at work in Tomaslava Square, ostensibly painting a water-colour representation of the statue to the monarch whose name the square bore. The artist was their contact and would provide them with the address of a safe house.

'Leave me to make the contact and get the address,' Stefan told the others. 'Better if we make our own way to the square and aren't seen together. When I've found out where we've got to go, I'll give you a signal and you two can trail along behind at a safe distance.'

Stefan was the first to leave. Then, giving him a start of fifty metres, Mannion followed. Jamie, although he knew he must, was reluctant to leave Mara.

'I don't want to leave you,' he murmured, holding her close. 'Not like this. Not even knowing when I'll see you again.'

'I don't want you to go, Jamie. You're all I live for. But it's safer for you if you go and, God willing, it won't be for long.'

'Will you go back to Belgrade?' Jamie asked.

'Yes. But you mustn't. Not yet. That's where the police will be looking for you. They'll put a watch on your uncle and your mother. They'll probably watch me, too. You're safer here, in Croatia. Stefan's friends will look after you.'

'How will I get in touch with you? How will I know where I can find you, Mara?'

'Stefan will help you. There are ways. His friends are well organised now and will always find me for you – because they think highly of you. We have to trust them, even though they don't altogether trust me, because I'm not one of them.'

'I'll find you,' Jamie vowed. 'No matter what happens, remember I love you and I'll go on loving you to the day I die. Will you remember that . . . even if things go wrong?'

'You're the only one I want, Jamie. I've waited all these years. I'll go on waiting for as long as it takes. But go now, Jamie. Go. My love goes with you. Now and always.'

With one final kiss, he tore himself away. He hurried down the lane and she watched him turn the corner and take the same direction as Stefan and Mannion. He did not look back. She guessed that he had steeled himself not to, in case his resolution wavered and he came running back to her arms.

She returned to the car and sat in it, composing

herself. The effort of sending Jamie away had demanded no less resolution than Jamie had needed to go. Now she felt drained and, for the first time since she had undertaken her dangerous task, she felt afraid. Afraid of the future and its unreadable obscurity. She told herself that it was simply reaction to the tension and excitement of an eventful day. She had been on the go since the early hours of the morning and she had scarcely slept a wink in the past week.

It took her fifteen minutes before she felt calm and relaxed enough to drive. Then she drove the big roadster out of the city, stopping at its southern edge to buy petrol before heading at a sedate pace towards Karlovac. At Draganici, she stopped to buy food, which she ate picnic-style in the car, a few miles further on. It was late in the afternoon when she reached Karlovac. The certainty that something was wrong assailed her as she approached the Richtman house.

Two cars were parked in front of the house. One was a big official-looking limousine. The other was a police car. Mara immediately recognised it as the vehicle in which the local Police Chief went about his duties.

She drove past the two cars and through the arched courtway that led to the stableyard. She drove straight through the open doors of the stable, which served as a garage for the roadster. She covered the car with the dustsheet under which it had lain for most of the winter. Then she locked up the garage before entering the big house by the kitchen entrance. She went straight up to her room.

It was there her father found her, thirty minutes later. He was in a towering rage.

'You've been out in the Mercedes.' It was an accusation. 'Where have you been?'

She faced him calmly.

'I went for a spin up to Zagreb. When did you come home, Papa? I though you were going to be in Vienna for ages.'

'That's patently obvious,' he snapped. 'Otherwise, you would not have dared to do what you've done. You've gone too far this time, Mara!'

'What am I supposed to have done?' she asked innocently, but fear made her voice wobble.

'I've just had a visit from the Chief of Police. The Belgrade police have been trying to find you and wanted to know if you had come back for Easter.'

'Why should the Belgrade police be interested in me?' she asked, trying hard to affect an air of indifference.

'Don't pretend you don't know,' Richtman flared. 'The police may be stupid, but I'm not. I can put two and two together. I can guess why you wanted the Mercedes. As soon as I was told what had happened, I *knew* you were involved.'

'Involved in what, Papa?'

He struck her across the face with his open hand.

'Don't try to come the innocent,' he snarled. 'Have you no thought of the harm that a scandal could do to me?'

She reeled from the blow but, cheek stinging, she faced him, unrepentant.

'I don't know what you're talking about,' she maintained. He hit her again.

'Liar!' he shouted. 'Three of your friends escaped from the prison in Lepoglava, this morning. Don't try to tell me that you know nothing about it or didn't have a hand in it in some way. I'm not a fool, Mara. I suspected something the minute I got here. Your mother had no idea where you had disappeared to – but the servants heard you taking the Mercedes out. At half-past two in the morning!' He snorted. 'For a spin to Zagreb! I ought to whip you, you silly little bitch!'

She stared at him defiantly.

'What did you say to the police?'

'I told them nothing,' he snapped. 'But that doesn't mean they won't start putting two and two together

173

themselves. And when they do, they'll come back here to ask where it is you went in the middle of the night. They'll be asking more questions . . . questions that I have no intention of answering, and questions that you will certainly not be answering. Because you won't be here to answer them!'

'What do you mean, I won't be here?'

'Exactly that. You're leaving! We all are – you, your mother and me. And there's going to be no argument. You will do as you're told – even if I have to beat some sense into you. Which is what I should have done years ago.'

He moved towards the door and looked back at her from the doorway.

'You have half an hour to pack your things. If you're not ready then, you'll go as you are.'

'Where are we going?' she asked, her voice trembling.

'Vienna,' he said shortly. 'That's where my work is now. And where it will be for the foreseeable future. I'm closing this place up for the time being, so pack as much as you need. You won't be seeing it again for a year or two.'

He went out, leaving her to stare at the closed door. She heard the key turning in the lock. He was taking no chances on her disobeying his orders.

The safe house was close to the main Belgrade-Ljubljana road. The front was a café – used mainly by long-distance hauliers – and the main premises, incorporating cheap hostel accommodation, extended back from the café front in a straggle of single-storey buildings that seemed to have been added piecemeal from time to time, eating into a swatch of waste ground that served as a parking area for trucks and other transport. What had been a stabling yard was now almost entirely enclosed by a warren of outhouses.

Jamie, Stefan and Mannion were installed in a room

well to the rear, and advised to remain there, out of sight. They received this instruction from the taciturn widow who presided over the café and adjacent property with beady-eyed ill humour. The age of this black-clad crone was difficult to determine. Her work-worn hands testified to a life of toil, but the grey wisps in her hair and the severe lines in her face may have been premature, making her look much older than she actually was.

In spite of her forbidding exterior, the three fugitives warmed to her within an hour of their arrival, when she came to their room with a tray of food. After prison fare, the meal she set before them was like food for the gods: strips of lean succulent pork, a platter of fried eggs, fresh-baked bread, butter, cheese, pickled onions and mugs of hot, sweet coffee.

She scorned their thanks, commenting that even dogs must eat, and advised them to make use of the adjacent bath-house before contaminating her blankets with their prison stink. Before she left, she warned them to expect visitors – but not until after dark. Someone from the Party would be coming to see them. Someone important.

In the event, no one visited the room where the fugitives were closeted. Instead, the fugitives were summoned to a room behind the café. The widow ushered them into a private parlour, where half a dozen men were seated around a table.

'Which of you is Stefan Markovic?' The question came from a handsome man of about forty, who was seated at the top of the table. From his manner and bearing, he was clearly the leader of the group. He had a neat, scrubbed look and, in his dark well-cut suit, starched collar and tidily knotted tie, he had the air of a prosperous business executive. Stefan faced him over the heads of the seated group.

'I am Stefan Markovic.'

'You have good friends in Belgrade,' said the man at the top of the table. 'If I had known about this plot of yours to escape from prison, I would have forbidden it. The Party has other priorities. I am surprised that our comrades in the prison at Lepoglava sanctioned your escape.'

'They didn't,' Stefan replied. 'We did not take the prison committee into our confidence.'

'Then you are guilty of grave indiscipline,' the man said severely. 'Our revolutionary aims can only be achieved by Party unity. If it was in the interests of the Party and the solidarity of the comrades who are still in Lepoglava that you endured imprisonment there, your duty was to have remained there.'

Stefan held back the angry reply that hovered on his lips.

'In prison, one can talk revolution and die dreaming about it. Outside, one can do something about it.' Stefan smiled bitterly. 'The prison committee would have found political reasons for not sanctioning our escape plan, but that is not entirely why we didn't ask their approval. By keeping them in the dark, we hoped to save them from possible reprisals – '

'You delude yourself,' the group's leader interrrupted. 'The authorites will take reprisals against every prisoner in Lepoglava because of what you have done. They will make life very hard for the comrades you have left behind.'

Stefan shrugged.

'If that happens, we regret it,' he said. 'But the Party faithful we left behind may also be grateful to us. We . . . my two friends and I were a constant embarrassment to them. As long as we were in Lepoglava, we stood in the way of any harmony between them and the other politicals – especially the Croat nationalists.'

The man at the head of the table considered this. He nodded thoughtfully.

'It has been our policy in prisons to show some kind of solidarity with other politicals who have fallen foul of the

Regency Government. A revolutionary of the Right is still a revolutionary. Why should you come between our comrades and the nationalists if the party line demanded a common front?'

Stefan glanced towards Mannion, whose impatience at the proceedings was beginning to show.

'My friend here was attacked more than once by Pavelic supporters. His grandfather was murdered by nationalists.'

'Ah, the American?' said Stefan's questioner, with a glint in his eye of dawning understanding. 'I have heard about him.' He frowned. 'But he is not a revolutionary. Not even a political. Why should his troubles be the Party's concern, or yours?'

'Because he is my friend,' Stefan stated firmly, with the air of one who has said it all.

'Was it because of him that you had your sentence increased?'

'The nationalists would have killed him if Jamie and I hadn't stood by him. There was quite a fight. They added three years to our sentences.' Stefan smiled. 'The nationalists all got three years, too – but there were seven of them, only three of us.'

For the first time since they had entered the room, one of the other men seated at the table spoke. He was younger than the group leader, dark-haired, with bright intelligent eyes.

'You were lucky to get only three years,' he said to Stefan. 'When I was inside, a friend of mine got a year added to his sentence for singing. Singing! Can you imagine that? For fighting, they would have given him twenty years!'

The group leader smiled tolerantly at this intrusion of his dialogue with Stefan. He said:

'My Montenegrin friend knows what it is to suffer in prison.' He made a gesture with his hands. 'All of us round this table know. We've all been inside at one time or another.' He gazed questioningly at Stefan. 'But we adhered to party discipline. We endured, together. We did not seek freedom for one, or for two. Not if it did not mean freedom for all.'

Mannion could keep silent no longer.

'Just who the hell are you guys?' he demanded. Ignoring the warning look that Stefan shot him, he remonstrated with his friend. 'Well, who are they? Are they on our side or not? The way they're talking, they make it sound like it wasn't the comradely thing to do, breaking out of that stink-hole, that the big-shot thing to do was to rot in there for the rest of our lives!'

'Please, Brad,' Stefan murmured, cautioningly. 'You are not one of us. You do not understand. . . . '

'You're goddamned right, I don't understand!' Mannion said heatedly. 'We get out of that stink-hole to help you fight your goddamned revolution, and that guy there treats you like you're some kind of heretic and he's the Spanish Inquisition. You don't need to apologise to anybody for what you've done!'

Mannion's outburst brought the Montenegrin to his feet.

'Please keep your voice down,' he demanded with quiet vehemence. 'Just remember that your presence here represents a considerable danger to all of us in this room – and some of us have a great deal more to lose than you. We were not party to your escape, and we are not unsympathetic to it – but it concerns us now, because our organisation has already been involved and will continue to be involved, whether we like it or not.' He stopped, breathlessly, at a nod from the group leader, who had remained quite unflustered at Mannion's heated words.

'Our comrade from Montenegro is right,' the group leader said quietly. 'We are not unsympathetic . . . we understand more than most how desperate you were to escape from Lepoglava. It did concern us, however, that the Party organisation was used without any reference being made to the Central Committee. It could have had damaging consequences – the left hand not knowing what the right hand was doing. Although, my American comrade, you are not one of us, I am sure you are intelligent enough to understand.'

Mannion flushed.

'I'm sorry,' he muttered. 'Maybe I spoke out of turn. I just thought you were being pretty hard on Stefan. He's been through enough.'

The man at the head of the table smiled.

'His worth is well known to me,' he said. 'We could use more like him. The struggle is just beginning. . . . '

Mannion and Jamie exchanged looks. Mannion returned his gaze to the man facing him from the top of the table.

'Stefan's fight is our fight,' he said. 'Maybe you could use a couple of volunteers.'

The man at the table considered this. A faint smile played about his lips.

'Is it the fight you hunger for?' he asked. 'Is it the struggle? Or is there something more? We seek more than freedom and justice for our people. We seek an end to the capitalist system. We seek to establish the rule of the proletariat. Our aims may not be realised in our lifetimes, but that does not deter us. All that matters is knowing that what we begin, others will be able to finish, that what we start cannot be stopped. Our job is to provide the unquenchable sparks, the first flames that will spread like a prairie fire and destroy the old, so that the new can be built.'

Mannion grinned.

'When I was in prison, I heard plenty about Lenin and the proletariat and how stinking the capitalist system was, and I'm not saying that what you guys believe is right or wrong. But I'd better say right now that all those study classes on Karl Marx and collective farming that your guys organised in the jug bored the pants off me. Politics is something I just can't get worked up about. I was raised a Democrat and, though maybe you're not, you guys are maybe the nearest to Democrats this country's got – and if you want to give the ordinary people a squarer deal than they got right now, it's OK by me. I'm with you, and I reckon Jamie is, too.'

Mannion's homily caused a mixture of reactions around the table. The most common was goggle-eyed consternation, as if he had given utterance to blasphemies. The group leader seemed slightly bemused. The Montenegrin was having difficulty keeping a straight face, but he broke the silence.

'One cannot fault our American comrade for lack of candour,' he commented drily. 'One might have reservations about entrusting him with propaganda work for the Party, but there are other ways in which he can serve our cause. Our present policy permits us to accept as *for* us, those who are not against us in the struggle against Fascism.' He turned to the group leader. 'We need all the friends we can get, Comrade Secretary, wouldn't you say?'

There was just a hint of reproach in the look that the group leader bestowed on the Montenegrin, but his words held none.

'You are the theoretician,' he said. He shrugged his shoulders. 'There has always been flexibility in our choice of friends, if not in our aims. I think we can spare ourselves discussion at a theoretical level. The practical is what is important.'

He stared down at the three fugitives, and gave a little smile.

'Forgive me, my friends, if we have seemed less than welcoming, but your daring escape took us all by surprise at a time when we had our minds on other things. Curiosity – and a natural anxiety that Party discipline might have been flouted – prompted us to call you before us like this. These things are sometimes necessary – to clear the air, you understand?' He beamed at them avuncularly. 'The air is much clearer now. You have shown yourselves to be brave and resourceful, and that convinces me that this is not a time for inquests or recriminations. We, all of us, have work to do.'

With this little speech over, the dapperly dressed man indicated that it was time to leave. Before he did, he shook hands in turn with Stefan, Jamie and Mannion, offering each a brief body hug with his free arm as he did so. His companions followed suit. Finally, only the Montenegrin remained.

'Comrade Secretary Tito has asked me to take charge of you,' he told the trio.

'Tito?' echoed Mannion. 'Was that the guy who did all the talking?'

The Montenegrin laughed.

'It was unusual for him to be so loquacious. He prefers to listen and let others do the talking.'

'A funny name – Tito,' Mannion observed.

'It was his nickname,' the Montenegrin said. 'From his way of giving orders. He really is a man of few words. When he wanted something done, he just said "ti-to" . . . you – that. Now, he uses the name.' He smiled. 'None of us use our real names any more. The police know them too well, unfortunately.'

'What do we call you?' Jamie asked.

'You can call me Djordje,' the Montenegrin said. 'That's how I'm known in the Party. And, on the subject of names, we'll need to get names for all of you. You're going to need identity papers before you show your faces outside these walls.'

'Will that be difficult?' Stefan asked.

Djordje grinned.

'No. Our Zagreb organisation have the best passport forgers in the business. I'll have papers for you by tomorrow. They'll deliver in double-quick time – if only to make amends for letting you three know about this safe house.'

'Why should they have to make amends for that?' Mannion wanted to know.

'Your escape should have been approved by the Central Committee. Somebody should at least have told them it was happening. We can't afford the luxury of freelance operations – even if they are as successful as yours. You must have used bourgeois contacts as well as Party activists – and that can be dangerous.'

'The people we used outside the Party we could trust,' Stefan said.

The Montenegrin frowned at him.

'We don't trust anyone outside the Party,' he said. 'You'd better remember that in future. We may not throw out the people who helped you get out of Lepoglava but don't think they won't be censured.'

'I'm sorry about that,' Stefan admitted. 'It was my fault, not theirs.'

Jamie, who had become increasingly bored with so much talk of Party discipline and the animosity it seemed to arouse, said impatiently:

'Can't we talk about something else? I'd like to know where we go from here.'

'Me, too,' chimed in Mannion. 'I got more than the police to worry about in this neck of the woods. This is nationalist country – and those guys have sworn to get me. All three of us are probably on their hit list.'

Djordje smiled.

'We'll be gone from Zagreb tomorrow night. I'm taking you back with me to Belgrade. That's where things are happening.'

'Belgrade?' It was Jamie who spoke. 'Won't that be rather risky? They're bound to be looking for us there.'

'I've been dodging Belgrade cops for five years,' Djordje said. 'It's something you'll have to get used to – being an illegal. But the city's safer than anywhere else.

It's full of illegals. And you can lose yourself there. Not like the country or in the mountains. A stranger stands out there. The cops would have you in no time.'

The thought of returning to Belgrade so soon filled Jamie with a fluttering excitement. It did not arise from fear. The knowledge of the attendant risks stimulated him, made him feel more fully alive than at any time during his six-year incarceration. The coming-alive process had started when he and the two others began to plan their escape. Now, after less than twenty-four hours of freedom, the process had accelerated dramatically, so that his senses tingled with the elation of it.

Their years in prison had not made Communist revolutionaries of either Jamie or Mannion, although this was not through want of trying by Stefan and the dedicated Marxists who made up the majority of Lepoglava's political prisoners. Despite the discipline and rigours of the prison regime, the Communists organised their devotees' lives with a fervour and thoroughness that allowed them to operate like a state within a state. They rebelled against the prison authorities as a solid mass when it was politic to do so, and they cooperated with these same authorities when it was politic to do so. Education figured highly on the Communist in-prison programme: political education, that is. Prisoners who arrived in prison with only a hazy idea of why they had opposed political or social injustice emerged as highly motivated and thoroughly indoctrinated Communists, graduates of a university in revolution – a university that flourished as a direct result of the Government's determination to suppress ideas it feared. By putting its opponents in prison, the Regency Government thus unwittingly conspired in proliferating the philosophies it sought to destroy.

Unlike other Communist movements throughout the world, the Party in Jugoslavia did not derive from the workers in industry and the semi-literate masses. It

183

came, instead, from a more affluent class: poets, writers and intellectuals who were disturbed by the denial, to so many of their countrymen, of the right to a voice in their own affairs. Thus, when the dictatorship sought to destroy the Communist movement, of the hundreds who were jailed, many were educated men, rather than miners, boilermakers and factory hands. Most were home-grown Communists rather than Moscow-trained and – although they revered the dictats that came their way from the Kremlin – their vision of revolutionary socialism was peculiarly Jugoslav in character; it owed more to the history of the South Slavs and their long periods of oppression by foreign invaders than to subjugation by their own rulers. That was a new phenomenon, and it had occurred when the new Russia represented a mystical Utopia to Jugoslavia's revolutionary dreamers. In the way that England's romantic poets had hailed the French Revolution as the blessed dawn of a new enlightened age, so the poets and scholars of Jugoslavia had hailed the Russian Revolution. Both were far enough away from the horrors of the reality to be undisturbed in their dreams of liberty, equality and fraternity for mankind.

Suppression and imprisonment did not dilute the enthusiasm of Jugoslavia's Soviet-inspired revolutionaries for their cause. It merely concentrated the intellectual cream of the country's Communist movement in prisons. There they organised themselves anew, turning the jails into centres of further education and tutoring a steady stream of willing pupils in the arts and science of world revolution.

Exposure to these indoctrinating influences did not make converts of Jamie and Mannion – perhaps because both had seen life beyond Jugoslavia's frontiers. And, because their lives had not been totally conditioned by the Jugoslav experience, neither could easily swallow – as their fellow prisoners did – that Soviet Russia was the heaven on earth that the Jugoslav idealists made it out to be. Their reluctance to accept the idea of a Russian Utopia was never more marked than at the time of Stalin's purges, which had the prison's Party propagandists turning terminological somersaults in their defence.

Several leading Jugoslav Communists who had escaped to Russia were among Stalin's victims, and this created crisis among the theoreticians and die-hard activists in Lepoglava. They finally performed acrobatics with dogma and indulged in much ideological agility before convincing themselves and the rest of the Party faithful that the sin of 'factionalism' and other errors had earned the purged unfortunates a fate they deserved.

Jamie and Mannion remained on the sidelines while their fellow prisoners agonised over the deviations of Stalin's victims. They did not allow their reservations about Communism to impair the genuine friendship which existed between them and the Communists and, indeed, they cooperated willingly in the education programme which the Communist prisoners devised. Both were in demand as teachers of English and as translators of the Marxist tracts and journals that found their way into the prison. The political lectures and debates which were a feature of prison life tended to bore both Jamie and Mannion, but they participated wholeheartedly in other Communist-run classes. Both men learned German and Russian from prisoners who were first-class tutors and both found that intense study offered a worthwhile antidote to the monotony of prison life.

If Jamie and Mannion held themselves back from the Jesuit-like zeal for Communism which characterised so many of their fellow inmates, there was one area of agreement where they stood shoulder to shoulder with the revolutionaries. The circumstances of their imprisonment – and the denial of justice – had filled both men with a loathing of the regime responsible. They promised each other that if they ever won their freedom, it would be spent in mortal combat with the corrupt and brutal forces that governed Jugoslavia. And, if that meant allying themselves with Stefan and his Communists – whom they saw as the bravest and most incorruptible of the Regency's enemies – they would gladly do so.

It was this promise that had prompted Mannion to offer his and Jamie's services to the man called Tito, albeit with an element of bravado. They had pledged themselves to Stefan and his fight primarily because Stefan's sworn enemies had singled them out for persecution – and prison had merely sharpened their hatred of a system that they saw as wholly evil. They had needed little encouragement from Stefan to hold on until the day when they could strike back at the monster that had deprived them of their youth and liberty.

Paradoxically, Jamie's survival in prison had been nourished by love and hate. The stimulant of Mara's love had sustained him on the one hand, filling the moments of extreme loneliness – of which there were many. Hatred of the regime whose brutal power had separated him from Mara had hardened his determination to endure the daily misery which he and its other victims suffered. His love and his hate had kept him going, developing side by side until the vision of their fulfilment had fused and become inseparable. The fulfilment of one became dependent on fulfilment of the other. He wanted nothing more than to live the rest of his life in peace and freedom with Mara – but how and where and when would this be possible in a land where the innocent could expect neither?

What had happened in the rest of Europe while Jamie was a prisoner of the Jugoslav state awakened the dormant militancy within him. The news reaching him in prison – most of it already filtered by the government-controlled press in Belgrade – stirred the Briton in him to both anger and pride: anger at official Jugoslav admiration for the Nazi conquests of France and the Low Countries and the defeats inflicted on Britain: pride that bombed and battered Britain was still holding out against Hitler's hordes. The growing pro-German stance of the Jugoslav Government heightened Jamie's enmity to it and made him feel more isolated than ever from the one place that might have provided freedom for him and Mara – his father's homeland, his own homeland. More and more he had felt a prisoner in the enemy camp – a feeling that was only partly ameliorated by the sympathy that most of the Communist prisoners professed for Britain's fight against Hitler and Mussolini, in spite of official Party statements that it was a war between two imperialist powers and of no interest to Communists.

Jamie was acutely aware of how his life had hinged on his mother's decision to make her home in Jugoslavia.

'If we had stayed in Scotland,' he had confided in Stefan on more than one occasion, 'I would not have been rotting in this prison. I would have been fighting the Germans in Africa or piloting a fighter against the bomber formations they're sending over London.' His inability to contribute to the distant war provided him with another reason for hating the regime that had robbed him of that privilege – especially when that regime, with every passing day, resembled more and more the Nazi tyranny with which it was so friendly.

When the war was discussed, no one was more openly pro-British than Stefan, who argued fiercely with the Party theoreticians about the morality of the Hitler-Stalin pact, which had allowed Germany to wage war on the rest of Europe. He found it hard to swallow the Moscow line of registering opposition to the war in those countries threatened and overrun by the Nazis, at a time in history when Hitler and Mussolini were promising the obliteration of the Communist menace from the face of the earth.

Stefan submitted to the Party line on this vexed question but, privately, he sought to assure Jamie that there must be hidden reasons for Stalin's refusal to oppose the triumphant Germans. He argued that it was only a matter of time before the Communists everywhere would be drawn into the armed struggle against Fascism, and nowhere was that more likely to see its beginning than in Jugoslavia.

'The closer the Regency tries to align this country with Hitler,' he prophesied, 'the nearer they will bring the people to open rebellion. Then you and I will be comrades-in-arms, Jamie. Our fight will be the same fight.'

Mannion, no less than Jamie and Stefan, longed for the freedom that would bring an opportunity to fight. He, too, wanted to translate his anger and frustrated energies into positive action against the forces that had combined to deprive him of his liberty. The Croat nationalists, who had promised him death if he ever got beyond Lepoglava's walls, made it all too easy for him to accept that all that freedom would bring him would be a fight for survival. And no single group was more vociferous than the nationalists in support of the pro-Nazi elements in the Jugoslav Government. Mannion, therefore, had no difficulty in identifying Stefan's fight and Jamie's as his own. Only Stefan, however, had the support of an organisation outside prison through which they could channel their energies and lust to fight back.

The practicalities of how they contributed to Stefan's revolutionary cause remained rather vague and fanciful when the three could only talk about their freedom. When that freedom became a reality, it was not until they were talking with the Montenegrin known as Djordje that they realised how unrealistic their preconceptions had been.

It was Djordje's announcement that he would smuggle them into Belgrade that brought them face to face with practicalities. They had had notions of forming armed bands in the mountains as a means of harassing the Nazi-flavoured Government in Belgrade. They'd had wild ideas about trekking through Macedonia to Greece and linking up with the Greek forces resisting Italian aggression in Albania. Such notions died, without debate, in the moment that Djordje named Belgrade as their immediate destination and the place where they would join battle against the forces of oppression.

'We have numbers in Belgrade now,' Djordje told them, 'and the time is near when we will bring them out on the street to demonstrate the anger of the people at the way the country is being led.'

'Things must have changed a lot in six years,' Stefan said ruefully.

'Things have changed a lot in the last six weeks,' Djordje replied. 'I have been urging Tito and the Politburo to leave Zagreb and come to Belgrade in readiness.'

'In readiness for what?' asked Stefan.

'The lid blowing off the pot,' Djordje said, with relish. 'All the indications are that Prince Paul and his gang are ready to sign a pact of friendship with Hitler and Mussolini, and not even the bourgeois parties are going to stand for that. The whole country will rebel. You have escaped from prison at the right time, my friends. Our hour is near.'

His excitement rubbed off on the three fugitives.

'Do you think it will come to civil war?' Jamie asked, strangely exhilarated.

'Perhaps yes, perhaps no,' said Djordje. 'What matters is that the whole tide of opinion is running against the Regency, and we must be at the front of any popular uprising to overthrow it. We cannot be seen to be also-rans, tailing on behind a bunch of right-wing

189

Serbian patriots who are fed up with the way Prince Paul is grovelling to Hitler. If they take control, Hitler's panzers will be rolling on Belgrade before you can blink – and that's the last thing we want.'

'Why?' protested Jamie. 'Why should you not want to fight the Nazis? They're not going to sit and applaud if you bring down Prince Paul and hoist the red flag over Belgrade.'

'Jamie's right,' said Stefan. 'If Prince Paul is kicked out, war with the Germans will be inevitable. You can't bring one government down because it wants to deal with the Germans and then, in the next minute, make a deal with them anyway. The Germans would laugh in your face and the people wouldn't stand for it.'

Djordje sighed impatiently.

'Who said anything about doing a deal with the Germans? That wouldn't keep their panzers out. They're not going to be frightened of us, but they would think twice about invading if we had Russia behind us – if we had a mutual-protection pact with the Soviet Union. That's what would keep us out of the imperialists' war – a friendship treaty with Stalin. And we are the one party in Jugoslavia who could get such a pact.'

'Peace at a price?' Jamie commented, in a tone that made Djordje look at him sharply.

'Our movement is the creation of the Soviet Union,' said Djordje. 'And the Soviets will do all in their power to protect that creation – from the Fascists, and from the British imperialists, whose agents are so busy in Belgrade at this moment, trying to stir us into war. It is war that demands a price we will not pay – not peace.'

From the way Jamie pursed his lips, Stefan could tell that he was in the mood to argue at some length with Djordje, and it seemed the wrong time and the wrong place. He headed him off.

'It seems to me we're all running away ahead of ourselves,' he butted in brightly. 'Prince Paul's still in

190

charge in Belgrade and we're talking as if he's going to pack up and sail off down the Danube as soon as we say the word. Let's take one thing at a time, eh? Last night at this time, we were worrying about getting out of Lepoglava, so let's leave something for us to worry about tomorrow, when we've all had a good night's rest.'

The others needed little persuasion to seek less contentious topics of conversation. Djordje was already regretting speaking so freely in front of Jamie and Mannion. He was usually much more guarded. He made a mental note to take greater care in future and not to let his tongue get carried away by the pulsing excitement he felt at impending events. It was hard not to be excited, however. Never in the years since he had become a committed Communist had he known an optimism such as that now holding him in thrall. Now, at last, he could see light ahead, an indication that the long dark tunnel of underground battling was to be rewarded with a sight of blessed day. He was impatient for it.

When he returned to the widow's café the following day, it was to find the three fugitives from Lepoglava as eager as he was to be on their way to Belgrade. The tensions of the previous evening had given way to new tensions. There was no speculation about war and peace in the aftermath of a Regency regime that had still to fall. That was set aside for the more expedient problem of journeying to Belgrade without falling foul of the ubiquitous arms of the police.

In the event, little difficulty was encountered. Armed with very authentic-looking identity papers, the fugitives travelled independently on the same train but got off at the stop before Belgrade. They travelled into the city on a country bus, arriving in early afternoon. It was to find a city agog with news of a Government announcement. The police were conspicuous by their absence, oddly keeping a low profile as excited groups of citizens thronged the streets.

Everywhere, ordinary people were expressing anger and agitation at the news they had heard. Serbian pride had been outraged. Hitler had shaken his sabre at Prince Paul and his Goverment, and the cowardly Regent had fawningly submitted to the German dictator's demands. Jugoslavia had signed a Tripartite Treaty of Friendship with Germany and Italy.

Djordje was jubilant when the three fugitives met up with him again at a safe house in Molerova Street.

'We have work to do, my friends,' he proclaimed. 'Our hour has come.'

2

Blitzkrieg

Jamie lay awake long into the night. The wind had got up and somewhere, at the far side of the house, a window shutter was banging relentlessly against its casement. Inside the room, Mannion snored gently and Stefan coughed in his sleep, but neither these sounds nor the extraneous banging were the causes of Jamie's wakefulness. They scarcely intruded on the restless working of his mind.

Mara filled his thoughts. He wondered if she, too, was already back in Belgrade and lay sleepless, not too far away, thinking of him. The events of the day – 25 March 1941 – had filled him with hope that he would be able to see Mara much sooner than he had believed possible. And his mother and Uncle Milan, too, for that matter. The hope had been born of the growing confidence with which he and his two friends had been able to move around the city. There had been no need to skulk in doorways and creep around furtively to escape the notice of the police. They had moved about openly and those police whom they had glimpsed had shown not the faintest interest in them. It had all been so different to what he had expected.

He had visualised posses of police scouring the city just for them. He had expected to see newspapers with their pictures on the front pages; posters with rewards offered for the recapture of the three notorious escapers. Instead, it was as if their jailbreak had never occurred – or at least, gone unnoticed. It seemed too good to be true that the big news of the day – the sensational signing of the Tripartite Pact – had rendered their recapture by the police an irrelevance. And yet, that was exactly how it looked. So mild was the police reaction to the widespread demonstrations of contempt for the Regency Government, it seemed that, for once, the forces of law and order were in sympathy with the public display of affront to Serbian pride.

Djordje exulted in his belief that the hour of the Communists had come but Jamie and Mannion saw little evidence that the mood of rebellion permeating Belgrade was either Communist-inspired or Communist-led. A Party worker had been delegated to take the three fugitives to a house in Zemun for the night and, on the way, they encountered several street gatherings where speakers were haranguing modest crowds to protest against the Tripartite Pact. The three men and their guide made the journey by bicycle and, although they did not stop to listen to what was being said, it was apparent that these protest meetings were far from being Red in character. The Jugoslav flag was very much in evidence and the colours and banners displayed proclaimed the slogans and sentiments of Serbian nationalist movements that were traditionally right-wing and bourgeois at heart. The audiences encouraging the speakers represented all sections of society, but it was noticeable that army officers in uniform were well to the fore, and the obviously affluent stood shoulder to shoulder with artisan neighbours.

These gatherings were confined to the city. Passing over the Sava into Zemun – a town that was a drab industrial adjunct – Jamie and his companions left the excitement behind. Zemun was quiet, the streets strangely deserted – as if its hard-working citizens had better things to do than involve themselves with the volatile moods of the capital on the other side of the river.

The house to which they were taken was as unpretentious as the neighbourhood in which it stood. The

fugitives bedded down on the floor without complaint –
they had been prepared for much less than the luxury of
a roof over their heads in exchange for their prison cells –
but sleep eluded Jamie.

He envied Mannion's gift of being able to drop
unconscious as soon as he stretched himself out. Indeed,
Jamie had frequently marvelled at the way the American
accepted all his misfortunes, including self-imposed
exile, with cheerful equanimity. He seemed to have shut
himself off from his past life in the States as if it had never
existed, expunging it from his mind as if the path his life
had taken demanded forfeit of all thought about it. He
refused with equal resolution to contemplate the future
in terms of courses to be steered. Voluntarily severed
from his own past and his own future, he was content to
identify his own immediate destiny with the demands of
Jamie's and Stefan's. In prison, all three had drawn
strength and a closeness of spirit from the arrangement,
and Mannion was happy to go along with it until one or
the other of his friends chose to go his own way.

It occurred to Jamie, as he lay sleepless, that Mannion
– like himself – felt obliged to repay Stefan's Communist
friends for their freedom by giving them active support.
He and Mannion were motivated by real gratitude and
the knowledge that escape from Lepoglava would have
been impossible without the Communists and the help
Mara had received from them. Jamie knew, however,
that Mannion shared the strange uneasiness he felt in
this obligation. He was uncomfortable with people like
Djordje, feeling almost guilty that he could not share the
man's fanatical certainties in the righteousness of his
creed and the exclusiveness of its truth. There was a
feeling, too that Djordje – although he was prepared to
tolerate Jamie and Mannion for the moment, as useful to
the cause – would abandon them without compunction if
it became expedient to do so.

Jamie's unease stayed with him until sleep overtook

him and his troubled thoughts gave way to troubled dreaming. He was awakened at six by exhortations from Mannion and Stefan to rouse himself. There was revolutionary work to be done.

The nature of that work was a source of amusement to Mannion, but not to Stefan. They were to deliver leaflets by bicycle to three addresses in Belgrade, for distribution to public gatherings later that day. The leaflets – Communist Party declarations condemning the Tripartite Pact – had been run off at an illegal printing press somewhere in Zemun during the night and delivered to the safe house before dawn.

'What do you find so funny?' Stefan asked Mannion reproachfully, as the three were packing the leaflets into workers' tool bags.

'They want us to be paper boys,' Mannion replied, apparently tickled by the idea. 'It's not what I expected. I thought we would be manning barricades or storming a police post . , . not this.'

'You won't be laughing if we're caught with this stuff,' Stefan pointed out. 'Being a paper boy, as you call it, got me five years the last time. This time, they'll put us away for the rest of our lives if the cops get hold of us.'

'You think I don't know it?' Mannion came back ruefully. 'That's what's so crazy. We're risking our necks for this propaganda when we could be doing something that really matters. This stuff isn't going to start any riots in the street.'

'Rioting won't achieve anything,' Stefan retorted. 'We have to win the minds of the people. We have to let them see where the Party stands. Otherwise, they will not support us when the time comes to act.'

Mannion shrugged.

'I thought the moment to act was now. The whole place is stirred up. You saw what it was like last night – all the flags and the shouting. Seems to me that what the Party is doing is jumping on somebody else's bandwagon, when what they ought to be doing is leading the parade.'

Stefan scoffed at the suggestion, but the events of the next forty-eight hours tended to confirm the shrewdness of Mannion's assessment.

They split up to make the leaflet deliveries in Belgrade, travelling into the city early, mingling in the stream of workers crossing the Sava from Zemun. Afternoon found them back at Djordje's headquarters in Molerova Street, where there was more bicycle messenger work to be done: passing the word to Party cells of public protest demonstrations planned for the evening.

Stefan, buoyed by the freedom with which all three had moved about Belgrade and by the seeming indifference of the police, was all for taking part in the protests and was happily surprised when Jamie and Mannion agreed, albeit they had different reasons. Mannion wanted the action, the involvement. Jamie nourished the hope – which had kept him company throughout the day – that, somewhere on the city streets, he would catch sight of Mara.

Djordje was pleased that Stefan's friends wanted to identify themselves in public with Communists and Communist sympathisers.

'If the police do recognise you and try and take you, we'll give them a fight,' he promised. 'There will be enough of us.'

In spite of his brave words, the crowds that rallied behind the red flags could be measured in hundreds rather than the thousands he had hoped for. It was the intention to converge on the city centre from three rallying points but, in the event, the public protest fizzled out. Jamie and his companions were in a group of several hundred that advanced down Queen Maria Street but found their way barred by ranks of police, spread across the road.

Djordje was fuming. He had expected a tussle with the police but he had also expected a crowd that was vast enough to intimidate them. He did not have it. Fear of the police – or perhaps long memories of their brutal methods of dispersal in the past – had kept too many Communist sympathisers in their homes. Djordje cursed their cowardice.

The confrontation was an anticlimax. The police were polite, almost friendly. They let it be known that the crowd could advance no further and appealed for its orderly dispersal. The protesters, arguing amongst themselves, turned back the way they had come and dispersed.

Jamie, Mannion and Stefan returned to where they had left their bicycles, all feeling strangely deflated by the turn of events. They cycled back to Zemun, to await further instructions from Djordje for the morrow. Their hosts, a railway worker and his wife – who were anxious for news about what was happening in Belgrade – shared their disappointment, and alleviated it by supplying their first hot meal of the day and some heady wine to wash it down.

The three were up early the next morning and taking turns to wash and shave in the tiny closet bathroom when the railwayman's wife came running from the kitchen in great excitement. They followed her into the kitchen, where her husband had his ear against the speaker of a small battery-operated radio.

Atmospherics crackled from the set, but not enough to render unintelligible the firm young voice that was speaking.

'What is happening?' Stefan demanded.

The railwayman shushed him but, seeing the impatience and bewilderment on the faces staring at him, offered a terse explanation:

'It is Prince Peter – King Peter now! He has deposed his cousin, Prince Paul, and appointed a new Government. The Army is behind him and he is asking for the support of the people.'

It was not yet eight-thirty in the morning when they reported to Djordje's headquarters. The apartment building buzzed with comings and goings, as if, somewhere inside, it housed an illicit betting office and there had been a sudden rush of its furtive clientele. An air of bewilderment, almost panic, prevailed as Djordje dealt with a stream of callers – all seeking direction as a result of the *coup d'état*.

Djordje stared in dismay at the fresh supply of anti-Pact leaflets which the three fugitives from Lepoglava had brought from Zemun.

'They are useless now,' he wailed. They were yesterday's propaganda sheets, and the events of the night had made them obsolete. Djordje vetoed their distribution. New leaflets would have to be printed, and he had already been at work on how they would be worded – but he was reluctant to send the copy off to the illegal press for printing before consulting other members of the regional committee on what line the Party should take.

Djordje himself had no doubt. He was all for rallying the Party behind the new anti-Nazi Government and giving it a chance to show that it was as liberal and democratic as it claimed to be in its overthrow of the Regency. Djordje advocated massive public demonstrations to indicate Communist support for the new patriotic regime and the right to a leading role in it. Their banners and their slogans, while hailing the new patriotic unity, must demand more democracy in government and – as a deterrent to Nazi aggression – closer ties and a treaty of friendship with the Soviet Union.

For all his certainties on what the Party line should be, and for all his confidence that he could carry the Belgrade members with him, Djordje still hesitated from issuing the directives that would have mobilised Communists to demonstrate that morning. He waited for the agreement of at least some of his regional committee colleagues to his plan of action. But they were proving hard to find. They, it seemed, were all out on the streets – looking for him and each other. He grew more frustrated as the morning wore on.

Stefan, for one, was acutely sympathetic with the Montenegrin in his dilemma. Every minute lost saw the floodtide of opportunity slipping away. So it seemed to the seething Djordje, and so it seemed to Stefan. And it stemmed from the injustice of the outlawing of the Communist Party all those years ago: the injustice that had driven them underground and compelled them to operate from secret and constantly changing locations. Never had their seriously disadvantaged state of illegality exacted a more severe penalty than this morning.

Even Jamie and Mannion sweated a bit for Djordje, although they were able to take a more detached view than Stefan, being less dazzled by the Soviet model of revolution. It seemed to them that Djordje's colleagues in Belgrade – and the ruling Central Committee in Zagreb – had been caught napping by the bloodless *coup d'état*, which had ended the Regency. In this, however, they were perhaps being a little unjust; they were unaware that, only the previous day, Djordje and his Belgrade comrades had again appealed directly to Tito to bring the Central Committee from Zagreb to Belgrade, where the action was. They wanted Tito and his Politburo to sense the mood of the people and be in a position to exploit it to the full.

It was, however, to take the stunning shock of the coup to shake the Central Committee into moving to Belgrade. Even then, events were to occur at a speed that outpaced their ability to act.

As cycle couriers, Jamie, Stefan and Mannion made

themselves useful to Djordje during that historic morning of 27 March but, for the most part, the time was spent waiting for errands to be given. Excluded from Djordje's discussions with cell leaders, who arrived in a steady stream, they began to feel that they were getting in the way.

It came as a relief, therefore, when Djordje announced that he had to go out and that there was no point in them hanging around any longer. He made it clear that the trio's obligation to him to put themselves at his disposal while they were dependent on him for refuge had been overtaken by other priorities.

'You were a long time in Lepoglava, comrades,' he said, 'and you must have lots of friends and loved ones you're longing to see. Go and see them. Now, when you've got the chance. The heat's off. The cops aren't touching our illegals. They'd probably be lynched if they tried.'

'But don't you need us now?' protested Stefan. 'Doesn't the Party need us?'

'Of course it does,' Djordje assured him, with a smile. 'It needs every man it can muster. But it can get by without you for a day or two. God knows, you've earned a break. Nobody expects you to jump straight back into the scheme of things.'

Stefan was not fully convinced, but appeared mollified when Djordje told him that the Univeristy cell, with which he had operated before his arrest in 1935, was still flourishing and would welcome him back. He told Stefan how to make contact. He diffidently suggested, too, that as a precaution against the outside chance that police activity might be renewed, the trio should split up.

He shook hands with Mannion.

'Good luck, my American friend. You're safe from Pavelic's thugs in Belgrade, but if you ever want to kill a few, it's OK with me. I've always detested them.'

Then Djordje shook hands with Jamie and wished him good luck.

'We, in the Party, will always honour you,' he said. 'We do not forget that, although you were not one of us, you were tortured and suffered for us and did not betray us.'

In parting, Djorde good-humouredly advised all three that if, that evening, they were not compensating for their years of celibacy with three of Belgrade's beauties, they would be more than welcome at the public rally at Vuk's Monument, called by the Party for eight o'clock.

'It's more like a carnival than a revolution,' Mannion observed. He was in high spirits, as were Jamie and Stefan, infected by the euphoria that gripped Belgrade. The taste of a new freedom was heady in the air. A beautiful spring day became an historic one as the capital's jubilant citizens took to the streets in greater and greater numbers to hail the *coup d'état* which, overnight, had removed the pro-Nazi Government.

To none was the taste of freedom sweeter than to Jamie, Stefan and Mannion. Since their parting with Djordje, they had walked and walked, revelling in the pleasure of being able to roam wherever they pleased with apparent impunity. Belgrade had a smile on its face. The national flag was again everywhere in evidence: borne on the shoulders of happy patriots, fluttering from windows and above doorways, worn like cloaks by cavorting girls.

The three witnessed occurrences which, only days before, would have been unthinkable. Near the railway station, a squad of gendarmes looked on indulgently as a dozen workers marched down the street behind a red banner, chanting: 'War before the Pact.' Elsewhere, troops of police applauded when youngsters hauled down the Nazi flag from the German Tourist Bureau – a euphemistic label for a known propaganda centre – and burned it in the street.

Their wandering brought them at last to a café near

the Sava docks, where they could discuss the implications of their new freedom at leisure. The café was Stefan's choice. He knew the owner to be a Party sympathiser, and there was a wariness in Stefan, still, of this intoxicating liberty. Nevertheless, even Stefan was unprepared for the enthusiasm of the welcome accorded him by the café owner and his wife. They received him as if he had returned from the dead. Jamie and Mannion – as his friends – were greeted with comparable warmth. Hugs and tears were the order of the day.

It transpired that the café owner had feared the worst for Stefan, after hearing rumours of his arrest in 1935. Now, he was overjoyed to see him alive. He happily assumed that Stefan and his two friends must have been released from prison on the Ada Ciganlija only that morning. Stefan's blank reaction to this assumption puzzled him.

'You have not been released from the island?' he asked.

'No,' Stefan replied. 'What made you think we were?' The man stared at him.

'They have freed all the detainees on the island. It was one of the young Prince's first acts as King – to release all political prisoners. They've emptied the Glavnjaca jail, too. I thought you must have come from one or the other.'

'We got out a few days ago . . . but we're trying not to broadcast the fact,' Stefan cautioned. He did not elaborate further. Instead, he asked the café owner if his wife's cooking was still the miracle he remembered. The man smilingly assured him it was and, minutes later, supplied the proof.

Dishes of steaming *djuvec* were set before the trio. Even Jamie was prepared to concede that his Uncle Milan's housekeeper, old Lucija, could not have done better. The rice stew, with its generous portions of chunky meat,

203

was rich with tomatoes, peas, beans and carrots and spiced with peppers. It was both delicious and filling.

'It sure beats Lepoglava hash,' was Mannion's verdict. 'Now, all we got to worry about is where our next meal is coming from!'

'Come home with me,' Jamie said. 'Both of you.'

'No, Jamie. We cannot put your family at risk.' Stefan spoke softly. He stared at his friend with troubled eyes. 'I know the heat seems to be off, but maybe we should wait and see how things are. Maybe we should wait and see if the amnesty for politicals included us. We broke out of prison, remember.'

'Djordje said we should split up. Is that what you suggest?' Jamie regarded Stefan with an air of disappointment.

'It might be the wise thing to do,' Stefan said.

'You want to fight your revolution all on your own?' Jamie's voice betrayed a bitterness he did not intend.

'If you want to put it that way, yes,' Stefan replied. 'But I wasn't thinking about me. I was thinking of what's best for you and Brad. I'm committed to Communism, Jamie – by choice. But you two are not, and that's what makes a difference. I can't ask you to come down the road I've chosen. That's a choice you have to make for yourselves – and not for the wrong reasons. You have to be as sure as I am that it's the right road.'

Jamie considered this unhappily.

'You know we feel the same way as you do about a lot of things,' he said. 'What bothers me – and it bothers Brad, too – is the blind faith you put in Russia . . . in Stalin, as if he was some kind of god.'

'He's the only hope this country has,' Stefan said fiercely.

'That's just the point, Stefan,' Mannion interjected softly. 'Jamie and I are worried that you and guys like Djordje are pinning too much hope on Stalin. You could be in for a mighty disappointment.'

Stefan's expression hardened.

'I don't want to argue about it, Brad.' He shrugged. 'Let's just say that it confirms the point I was making – that I can't ask you to come down the road I have chosen. It is wiser that we separate now, as friends. Nothing will ever change that. No man could ask for finer brothers than you have been to me.' He blinked at Jamie. 'You, Jamie – it has cost you so much . . . just because you knew me, and because you stood by me. I have a debt to you that I can never repay.'

A sudden warmth towards Stefan flooded Jamie in remembrance of a two-way bond of strength and hope that had been forged out of much suffering. He managed a tremulous smile.

'We've always stood by each other.' He grinned at Mannion. 'The three musketeers. . . . '

'All for one and one for all,' said Mannion, grinning back. He made a rueful grimace. 'If anyone's the odd guy out, it's me. I got no ties, no place in particular to go – but you guys don't need to worry about me. Everybody – except maybe our old pal, Djordje – seems to think that it's only a matter of time now before Hitler marches on Belgrade. If there's going to be a war, I might as well be in it. The Army's not going to be so goddamned fussy that it draws the line at having ex-cons. It's going to need every man it can get.'

Jamie and Stefan looked at Mannion in surprise.

'You'd join the Army?' Stefan asked, in a shocked tone.

'Sure. If they'd take me,' Mannion replied. 'You got any better ideas?'

Further discussion on the matter was postponed by the arrival of a newspaper seller, with a special edition. They purchased a copy and crowded round Stefan to read it. The front page carried a large photograph of Jugoslavia's new monarch, seventeen-year-old King Peter, and carried the full text of the proclamation to the people, which he had broadcast at seven o'clock that morning. There were also details of the *coup d'état*.

Cvetkovic, the pro-Axis Prime Minister who had gone to Vienna to sign the Tripartite Pact aligning Jugoslavia with Germany and Italy, had been arrested on his return to Belgrade and taken to Air Force Headquarters in Zemun. There, he had been confronted by General Simovic, the Commander-in-Chief, and General Mirkovic, the Air Force Commander, who had demanded and received his resignation. In addition to the Prime Minister, the Foreign Minister and a number of senior military officers had been arrested. The conspirators had had the support of Army officers in Belgrade, Skopje, Zagreb and Sarajevo – nearly all below the rank of colonel – and had effected their takeover without a shot being fired.

The Regent, Prince Paul – on his way to Zagreb while rebel troops of the Royal Guard sealed off the Royal Palace in Belgrade – had been presented with a *fait accompli* on arrival at the Croatian capital. He had been informed that, under General Simovic, a new all-party Government had been set up in the name of King Peter the Second. The deposed Regent had been given twenty-four hours to return to Belgrade, collect his family and such effects as they needed, and leave the country. It was believed he would seek asylum in Greece.

The newspaper announced that next day, Saturday, March the twenty-eighth, King Peter would attend a divine service of dedication and thanksgiving at Belgrade Cathedral. There was no mention of an amnesty for Communists, but prominence was given to the Serbian Democratic Party and the part it had played in welding an all-party front against the Regency. It had campaigned for the release of all political prisoners, and this was one of the declared aims of the new Government, which was likely to be implemented quickly.

'Hey, will you look at that? Looks like we weren't the

only ones that bust out of jail,' said Mannion, gleefully pointing to a box in the centre spread of the newspaper. The item reported that young King Peter, who had been a virtual prisoner of his cousin while the Regency Government reigned, had escaped from Prince Paul's ring of guards by shinning down a drainpipe. 'If the King can get away with it, why not us?' Mannion concluded.

'He didn't shoot one of Luk's agents,' Stefan commented, with a wry smile.

'Give him time.' Mannion grinned back at him. 'Maybe he'll have them all shot now.'

'I would become a royalist overnight if he did.' Stefan's tone implied no danger of that likelihood. He admitted grudgingly: 'Still, he's made a good start. I would have been more impressed if his new all-party Government had had a few Communist ministers.'

'Your big shots will have to come out in the open first,' Mannion said.

'They will,' Stefan said with conviction. 'If the time is right.'

'And us?' asked Jamie. 'Do we take that chance?'

'I say we take no chances. What do you say, Jamie?'

'We took a chance coming to Belgrade. Now that we're here, I want to go home – even if it's just for tonight. Uncle Milan will see we're all right.'

'And you, Brad?' asked Stefan. 'Do you want to go with Jamie?'

Stefan's stare seemed to make Mannion uncomfortable, as if he was being obliged to make a choice between his two friends.

'We've got to do something,' he said. 'Yeah, I'll go along with Jamie if he wants to see his folks. I never had a real chance to thank his uncle for all he did for me. Now, might be as good a time as any.'

'You've changed your mind about trying to get into the Army?'

'I haven't made up my mind about anything yet,' Mannion replied, defensively. 'Right now, I'm happy to go along with Jamie.'

'You come too, Stefan,' Jamie urged. 'Let's stick together.'

'No, my friends. Sooner or later we would have had to part company. Better that we do it now. Without arguments . . . without bad feeling.'

There were no bad feelings when they separated, only regret on the part of Jamie and Mannion that Stefan's priestly attachment to his gods of revolution should make him want to go his own way, leaving them – it seemed – to pursue less noble and more self-indulgent ends.

A festival atmosphere still gripped the city in late afternoon as Jamie and Mannion made their way through the thronged streets. It lifted Jamie's heart to see how prominent among the flags bedecking the buildings was Britain's Union Jack. It fluttered everywhere, as did the Tricolor of France, alongside the Jugoslav national flag, as if to proclaim newfound Serbian pride in the Alliance that had fought the Austrians and the Turks.

The pair were waiting for a tram when a car suddenly braked, only yards away. Jamie – his eyes on a band of Serbian nationalists, who were marching along, chanting 'War before slavery' – did not glance at the man who emerged from the stopped car until only a pace separated them. When he did, recognition was instant. Jamie's heart almost stopped. His impulse was to run, but he remained on the spot, paralysed, his knees like jelly.

The face smiling at him was Luk's. The hand that reached out to rest on his shoulder was cautioning rather than restraining.

'Don't run, young comrade. So you got back to Belgrade? I congratulate you.'

Jamie remained rooted to the spot. Beside him, Mannion – suddenly alert and sensing danger – had bunched his fists.

'Don't look so scared,' Luk said. 'I'm not rounding up Reds today. I only stopped to make sure that you were who I thought you were. How long has it been. . . ? Five, six years? You have changed, but I do not forget a face.'

'Then you have me at a disadvantage,' Jamie said, and affected puzzlement. 'I don't think I know you, sir.'

Luk laughed uproariously.

'You still have your manners, I'll say that for you,' he conceded mirthfully. 'But not knowing me! Please. Did I make so little impression on you the last time?' His gaze took in Mannion. 'Ha! And this is the American . . . the one who shot Banjo. What a pity he did not make a better job of it, eh?'

Still, Jamie stood, poised for flight but unable to take the first step, bewildered by whatever game the secret police chief was playing. Had Mannion and he been trapped? Did Luk have men all around, waiting to pounce at the first sign of flight?

Luk seemed to enjoy the uncertainty his sudden appearance had provoked.

'You're trembling like a couple of rabbits,' he chided. 'I should be flattered that I am able to inspire such fear, but I meant what I said. I saw the pair of you standing there, bold as brass, and I just couldn't pass by. . . .' He smiled as Jamie continued to glance nervously about him. 'Nobody's going to jump on you,' he said. 'If you think that Banjo's going to materialise out of the road and cart you off to the Glavnjaca, you're wrong. Banjo isn't going to be troubling anyone for a long time, I'm happy to tell you.'

Jamie stared at Luk, with the first ray of hope stirring within him that the secret police chief did not, after all, present a threat to his and Mannion's freedom. He was aware instinctively that Mannion – as poised and as ready as Jamie for flight – was on the point of desperate action. Partly obscured from Luk by Jamie's body, he was reaching inside his jacket for the gun that had been tucked in his waistband since the escape from Lepoglava. The brush of his arm against his back was sufficient to warn Jamie of the intention behind the surreptitious movement. Jamie backed into him, gently jogging his friend with an elbow as an indication to stay his hand.

'Should we be interested in this Banjo?' he asked Luk, with a calm he did not feel. The care in his choice of words seemed to amuse Luk.

'If anyone should be interested, it's you,' he said. 'He gave you a bad time and he's the one you can thank for the stretch you got in Lepoglava. He's the one who stitched you up.' He smiled. 'I gave you a pretty hard time myself, but I might have gone easier if I had realised at the time how good Banjo was at bending witnesses. He was a lot smarter than I gave him credit for.'

'You speak of him in the past tense,' Jamie said, feeling bolder. 'Has something happened to him? Is he dead?'

Luk laughed.

'Dead? Damned few would mourn him if he was – but no, he's not dead. He just backed the wrong people, that's all. And he was too ambitious . . . too ambitious for his own good. He thought he could take my job.' Luk contemplated the folly of such ambition with an air of sadness. It dawned on Jamie as he did so that the secret police chief was more than a little drunk. He swayed gently on his feet and as if to confirm Jamie's impression, emitted a sigh that betrayed breath reeking with alcohol.

'Here comes a street-car,' Mannion announced. To Jamie, it sounded like a challenge to Luk; inviting the police chief to prevent them boarding it. But Luk waved them away.

'Take it,' he told them. Again he swayed, and beamed with apparent pleasure at the sight of the approaching tram. Its front was decorated with a billboard photograph of the boyish King Peter, and twin staff-mounted Jugoslav flags had been fastened on either side of the driver's cab. Flag-carrying passengers were hanging precariously to the flanks of the tram and shouting boisterously.

Jamie and Mannion needed no second bidding from Luk. They made for the crowded step of the tram. Securing a foothold Jamie glanced back. Luk had not moved, and now the secret police chief raised both arms and shouted in a piercing voice:

'Long live King Peter! Long live Serbia!'

His exhoration brought jubilant acclamation of patriotic sentiment from the flag-wavers around Jamie and Mannion. Luk repeated his shouts as the tram moved off and gathered speed.

He remained where he was, flushed with a wellbeing for which a half-bottle of brandy was only partly responsible. He had much to be satisfied with on this day of national joy. He had played no small part in making it possible, even though his involvement had started fortuitously – as a result of Banjo going over his head and trying to discredit him in the eyes of the old palace guard. It had been a shock to discover that the old guard were ready to discard him in favour of his treacherous underling – but the discovery, in time, had made it all the easier for him to put his expertise and cunning at the disposal of the plotters who wanted to depose the old King's first cousin, the Regent, and put young Peter on the throne. As a King's man and a Serb who considered himself a patriot, Luk had been agonising over exposure of the anti-Regency clique when discovery of Banjo's treachery simplified the making of choices. He had joined the plotters.

Now, Banjo was locked up safely in the Glavnjaca and

finding out what it was like to be on the receiving end of rough justice. Well, he deserved all he got. It was odd that, within hours of having placed Banjo under arrest, he should come face to face with one of his former lieutenant's victims. The student with the strange name, Jamie Kyle, he remembered with remarkable clarity. It would be an exaggeration to say that the youngster's face had haunted Luk: it had stayed with him in a puzzling way, something misunderstood, as if a question mark hung over the mental image.

Luk could recall in detail the interview he had had with the boy: his protest of innocence and his stubborn refusal to name names. Luk had felt a strange sympathy for the boy. All of this had come flooding back when news of the Lepoglava jailbreak was flashed to Belgrade HQ. Luk's first reaction had been one of astonishment that the boy was still in prison after all this time. A requested report had revealed that the boy and the two who escaped with him had had three years added to their sentences because of a stramash with Pavelic supporters among the inmates.

This information had, if anything, earned plus marks for the three offenders from Luk. Pavelic and his Fascist thugs were top of Luk's hate list. They and their like had assassinated the old King in Marseille. They were a far greater menace than the Communists, who had not so far descended to assassination and blowing up passenger trains to further their aims. Indeed, the Reds were a highly moral lot compared with the Croat nationalists. What Luk couldn't stomach about Reds was their worship of Russia and the Russians. A Soviet-oriented Serbia was as repellent to him as a Serbia ruled by Habsburgs or Turks.

Hunting for the three escapers from Lepoglava had not figured highly among Luk's priorities. The Regency had not gone soft on Communists and their fellow travellers, but Luk himself had ceased to regard them as

212

a threat in Belgrade. He was a great deal more concerned with the violent German-loving elements with whom the Regency seemed to be getting on better terms. It rankled with Luk that the Regency's fear of the Fascists dictated a kid-glove policy to those whom he classed as the country's most dangerous enemies. In Croatia, the situation was ready to boil over, with the Fascists taking over and thumbing their nose at Belgrade.

The escape of a couple of Communists and a Pavelic-hating American had not, therefore, become a burning concern with Luk. He had instituted inquiries of a routine nature, which had yielded nothing. The prisoner Kyle's relatives had been contacted. His uncle, a respected businessman, had clearly been surprised by the jailbreak and obviously had no prior knowledge of it. It had also ocurred at a time when he was distracted by the illness of his sister, the escaped prisoner's mother, who was in the Queen Maria Hospital and likely to be there for some time.

An attempt to locate the girl who was the known associate of all three escapers had also proved fruitless. She had not been in her apartment for a week and was believed to have returned to the family home near Karlovac. A neighbour had volunteered the information that the girl was not expected back in Belgrade until after Easter. Associates of the prisoner Stefan Markovic had also been questioned without success. Luk had quickly relayed the little information available to Zagreb, passing the buck back to the authorities in Croatia, where the escape had occurred. He had then devoted his attention to more pressing priorities – of which there were many. Not least was the part he would play in the overthrow of the Regency.

How ironic that on the day that he believed would be one of historic significance for Serbia and Jugoslavia, he should encounter two escapers who – he had at one time believed – posed a serious threat to the state. Watching the flag-festooned tram that bore them away, Luk marvelled at his own capacity to misjudge the proportion of things. It did not trouble him that his zeal in the past might have made him an accessory to – if not the instrument of – one or many miscarriages of justice. All that mattered was the protection of the state. He did not see it as an act of self-preservation, which it also was. Luk could draw no distinction between the state's interest and his own.

Thus, the state's injustice to Jamie Kyle and Brad Mannion in the past was as unimportant now as any present need to curtail their liberty. If they had offended against the Regency regime – or vice versa – it could be forgotten. Because the Regency was no more. It had passed forever into history and would remain there, unmourned.

As Luk stared after the departed tram, he repeated almost inaudibly the words he had shouted only moments before: 'Long live King Peter! Long live Serbia!' He felt a silent welling of pride within his breast that, again, he could truly call himself a King's man. He recalled the anger that had filled him on that faraway day in the Prefecture in Marseille when he had watched the old King die. A new anger filled Luk now: an anger at the homicidal forces that had contrived the old King's death and would now, in their wrath, unleash themselves against the new.

Luk braced himself in the warm spring sunlight, soberly aware that the new King and all those dedicated to the day-old monarchy's survival would not have to seek enemies – for they were legion. In addition to those within – which would be Luk's immediate concern – there were the enemies without: the armed hosts gathered in Austria, Hungary, Romania, Bulgaria, Italy and Albania, and ready to march on Belgrade.

A second tramcar went rattling past Luk as he

returned to his car. He watched its progress. It, too, was bedecked with flags and crowded with noisy celebrating citizens. This time, Luk shouted no patriotic slogans but stared morosely at the spectacle.

'Rejoice while you can,' he murmured softly. 'Tomorrow, you may be weeping.'

Ten days were to pass before Belgrade's joy turned to grief. On the same day that Jamie Kyle was being happily reunited with Uncle Milan and learning that his mother was in hospital, the author of the grief to come was convening an emergency meeting of his military commanders, some six hundred miles or more to the north. The leader of the German people, Adolf Hitler, was noted for his rages, but the fury he displayed on that March evening in 1941 surpassed any that his close associates had ever witnessed.

In the heat of his anger, he made the decision that was to cost him the conquest of all Europe, from the Atlantic to the Urals, and number the days of the Third Reich. His greedy eyes already fixed on Russia and with his armies marshalling in Poland, Czechoslovakia, Hungary, Romania and Bulgaria for the great attack, he became almost apoplectic at the news of events in the Jugoslav capital. His personal envoy had been spat upon and jeered by ranting crowds, the Nazi flag had been burned in the street, and the Prince Regent and his ministers had been ousted by a military clique.

Only three weeks previously, Prince Paul had met Hitler at the Berghof and given the Fuehrer the assurances he wanted about the unhindered passage of troops across Jugoslavia. He had even offered Prince Paul the territory of Salonika as an inducement to joining the Axis powers. And, only two days ago, Hitler and his Foreign Minister, von Ribbentrop, had gone personally to Vienna to co-sign the Tripartite Pact with Jugoslavia's Prime Minister and Foreign Minister. Now, the

Prince Regent had been ejected in favour of a schoolboy, and the rebel officers had scrapped the treaty before the ink on the parchment was dry!

Hitler lost no time in summoning his Army chiefs to the Chancellery in Berlin to consider the emergency created by the Jugoslav *putsch*. It seriously upset his plans to invade northern Greece from Bulgaria and thus secure his southern flank before invading Russia in May.

'These upstart Slavs must be taught a lesson that they'll never forget!' Hitler thundered at his generals, his temper not improved by the late arrival at the Chancellery of three senior members of his team. Field Marshal von Brauchitsch, the Army's Commander-in-Chief, General Halder, Chief of the General Staff, and von Ribbentrop, the Foreign Minister, had rushed to answer the Fuehrer's summons but did not reach the Chancellery until half an hour after the meeting was scheduled to start. They had to endure angry tickings-off for their tardiness before getting down to the business in hand – not that they were allowed to make much contribution. Hitler had already decided on how the Jugoslav impertinence should be punished.

'Jugoslavia must be destroyed!' he declared. 'As a nation, it will cease to exist. Its military strength will be dismembered. I want these Slavs crushed with unmerciful harshness! And I want it done without warning. There will be no exchange of diplomatic messages, no ultimatums delivered. We shall strike and we shall destroy!'

He turned to Goering.

'I want the Luftwaffe to revenge the insults we have suffered in Belgrade. The city is only a short distance from our airfields in Hungary and will be the first target of our bombers. I want wave after wave of attacks to reduce the city to rubble and ashes.'

He turned to Keitel and Jodl.

'It is my intention to force a way into Jugoslavia as our

216

bombers destroy the capital, and your task will be the annihilation of the Jugoslav Army. I want the military plans worked out immediately . . . tonight!'

He turned to Ribbentrop.

'In due course, you will inform the loyal signatories of the Tripartite Pact of our intention to destroy Jugoslavia. War against the Slavs should be very popular in Italy, Hungary and Bulgaria, because each of them can expect a share of the spoils. I shall give the Banat wheatlands to the Hungarians, Macedonia to the Bulgars, and the Adriatic coastlands to Italy. We shall give the Croats their independence – under our protection, of course – and keep Serbia for ourselves.'

Hitler then announced the codename he had chosen for the crushing of Jugoslavia – Operation *Bestrafung*. He thought the name – meaning 'punishment' – was particularly appropriate. He saved his final – and perhaps the most fateful – announcement for the effect of the Jugoslavian crisis on the operation codenamed *Barbarossa*: the invasion of Russia.

'The beginning of *Barbarossa* on fifteenth May will have to be postponed by four weeks,' he told his assembled generals. They offered no dissent. But the same generals, later in the year – when the German armies were hammering at the gates of Moscow but stalled by the early advent of winter – were to rue that four-week delay with bitterness.

The bombers came out of a clear blue sky from the north. They followed the track of the Danube, homing on the beaconlike pile of the Kalemegdan at the broader river's junction with the Sava and then sweeping like skeins of geese across the city. Belgrade lay defenceless below them. Jugoslavia had more than half a million men under arms, but not a single anti-aircraft gun was deployed in defence of the capital. The bombers flew in low, and unmolested. Flight after flight sent their cargoes of death raining upon the densely packed city below.

Jamie and Mannion were at breakfast when the first thunderous explosions came booming across the city, rattling the windows of Milan Alexandrovic's house and shaking the doors. Only minutes earlier, Jamie's uncle had called out a cheerful goodbye as he had left for eight o'clock Mass.

The two men raced out to the street, followed by an agitated Lucija, who was calling on the saints in heaven to protect them all from whatever cataclysm had descended on them, this Sunday morning. Looking skywards, they heard and then saw the tight formations of two-engined aircraft that came into view, bearing south on an unwavering course at a height of a thousand feet. A tide of rolling explosions followed in the bombers' wake, rushing towards the watchers in the street and threatening to engulf them.

Grabbing Lucija unceremoniously, Jamie forced her down in a sprawling huddle beside him, close to the wall of the house. Mannion joined them, unnecessarily urging them to keep their heads down as a house erupted in a fountain of masonry only five hundred metres away and blasts of sound reverberated upon their ears from all around. A pattern of rapidly successive explosions rolled on and passed them like an unwinding carpet, creating a sandstorm of swirling dust and curling smoke. The clouds carried with them the stench of high explosive, acrid and suphurous.

Still the bombers came – but the weight of their attack seemed to be concentrated on the heart of the city, with the outer reaches and suburbs spared the worst of the merciless pounding. Lucija did not want Jamie and Mannion to leave her, but Jamie insisted they must. His thoughts were for his mother, recovering from surgery in the gynaecological ward at the Queen Maria Hospital in central Belgrade. The area was being blanketed by bombs.

218

'We'll find Uncle Milan and bring him back to you,' Jamie promised the old woman, 'but I've got to see if Majka is all right and see if we can bring her home. The hospital will have to be evacuated if this goes on.' He dared not voice the thought: if it is still standing.

'What has happened to Milan? Why hasn't he come home?' Lucija wailed.

'He will have taken shelter. You saw how bad it was. He's probably on his way right now.' Jamie's attempts to reassure the old woman were only partly successful. In the end, Mannion offered to stay with her while Jamie went in search of Milan.

The tiny church of St Podgorica, which Milan attended most Sundays, was only fifteen minutes' walk from his house. It was a quaint wedding cake of a building, sandwiched in the middle of a row of shops. Making his way there Jamie broke into a run, hurrying past scenes of devastation that numbed and bewildered his mind. What had been a familiar landscape was no longer so. Rows of buildings that had been landmarks had ceased to be recognisable; here and there a skeletal shell remained, and elswhere a gap yawned above a disarray of rubble from which the dust and smoke still swirled. It was a world inhabited by grey dishevelled spectres who wandered dazedly about, weeping and calling for loved ones. Other dust-grimed spectres exhibited frenzy in the midst of the devastation, tearing at the rubble mountains with bare hands as they sought lost families in the wreckage of their homes. There was no sign of organised fire, rescue, or medical services; no cohesion in the attempts to aid the injured and the buried.

Jamie stopped only once, to help a weeping woman with a child in her arms. He drew back in horror; there was nothing he could do. The woman was uninjured but her child was dead.

Jamie hurried on, hoping against hope that he would meet his uncle coming the other way. His hopes died when he realised that he had reached the street where the pagoda-like tower of the St Podgorica Church had been a conspicuous fixture. It was not there. The arch of the doorway still stood, but the roof and tower had disappeared. All the buildings on that side of the street had been flattened, leaving only a façade of crumbling brickwork, with the stout pillars of the church doorway the only recognisable feature.

In the vicinity of the church were about dozen people, some clambering in the ruins. Jamie arrived to find a human chain busy in the task of lifting dead and wounded from the spaces amid fallen roof beams. Somewhere inside, the voice of a trapped woman was crying pitifully to be helped. Each agonised cry was weaker than the last.

There was no access through the doorway. It was heaped high with rubble. He joined the human chain struggling in the sloping jumble of masonry to lower a grievously injured old man to street level, and helped in the manoeuvre. The man was fully conscious and kept appealing to his rescuers in gasping sobs to save his Sofije. It was apparently his Sofije whose cries could be heard. A dust-encrusted rescuer, his eyebrows and moustache caked with mortar, met Jamie's eyes with a bleak gaze.

'They cannot free the woman,' he murmured. 'She has half the roof on top of her.' He looked angrily at the sky as a fresh roar of explosions erupted in continuous tumult, no more than two miles away but sounding frighteningly close. 'God curse the devils!' he shouted, as the heavy drone of aircraft engines filled the sky in succession to the hollow thunder of bursting bombs.

Jamie told the man that he feared his uncle, Milan Alexandrovic, might have been in the church when it was hit – did he know him? The man shook his head but pointed to a bearded giant directing the rescuers from the top of the rubble.

'Perhaps the priest will know,' he said. 'You'd better ask him.'

Jamie clambered up the rubble mountain to where the priest was bellowing instructions to three men who were trying unsuccessfully to move a huge slab of concrete. Somewhere below, the woman called Sofije was still begging for help. The priest glared wild-eyed at Jamie, seeming not to hear his question about his uncle. Then, without answering, he turned and plunged down amongst the debris of the church's interior. Shouldering aside one of the men who was trying to move the massive slab, he began to heave at the obstruction with the fury of a man possessed. Exhorting the others to lend their strength, he strained with his great shoulders and arms until it seemed his eyes would pop from his head with effort. But the object was immovable.

Jamie had moved down to lend his own weight, but there was insufficient room for a fifth body to be brought to bear. He stood back as the fierce-eyed priest finally gave up and subsided with a groan of despair on a fallen beam, head in hands. He looked as if he had been hauled through an ash-heap, headfirst. His hair was awry and greyed like his cassock with dust. He turned an anguished face to heaven and cried out:

'O, God, why didst Thou take so many of my flock and spare me?'

The miracle of the priest's survival was not apparent to Jamie, although evidence of its nature was there to be seen. The altar area, although strewn with ikons and some debris, was remarkably undamaged amid the collapsed masonry and fallen roof beams all around. From this island, the priest had stepped, unharmed but for a scratch or two, when the rest of the church of St Podgorica had disintegrated all around him. But the giant clergyman derived no comfort from his miraculous deliverance. He was drawing in great gasping breaths – a sign of how drained his labours had left him – when he

221

became aware of Jamie's anxious scrutiny. He displayed his large blackened hands, as if they offended him.

'Strong hands are not enough,' he said. 'We need tools . . . lifting equipment. Do you know where we can get them?' The fierce eyes burned at Jamie.

'I'm sorry, I don't know.'

The priest suddenly got to his feet.

'Then we must try again with our hands – the tools God gave us.' He turned his attention again to the slab, sliding torn fingers below its projecting end and embracing it with his arms and body. He tried again to move the obstruction sideways. Another of the rescuers moved to help him, but hesitated, his head cocked to one side.

'She has gone quiet,' he said. Even the priest stood back as all of the little group froze, listening. The cries from below had stopped. There was nothing to be heard. One of the men crossed himself.

'She has gone,' he said. 'I heard the rattle. It was the last sound she made.'

'How can you be sure?' the priest demanded angrily.

The man looked at him reproachfully.

'I have heard it many times, Father. I know the sound too well.' In a gentle voice, he added, 'There is no more we can do here. We should see to the living.' He turned and began to climb out of the rubble but stopped when the priest asked where he was going.

'To see if my family are still alive. I was only passing when. . . .' He shrugged and left the rest unsaid. Without another word, he climbed over the top of the rubble slide and disappeared from view. The other men followed him silently, leaving only Jamie and the priest.

'Why do you stay?' the priest asked Jamie glumly.

'My uncle . . . Milan Alexandrovic. Do you know if he . . . ?' The priest let him get no further.

'Milan is dead,' he said flatly. He turned his eyes towards the mountain of debris that was heaped towards the door of the church. 'He was in his usual place, by the pillar. We heard the aeroplanes. He caught my eye – perhaps he wanted me to stop the Mass. I didn't stop, only paused, and then . . . then it all happened so quickly.' He lowered his head and Jamie saw the great shoulders heave. He realised that the priest was silently weeping.

Jamie left him there, alone and weeping in the ruins of his church amid the buried dead of his flock, who had come early on an April morning to celebrate the joy of the Resurrection.

By mid-morning, the bombing had stopped. Jamie and Mannion walked, picking their way through the crowds of people fleeing from the city, towards the centre of the devastated Jugoslav capital. It was like exploring a planet that existed only in nightmares. Palls of smoke drifted up from countless fires that blazed unchecked, and everywhere the eye looked the scene was one of destruction and ruin.

On every one of the ten days since their encounter with Luk, Jamie – with Mannion trailing companionably at his heels – had searched the city for a trace of Mara. But, it seemed, she had vanished from the face of the earth.

She had not been near her apartment in weeks, and none of her friends and acquaintances were able to provide a clue to what might have happened to her. Jamie had even made a long-distance telephone call to the Richtman home in Karlovac in an effort to solve the mystery – only to be told by an operator that the line had been disconnected.

Jamie became more and more concerned for Mara's safety as each day passed and it became plainer – although he was reluctant to admit it – that she had never returned to Belgrade. His unease had taken the joy out of his new freedom. The sole compensations were the warmth with which Milan had welcomed both himself and Mannion to his home and relief at discovering that his mother's incapacity, while demanding several weeks of hospital care, was not unduly serious. He was able to visit her every day in hospital. The visits had become a part of his daily pilgrimages to the city in search of Mara.

But this Sunday morning was different. The object was to make sure that his mother was all right and to bear the unhappy news of her brother's death, which made a grim journey even grimmer.

In King Milan Street, soldiers were trying to clear the carriageway of a tram that had been blown off its rails and lay on its side. The wrecked vehicle was obstructing the flow of cars, handcarts and horse-drawn wagons, loaded high with furniture and other possessions, which were seeking a southbound exit from the city. Heavy smoke drifting up from the Royal Palace indicated that it had not escaped from the hour-long bombing by the Luftwaffe. Nor had the Queen Maria Hospital.

The area in the immediate vicinity of the hospital had suffered so badly that Jamie knew, when he and Mannion were still some distance away, that he need not nurse expectations of finding it intact. The nearer they got to it, the faster his hopes of finding his mother alive vanished. The two-storey building, at the head of a cul-de-sac formed by neat terraced houses, was hard to identify from memory of its location,. Little remained of the twin terraces of houses: only a gable here and a wall there, with gaps where the windows had been.

The hospital itself had no frontage. Gone was the arched tunnel to the interior courtyard, and gone was the entire two-storey block through which the tunnel had run. Only a mountain of rubble remained. It had spilled across the interior court and, revealed beyond was the shell of the rear part of the hospital, previously invisible from the front. The approach was almost unrecognisable as a roadway, having been rendered impassible by deep six metre-wide craters. A small knot of people had gathered at the entry to the cul-de-sac, where a fire engine was parked. Its crew were engaged in the task of moving the people away.

'Gas,' said Mannion, sniffing the air, which was heavy with the pungent odour. It was escaping from a fractured main.

'Keep back,' a fireman warned Jamie testily. 'The area must be cleared.'

'My mother was in the hospital,' Jamie said, advancing until the man barred his way. 'A patient . . . first-floor front – the gynaecology ward. I must get through.'

'Nobody gets through,' the fireman said. 'There's gas. I'm sorry about your mother, but there's nothing you can do now. There's nobody alive in there. We got three girls out – nurses – but they were in a bad way. I don't think they'll last. For the rest, at least it was quick – all over in seconds.'

Even as he spoke, a siren began its caterwauling somewhere in the city. Through its eerie sound came the deep heavy-throated throb of aircraft engines. It had just turned noon and the first waves of Luftwaffe bombers were returning to resume their barbarity of the morning. They were to keep returning, morning and noon, for three days – by which time the rape of Belgrade was considered complete. On the third night, less than thirty thousand peoople remained in the city – a tenth of its population. Nearly forty thousand were dead or grievously wounded. The rest had fled.

3

No Way Back

Not a waking hour passed without Mara thinking of Jamie, wondering if he was safe, wondering where he was, wondering if he was enduring the same agony of mind that tormented her. She consoled herself with memory of his farewell words to her in Zagreb: his promise to go on loving her until the day he died and his plea to remember that, even if things went wrong.

Well, things had started going wrong with a vengeance. She doubted if she would ever be able to forgive her father for the way he had virtually abducted her to Vienna. It was not as if he had acted out of concern for her. His only concern was that her activities would prove an unwanted embarrassment to him in his new eminence as some kind of diplomatic fixer.

Mara had shown a passivity to her father's wishes that she did not feel. She had allowed herself to be whisked north across the Austrian border because, at the time, no prudent alternative was open to her. She had been acutely aware that any rash act on her part might endanger Jamie. It had been a shock to discover that the police were on to her so quickly, and she was far from confident that she would be able to withstand intensive interrogation. She was under no illusion about the methods used by the police to make people talk. Under the circumstances, Vienna was as good a place as any to be until the hue and cry for the escaped prisoners had died down. She could return to Belgrade at a time of her own choosing – and without prior consultation with her father. In the meantime, she would allay his suspicions by acting the part of contrite and obedient daughter.

The manner of her parents' living in Vienna came as a surprise to Mara. Her father conducted his affairs from a huge house in a leafy, almost rural part of Hütteldorf – although what his precise function was and for whom he worked was not clear to Mara. Officially, he was a representative of the Belgrade Government, but he seemed to function quite independently of the Jugoslav Embassy and accredited diplomatic staff. He frequently entertained luminaries of the German and Austrian foreign service and, from the deference he accorded these gentlemen and his anxiety to please them, it might have been concluded that it was their interests he served more faithfully than Jugoslavia's.

Richtman certainly entertained lavishly and often, and expense never seemed to be an impediment. The big house in Hütteldorf was staffed by an impressive array of servants and the household functioned with a *fin-de-siècle* style that recalled the days of Habsburg opulence. In Mara's eyes, it was all rather passé and decadent – although it was totally in keeping with the yearning her parents had always shown for the former days of Empire and its departed glories.

Having espoused the role of dutiful daughter as a means to an end, Mara found herself shopping for an evening gown on her very first day in Vienna. Her father was giving a special dinner party that evening and he had made it very clear to her that her attendance and good behaviour were obligatory. In spite of all his misgivings about her, he wanted to show her off. Mara acquiesced, therefore, when her mother insisted on taking her to a couturier to be suitably robed. The dressmaker had modest mews premises off Hütteldorfer Strasse and could be relied on to fit Mara into one of her creations on the spot.

Her mother was much more excited about the expedition than Mara, happily believing that the new dress –

which was to be a parental gift – would be the final healing of the breach between father and daughter. With her mother's encouragement, Mara opted for a virginal white sheath which seemed to have been moulded to the contours of her firm young body.

Later – with her hair swept up and with a black choker adorning her elegant neck she knew that she had never looked better. But she derived no pleasure from the knowledge, dreading the prospect of making polite talk to her father's guests while her heart was elsewhere. There was only one person in whose sight she wanted to be pleasing – and he was far away. Regret gave a sad-eyed regality and a haunting wistfulness to her beauty.

It was by accident rather than design that her appearance among the assembled dinner guests constituted a minor sensation, stopping conversations dead in mid-sentence and attracting every eye. Reluctance to face a full room of strangers – rather than desire to draw attention to herself – was the reason why Mara delayed until the last minute before making her entry. The drama of that entry was heightened by having to descend the broad staircase that opened into the rather baroque grandeur of the galleried hall, where drinks were being dispensed.

Suddenly the object of every eye as she stood on the staircase, Mara was tempted to turn and run. The admiring silence prevailed until she reached the bottom of the stairs. There she was the centre of attraction. Everyone wanted to know who she was. The revelation that she was the host's daughter caused almost as much sensation as her entry. Her father was good-naturedly chided by all and sundry for having concealed, until that moment, the existence of a beautiful daughter. Everyone wanted to know where she had been kept hidden.

Both father and daughter were mercifully saved the need of too much explanation by a servant's timely announcement that dinner was about to be served. Mara found herself being escorted towards the dining room by a middle-aged overweight stranger who introduced himself simply as Hans, from Bavaria. He was talkative and had the disconcerting habit of licking his thick sensual lips whenever he was about to speak. He reminded Mara of a Doberman her father had when she was a little girl: a dog of voracious appetite and unpleasant temperament. It had licked its chops with the same salivating relish as her dinner companion.

From the moment she sat down at table, Mara became aware that the dinner had some celebratory significance of which she alone seemed to be in ignorance. The meal was well under way before she plucked up the courage to ask her lip-licking neighbour to enlighten her.

'You mean you have no idea what took place in Vienna today?' The plump Bavarian's eyes were round with astonishment.

Mara confessed that she had no idea. She and her mother had gone shopping but they had neither seen nor heard anything out of the ordinary. The Bavarian seemed to find her innocent confession highly amusing. He chortled with glee.

'Isn't that so like a woman!' he exclaimed happily. 'She is so preoccupied in shopping for falderals that history can be made without her ever being aware of it! Did you not know that the Fuehrer was in Vienna today? He came here specially to meet your Jugoslavian Prime Minister.'

'Did he?' Mara said, trying hard not to show that she was less than thrilled. As far as she was concerned, Adolf Hitler was a power-crazy gangster who ought to have been drowned at birth and Dragisa Cvetkovic was a weak-kneed traitor. They were welcome to each other.

She listened with chill gripping her heart, however, as the Bavarian regaled her with the news that, at a special ceremony, Hitler and Cvetkovic had signed a treaty which made Jugoslavia the ally of Germany and Italy.

'This is a proud day for your father,' the Bavarian prattled on, oblivious of the effect of his words. 'A day he has worked for, as we have all done behind the scenes. . . . A day when all Croatia can rejoice, for it is only a matter of time now before the new order is established.' He laughed. 'Although your father might put it differently – the old order restored.'

Mara thought she was going to be sick. Her gorge rose and she gagged on the morsel of pork that she had just forked into her mouth. She forced it down unchewed. Heat flooded her face and, with it, a rising nausea.

She rose hurriedly from the table, napkin raised to her mouth.

'Excuse me, please.' She glanced anxiously up the table. 'All of you . . . Papa.'

She turned and fled, causing the company to suspend eating and conversation. Every eye followed her hurried progress from the table to the door.

'What is the matter with her?' someone asked.

'One minute, she was all right. The next, she was unwell.' It was the Bavarian who spoke. He seemed aggrieved to have lost his audience.

'Perhaps I should go to her,' Mara's mother suggested, half rising.

'No,' Richtman commanded from the top of the table. 'The servants will see to her. Let her be. She will come back if she feels up to it.'

He was secretly relieved that Mara had left the table. He had been sweating blood ever since he saw Hans Lohr grab her as a dinner partner, fearing that Mara might, in conversation, come out with some of the political claptrap sentiments that would have gone down well with her Bohemian friends at Belgrade University but were likely to give Lohr a seizure. Lohr was a high functionary in the Nazi Party and reputed to enjoy Hitler's confidence. He was also a vindictive man. He was not likely to be in the least amused if his host's daughter started spouting cliché-ridden Marxist jargon at him or airing her half-baked views on democracy and a free society.

So relief filled Richtman at his daughter's sudden departure from the table. With hindsight, he realised that it had been a mistake to compel her to attend. She had certainly adorned the small gathering, and the tributes he had been paid for siring such a beauty pleased him mightily – but his pleasure was tempered by the private knowledge that he did not altogether trust this lovely daughter of his. She had been docile enough since, in his anger, he slapped her in an effort to make her come to her senses – which was encouraging. It re-inforced the belief that he should have taken a hard line with her long ago. At the same time, that very docility was disturbing. She had always been a rebellious child, and docility did not sit naturally on her. It was hard to tell if the fire had been quenched or if it still flickered quietly on a low flame. The fact remained that Mara would have to become reconciled to being part of the family again. She would have to realise that her wild Bohemian days were over and the knot that tied her to her Belgrade friends had been severed forever. Just as surely as Mara's ties with Belgrade had been cut, so, too, would Croatia's ties with Serbia soon be cut. Then the Richtmans would come into their own.

Mara's despair at the knowledge that her father and his friends had been actively engaged in allying Jugoslavia to Nazi Germany reached its nadir on the day after the dinner party. That Jugoslavia should have signed a treaty was bad enough; what disgusted Mara more than anything was the realisation that her father and his clique did not view the treaty as their final goal, but as a mere stepping stone to an unspecified objective. It was not clear to Mara what this objective was, but the fact that it had Nazi backing was enough to fill her with dread.

As quickly as Mara's spirits had sunk, so they rose again within forty-eight hours – when the Austrian capital was given the news of the Jugoslav *coup d'état* which toppled the Regency Government. No matter that the Viennese press and radio reported the event with a Nazi slant, condemning the rebels as Anglophile gangsters and screaming of treachery, Mara glowed with inner pride over what had happened in Belgrade. It gave her quiet satisfaction, too, to witness the chagrin of her father and his Nazi friends, who met in endless crisis meetings at the big house in Hütteldorf. Her father's parties and entertaining continued, but they did not conceal the panic and acrimony in the air. There was much shouting and argument behind locked doors.

Mara made no display of the new optimism that filled her. She maintained the pretence of docility, while privately laying the plans to escape from the house in Hütteldorf and make her way back to Belgrade. Train services between the capitals had not been interrupted because of the *coup d'état*, so she resolved to make her escape by train. First, however, she had to lull her parents into a false sense of security. Especially her mother, who seemed reluctant to let her out of her sight. Mara guessed that her father was behind this vigilance.

If Mara wanted to go into the city, her mother always insisted on accompanying her. So Mara instigated a way to be free of her mother's company for part of these visits. She would go the the cinema while her mother went shopping or to the hairdresser's, and they would meet up again in time to return to Hütteldorf in late afternoon. It was Mara's intention, on a chosen day, to linger only minutes in the cinema and, by the time that the film was over, to be well on the way to Belgrade.

On the fourth day of April, Mara executed a dummy run: going into the city with her mother, leaving her at the cinema door and taking a seat inside, then leaving almost immediately to time the short journey to the railway station. She found that she could catch the three p.m. express for Belgrade with a comfortable leeway of fifteen minutes. She became consumed with the need to put her escape plan into operation at the earliest opportunity. That presented itself on the first day that the chosen cinema changed its programme – the following Monday, 7 April. She decided that that would be the day.

A fever of excitement gripped her throughout the weekend. It lasted until just after midday on Sunday, when she returned from church with her parents. Her father switched on the radio, to listen to the world news while they ate lunch. At first, the newsreader's words made no sense to her. She was only half-listening, being preoccupied with her private plans and the need to put in twenty-four more hours without arousing suspicion. Then she heard the word 'Belgrade', and she listened with mounting horror to the voice on the radio.

. . . the city lay in flames after wave upon wave of Luftwaffe bombers pressed home their attack with determination and precision. As part of *Bestrafung*, the Fuehrer had ordered Operation *Strafgericht* to be carried out ruthlessly as an open expression of international affront at the treachery and duplicity demonstrated by the rebel Jugoslav regime in its rejection of friendship and peace with its Tripartite Treaty neighbours. Now, the so-called Jugoslav nation will be made to pay the price of meeting neighbourly goodwill with odious betrayal. At dawn today, the armies of Germany and her faithful allies began crossing the borders of Jugoslavia and will crush all opposition in their path. The Hungarian Third Army is thrusting south in the vicinity of the Rivers Danube and Tisa, while further west, German Panzers have crossed the Drava into Croatia in a two-pronged attack. Second Army units under General Weichs are driving south from Austria into Slovenia and Croatia while, on the Adriatic coast, the Second Italian Army, under General Ambrosio, is striking south from Fiume and east towards Ljubljana. In the south, Italian divisions have entered Montenegro from Albania and are driving on Dubrovnik. In Macedonia, German Panzers and elements of the Bulgarian Army have struck westward in three separate thrusts. At two other points, General Kleist's First Panzer Group have crossed into Serbia and should soon be occupying the town of Nis and other strategic points in the Morava valley. Further north, two columns of motorised Wehrmacht troops have made a lightning attack towards Belgrade from Romania and are within ninety kilometres of the city. First reports indicate that total surprise was achieved and advances are proceeding according to plan. . . .

Mara listened to the chronicle of infamy, numbed by what she was hearing. There would be no trains running from Vienna to Belgrade tomorrow: that was a certainty. There would be no way back to Belgrade for a long, long time. But that setback to her plans paled to insignificance in the shadow of the crime that was being committed against Jugoslavia and its people.

With shock, Mara stared along the table at her father, and revulsion filled her at the realisation that he was happy and excited by the news. He was still listening intently to every word from the radio but he could scarcely contain himself, and his eyes were bright with rapture, as if he were listening to a symphony of sublime emotional appeal.

'It is wonderful!' he cried as the news bulletin ended and stirring martial music blared from the set. 'This will teach these dogs in Belgrade a lesson. A quick German victory will be our victory.'

'You disgust me!' Mara hurled at him from the far end of the table. She stood up, her lovely face white with anger, her whole body trembling. 'It is *your* country that is being bombed . . . *your* people who are being killed and maimed by these butchering Nazis! And you sit there and applaud!'

Richtman's delight faded and he stared at Mara, fury mounting.

'Don't you dare speak to me like that! You don't know what you're talking about. *My people! My country*! What do I have in common with those arrogant Serbs who have sat in Belgrade and taxed us out of existence? Or with half-savage Montenegrins who are still living in the Middle Ages? Or illiterate Macedonians? I am a Croat. *We* are Croats.'

'I am a Jugoslav!' Mara cried. 'We are Jugoslavs!'

'*You* are a child. And a particularly stupid child at that!' Her father rose to his full height and glowered at her with anger-filled eyes. 'Weren't you listening to the radio? Didn't you hear what was said about Croatia? How the German soldiers are being greeted by the people with open arms?'

Mara had not heard that, but she did not dispute it. Propaganda, probably. There had been no shortage of that mixed in with official communiqués.

'I heard that Belgrade was in flames,' she stormed. 'I suppose the Germans are bombing it out of kindness!'

'Belgrade is a cesspool!' her father retorted angrily. 'If it is wiped off the map, it is all it deserves!'

'*Ja, mein Fuehrer*! Of course, *mein Fuehrer*! Forgive me if I forgot for a moment how fond you were of mass murder.' Mara was shaking with anger, her voice shrill.

'Go to your room!' Richtman ordered. 'And stay there!'

Mara glared at him defiantly, hating him. She realised that argument was futile. Nor was there going to be any support from her mother, who had not opened her mouth but sat there, throwing her reproachful little looks. Mara summoned a measure of calmness.

'As you wish,' she said. She walked towards the door. There she paused and turned to face her father. She raised her arm in the Nazi salute.

'*Heil Hitler*!' she sang out, her face impassive. Then she turned and left.

She was lying fully clothed on her bed, ten minutes

later, when her father came to her room. He wore a look of suppressed fury and in his hands he held his riding crop.

'I am going to teach you a lesson you'll never forget,' he announced, and seized her by the hair. With a twist of his wrist, he turned her over so that she lay on her stomach, her face muffled into the pillow. Her disbelief was total. She was a woman of twenty-four years, and her father was intending to beat her.

Humiliation filled her as she felt her light cotton frock flicked from her thighs by the handle of the crop. Then a hand inserted itself at the waistband of her panties. There was a tug and the flimsy garment ripped as it was torn off, exposing her buttocks and stockingless legs. The grip on her hair was excruciating. She closed her eyes, tears burning at the corners as she tried to shut out the horror of what was happening.

She felt her father brace himself as he raised the crop high above his head. Then there was his grunt as he brought it flashing down across her bared backside. Pain, like a line of fire, shocked to her brain as the thin corded whip bit into her flesh with a sharp swish of sound. She cried out, a choked gasp of shock at the violation as much as a cry of pain. She bit with her teeth into the softness of the pillow, effectively gagging herself, determined to betray neither her terror nor pain.

Richtman brought the crop down again and again. Mara lay limp in his grip, making no struggle and uttering no sound. A spontaneous shudder of her body was her only reaction to each successive blow. The beating slowed and finally stopped, as if its perpetrator, getting no squeals and cries for mercy, lost resolution for the task.

Richtman let go of her hair and stood back from the bed, breathing heavily.

'Now you know what to expect,' he mumbled at her. 'You will show a respectful tongue or you will get the same again. And you will stay in this room until I give you permission to leave it. Am I understood?'

She made no reply; she lay with her face buried in the pillow, unmoving. Moments later, she heard him go out and slam the door. Only then did she give way to the pain and humiliation, weeping softly into the pillow. She wished she were dead.

For days, Mara stayed in her room, vowing to herself that she would die there rather than ask her father's permission to leave it. Her mother came to her several times and begged her to ask her father's forgiveness, so that some kind of normality could be restored. Mara was contemptuous of her mother for believing that it was she who should seek forgiveness and not her father – and she steadfastly refused.

Then, on two occasions, Richtman himself came to the room, carrying the crop with which he had beaten her. But he did not use it a second time. He lectured her on her obstinacy and tried to tell her that he had disciplined her severely for her own good. On the second visit, he announced that she need no longer consider herself restricted to her room, but she was not allowed to leave the house and gardens without permission. He let her know that it was silly to sulk in her room when the weather was so fine. She should be enjoying the spring sunshine.

Mara simply stared at him, dumbly impassive. She did not offer a word in reply.

Her self-imposed isolation had gone on for more than three weeks when she had a surprise visitor. She had taken to writing verse – of rather introverted and gloomy character – and was busy at it when she looked up to see Petar standing there. He had knocked softly and entered and, now, he stared at her, the blue eyes beneath his wavy blond hair soft with concern.

'What's this I've been hearing about my little sister?'

he asked, with an attempt at cheerful impishness. He
held out his arms and, with a little cry, she ran to them.
He held her, patting her shoulder comfortingly as she
sobbed against his chest. Then he gently forced her face
away from his body and dabbed the tears from her
cheeks with a handkerchief.

'You'll have my new uniform all stained,' he complained teasingly. 'Now, tell me what this is all about.
Mama says you've been mumping in your room for
days.'

Mara blinked a tear away.

'Did she tell you why?'

'She said you had a row with Father.'

'He thrashed me . . . with a riding whip.'

'You – You're joking?'

Mara pulled up the back of her dress to show her
thighs.

'Does that look like a joke?'

Petar stared at the livid weals that disappeared below
the white of her panties. His expression was thunderous.
He stretched out a tentative hand to touch the bruised
flesh and darted a look at her.

'May I look?' he asked.

'If you want to. I'll pull off my pants. You've seen my
bare bottom often enough.'

'No.' He stopped her. 'There's no need for that.' He
moved the hem of the panty-leg upwards, exposing the
heavier density of criss-cross weals on her buttocks. He
dropped the garment quickly again and made her cover
it with her frock. His blue eyes were ablaze with anger.

'I'm going to murder him for this!' he growled through
gritted teeth. 'I'm going to damned well murder him!'

'No,' Mara said. 'You'll do nothing.'

'I'm not going to let him get away with this. Dammit,
Mara, you're an adult woman – not one of his rogue
hunting whelps that he can take a whip to ! My God, it's
sickening!'

'You'll do nothing, Petar,' Mara said firmly. 'What happened is on his conscience now, and he knows it. Let him suffer.'

'He has no conscience,' Petar snorted. 'He needs a taste of his own medicine.'

'Please do nothing,' Mara pleaded.

'We'll see,' Petar said. 'I'm making no promises. What brought it on?'

'I called him "*mein Fuehrer*" and shouted "*Heil Hitler*" at him.' She began to tell him about the incident, but broke off and stared at him.

'That uniform you're wearing, Petar. . ?'

He straightened his shoulders and thrust out his chest.

'It's smart, isn't it?' he said brightly. 'It's the new field style, straight from the factory. Do you like it?'

'Isn't it German?'

He snapped her a salute.

'Of course. And didn't you notice?' He touched his lapel. 'It's *Oberleutnant* now. I've been promoted.' His smile faded as he saw her expression. 'What's wrong, Mara. Why are you staring at me like that?'

'You are a Jugoslav officer, Petar. You're wearing a German uniform and *you are asking me what's wrong*?'

Her accusing eyes perplexed him.

'Mara, I've been attached to the German Army for months. I know it was temporary attachment at first, but the Divisional Training Commander at Wehrkreis Eighteen wangled my release from Belgrade. It was the only way I could stay on. If I'd gone back, I would have been posted to some godforsaken barracks in the wilds of Macedonia where nothing ever happens. I wanted to do some real soldiering, to see some action . . . and the officers I was with were a great bunch of fellows. I wanted to stay with them – I didn't want to be left behind when they went off to fight.'

'Petar, they've been fighting Jugoslavs! *Our people*!'

Petar shrugged sheepishly.

239

'I had qualms about that – when I heard about the *putsch*. The last thing I wanted was to be fighting old friends from the academy in Belgrade, but Simovic must have been crazy to stage a rebellion when he did. Tearing up the treaty with Germany was an act of madness. You can't spit in the face of the greatest military power in the world and expect them to shrug it off. It was asking for trouble. And what has it achieved? Absolutely nothing! Simovic and his Serbian hot-heads caved in like the windbags they are.'

'What do you mean, Petar? Caved in?'

'Don't you read the newspapers, Mara? Don't you know what's been happening while you've been hiding in your room? Our people – as you call them, Mara – didn't want to fight the Germans. The Army threw in the towel without a fight. Jugoslavia doesn't exist any more. It has been cut up into little pieces and the vultures we had for neighbours are all getting a piece of the pie.'

Mara found it hard to digest what Petar was telling her.

'You mean that the fighting has stopped?'

'It never really got started, thank God. The young King got out while the going was good. So did most of his ministers. The blitz on Belgrade was enough to start the rot. It was a pity about poor old Belgrade getting the worst of it – but at least it made things mercifully quick. Better than a long-drawn-out meaningless war with the same result in the end.'

'How can you be so calm and unfeeling about it, Petar?'

'I'm a realist, Mara. I have feelings like everyone else, but I don't allow them to blind me to realities. I'm a soldier, and soldiering is the only thing that really interests me. A soldier doesn't question where he has to go or what he has to do. He just does what he's told as honourably as he can and he asks no more than to be

240

judged on his conduct as a soldier. Moral and political judgements are the province of others . . . I want no part of them.'

'But you have to make moral and political judgements, Petar,' Mara protested. 'You can't separate yourself from the rest of mankind just because you wear a uniform. You took an oath to serve Jugoslavia.'

'But I was released from it. If I hadn't been, I wouldn't have taken the Wehrmacht oath to serve Germany and the Fuehrer. That doesn't make me a Nazi or a member of the Nazi Party. The Army isn't political —'

'It makes you do the next best thing,' Mara interrupted. 'The Army does what Hitler orders it to do.'

'Perhaps,' conceded Petar, 'but it keeps him in check, too. I know. The men that I've lived with and worked with are good men and honourable men, with a code of behaviour that makes it a privilege to serve with them, and belong. They're not the bullies and thugs that British propaganda makes them out to be.'

Tears glistened in Mara's eyes.

'Oh, Petar, what is going to become of us? We see things so differently. . . . I don't think I could bear it if I were to lose you the way I seem to have lost everything else. I've got nothing to hang on to any more. I feel utterly lost.'

He put an arm round her shoulder.

'Come on, Mara. Cheer up. You'll always have me. Nothing's ever going to come between us. I'm still your big brother under this uniform that you don't like. I love you the same as I always did and I always will.'

She clung to him, confused and unhappy but comforted. Next to Jamie, she loved Petar more than anyone in the world, and never had she needed him more.

'Save me, Petar,' she appealed to her brother tearfully. 'Help to get me away from this place.'

'I'll do what I can,' he promised. 'We'll talk about it

241

later. I thought that, this afternoon, we might take a walk down by the Schönbrunner Schloss. They say that the Tiroler Gardens look a treat at this time of year.'

'What about Papa?' she asked fearfully.

'I'll take care of Papa,' Petar promised.

And he did. Mara did not witness the confrontation that took place between Petar and his father, but it was the talk of the servants' quarters for weeks to come. Raised voices coming from Richtman's study had been heard by a housemaid working in an adjacent room, and she had listened, agog.

She had heard Petar threaten to strangle his father with his own hands if, ever again, he dared to lift a finger against Mara. There was more, much more, but the culmination had been the pitiful sound of the master pleading with his son not to turn against him and promising him the earth in return for forgiveness and a second chance.

The outcome was that a distraught Richtman had gone to Mara and apologised to her for his treatment of her. He had presented himself to her with the woebegone air of a player overacting the part of a penitent sinner in an undistinguished tragedy. She had received the performance with wordless contempt, making no comment even when he indicated that he would place no further restriction on her movements – she was free to come and go as she pleased.

Petar had a week's leave, and much of it was spent with Mara in search of a solution to the problems which beset her. A return to devastated Belgrade – now under German military control – was out of the question. Even more unthinkable to her was the prospect of continuing to live with her parents. The solution, arrived at with Petar's help, was not the ideal one as far as Mara was concerned but an acceptable stopgap. She found a surprisingly well-paid job as a translator with a publisher, who had offices on the far side of the Danube in Florisdorf, and also a place to stay. A girl friend of Petar's was vacating her tiny furnished apartment in Kaisermuhlen and Mara was able to get in first, ahead of the competition, and secure the tenancy.

She moved to Kaisermuhlen on the same day that Petar rejoined his regiment. Mara wept when she kissed her brother goodbye, not wholly reconciled to the fact that he had chosen to serve in Hitler's legions, but comforted to some degree by the knowledge that the bond of love that had tied them from childhood was deeper and stronger than ever. It transcended all differences and doubts.

Other soldiers boarding the same train were bidding farewell to their sweethearts as Mara lingered with Petar. The scene stirred a mixture of emotions in Mara, bringing home to her that her brother's profession was war and that it could claim his life. He had told her that his unit had been ordered to Romania 'for manoeuvres' – but the gleam in his eye had suggested that something much bigger than playing at war was afoot. There, on the railway station, she had a sudden insight into the truth. Russia! Was that sleeping giant the next in line for conquest by the madman in Berlin? The thought terrified her – not for the wider implications but because she might never see her beloved brother again.

She watched his train pull out of the station, with tears of anguish rolling down her cheeks. That night, alone in her tiny apartment, she wept some more for Petar and cursed her loneliness and her impotence to control events. She prayed to God to protect Jamie. Could she not be given a sign that Jamie was still alive and somehow reaching out in thought to her? Where was he? Was he already dead, swept away by the Panzers that had vanquished Jugoslavia in a week?

4

Black Mountain

Jamie lay on his back, looking up at the night sky. The concave of the heavens was a sea of deepest purple in which the stars swam like glittering diamonds. Here in the mountains, the stars seemed to dip lower to the earth and the very air had a sweeter, sharper quality.

It was another world, up here in the Crnagora: the starkly beautiful world of black moutain, from which the land derived its Italianate appellation of Montenegro. To Jamie, it was almost like another planet: a land of barren moonscape solitude and pathless heights, furrowed here and there by wooded valleys and precious life-giving streams. Its scattered villages were peopled by a hardy breed that reminded Jamie of the proudly independent inhabitants of Scotland's remote glens – those who had not been driven to more benign meadows by the harsh inhospitable uplands of their birth. Here, too, the clan system prevailed – as it had flourished in Scotland before the Jacobean upheavals – and, with it, the traditions of a fierce warrior race and the atavistic mores of tribal society.

It had been some deep atavistic stirring within Jamie that had brought him to Montenegro. Something in the ancestral blood, a savage instinct that only violence could expiate, had wakened in him – triggered by the still vivid horror of Belgrade's destruction and the shock of losing his mother and his Uncle Milan in a single morning. Adding to his frenzy was the bitterness that was the legacy of six wasted years in prison and the cancerlike frustration of separation from Mara, with its black despair of not knowing where she was or what had happened to her.

Stefan – stretched out on the ground, not far from Jamie – grunted in his sleep, momentarily distracting Jamie from his contemplation of the stars. Jamie smiled to himself, recollecting that his sleeping friend was the moving force behind the Montenegrin adventure. There are guns in Montenegro, Stefan had declared on that day in Belgrade when he had come back into Jamie's life. Lots of guns! If you want a gun and you want to fight, Montenegro is the place to be!

Jamie had wanted to fight. More than anything, Jamie had wanted to fight. His whole being had cried out for action – any kind that would appease the blackness of mind that so unsettled him. In Belgrade, he had felt like a snared animal, trapped and powerless in a forest that was ablaze, with nothing to do but wait until the flames engulfed him. Belgrade! Eons seemed to have passed since Belgrade – but it was only weeks. What a journey it had been! And so much had happened along the way!

Jamie's thoughts returned to Mara, and the day when he had thought she was dead. That was in Sarajevo, during the short stopover on the two-legged train journey from Cacak, in Serbia – where they had boarded the train – to Mostar, in Hercegovina. In Sarajevo, they had to change stations as well as trains – the mountain line into Sarajevo was narrow-gauge – and this meant a delay of some hours in the city. Those were anxious, nerve-racking hours for Jamie and Stefan. They were uncertain how their forged identity papers would withstand the scrutiny of the Croatian militiamen who were keeping a watchful eye on arriving and departing rail travellers. These militiamen – members of the Ustashi, as Pavelic's Fascist paramilitaries were called – were not conducting identity checks, however, and Jamie and Stefan strolled past them with a nonchalance that belied the racing of their hearts.

With other passers-by, the two men stopped to read a large public notice displayed on a board. The poster announced the execution in Zagreb of a dozen unfortunates, who had been put to death in retaliation for the murder of a police agent. The third name on the list of hostages registered with Jamie like a blow between the eyes. It was *Richtman*. Mara's surname! His immediate shocked reaction was to conclude Mara must have been arrested in Zagreb or Karlovac as a result of the prison break, and that she must have been in police custody while he was safe in Belgrade. In his haste to believe the worst, Jamie discounted the fact that the Richtman named on the list was not preceded by the initial 'M', for Mara. The name Richtman was rare enough in Jugoslavia to preclude the hope that it was not Mara who had been executed. They had simply got the initial wrong.

It was Stefan who pulled Jamie away from the poster and convinced him, eventually, that the Richtman who had died had not been Mara, but a man whom he knew personally – a leading member of the Communist Party. All the names on the list were of prominent Communists. Didn't Jamie remember any of them? He ought to have done, because nearly all of them had been fellow prisoners of Jamie's in the prison at Lepoglava.

Jamie apologised for becoming so agitated, aware that his reaction to the poster announcement had not gone unnoticed – and the last thing that he wanted to do was draw attention to himself and Stefan. He felt ashamed of having so hastily jumped to conclusions. It was symptomatic, however, of the fever of anxieties that gripped him whenever he thought of Mara – which was a hundred times a day. Not knowing where she was or if she was safe was an agony.

The poster in Sarajevo was the first indication Jamie and Stefan had been given that, unlike the political prisoners in Belgrade, the inmates of the Lepoglava prison had not been freed at the fall of the Regency

Government. The failure of the prison authorities at Lepoglava to implement the new regime's amnesty and release political detainees was, indeed, to have fatal consequences for most of the prisoners with whom Jamie and Stefan had served time. Nearly all were to fall victim to Pavelic's death squads, who began a reign of terror in the wake of the German invasion of Jugoslavia.

The city of Zagreb had fallen to the Germans without a fight, within four days of the invasion, and the Croatian Fascist Ante Pavelic had wasted no time in capitalising on the arrival of his Nazi allies. With Hitler's blessing, he had, that same day, declared Croatia an autonomous state, independent of the Kingdom of Jugoslavia – and he had appointed himself Head of State, with dictatorial powers. Then he had released his indisciplined Ustashi on the countryside to assert his authority and free the Germans of the burden of policing their conquered territory.

The knowledge that Pavelic ruled in Croatia accented the hazards which Jamie and Stefan knew they would have to face on the long journey to Montenegro. They knew they could expect trouble from the Ustashi as soon as they passed from Serbia into 'independent' Croatia. It was with some trepidation, therefore, that they joined the cross-border train at Cacak, for they had no idea what kind of conditions awaited them on the other side of the mountains. The tedious and relatively uneventful nature of the train journey did nothing to allay their uncertainties, which kept them company every mile of the way.

There was no inspection of identity documents or luggage search at the 'new' border – in fact, the old border that had once delineated the Austrian Empire's boundary with Serbia – but there was a nail-biting wait of two hours in the little mountain station that marked the frontier. No Ustashi appeared out of the night to search for anti-Fascists among the passengers. For all that, Jamie and Stefan never felt free from anxiety until long after they had changed trains at Sarajevo and passed far beyond Mostar – out of Ustashi-controlled territory and into Italian-occupied Montenegro. Nor did most of the Serbian passengers on the train. Every little station along the way saw its quota of Bosnian-born and Croatian-born Serbs board the train, and each had tales to tell of butchery and massacre by the Ustashi in the villages to the north.

Many of these simple peasants, adherents of the Orthodox Church, had been traumatised by their experience of brutality at the hands of the pre-dominantly Muslim Ustashi. They could scarcely bring themselves to speak of the appalling terror that had descended on their villages. They had escaped in ones or twos, often constituting the only survivors from communities a thousand strong. They had seen their families and friends – men, women and children – rounded up and bayoneted or clubbed to death, the bodies tossed into gullies and ditches. Here and there, the blows and wounds had not caused death and the victim had wakened in a pit filled with corpses. It was survivors such as these who had found their way to the railway and the train that carried Jamie and Stefan to Montenegro.

Now, the mountain was Jamie's bed and the Montenegrin sky was his roof. As he lay staring at the stars, he was touched again by the horror of the recitals of atrocity he had heard. It gave him comfort to feel, against his body, the unyielding hardness of his recently acquired M1924 rifle. There was a satisfaction in its possession: a security and purpose that he had not known in Belgrade. Belgrade had been a city of the dead, a city emptied of its people, where to venture on the streets was to invite a bullet from trigger-happy police, who seemed to think that the only survivors of the bombing were either looters or fifth columnists.

Stefan had been right. There *were* plenty of guns in Montenegro – and it had not been difficult to obtain one. Here, the boy children were weaned on firearms and were expert shots at the age of twelve. No hill peasant was dressed without his rifle. The Montenegrins acquired weapons like magpies, with caches all over the place: rifles stolen from the Italians or obtained by the wagonload from disbanding units of a Jugoslav Army that no longer existed, officially.

It was Djordje, the Montenegrin who was a leading light in the Belgrade Communist hierarchy, who had pointed Stefan in the direction of Montenegro and told him whom to contact.

'The people will rise,' he promised Stefan. 'Not just the Communists . . . the entire population. They'll make life as difficult for the Italians as they did for the Turks in my father's day.' Djordje himself was intending to go to Montenegro, to stir things up, and he was encouraging other Communists to do the same. He wanted them at the front of any popular uprising. The only native political group likely to oppose a rebellion against the occupiers was the Montenegrin separatists – the so-called Greens. Mussolini had promised them independence from the rest of Jugoslavia and restoration of the old-style Bishop-Prince rule. 'But we'll sort out the Greens,' Djordje had said. 'They're just an opportunist minority with an eye on the main chance.'

So Stefan was on his way to Montenegro when he found Jamie and Mannion again. It was not a chance meeting. He did not want to leave Belgrade without trying to find out if his two friends had survived the bombing.

He went to Milan Alexandrovic's house. There, he found Jamie and Mannion preparing to get out of Belgrade, too. Neither had any firm idea of where they would go. They simply resolved to get out before the

249

German troops marched in and hoisted the Nazi flag over the Kalemegdan. Old Lucija would not be budged. She was determined to stay on in Milan's house, come what may – but she was adamant that Jamie and Mannion must go. As young and fit men, their duty was with the Cetniks, who would surely be banding together in the mountains to continue the fight against the Germans.

Stefan's arrival settled matters for Jamie and Mannion. He gave them a specific objective: Montenegro, where there were guns to be had and opportunities to use them against the invader.

The three men made their way south from Belgrade on foot, but using any form of transport on which they could scrounge a ride: horse-cart, ox-cart, an old autobus that broke down every couple of miles, and an ancient baker's delivery van that was even less mechanically reliable and had finally to be abandoned. By slow stages, they progressed to the town of Cacak, where they encountered Stefan's brother, Marko. It was a fateful meeting – because, as a result of it, they parted company with Mannion.

Although, by then, the Government had capitulated, Marko was still in uniform, wearing the blue-piped yellow epaulette and metal stars of cavalry lieutenant. He revealed that he and many others had ignored the order to surrender to the Germans and had established a Cetnik military command in the hills around Cacak. Overjoyed as Marko was to see his brother, he seemed even happier to find out that Jamie and Mannion were his travelling companions. The last thing he had expected to find in the sleepy little town on the banks of the western Morava was an English speaker who was fluent in Serbo-Croat. And lo, the good God had provided not one, but two! He could not believe his luck.

He explained that, for the past week, his colonel had been sending out in all directions for a proficient English

250

speaker to help maintain the radio link they had established with Britain's Middle East Headquarters in Cairo, by translating the heavy volume of communications they were receiving. At their mountain base, they had been dependent for this work on a former attaché at the British Embassy in Belgrade, but his man – who was elderly – had taken ill and died. A replacement was impossible to find. Now – Marko had made it clear – either Jamie or Mannion was the answer to his colonel's prayers. He hoped one or the other would volunteer, because his colonel was the kind of man who would think nothing about press-ganging a suitable candidate.

'Why can't we all join up with you?' Mannion asked. 'We all want to fight.'

Stefan's brother hummed and hawed. Mannion's suggestion clearly embarrassed him. In the end, he admitted that Stefan was the stumbling block. He stared apologetically at his brother.

'You're a Communist, Stefan. And you're known to be a Communist. The Colonel wouldn't have you within a mile of his camp. I'm sorry.'

'All I want to do is fight Fascists,' Stefan insisted.

'We all do,' Marko replied. 'The Colonel, too. Believe me, he hates the Nazis as much as you do. But he's an old-fashioned monarchist down to his socks and he thinks Stalin's as big a monster as Hitler. I tell you, he wouldn't have you on the base. I've had a hard enough time living you down as it is.'

'I'm sorry you're ashamed of me,' Stefan said testily.

'I'm not ashamed of you, Stefan,' Marko protested. 'You're my brother and I love you. We just see things differently when it come to politics. It doesn't make any difference to the way I feel about you.'

The matter remained unresolved and the three stayed on in Cacak while Marko went off into the hills to consult his colonel. Jamie and Mannion were both for pushing on to Montenegro, but Stefan stayed them. He had promised his brother that they would hang on in Cacak for a few days , if only to say goodbye on his return.

Marko returned. But not alone. With him came the person who was to make all the difference when it came to deciding who went on to Montenegro: whether it was the 'three musketeers' who had endured Lepoglava together, or only two.

Jamie and his companions were sleeping rough – the weather was clement – in the ruins of an abandoned monastery, some distance from the town. They had chosen it as a camp site for its hidden seclusion, as the original occupants had in the days when Turkish swords made the preservation of the Orthodox religion a high-risk activity. Once a day, the three ventured into Cacak for provisions and any news they could glean of events in the world beyond. Then they returned to the hillside, believing that their hiding place was known only to them.

That illusion was shattered on the day of Marko's return. In mid-morning, they were laundering their clothes at the stream which flowed past the ruined monastery when, almost simultaneously, they realised they were being observed. Looking up, they saw the two riders watching them from a rise, only a hundred metres away. Horses and riders were motionless, like statues, with the sun behind them – tall silhouettes. They did not recognise Marko until he wheeled his mount to bring it in a circling run down the slope towards them. The second rider followed suit. Jamie blinked in surprise at the realisation that it was a girl: an exceptionally good-looking girl, with short raven hair that was slightly tousled by the wind.

'Marko!' Stefan shouted. 'How in heaven's name did you manage to find us?'

Marko laughed.

'Nobody moves this side of the Sumadija without us

knowing. Our spies in the town told us you were here.'

The girl dismounted and stared at Mannion with frank interest. Mannion, a smile playing at his lips, was reciprocating the scrutiny.

'Do I pass your inspection?' the girl asked, with a teasing laugh.

'Ten out of ten,' Mannion replied. 'I was about to ask you the same question.'

Again she laughed softly.

'Marko said you were handsome and that I would fall in love with you at first sight.'

Mannion grinned.

'And now you've seen me?'

She laughed again.

'He did not tell me that you had such wicked eyes.'

'They go with my wicked heart. Marko didn't tell us anything about you. Not that I blame him. He would have had a hard time keeping me away. . . .'

Mannion and the girl had become so entranced with each other that the others simply looked on with amusement, shamelessly eavesdropping on an encounter that had the makings of a mutual admiration society.

'You have made a conquest, Lela,' a grinning Marko finally intervened and, with a wink at Stefan and Jamie, he surrendered the reins of his horse to Mannion and suggested that he and the girl might water the animals and find a place to tether them. 'It will give you a chance to get acquainted,' he added mischievously.

'We've got bad news for you,' Stefan warned Marko, when Mannion and the girl had wandered off upstream with the horses. 'Brad and Jamie are coming with me to Montenegro. Your colonel will have to get somebody else to do his cipher work.'

'Do you think so?' Marko asked, slyly. 'I told you that he wasn't the kind of man who took no for an answer. He could use force. After all, we are fighting a war – and this is an emergency.'

'You're bluffing, Marko. Are you trying to tell me he would try to kidnap Brad or Jamie?'

Marko shrugged.

'I hope it won't come to that. One volunteer is worth twenty conscripted men. All the same, I'm glad you and your friends did not try to leave Cacak. You would not have got very far.'

Stefan stared at his brother in disbelief.

'Who would have stopped us?'

'This is Cetnik country, Stefan,' Marko said. 'We control it. I'm not trying to threaten you in any way . . . I'm just stating the facts of life.'

'Then it's Jamie or Brad you have to convince, not me. They want to fight Fascists, not sit around on some mountaintop translating English signals!'

'We don't carry passengers,' Marko replied. 'Whoever comes with us will have to soldier like the rest of us, even if he's part of the headquarters strength. We'll be on the move a lot, hitting the enemy where and when we can – and that'll mean long night marches and fighting enough for any man.'

'But you have no place for Communists in all this fighting you're going to do?' Stefan inquired with an ironic smile.

Marko shrugged his great shoulders, avoiding Stefan's eyes.

'I'd take all three of you if I could. But it's not up to me.'

'It's not up to me either,' Stefan declared. 'It's up to Brad and Jamie to decide what they want to do.' He looked questioningly at Jamie. 'Do you want to go with Marko, Jamie?'

'I'm going to Montenegro,' Jamie replied firmly.

Marko smiled.

'That leaves the American.'

'And he's not interested.' Stefan's comment was delivered with a challenging smile.

'Maybe I can persuade him,' Marko suggested.

'You're welcome to try,' Stefan replied, and smiled at Jamie. 'Don't blame us if he tells you to go to hell.'

'I won't,' Marko promised, and observed, 'At least he seems to have hit it off with Lela. They're taking a long time to see to the horses.'

Stefan laughed.

'So that's why you brought the girl! You thought you could seduce him?'

'Heaven forbid!' Marko snorted, disclaiming the notion and mirthfully accusing Stefan of crediting him with a guile he did not possess. 'All the same,' he added, appreciating the possibilities, 'she is a stunner, isn't she? She only came along out of curiosity. She's our radio operator, and I've been teasing her for days about the handsome American I'd found to take the place of the old Englishman who kicked the bucket. I'm sure she thought I was making it up about this Yank who looked like Clark Gable and spoke our language with a funny accent.'

'They *are* taking a mighty long time,' Jamie commented.

Marko found his sudden concern amusing.

'Getting worried, are you?' he inquired mischievously, enjoying the situation. 'Never underestimate the power of a woman. I should have thought of it myself . . . I just never imagined Lela as being our secret weapon. She's the wrong type – too strait-laced. She certainly put me in my place when I tried to romance her.'

This confession drew a smile from Stefan.

'Knowing you, big brother, I'm not surprised. You probably weren't very subtle in the way you went about it.'

'I'm not the only one she's slapped down,' Marko confided ruefully. 'As for subtlety, Lela's been among men too long to expect it. She's just like one of us. We've never made any concessions because she's a woman –

and she takes it all in her stride. You should have heard the ribbing she got when that stuffy old Englishman died. We told her she'd worn him out – that he'd had palpitations from looking down the front of her shirt.'

Mannion and the girl eventually returned, looking like conspirators.

'You two took long enough,' Marko commented, casually.

'Lela. . . .' Mannion spoke the name self-consciously. 'Lela's been telling me about your setup.'

'Oh?' Marko sounded almost uninterested. 'Too bad you're set on going to Montenegro.'

The look Mannion darted at Jamie and Stefan was troubled.

'I didn't know that anything had been settled. That's why we've been hanging around here instead of being halfway to Montenegro.'

'It's your decision, Brad,' Stefan quickly assured him. 'I talked you and Jamie into going to Montenegro and I'll go on alone if I have to – but I'm not twisting anybody's arm. I won't hold it against you if you want to stay with Marko.'

'And you, Jamie?' Mannion's troubled eyes turned on Jamie.

'You're a free man, Brad. You don't have to go on with us if you want to stay.'

'No hard feelings?'

'None at all.' Jamie uttered the words without a sign of the disappointment that coursed through him. He didn't want Brad Mannion to go. They had come through so much together, come to depend on each other so much. Jamie knew that it was selfish to think that way but it hurt, nevertheless, that Mannion could walk away so casually from so total a comradeship.

Looking back, Jamie wondered often if – in his anxiety not to betray his feelings or influence the American – he had sounded indifferent to whatever Mannion chose to do.

What shook Jamie and Stefan more than anything and what they found hard to accept was that Brad should desert them for a girl of a few minutes' acquaintance. It was so unlike him. He was the last person on earth likely to have his head turned by a girl. It wasn't that he was averse to female company; he could be a real charmer when he set his mind to it. But he always gave the impression that the woman had not been born who would put her brand on him, that lasting relationships with the female of the species were slow death to the man who valued his freedom. And, yet, in the twinkling of an eye, he seemed to have succumbed heart and soul to this girl Lela.

On the eve of his departure to join forces with Marko and his colonel, Mannion bared some of that soul to Jamie. Marko and Lela had ridden off towards Cacak in mid-afternoon, with the promise that one or the other would return next day with a mount for the American. Stefan – his chest troubling him, as it frequently did – had turned in early, while Jamie and Mannion lingered beside the embers of their campfire. Jamie, still a little aggrieved that Mannion had decided to quit them, chided his friend on the suddenness of that decision. Wasn't he being a bit impulsive?

'Maybe,' Mannion conceded, and went on to tell Jamie that his whole life had been dictated by impulses – some wise, some unwise – which, one way or another, was the reason why he was now camped on a Serbian hillside and about to throw in his lot with a bunch of fugitive cavalrymen.

Impulse had made him shoulder his father's commitment to revenge. Impulse had made him confront Graz in Belgrade, and had landed him in prison. His impulses, he said, were his instinct to do the right thing at probably the wrong time.

'But I never look back,' he told Jamie. 'If I did, I'd probably go out of my mind. The only view I get, looking back, is all the bridges I've burned.'

'You've never burned one before for a girl,' Jamie said.

Mannion did not reply immediately. He seemed to give a lot of thought to Jamie's remark.

'You know, Jamie,' he confided eventually. 'I've always envied you . . . envied the way you felt about Mara. I thought there was something missing in me, because I couldn't feel that way about any woman . . . I didn't think the woman existed who could make me think she had some magic that made her different from all the rest. To me, a dame was just a dame, and a guy could have his pick any time he wanted.'

'Not in Lepoglava!' Jamie reminded him.

Mannion laughed.

'Hell, no,' he agreed, 'but in Lepoglava, you learned to do without a lot of things. You did without a smoke when you would have given an arm and a leg for one. You never saw a T-bone steak, smothered with onions, or ate your meals off white linen. You couldn't get an ice-cold beer when you were dying of thirst. You learned to live without these things – and dames were just the same. They were just something you missed and maybe talked about, because they weren't available. That was where you and I were different. I missed dames in general, full stop. You missed Mara, because she was special.'

'Are you trying to tell me that this Lela is special, Brad?'

'She's special all right, Jamie. Very, very special. She's not like any woman I've known before – and I've known a few. Just meeting her like that, today . . . the way she rode up and stared at me like she had just found a shiny new silver dollar. It was like a miracle, like I was being given a chance that might never come my way again. She's the only reason I would quit you guys, Jamie . . . I don't give a goddamn for Marko or his goddamn colonel, but Lela – she's special. For her I'd

258

walk to the ends of the earth. Where she is is where I want to be. Not another goddamn thing matters.'

Next day, Lela rode into their camp, leading a second horse. The farewells were brief. Then Mannion – a far from expert horseman – rode off with her. Jamie and Stefan walked down into Cacak and, later that day, boarded the train to Sarajevo.

It surprised Jamie and Stefan how freely they were able to move around in Montenegro. In the towns they passed through, they became accustomed to the sight of Italian soldiers in the streets, without feeling threatened by them. Even Montenegrins admitted that the behaviour of the occupying troops towards the civilian population was exemplary. In spite of this, the Italians were universally despised, just for being there. Away from the towns, there was not an Italian to be seen. As a consequence, the outlying hill villages and lonelier communitites had become mustering points for little armies of rebellious Montenegrins eager to bear arms against the invader. The fiery cross had gone out and it was to the traditional clan seats that the scattered sons and cousins of the tribe returned to undertake war as a matter of family obligation. There was no unification of command or sharing of particular objectives. It was up to each clan to make life as disagreeable as possible for the invaders in whatever way they chose. It was hoped that the sum total of these diverse and unconnected demonstrations would encourage the Italians to go home to Italy.

It was in the town of Podgorica, thirty-five kilometres from the Adriatic coast and less than twenty from the mountains of Albania, that Stefan located a cousin of Djordje's, a local Communist activist. He was acting as an unofficial recruiting agent for the clan-oriented rebel bands that were assembling in the mountains. The Party had no control over these armed groups, but it had faithful supporters in most of them – and Djordje's cousin was doing his best to ensure that Communists occupied positions of leadership. He was aided in this by a sudden upsurge in popularity for all things Russian – including Communism – by the German invasion of Russia on the twenty-second of June. Czarist Russia had been the traditional champion of the Serbian-Montenegrin idea and Orthodoxism, and, it seemed, the fates of Russia and Montenegro were to be interwined again.

Ironically, it had taken the German invasion of Russia to prod the Communist leadership in Jugoslavia into issuing orders for armed resistance against the Axis forces of occupation. Until that time, no directive had come from Moscow on the subject, and the only guerrilla activity against the occupiers had come from Jugoslav Army officers, who had organised Cetnik-style harassment throughout Serbia. Once the Russian homeland was under threat, however, the Comintern in Moscow had sanctioned Communists throughout occupied Europe to form sabotage and guerrilla groups.

Djordje's cousin in Podgorica directed Stefan and Jamie to a clan rallying point in the mountains above the Moraca River, a high treeless plateau dominated by a craggy pillar called the Devil's Rock. Nearly a hundred men were camped in the shadow of the crag and its dark shape was like a finger thrust out into the starry heavens. It was a strange and haunting place, timeless in its overpowering remoteness.

As Jamie recalled in his mind the events that had brought him to this high wilderness, he was seized by a crushing awareness of his own insignificance and the shortness of his own life compared to the everlasting grandeur of this tiny corner of the Crnagora. Ten thousand years ago, the Devil's Rock had pointed its dark finger at the sky, as it did tonight. Ten thousand years from now, it would do the same – long after Jamie's generation and successions of following generations had returned to dust.

Jamie was strangely comforted by the thought. Three score years and ten – man's expected optimum – was no more than a heartbeat in eternity. So what if it was cut short, with two-thirds of its expected course to run? The difference was negligible, gone in a flicker of an eye. As Jamie lay, unsleeping, it allowed him to accept the unacceptable – that tomorrow might be the day he died.

He was dreaming of Mara when the sun woke him. Stefan was already awake and rolling his blanket into the sausage shape which would allow him to sling it over one shoulder and attach it like a bandolier at his waist.

'Better shake yourself, sleepyhead,' he advised Jamie cheerfully. 'We march in twenty minutes.'

The camp had come to life. Jamie folded his own blanket and draped it, plaidlike, across his shoulder, the Montenegrin way. Only the previous day, a peasant uplander with a gnarled face and magnificent moustache had schooled him in the uses of his blanket: as a padded rest on rock when firing his rifle; as a camouflage canopy over head and shoulders; as a loose garment that bore the buckled bite of his haversack strap on his shoulder; as an armshield in close combat with knife or bayonet. The friendly veteran was typical of the clansmen who had found their way to the Devil's Rock, making Jamie and Stefan welcome as well as showing intense curiosity about them. The fact that two such well-educated men had journeyed all the way from Belgrade to fight Fascists earned the pair respect and approval.

It was a motley band that had gathered on the high plateau. Now, in twos and threes, from their sleeping places in the open, they began to assemble round a rocky platform at the base of the Devil's Rock. Here, a group of half a dozen elders had been holding a council of war and were ready to pronounce on their deliberations. Stefan and Jamie moved with the drifting tide towards the rock

261

as one of the leaders advanced to its edge to address the assembly.

He wore a drab town suit and collarless shirt. A brimless black Montenegrin hat was pulled down over his straggly grey hair. He peered at the men below him through thickly glassed steel-rimmed spectacles. Jamie recognised him as the Communist official to whom he and Stefan had reported on arrival at the Devil's Rock.

'Comrades,' the man began, 'you know me and the party I represent. My struggle and the Party's struggle has been the people's struggle. Today, that struggle becomes a war – a war which has the support of every Communist in the Crnagora and the organisational apparatus that we have built here. We built that apparatus in the name of revolution. Now we offer it to the people in the name of liberation. Through us, the call from the fathers of your people has gone out – and you have answered it, because you are the sons of your fathers and prize freedom before life.'

A cheer greeted the declaration.

'Comrades,' the speaker went on, 'we are of many parties here – but we are of one family! We are *Montenegrins!*'

This earned a bigger cheer. The speaker waited for silence.

'Montenegrins and kinsmen,' he continued, 'in Cetinje yesterday, traitors to our land had the audacity – under the protection of Italian guns – to declare this, our beloved country, to be an independent sovereign state.' The speaker savoured the puzzled silence that greeted this announcement. Then he roared the three words again: 'Independent sovereign state!' Every syllable was articulated with scorn as he added, '*Whose destiny is to be united forever with the destiny of Italy!*'

Angry cries rose from the gathering.

'Death to the Italians!'

'Death to the Fascist-loving Greens!'

The orator waited for the shouts to subside.

'Comrades, the Greens have joined hands with the foreign invaders to impose on you what they call a form of constitutional monarchy . . . Mussolini wants to give you a king!'

There were cries of 'No! Never!'

'My friends, I ask you – who wants an Italian lickspittle as king in a land where all men are born equal . . . and all men are kings?'

Laughter and more shouting greeted the rhetorical question.

'Comrades and kinsmen,' the orator went on, 'we Montenegrins do not like to hurry. When there is work to be done and we are asked why we do not begin it, we say, "*ima vremena*" . . . there is time. Yes, my friends, there is time. There is always time. But for the work that now awaits us, the time has come. The time is *now*! The time has come to make our land free! The time has come to throw out the foreign invaders who want to turn Montenegro into a vassal state with a Fascist overlord! The time has come to fight again as our fathers fought the Turks! The time has come when we will be free, or we will die!'

A bedlam of cheering and shouting erupted as the grey-haired Communist gave the clenched-fist salute and then modestly backed away from the front of his rocky platform. His place was taken by an erect seventy-year-old of dignified bearing, a clan elder. He spoke briefly but to the point. Like the Communist, he appealed to the national and family loyalties of the assembled men. He stressed that all shades of political opinion had answered the call to fight, and he called for unity of purpose. He declared that, united, they would drive the invader from the land. Then he introduced a bearded giant in officer's uniform – a major in the Royal Army who had distinguished himself in the brief campaign against the Italians around Lake Skadar. He was the unanimous choice, as a son of the clan, to command the volunteers who had answered the call to arms – and he, too, had a few words to say.

He made it clear that he intended to organise his audience on military lines and that discipline and attention to orders were priorities. They would learn to fight as a disciplined force, like soldiers – not a trigger-happy rabble. A first essential was the acquisition of automatic weapons, grenades, field guns, ammunition, stores – and, with that in mind, he had selected their first objective. It was the military outpost that the Italians had established near the village of Bioce, in the Moraca valley. The post was strategically situated on the main road from Podgorica to Kolasin, in the interior, at a point where it was met by the road from Pelev Brijeg. It not only commanded the road junction but the bridges over the Moraca River and its tributary, the Mala, whose confluence it overlooked.

'We attack tonight, after dark,' the Major announced. 'But now, we march! We have a long way to go.'

And march they did. On tracks which allowed only single file, they trekked in a long serpentine chain along the high reaches. With the sun at its zenith, they rested and each man ate from the meagre provisions he carried. Late afternoon found them on the wooded heights above the confluence of the two rivers.

In a high tree-screened gully, the Major split his force into three sections: approximately forty men in two of them and thirty in the third. He himself took command of one of the bigger sections. Two former royalist officers – both young men – were detailed to lead the other two groups. Jamie and Stefan were allocated to the smallest group and were dismayed to find that it had not been allotted an attacking role. Instead, it was assigned the task of mounting roadblocks – three in all – to cut off any traffic to and from the Italian post.

Their officer was a sunny-natured young man, no

older than Jamie, to whom all of life seemed a huge joke. His eyes had a permanent twinkle and, like the Major, he sported a full beard – which he had vowed not to shave off until the last invader, Italian or German, had been kicked out of Jugoslavia. His name was Mihailo Dudic. None was more disappointed than he that his section would not be leading a frontal charge against the Italians, but he quickly recovered his sense of humour, taking some consolation from the fact that he and his men would be the first to test the alertness of the Italians. The Major wanted the three approaches to the post to be cut off before he launched his attack.

An hour of light remained when Dudic led his silent column down the wooded slopes of the valley's west side. He seemed to have an intimate knowledge of the terrain and was quietly satisfied when they reached the road about two kilometres up the valley from the Italian post. There, choosing the site, he left ten men to man an ambush point. He led the remainder south along the road for a short distance before signalling them once more on to wooded hillside.

Further on, Dudic stopped the column and, from a grassy vantage point, studied the land below through binoculars. Rising, he grinned at Jamie, who had been at his elbow, and invited him to take a look at the enemy post.

It lay below, on a knoll above the meeting place of the rivers. A fort had once stood at the highest point, but now only the crumbling foundation walls of that mediaeval construction fringed, like a tonsure, the bald summit of the knoll. Slightly below the once fortified summit, stood the boxlike concrete shapes of the Italian position: a single-storey main block, long and low and probably housing sleeping quarters and other offices and, nearby, the smaller shapes of blockhouses and storage sheds. There was no sign of life but, from somewhere below, the plaintive notes of a strummed mandolin rose on the evening air.

'Listen,' Dudic said softly. 'Some homesick soul wishes he were back in Napoli.' He glanced at his watch. 'Two hours from now, he'll be wishing he'd never seen the Moraca River!'

He led his men along the hillside, circling the Italian post and working lower; then waving them to cover as the bridge over the Moraca came into view. Some distance down the road, beyond the bridge, was the village of Bioce. There were no sentries guarding the bridge and none visible around the Italian camp. Dudic waited for the light to fade from the summer sky before sending the twenty men over the bridge, three at a time.

On the far side, he detailed ten – including Jamie and Stefan – to get off the road and stay out of sight. He ordered the remainder to follow him. Dudic returned about twenty minutes later, having crossed the bridge over the Mala and established a second ambush point a little way up the twisting road to Pelev Brijeg. He led Jamie and the others through the village of Bioce – in which not a soul stirred – and out the other side. They marched at a brisk pace down the Podgorica road for half an hour before Dudic indicated that he had found his third ambush point: at a sharp bend, with the river on one side and on the other a steep incline that gave an uninterrupted view of the road from the south for five hundred metres. He ordered rocks and fallen timber to be manhandled into the road to form a barrier. This was located above the bend, so that it would not be seen by northbound traffic until it was reached.

Four men were left behind the barrier, with their rifles. Jamie and Stefan were among the half-dozen to take up firing points on the slope commanding the road. Dudic chose his own vantage point on a shoulder of rock, a few metres above Jamie.

'Keep watching the road,' he called down to Jamie. 'If the caribinieri send reinforcements from Podgorica when the shooting starts, this is the way they'll come.'

The shooting started just after midnight. It erupted from the far side of Bioce with startling suddenness, taking Jamie by surprise even although he had been waiting for it for a seeming eternity.

'Did you ever hear sweeter music?' Dudic called down exuberantly.

Volleys of riflefire continued to echo from higher in the valley, but hopes that the Italian post would be overcome in a quick battle were dispelled when the rattle of machine-gun fire contributed to the clamour and the whine and clunk of mortar bombs sounded in the night. The Montenegrins had neither machine-guns nor mortars – and that meant the Italians were hitting back hard.

Jamie could hear Dudic fidgeting and moving about on the rock above. Frequently he gave voice to an expletive, when the mortar or machine-gun fire sounded particularly intense. He was clearly torn by impatience to know what was happening up at the Italian post, and the ferocity of the defenders' fire worried him. After two hours, it was still flaring up at regular intervals with undiminished intensity.

'Maybe our people need help up there,' one of the Montenegrins on the road shouted up to Dudic.

'We stay here!' the officer roared down at the man. 'These are our orders!'

They heard the labouring truck engines from lower in the valley before they saw the wink of headlights, broken and diffuse, through distant trees. The lights took on a steadier shape and glow as the vehicles reached a five-hundred-metre straight stretch below.

'Hold your fire until they're right on top of you,' Dudic shouted to the men behind the roadblock. 'Then let them have it!'

There were three vehicles in the convoy: two open trucks, packed with riflemen, and an armoured car with the barrel of a 20 mm cannon poking from its squat

267

turret. Unaccountably, the armoured car was not leading the way but bringing up the rear. The first truck rounded the bend and foundered on the rocks barring its path like a stricken whale. One front wheel rode up on the obstruction while the other lodged firmly as it encountered immovable rock. The truck tilted dangerously, throwing the occupants of its rear in a struggling heap towards the tailgate. Simultaneously, the Montenegrins behind the barrier – standing upright and firing from the shoulder – unleashed a fusillade of shots at the windscreen of the stranded vehicle.

The second truck, travelling much too close to the leader, only avoided a collision by slewing left towards the river and stopping. Jamie, eaten with tension, found release as he aimed his rifle at the troops in the second truck and pumped bullets at the tightly packed mass of struggling bodies. From the other positions, bullets poured on the shocked Italians with a fury that belied the size of the tiny ambushing force. Dazed and bewildered by the jolting standstill, even those Italian soldiers with the will to fight were thwarted by the press of humanity around them. Those who escaped from the carnage of the trucks and leapt to the ground were still exposed to the unrelenting crossfire that was being directed at them by attackers they could not see. A number managed to bring their rifles to bear, but they fired haphazardly at the dark hillside.

The first sharp fury of the engagement passed, leaving the two trucks tenanted by only dead and dying – perhaps forty or more in number. A dozen Italian soldiers had dropped below the road, towards the river, where they were being picked off by the Montenegrins who had been manning the roadblock. The latter had scattered from behind the barrier and were stalking the terrified survivors from the road, who were blundering around blindly in search of safety.

Survivors from the second truck had retreated down

the road to gain the cover of the armoured car, which had halted thirty metres away and had taken no part in the action. The cannon turret had not deviated from the fore and aft position and the co-axial machine-gun – sited forward of and just below the turret – had remained silent. This phenomenon had not escaped the interest of Dudic, who dropped down beside Jamie and crouched beside him.

'What a prize that Autoblinda would be!' he exclaimed excitedly, peering at the armoured car through his binoculars. 'Do not waste your bullets on it. Look at them down there. What are they doing – fighting to get into that tin can? Or out?'

Jamie could not make out what was happening on the far side of the armoured car, where several Italian soldiers who sought the protection of its flanks were milling about. The metal side door had been pulled open and a struggle was taking place but, as Dudic had observed, it was impossible to tell whether the driver was being hauled out and resisting, or others were trying to get in. In spite of the officer's warning about wasting bullets, Jamie took careful aim and fired at the bobbing helmets. The single shot had effect. All the heads ducked out of sight.

'You got one of the sphagetti-eaters!' Dudic roared approvingly, lowering his glasses. 'That's given them something to think about. Let's get down there while they're still eating mouthfuls of dirt!'

With that, he went slithering down the slope towards the road, giving voice to a bloodcurdling war shriek, which, if nothing else, gave some intimation to the other Montenegrins on the hillside of his intentions. Jamie followed him, heart thudding against his ribs – more fearful of breaking his neck in his headlong descent than of Italian bullets.

Dudic seemed intent on charging the armoured car, scarcely breaking stride as he reached the road. A fresh battle cry died, half-uttered, as a shot rang out – and he completed three spinning strides before falling.

Jamie, careering down the slope, saw him fall and, fighting to control his own descent, arrested his momentum in the final strides that would have carried him into the roadway. He fell belly down, in a slide on the gravel-strewn verge. A shadow moved near one of the armoured car's platelike wheels as he manoeuvred the butt of his rifle against his shoulder. He fired without sighting and was rewarded when a scream of pain gave proof of a lucky shot. The shadow materialised in the shape of a man detaching himself from the greater shape of the armoured car. The wounded Italian seemed to be trying to get to his feet but was impeded by lack of control in one leg. The rifle he had been holding went spinning away from him, clattering noisily on to the road, while he fell on his hands and knees. Jamie fired a second time and the shape collapsed in a sprawl.

A second shape appeared – a man kneeling on one knee. There was muzzle flash as he fired the weapon at his shoulder. The bullet screamed over Jamie's head, and he heard its ricocheting flight off rock. Sucking in his breath, Jamie sighted and fired. The shadow dissolved with a faint cry and the flail of an arm that sent a second rifle clattering against the plated bonnet of the armoured car.

Jamie rose to one knee and sent two more bullets whining off the metal flanks of the stationary vehicle. There were shouts as two figures, then another three, emerged from the lee of the armoured car with their arms held high. It took Jamie a moment to comprehend that the enemy soldiers were frantically appealing for a cessation of fire: they wanted to surrender.

He rose and advanced towards them, keeping them covered. He motioned them out into the middle of the road, uncertain what to do next. His relief was considerable when two figures glided out of the dark and joined him. One of them was Stefan. They willingly took charge of the prisoners while Jamie went off to find Dudic.

He was still lying where Jamie had seen him fall – and Jamie was sure he was dead. His face and hair and beard were covered in blood and he seemed not to be breathing, but Jamie detected a heartbeat. It seemed steady and strong.

'Can I help?'

The voice at his shoulder startled Jamie. He looked up and recognised one of the Montenegrins who had been manning the roadblock: a tall gangly man of about forty, with a droopy moustache and fierce burning eyes.

'His head's all bloody but he's breathing,' Jamie said. 'I'm frightened to touch him in case I do more damage. Do you know anything about head wounds?'

'I'm a doctor,' the other said, and gently moved Jamie out of the way. Jamie let him take over, open-mouthed with astonishment. He had taken the man to be an illiterate mountain peasant. The lesson was salutary. He was never again to assume anything about Montenegrins from appearances.

Although the sound of desultory firing still came from above Bioce, the brief battle at the bend in the Podgorica road was over. It had been more of a massacre than a battle. Dudic – whose scalp had been grooved by a bullet – was the only Montenegrin casualty. The Italian losses were forty-seven dead, seven wounded and eleven prisoners.

Jamie, who felt he had not done anything particularly heroic, was embarrassed to be hailed by his comrades in Dudic's section as a kind of super-warrior. Hadn't he captured an armoured car single-handed, killing at least two men and forcing five more to surrender? Hadn't his brave action virtually ended the battle, causing all those Italians still resisting to throw down their arms?

Well, that was not quite the way that Jamie saw it. He had simply followed Dudic down the hill and reacted by

271

following an instinct of self-preservation. It had to be remembered, too, that the armoured car played no part in the action. Its guns had never been fired. Indeed, the Italians in its vicinity had been fighting amongst themselves, trying to get into it – not to prolong the battle but to get the hell out of it and back to Podgorica!

It was the driver of the seven-ton Autoblinda who supplied Jamie with the full story. Had the armoured car been leading the three-vehicle convoy into the ambush, instead of bringing up the rear, the battle might have had a vastly different result. In normal circumstances, the Autoblinda would have been in front – but the circumstances of its departure from Podgorica had been anything but normal.

When the garrison commander received the emergency message from the post above Bioce that it was under attack, the crew of the Autoblinda could not immediately be located. When they were, they were found to be dead drunk. In the meantime, two platoons of riflemen had already been despatched towards Bioce. A spare driver for the armoured car had then been found and sent off in pursuit of the two trucks, with orders that it be crewed from one of the l.m.g. sections in the trucks.

Unfortunately, this order was never carried out. It was not even delivered to the officer in charge. The armoured car caught up with the trucks only a few kilometres short of the ambush point, but was forced to tail behind them. The drivers in front refused to stop, and the armoured car was given no opportunity to pass.

Pressed to recount the story – as, subsequently, he often was – Jamie never failed to give the full facts and play down the idea that his capture of the armoured car had required exceptional heroism. The story illustrated for him the ironic absurdity that is so much a condition of war: how battles are won or lost on a fickle set of circumstances that defy prediction. Hardly anyone ever believed his account. It was accepted as entertaining –

he told it in a self-mocking way as, understandably, a shy and modest hero would – but his version did not tally with that of several eyewitnesses whose accounts of the action on the Podgorica road circulated throughout Montenegro far in advance of Jamie's. Jamie's listeners *knew* that the battle had turned on the ability of the guerrillas to neutralise the Italian armoured car, with its rapid firing cannon and murderous machine-gun – and hadn't Jamie, single-handed, stormed it with only a rifle, killing several men and compelling the vehicle's crew to surrender?

Once a folk legend is born, it is not allowed to die. It is nourished by many tellings and grows and grows. The capture of the armoured car was, however, only the prelude.

In the aftermath of the victorious ambush, Jamie's euphoria lasted less than half an hour. It did not survive the victors' attempts to clear a passage for the armoured car through their roadblock, a task that first entailed removal of the trucks.

Up on the hillside, firing at the trucks, Jamie had experienced a kind of joy. There was none in him when he came face to face with the butchery for which he and Dudic's section were responsible. Guilt and nausea, in equal measure, filled him at the sight of the Italian dead: the repose of young faces, strangely boyish in death; the horror of bodies with obliterated faces.

They hauled the trucks off the road and set fire to them. The decision was taken by common consent. It was unanimous. The decision to award Jamie the star prize of the night's contest was also made by common consent. He was given command of the Autoblinda. After all, he had captured it. Dudic, who might have had different plans for the armoured car, was still incapacitated and was not consulted.

Jamie welcomed the unexpected responsiblity of the

Autoblinda, which freed him from the grisly task of making funeral pyres of the dead-laden trucks. And no one objected when he nominated Stefan as driver – least of all Stefan. With the eager help of the Italian driver, they familiarised themselves with the operation of the Autoblinda and its armaments.

By sunrise, they had achieved a degree of mastery over the formidable little war wagon. By then, Dudic had recovered his senses, if not his energy, and was sitting up and trying to bring his concussed brain to bear on the events of the night. The process was, surprisingly, accelerated by the renewal of heavy firing from above Bioce. The attack on the Italian outpost was obviously going a lot less smoothly than had been anticipated.

'Maybe they need that Autoblinda a lot more than we do,' someone suggested to him. It was then that it sank through to Dudic's befuddled mind that the armoured car had been captured intact. He became positively ecstatic when he was told that Stefan and Jamie had driven it up round the roadblock and had got the hang of its weaponry.

'Then they must take it through the village,' Dudic declared. 'The Major must be told we have such a magnificent weapon.' He despatched a runner immediately to warn the Major of its imminent arrival. 'Now,' he announced, 'I must inspect our prize and congratulate the bravo who won it for us.'

Helped by the doctor – Dudic was still weak and groggy – the wounded officer made his way along the road to where Jamie and Stefan were showing off their new toy to the Montenegrin who had drawn the job of guarding the prisoners. The Italians were sitting glumly at the roadside, some way off, watching two of their captors sorting through the huge pile of rifles and other weapons that had been salvaged from the trucks.

Dudic's eyes lit up when he saw the booty.

'Tell the men they can have their pick,' he said to the sorters.

'They already have,' he was told, with a broad grin. 'My cousin Bogdan bagged the two machine-guns – one for him and one for me. He and my brother took them up to cover the road . . . in case we have more visitors from Podgorica.'

'We should have kept the trucks,' Dudic said, with a sniff, a trifle put out that his wishes had been anticipated. 'To carry all that stuff, and us!'

The man sorting the weapons shrugged.

'The tyres were all shot to ribbons and one had a broken axle. The trucks were no use to anyone.'

Dudic grunted and moved on. His displeasure vanished as Jamie gave him a guided inspection of the Autoblinda. At the end of it and much to Jamie's embarrassment, the young officer seized him in a warm embrace, face beaming, and commended him for his bravery and enterprise. Stefan watched, smiling at Jamie's discomfiture. Dudic looked like a fearsome corsair, with his bushy beard, bruiser's face, and hair curling from below the turban-like wrapping which the doctor had put on his head.

'Now you must show the Major and the others what this little beauty of ours can do,' he told Jamie. 'With its armour and its firepower, you'll be able to drive right through the front door of the Italian barracks.'

And that, in a nutshell, was a fair assessment of the task allotted to Jamie and Stefan when they drove up through Bioce and made contact with the main guerrilla force. They found the Major bitter and disappointed that his eighty attackers had been unable to penetrate the Italian post during the hours of darkness. The Italians had reacted speedily and efficiently to the first attack and had kept the Montenegrins at bay ever since. Now a stalemate situation prevailed, with the attackers besieging the post but unable to get close to it without being cut down by the machine-guns of the defenders.

Since first light, the Major had been considering

abandoning the attack altogether because of the number of Montenegrin casualties suffered during the night. The Italian mortars had – either by shrewd guesswork or good luck – all but decimated one group assembling for attack, and the machine-guns had wiped out another infiltrating from the river. Less than fifty of the eighty-strong force remained, and they had been reduced to sniping at the Italians from a distance. The Major had been praying to God for the gift of just one artillery piece with which to soften the defenders up. The Autoblinda, if not the answer, was the next best thing.

The passage over the Moraca bridge proved uneventful. All the way to Bioce, Jamie had complained to Stefan of the rather weaving course of the armoured car, which proved particularly unnerving on bends. 'It's the steering on this damned thing, not me,' Stefan assured him. 'It has a mind of its own.' So Jamie kept a discreet silence on the bridge as they crossed, yawing dangerously close to one parapet and then flirting with the other. It was possible that the Autoblinda's steering was every bit as tricky as Stefan said it was. All things considered, he was doing remarklably well when – as Jamie knew – the only thing he had driven in years was the tractor on the Lepoglava prison farm.

Stefan gunned the Autoblinda up the gradient away from the bridge, negotiated the slight bend and then slowed to a stop on a crest that gave an open view of the knoll and the squat concrete bunkers of the Italian post.

'Be ready to reverse in a hurry,' Jamie called down. 'They're not going to be pleased when they realise we're not on their side!' He swung the turret round to sight on the nearest blockhouse. The turret was like an oven and he could feel sweat running down his back. He pulled the trigger of the cannon, aiming at the dark rectangle of gun-slit. The results were encouraging, if not spectacular. He saw a line of deep scars appear, gouged from the face of the blockhouse like bites in a cheese. A wisp of grey smoke issued from the gun-slit, becoming blacker and increasing in volume.

Jamie raked the long rectangle of barracks building. This lacked the tough-walled thickness of the blockhouse, possessing only a concrete-washed skin over tawdry brick that disintegrated as the exploding shells burst through it. Huge holes appeared in the walls, marking the track of the raking fire.

Riflemen on the flat roof of the building began to return the Autoblinda's cannonade. They were joined by a machine-gunner, whose first burst peppered the armoured car and battered like hail against its flanks.

The source of this racketing hail was a second blockhouse. Jamie targeted on it, again aiming at the firing slit. The blockhouse seemed to tremble and crack from an internal explosion, and a rush of black smoke and orange flame spewed from its narrow mouth. The machine-gun's chatter ended abruptly.

Jamie turned his attention on a canvas-topped truck. This had the most specatacular result of all. The jerry cans of fuel loaded in its back blew up in a fountain of flame, setting fire to one end of the barracks building and showering the riflemen on the roof with a rain of liquid fire. It was then that Jamie's cannon jammed.

'Let's get out of here!' he bellowed down to Stefan, but there was no immediate response from below. Then came an excited shout.

'Look Jamie, look! They've had enough!'

From a window of the barracks, a white shirt, tied to the barrel of a rifle, was being waved. The Italians had surrendered.

The legend that was to attach itself to Jamie's name, which had begun with the capture of the armoured car on the Podgorica road, was thus sealed in a brief fury of cannonfire that frightened Jamie in its easy success. It was as if the gods had conspired to vanquish his enemies and allowed him to be the recipient of the homage and glory that was rightly theirs – all for their own silent amusement. The joke would be complete when the frail mortal they had favoured was confronted by tests, and had nothing on his side but his own puny resources.

The conviction stayed with Jamie, therefore, that the folk-hero image that he acquired that day on the banks of the Moraca was false. He was too much aware of his own limitations not to fear the day when those limitations would be cruelly exposed. That awareness, nevertheless, was to act on him like a goad, compelling him to drive himself on beyond where he thought his limits reached.

The name the Montenegrins gave him was an uneasy burden. He was no longer the 'English Serb'; in one short day, he had earned the title 'Tiger of Bioce'. To his face, he was addressed simply as 'Tiger'.

He came to accept it with the joy of one compelled to wear a hair shirt.

5

Retreat

The mists which had lowered on the high hills after sunset crept lower into the steep cleft of the Upper Moraca valley during the night. Damp dewdrop tears hung like myriads of pearls on the grey stone crags, deposited by the chill moisture-laden clouds that swirled gently from the canyon's heights to drift down and swim, wraithlike, amid the rocky hollows and gorged banks of the river's shining thread.

Even with the coming of the dawn and a slight lifting of the clinging mists, a forbidding bleakness remained. That bleakness added to the sullen misery of the two dozen men camped in the shallow caves about the river's edge. They were all that remained of the hundred-plus guerrilla force that had descended on Bioce and won a stirring victory over the Italians. The euphoria of that occasion had long passed.

News of similar victories all over Montenegro had kept spirits high for some days but the absence of any coordinated strategy in the wake of these successes – and a swift military response from the Italian Ninth Army – had sapped the morale of the irregulars who won Bioce.

The scale of the uprising and its success seemed to have surprised not only the Italians but those who had worked hardest to foment it. Having started a conflagration, they found that they had neither the authority nor the organisation to control it. The Communist Party had quickly set up a supreme command – a committee weighted, but not too heavily, with non-Communists – but its orders took a long time to filter down to the assorted rebel forces in the field and were frequently ignored.

Consternation and confusion certainly greeted the first orders emanating from the new command in the wake of the initial successes, which had virtually wrested from the Italians all control of the Montenegrin hinterland. In the moment of victory – it seemed – the rebel command wanted to disband its nondescript battalions and send them home to the villages and scattered communities whence they had come. They were ordered to cache the arms and food plundered from the isolated Italian garrisons that had been overrun, and organise themselves into small, easily mobilised units which could be called into action at short notice.

Still heady from their success, the rebel clansmen were outraged by what they saw as an abandonment of all they had won. Having rallied in their thousands to fight, they wanted to go on fighting – not scurry home and put their rifles away. The victors of Bioce did not disperse. They wanted to storm into Podgorica town, where the hills of the Moraca valley gave way to the dusty plain that stretches south to the inland sea of Lake Skadar. Their enthusiasm to drive on Podgorica with the captured armoured car in their van was not shared by the Major, who was acutely aware of the limitations of his untrained warriors.

As if to demonstrate his disdain for advice from unqualified amateurs, he ordered the Autoblinda to be stripped of its guns and the vehicle itself rendered inoperable. This was done by running it into a steep ravine. Jamie watched it plunge fifteen metres to finish upside down on the rocks of the gorge floor, with feelings of relief. Both he and Stefan were glad to be free of the prize to which they had fallen heir. The novelty of crewing the machine had quickly worn off with experience of the suffocating heat of its claustrophobic interior. Added to that was their intense distrust of the vehicle's defective steering, which they were sure would have resulted in them ending up like corned beef inside seven tons of scrap metal.

Deaf to the mutterings of the Montenegrins at his wasteful destruction of the armoured car, the Major led them over the hilly tracks from the valley of the Moraca into that of the River Zeta, which joined the Moraca near Podgorica. They camped on high ground, while scouts were sent up the Zeta towards Danilovgrad to investigate the situation there. From the direction of the town had come frequent bursts of small-arms fire, a sign that the Italian garrison was still holding out. The scouts confirmed that the Italians were, indeed, still putting up a fierce resistance, so the Major marched his sixty rifles to join the siege. As they approached in a body along the east bank of the river, following the railway line that ran from Podgorica to the high-plateau town of Niksic, they had had their first taste of artillery fire. Unaware that an Italian 75-mm battery was sited above them, their first warning of its existence was a shell-burst near the middle of the column, which killed two men.

They remained four days at Danilovgrad, taking part in one unsuccessful assault on Italian positions and then having the satisfaction of securing the hill occupied by the troublesome artillery. They were poised for a final desperate assault on the garrison troops when, un-accountably, the Italians surrendered.

'Look at them!' a comrade of Jamie's roared, as a thousand Italian soldiers laid down their arms and paraded with hands in the air. 'Someone must have told them that the Tiger of Bioce was here!'

Spirits still high, and with the Major not displeased with the way his men had behaved under fire, they had returned along the Zeta valley to watch for Italian troop movements in the vicinity of Podgorica. Reports had come in that enemy reinforcements were assembling there in large numbers, having arrived from Albania along the Shkoder road and by flotillas of small craft that brought them twenty-five kilometres up Lake Skadar to land them on the Montenegrin shore.

Little seeking was required to confirm these reports. Almost immediately, the small guerrilla force found itself on the wrong end of an offensive designed to crush the uprising and teach the Montenegrins a lesson. The Italian Supreme Commander, General Birolli – appalled at the loss of his inland garrisons – had ordered his Ninth Army to fan out in strength from Podgorica and extinguish all armed resistance.

Encamped on a hillside above the Zeta, Jamie and his comrades were spotted by a low-flying Italian scout plane and got a taste of things to come when two fighter-bombers strafed and bombed the hill. They had been watching the road on the far side of the river, puzzled by the sight of a procession of peasants – old men, women and children, carrying bundles and herding a variety of farm animals – heading towards Danilovgrad.

The strafing planes caused no casualties but created a vestige of panic in the guerrillas, who felt naked and defenceless on their exposed hilltop. Some bolted down the slope for the cover of trees, lower down. When the aircraft had disappeared, the Major's attention was drawn to spirals of smoke to the south by an agitated observer, who declared that his home village lay in that direction and that something terrible must have happened there to cause such dense smoke.

Fifteen minutes later, the guerrillas gained their first sight of the approaching Italian column. It was moving at snail's speed and with great caution. Armoured cars and trucks led the advance along the road, which skirted the river's far bank. Green-trousered infantrymen, in single file, were progressing slowly in a flanking position along the valley's distant slope. On the near side of the river were more flanking outrunners, following the track of the Podgorica-Niksic railway.

The column halted short of a straggle of humble peasant houses, a hamlet of simple wooden dwellings on a rise above the road, and in moments flames and black smoke could be seen rising as every building was torched. The spotter plane then returned, following the course of the river down from Danilovgrad and passing the guerrillas' hilltop at almost eye level. Some of the Montenegrins loosed off a fusillade of shots at the aircraft, causing it to bank away swiftly. It circled in the vicinity of the column, and the reason soon became clear. Distant puffs of smoke signalled the opening shots of a sustained artillery barrage that raked the guerrillas' hilltop with deadly accuracy. Huge clods of earth and great fountains of stone and rock erupted all around Jamie and his comrades.

It was too much for most of guerrillas who had remained on the hilltop after the bombing and strafing. They fled from the bursting shells. The Major shouted at them to hold their positions and lie low where they were, but his shouts were either unheard in the thunder of exploding shot or ignored. Standing erect and bellowing frantically for courage and not cowardice to be shown, he died in mid-exhortation, his body blown high in the air in an explosion of earth and stone that left a shallow scorched crater.

Dudic took command, but the force he remustered, some kilometres distant from the long-abandoned hilltop above the Zeta, was less than thirty strong. Most were very young men who had answered the Communist call to arms. Some were far from happy at having stayed to carry out Dudic's bidding. They shared the feelings of those who had refused to remain: that their place now was in their home villages. Defence of their own homes was their first priority if, as seemed certain, the Italians were burning every village in their path.

Dudic did not try to detain those who wanted to return to their own homes. He understood their feelings and he knew he had no more power to stop them going than he had had to stop those who had already deserted without any intimation of their intentions.

Jamie and Stefan were bewildered by the turn of events. Unlike the Montenegrins, they could not run off to their homes and families because they were at risk. Home and family were luxuries that had ceased to exist for the two young exiles, with the result that they felt embittered by the desertion of so many comrades. Jamie was the more bitter of the two; filled as he was by a constant yearning for Mara and acutely aware that his own personal desires had been set aside to join the Montenegrin fight. He felt envy for those Montenegrins who could just quit and go home because, they said, their loved ones needed them. Jamie needed and wanted Mara more than anything in the world but he did not even have the consolation of knowing that she was alive. That uncertainty lived with him as a constant torment, making it no easier to remain undismayed by the melting away of the rag-taggle army that had become his home and his hope.

A runner, whom the Major had despatched to Danilovgrad to give warning of the Italian column, found Dudic's depleted party in late afternoon, on his return. He carried orders, which advised against any attempt at frontal opposition to the Italian force and contained the instruction to return to the Moraca valley and harass any attempted enemy incursion towards Kolasin. Dudic smiled wryly at the admonition to avoid frontal opposition to the Italian column in the Zeta valley, which he reckoned was the spearhead of an entire division. He had already shed any illusions he might have had about the ability of the makeshift Montenegrin army of hillmen to face a modern well-equipped army head-on – especially one with air support and a monopoly of heavy weapons.

They reached the Moraca's wooded valley before

nightfall, only to find that another Italian column was camped below Bioce, having advanced at a leisurely pace from Podgorica. Wary of attacks from the hills, the Italians had taken time to secure their flanks. During the next three days and nights, they edged slowly up the valley, reoccupying Bioce and the post at the crossroads in spite of hit-and-run raids by Dudic and his men.

The fourth night found the little band high in the valley, camped in caves by the river's edge and shivering with cold as the chilling mists rolled down the grey walls of the canyon to invest all they touched with icy penetrating damp. Gone was the élan with which the men had first marched out to fight. Gone was the heady thrill of victory. As they had retreated further and further up the valley and as their nuisance raids on the enemy had seemed to have less and less effect, so their spirits had flagged. Now, the mist and the cold added another dimension to their misery. It seemed to them that the Italians were deliberately stalling in order to prolong that misery. The cagey enemy had paused at Bioce, re-establishing the strongpoint that overlooked the road and river junctions, showing little inclination to push up the road to Kolansin. Even now, their most forward unit had dug in less than two kilometres up the valley from the crossroads.

Dudic, Jamie and Stefan shared a looted can of sardines for breakfast. The young officer had taken to consulting the pair more and more as the band's morale deteriorated and mutinous mutterings increased among his fellow Montenegrins. Now, Dudic was weighing up the value of another nuisance raid on the Italians in the hope that it might discourage them from venturing any further up the road to Kolasin.

'If the Italians decide to push up the road to Kolasin, we're not going to be able to stop them,' Jamie said. 'They must have a couple of thousand men down there. And I don't think our sniping away at them is going to make much difference. When they're ready to come, they'll come.'

'My orders were to harass them,' Dudic said.

'And whoever gave those orders seems to have forgotten we exist,' Jamie said, with a hint of bitterness. 'Do they know there are only about twenty of us left, and that we'll be reduced to throwing rocks at the Italians if we don't get ammunition from somewhere pretty soon?'

'Dynamite would be more useful,' Stefan put in. 'We could be blowing up chunks of the road, blocking it with landslides. That would slow the Italians up. They're not going to sit around in Bioce for much longer.'

'Maybe I should send a messenger to Kolasin,' Dudic said thoughtfully. 'There must be somebody there who knows what's going on. . . .' He broke off at the sound of a birdlike whistle from a crag high on the hillside above. It was an alarm signal from one of the lookouts. There was a scurry while men grabbed their weapons and ran to conceal themselves on the rocky slope above the road.

They expected danger to materialise from the direction of Bioce, but it was from the north, not the south, that the sound of a truck engine was heard on the road. It lumbered into view round a bend, almost ghostlike in the thin swirls of mist. A red flag fluttered beside its cab, and it was laden with oddly garbed armed men, who filled the rear and were perched on the running boards and mudguards.

Dudic emerged and walked along the road to meet the truck. He was joined by others from the hillside as they realised that the newcomers were friends. Greetings were being exchanged when the clip-clop of horses' hooves announced additional arrivals from the direction of Kolasin. Three mounted men were each leading two horses in tow. It was Jamie who recognised one of the riders as the Montenegrin he had first seen at Tito's side in Zagreb: the man he knew as Djordje. Jamie raised his rifle as a kind of salute.

'Greetings, Comrade Djordje.'

Recognition was not mutual. The rider stared long and hard at Jamie. Then the eyes gleamed and beaming delight crossed Djordje's face like a sunrise. He leapt from his horse and seized Jamie in a two-armed embrace that took Jamie's breath away. Stefan arrived to compound the Montenegrin's delight and was embraced with equal fervour. Djordje's pleasure at meeting Jamie and Stefan again was exceeded only by his pride at the circumstances in which he had found them: fighting for his own beloved Montenegro. That pride and pleasure grew when Dudic joined the reunion to regale the high-ranking revolutionary with an account of the exploits of the pair, whom he now regarded as his lieutenants. Jamie groaned with despair when Dudic revealed his nickname 'the Tiger of Bioce' and gave the legend a few more arms and legs than it had had before.

'Our shepherds will be composing tunes on the *curlik* in your honour,' Djordje told Jamie, slapping his back. 'They will sing your name at campfires for a hundred years!'

Although he was not unduly forthcoming on the subject, Djordje revealed that he had been given a roving commission by the supreme command to assess the general situation and introduce some cohesion to the rebel army's efforts. He admitted that administration had been fraught with problems and that the spontaneity and size of the popular uprising had caught its leaders on the hop and without any clear idea on how to direct it. Now that a command structure was taking shape, however, its ability to function had been bedevilled by the new Italian offensive, which had had a devastating effect on the unity and morale of the Montenegrin peasantry.

'We never wanted a frontal war with the Italian Army, but that is what it has become,' Djordje said. 'And it's the kind of war we can't win, because we can't

287

fight it on equal terms. Somehow, we've got to disengage . . . pull in our horns and save our men and our guns to fight another day on ground that we choose.'

'Is that why we were told to disband on the day we took Bioce?' Dudic asked. 'We took no notice of the order. We thought it was crazy – a mistake.'

'The order was countermanded almost as soon as it was issued. But that was only because it caused so much bad feeling. The sensible thing would have been to carry it out. That way, we might have kept our army intact, even if it was an unseen army. Instead, it began to disintegrate when the men heard that the Italians were burning their homes and villages and turning their women and children out on to the hills.'

'We know all about that,' Dudic said. 'A lot of our men just cleared out. You can see what's left.' He smiled. 'They're young, unmarried men. Mostly Communists, like yourself.'

'We Communists are realistic when we are fighting for our lives,' said Djordje. 'We are prepared to lose them and expect no mercy from our enemies. By the same token, we expect no mercy for our homes. What our enemies burn and destroy, we shall build again. It is the survival of our ideals that matters to us – not us or our possessions or houses made of bricks and mortar.'

'You've come from Kolasin. How are things there?' Dudic asked the question blandly, having no wish to get into a political discussion with this man, who – he suspected – was probably fanatical in his views.

'The people in Kolasin are on edge,' Djordje said. 'It is to be expected, I suppose, with the Italians so close. But the situation has shown us who are our friends and who are our enemies.'

'In what way?'

'Some of the worthy citizens are proving less than worthy. They are blaming everything that's gone wrong on us Communists and are ready to side with the Italians if it means saving their town. They are cowards and Fascists and, if I had my way, I'd shoot every one of them out of hand. But that's too simple a solution. It's the Fascist way of doing things, not ours. We've got to convince the doubters and the waverers that we're fighting for the freedom of *all* the people. We Monte-negrins have got to stop fighting each other and stand shoulder to shoulder against an enemy who'll make slaves of us all if we don't'

As Djordje spoke, Dudic kept nodding his bandaged head fiercely in agreement.

'I have felt that from the start,' he said. 'We're all in this together. It's a patriotic war. Although. . . .' He frowned, hestitating to say what was on his mind.

'Although what?' Djordje prompted him.

'The men who stayed with me. . . .' Dudic spoke with diffidence. 'As I told you, they're Communists, and they've done everything I've told them. But they resent me. They resent taking orders from me.'

'Because you are a royalist officer?' Djordje smiled. 'Perhaps they do not quite trust you because you do not quite trust them.' He shrugged. 'All of us must make allowances. Your generals did not do the Royal Army a service when they surrendered to the Germans. You must not blame our young fighters if the thought crosses their minds that all royalist officers are of the same gutless breed.'

Dudic bridled like an angry terrier.

'May God rot them if I ever gave them occasion to think such a thing.'

Djordje grinned and was quick to assure Dudic that he was merely making a point. He had no doubt that Dudic was as brave as a lion. Indeed, he had been quietly assessing Dudic and liking what he saw.

'Perhaps,' he said, 'we two could set an example for the others by showing the kind of unity that's needed. How would you like to serve with me?'

Dudic stared at him, eyes wide with surprise.

'What about my men . . . the job we were given? On whose authority. . . ?'

'I have the authority. And don't worry about the men or the job you've been doing. The comrades from Kolasin will take over here and will be responsible to the command we've set up in the town. Your men can go back to Kolasin in the truck.'

'And me?' Dudic asked. 'What do you want me to do?'

'Advise me,' Djordje said. 'You have been trained as a soldier. You know about fighting. I am only an amateur – although I've been learning fast . . . about what is militarily practical and what isn't. What I *have* been trained to use is my mind. And wars are won as much by brains as by brawn.'

'I have a reputation for recklessness,' Dudic said with a smile.

'And I for cunning,' Djordje replied. 'Perhaps we shall complement each other. There is a time to play the fox and a time to be bold. So, what do you say? Are you bold enough to be the military brain that I shall pick like a crow?'

'I'm bold enough,' Dudic said, infected by Djordje's sense of purpose. A frown darkened his face, however, as he caught site of Jamie and Stefan standing a few yards away. The pair had discreetly moved out of earshot, in deference to him, when he intruded on their conversation with the high-ranking Communist. Djordje saw the frown.

'No second thoughts?' Djordje asked sharply.

'No . . . no,' Dudic murmured. 'New ones.' He was remembering his own need to pick the brains of Jamie and Stefan. To Djordje, he explained, 'It was what you said about brains being as important as brawn in winning wars. It occurred to me that if I go with you, I'll be losing two men who have been a real tower of strength. They're thinkers – more brains between two of them than you're likely to find in an entire platoon of conscripts. But you seemed to know them. You were talking to them.'

Djordje grinned.

'You won't be losing them. I intend to take them with us. They're old friends from Belgrade. You don't need to tell me that Stefan Markovic has a fine mind: I know it. They say he has real genius as a writer. The other one's interesting, too – half Serb and half wild Scottish Highlander. I thought he was the quiet scholarly type but now they call him the Tiger of Bioce, eh?'

Dudic was pleased that he would not, after all, be parting company with Jamie and Stefan. In his eyes, they were outstanding officer material, and it was reassuring that Djordje, too, seemed to appreciate their worth.

'Did you know them at the University in Belgrade?' he asked Djordje.

The other laughed.

'No,' he roared. 'They had just graduated from Lepoglava when I knew them. The prison, that is! They went over the wall!'

'They were in prison?' Dudic's face was a study in astonishment.

'Yes. Didn't you know?' Djordje laughed again. 'Obviously, their education was a great deal more extensive than you realised.' He left Dudic to ponder while he went to break the news to Jamie and Stefan that he had plans for them.

Approaching them, he recalled that there had been three escapers from Lepoglava. The third was a bit of an oddball, an American, who had spouted something marvellously funny in front of Tito about the Jugoslav Communist Party being the next best thing to the Democratic Party in the States. Djordje searched in his mind for the American's name. Then it came to him.

Mannion – that was it. Yes – Mannion. Djordje wondered what had become of him.

Mannion was getting very wet.

The weather system responsible for the tumbling masses of cloud that shrouded the mountainous Moraca valley region in dripping mist was the cause of equally inclement conditions over central Serbia, some two hundred and fifty kilometres to the northeast. For some days, Serbia had been wilting under high temperatures and stifling humidity, but now that succession of hot rainless days was ending with booming thunderclaps and sudden downpours of tropical intensity.

Mannion ignored the drenching rain that had already saturated his shirt so that it stuck to his back like a second skin. He was concentrating on his view of the fallen bridge, trying to shield the binoculars from the rain with one hand and straining his eyes to penetrate the torrent. A sudden easing of the rain improved visibility, allowing him to study the remains of the bridge.

Great wooden spars littered the shallow stream of the river, wedged among the rocks that protruded above the current's swirl. German soldiers – some caped against the rain, some naked to the waist – were working to retrieve the more substantial beams. Some were wading in the river and had attached the tackle of lifting gear to a heavy timber. As Mannion watched, the lifting operation began. Rope had been reeved through the block of a tripod derrick at the bridge's rocky landfall and hooked to the towing bar of a truck. The truck edged forward, taking the strain of the rope and then, slowly, the scorch-blackened beam was hauled from the water.

Mannion passed the field glasses back to Stefan's brother Marko, their owner, who was crouched beside him. They were on a mossy escarpment of rock that jutted from a wooded bluff, some twenty metres above the river and a mere three hundred metres upstream from the toiling Germans.

'They'll have the bridge back in operation by tomorrow,' Mannion said with disgust.

'But not the truckload of men who were crossing when we blew it,' Marko observed, rain dripping from his shaggy beard.

Mannion's eyebrows lifted at Marko's use of the first person plural. *We* indeed, he thought. Marko had been in the village – a good three kilometres from the bridge – during the bridge-blowing operation and had been ten or twelve kilometres away in the hills when the charges were ignited. One man had crawled around in the timber supports of the bridge, laying the charges. And the same man had run the detonating cable up the road and on to the hill and had waited four uncomfortable hours for the truck to appear, before blowing it and its occupants to kingdom come. That man was Mannion.

He did not, however, grudge Marko's collective 'we' in his reference to the bridge's destruction. The others had played a part. Thirty men had temporarily occupied the village and sealed off the road on either side of the bridge so that the explosives could be put in place without hindrance. It had not been a one-man show. But one man had done all the hard work – at some considerable risk – and that entitled Mannion to some proprietorial feelings about the bridge's demolition. He bore no resentment that Marko and others should claim part of the glory for what had been a team effort – but it did rankle a little that his own contribution had demanded all of the labour and most of the sweat.

Two months with Marko's Cetnik company had wrought changes in Mannion. A tough resilience and ready adaptability to unkind and unexpected circumstances had aided him in the past to cope with the cruellest blows of fate. He had not bemoaned misfortune but had accepted it as the chance consequence of his own deliberate actions. It was not his nature to look back in anger and wonder where he had taken the wrong turning. He knew where and when he had made that turning, and why – and there was no point in crying over it. Better to concentrate on the stony way ahead than the road you had come. It was a source of wonder to him, therefore, that his voluntary departure from the path he had shared with Jamie and Stefan – a significant turning point – had not tempted the malign fates to intervene and punish his wilful disregard for their power. Not once had he regretted following the dictates of his heart and chasing a dream – because the substance of that dream had materialised in a manner that exceeded all his wildest expectations. In the joy of loving and being loved, Mannion found a happiness that he had not known was available to mortals. And the experience had changed him.

The happiness of loving Lela and being loved by her was absolute. But the very circumstances of the life they shared gave that happiness an awesome fragility. Its sweetness was sharpened by danger, every second made a hundred times more precious by the knowledge that it was borrowed from a store that could run out within hours.

When Mannion rode off with Lela, leaving Stefan and Jamie at the camp near Cacak, he was excited by his own impetuosity: stimulated by a spirit of recklessness and the need to venture into new and unknown territory. It was as if, having drifted along with Stefan and Jamie – following rather than being led – he had been seized by the need to choose his own direction in life, to reassert that streak of individualism that was so much a part of him. Tagging along with Jamie and Stefan, he had lost control of his own destiny and he had known that only by breaking with them could he win it back. Lela – and the way he had felt about her from their very first meeting – had supplied the sense of purpose he needed to begin a new chapter in his life, and had provided the opportunity.

He put the past firmly behind him. What had gone had gone. Belgrade, Lepoglava, his friendship with Jamie and Stefan, all were ancient history, closeted away as securely as his memories of America. He did not know what to expect when he rode off into the hills around Cacak with Lela. Nor is it likely that he could have forecast the outcome.

The first surprise was his discovery of the size and composition of the Cetnik community over which Marko's colonel ruled. Mannion had anticipated a tight-knit military unit, living rough in caves on some inaccessible mountaintop. He was right only on the difficulty of access to the Cetnik headquarters. The monastery, which was its centre, and the straggle of wood and stone houses nearby, were hidden and remote: far from any roads and reachable only on horse or by foot.

Men, women and children inhabited the monastery – soldiers and civilians – a microcosm of well-heeled city society. The order of priests whose monastery it was had a presence of half a dozen Orthodox clergymen of varying ages, several of whom wore cavalry boots and carried guns. Serbian national identity had sprung from adherence to Orthodoxy, and the rites of religious observance were as much part of the Cetnik community's life as guerrilla warfare.

It took Mannion very little time to realise that his main qualifications for recruitment to the Cetnik strength – his dual fluency in English and Serbo-Croat – did not equip him for the task expected of him. The Cetniks *had* established short-wave radio contact with the British in Cairo, but all outgoing traffic ceased with the death of the fugitive embassy official, whose knowledge of the ciphers involved had died with him. He had left behind two notebooks full of handwritten tables of alphabetic and numeral sequences and copious *aides-memoire*, but these would have baffled even a trained cryptologist.

The notebooks undoubtedly contained the codes and callsigns used to communicate with Cairo and must have been copied from a British Foreign Ministry manual, but they had been disguised in a manner that would have made them comprehensible only to the copier – presumably as a guard against them falling into the wrong hands.

After the embassy official's death, the Cetniks were still able to raise Cairo, but what came back over the air waves in Morse were strings of five-letter groups that were quite undecipherable.

Mannion's knowledge of English was no help in translating these puzzles, and he had to face the fact that all he represented to the Cetniks was another mouth to feed. Only by chance was it discovered that he had a value to them of far greater significance than ever hitherto expected.

This occurred when, out of curiosity, he was examining the construction of the monastery building and was lost in admiration of the skill that had gone into its erection in so forbidding a location. Shielded on one side by sheer rock face and perched above a drop well over a hundred metres, it blended naturally with its surroundings, becoming part of the landscape. From afar, it was invisible, merging with the face of the moutain; at close quarters, the engineering skill with which that effect had been achieved was mind-boggling. This was no monolithic Manhattan wonder of steel and concrete raised in a year with modern know-how, but the product of a so-called primitive time – it had stood for more than six hundred years, a monument to man's spirit and ingenuity.

Some Cetnik officers observed his interest, and their suspicions were aroused. They questioned Mannion, whereupon he explained his great admiration for the skill of the thirteenth-century builders who had constructed the monastery on a site that offered such a challenge. As someone who had worked in the construction business – he said – he was truly impressed.

It was at this point that the Cetnik officers took a sudden and excited interest in Mannion and his past. He found himself admitting that he had studied structural engineering in college in New York and that he had had three years' practical work in the construction industry.

Did he know about the construction of bridges? Yes, he knew something about bridges and how they were built. What about explosives? Yes, he knew something about explosives, although he wasn't an expert. Often in New York, when demolition was taking place on a site that was being developed, it had been necessary to use explosives in the clearing operation.

Expert or not, before the day was out, Mannion found himself conscripted to become the Cetnik command's chief engineer and sabotage officer – in succession to a much-relieved cavalry officer whose two previous attempts at blowing bridges had left them virtually undamaged. Dazed as he was by this surprise development, it was by no means the most unpredictable outcome of his decision to join up with the Cetniks.

Mannion had not foreseen, when he parted company with Jamie and Stefan, that within ten short days he would be a married man. But the desire of Mannion and Lela for each other was such and the need to declare it openly to the world was so strong that the days preceding the ceremony seemed an eon in passing.

The entire Cetnik community took part in the celebration. Mannion and Lela took their vows before an Orthodox priest, who was resplendent in white robes intricately threaded with gold. Before the iconostasis in the monastery church, they pledged their love until death and, later, they joined the surprisingly lavish feast organised in their honour. Wine flowed like water at this outdoor *slava*, and the priest blessed and cut the special *kolac* before the huge family cake was distributed for all to eat.

The festivities went on long into the night, with dancing of many variations of the *kolo* to the music of bagpipe and flute. Mannion and Lela stole away from the merriment at its height and retired to Lela's cell-like room in the monastery, which, until that day, she had shared with an elderly woman who was the mother of one of the Cetnik officers. There, Lela shyly gave herself to Mannion, and they slept naked in each other's arms for the first time.

Now, in every minute that he spent apart from Lela, Mannion's mind soared with joy at memory of their lovemaking, and part of him longed for the moment when he again held her in his arms. As the rain continued to spatter on his shirted back and he watched the German soldiers repairing the bridge, it was Lela who occupied his uppermost thoughts. She seemed to thrive on the danger which daily they both shared. This was the only source of argument between them. Lela was in the habit of gathering intelligence for the Cetnik commander, visiting towns and villages to contact the wide Cetnik network of spies and informers. It had been on one such excursion that she met Mannion, near Cacak – and she frequently reminded him of the fact when he tried to get her to opt out of such missions. She looked on the intelligence-gathering as an extension of her job as radio operator – a job which had made little demands since the death of the Englishman. And she was, after all, a soldier in the Cetnik cause – she was wont to remind Mannion – and risk-taking was part of a soldier's life.

Much as Mannion argued, he made no headway with his fiercely proud bride on the matter, and she continued to gather the information which allowed Mannion and his Cetnik comrades to carry out their frequent forays to ambush German troops and blow up bridges used by their convoys.

The bridge below his and Marko's observation point was the third that Mannion had successfully demolished. Its destruction gave him the greatest satisfaction because he had looked on the first two almost as trial runs: vehicles for learning his newfound trade as sabotage officer. The Cetniks had considerably more faith in his aptitude for the job than he had himself – but he had learned a lot on the first two operations that had helped with the third.

Now, as he watched the German engineers at work on the bridge below, it was hard to contain his dismay at their method and efficiency. He had no doubt that, by next day, they would have a new bridge in place across the river and that it would be every bit as strong and functional as its predecessor.

'Have you seen enough?' Marko asked him. 'We don't want to be late for Lela.'

Mannion did not need reminding about Lela. He was a great deal more worried about her than he was about the bridge. He had not wanted her to go down into the village, with so many Germans swarming all over the place. Their presence was due entirely to the bridge sabotage, and the chances were that they would be suspicious of everybody and trigger-happy.

She had laughed at his fears.

'If they look twice at me, it won't be because they think I'm a saboteur!' she had said lightly.

'That's some consolation,' Mannion had complained. 'It's bad enough worrying that they'll shoot you, without going out of my mind wondering if they're going to rape you!'

But she had gone, despite his worries and his strictures, unaware of how fetchingly beautiful she looked to him in the patterned peasant skirt and loose three-quarter-length waistcoat. To give verisimilitude to her role, she was bent almost double under the bundle of firewood they had gathered for her, and which she was to deliver to a sympathiser as if she were one of the family.

Mannion and Marko left their vantage point and made their way to where they had left the horses – their own and Lela's. Then they walked the horses through the woods to a clearing that was only a short distance from the road which twisted downhill into the village. This was the rendezvous to which Lela had promised to return by midday.

They were early, and the rain had stopped. They stripped off their shirts and tried to dry their sodden equipment. Mannion cleaned his rifle and oiled it. Midday came and went, and there was no sign of Lela. Leaving Marko with the horses, Mannion went to scout the road. From a thicket-covered bank, he found a perfect view of the village and the road that wound up towards him. It was deserted, as the village seemed to be. The only sound was of distant hammering, coming from beyond the village, from the direction of the river and the fallen bridge.

The minutes dragged by. Mannion waited, watching, seething with anxiety for Lela. If anything had happened to her . . . . Anger boiled in him: anger at the Colonel and his coterie of senior officers, who used her so casually as a go-between because they believed a woman was less likely to attract attention than a man. Lela, with her looks, was the kind of woman who would attract attention anywhere! Why didn't the Colonel and his chums shave some of the hair off their faces and do their own goddamned spying? Their beards were the give-away, they said. The Germans knew the fighting Cetniks had sworn to go bearded until their country was liberated, so they arrested bearded men as a matter of principle.

The Cetniks were amused at Mannion's over-protective attitude towards Lela, which they seemed to think stemmed from a jealous husband's reluctance to let her out of his sight. And, mischievously, Lela encouraged their jokes, using them as a lever to make Mannion think that he was being faintly ridiculous. Her information-collecting sorties, she claimed, were as harmless as shopping trips and, indeed, she frequently used them as such.

Well, there was precious little shopping to be done in the village down below. Maybe, on trips to the small towns she had visited, Lela had been able to preserve some anonymity because there were plenty of people on the streets – but not down there in a place that was scarcely big enough to boast a hundred inhabitants. It would only need one of them to point the finger at Lela as the stranger in their midst and she could be in trouble. Some of the villagers had not taken it at all kindly when the Cetniks rode in and took the place over in the middle of the night. Nor had they been happy at the destruction of *their* bridge. They were all for the Cetniks blowing up bridges – but why *theirs*? What was so important about *their* bridge?

The truth was that although the Germans used the bridge a lot, they did not take the trouble to guard it, making it a relatively soft target. Well, as sure as God made little apples, Mannion thought, the Germans would be guarding the rebuilt bridge in the future. And, if nothing else, the Cetniks would have accomplished one legitimate objective of their sabotage: to compel the enemy occupying forces to spread their thin resources wider and wider.

One o'clock passed and still Lela did not come. By then, Mannion had become restive enough to be con-templating the desperate measure of going down to the village to look for her. Only the fear that so rash an action could be self-defeating deterred him. If Lela was perfectly safe but biding her time, he could screw everything up by throwing caution to the wind. He decided to wait thirty more minutes.

Less than ten had gone when he was suddenly alert to movements in the village. He could hear activity, rather than see it, because his view was restricted by a house at the high end of the village which hid a bend in the road. Shouted commands echoed up to him, mingling with other sounds: doors being slammed, a motor revving, muted traffic noises.

A military staff car came into view on the road, emerging from the bend hidden by the view-obscuring house. Two German officers sat in its open back. Mannion instinctively retreated deeper into his covering thicket, showering himself with droplets from wet leaves as he did so. He gripped his rifle in readiness, but the car only came a short distance up the hill towards him. It stopped and the two officers got out, abreast a flat shelf of stony hillside. The Germans seemed to be arguing, their voices carrying to Mannion. The argument was short-lived, won apparently by the man in the darker uniform – presumably the senior of the two.

The other officer, the set of his head and hunch of his shoulders depicting anger and resentment, returned to the road and strode off to the village. The officer in black watched him go, disdainfully. He returned to the car, climbed in the back and lit a cigarette.

The German made a tempting target for Mannion. He was unmissable, at a range of three hundred metres. Mannion put aside the temptation. There was Lela to think of. He tried to construct a meaning from the altercation he had witnessed – but he could think of none. It was illuminating in one respect. Mannion had thought that German soldiers did what they were told, immediately, and without question. Clearly, that was not always the case. He felt a wayward pang of sympathy for the enemy officer who had gone stomping back to the village on foot. In any argument, Mannion's sympathies always went to the little guy who tried to buck the system.

Five more minutes passed. Voices carried up to him from the village: shouts and wails, women screeching. There was the sharp report of a single shot being fired – then an ominous silence.

A big German Army truck appeared on the road, labouring on the gradient above the end house. The officer in the staff car got out and waved it down, directing it to turn across the road, blocking it. Then a procession on foot appeared. A dozen German soldiers were herding a group of villagers: elderly men, most of them, but two women, too. The women were old and walking very slowly.

Mannion held his breath, not knowing what interpretation to put on the scene but instinctively uneasy. He was relieved that Lela was not in the group being herded up the road. The officer in black shouted an order and the soldiers shepherded the villagers off the road to the open hillside near the big truck. Then the soldiers were ordered back down the road towards the village, where a small crowd had appeared: more villagers – men, women and children. They were silent, cautious, as if reluctant to venture further than the village limits. The soldiers, hurrying down the hill, made sure they did not venture further. Forming a line across the road, they motioned the newcomers back towards the village. Mannion's heart leapt when he saw Lela amongst the group. She was one of several women who backed down the road, then halted and faced the Germans in a sullen line, as if intent on no further retreat. The Germans halted too, not forcing the issue.

Mannion's attention was so taken up with Lela and the confrontation at the village end that the sudden burst of machine-gun fire from the draped rear of the truck almost made him jump from his skin with shock. Eyes

303

popping from his head, his gaze was jerked back to the flat shelf of open hillside, where the huddle of elderly villagers went down like ninepins and now lay in a convulsing heap. A second burst of fire ended the convulsions. From the edge of the village a great wail of angry grief issued from the watching crowd.

Numb with disbelief and horror, Mannion sighted his rifle on the black-uniformed officer, but his hands were trembling so fiercely that the weapon was wobbling like a live thing. He lowered it again, assailed by the sudden certainty that a single shot from him would merely provoke an even greater massacre, and the victims would be Lela and the villagers clustered below. He had to force himself to relax his grip on the rifle, so consuming was his anger and so compelling was the urge to use it. Eyes burning with hatred, he saw the black-clad officer return to his car and light another cigarette. Then the staff car was manoeuvring to face back down the hill and bumping off the road to make its way round the truck. Horn blaring, it coursed down towards the village, forcing a way through the German soldiers and past the now silent crowd of villagers. It was followed by the truck. Then the soldiers on foot disappeared into the village, thrusting past the cluster of Serbs who stared at them with silent loathing.

A stream of villagers now ran up the road to the killing ground to gather in anguish around the fallen bodies and claim their loved ones among the dead. The sound of pining echoed on the hillside.

Mannion saw Lela amongst the grieving figures. She offered a comforting arm to a stout woman in black, and Mannion saw the woman's angry rejection of the arm and heard her voice raised in anger. Lela retreated, hesitatingly at first and then hurrying as other mourning women shouted at her. She came up the road, half-running, and Mannion scrambled towards the road, slipping and sliding on the wet ground, to meet her. She was distraught, weeping, and breathless from her exertions.

Mannion held her briefly, hushing her incoherent attempts to explain her tears.

'I saw what happened . . . everything! Don't try to speak now,' he urged her, and guided her away, half-carrying her. Deep in the cover of the trees, he allowed the pace to slow. Then he walked her, supporting her with one arm while he murmured endearments and tried to comfort her. By the time they reached the clearing, she had recovered some composure.

Marko, taut with anxiety, bombarded them with questions. He had heard the shooting. He blanched when Mannion told him tersely that the Germans had gunned down a dozen or more villagers in cold blood.

'It was because of us!' Lela cried out. 'Because of the bridge! Because their soldiers were killed! The people in the village were given until noon today to hand over the saboteurs.' Tears flooded Lela's face as she tried to continue. 'Oh, Brad,' she sobbed, 'we brought it on those poor people. They could have betrayed me. . . .'

'I know, honey, I know.' Mannion held her, trying to comfort her and, at the same time, feeling an icy prickle of stark dread at how close he had come to losing her. Silently, he offered a prayer of gratitude for those brave angry people down there in the village. They had allowed the slaughter of their loved ones rather than betray Lela – but how tempted they must have been to hand her over to the Germans! No wonder that those women had rounded on Lela in anger when confronted with the grisly reality of the price of their silence.

Mannion, Lela and Marko made the long ride back to the monastery camp in near silence. There, the news that the Germans had shot so many innocent people as a reprisal for the attack on the bridge was received with shock and misgiving.

No one was more deeply shaken than the cavalry

Colonel who commanded the Cetniks. He wept openly when Lela reported all that had happened, and Mannion supplied his own eyewitness account.

'What kind of monsters are these who would do such things?' he asked and, looking very old, went off alone to the monastery church to pray for the dead and seek divine guidance on how to fight a war against the murderers of civilians. An hour later, a messenger arrived from the town of Kraljevo to say that the Germans were posting notices all over the region with warning of dire punishments for Serbian acts of terrorism. In future, for every German life taken in terrorist acts, one hundred Serbians would be shot in reprisal.

One man without any illusions about the depths of barbarity to which man could sink in war was Aleksander Popovic. At the age of thirty-one, he had had his fill of war and killing and had decided that he wanted no more for as long as he lived. It mattered not to him that he was a national hero and that, if he stayed on in the Army, he was almost assured the highest rank attainable. So, in 1919, at the height of his fame, this hero of countless battles against the Turks had retired to a remote valley of Montenegro, not far from the Albanian border, to live a reclusive existence. Over the years, a succession of political parties had tried to woo him away from his high wilderness home, anxious to capitalise on his name and the heroic legend attached to it.

Popovic had rejected them all, with the finality of a man who had discovered the secret of true tranquillity and knew that it was dependent on the distance he could keep from the human race and its follies. Neither silver nor gold nor the promise of position and power could lure him from his spartan solitude, where nature and the elements were at once man's only enemy and his abiding consolation.

In spite of his chosen isolation – or perhaps because of it – the more enshrined he became in Montenegrin folklore as a great warrior hero. His withdrawal to a region that was more the haunt of the wolf and the bear than man's, merely added an aura of mysticism to the magic of his name. Only one thing, it was said, would bring the old warrior down from his lair. And that was the imperilment of his country's freedom and a national call to arms.

But the Royal Army did not call him out of retirement when Jugoslavia was invaded by the Axis powers. This oversight was not repeated by the invading Italians, who knew all about Popovic and were aware of his value as a figure round whom resistance to their rule might be rallied. Failing to win his voluntary cooperation, the Italians arrested Popovic and brought him down under carabinieri escort to the town of Berane. There, he was held in custody but only briefly. He killed his guard – a Muslim militiaman – with his bare hands and escaped. The Italians put a price on his head, but Popovic was still at large when the hunt for him was overtaken by more significant events – notably, the general uprising which swept Montenegro and crushed the Italian garrisons in the interior.

'And now you want to find Popovic?' It was Stefan who put the question to Djordje. They had stopped to eat a simple lunch and were waiting for the rain to slacken before they continued their journey. Their shelter was a large rocky overhang, just off the steep stony road that led from the canyon of the Moraca River and across the mountain to the Tara River, further east. Djordje, his two escorts, Jamie, Stefan and Dudic were sitting in a half-circle on a shelf of dry rock; the horses stood in a passive group nearby. Djordje had been relating Popovic's history, by way of enlightening the others on his immediate plans.

'Our People's Army needs men of Popovic's calibre to

307

command them in the field,' Djordje said, in reply to Stefan. 'Just to have him on our military staff would be an inspiration to our men. My own father fought under him and said he would have followed him to hell. Even the Turks respected him, feared him – and there were damnéd few enemies put the wind up Johnny Turk.'

'The Turks still hate him,' Dudic commented. 'He paid them back in kind. They say he outdid the Turks in cruelty – and that takes a bit of doing. They've never forgiven him.'

'Well, it's never bothered him, living where he chose – so close to Albania,' Djordje said. 'The Gegs rule these mountains, and killing infidels is a sport to them.'

Dudic smiled.

'They say he lived where he did so that he could spit across the border at them.'

Djordje laughed.

'I heard it differently. I was told that it was because he could stand on top of a mountain and let them see him pissing in the direction of Mecca.'

The rain eased to a swirling drizzle and the little party moved on, descending from the highest point of the road to reach the west bank of the Tara and follow it north.

Neither Jamie nor Stefan numbered horsemanship amongst their accomplishments but, before the day was over, they had painfully acquired sufficient skill to give a passable imitation of a pair born to the saddle. They were agreed on one point: that if it was to be their lot to traverse the lofty wilderness tracks of Montenegro, it was infinitely preferable to do so on the back of a horse than on foot with a thirty-kilo pack on the back.

Both men had been agreeably surprised by Djordje's invitation to accompany him on his travels, although puzzled by his vague explanation of the role they had to fill. They had concluded that they were expected to be additional bodyguards.

'I need a few more guns around me,' Djordje had said.

'Who knows what we'll find on the other side of the mountain?' It was the first intimation he had given them that he intended to cross the Moraca and go east. This had meant going downriver for some way, in order to find a crossing place – and the one they had found was perilously close to the advance Italian positions above Bioce.

Indeed, they had come under riflefire from Italian lookouts after they crossed the river and were ascending the slope above the east bank. Fortunately, they had been heading away from the Italians, back up the valley, and had been able to get quickly out of range. Soon, they had reached the road that twists from Bioce out of the Moraca valley and then down to the Tara.

A hazy afternoon sun was blinking through watery clouds when the six horsemen reached the Tara. The road was no more than a stony track along the Tara's banks. It followed the course of the river, crossing and recrossing it where the steepness of the gorge denied passage on one side or the other.

Making good progress along the dozen kilometres with the river in company, they reached the small town of Matesevo. They halted only briefly, so that Djordje could glean information on the situation further east. None of it was good.

An Italian column was driving westward from the city of Pec through the great Rugovo Gorge, and there had been fierce fighting around the Cakor Pass. The Montenegrins were slowing the Italian advance but could not stop it. They were being forced back all the time.

The news from Berane, a little to the north, was equally depressing. There, when the Montenegrins rose, the local Muslims had taken the side of the Italians and unleashed a reign of terror on their Orthodox neighbours.

The party took the road east out of Matesevo, keeping

up a brisk pace in spite of the little groups of refugees heading in the other direction. Two hours later, stark little clusters of stone and wooden houses came into view – the town of Andrijevica.

'We'll spend the night here,' Djordje announced, to the great relief of Jamie and Stefan, who had done more than enough riding for one day. While they saw to the horses, Djordje went off in search of clues to the whereabouts of Aleksander Popovic. He was in luck. Popovic had spent three days in Andrijevica after his escape from Berane, hiding out at the home of a veteran soldier who had lost an eye in the war of 1912. The veteran had been reluctant to say very much about the present whereabouts of Popovic until Djordje revealed his reason for wanting to find him.

'Will he join our fight?' Djordje asked the old soldier.

'He is only waiting to be asked,' the man assured him. 'He would have served in the ranks, if necessary, when the war first started – but the call he expected from the Army did not come. I'm too old at fifty-five, he told me. Can you imagine that? Too old at fifty-five! I tell you there's a lot of fight in him yet, and all it needs is somebody like you to tell him that.'

'I will if I can find him,' Djordje said.

'If you go to the right place, he will find you,' the old man said with a twinkle in his eye. 'Do you know his lair on the mountain?'

'Is he there? Is that where he is?'

'He will not be far away. Go there. He will find you. But be careful. Others have been looking for him, too.'

'Others?'

'Turks. The man he killed in Berane was a Turk, the son of a chief in the Geg country. They have sworn to give Colonel Popovic a lingering death.'

'And does he know this?' Djordje asked.

'He knows, all right. He said he would be ready for them. He made a joke of it. . . . If Allah wills it, he said, I will die at the hand of the Turk – because I sent plenty of them straight to Paradise – but I will die on my own mountain and send a few more souls to Paradise first.'

'Has he many men with him?'

The one-eyed veteran laughed.

'No, unless you count that hoary old villain who's been his servant since his Army days. And he's seventy if he's a day. There has always been just the two of them up there . . . and never a woman. The Colonel had a wife and a baby son – but the Turks butchered them in the other war. He never married again.'

Armed with a map drawn by the one-eyed veteran, Djordje and his coterie of five rode out of Andrijevica in the early-morning light of a day that promised to be warm. The clouds were high, fleecy-white, sailing across the mountaintops like convoys of galleons. The riders had the gushing River Lim for company. As they rode down the valley road, the crash of artillery fire rumbled ominously from the east.

'Italian guns,' Dudic informed the others. He gauged the distance at anything up to ten kilometres – but they sounded much closer. A family of peasants, pushing a cart containing their worldly possessions, told the riders that the Montenegrin defenders had been unable to hold the Italians at the 1500-metre-high Cakor Pass. Soon they would be coming down this very road.

At the village of Murino, the travellers encountered weary remnants of the force who had been fighting the Italians. They had acquired a small field gun, from which the firing pin had been removed, and a blacksmith was trying to improvise another. They also had a supply of shells for the fieldpiece but these were minus the nose detonators.

'What's the point of firing shells that won't explode?' Dudic asked an officer working on the gun, an ex-Royal Army man, like himself.

'Because the noise of that gun going off will make us

311

feel better!' the officer said, with a grin. 'It's the only artillery we've got!'

For some reason, the encounter cheered the six riders up as they headed south, away from the Cakor road. They followed a tributary of the Lim for some distance before crossing it on a wire-rope bridge that had a planked walkway. The bridge swung alarmingly as the horses were led across, one at a time. The animals were reluctant to set foot on this swinging catwalk but, once they had been persuaded to do so, they nimbly picked their way to the other side.

Their track – barely recognisable as such – now led east and steeply upwards until its snakelike course wound away to the right to follow the contour of the mountainside. Below them, the ground dropped away to lush grassland watered by streams which ran into Lake Plav: a shimmering turquoise lagoon, some kilometres to the southwest. Looking back over their shoulders, the riders could see the lake, its placid blue surface like a stretch of fallen sky, laid flat like a mirror below the towering peaks of the massif.

The lake soon became lost to view, shut from sight by breathtaking heights as they entered a valley. They identified from their crude map the confluence of two rushing mountain streams. The track they had to follow was the most southerly of these – and they did so, more in hope than in certainty, because it seemed to lead straight to a canyon end and impassible mountain. A kilometre further on, however, they found that the stream bent away from the rockface at right angles and was issuing from a valley that had been hidden from their sight. It was entered by a precipitous defile, whose narrow gloomy bottom the sun never reached.

Emerging on the far side, the riders found themselves in a pleasant grassy valley, its steep slopes clothed by woods rising to craggy pinnacled grandeur. They knew they had found the valley where they would find

Aleksander Popovic or – as the veteran in Andrijevica had warned them – Aleksander Popovic would find them.

'What now, comrade?' Dudic asked Djordje.

'We'll rest here and wait,' Djordje said. 'If the old man was right, Popovic will come to us.'

'How will he know we're here?'

'I don't know. The old man said he would.' Djordje smiled and looked up at the craggy top of the ravine through which they had passed. 'Perhaps these ravens up there are his warning system. They're making enough noise.'

Dudic frowned.

'I don't think they're interested in us. Sounds as if they're fighting over a rabbit or something. I think I'll go and take a look.'

Djordje raised no objection. It would be possible to see a long way up the valley from the crags; perhaps even spot the location of Popovic's house. Dudic took Jamie with him.

It was easy climbing but hard work. Both men were sweating profusely long before they reached the top. They found themselves on a grassy plateau strewn with boulders and patchy shrub. What struck them immediately, however, was the spectacular view, not only of the hidden valley but back down the route of their trek.

The ravens scattered, screeching, at the approach of the two men. The place where they had been feeding was partially hidden by a boulder the height of a man. Curiosity took Jamie forward, ahead of Dudic. He stopped in revulsion at the sight of the carrion on which the birds had been feasting.

It was a man – or had been a man. The bearded face was eyeless. The head had been half-severed. And the body had been ripped open from throat to belly.

6

War Without Mercy

Jamie turned away from his grotesque discovery. Apalled by the sight of the corpse, his stomach was turning over at the stench assailing his nostrils. He waited for Dudic to complete his own horrified examination. This did not take long. Hand over his nose and mouth, he rejoined Jamie – upwind of the putrefying horror.

'The old man who stayed with Popovic? Do you think that's who it is?' Jamie asked the question, fighting a desire to gag.

Dudic nodded.

'It must be. Holy mother of God, he's not a pretty sight!' He pondered the immense views from the plateau, as if working something out. 'This place. . . . If that ravine over there is the only way in, the old man must have been a lookout. Perhaps he and Popovic took it in turns to watch, so that they were never taken by surprise . . . .'

Jamie's eyebrows lifted.

'Somebody must have taken the old man by surprise. How?'

Dudic shrugged.

'Who knows? Old men get tired. They fall asleep. On the other hand, if whoever did it knew he was here and came visiting by night. . . .'

'Turks?'

'They certainly weren't friends. And my bet is that they're still not far away.'

'How can you tell?' Jamie asked. 'From the smell, he could have been lying there a week.'

'Not in this heat. And the buzzards and the flies have hardly started on him. You'd know if you'd seen what they can do to a sheep in a week.' He stared grimly at Jamie. 'That poor devil was alive at this time yesterday. My guess is that he was killed in the early hours of this morning. Last night at the latest.'

'Then we'd better tell the others. . . . ' Jamie's voice trailed away. 'Good God, look!' Dudic turned to stare in the direction of Jamie's pointing hand. From the top of the hidden valley, a cloud of black smoke was rising above the treetops.

A hurried conference was held when the pair climbed down from the ravine's top to rejoin the others. The discovery of the old man's body and the telltale smoke from further up the valley did not augur well for the fate of Popovic. It was Dudic's theory that a raiding party of venging Turks had come to the valley with the specific purpose of killing Popovic and his retainer. How big that raiding party was could not be estimated, but its existence so close posed a very real threat to the band of six. Dudic was sure of only one thing: that the raiders had entered the valley by the same route as themselves – having taken care of Popovic's lookout first – and they would leave the same way, via the defile.

Djordje, faced with the decision-making, considered his dilemma. He could abandon his mission to Popovic and make haste back to Andrijevica, with every chance of being seen by the raiders and pursued. Or he could wait for the raiders to leave and either ambush them or let them pass, depending on the size of the raiding party. But even these alternatives posed problems. If they allowed the raiders to pass, it would put the raiders between them and their own path to safety.

'We wait for them in the ravine,' he said. 'We do not let them pass.' He looked towards Dudic, eyebrows raised questioningly. 'What does the military expert say to that?'

'It is a bold decision,' Dudic said with a smile. 'For a cunning man.'

They concealed and tethered the horses beyond the narrow defile and then returned to climb the ravine's precipitous sides to choose ambush points with care. The hollows and ledges of the ravine's twin faces provided an abundance of ideal locations. Dudic directed the choice, three to each side, and disposed to create the most effective crossfire. Then the waiting began.

It was a disciplined waiting, as Dudic had demanded it should be: no friendly calls from one position to another to ease the tedium or the nervous strain. Each man had the company of his thoughts; each his separate measure of fear or comfort. For none did the minutes rush by. The passage of each was drawn out. Only when measured in decades does time fly – and only then when they have gone.

The end of the waiting came suddenly. From sunlight beyond the ravine came the sound of voices: an un-restrained cackle that was almost boisterous in its humour and lack of caution. The newcomers came on foot. They walked with the brisk loping stride of hillmen. They wore the baggy pantaloons and balloon-like shirts of the Muslim, and favoured a variety of headgear – from turban-like swathe to brimless cap. In their midst were two mules, with loads that included a leather armchair as well as other household utensils. The men were festooned in arms: rifles, pistols, knives. One man had a handsome sword draped from his neck – the kind of sword that a Serbian officer might have carried on ceremonial occasions.

Jamie counted thirteen men in the straggle entering the ravine and held his breath in expectation of more to come. But none came. The procession had reached the middle of the defile when Dudic opened fire. It was the signal the others had been waiting for. The gorge echoed to the chorus of rapid fire from the six rifles. There was scarcely a cadence between the emptying of six magazines and an encore. In thirty seconds, it was all over. Thirteen bodies sprawled on the narrow riverbank below. Only the mules lived, but both had gone down under the hail of bullets and were screaming pitifully. Djordje, the first to descend, ended their braying with two pistol shots.

When the others joined him, he was holding the ceremonial sword, which he had retrieved from the body of the man they took to be the Muslims' leader.

'Colonel Popovic's sword?' Dudic asked him.

'I'm afraid it could be,' Djordje said grimly. 'Something tells me we are not going to find him alive.'

But Aleksander Popovic was alive when, an hour later, they did find him. Alive, but so near to death that it did not matter. He was beyond their aid, having passed beyond the screaming and the groaning of agony that he had endured alone, his life strung by a thread in a fitful limbo of fainting and near fainting.

The six had ridden up to the high end of the valley, towards the smoke that Jamie and Dudic saw earlier. Its source was not difficult to find. Drifting smoke filled their nostrils as they followed the stream up through the woods. It had led them to what remained of Popovic's house. Fallen rafters still burned in the charred debris. Little else was left of what had been a substantial timber dwelling. The outline of four rooms could be seen from the rectangles of blackened stone that marked the wall bases.

On the grassy bank that fronted the house were scattered some of the old warrior's possessions that had not been plundered by the Muslims: photographs of his dead wife and child, their frames smashed; a large cabinet gramophone, its sides kicked in and its winding handle wrenched out.

And there, too, was Aleksander Popovic, scourge of

317

the Turks. He had been spreadeagled on the table from his own kitchen, his wrists and ankles roped to the corners. And he had been impaled. A stake – wandlike in girth and whittled white – had been driven into his naked body at the groin, and it protruded at his neck. The obscene cruelty of it was such that they could scarcely bring themselves to look upon the horror.

It was Djordje, his handsome face pale with shock and revulsion, who made the discovery that Popovic was still alive. The old warrior's misted eyes fluttered open and he tried to speak. But the sounds that burbled from his blood-flecked lips were incoherent. Only his eyes spoke, and the message was unmistakable. They flickered from the pistol, which Djordje had drawn on their cautious approach to the house and still held in his hand, to Djordje's face – and they contained a look of agonised pleading.

Djordje nodded, understanding. Tears coursed from his eyes.

He moved to one side and, placing the muzzle of his pistol to Popovic's ear, he pulled the trigger. Then he turned away, his face ravaged, to stare sightlessly across the magnificent vista which, for twenty years, had greeted Popovic from his front door. Below the house and the saddle on which it was perched, the land dropped in a precipice, and beyond was a spectacular panorama of the Prokletije range, where it extended deep into Albania. Djordje did not see its beauty. He seemed to sense the stares of the five men who had witnessed what he had done; they were grouped behind him in a half-circle, only a short distance away. He turned on them, eyes blazing.

'I had to do it!' he shouted. 'It was the only merciful thing!'

But there was no accusation in the staring eyes, only compassion. It was Dudic who spoke.

'It took courage to do what you did, Comrade Djordje.

318

More than I've got. We know you acted from humanity.' He looked round at the others. 'Do I speak for all of you? Is there one of you who would not have done the same in the name of mercy?'

'It was a kindness,' Stefan said, his voice not much more than a whisper. 'One of us had to end his suffering.'

'None of us blame you,' Jamie said. 'I think it was what he was trying to say . . . the way he looked at you . . . to make it quick.'

Until they came upon the awful spectacle, Jamie had felt uneasy about the slaughter of the Muslims in the defile. They had been shot down without a single reservation being expressed. It was assumed that one of their number had killed the old man above the ravine and that they were hostile – but they had not been given the opportunity to demonstrate that hostility.

Now, Jamie could feel only loathing for the dead Muslims, the authors of the lingering torture that had been inflicted on Popovic. No wonder Uncle Milan had never lost his hatred of the Turks. Their barbarity was unforgivable.

He could think of nothing else as they set about the task of burying Popovic. He relieved his feelings by voicing his outrage.

'Now you can begin to understand the kind of hatreds that bedevil our country,' Stefan told him. 'They are bred in the bone.'

'He's right,' Dudic said. 'He's a Serb and should know. It's the same with us, who are Montenegrin by birth and Serbian by tradition. We have never had any difficulty in hating Turks. They've been giving us reasons for hating them for four hundred years. What they did to Popovic today is only a sample. It used to be their favourite way of executing infidels.'

'It's barbaric – as bad as crucifixion!' Jamie declared angrily.

'The same kind of death,' Dudic said. 'In the old days,

the Turk executioners were supposed to be an elite. Their skill was judged by the length of time it took their victims to die. If they skewered a Christian and it took the poor beggar less than three days to die, they were considered to have botched the job.'

Jamie shuddered.

'I just can't grasp the mentality of people who are capable of that kind of cruelty,' he said. 'It's beyond forgiveness.'

'And forgetting,' said Dudic. 'An aunt of mine was made to stand and watch while the Turks flayed her young brother live. She said that she would carry the sound of his screams to her grave and that her hate for the Turks would still be with her on the day of resurrection.'

'The Turks are not the only ones who kill and torture one minute and bow to their God in the next, ' Stefan reminded them. 'All religions are the same, with Christianity no better than the rest. How many heretics have been burned, or disembowelled, or had their eyes put out in the name of a loving Christ?'

Dudic smiled tolerantly.

'Blame man, not the God he worships, comrade. Your Communism is a religion, too, and every bit as capable as all the others of tearing the bowels out of non-believers.'

'If Communism is a religion, then it's the only one in sight that will save Jugoslavia!' Stefan retorted passionately. 'We draw no boundaries. It doesn't matter to us if a man is born Turk or Christian, Orthodox or Catholic, Buddhist or Muslim. . . . Our faith is in the brotherhood of all peoples and their entitlement to freedom and justice.'

'We all want freedom and justice,' Dudic said, reasonably.

'But we'll never have it until we have created a new society,' Stefan argued. 'The kind of society that only revolutionary socialism can bring.'

Dudic, who had become used to Stefan's seriousness and liked him, in spite of it, grinned broadly.

'We've a lot of soldering to do before that day comes,' he said. With a twinkle in his eye, he added, 'But who knows? If this war lasts long enough, you'll maybe make a convert of me yet.'

They buried Aleksander Popovic in the shallow grave they had scooped from the hillside with improvised tools. When it was done, Djordje plunged the old warrior's ceremonial sword into the soil at his head, while the others flanked the grave in a solemn line.

'Sleep well in the land you loved,' Djordje said, staring at the ground, and bowed his head once in salute. He nodded towards Dudic, who brought himself stiffly to attention and saluted. Still at the salute, Dudic gave the order to fire one round. Four rifles pointed at the sky and the mountains echoed to the sound of a single volley.

They rode away from the valley top in silence. It was evening before they reached the swinging bridge, and light was fading from the sky when they rode into Murino. The village was packed with refugees and guerrilla fighters who had fallen back before the advancing Italian army.

The entire civil population of the villages along the Lim was, it appeared, being evacuated ahead of the Italian advance. With their cattle and possessions, most of these refugees had crossed to the west bank of the river and were streaming through Andrijevica and Matesevo towards Kolasin. The villages they had left could be seen from Murino; orange tongues of flame and pillars of smoke signalled that the Italians had passed through and had not spared the humblest dwelling from the torch. Fanned out, ahead of the Italian motorised units on the road and forcing the Montenegrin guerrillas to concede the high ground, were Muslim hillmen from Albania, who swarmed over the inhospitable terrain in their hundreds. Supported by Italian artillery and free to plunder and loot as they came, these fierce tribesmen needed little encouragement to wage war on their traditional enemies and neighbours – and seldom had the odds been so heavily stacked in their favour. Wherever the Montenegrin resistance proved too stubborn to overcome, they only had to call up the heavy guns to blast their enemies from their path.

Djordje conferred with the royalist officers who were directing the fighting and trying to cover the retreat of the fleeing villagers along the Lim valley. He was unable to offer them much comfort and he derived little from their comments. They were critical of the Communists, whom they blamed for starting the uprising without sufficient thought about how it was to be conducted. Now the fighters who had rallied to their support were paying the price of their mismanagement. The defenders of Murino had no intention of slackening their fierce resistance to the Italian column – but they were angry men, bitter in the knowledge that they were in a no-win situation.

It was a return to Murino much different to the one Djordje had envisaged; with Popovic riding at his side, they would have demonstrated the unity needed to make Montenegro free, and the very sight of Popovic in battle harness would have been an inspiration to all. Instead, news of the old warrior's death had the opposite effect. It was taken as a sign that the battle, if not already lost, was one that could not be won.

The Lim valley was no place for those who had no direct part to play in opposing the inexorably advancing Italians and their Albanian mercenaries. So, Djordje and his men did not linger. They kept on towards Kolasin.

Jamie, Stefan and Dudic – whose liking and respect for Djordje had increased since their meeting on the Moraca – detected more than fatigue in the tired droop of his shoulders as he rode ahead of them along the west bank of the Lim. They knew that the criticism voiced at Murino had upset him and that it had come at a time when his sense of failure over the quest for Popovic was acute.

'It has been a bad day,' Dudic said to the others, keeping his voice low. 'He has taken it to heart. He was really counting on Popovic, and coming all this way for nothing has knocked the stuffing out of him.'

'It wasn't his fault that the Turks got to Popovic before we did,' Stefan said. 'And I'm not convinced that one man – even one as legendary as Popovic – was going to make all that much difference. A couple of field guns would do more for morale than a hero figure from another war.'

'In the short term, perhaps,' Dudic conceded. 'But it was the *idea* of Popovic that Comrade Djordje was staking so much on. He knows that no battle is lost while men still have an idea to follow – and Popovic was an idea that *all* Montenegrins could follow . . . a national figure above politics of the right or left. Now Comrade Djordje has lost the figurehead we needed to hold us all together, and he sees the unity we had disintegrating. He must be sick with despair. I know just how he must be feeling.'

'Do you?' Stefan queried, regarding Dudic with surprise. 'You think very highly of him, don't you?'

Dudic laughed.

'And you think I shouldn't? Because he's a dyed-in-the-wool Communist and I'm not?' Dudic made a flourish with his hand, dismissing the idea that political differences mattered. 'Comrade Djordje is a patriot and he has vision. I admire him very much. He knows that we Montenegrins can be our own worst enemies.'

'I'll ride with him,' Jamie volunteered. 'Maybe all he needs is somebody to cheer him up.' He jogged his mount forward to catch up with Djordje, ignoring Stefan's and Dudic's comments on the unlikelihood of his gloomy conversation cheering up anybody.

Djordje, despite the dejected way he was slumped in the saddle, greeted Jamie with a smile, quickly dismissing the notion that he would prefer to ride alone.

'What are they tattling about back there?' he asked Jamie. 'Is it me?'

'Nothing you wouldn't have been flattered to hear,' Jamie assured him. 'They were talking about Popovic – the disappointment you must be feeling after all the hopes you had.'

'Disappointment is putting it mildly,' the Montenegrin confessed. 'Finding him like that was a disaster, although not all our people are going to see it that way. In the Party, I mean. Some were totally opposed to me seeking out Popovic or anyone else whose reputation was made with the Royal Army. They're blind, of course. If we're going to have an army, we need professionals to run it.'

'I would have thought that was only common sense,' Jamie commented.

Djordje smiled wryly.

'Unfortunately, that's a commodity that can be as hard to find in members of the Communist Party as it is anywhere else. And you heard the officers back there in Murino, blaming all their troubles on the Communists. Nobody seems to realise that we're all in this together and that it's a war to the death – a war without mercy. And it's only just begun.'

'Things are going badly,' Jamie said, aware as he said it that the observation was scarcely uplifting. Perhaps Stefan and Dudic knew him better than he knew himself: that he was the wrong person to try to cheer anyone. Djordje responded, however, with a steely optimism that belied the tired droop of his shoulders.

'Things are going to get a great deal worse,' Djordje promised, with a smile that was at odds with such a prophecy. 'But I tell you this: we shall win. Never doubt that. Never stop believing it. We shall win!'

Proclamation of the belief seemed to lift Djordje. He sat more erect in the saddle, and he seemed to shed his fatigue. Jamie felt his own optimism rise. He grinned at Djordje.

'We never died of winter yet,' he said. The aphorism was foreign to the Montenegrin, puzzling him momentarily. It was a strange thing to say in high summer. But the drift of what Jamie meant filtered through to Djordje. The winters of the Crnagora could be awesome, but the people of Montenegro survived them, as little subdued by them as by the Turk or any other foreign invader.

'You are right, my friend,' Djordje agreed, almost gleefully. 'We Montenegrins know all about winter and how harsh it can be. We know how to endure. We must not lose heart because, for the moment, the Fascists have us on the run. We must endure defeat now as we endure the first snows of winter, and we must not delude ourselves that the winter we face will not be long and hard. But we will see it out, eh? We will see it out.'

'Oh, we'll see it out,' Jamie affirmed, scarcely aware that in his fierce resolve to endure whatever lay ahead he snarled the words. This war was like Lepoglava all over again – only worse, because it was a sentence of indeterminate length. But it had to be endured. Only when it was over could life begin to take on any meaning. With Mara. He had shut from his mind any other prospect, because none bore thinking about. Deep within him he had to nourish the spark of hope, keep alive the conviction that he and Mara were meant to survive, for each other.

If that hope should ever die, Jamie knew that he would die with it.

Jamie was seldom far from Mara's thoughts. So much did he fill them that each day brought its own special agony of despair. Every empty minute was torture. She did not want to contemplate a future and a life which did not have Jamie at its centre. Without him, life was an exercise in existence – a meaningless purgatory. So she clung with a tenacity that bordered on unreason to the hope that he was alive and that they would be reunited. Her hope received no nurture from events. Indeed, every day that passed seemed to conspire to push fulfilment of that hope further and further from reach.

Vienna basked in the high summer of Nazi success. As the German war machine rolled, seemingly unstoppable, across the steppes of Russia, and the rest of Europe lay in thrall to the Nazi warlords, Mara was given no food for hope, no matter where she looked. From every side she was bombarded by sounds and signs that proclaimed the substance of Hitler's boasts of a thousand-year Reich – and the death of all her own dreams. Yet she could not let her dreams go. They were all she had. The nightmare was living.

As the summer passed, she sought escape from the nightmare in her work. Only by total absorption in something else could she hold at bay her longing for Jamie and the despair it aroused. But soon work alone was not enough. The empty hours were a torment. The silence of her lonely room mocked her, crushing hope and dismissing her dreams as fantasy, as self-delusion.

Had she chosen, she could have lost herself in a hectic social life. Men, attracted by her beauty and the rather sad aloofness that heightened it, propositioned her with a frequency that others would have found flattering. In the office and in the restaurant where she ate most evenings, she parried the overtures that came her way with a firmness which brooked no misunderstanding.

It was one would-be suitor who, early in July, provided Mara with one avenue of escape from the empty hours that she found so hard to endure. A young German Army doctor, he accepted her rebuff to his advances philosophically, but it did not make him abandon his interest. Denying, of course, that he had an ulterior motive, he tried to recruit her to the nursing reserve being formed at the hospital where he worked.

At the time, a drive was being made in Vienna to mobilise civilians into all kinds of war work, and the formation of a new nursing reserve was part of it. Women were being invited to become part-time members of the Army Nursing Corps and undergo training, so that already trained nurses could be released for service at the war fronts. The idea of such work had two-fold appeal to Mara. It would not only fill her loneliest hours and give outlet to the compassionate side of her nature, it would reduce the pressures constantly being made on all women of her age to identify with the war effort. Better, she thought, to volunteer for work of a merciful character than be conscripted to a more combatant service – working directly in air defence, perhaps, or making munitions.

So Mara became a nursing cadet, working from six p.m. to midnight five days a week attending special classes or doing relief duties on Saturdays and Sundays. On top of her job with the publishing firm, it meant that she seldom got to her bed before two in the morning and, by then, she was so physically and mentally tired that she slept as if she had been sedated.

On the last Wednesday in July, she finished work early – for once not too dismayed at having two hours to spare before she changed into uniform and reported to duty at the hospital. She would have a leisurely bath, a bite to eat, listen to the radio for news and still have time to walk the two miles to the hospital – a change from rushing and joining the sweaty five-thirty crush on public transport. She arrived at her little apartment in Kaisermuhlen to find her mother sunning herself in the tiny border garden.

'Mama, what brings you here?' Mara concealed her dismay. She had not seen her mother for a month and had not missed her fussing ways and attempts to persuade Mara to visit her father.

'Your father and I are leaving Vienna,' Mrs Richtman announced fretfully. 'I had to see you. I worry so much about you, living here all on your own.'

They were sitting over coffee in Mara's tiny apartment before the older woman explained the purport of her visit.

'We are going back to Croatia, Mara. Your father has been given an important new post in Zagreb, and it will break his heart if you don't come with us.'

Mara regarded her mother sceptically.

'Papa will break his heart, will he? Does that mean he doesn't get the job unless he has a daughter in tow?'

'Mara! How can you say such a thing? Your father loves you.'

'He just shows it in peculiar ways,' Mara said. 'He's a monster, Mama, and you know it. For the life of me, I just can't understand why you've put up with him for as long as you have. He treats you like a doormat.'

Mrs Richtman flushed.

'Your father and I understand each other. He has always been forceful. . . .'

Mara smiled at the understatement.

'Was it his idea that you came to see me?'

The direct question flustered Mara's mother.

'Does it matter whose idea it was?'

'So it was your idea, Mama. You still think you can make peace between us?'

'It's wrong for a daughter to hate her father,' Mrs Richtman said tearfully.

Mara rose and put an arm round her mother's shoulder.

'I'm sorry, Mama. I don't want to hurt you. But don't you see? I can't pretend to have feelings I don't have . . . not even for your sake. I don't feel the way I do about Papa just because of what he did to me. I can even admit that there was some truth in what he said – that he had let me get my own way for too long. But I can't change now, and neither can he. And it's what he is and what he does and what he represents that I can't stomach.'

Mrs Richtman was little comforted by her daughter's words. Didn't Mara realise how important a man her father was? Didn't she understand that, as Provincial Political Officer with the new Croatian Government, he would enjoy ministerial rank and wield great power and influence? Didn't Mara want to share the prestige and privileges which would come to the family as a result of her father's position?

The more her mother talked, the more Mara realised that there was a communication gap between them of unbridgeable width. Her mother did not even begin to comprehend the scale of values that separated them. She assumed that Mara's ambitions and expectations from life were identical to her own, and Mara found it impossible to get it through to her that they even differed in the slightest.

It came as a relief when Mrs Richtman, sniffing back the tears, finally admitted defeat and left. She had been greatly mollified by Mara's revelation that she had joined the nursing reserve and was due on duty at six, seizing on the excuse of such important war work as the reason why Mara could not possibly leave Vienna.

'Your father will be very proud of you,' were her parting words to Mara.

It was only when her mother had gone and she was rushing round frantically to get out in time for duty that Mara had her first misgivings over so readily rejecting the opportunity to go to Zagreb. She had only been marking time in Vienna, waiting for the chance to return to Jugoslavia and Jamie. Now she had scorned that chance with scarcely a moment's thought.

But the more thought she gave the matter, the more she convinced herself that she had made the right decision. If she were to find Jamie anywhere, she reasoned, it would be in Belgrade, not Zagreb. But that was not the most compelling reason for rejecting the chance that had come her way. The stumbling block was her father and the new post he was getting. It seemed to Mara that the Nazis were rewarding him for his services by making him some kind of gauleiter – and the thought of being in any way beholden to him was anathema to her.

To take her mind from the possiblity that she had made a mistake, she tuned in her radio for the late-afternoon news roundup. Most of it was taken up with boasts from the Eastern Front and claims that half a million Russian prisoners had been taken and more than ten thousand Red Army tanks had been destroyed. The only mention of Jugoslavia came at the end of the bulletin. It was brief and gave no indication of how the country was reacting to foreign occupation. The broad-caster announced with suitable solemnity that General Ludwig von Schroeder, former head of Germany's civil defence, had died as the result of injuries sustained in an air crash near Belgrade.

Mara switched off the set, wondering why she wasted her time listening to news bulletins. So much was propaganda. And yet she knew that tomorrow and the next day and the day after that, she would tune in just as avidly, in the hope of more than a mention of Belgrade. Had the Jugoslavs quietly knuckled down to the invaders of their soil with the docility of lambs – as the meagre information filtering through seemed to suggest? Knowing her people as she did, Mara found this hard to believe. She lived in expectation of tumultuous happenings: news that the Serbs and Croats and Bosnians and Montenegrins and the Slovenians and the inhabitants of the Dalmatian littoral had risen in their thousands and thrown out the invaders.

But was that just another dream? A dream as tenuous

and slipping from reach as the dream for Jamie and herself of the joy of love fulfilled?

The three days Mannion spent in Kragujevac passed like a dream. But it was not a dream – more like a honeymoon. The run-down little hotel might not have been everyone's idea of paradise, but for Mannion and Lela it was the nearest thing to heaven on earth. In the intimacy of their room, they soared to new heights of delight in their lovemaking. The world beyond their big brass bed and the four walls that contained it ceased to exist. They exulted in the joy of lying in loving embrace on snow-white sheets, of eating simple but sumptuous meals from a linen-spread table and china plates, of luxuriating in the warmth of a scented bath.

Mannion had won a victory in being allowed to accompany Lela into Kragujevac on her latest mission – not because the Cetnik commander had deemed she needed her husband's protection but because Mannion needed a new supply of detonators and insisted on collecting them himself. Kragujevac was the source of most of the arms and ammunition being smuggled to the Cetniks in the hills. They came from the ordnance factory in the town. The sophisticated operation had been going on for some time under the noses of the German garrison. Not only was a constant supply of the factory's output being diverted directly to the Cetniks, but not a single item left the factory without the Cetniks having advance knowledge of where it was going and when it was being shipped. A number of ammunition trains had been mysteriously derailed and plundered as a result.

Although German suspicion was aroused, their over-stretched security forces were too thin on the ground to detect the nature and scale of the deception taking place.

It took Mannion only a few hours in Kragujevac to accomplish all he had to do there. He obtained the detonators and they were cached on a hillside outside the town, ready to be collected when he and Lela departed. Lela's business took longer. Her orders were to remain at the little hotel – it was owned by a Cetnik officer's sister – and await the arrival of an officer from the staff of Colonel Draza Mihailovic, leader of the Cetnik resistance movement and the man who was trying to establish overall command of the Serbian guerrillas. Mihailovic had made his headquarters in the mountains, on Ravna Gora.

After three days, the man from Mihailovic's headquarters had still not appeared – but his failure to do so brought no complaints from Mannion. These three days with Lela had been a gift from the gods – the honeymoon they had never had when they married at the monastery in the hills – and Mannion was content to let these stolen days of happiness go on indefinitely.

The small garden at the rear of the hotel was both sheltered and secluded, and it was to its sunniest corner that Mannion repaired to wait for Lela, enjoying the autumnal warmth of the September sun, the lazy hum of insects. He had not a care in the world.

'You are under arrest.'

The voice jolted him awake and out of his sprawled repose in the wicker chair. He blinked his eyes open to stare up at the grinning grey-haired man who stood a few feet away. Lela was at his side, grinning broadly.

'I would introduce you,' Lela said, 'but I believe you've met.'

Mannion stared at the man without recognition.

'Belgrade,' the other prompted. 'In April. You and your young Communist friend were hurrying to catch a tram, if I remember correctly.' Luk had the kind of memory that seldom functioned incorrectly. Mannion's took a little longer, but it clicked over now, placing the stranger. He looked different: hatless and wearing an open shirt.

'Your name is Luk?' Mannion murmured. 'Secret police. . . ?'

'Not now,' Luk said. 'And I'd be grateful if you didn't mention it. I still have enemies.' He smiled. 'I knew it must be you as soon as your wife said you were American. Two crazy Americans running around loose in Serbia would have been too great a coincidence. I believe you have become dept at blowing up bridges.'

Mannion shrugged.

'And you?'

'I had to leave Belgrade rather hurriedly,' Luk said. 'But I stay active. We must all make use of what talents we have.'

'He has come from Ravna Gora,' Lela enlightened Mannion. 'He is the one we've been waiting for.'

'From Colonel Mihailovic's headquarters,' Luk added. 'I have been moving from group to group on the Colonel's orders. Communications have been bad – too many freelance operators and no organised strategy. Colonel Mihailovic wants to change all that – build up a proper chain of command and introduce a bit of military order and cohesion to fighting the Germans. He's in charge, and he wants things to be done his way.'

'That seems reasonable enough,' Mannion said. 'It's a funny kind of war. Too many chiefs and not enough Indians. It's time somebody took charge.' He smiled at Luk. 'I say good luck to you.'

'I'm going to need it,' Luk said, a trifle wistfully. 'From what your wife tells me, your own commander will toe the line – he's been worried about German reprisals. But some groups don't give a damn about the consequences of their actions. They don't seem to realise that we can't exist without the help of the civil population, and that we'll lose their support if it's the civilians who are made to pay every time we blow a bridge or derail a train.'

The gist of the message which Lela and Mannion were

charged to take back to their own Cetnik company was that future operations were not to be carried out except on the sanction or order of Colonel Mihailovic's military staff. There were also details of how direct communications with the Ravna Gora HQ were to be set up, but these seemed almost incidental. The transmission of Luk's intelligence was significant to Mannion and Lela only on a personal level. For them, it meant that the honeymoon was over.

It was Luk who provided them with the excuse to stay one more night at the hotel. He wanted them to sit in on a meeting he was having that night with two leaders of the anti-Nazi resistance in Kragujevac.

'They've got some wild notion that if we can help out with a couple of hundred men, they can wipe out the German garrison and take over the town,' Luk said. 'Maybe you will help me talk some sense into them. We don't want the Germans rushing reinforcements down here from Belgrade and closing everything down. Kragujevac's our arsenal and we want it to stay that way.'

'If they won't listen to you, they're not likely to listen to us,' Mannion pointed out.

'Why shouldn't they listen to you?' Luk countered. 'Your Cetniks in the hills need the weapons and bullets you get from this town. What good will you be if your supply is cut off?'

The meeting was held in the hotel-owner's private sitting room. Luk, Mannion and Lela were already there when the two local men were shown in. Their arrival provided Mannion with the first of several surprises. One of the men was a swarthy thickset giant with a drooping moustache, and Mannion recognised him instantly. He was an ex-prisoner from Lepoglava and had shared the hard times there with Mannion for three years, before being released in 1939. His name was Ivan and his face lit up like a harvest moon when he saw Mannion.

The American found himself embraced in a bear hug, while Ivan showered him with a verbal barrage of delight and surprise. How good it was to find an old friend! And here in Kragujevac of all places! How well he looked! But what a surprise to find him as emissary from the Cetnik Colonel at Ravna Gora when he had expected a royalist officer!

When Mannion gently disentangled himself and tried to indicate that Luk and not he was the emissary of the Cetnik Colonel, the joy on Ivan's face disappeared. Ivan stared at Luk, seeing him for the first time, and recognition was not only immediate but mutual. Anger darkened the big man's face.

'You!' he growled. He turned to Mannion. 'What is this jackal doing here?' He was breathing hard, like a man on the brink of fearful violence. He listened in disbelief as Mannion explained that Luk was Mihailovic's representative and that he and his wife, Lela, were operating with another Cetnik group – to which they would be returning next day.

Luk was unruffled by Ivan's show of anger. He remained seated at the table, toying with the wineglass in his hand. Then he pushed the wine bottle before him across the table, followed by two empty glasses.

'Calm yourself, Ivan,' he advised, stony-faced. 'You would have seen less of trouble in the past if you had been able to control that hot head of yours. Now is not the time to rake up old differences.'

'Old differences!' Ivan turned to the others, eyes blazing. 'Do you know who this whore's son is? He was running the secret police in Belgrade the last time I saw him. His thugs beat the hell out of me six nights running because I wouldn't betray my comrades!'

'We're on the same side now, Ivan,' Luk said wearily. 'Save your hate for the Nazis, not for me. What happened in Belgrade is water under the bridge.'

Ivan was in no mood for forgiving or forgetting.

'I swore that if I ever got the chance I'd kill you,' he snarled, towering menacingly over Luk, 'and nothing's happened to change my mind. I'd be doing the world a favour if I wrung your traitorous neck right now!'

No one in the room was in any doubt that the big man meant every word, Luk least of all. The revolver that suddenly appeared in his hand was testimony to that. He had whisked it from the waistband of his trousers and he pointed it at Ivan's face.

'If anybody does any killing around here, I'll be the one who does it,' the former secret policeman warned. 'But don't make me do it, Ivan. I came here to talk because we're fighting a war . . . a war that we're not going to win unless we Serbs bury old hatreds and concentrate on the real enemy. Now, do as I say and sit down. Pour yourself a glass of wine and we'll sit round this table and talk like reasonable men.'

Ivan was far from persuaded, but the gun pointed at his face and the coaxing of his companion conspired to bring about a cooling in his belligerent attitude. He backed down and accepted the wine which his companion poured for him. Eventually, he agreed to talk about the mission that had brought Luk to Kragujevac from Ravna Gora. He made it plain, however, that the truce he was prepared to observe was not to be taken as a sign of any weakening in his desire to see Luk dead.

With Mannion and Lela relegated to the role of nervous specators rather than participants in the subsequent discussion, Luk outlined the reasons why no Cetniks under Mihailovic's command could be committed to any attempt to take over Kragujevac. He also stated Milhailovic's hope that all groups engaged in anti-Nazi activities would regard the Colonel as the national leader and take orders only from him, so that the efforts of all could be coordinated in a single planned strategy. Luk's words were greeted by Ivan and his companion with a mixture of outrage and unconcealed hostility. The arguments raged back and forth across the table.

Ivan told Luk forcibly that the people of Kragujevac were not about to start taking orders from a bunch of Army officers hiding out in the mountains who were only interested in preserving their own status and privileges. The resistance in Kragujevac had its quota of nationalists like Mihailovic, but it was composed of all political colours: Communists like himself, Democratic Socialists, Liberals. They crossed the whole political spectrum and they knew the local situation better than anyone. They were the ones who were living every day in a state of occupation and knew best how to deal with it.

'We want to be free of the Germans,' Ivan declared, 'and if you won't help us get rid of them, we'll do the job ourselves! Have you see their garrison troops? Old men, most of them. They've had to send all their best soldiers to Russia, and what they have left can easily be defeated.'

'Suppose you can take the town,' Luk conceded sourly, 'how long do you think you'll be able to hold out when they send their bombers to flatten every house and they bring their tanks south from Belgrade?'

'We are strong in Kragujevac. We have plenty of men and we have plenty of weapons. We are not afraid of the consequences. And our comrades in Kraljevo are with us. They are ready to strike when we do.'

Nothing that Luk could say had any effect on Ivan and his companion. They were determined to take positive action against the Germans, whether Colonel Mihailovic and his military command approved or not. Luk pleaded for time.

'At least, let me let Headquarters know what you intend,' he begged the two men. 'If they know you're determined to go through with this, they may decide to support you.' He shook his head gloomily. 'But I can't see them doing that. Colonel Mihailovic and his staff believe that time is on our side and that we must employ a long-term strategy. He wants to go on building an army in the mountains, training it for the day when it can take decisive action. He believes that direct confrontation with the Germans now would be a mistake . . . it would be inviting massive retaliation while we are still weak and unorganised. He believes that while we grow stronger, the enemy will grow weaker. He will become sapped by his war against the Russians when winter sets in – '

'Not if you believe their boasts on the radio,' Ivan interrupted. 'They say they will be in Moscow in a month.'

'But already the first snows have fallen in Russia,' Luk countered. 'In September! Hitler may find Moscow no more hospitable to his armies than Napoleon did before him. Winter may be Russia's great ally – and it could be ours, too. By avoiding action with the enemy now and letting him overextend himself, we can save our resources for when it matters.'

Luk appealed to Mannion and Lela for support in the argument but neither felt qualified to offer it. Mannion's experience of the Cetniks had left him with the belief that there were too many chiefs and not enough Indians, and in this respect he was with Luk in believing that coordination under a single command was needed if the guerrilla war was ever to have more than a nuisance effect on the Germans. At the same time, he had some sympathy for Ivan and those townspeople who bore the brunt of occupation and were anxious to shake off the shackles.

It was Lela, with her woman's common sense, who sought moderation on both sides. Taking care to favour neither one point of view nor the other, she suggested second thoughts on both sides. Ivan and his colleague should go back to their people and tell them what Colonel Mihailovic was attempting to do, while Luk returned to Ravna Gora and explained the dissatisfactions of the people in Kragujevac and their impatience for action.

'I do not trust this man to speak for us,' Ivan immediately complained, looking fiercely at Luk.

'Then come with me and speak for yourself,' Luk invited.

'Alone? Do you think I'm crazy?' Ivan was scornful.

'Bring as many friends as you like, if it will make you feel safer,' Luk said. 'You have nothing to fear. I guarantee you will be well received at Ravna Gora.'

To Mannion's surprise and Lela's relief, Ivan agreed. Neither was comforted, however, by the attitude of both Luk and Ivan when the meeting finally broke up.

When he was leaving, Ivan confided to Mannion, 'What has happened tonight will make no difference to what we do in Kragujevac. Nothing has changed.'

Luk was no more optimistic.

'If that hot-head doesn't show a lot more respect for Colonel Mihailovic than he showed to me, he could find himself in a lot of trouble when he gets to Ravna Gora,' Luk told Mannion and Lela when the two Kragujevac men had left the hotel.

'But you gave him your personal guarantee,' Lela protested.

'I meant it, too,' Luk replied. 'But Ivan is a fool if he thinks he can dictate to the staff on Ravna Gora. They look on themselves as the only authority in this land, in the King's absence, and they're not going to argue the toss with anyone who challenges that authority. That includes me. They might come to the conclusion that if Ivan won't do what he's told, he's committing treason.'

'They wouldn't harm him ... would they?' Mannion's question was offered lightly, conveying that not even he took it seriously. But Luk's grim expression showed no sign that he regarded it with levity.

'They're professional soldiers on Ravna Gora,' he

said. 'They don't wrap traitors in cotton wool. They give them a quick trial – and then they shoot them.'

Lela awoke to find the other half of the bed empty, although it was still warm from Mannion's body. She sat up, alarmed, and then sighed with relief as a movement by the window caught her eye. Hands on the broad sill, his weight on his arms Mannion stood in arched pose, staring thoughtfully out into the night. Moonlight glistened on his naked shoulders.

'Come back to bed,' Lela called softly. 'You'll get cold.'

She held out her arms to receive him as he padded across the space to the bed. She shivered at the first delicious touch of his hands on the flesh of her back but was surprised at the ferocity with which he pulled her to him, crushing her breasts against his chest.

'You're hurting me,' she reproached him softly. 'What has happened to my gentle lover that he is so angry?' He was quick to show concern, reducing the fierceness of his grip and murmuring an apology as he slipped into bed beside her. She made way, drawing him in and then tumbling over him so that she lay on top. She kissed his stubbly chin. 'What is the matter, my darling? Couldn't you sleep?'

'I *am* angry,' he confessed. 'But not with you, sweetheart – with what happened last night.'

'There is nothing more you can do,' she told him, moving her hips so that her stomach and thighs rubbed gently against his. 'If you warn your friend Ivan against going to Ravna Gora, it could make things worse than they already are. The man you call Luk gave you his word of honour that Ivan would not be harmed.'

'What if he can't keep his word? What if Mihailovic overrules him?'

'Mihailovic wouldn't do that. Not if Luk has as much influence with him as he says he does.'

340

Mannion sighed.

'All Luk said was that his friendship with the Colonel goes back a long time, that Mihailovic was in Military Intelligence while Luk was in the political wing, rounding up poor saps like Ivan and me for the dictatorship. That doesn't mean to say that Mihailovic will do what Luk asks him to do.'

'He's a Serbian officer, Brad. Like my father, and his father before him. They have a code of honour. They will not go back on a promise made on their behalf.'

'I just hope to God you're right,' Mannion said.

'I know I'm right, darling,' Lela murmured. 'Don't let it spoil our last night here. It has been such a happy time.' As if to remind him, she opened her legs, enveloping his manliness in the moist folds and furry softness below her thrusting belly. A groan of ecstasy escaped her as Mannion responded, roused to new passion and eager for that bodily fusion that excludes all from mind but the exploding rapture of its wonder.

The night was cool and Luk fastened his sheepskin jacket more closely about him. He was breathing heavily. The track up the hillside was steep and he could feel his heart thumping away in quick time. The years were telling on him now, he knew. He was of an age when he should have been taking life easier – but the reverse had happened when he joined up with Mihailovic at Ravna Gora. He had walked or ridden hundreds of miles, helping to organise the intelligence framework that kept the Colonel informed. All the trekking he had done should have made him fitter and tougher, Luk reckoned. But it hadn't. It was burning him out. He was perpetually tired, both mentally and physically, and there were times when he just wanted to lie down and die. He was strangely sick of life. Perhaps it would have been different if he had led a more normal kind of life – if he had married and had children.

Such thoughts were a sure sign that he was going soft. He was paying now for all those years of being hard: the original unbreakable man. He had always fought to win and he had never cared how. His motto had been 'Fear God and trust no man', with the rider that God didn't frighten him all that much.

God didn't frighten Luk half so much now as his own changing nature, and the discovery that he was not made of granite. He wanted to trust people when all his instincts told him that it was an investment that paid no dividends. More than that, he wanted people to trust him. It hurt him when they did not.

Even Draza Mihailovic had not been sure of him at first. It had taken him some time to overcome his initial distrust, but Mihailovic had always been a loner, a bit of a square peg until he became Director of Military Intelligence. Secrecy and clandestine activity were right up Mihailovic's street. Temperamentally and intellectually, he made a much better spymaster than he would ever be an army commander.

In Kragujevac, Luk had been hurt by the hot-headed Ivan's show of hatred for him. It was a sign of Communist small-mindedness. Once a class enemy, always a class enemy. At one time, Luk had respected the Communists because their zealotry and unwillingness to compromise had equalled his own – but not now. They had not lifted a finger to defend Jugoslavia against the Nazis *until Russia had been attacked*. What kind of patriotism was that? Didn't they give a damn for their *own* country?

Yes, Ivan was sadly typical. In a game that was over and done with, he and Luk had been on different sides and bound by rules that no longer applied. The battle lines had been redrawn and old rivalries shed since then, as Ivan should have accepted. It was a new game for far bigger stakes and its name was survival.

It had been a victory of sorts to get the Communist to

agree to consult Mihailovic before making any ill-considered attack on the Germans in Kragujevac. In spite of the fears he had voiced to Mannion, Luk was hopeful that Ivan's visit to Ravna Gora would not be a disaster. Mihailovic had already had talks with the Communist leader, Tito, and they had gone well. Ivan might be encouraged to exercise a little caution. He would surely think twice before fouling up the accord his Party boss had established with Mihailovic – or he would be in trouble with his own people.

Luk stopped twice to rest as he made his way up the hill track. He wondered how many men Ivan would bring to the rendezvous. Half a dozen? More? There was no saying. It depended on how many guns it took to make Ivan feel safe in the lion's den. He certainly wasn't going to frighten the Cetniks at Ravna Gora, no matter how many he brought. Luk had tried to impress on Ivan that a show of force would be futile and that it would be stupid and wasteful to make the journey with more than one escort but he was unsure if Ivan had been convinced.

The rendezvous was a hilltop shepherd's hut. It was there Luk had left his own Cetnik guide, with their pack-mule, before going down into Kragujevac. The guide was an old man, much older than Luk, but the years sat lightly on him. Luk was looking forward to seeing him again. There was something rock-solid and reassuring about the old man's company. The world seemed a calmer, more orderly place in his presence.

The last part of the climb was the steepest. Picking his way carefully in the bright moonlight, Luk heaved a sigh of relief as he reached the top and a grassy plateau stretched before him. The dark shape of the hut was etched sharply against the sky. Chest heaving from his ascent, he stumbled towards it. He was still forty metres from the hut when a single shot rang out.

Luk felt surprise and shock as the pain struck him, stopping him in his tracks. The blow on his chest had the force of a mule's kick, sending him a pace backwards before all strength disappeared from his legs and he collapsed. A roaring filled his ears as he lay flat on his back, trying to comprehend what had happened to him. The roaring seemed to come from within his own head, although he was making no conscious sound. He was suffocating, unable to breath, his chest in the grip of a tightening band of steel that was squeezing and squeezing and filling his mouth and nose with foaming liquid.

He did not see the two shadows that detached themselves from the black shape of the hut. The two men who approached the fallen body were both armed. The shorter of the two – a stocky man – still held the rifle from which the shot had been fired. The other – a giant – held a revolver in his hand.

'Is he dead, Ivan?' asked the man with the rifle, stopping and letting his companion inspect the body.

'Not yet,' said Ivan, staring without pity at the blood gurgling from Luk's mouth and nostrils. He pointed the revolver at the pale face on the ground and pulled the trigger. The sound of the shot seemed to reverberate across the plateau and echo in the hills. Ivan walked away to rejoin the man with the rifle.

'Well, comrade, I promised you revenge for the torture you suffered in Belgrade. Are you satisfied?'

'I'm glad it's over,' the other said. 'I've waited a long time for justice.'

'As I have,' Ivan said. 'The world is well rid of that jackal. He wasn't so tough after all, was he? And not so clever, either. The fool must have believed that I would go to Ravna Gora with him.'

'What about the others he met in town, the woman and the man?'

'The American and his woman? They left Kragujevac yesterday morning. But we don't need to worry about the American. He was with me in Lepoglava. He knows what a bastard Luk was and he won't lose any sleep over this. He'll never know about it, anyway.'

'Was it really necessary to kill the old man too, Ivan? He did us no harm.'

'He was a royal lackey, like all damned Cetniks. We had no choice if we were going to get Luk.'

'And the mule, too? Did we have to kill the mule? We could have got a good price for it in town.'

Ivan snorted.

'Now you're talking like a goddamned capitalist. I'm beginning to regret I let you in on this.'

'Why did you, Ivan?'

'Because you're a Party man and this was a Party matter. Luk was an enemy of the Party and we executed him.'

'What if Mihailovic tries to interfere again, Ivan? What if he sends somebody else to us with orders not to attack the Germans without his say-so?'

Ivan laughed.

'He'll be too damned late, that's what! Mihailovic won't be so bossy when he hears we've taken back Kragujevac and Kraljevo from the Germans and the towns are ours! We'll see who's boss then! I tell you, comrade, two weeks from now we'll be running the show. We'll be top dogs!'

Unfortunately for Ivan and his powers of prophecy, events were to prove him wrong. In two weeks, Ivan was to be as dead as Luk, and the deeds would have taken place that would write the names Kragujevac and Kraljevo large in the Book of Infamy.

The Cetnik Colonel who commanded the company encamped at the monastery announced to Mannion, Lela, and Marko and the others the news of events in Kragujevac. Within minutes of a messenger arriving from Cacak, the Colonel had assembled the entire community. He addressed them in a voice that shook with emotion.

In spite of the orders of Colonel Mihailovic – recently

345

appointed Minister of War by King Peter's Government-in-exile – brave but misguided patriotic elements in Kragujevac had enticed German Army units into battle. The attacks by the Serbian patriots had been repelled. They had scattered after inflicting a relatively small number of casualties on the enemy. The Germans had admitted the loss of fifteen men and twice that number wounded.

As a consequence, they had reinforced the town and inflicted a terrible punishment on the citizens. As a reprisal, the German commander had ordered the execution of every male in the town over the age of fifteen. Five thousand men and boys had been rounded up and shot in batches of one hundred. The massacre had been accomplished in the course of one day.

At Kraljevo, as a result of another unsuccessful skirmish with German troops, fifteen hundred men and children had been shot in reprisal.

By the time that the Colonel had finished speaking, most of the women and not a few of the men were weeping openly. Mannion bore Lela away, trying to comfort her in her tears, but he had no words to staunch the shock and horror that he, too, shared.

'We'll avenge them, Lela, every man and child!' he vowed, but it only brought from her a woeful, 'No, no, no.' How could you fight such an enemy, if his answer was to slaughter the innocents by the hundred and thousand? What weapons were any use against such terrible retribution?

Mannion could give her no answer. His mind rebelled against submitting to such evil – but what was the alternative? One either had to submit or fight. Submission would only perpetuate the evil, not end it. Better to die. Yes, better to die, fighting it. Fighting it with every muscle and sinew. With every breath. There could be no compromise. It was a war without mercy. War to the death.

7

The Seeds of Fratricide

Jamie would have liked to talk to the British officer, but he was never given the opportunity. Indeed, Djordje went out of his way to impress on Jamie that any contact between him and the scholarly-looking Lieutenant-Colonel Hudson could endanger the officer's life. Jamie was astonished, angered even, but he promised Djordje to stay quiet about his own British connections and avoid conversation with the Briton. He knew that Djordje had not given the warning lightly. The Montenegrin was genuinely alarmed by the reaction of some of his Communist colleagues to the arrival at their mountain headquarters of the first British military mission to Jugoslavia, in the company of representatives of the Royal Government-in-exile.

'It's like this, my friend,' Djordje said. 'Some of our command are of a mind to kill our visitors because they do not trust them. I do not think the Englishman means us any harm, but it's not us that he is seeking in Jugoslavia. He is under orders to make contact with the officer nationalists who are holding out in Serbia, and the man who leads them – Draza Mihailovic.'

'We are all allies,' Jamie protested. 'I'm British, but your Communist friends accept me. Why not this man?'

'Being British doesn't count for anything,' Djordje cautioned, almost apologetically. 'The Party looks on Britain as an imperial power, a country that's as inimical to Communism as Italy and Germany. Her only saving grace is that she is now the ally of the Soviet Union. At least, that is how some of my people see it. They are highly suspicious of a British monarchist officer coming here with a party of Jugoslav monarchist officers who represent a cowardly clique that surrendered the Army and ran away and left the rest of us to stew.'

'And you are suspicious of this British officer, Djordje?'

'No, I have received him as a friend, in goodwill . . . as most of our command has.'

'But you won't allow me to talk to him?'

'It could be dangerous, comrade. There are those who would be quick to put the wrong construction on it. The Englishman has been asking many questions about how many men we have and where they are deployed and how well armed they are. We have told him nothing. If he is seen talking to you, his own countryman, it will be said that he is ferreting from you all the secrets that we have held back. It will confirm the fears that he has only come to spy on us.'

'But that's ridiculous,' Jamie protested.

'Perhaps,' Djordje conceded, 'but do not doubt the dangers. It could earn the Englishman a bullet in the back of the head. And not only him. You could be the victim of the same paranoia. I don't want anyone pointing the finger at you and calling you spy.'

So Jamie accepted the caution and avoided the British officer – more out of respect for Djordje than for any other reason. Since the fall of Kolasin and during the troubled weeks that followed, Jamie had come to regard Djordje as one of the few men in the Communist leadership who offered real hope for the disintegrating rebel forces. He was as unshakable as ever in his devotion to Communism, but he was not as blindly dogmatic and narrow as some of his colleagues. He was humane and reasonable: qualities that were not always conspicuous in the die-hards around him. He was wise and far-sighted in situations where others, ruled by hair-trigger emotions, gave no thought to the consequences of their actions.

The Italian Venezia Division had entered Kolasin early in August and the guerrillas had been driven into the inhospitable mountains to lick their wounds and count the cost of defeat. While the Italians regarrisoned all the towns and communication points that had fallen to the Montenegrins in the first week of rebellion, the rebel leadership – searching for reasons for their defeat – took to feuding with each other and looking for scapegoats. Old clan rivalries reasserted themselves, political splits appeared, and summary punishment for apparent treachery created chasms where, before, there had been mere cracks in the unity.

A consequence was that in some hill villages where the guerrillas had previously found support and a warm welcome, they now encountered hostility and suspicion. Much as this dismayed Jamie, he was just as uneasy in villages where the guerrillas were well received, not because of the friendship displayed but because of the villagers' boasts that they had been settling old scores in the neighbourhood. The sullen resentment found in one village was usually due to the death of one or more of its inhabitants at the hands of politically motivated rivals from the next.

In Jamie's view, Djordje was one of the few Communists with authority to condemn the senseless killings and argue the need for a tolerance that superseded clan and political loyalties. He alone seemed to realise that every incident that impaired the fragile unity of his makeshift little army was a grievous self-inflicted wound, and he talked himself hoarse trying to preserve that unity.

He was also a moderating influence with local commanders, who felt no obligation to be governed by the normal rules of war in their treatment of prisoners. Communist veterans of the Spanish Civil War in the guerrilla ranks had no compunction about shooting all captured Italian officers as a matter of course – and their

349

men, too, if they became an unwanted encumbrance. Djordje intervened several times to prevent the summary execution of Italian officers, persuading the local commanders to trade them for their own men taken by the Italians, instead. Usually, the nearest garrison commander was only too happy to make such an exchange.

Unfortunately, such events became rarer and rarer and finally ceased as the war became progressively more bitter and mercy was interpreted as weakness.

September was more than halfway through when the joint British-Jugoslav mission made its surprise appearance in Montenegro. Lieutenant-Colonel Hudson and the two Royal Jugoslav Air Force officers who accompanied him landed from a submarine on a deserted strip of Montenegrin coast near Petrovac and successfully made contact with a Communist guerrilla group in the mountainous littoral. It took a week to guide Hudson and his companions through Italian-held territory to the mountain headquarters of the Montenegrin Supreme Command, west of the Moraca valley.

Jamie shared in the general excitement that surrounded the small party's arrival and was sure that he would be called on to act as interpreter for the Englishman. The call never came. Hudson's command of Serbo-Croat was peerless and he needed no interpreter. Jamie was disappointed. His disappointment turned to chagrin, however, when Djordje sought him out and extracted his promise to avoid any communication with his fellow countryman.

'It is diabolical,' he confided to Stefan. 'Your Communist big shots can't see a shadow move without thinking it's a fifth columnist or a traitor who's in cahoots with the Italians. They'd suspect their own grandmothers.'

'So would you, Jamie, if you had been hounded all your life by the secret police and their informers. They have learned the hard way that nobody outside the Party can be trusted.'

'Even me, Stefan?' Jamie challenged.

'Even you, Jamie. Djordje apart, they don't know you as I know you. You have their respect but you'll never be completely trusted by them until you commit yourself to Communism as whole-heartedly as you're committed to fighting Fascists. So long as you choose to stay outside the Party, Jamie, some of our people will always put a question mark beside your name. There will always be doubt about you.'

'Maybe that's just what holds me back, Stefan. I don't have your conviction, or Djordje's – your blind faith. Doubt is a two-way thing. I have doubts, too. Not just about Communism – but about all ideologies, and the right of any of them to own me, body and soul.'

'Maybe you should start your own political party,' Stefan chided him, and chuckled at the thought. 'That would really set us off in opposite directions, eh? Me, labouring for the day when we Communists could build a new Jugoslavia and proclaim a one-party state . . . and you, turning your back on the world and declaring a one-man party.'

'I could do worse,' Jamie said, and his smile was as broad as Stefan's. 'The more I see of Montenegro and its politics, the more I become convinced that I'm the only sane person left on earth.'

Although the Communist-weighted Supreme Command felt slighted by Hudson's determination to contact Mihailovic and deal only with him, they decided in the end to do all they could to help the Englishman. They would supply mounts and packhorses for him and his party, and lay on escorts and guides for the journey to western Serbia. They even returned the Englishman's radio, which had been mysteriously 'mislaid' by his Communist hosts at the mountain HQ.

Djordje was a much relieved man when he relayed

news of the Supreme Command's deliberations to Jamie and Stefan. He saw the decision as a victory for common sense – although, as far as he was concerned, it had its price. The hard-liners had bowed to Djordje's moderation on how the Allied Mission should be treated, but they had used another pressing matter to get Djordje out of their hair for the immediate future.

This had come about because of an avalanche of directives and demands descending on the Montenegrin Command from Tito's headquarters in Serbia. Some of the missives were highly critical of the Party leadership in Montenegro, accusatory in tone and showing little understanding of the situation. It was decided that someone had to acquaint Tito and his politburo of the facts – and the hard-liners had no hesitation in nominating Djordje for this unwelcome task.

'I shall be leaving for Serbia in two days' time,' he told Stefan and Jamie.

'Alone?' Jamie asked.

Djordje shook his head.

'I shall be taking one man with me.'

Neither Jamie nor Stefan doubted that Dudic would be the automatic choice. They were taken aback when Djordje told them that Stefan would be accompanying him. Stefan's crestfallen look did not escape the Montenegrin.

'The idea does not seem to please you?'

'I'm flattered, of course,' Stefan said unhappily. 'It's just that Jamie and I . . . we have always been together.'

His concern seemed to amuse the Montenegrin.

'Sure. Like Tweedledum and Tweedledee – where one goes, the other goes.' He smiled broadly. 'Don't worry, comrade, I have no intention of breaking up my little team. You won't be apart for long. If all goes well, we shall meet up again at Tito's headquarters in Serbia. In the meantime, Lieutenant Dudic and you, Comrade Jamie, will be going on a journey, too.'

Jamie stared uncertainly at Djordje.

'A journey?'

'To Cetnik country,' Djordje said. 'To Ravna Gora, where the royalist officers have their headquarters. You will travel ahead of the Englishman, Hudson, and the escorts we are providing. I don't want anything untoward to happen to your countryman – either by accident or design. Do you understand?'

'I'm not sure I do,' Jamie said.

'We have promised the Englishman that we will get him to Mihailovic. It's important that we keep that promise. I don't want him to be ambushed by any of our people by mistake or through ignorance of the importance we attach to our promise. Nor do I want him and his party falling foul of any bandit Cetnik group who are scalp-hunting for the Germans or the Italians – as I'm told some of them are. You and Dudic will act as pathfinders for the scouts with the main party, and it'll be your job to warn them if there's unsafe territory ahead. They'll be moving by night, because we think it will be safer for them. You'll be moving ahead of them by day.'

'Why Dudic and me, Comrade Djordje?' Jamie asked. 'I thought I had to steer clear of the British Colonel.'

'You would still be well advised to do so. It is a measure of the respect in which you are held that you've been chosen. Everyone knows that the Tiger of Bioce is above the clan feuds that bedevil us; you'll get unhindered passage for yourself and the Englishman's party, where others would not – anywhere in Montenegro. Dudic's been picked because he knows the mountains, and he'll be your passport when you reach Cetnik country. His being a royalist officer should count for something.'

In the event, it was to count for much less than Djordje hoped.

*

353

Encompassed by magnificent mountain scenery, the town of Uzice was a revelation to Stefan and Djordje. It was not the town's superb situation nor its spectacular environment that took their breath away but the visible signs on every hand that, here in the heart of western Serbia, the red banner had been raised and Communism reigned. After the primitive conditions of the Montenegrin headquarters encampment, those enjoyed by the Communist leadership in Uzice bordered on the wondrous.

The two men had had a relatively uneventful journey out of Montenegro. They had left their horses in the care of a local command on the far side of the Zlatibor mountains and had enjoyed the doubtful comfort of an open truck for their last fifty kilometres of the tortuous route to Uzice. To Djordje and Stefan, it was a thrill to see the streets filled with khaki-uniformed soldiers wearing the red flash of Communism. Some fifteen hundred of them, well-armed and smartly turned out, had occupied the town and taken control of every aspect of its life. So visible was their presence that they seemed to outnumber the indigent population, whose role had been reduced to that of dazed and uncomprehending bystanders.

Tito had made his headquarters in the National Bank, a substantial building, and it was to this well-guarded fortress that the truck delivered Djordje and Stefan. They were suitably impressed.

'All this puts our efforts in Montenegro in the shade,' Djordje confided to his companion, rather wistfully. 'It makes me feel like a poor relation. I expected the Central Committee to be living in caves – nothing like this.'

Djordje's hopes of an immediate interview with Tito were thwarted by a dark-haired young woman who introduced herself as the Communist leader's personal secretary and made it clear that no one, but no one, got within a mile of the exalted presence without her sanction. She was a good-looking woman who might have been described as pretty, but for a sharpness of feature emphasised by a sourness of manner and bossy rudeness that made Djordje's hackles rise.

'I happen to be a member of the Central Committee,' he informed her coldly. 'If you will just tell the Secretary-General that I'm here, I think you'll find that he won't keep me waiting.'

'I don't care who you are,' the woman replied haughtily. 'The Secretary-General is in conference and cannot be disturbed. If you care to leave your name and tell me where you can be contacted, you will get a call if the Secretary-General wishes to see you.'

'Will I, by God?' Djordje was controlling his anger with difficulty.

'If your business warrants it,' the woman stated imperiously. 'Is it a military matter or a Party matter?'

'Does it make any difference?' Djordje asked icily.

'An obvious one,' the woman said, her stare frigid. 'Do you wish to see Comrade Tito in his capacity as Party Secretary or in his capacity as Army Commander? There is a distinction, you know.'

'I should like to see him in both capacities,' Djordje said.

'And where can you be found?'

'Right here!' Djordje snapped. 'I'll wait!'

'You may have a long wait,' the woman retorted and, turning on her heel, flounced off into an inner room. Djordje stared after her, fuming.

Stefan, a spectator to the confrontation and tempted to see the funny side, did not betray his amusement by smiling. Tactful sympathy seemed more prudent.

'Snooty bitch,' he commented. 'Imagine waking up to that in the morning!'

Djordje's opinion promised to be even more colourful but it died, strangled in his throat, at the interruption of a man who had been quietly sorting through bundles of news-sheets at a nearby table. He wore a neat civilian suit, but the red armband on his jacket proclaimed him to be some kind of Party functionary.

'Watch what you say about Zdenka,' he warned.

'Is that what they call that cow?' Djordje said testily. The man smiled.

'Her Party name. I knew her when she was small. She was plain little Davorjanka Paunovic then. She has come up in the world.'

'What is she to the Secretary-General?' Djordje asked.

'You heard her. Personal secretary.' The way the man spoke the words made Djordje look at him sharply.

'She is more than that to Tito?'

'What do *you* think, comrade? What's the point of being Secretary-General if you can't have someone to keep you warm in bed – especially if your wife's trapped in German-held territory? All the Central Committee have their floosies to follow them around . . . I beg your pardon – personal secretaries.'

Djordje and Stefan exchanged shocked looks. Both set store by the puritan zeal that had prevailed in the Party since the new morality swept through it in the thirties. Bohemian attitudes had been purged in the belief that moral as well as political leadership had to be shown by Communists.

'You had better watch your tongue,' Djordje advised the man.

'Oh, I know when to hold it,' he replied complacently. 'I only spoke because your friend called Zdenka a bitch and made it plain he wouldn't fancy waking up next to her in the morning. Neither of you seemed to know that it's the Secretary-General who wakes up beside her most mornings. He doesn't take kindly to people calling her names. And don't think she isn't as powerful as she says. She runs this place.'

'She said the Secretary-General was "in conference". What was she talking about?'

The man shrugged.

'It's a meeting to plan the October Day parade – you know, like they have in Red Square in Moscow – here in Uzice, with the Secretary-General taking the salute. The meeting will go on for hours yet. Where are you staying?'

'Nowhere,' said Djordje. 'We've just arrived from Montenegro.'

The functionary took them to another functionary, who found the pair places to stay. Djordje, as a member of the Central Committe, was given a room at the Palace Hotel. Stefan, without that rank, was billeted in a church with a guerrilla unit composed mainly of students who had escaped from Belgrade. They did not call themselves guerrillas, however. They styled themselves 'Partisans', in the Russian style. There was no equivalent word in Serbo-Croat. The nearest meant 'supporter', as might be applied to followers of a football team. In the days to come, the term Partisan was to become wholly identified with the Communist-led fight for Jugoslavia's liberation.

Later that day, Djordje did get to see Tito and was invited to dine with him at the table reserved exclusively for members of the Party leadership. Stefan was left to his own devices but was at the Palace Hotel, early next morning, to report to his chief. He found Djordje in a disturbed mood. The reason for it was his experiences of the previous evening.

'I was appalled,' he confessed to Stefan. 'Tito welcomed me like an old friend – but he has changed. He was always a little vain, but he has put on airs. He thinks of himself as a General now, as well as Party leader. I've always thought that the jobs should be separate – a civilian to run the Party and a soldier to run the Army. But he sees nothing wrong in taking on both jobs at once and running everything his way.'

'What's wrong with wearing two hats?' Stefan asked. 'The Army should aways be subservient to the Party.'

Djordje smiled.

'Tito seems to like his Army hat. It's a Russian *pilotka*, with gold all over it. God knows where he got it. Or the fancy-looking limousine he runs around in. By God, he and his crew know how to look after themselves. Having dinner with them was like eating at the royal court: the king at the top of the table and everybody else jealous as hell of where they sit. I thought I wasn't going to get a seat at all, you should have seen their faces when Tito asked me to sit next to him.'

'That was never a problem in Montenegro. Rank, I mean,' Stefan said.

Djordje nodded agreement.

'We all counted the same. Everyone is equal under Communism. Or so I thought.' He frowned. 'The politburo don't have the faintest idea of what we've been going through in Montenegro. And they don't seem to care. This is the only front they're interested in – their own. A month ago, they sent us a directive demanding us to send three thousand men to them immediately. Three thousand men! They asked me last night why we hadn't sent them – and I told them! It didn't go down very well.'

'Maybe I should have been there to give you moral support,' Stefan said lightly.

'We would still have been outnumbered. I took a lot of stick. They all had a piece to say about the Montenegrin Party's errors and where we had gone wrong. Now they think that everything will be fine if a few heads roll in Montenegro and they send in some heavy-handed new broom to restore a bit of Party discipline.'

'What did they have to say about the Englishman, Hudson?'

'Tito wants to meet him after he has seen Mihailovic. We have had trouble with the Cetniks in Serbia. Mihailovic has no control over them and yet he seems to think that we should take orders from him. It's a mess.'

'What about your own position, Comrade Djordje?'

'What happens to me is the least of my worries,' Djordje said wearily. 'It's what happens to my country that concerns me. It's Montenegro all over again – too many people thinking the war has been won before it has even begun. The Germans aren't going to sit back and applaud while we take one undefended town after another. And yet all our people can think of is staging an October Day parade! We should be digging ditches and building barricades and tank traps for the day when the German Army wakes up, Comrade Stefan. Because that day is going to come, comrade. It's going to come! And God help us when it does!'

Jamie and Dudic knew they were being watched. Since early morning, when they started down the long valley, both men had felt the presence of watching eyes. Only once were they given visible evidence that they were not alone. Looking back, they saw a lone horseman, carved like a sculpture on top of the hill they had just descended. The rider remained stationary against the skyline for fully ten minutes. Then, when they looked back – as they did frequently after spotting him – he was no longer there. Nor was he anywhere in sight.

At midday, they halted, to eat meagrely and replenish their water bottles from the sparkling stream that coursed down the valley. Their feeling of being watched intensified and, this time, they saw their watchers, who made no attempt to conceal themselves. There were six of them, all on horseback, high on the far side of the valley. Their mounts were immobile and the six sat there, hunched in the saddle, just staring down at the two men on the stream's bank.

'Your Cetnik friends give me the creeps,' Jamie told Dudic. 'Why don't they come down and introduce themselves instead of sitting up there like that? They're like vultures weighing up their supper.'

'We're trespassing on their territory,' Dudic said. 'They're maybe just wondering who we are.'

359

'They know,' said Jamie. 'The tom-toms will have told them – the same as it was on the way to Ravna Gora. There wasn't a village we touched where the people didn't know all about us in advance. They knew who we were, where we were going, and why.'

'News travels fast in these parts. Nobody gave us any trouble.'

It was true. At first – in Montenegro and, later, in Serbia – their news that a British Army officer was close behind had created great excitement among the peasant communities. Hudson's progress had not only been unimpeded, it has been everywhere met with unreserved goodwill. Jamie and Dudic had not gone all the way to Mihailovic's headquarters on the high plateau of Ravna Gora. Their mission had ended after contact with a troop of Mihailovic's regulars, who took over escort duties of Hudson and the exiled King's representatives. Now, the two men were heading for Uzice. Twenty-four hours ago, they had parted company with the Montenegrin escorts who had accompanied Hudson's party. Jamie had felt uneasy ever since. He did not like the silent observation of their movements.

After their short break, their track led them through woodland. October sunlight filtered through the trees, dappling a path that had been used by others. The soft turf was pitted with recent hoof marks.

They emerged from the woods on to a high meadow, where the valley elbowed and presented them with a view of a hillside village, two kilometres distant. The land between was hidden by the meadow's far edge, which rose away from them to form a ridge. They cantered across the grassland towards it.

It was Jamie, glancing back over his shoulder, who saw the following horsemen. They came out of the woods in file but extended to advance abreast, quickening speed with the clear intention of closing on Jamie and Dudic. Jamie's shouted warning was unnecessary.

Dudic was already slowing his mount to a gentle walk and drawing Jamie's attention to the ridge.

There, more riders had appeared and, here and there along the ridge, other men on foot. They were spread out along the far edge of the meadow: three mounted and perhaps a dozen without horses. The men on foot carried their rifles at the port or crooked on an elbow, ready for use, and there was menace in the way they halted and awaited Jamie and Dudic.

Jamie slowed his horse, as Dudic had done, and kept advancing abreast of him at a walk. The six riders behind had slowed and they, too, were walking their mounts, some sixty or seventy metres to the rear.

'I don't like this,' Jamie muttered to Dudic.

'Maybe they think we're spies,' Dudic replied, grinning. 'Leave the talking to me, Jamie. And if the worst comes to the worst, be ready to go like the wind.'

They reined to a halt, twenty paces from the waiting men. There was the click-click of rifle bolts being cocked, and no welcome on the sullen faces of the riflemen. From higher on the hill, an officer on a white horse wheeled his mount down the slope towards the two strangers. They took him to be an officer, at any rate, although his uniform was a mixture of regulation dress and personal foible. He wore a black woolly rimless hat, whereas most of his men sported the khaki variety. He was heavily bearded. He rode up and surveyed Jamie and Dudic arrogantly.

'This is as far as you go,' he said peremptorily, addressing Dudic.

'We're friends,' Dudic said. 'We're going to Uzice on orders from our command. Colonel Mihailovic's command at Ravna Gora has guaranteed our safe conduct.'

The officer laughed.

'Colonel Mihailovic does not command here. I do. And I say you go no further. Yesterday, you were camped with the Reds who brought the English officer from Montenegro. Why did you leave them?'

'I told you. We are under orders to report to Uzice.'

'Communist orders? Only Communists are welcome in Uzice.'

'Our commander is a Communist – but that is nothing to us. He and we are soldiers in the National Army of Liberation. Politics is secondary to the war we are fighting against the invaders.'

The officer laughed again.

'Tell that to my men. Two weeks ago, we occupied Uzice and declared it a free town. But two days later, the Communists moved in with their red flags and took over everything – the school, the town offices, the hospital, the bank and all its money, the arsenal. They started ordering our people about – told us that we must take our instructions from them or get out.'

Dudic frowned unhappily.

'I am sorry. I thought there was supposed to be an accord. . . .'

'Accord!' The officer snorted. 'They are Soviet puppets, AntiChrists, and they mean to wipe out everything Serbia stands for.' He stared hard at Dudic. 'Your beard is the beard of a Cetnik and you wear the tunic of a royal officer. Is it by choice you serve this Communist commander you talk of?'

'I serve my country – not a political cause. I am a soldier.'

'Then join us. Fight where you belong. You have come at the right time. We are going to teach the Reds a lesson they won't forget in a hurry.'

Dudic's face was impassive. 'May I ask how you intend to do that?'

The officer smiled.

'That village over there, on the hill . . . some Reds moved in yesterday and kicked out the half-dozen men we had left there. Today, we intend to show them whose territory this is.'

362

'You intend to talk to them? Warn them to leave?' The officer laughed uproariously.

'Our bullets will do the talking. Are you with us?'

Dudic glanced at Jamie's tense face.

'What do you say, Jamie? Do you wish to kill Communists?'

'I would prefer to kill Italians or Germans,' Jamie said.

'Are you with us?' the officer repeated.

'What if we are not?' Dudic inquired. 'What if we choose not to kill our fellow countrymen?'

'You will find out what we do to traitors.' The officer turned to the men covering Dudic and Jamie with their rifles. 'Take them! he commanded. 'We've had enough talk.' Four men advanced, with the clear intention of pulling Dudic and Jamie from their saddles.

'Ride!' Dudic shouted at Jamie. 'Make for the village!'

Jamie needed no second bidding. He dug his heels into his horse's flanks. It reared and surged forward. Dudic's mount, too, leapt forward, scattering the four men in all directions and causing the officer's white horse to react violently with fright. The ridge of the grassland had concealed the rocky hollow that lay beyond, and it was into this saucer of rough ground that the fugitives hurtled, momentarily hidden from the riders who set off in pursuit. The hollow was full of Cetniks. Most were sitting on the ground, rifles beside them or stacked nearby in tripods.

The men in the hollow leapt to their feet in confusion at the appearance over the brow of two horsemen, who careered among them and were no sooner past when they were followed by half a dozen more. The riflemen, who had been spread out along the ridge, recovered from their initial bewilderment and sent a hail of bullets after Jamie and Dudic. The latter parted company as they both changed course to avoid a group of bewildered Cetniks who were falling over each other to get out of the path of the charging horses – Dudic going left, Jamie veering right.

Jamie's course took him to the shallower end of the saucer and over its gentle slope on to mossy ground where birches grew, presenting both cover of a kind and obstacles to be negotiated. Dudic was nowhere in sight. He had failed to crest the higher slope out of the hollow. Almost at the top, a single bullet had pierced the flesh of his thigh and another had wounded his horse. Rider and horse had toppled and tumbled back down the slope. Jamie saw none of this, intent only on headlong flight and staying in front of two Cetnik riders who seemed to be gaining on him with every stride of their mounts. He changed direction several times as the density of the trees increased and he sought a more open track.

Suddenly, there was open ground before him and he was hurtling across it, his target a distant ribbon of track on the far side of the valley and the wooden bridge at its foot. Above and beyond, he could see clusters of grey dwellings and wisps of smoke spiralling from kitchen fires.

The ground banked steeply down towards the bridge, but fear kept horse and rider surging forward at a dangerous speed. Glancing back, Jamie saw two riders, then a third, break from the trees. They paused briefly, before sighting him and wheeling in pursuit. His lead was no more than three hundred metres.

Across the bridge, hooves pounding a tattoo on the wooden planks, Jamie's horse slowed at the steepness of the firm but rough road that led to the village. He slid from the saddle, hauling his rifle from the scabbard. His sweating horse, glad to be relieved of its burden, trotted a few paces and stood, waiting.

Kneeling in the middle of the road, Jamie aimed and fired as the first Cetnik reached the bridge. He seemed to be plucked from his saddle and fell on the broad plankwork, causing the other two riders to rein sharply to avoid trampling him. One of the Cetniks dismounted and, using his horse as a shield would have returned Jamie's fire if he had been given time to sight his rifle. Jamie's second bullet hit him between the eyes. He slid from sight down the brown haunch of his skittish horse to lie motionless below it.

The third Cetnik, surveying his dead comrade, seemed not to favour the changed odds and raced back the way he had come. Jamie let him go. He stared after the rider, his body trembling with reaction. Sick with the knowledge that he had killed two Serbs, he tried to convince himself that it was necessary. And settling on his mind and numbing all other thought was a terrible anxiety for Dudic. Where was he? Why did he not come?

Jamie scanned the distant trees, willing the sudden appearance of the Montenegrin officer, expecting with every second the welcome sight of galloping horse. But Dudic did not come. The minutes passed and still he did not come.

The footsteps behind Jamie made him whirl in surprise. He found himself staring into the muzzles of four rifles. Their owners – two men and two girls in their late teens – wore red flashes on their khaki tunics. The men were hatless, their hair cropped short and their cheeks clean-shaven. Their expressions showed more curiosity than hostility.

One of the girls advanced and asked a question. Jamie stared at her. She repeated it. Why were his eyes wet with tears? Was it because he had shot the Cetniks on the bridge? Jamie could only stare at her dumbly, unable to find the words to explain his emotions and why they had bubbled up in that instant. The newcomers had surprised him in the moment when the certainty assailed him that, no matter how long he waited, Dudic was not going to come riding into sight. Brave, smiling Dudic was dead. The thought filled him with the same sense of shock and loss he had felt as he had stood in the ruins of

St Podgorica Church in Belgrade and known that Uncle Milan lay somewhere below the rubble.

There were fifty or more Partisans in the hillside village. The four who had found Jamie took him back there to tell his story to the craggy-faced Spanish Civil War veteran who was their commander. The Partisans' occupation of the village was only a temporary one: a foraging sortie from their encampment near the town of Pozega. A string of ox carts was laden with the vegetables and other produce from the surrounding district.

'We have paid good prices for all we have taken,' the Commander told Jamie. 'Not like the damned Cetniks we found here – the ones you heard about from the lot who ambushed you. They took what they wanted at the point of a gun. We pay for everything in silver.'

'Do you think the Cetniks will attack the village?' Jamie asked.

'They're welcome to try,' the Commander said. 'Thanks to your warning, we know how many to expect – and we're ready for them. We didn't know what to make of the shooting we heard earlier on – when you and your comrade made a break for it.' He gave a puzzled shake of his head. 'What kind of soldiers are they? It was stupid of them to start popping off at you like that and give away their presence. We had no idea there were so many of them so close. They must know now that they have no chance of taking us by surprise. If they've any sense, they'll leave us alone.'

But the Cetniks did not leave the Partisans alone. Nor did they display any great military acumen when, an hour before sunset, they attacked the village. There was no feint to disguise the direction of attack; they made a concerted rush from the woods below the village, across open hillside. A single volley from the waiting defenders was enough to send the atackers scurrying back whence they came, leaving eight or nine dead or wounded on the open hill. Nor did they have any stomach for continuing the fight at long range. They scattered through the forest in headlong flight. They were pursued, cautiously at first, by little groups of Partisans who emerged from their defensive positions, and then with all caution gone as they realised that the Cetniks were fleeing in disorder. The flight of some was short-lived. Hands raised to indicate surrender, they came from the woods to meet the Partisans, denouncing their leader as a madman and claiming that they had no wish to fight brother Serbs. The rout was total, and before long more than thirty prisoners had been rounded up and were swearing in earnest tones that they wished to be recruited to the Partisan cause.

Jamie, hopeful that he would find some indication of what had happened to Dudic, attached himself to a party, twenty-strong, that crossed the valley stream and combed the wooded bank for fleeing Cetniks. They came after a time to the hollow where the Cetniks had been camped. It still bore the signs of recent occupation: discarded tins and a surprising number of empty wine bottles.

Nearby, they found Dudic. He was hanging by a rope from the bough of a tree, head slumped on his chest and one trouser-leg stained with blood from a bullet wound that had not been treated.

Light was fading from the sky as Jamie stared at the gently swinging corpse, his mind raging against the senseless cruelty it proclaimed. Was there no end to it in this land of madness?

The four riders were hunched stiffly in their saddles, heads bowed against the driving rain. The flinty road was pitted with puddles and the clip-clop of the horses' hooves echoed with a splashing resonance as they scattered spray with every step.

Mannion rode behind the Partisan officer who was leading. Marko and the Cetnik Captain – a fiercely volatile man called Nikolic – followed, almost abreast. They reined briefly at the high bend of the road where the village below came into view. If the sight of their destination offered any comfort, they showed no sign of the fact. No words were spoken. They headed down the steep slope in file, their mounts stepping cautiously to avoid slipping on a surface made treacherous with running rivers of mud and gravel.

Glancing to his left, Mannion shuddered involuntarily. There, on a flat shelf of open hillside, the Germans had gunned down fifteen villagers in reprisal for the bridge he had blown. Even now, three months after the event, revulsion filled him at the wanton barbarity of the killings. Vivid memory of it was edged with guilt. His had been the deed that had provoked the atrocity. He recalled with startling clarity the moment when he had held the black-uniformed German officer in the sights of his rifle. His temptation to fire had been strong but his fear of endangering Lela had been stronger. Would it have made any difference to the outcome if he had pulled the trigger? The question had often haunted him. It haunted him now.

The village looked no different today from on that other day. It had been raining then, too. Warm summer rain. Not this icy torrent that stung the face and numbed the hands with its biting chill. As he gentled his horse down the slippery gradient, Mannion tried to turn his mind from the horror that the rain-swept landscape evoked. The thought that at least Lela was far away from this place of grief consoled him. She had been spared its reminders. He was thankful that, for once, she was safe and sound within the walls of the Cetniks' monastery fastness; thankful, too, that the need for her intelligence missions had ceased. The nature of the war had changed in the last month with an improvement in communications with Ravna Gora.

It was fitting, Mannion thought, that Lela was more or less permanently confined to the Cetnik base with the other women. She had their unborn child to think about now. The knowledge that she was carrying his child had filled them both with a wonderous awe, a fragile fluttering joy that was like no other feeling. The fears had come later: the fears and the mind-numbing uncertainties. Into what terrifying kind of world would their child be born?

Mannion dragged his thoughts away from Lela. The Partisan officer was cantering ahead to meet a huddle of men who had emerged from the lee of a house, where a guard post of sorts had been set up. They greeted the Partisan officer with clenched-fist salutes and jocular commiserations on his rain-sodden look. His replies made light of the weather and his discomfort. These were his own people and he was clearly happy to be back among them.

He and his Partisans had been in possession of the village for two weeks now. They had occupied it after a brief and bloody fight with the small detachment of Germans who had been dug in around the rebuilt bridge, on the village's far side.

The Partisan intrusion into territory that the monastery-based Cetniks considered their domain had at first enraged Mannion's Colonel and some of his officers – but they had held their fire in check. The villagers had, to the surprise of the Cetniks, welcomed the Partisans as liberators. The welcome was all the warmer for Partisan assurances that it was not their intention to pass through, but to stay and defend the village and its bridge. The villagers' rapport with the newcomers had a chastening effect on the Cetniks. There was no conflict between the rival forces.

Indeed, an order from Mihailovic in Ravna Gora – to strive for harmony between Cetniks and Partisans – persuaded Mannion's Colonel to suppress his anti-

Communist inclinations and establish a working relationship with the Partisan commander. In consequence, a degree of cooperation – although uneasy – was achieved in the region.

It was in this spirit of cooperation that the Partisan commander rode, unescorted, to the Cetniks' monastery base for a crisis consultation with the Colonel. And it was a result of that consulation that he now returned to the village in the company of Mannion, Marko and the captain, Nikolic. The crisis, which neither Cetnik nor Partisan commander could ignore, had arisen with the threat posed to both their forces and the entire area by a rapidly approaching German army.

In mid-October, in the wake of the mass murder of thousands of the citizens of Kragujevac and Kraljevo, the Germans launched a major offensive with the aim of suppressing all opposition in central and western Serbia. They assembled in force in the garrisoned towns of Valjevo, Kragujevac and Kraljevo and were driving south and west into the green hills of the Sumadija and along the valley of the western Morava River towards Cacak and Uzice.

During the late summer months, a huge quadrant-shaped area of western Serbia – with the town of Uzice at its centre – had been freed of German occupation. Now, from key points on the quarter-circle perimeter of the quadrant, the Germans were advancing on the centre, making four main thrusts down the radii and spreading out from these spearheads to form an arc-shaped front. Their intention was to squeeze the Serbian forces tighter and tighter before this shrinking arc until they were all bottled up in Uzice with the mountains at their back.

The immediate problem facing the Partisans in the village with its rebuilt bridge was the consequences of its abandonment. Their commander – in spite of his promise to the villagers – had come to the conclusion that the village was untenable, even with Cetnik help, and that the bridge should be destroyed. Mindful, however, of the German reprisals when the Cetniks had destroyed the bridge, he was anxious to have Cetnik accord with whatever action he took. He kept to himself an additional fear. He new that when he did withdraw from the village, his path of retreat was across Cetnik country – and the last thing he wanted when he pulled back was harassment from Cetniks as well as from Germans.

It was, therefore, some relief to him to discover that Mannion's Colonel agreed it was futile to defend either the village or the bridge; they could hope to delay the Germans only by destroying the bridge. If they tried to defend the village, it would be no more than a gesture – and this made no military sense. The Colonel insisted, however, that the people of the village could not be abandoned to German wrath. They would have to be persuaded to leave their homes and evacuate with such possessions as they could carry.

The Colonel suggested that in order to demonstrate to the villagers that Cetniks and Partisans were in unison over the matter, the task of blowing the rebuilt bridge should be entrusted to his own expert. Furthermore, one of his officers – a Captain Nikolic – would go to the village to explain to the residents why they must leave their homes and seek refuge in either Cacak or Uzice. Nikolic was the ideal choice, if persuasion was going to be necessary, because he had a cousin there who was one of the most influential members of the community.

Mannion, the Colonel's bridge-blowing expert, accepted his assignment without fuss. He made only one request: for the assistance of one man. It pleased him when Marko volunteered for that honour. He was less pleased when he discovered that Nikolic would also be riding with them. He did not like Nikolic, or his arrogant manner. It was a personal thing. There had been bad blood between them ever since the Captain made a pass at Lela. Mannion might never have found out about it but for his persistence in wanting to know why Lela kept making excuses to avoid being in Nikolic's company. She seemed to panic whenever he appeared and, finally, she had confessed why. Mannion, furious, had sought out the Captain, and it was not Mannion's fault that they didn't come to blows. Nikolic had apologised abjectly, blaming too much wine for what he claimed was an isolated incident of innocent flirtation. Mannion had not forced the issue further. Thereafter, however, he had made no attempt to conceal his dislike of Nikolic. The Captain, in turn – while always presenting a bluff friendliness to Mannion's face – never lost an opportunity to disparage the American behind his back. Aware of this malicious tittle-tattle, Mannion ignored it.

Only to Marko did Mannion make any comment about the disagreeable fact that Nikolic would be riding with them on the bridge-blowing mission, and that was just to point out that the Captain was an odd choice for a job that would require tact and diplomacy.

'It's like sending an arsonist to put out a fire,' he said. 'I'd feel a lot safer without him. He's a loudmouth and a bigot, and the last person on earth I'd send anywhere near the Communists. He only needs to open his mouth and he'll get us all lynched.'

Marko's fears were well justified. Within minutes of reaching the village and being invited to a meal of hot food in the Partisan commander's quarters, Nikolic was voicing his opinion of the Partisan army on this, his first sight of its members – and none of it was complimentary. The guard post was wrongly sited, the men were sloppy and too familiar with their officers, and as for that ridiculous saluting with clenched fists. . . .

The Partisan officer stared at him, eyes bright, without emotion.

'My men may have ragged coats and leaky shoes, and perhaps they do not have the fine manners and fine plumes of professionals . . . but they know how to fight and they know how to die.'

'They probably know the braying of an ass, too, when they hear it,' Mannion said, looking daggers at Nikolic. 'At times it sounds uncannily like Captain Nikolic's voice.'

It took a moment for the insult to penetrate the wall of disdainful superiority. Then the blood rushed to Nikolic's face as comprehension was followed by anger. His hand flew to the pistol at his belt, but halted there. Nikolic hesitated as he met the challenging glare in Mannion's eyes.

'Damn your foreigner's impertinence!' he blustered. 'I've had men in irons for less! I'll have you broken!' For all his fierceness, the threat sounded feeble.

'Just shut your goddamned mouth,' Mannion growled. 'We're here to do a job, and the sooner you remember that and stop talking down your patronising nose, the better!'

But Nikolic was in no hurry to stop talking.

'You're a witness to this, Markovic,' he burbled on, drawing in Marko. 'You heard what he said. I'll have him disciplined and you'll back up my report when we get back.'

'Like hell I will,' Marko said vehemently. 'You're trouble, and you always have been, so don't expect any help from me. And don't expect any from the Colonel when we get back. He's wise to you and that poisonous tongue of yours. He wouldn't give a goddamn if he never saw you again.'

Nikolic faced them like a cornered animal.

'Damn you both!' he snarled.

He sulked like a petulant child, refusing the bowls of steaming soup brought to them by the Partisans, while the others drank theirs with relish. Mannion and Marko were about to set off to the bridge, when the Partisan who had been sent off to collect Nikolic's cousin returned in a rather agitated state. His commander asked him why he had returned alone, which increased his agitation.

'This man . . . the one you wanted – he is the one the village people said was a traitor . . . the one who bargained with the Germans and spoke against us.'

Nikolic was all ears now. He rose from the corner where he had been sitting staring out of the window at the rain.

'What is this you are saying? Where is my cousin?'

The Partisan officer faced him. His expression was gravely apprehensive.

'You will have to persuade the villagers to leave without your cousin's help.' He hesitated, plainly troubled. 'It was as you heard. He made deals with the Germans and tried to rally the people here against us.'

'Where is he?' Nikolic demanded, his voice shrill.

'He was tried and found guilty. Him and two others. They were executed.'

Nikolic's eyes bulged and seemed ready to burst from his head. A pining cry of disbelief burst from his throat.

'You bloody murderers!' he shouted. 'My cousin was a patriotic Serb, and you and your criminals murdered him!'

'He was no patriot,' the Partisan officer replied, anger in his own voice. 'He condemned himself from his own mouth. He denied nothing . . . regretted nothing. The Germans murdered fifteen people in this village and yet he still defended them, claiming that they were Serbia's friends and that the Partisans and Cetniks who opposed them were the real enemies.'

'He was right!' shouted Nikolic, beside himself with rage. 'You're rabble! Murdering rabble! I'd sooner fight with a German at my side than scum like you!'

The Partisan officer's face blanched, his drawn lips white with suppressed rage. His silence was the silence of a man retaining an exterior calm while boiling inside. He held out a hand in restraint, in a signal to one of his men near the door who had raised his rifle and cocked the bolt – the only sound to disturb the charged silence in the room. Mannion and Marko were frozen near the door, heads half-turned and shock etched on their faces.

Nikolic caught their looks.

'That goes for you, too,' he snarled. 'And that senile idiot who sent us here while he hides behind thick walls with his priests, weeping and praying for the salvation he'll never see.'

'Your tongue's running away with you again, Captain,' Mannion warned softly. 'If that guy over there was to put a bullet in you, I don't think I'd blame him.'

'Tell him to go ahead,' Nikolic invited, with bravado. 'Murder is probably all these goons know.' He turned to taunt the Partisan officer. 'Well, aren't you going to tell your man to shoot?'

The Partisan officer drew in his breath, as if summoning the last reserve of his self-control. When he spoke, his voice was calm but its tone was icy.

'You came here under the promise of my protection. I suggest you now leave before it is withdrawn. The kindest interpretation I can put on your words is that they have been provoked by shock. I did not realise that one of the traitors we dealt with was your cousin – the name meant nothing.' He drew another deep breath before adding tersely, 'Just go. While you can.'

Nikolic sniffed contemptuously, with a toss of his head.

'Don't expect my gratitude,' he scoffed. 'You may live to regret your charity.'

He strode past Mannion then turned and faced him. 'You may regret it, too. And that little whore you call your wife.'

Mannion lunged after him as he made for the door, but Marko restrained him.

'Let him go, Brad. The only fighting he's good for is with his mouth.'

Mannion shook himself free and stumbled after Nikolic, but the delay had afforded the Captain a good start. He was mounted and wheeling his horse out of the yard, where it had been tethered, before Mannion had shaken off Marko. At the sight of Mannion, Nikolic pulled his pistol from its holster and, swivelling in the saddle, fired wildly in his direction. The bullet whined off the stone lintel of the doorway behind the American. Mannion flung himself in the mud as a second shot screamed past his head. When he recovered, it was to the sound of galloping hooves as Nikolic urged his mount through the centre of the village at breakneck speed.

Marko, who had seized the rifle of a startled Partisan guard, aimed the weapon at the fleeing rider. But, in the moment of firing, a swift blow knocked the rifle upwards and the shot flew harmlessly in the air. Marko stared in astonishment at the Partisan officer who had followed him out and whose action had deflected his aim.

'That son of a rat will make mischief for us,' he protested to the Partisan.

'My men will stop him at the bridge,' the Partisan said. 'That's where he's heading. If he's to be returned to your Colonel, it will be alive. After that, it's the Colonel's decision whether or not he stays that way.'

But the Partisans did not stop Nikolic at the bridge. Nor did they stop him two kilometres further along the road, where forty of their men were occupying dugouts beside and above the road and watching the movements of German motorised units on a distant hillside. The Partisans, intent on their front, were taken by surprise by a single rider's approach from the direction of the village and by his failure to stop when some of their number stepped out into the road to greet him and investigate his haste. He swept past them and was last seen galloping headlong towards the enemy.

Mannion was crouched in mud on the riverbank below the bridge, placing the first charges, when they heard the rattle of machine-gun fire. Marko, handing him sticks of dynamite from a box wedged between his knees, cocked his head to one side, listening.

'We're not going to have as long as we thought,' he observed in a sad voice. 'Our Partisan friends said the Germans were miles away and didn't seem to be in a hurry.'

'Well, they're not miles away now!' Mannion commented with feeling. 'I just hope they can be stalled long enough for us to finish the job.'

The firing continued unabated while they worked feverishly. The Partisan commander had warned them that the forty or so men posted as the village's first line of defence, a couple of kilometres along the road to the northeast, could not be expected to present a serious obstacle to the Germans. His orders to them had been to slow the enemy as best they could, giving ground slowly to avoid encirclement and making the Germans fight for every metre of road to the bridge. In the meantime, he had ordered the villagers to evacuate their homes. Most had been only too willing to leave while the going was good, but a number had steadfastly refused to take such a drastic step. Even they were to change their minds as the day progressed. A factor was the sound of firing when the van of the approaching German column encountered the Partisans guarding the road approach to the bridge. More decisive, however, was the sudden appearance out of the north of three Junkers 88 fighter-bombers. The aircraft made no attempt to hit the bridge but concentrated their bombing and strafing attack on the village itself.

Mannion's first indication of this unexpected development was the sudden roar of aircraft engines and the earth-trembling blast of bombs exploding, a kilometre away. Perched precariously under the bridge, a couple of metres above the rushing torrent of the flooding river, he halted briefly from his work and commented on the uncomfortable proximity of the bursting bombs. Marko grinned at him.

'We're in the safest place,' he observed. 'This bridge will be the last place they want to hit. My guess is they'll want it in one piece.'

The raid was brief but terrifying for the people remaining in the village. Flying low, to remain under the grey cloud base, the warplanes made several swooping attacks before climbing away into the overcast. The house where the Partisan commander had established his headquarters was one of many reduced to smoking rubble, but the most costly loss was that of four trucks parked nearby: the Partisans' entire complement of motor transport. Providentially, the Partisan commander and his small entourage had quit their headquarters before it was hit.

At four in the afternoon, the bridge was successfully blown while, only a kilometre away, the Partisans, fighting a stubborn rearguard action along the road, were still instilling caution in the troops spearheading the German advance.

Night was falling as the last Partisan units were withdrawn across the river, which had risen dangerously with the autumn rains. Wet and silent, they trooped through the village, where Mannion and Marko directed them round a section of roadway which they had mined with buried charges and primitive pressure detonators. The abandoned village was eerily quiet as the pair made their way past bomb-shattered houses to the mustering point on its far side. There, the Partisan commander was waiting for them.

'So far, so good,' he greeted them. 'Thank God for the night.' There had been no sign so far that the Germans beyond the river were aware that the Partisans had quietly abandoned their positions. Now, however, the night erupted with the distinctive racket of mortars as the Germans rained bombs on the hill above the wrecked bridge. The Communist officer smiled wearily. 'Now it's only a matter of time before they find that they're wasting their ammunition on rabbits.'

'Maybe they'll wait for the morning before they come this side of the river,' Mannion suggested hopefully.

'Maybe they will but maybe they won't,' the officer said. 'Either way, I'm taking no chances. I don't intend to tangle with Hans if I can help it. My job is to extricate the men I've got left, so that we can all live to fight another day. Manpower is the most precious commodity we've got, and I don't intend to waste ours fighting battles we can't win.'

He reasoned that the Germans, advancing in steam-roller fashion along the arterial roads, would be only too pleased to flatten all opposition in their path – and that they had the strength to accomplish this. He had no intention of obliging their generals by lying down in their way.

'Let them have the roads,' he said. 'God knows, they're few enough and bad enough. But if they want *us*, let them follow us into the mountains and forests, where their armoured trucks and heavy guns can't move. That'll even out the odds.'

While it was still daylight, he had directed evacuees from the village and a Partisan group with wounded to avoid the road – where they would be at the mercy of strafing aircraft – and head overland towards the Cetnik monastery. Now, with the Germans pounding the abandoned positions above the wrecked bridge, he led the remainder of his force along the route taken by the refugees, away from the road.

The tracks, through forest and along steep hillsides, were almost impossibly difficult in darkness, but by dawn they were more than ten kilometres from the vacated village and within sight of the crags where the Cetnik base was located. Marko had some reservations about the welcome they might expect.

'The Colonel is going to have a fit when his hidey-hole is invaded by this lot,' he confided to Mannion. 'It's one thing cooperating with the Communists, but something else again having them crawling all over his sanctum sanctorum.'

'He might be glad of the reinforcements,' Mannion replied. 'Especially if the Krauts divert a couple of infantry companies to look for us.'

'That would really make the Colonel pop his cork. The old boy thinks the Germans wouldn't find his eagle's nest if they looked for a hundred years.'

'So Lela's always telling me,' said Mannion. 'But I wouldn't bet too much money on it. Even if she does quote Victor Hugo at me.'

Marko's eyebrows lifted. 'Victor Hugo? Should I know him?'

Mannion laughed. 'Not you, Marko. But your brother Stefan sure would. I reckon he was deeper into French poets than you or me.'

Marko made a face. 'Did this poet write about Serbia?'

Mannion laughed again. 'No, but he wrote a poem about picking a flower for some dame he was crazy about . . . I wouldn't have known about it if I hadn't picked some flowers for Lela on the rocks, back of the monastery.'

'You picked flowers?' Marko's grin was of the ear-to-ear variety. 'I didn't think you were the flower-picking type.'

Mannion grinned back.

'Never judge a book by the cover, Marko. Me, I'm a very romantic guy, deep down.' He cocked an eye at his companion. 'And what's wrong with a guy picking flowers for his wife?'

'Nothing. Nothing at all.' He shrugged his great shoulders with an air of mystification. 'I'm just wondering what it has to do with our headquarters and the chance of the Germans ever finding it.'

'Because of our little hideaway's inaccessibility,' Mannion explained. 'The same as the place where this guy Victor Hugo picked his flower. A place, he said, that only the eagle knew and only the eagle could approach. The kind of place that nobody would find in a hundred years.'

Comprehension dawned on Marko's face like a sunrise. 'Ah, I see!' he exclaimed, and then his face darkened. 'But there's a snag. A place like that is only difficult to find if there's only one person who knows about it and doesn't tell anyone else where it is. I'm not thinking of eagles . . . I'm thinking of rats.'

Mannion shot a look at his companion.

'Any rat in particular?'

'A rat called Nikolic,' Marko said, his face grim. 'I've been wondering why it was that the Germans stopped puddling about and came belting towards us yesterday, why they suddenly decided to send three aircraft up in poor flying conditions to bomb a relatively unimportant village. Was it because somebody told them that we were about to blow up that damned bridge and it was time they got their skates on?'

Mannion's face darkened. 'Surely not even Nikolic. . . ?'

'That son of a bitch is capable of anything!' Marko interrupted fiercely. 'It's too much of a coincidence. It all happened too quickly. With you or me, the Germans would have had to beat the hell out of us to tell what we knew, but Nikolic would have been running off at the mouth to them before he was out of the saddle – anything to save his own miserable neck!'

'We can't be sure,' Mannion said, but his light-heartedness of a few moments earlier had left him. He had been buoyed and happy at the knowledge that, in a few hours, he would be holding Lela in his arms. Now, the fatigue of three days with next to no sleep suddenly seemed to hit him.

The drone of distant aircraft did nothing to ease his misgivings. At the first sound, there was a bustle of activity as the uneven line of Partisans suddenly broke at a shout from their commander. Turning back from the head of the column, he jogged his horse along the straggle of weary men, urging them up from the open floor of the valley towards the firs and spruce that cloaked its slopes. They forced tired limbs to quicken as they loped for cover; rewarded for the effort, when they reached the trees, with the chance to sprawl and rest their bodies.

The aircraft, dots in the morning blue, passed over at height. On foot, the Partisan commander led his horse past his resting men to tether the animal beside the thicket where Mannion and Marko had tethered theirs.

'The planes are too high to be looking for us,' he said to the pair. 'But we'll take a break. The men are nearly all in.'

'Three Junkers 88s'' said Marko. 'Maybe the same three that hit the village yesterday.'

'Maybe,' said the Partisan officer. 'Who knows?' He stared at the sky. 'If it is the same lot, they've got other business this morning.'

Mannion, his eyes also searching the sky, was filled with a terrible foreboding as he concentrated his senses on the still audible throb of the aircraft engines. 'They're coming back,' he said. There was a perceptible change in the character of the droning sound – a quickening of throttle – and the tone grew louder. The three Junkers *were* returning.

They came back down the valley in line ahead at five hundred metres and wheeled in a one-hundred-and-eighty-degree turn above the fringe of forest where the

Partisans had taken cover. One moment, the black undersides of the wings, which spanned over twenty metres, were stark agains the blue of the sky, and then they tipped as the bombers turned and their shapes seemed to merge with the green of the far hillside.

The roar from three pairs of twelve-cylinder engines almost drowned the curse that Marko hurled at the gracefully wheeling aircraft. 'Damn their eyes!' he shouted, as they screamed away along the valley. 'They can't possibly have seen us!'

'It's not us they're interested in!' The words came from Mannion with a vehemence born of the intuitive realisation that was like a screaming voice in his mind. 'It's the monastery they're after!' He was already racing for his horse. Mounted, he paused only to throw a terse explanation in the direction of the astonished Partisan officer. 'I've got to know,' he shouted. 'I'll see from higher up.' Then he was urging his mount up through the trees and, in moments, was lost from sight.

His mind seething with premonitory dread, Mannion drove his horse right and then left as he angled his way up the incline through the trees. The animal was lathered in sweat when, aiming for a bright patch of light, he emerged into sunlight and a rocky saddle affording a panoramic vista of valley and mountain. Throughout the desperate climb, the sound of the bombers' engines had maintained a constant accompaniment, sometimes distant, sometimes close, spurring him and goading his fevered mind.

Dismounting, he clambered over rock, seeking a view of the tooth-shaped crag where the Cetniks had made their base. He had no difficulty picking it out. Around its distinctive summit, the three bombers were circling in a lazy arc, like eagles viewing their prospective kill. Eagles! The irony of the simile of eagles, and the romantic notions they had conjured scarcely half an hour ago, now welled in his mind like bitter gall.

The pilots in the wheeling planes had finished their runs to identify their target. They had considered their options on line of approach and altitude, assessing the difficulties and calculating the technicalities of achieving maximum effect. Now they made their attacking runs, safe in the knowledge that there would be no gauntlet of murderous flak to brave.

Mannion could not discern the actual monastery building, knowing only that it was part of the molarlike tusk of rock towards which the three bombers winged in steady flight. He cried out in impotent protest as shooting pillars of smoke and rock flew from the mountain face, followed by spewing avalanches of stone.

The horrendous spectacle lasted for less than five minutes, but every second was an agony for Mannion, knowing that, somewhere amid the cataclysmic horror he was watching, was the wife whom he had thought safe from any danger. Now it was over and the dustclouds from the cascading avalanches were beginning to clear, Mannion could see where the ancient monastery had been. A black area, from which smoke drifted, was new; as if part of the mountain had been gouged away from its face.

The three aircraft had not finished their day's work. They turned their attention to a new target: a hump of open hillside which lay between Mannion and the tooth-shaped mountain. The Junkers had climbed away to regroup on completion of their bombing runs; now they came diving down to swoop below the hilltops and speed down the valley at treetop level, cannons blazing. It dawned on Mannion what their target must be; the refugees from the village and the wounded, evacuated by the Partisans, had been caught in the open.

Mannion did not have to wait long to see the proof. The distressed survivors of the Junkers' parting attack were overtaken by the main Partisan force an hour after resuming their trek. Worse awaited them when they reached what had been the Cetnik base. Even locating it was difficult. Its approaches had been obliterated by avalanches from which the dust still rose. Of the monastery itself, there was no trace. It – and the eight-hundred-metre shelf of land supporting it – had slipped down the mountainside and been buried by massive rockfalls from higher up the mountain. The character of the mountain's face had been changed beyond recognition by the aerial bombardment and the avalanches it had triggered.

No survivors were found; only the mangled corpses of three men and a horse. Between a hundred and a hundred and fifty dead lay uncounted and irrecoverable below thousands of tons of rock.

Desolate and alone, Mannion searched for Lela on the mountainside, while the Partisans made camp in a sheltered gully a little way along the valley. He was still searching as darkness approached and Marko found him.

'Come away, old friend,' he coaxed. 'You must let her rest in peace. You will not find her.'

Mannion nodded dumbly. She was gone, her lovely body crushed and broken below these cursed rocks. And, within her, the child that would not now be born. The knowledge of his loss overwhelmed him, crushing him and weighing down on him as if it were he who was pinned in darkness below immovable granite.

He allowed Marko to lead him down the mountain-side and support him when he stumbled. He was almost unconscious on his feet, overtaken at last by three days and three nights with little or no sleep and by the shock of grief such as he had never known. He walked like an automaton, not knowing or caring where Marko led him. He was only vaguely aware of the cooking fire, past which he stumbled like a drunk, and of the earthy cave mouth where he sat on rock while Marko spread his cape and bedroll.

'Come on, my friend,' he heard Marko say. 'Rest is what you need, and God knows when we'll get the chance of it again.'

Mannion sank to his knees on the spread cape and tried, clumsily, to enfold himself in the blanket that Marko held out for him. He fumbled with it, using only one hand. And it was then that Marko saw that his other hand was clenched shut. Mannion was clutching something between fingers that were grimed and torn.

Marko gently prised the fingers apart. The broken stem and crushed white petals of a flower fluttered from Mannion's hand. Mannion watched them fall.

'It was growing on the mountain,' he said in a broken voice. His stricken soul was in the red-rimmed eyes of the upturned face, staring at Marko's. The face crumpled and looked down. Flames from the nearby cooking fire bathed the spread cape with flickers of dancing orange light. Against the dark sheen of the cape, the fallen petals lay like scattered snowflakes.

In the grey light of morning, the Partisans broke camp and marched away from the tooth-shaped mountain. Mannion and Marko were the last to leave that place of desolation. 'Join us,' the Partisan commander had urged them both, but had not sought a snap decision. He had left them to talk it over.

A scarlet rim of sun was peeping over the eastern hills when Mannion took his last look at the mountain. He stared at it for a long time. In the past, he had never looked back – but now, for the rest of his life, he knew he always would be looking back. And the image of that mountain would always be there, with the image of Lela. He would only have to close his eyes and she would be with him: the fragrance of her hair, her smile, the touch of her skin, the lovelight in her eyes. These would stay with him now. Forever. Always.

Marko waited, a little way off, as Mannion made his silent farewell. He said nothing when, finally, Mannion came cantering towards him. They exchanged quizzical little smiles and a nod of understanding. Then, wheeling their mounts, they rode side by side towards a distant sound, which neither could at first identify. It was only when they neared the file of men moving ahead of them that they recognised what they were hearing. The Partisans were singing as they marched.

8

The End of the Beginning

The days of the 'Red Republic of Uzice' – as disillusioned residents of Tito's headquarters town had dubbed it – were numbered. Djordje knew it when he telephoned a crossroads inn only a few miles from the town to talk to a Partisan colleague who was living there, and a German Army officer answered on the other end of the line. Only the day before, the crossroads had not been consideredd to be in imminent danger. Now it was in enemy hands!

Djordje was an unhappy man. Ever since his arrival in Uzice, he had tried to persuade the Central Committee to construct strong defensive positions in a ring around the town, in preparation for the German attack which he felt was inevitable. No one wanted to know, at least while the 'Front', as the confused battle lines were known, was nowhere near Uzice. More concern was shown for programmes of political education, the establishment of a propaganda press, and the norms of civil government than for what Djordje saw as military necessities. Some of the Central Committee got more worked up about the Cetniks than they did about the threat posed by the German Army.

Certainly, the Cetniks gave them cause. Accounts of their treachery and atrocities came in from all sides with a frequency that could not be ignored – but accounts of misguided Communist provocation *were* ignored. Impartiality was not the Central Committee's strong point. Tito, to his credit, had gone out of his way to reach for some kind of harmony with Mihailovic – but he did not hesitate to show the mailed fist when he felt the need arose.

He demonstrated this when the intelligence grapevine reported an intended Cetnik attack on a Partisan company which had occupied a number of hill villages and irked the local inhabitants by trying to politicise them. Tito moved in more men and pre-empted the Cetnik attack by striking first and vanquishing the Cetniks. There were more Partisan casualties in the battle than Cetnik, but Tito showed remarkable restraint afterwards. He did not shoot all the prisoners – as the Cetniks would have done if they had won. He executed only those who could not bring themselves to join the Partisan army. Only a few die-hard officers elected to die rather than change sides.

Djordje realised that what bedevilled the hopes of any real harmony between Partisans and Cetniks was the absence of a single leadership in the Cetnik ranks. Mihailovic, hermitlike in Ravna Gora, believed he was the supremo – because the exiled King had said so – but he had no control over half the *hadjuk* outfits who claimed to be Cetniks and operated like the bandit chiefs of old. Then there were the out-and-out Cetnik traitors, whom Mihailovic did not even consider enemies, as the Partisans did: the State Guard, raised by the puppet, Nedic, in Belgrade, and Ljotic's Volunteer Corps. Both organisations were indirectly, if not directly, controlled by the Germans. The amorphous nature of the Cetnik beast made it almost impossible to deal with. The Partisan movement, on the other hand, spoke with one voice and acted as an entity. And it had no difficulty identifying its enemies. If it had a notable failing, that lay in a consistent difficulty in recognising its friends.

Jamie's return to Uzice, with the news of Dudic's death, saddened Djordje beyond measure. The grisly end of the young officer epitomised, for him, the tragedy of his torn country: what he saw as a death-wish syndrome – an unhappy compulsion for fratricidal conflict at a time when the need for the brotherly union of all the South Slavs was greatest.

Djordje's general unhappiness was compounded when Tito vetoed his wish of an early return to Montenegro. Instead, he was allotted a vague role connected with Headquarters security and the gathering of military intelligence. The Central Committee, no less than the Command in Montenegro, were paranoid about the infiltration of fifth columnists, Axis spies and Cetnik *agents provocateurs* – and Djordje was given the job, loosely defined, of establishing a counter-intelligence office that was answerable directly to Tito, in his dual role as Party chief and Army commander. It was anathema to Djordje to have to work as a kind of secret policeman, but he was flattered, nevertheless, to be given a task that measured the high trust placed in him by Tito. Not everyone approved of Djordje's appointment and what appeared to be his patronage by the Secretary-General.

Tito's personal secretary, Zdenka, disapproved – because of the easy access to Tito it afforded Djordje – but Zdenka was jealous of anyone who had the ear of her master. Also unhappy was the Croatian Gubec – a Party zealot who had adopted the name of a celebrated South Slav revolutionary and martyr of another age, and who now saw himself as the scourge of all counter-revolutionaries and traitors. Gubec now found himself in a junior capacity and resented Djordje's insertion above him as a kind of overlord to his activities. Gubec had enjoyed power in the pursuit and elimination of enemies of the Party and brought a holy zeal to the office of avenging angel. It rankled with Gubec that the man who had been placed in authority over him was – in his opinion – of more fragile stuff and lacked the steel to do the job.

All Gubec's fears about his new boss were confirmed on Djordje's first visit to the prison in Uzice, where a variety of suspected Party enemies, traitors and informers were being held for examination. Djordje arrived with Stefan, his first lieutenant, and the two men were appalled to discover a number of prisoners with untreated injuries. Gubec could not comprehend their anger when he explained that the prisoners had come by their injuries under interrogation. Nor did he take kindly to the furious tongue-lashing Djordje gave him when he admitted that he, personally, had broken the fingers of the two most seriously injured men in an effort to extract confessions. Gubec could not understand why there was any need to go easy on two traitors just because they were ignorant hill peasants without a dinar to their name. They had made trouble for the Partisans, rousing a whole village against them with demonstrations and hostile speeches. How was he to find out who had put them up to it if he didn't get rough with them?

'And did they give you your confession?' Djordje demanded icily.

'No,' Gubec admitted. 'They persisted with their lies that they had not been put up to it . . . that it was all spontaneous and that they were speaking for the whole village. They were afraid of what would happen if the Germans came.'

'Did it occur to you that they might be speaking the plain truth?' Djordje asked.

'The Cetniks are behind them. The whole village is Cetnik. All the villages are Cetnik.'

'And they're wary of strangers,' Djordje agreed. 'Any strangers. We've got to win their trust, damn you. Not persecute them because they're afraid.'

Djordje went on to warn Gubec that he was going to change the way things were run. And he started by ordering the release of the two rather elderly hill peasants, after their injuries had been treated. To Gubec's dismay, more releases followed as Djordje and Stefan examined the charges relating to every prisoner in his custody. It seemed that a native of the region had only to make an indiscreet comment that was faintly critical of Communists or Partisan presence to be suspected of being in league with the Germans.

Prophesying dire consequences as the inevitable outcome of Djordje's leniency, Gubec reluctantly freed more than half the prisoners. When, on the very next day – 12 November – a huge explosion rocked the Partisan Headquarters in the National Bank, he reacted like a man who had been proven wholly justified by an act of divine wrath.

Tito and his staff – Zdenka almost gibbering with shock – poured out of the bank as ceilings collapsed about their ears, believing that an air raid had started. They stood amid the shards of glass blasted from the bank's windows, scanning the sky for a sight of a bomber that was not there. The explosion had actually occurred *underneath* the bank – in the vaults, where the Partisans had set up a makeshift ordnance factory.

When Djordje and Stefan arrived on the scene, it was to find engineers trying to seal off the underground chambers from the air in order to halt the spread of a raging fire. Below, explosions were still occurring as the flames reached boxes of bullets and grenades scattered in its path. Later, when the fire was spent and cries of sabotage were in the air, Djordje and Stefan began their search for the cause.

Inside the warren of vaults, they found huddles of corpses sitting where they had died, with handkerchiefs masking their mouths and nostrils. They had escaped the blast and the fire but had died of suffocation when the exits were sealed. It was impossible to calculate the number of dead because no one knew how many people had been working underground at the time. Nor was it possible to determine the cause of the blast. There was no evidence of sabotage, but much to suggest a tragic and predictable accident had occurred.

In the haste to produce arms and ammunition, even the most basic rules of industrial safety had been ignored. Electrical cables snaked all over the floors, unprotected and with threadbare wiring, joined here and there with no insulation. Powder and highly inflammable materials were stacked higgledy-piggledy wherever there was floor-room, close to sparking lathes and welding benches. It would have constituted an insurance inspector's nightmare.

Security against unwelcome visitors had been non-existent, with people going in and out at will, and this had precluded even the paranoid Gubec from shouting too loudly that the disaster was the work of Party enemies and saboteurs. Any accusations would have rebounded on his head because, until the previous day, he had been responsible for Headquarters security.

Djordje, acutely aware that it was a case of locking the stable door after the horse had bolted, instituted a card identity system. But even that was to be rendered a meaningless exercise by the march of events. Just how futile was brought home to Djordje on the morning that he telephoned a colleague and the call was answered by a German officer.

At Headquarters, he ran into Tito as he was about to motor out with the British officer, Hudson, to view the battlefront. And probably regale the officer with tales of the 1914 war, Djordje thought. In that conflict, Tito had been a soldier in the Austrian Army – fighting the Serbs – and he had served in the Sumadija campaign. Later, he had deserted to the Russians and become involved with the Bolsheviks, but he still liked to talk – unwisely, Djordje thought – of his soldiering days around Uzice. Tito seemed blissfully unaware of how his Austrian Army reminiscences set on edge the teeth of any Serb who happened to be listening.

Djordje did not get the chance to tell Tito about the telephone call. Tito had already come to the conclusion that Uzice was going to be difficult to hold, and he had ordered the evacuation to Mount Zlatibor of all Partisan staff and personnel not involved in defence of the town. He included Djordje in that number and charged him with the safe removal from Headquarters of Party records and other vital material. That included the Partisan treasure trove of nearly half a ton of silver coins. The money, contained in stout chests, had been appropriated from banks under Partisan jurisdiction.

By noon, the silver and several sacks of documents – a by-product of the Partisans' brief bureaucratic reign in Uzice – had been loaded into three trucks and were ready to leave. Jamie and Stefan rode shotgun on one. Djordje travelled in the cab of the second with Gubec and a couple of guards in the back. Their destination was the mountain village of Kraljeve Vode, where Tito had decided to locate his new headquarters.

The trucks became part of a steady procession trickling south out of Uzice on to the road that wound high into the Zlatibor range. Little knots of townspeople watched with sullen faces as they left, under no illusions about the sudden exodus. The brief day of the Red Republic was over, and Uzice was being abandoned to its fate.

From the high ridge, Jamie and Stefan had an eagle's-eye view of the road. It snaked in a great semicircle below them, appearing as a thread away to their left, looping all the way round the hill they had climbed, to disappear behind them. For some time now, they had been watching the approach of a dozen or more Partisans who had appeared on the hillside beyond the road and slithered down the steep slope towards it. Stefan had hailed the men and, with joy and new heart, it seemed, the group started climbing towards them as if their lives depended on their haste. The indication that was really the case came when the climbing men were only thirty or forty metres below the watchers' position. A sudden volley of firing echoed from beyond the far hillside. To the surprise of the men on the ridge – four of Gubec's men had joined Jamie and Stefan – one of the Partisans below turned and, waving his fists in fury, started screaming hate-filled obscenities at the hill opposite. His tirade was answered almost immediately by a burst of automatic rifle fire. Bullets whined off rocks in the vicinity of the enraged man.

It was one of Gubec's men who shouted and pointed to a gap that broke the outline of the facing hill: the precise place where the Partisans had first been seen. Antlike figures seemed to swarm from the gap, the scuttle helmets they wore somehow adding to the impression of busy insects. The six on the ridge opened fire with telling effect and maintained it while the Partisans below them scrambled desperately for safety.

One of the Partisans plumped down beside Jamie as he sighted on a German who had reached the road and was calmly directing others to a cluster of boulders which offered protection from the heights. Jamie's shot went screaming away crazily as a voice at his elbow said to him in English: 'Hello, old buddy. Fancy meeting you here.'

He turned on his side to stare into the gaunt eyes of a stranger. With a sense of shock, he recognised Mannion. He was about to speak, when Mannion pre-empted him.

'Later,' the American growled. 'Business comes first.' He eased himself into a lying position alongside Jamie, sighting his rifle. With deliberation, he began to fire. He was selecting his targets carefully among the German soldiers, who were moving methodically down the far slope towards the road without any regard for fire from the ridge. Mannion grunted with satisfaction each time he fired – a small signal of pleasure at the deadly accuracy of his shots.

From away to the left, a machine-gun suddenly chattered and the ridge was swept with the whine and scream of bullets ricocheting from rock. A scout car had appeared at a bend in the road, away to the left, and the fire was coming from the gun mounted on a frame beside the driver. From the road below came the shrill blasts of a whistle, then movement there and on the far hillside abruptly ceased as the Germans scurried for cover in a ravine-like dip below the level of the road. It was as if the ground had opened and swallowed them up. Nothing moved.

Mannion rolled over and slid below the ridge, behind Jamie.

'Now would be a good time to leave,' he announced. 'They'll wait for their buddies on the road to catch them up. That buggy with the gun on top is probably out front of a line of armoured trucks.' Light flecks of snow were swirling into their faces out of a leaden sky. Mannion glanced up. 'It's gonna be dark soon. With any luck, the Krauts'll call it a day.'

A thousand and one questions were bursting in Jamie's mind, but he said, 'What makes you think that?'

'The sons of bitches have been doggin' us for a week . . . all the way from Pozega.'

'It shows on your face. You look – '

'Washed out? Screwed witless?' Mannion gave a harsh laugh. 'We thought we'd be OK if we could get to Uzice. That was where we were gonna be safe! Everything was gonna be hunky-dory if we could just get to Uzice!'

'We left the day before yesterday,' Jamie said. 'Stefan's here.'

'So I see,' Mannion said, glancing over his shoulder. Some distance away, two men were hugging each other and exchanging emotion-charged greetings. 'Marko's here, too.'

'Are the Germans in Uzice?' Jamie asked.

'They're all over the goddamned place!' Mannion muttered fiercely. 'We never saw much of the town. We were running too goddamned fast. In one end and out the other! Jesus, we've been running ever since. I thought I was never gonna get up that goddamned hill. All we've been doing is fighting and running, fighting and running . . . it makes you go kinda crazy. Did you hear old Petrovic bawling at the Krauts?'

'It was a crazy thing to do. You could have been wiped out on that hill.'

'Maybe we would have all felt better if we had been,' Mannion said bitterly. 'We didn't want to leave the other guys. But the boss man said go – and we went!'

'The boss man?'

'The Big Chief. The Partisan capo. The guy who ran our outfit. He had half his leg shot away and he made us leave him behind in a gully just back of that hill over there. Him and twenty other guys, all wounded! He ordered us out at the point of a gun – those of us who were fit, that is. He told us to save ourselves, get the hell out of it, or he personally would put a bullet in our heads. And goddamn us, we went! We just walked away and left them for the Krauts!'

'You mean. . . ?'

'I mean,' snarled Mannion, 'that they're dead now! Every last mother's son of them! You must have heard the firing!'

Jamie winced at the anger in Mannion's voice. He remembered the sound of firing that had preceded their first view of Germans on the hill opposite. He winced again as Mannion asked him caustically, 'Where have you been fighting this war, old buddy? Didn't you know the Krauts don't take no prisoners?'

Jamie didn't reply. The joy he had felt at seeing his old friend again had gone and a strange pain had taken its place. It was Mannion who had soured things, with his scowling bitterness. That had been no part of the man he had known.

'Time we were moving,' Jamie said, as much to the

others crouched behind the ridge as to Mannion. One of Gubec's men nodded and voiced his agreement. He had slithered down from his vantage point.

'They've gone to ground below us,' he reported, 'and the weather's hiding us from that gunner.' A squally snow shower was swirling along the hillside and the gun-mounted scout car was obscured somewhere beyond it.

There was a warm greeting for Jamie from Marko when they came face to face, but the pleasantries took second place to the more urgent demands of the moment. The priority now was a speedy return to Kraljeve Vode, which was some kilometres away. Stefan and Jamie led their now augmented party down the hill to rejoin the road where it looped behind the west-facing slope. There was a risk that they might be quickly overtaken by German vehicles pressing along the road from the other side of the hill, but they banked on the Germans staying where they were until morning. Darkness came down like a blanket, suddenly, as if to confirm their wisdom in choosing the road – although even that had its hazards.

The first was a man-made landslide, the work of Partisan sappers, and the second was a great hole, where ten metres of roadway had been. This, too, was the work of sappers, who had blown up the road only that afternoon. Beyond it was a roadblock manned by Partisans, who fired at the newcomers – fortunately without causing injury – before identities could be established.

Once they were through the roadblock, the tension that had gripped the group fell away. Before, they had been silent, nerves on edge. Now, as they neared the mountain village, they felt safer. They chattered happily, Mannion's Partisan comrades speculating extravagantly on the food that might be available in Kraljeve Vode. The two brothers strode together, Stefan almost elated at the red patch Marko displayed on his coat. Did it mean that Marko had been converted to the cause of revolutionary socialism? The pair joked amiably about such an unlikelihood, displaying a close-ness and comradeship which, somehow, their past relationship had never allowed to blossom. Before, they had just been brothers. Now, they were brothers-in-arms.

Jamie, still nettled at Mannion's surliness towards him, marched alone – ahead of the others.

'Wait for me, goddamn you,' a voice called. 'Some of us have blisters.' Jamie waited for Mannion to catch up with him. 'I thought you guys were in Montenegro,' the American said.

'We were,' said Jamie, striding out again.

'You're sore at me?'

'Why should I be sore at you?'

'Because I sounded off at you, back there on that hill.'

'You've changed, Brad.'

'Yeah,' Mannion admitted. 'I've changed.'

'Do you want to talk about it?'

'No. It's nothing personal. I just don't want to talk about it. OK?'

'Whatever you want, Brad.'

'I don't want you to be sore at me. Just give me time, eh? Goddamn it, Jamie, when I saw you up there on that hill . . . when I saw it was you . . . I was so glad. I wanted to cry. Crazy, ain't it? I was chewed up inside. Well, I'm telling you right now so's you can laugh at it.'

'I'm not laughing, Brad. I was glad to see you. I never thought I'd see your ugly face again, damn you! I thought my eyes were playing me tricks. At first, I thought it wasn't you but just somebody who looked like you. You really are different.'

'We all change. I'm older.'

'Yes,' Jamie agreed. 'We're all older.' He recalled the night near Cacak, when they had last talked. 'How about your girl friend, Brad? Lela, wasn't it? Is she still special?'

When there was no immediate reply, Jamie glanced sharply at Mannion.

'She's dead, Jamie,' Mannion said, and the break in his voice was more eloquent than a hundred explanations. It said so much. In an instant, it conveyed to Jamie the immensity of his friend's hurt with such clarity that his empathy was like a cloudburst of pain. Jamie lived night and day with the fear that he might never see Mara again; fighting it. Hope was his only sustenance, the only weapon with which he could keep the unendurable at bay. And so Jamie suffered for Mannion, whose loss was fact and not fear of loss.

'I'm sorry, Brad,' he said, and the dark hid the tears that wet his eyes. They walked on in silence. They had reached the outskirts of Kraljeve Vode before the silence was broken. It was Mannion who spoke, his tone falsely light.

'You never did tell me what you guys were doing, sitting on top of that mountain back there,' he said. 'Did somebody send you out to look for strays and stragglers, or was it just a lucky chance you were there?'

Jamie laughed.

'It wasn't stragglers we were looking for, Brad. It was the big White Chief himself – Comrade Secretary-General Tito. He should have turned up at Headquarters yesterday but nobody has seen hide nor hair of him. The place has been in a right old panic.'

'God help him if the Krauts have got hold of him,' Mannion said. 'What about his bodyguards? I thought those guys never went anywhere without a big escort.'

'The Old Man's a law unto himself. The last time Djordje saw him, he was shooting off in his car with a British officer. That was in Uzice. There was just the Old Man, the officer and the Old Man's driver. They were going to take a look at the fighting – but we got a report that the car got shot up by a strafing plane.'

'Djordje?' Mannion echoed. 'The same guy we knew in Belgrade?'

'The same,' Jamie confirmed. 'You met Tito, too. In Zagreb. You gave him a lecture about the Communist Party being the next best thing in Jugoslavia to Roosevelt's Democrats, remember? Djordje often talks about it. He thinks it was priceless.'

Mannion was remembering.

'Was Tito the guy in the snappy suit? Looked like the president of the First National Bank and did a lot of talking?'

'That was him,' Jamie said. 'He's still a fancy dresser. Only now he's got a Russian cap with scrambled eggs all over it.'

'He wasn't old,' Mannion recalled. 'Why do you call him the Old Man?'

'Because he's Number One in the Party, I suppose. Everybody talks about him as *Stari* – the Old Man. But not to his face.'

Kraljeve Vode had become an armed camp. It was filled with Partisans and they were camped wherever they could get a roof over their heads. The village boasted three hotels, but headquarters had been established in a fine-looking villa whose owner was absent. It was in this crowded building that Jamie and Stefan found Djordje to report that their search for Tito had been unsuccessful. Djordje was dismayed and not a little alarmed when he learned how close the Germans were to the village. In spite of this, he went out of his way to arrange warm food and shelter for the weary Partisans with whom Jamie and Stefan had returned. The shelter turned out to be an empty truck – one of many parked in side tracks that gave access to houses off the main road – but even the cold interior of a truck was better than sleeping in the open.

The next day dawned dismal and grey, and with only

one note of cheer to lift the hearts of the Partisans. Their charismatic leader was safe and sound, having turned up in the middle of the night, looking rather the worse for wear. Mud-stained and grimy, he and the British Colonel – and the unit escorting them – had escaped a close encounter with a battalion of German infantry by crawling along a ravine and trekking to Kraljeve Vode. The morning, however, brought no other consolations. The military situation was grim and it took Tito and his staff little time to decide that their only course was to preserve their meagre resources of manpower and material by ordering a general retreat.

The order given, Tito and three members of his hierarchy climbed into a car and it drove off to the south. Jamie watched them go. The ready smile which usually softened and so transformed the Secretary-General's handsome face was absent today. He looked tense and strained. Inside the headquarters villa, the faces bore the same taut look. Already preparations for a quick departure were under way. Djordje confirmed what Jamie had already guessed: the Partisan army was in no shape to regroup and offer serious opposition to the advancing Germans. It would fall back through the mountains, all the way to Montenegro if necessary.

Jamie left the villa to find Stefan and break the news to him that their departure, this time, would not be in the relative comfort of a truck but on foot. Those trucks not needed for supplies – and the inevitable chests of silver coinage – were to be reserved for the seriously wounded, Party officials and noncombatant personnel. Those who were able to fight, would walk. Djordje had not objected when Jamie suggested that he and Stefan team up temporarily with the Partisan unit to which Mannion and Marko had attached themselves.

They were on the trail within an hour. They marched abreast: Jamie, Mannion, Stefan and Marko. They did not look back at the headquarters villa, where there was still much activity. Tomorrow or the next day, that house – the biggest and grandest in Kraljeve Vode – would be full of German officers flushed with victory.

Snow fluttered down from a grey sky, whitening the caps and shoulders of the marching Partisans and coating their eyebrows. Defeat had not dispirited them, and a night's rest had put new vigour into their tired bodies. One man started singing – and soon another took it up, and another, until the sound was welling up amongst the encompassing crags to the sullen sky.

Jamie felt his own spirits rise. It must have been like this in the other war, he thought. His father's war; his mother's war. They had faced the hopelessness of defeat, the misery of the Great Retreat – and yet they had come through. Their love had survived and, with it, him: already a seed in his mother's womb. It was as if he had come this way before, which, in a sense he had. That had been his beginning, as this endless march into nowhere was a kind of a beginning. He could feel it like a burning certainty, and he could feel the presence of Mara, as if she were with him and within him, willing him to keep faith, to endure – for her.

He became aware of Mannion beside him, singing in a raucous off-key voice. Their eyes met and Mannion grinned.

'Sing up, goddamn you!' the American bawled, and mouthed the words of the rousing ballad at Jamie in choirmaster fashion: 'There's a greenwood . . . by the Sava . . . where there stands an old oak tree. . . . And a girl sits . . . by that oak tree. . . . It's the girl who waits for me.'

Jamie had the tune better than Mannion, and he joined in, singing lustily. In his mind's eye, he could see the Sava and the botanical gardens below the Kalemegdan. And he could see the girl, waiting. The girl was Mara.

PART THREE
ANOTHER MOUNTAIN, ANOTHER RIVER

1

Autumn, 1943

It was a day without wind, one of those glorious
September days when the sun's warmth was like a kiss
on the skin. There was a languid glassiness to the Sava's
gentle flow; its dunny hue was bright with diamond
sparkles of glittering sunlight. The sight of it comforted
Mara. It goes on forever, she thought. Night and day,
summer and winter, always moving, never still, through
tempest and shine, times of sorrow and times of joy;
always changing and yet never changing, eternal.

Passers-by glanced at the girl, struck by her sad-eyed
beauty; impressed by it in spite of the trim uniform that
denoted her service to the occupying power. Few of the
Sunday promenaders displayed the hostility they invariably felt for the uniformed invaders of their city – but
this was not because the Red Cross insignia on Mara's
sleeve muted such hostility. Two years of foreign
occupation had taught the citizens of Belgrade how to
hate with impassive faces.

Mara's return to Belgrade was full of trauma. She was
unprepared for the scale of devastation that met her
eyes. And she was unready for the experience of feeling
and being made to feel alien in the city she considered
her true home. She could not explain, nor did she make
any attempt to try, that her uniform and her attachment
to a German military hospital did not signify approval of
the Nazi cause. They were the means to an end:
trappings that revealed no more of the woman and her
heart than a bus ticket.

In Vienna, her work as a reservist in the Army Nursing

Corps had been an escape from the despair of being separated from Jamie – an antidote to the impotence of exile. But she had kept her reasons to herself. Who would have understood, even if she had cared to explain? Ironically, it was the Army Nursing Corps that had provided her with the opportunity to end her exile. There had been a call for volunteers to muster a mobile hospital unit for service in Jugoslavia. Mara had leapt at the chance. Her hopes that, somehow, she would find Jamie had rocketed sky-high, and it was in a state of intense expectation that she returned to Belgrade. Then came the shocks.

A kind of normality had returned to the city since its devastation by the Luftwaffe. The trams still ran and the docks and railways were as busy as ever – but familiar landmarks had gone, whole streets had disappeared or were lined with mountains of rubble. Friends, too, had disappeared, with few clues to whether they were living or dead. Had they died in the apartment buildings, now ruined, where once they had lived – or had they fled? Mara had no way of telling.

She went out to the home of Jamie's Uncle Milan, to find it occupied by six German Army officers. They received her politely and suggested that their civilian cook, who had come with the billet, might know something about the previous residents. Old Lucija had become a crotchety and embittered woman, who did not disguise her contempt for her unwanted guests. Nor did she hold back her venom at the sight of Mara in her 'German Army' uniform.

'I'm a nurse, not a soldier,' Mara told her several times, but it did not stop the old woman from scathingly commenting on what she thought of traitors and turn-coats in general and Mara in particular. Nevertheless, she told Mara that Milan and his sister were dead and that, yes, she had seen Jamie.

'Where is he? Have you heard from him?' Mara pleaded. 'I must know.'

'He went to fight with the Cetniks,' Lucija crowed at her triumphantly. 'And if I knew where he was, I wouldn't tell you. Better he's dead than has anything to do with the likes of you.'

Other friends whom Mara traced were equally hostile to her; particularly two ex-students who had roomed with her. Both were Serbs, and Mara was stung to tears by their cold rejection of her as a 'Croatian whore'. It was bad enough to be called a whore without the national tag being attached to it. Croatian by birth she might be, but she had long since shaken off the prejudices and anti-Serb nationalism that went with her birthright. Most of her friends had been Serbs and it was their passion for freedom and justice and the Jugoslav ideal that had shaped her entire outlook and helped to create the gulf that separated her from her parents. Indeed, if she hadn't been more Serbian than the Serbs in spirit, she would not have been in the plight she now endured.

As she strolled in the garden walks beside the Sava and experienced the glancing appraisal of the other Sunday promenaders, Mara wondered if they were all judging her as her former friends had done. Did they see the uniform she wore and conclude that an enemy walked in their midst? It was another hurt to bear: to be hated on sight, not for what she was but for what she seemed to be.

She was approaching a bench seat where an elderly man was sitting, reading a newspaper. He glanced up, and there was recognition in his eyes before he hastily averted them. Hope suddenly lifted in Mara's breast. She recognised the man: a professor at the University, a liberal, well known for his sympathies for all things democratic. He had played a leading part in the campaign to have Jamie freed from prison. But he stared at her blankly in response to her eager greeting.

'Were you one of my students?' he asked, with an air of

bewilderment. 'I'm sorry that I cannot recall you. There have been so many.' He fluttered a hand apologetically. 'And my memory is not so good.'

'My name is Mara Richtman. You must remember me. You helped me raise money to free my fiancé from prison. You put me in touch with the people who helped in his escape from Lepoglava. . . .'

The man reacted as if he had been prodded with an electric probe. He shot up from the bench, looking around fearfully. 'You are making a mistake, young lady. I have never seen you before in my life.'

He would not listen to Mara. The more she pleaded, the more flustered he became, shaking his head and telling her he did not want to hear. Finally, he turned on his heel and hurried away, almost running. Mara stared after him, defeated. She knew he had been lying. He had recognised her instantly, in spite of the uniform. It was the uniform that provoked his lies and excuses about failing memory, of course. The uniform of a nurse, but it had been enough to frighten the life out of a man whom she had once considered brave – a moral giant! His fear filled her with disgust.

Mara continued her walk, unusually angry. Now, when the promenaders stole glances at her, she stared back at them, daring them to meet her gaze and feeling better when they quickly turned their eyes away. Damn you, she silently challenged them, think what you like!

The only happy thing that happened to Mara after her arrival in Belgrade was the return into her life of her brother Petar. He provided the only ray of brightness. His sudden appearance in Belgrade – only a week after her own return – was a small miracle for which she daily thanked God. They had corresponded all the time he was on the Eastern Front and during his long spell in hospital in Russia, after he was wounded near Kharkov. Then there had been a silence: a silence which Mara interpreted as confirmation of his forecast that he would

410

return to the Front as soon as he was fit. But he had not returned to the Front. He had been brought back to a training centre in Austria to await a new posting. And the new posting had turned out to be Belgrade.

The hard realities of war and more than one narrow escape from death had done little to dampen his sunny nature. Nor had they diminished his enthusiasm for the German Army. If anything, his pride in belonging to this martial brotherhood had increased. It disturbed Mara, but was not a subject of contention between them. Their affection for each other overrode all other considerations. Mara felt no hypocrisy over her love for Petar because, in personality and behaviour, he was the living antithesis of all she associated with Nazism. He was kind and gentle and honourable to such a degree that his pride in belonging to an army whose overlord was a Nazi seemed almost a mild eccentricity.

After her encounter with the professor who had chosen not to remember her, it was the prospect of meeting Petar later in the day that helped her to banish her ill humour. Somehow, he always managed to cheer her up and that – she acknowledged to herself, with a smile – was no easy job. For two weeks now, she had missed his morale-building banter and levity – he had gone off to Zagreb for a fortnight – and she realised that she needed it now as an opium addict needs the comfort of his pipe.

Mara was billeted in what had formerly been a hostel for female university students, and it was from there that Petar collected her in the early evening. He arrived in the company of a young Hauptsturmfuehrer who might have been an advertisement for the Aryan race: tall, blond, athletically built, and with clear blue eyes. Wolf Bleyer was an intelligence officer, attached to HQ staff in Zagreb.

'Wolf was at a loose end, so I asked him along to have

dinner with us,' Petar told Mara. 'He's a good guy. We cracked a bottle or two in Zagreb at his expense so I'm returning the compliment.' Petar escorted Mara down the path from the hostel to a dun-coloured staff car, where Bleyer was sitting behind the wheel. He leapt out at the sight of Mara and waited to be introduced.

'I don't know what your brother told you,' he said, 'but the only reason he asked me out to dinner was because he needed a chauffeur. I was available. I hope it's not an intrusion.'

'The more the merrier,' said Mara politely. Privately, she was sorry that she was not going to have Petar to herself. She hoped that the need would not arise to spell out to Petar's friend that she was 'not available'.

'He's right about us needing a chauffeur,' Petar put in chirpily. 'There's no point in having friends if you can't use them. These *Abwehr* boys can get anything they want, believe me. What do you think of him, Mara? He hasn't been in Belgrade five minutes and he can whistle up a car just like that!'

Bleyer laughed. 'If I wanted to walk everywhere, I would have stayed in the infantry.'

They drove out to a hotel that had once been famous for its Serbian cuisine. It had reopened recently under Croatian management as the Hotel Adlon. Its customers were mainly officers from the Army of Occupation, which did not displease Mara. It meant escape from the resentful stares of the native population. Petar was strangely subdued throughout their meal, and it was left to Wolf Bleyer to stimulate the conversation and provide an air of congeniality – a task he accomplished manfully, with a wit and charm that came easily to him. It was on his insistence that they ordered a bottle of cognac to accompany the jug of strong Turkish coffee with which they finished.

'You need cheering up,' he told Petar. 'I've never known you so dull.'

'I wish I was back on the Eastern Front,' Petar said gloomily.

Bleyer looked at him, askance.

'Maybe we'd better make that two bottles of cognac – and you'd better see the regimental psychiatrist in the morning. You're crazy!'

'I mean it,' Petar said. 'Life wasn't complicated out on the steppes, fighting the Ivans. It's different here.'

'But you're not fighting anyone in Belgrade. You've got a nice cushy desk job here.' Bleyer winked at Mara. 'He doesn't know when he's well off.'

'I won't be behind a desk forever,' Petar said. 'I wasn't sent to Zagreb to do two weeks' parachute training just for the hell of it.'

Bleyer's smile left his face.

'You're worried because you'll maybe have to fight Partisans?'

'Let's just say that I would rather fight anywhere else in the world than Jugoslavia,' Petar said.

'You don't need to apologise for it,' Bleyer said. 'I don't blame you for feeling the way you do. You know what I think about things.'

Petar looked across the table at Mara.

'Wolf says that if he had been born a Jugoslav, he would be fighting with the Partisans against the Ustashi and the Cetniks.'

Mara regarded Bleyer, eyebrows raised. 'And against the German Army, too?' she inquired softly. 'Isn't that strange talk for a Nazi?'

Bleyer smiled at her.

'For a Nazi, yes, it would be strange talk. But I don't happen to be one. I'm just an old-fashioned German who believes that governments should be elected by the people, and not at the point of a gun.'

'Then you are on the wrong side,' Mara said sweetly.

Bleyer smiled again.

'That thought has occurred to me frequently – but

413

please don't get me wrong. I'm a soldier, and a loyal one. I'll do what I'm told and I'll fight whoever I'm told to fight. That doesn't mean that I have to approve of everything that goes on – because a lot of it makes me downright ashamed.'

'Then surely you should do something about it,' Mara prompted.

The handsome young officer shrugged.

'I am only a very small cog in a very small wheel that's part of a very large and very complicated machine. I can only function as best I can within the limits I'm given. The machine I'm part of isn't even going to hiccup if I fall off, or even if the wheel on which I'm a cog falls off. It'll go on just the same.'

'What makes you sympathetic to the Partisans?' Mara persisted.

'I didn't say I was sympathetic to the Partisans,' Bleyer corrected her. 'What I said to Petar was that if I had been born in this country, which you and Petar were, I would be a Partisan, too.'

'Are you suggesting that we should change sides?' Mara asked, intrigued by this German.

Bleyer laughed softly.

'Heaven forbid,' he said. 'By language and tradition and lineal descent, you are as German as I am, and it's to your credit that you chose to wear German uniforms. I would think less of you if you had joined up with one of those ragtime Croatian outfits or Nadic's lot, who only seem to be interested in killing Jugoslavs – particularly Jugoslavs of a different religious persuasion.'

'The Partisans are Communist bandits and terrorists, according to the newspapers.' Mara's eyes challenged Bleyer's. 'But you seem to admire them. Are you a Communist?'

Bleyer laughed delightedly.

'I wouldn't last ten minutes in my job if I was,' he declared, smiling. 'Believe me, I detest Communism and

414

all it stands for. Please don't mistake my admiration for the Partisans as fondness for Communism. Besides, admiration is the wrong word . . . I have a healthy respect for the Partisans. Respect is the better word. I respect their integrity, their courage, their spirit of patriotism. They're more representative of Jugoslavia as a whole than any of the other assorted bunches who claim to be. That includes Germany's so-called allies. Pavelic's Ustashi are just barbarians, led by savages. Even the ones we've tried to train and incorporate in the Army. Ask Petar.'

Petar nodded grimly and, when he spoke, his voice was heavy with irony. 'The illustrious Kama Division – the celebrated Muslim SS. The Prophet's gift to the Third Reich . . . *sans* discipline, *sans* reliability, *sans* principles, *sans* honour.'

'A disgrace by any standards,' Bleyer agreed. 'They were sent to train in France and terrorised the country-side, stealing and raping. When we tried to sort them out, they mutinied and demanded to be returned home – where, apparently, they can rape and pillage to their hearts' content – and fight, of course; preferably against undefended villages with Christian inhabitants.'

'The trouble is that Pavelic was given too free a hand in Croatia,' Petar said. 'The Wehrmacht should have taken control in 1941 instead of letting the nationalists run riot.' He looked at Mara, who was listening, white-faced, taking in all they were saying. 'It shames me that people like our father have been given almost unlimited power to indulge their worst instincts . . . people one would have expected to have been guided by good Catholic principles. I can understand the Muslims hating the Serbs and their Orthodox traditions and wanting to wipe them out, but our Catholics are no better. Their hatred for the Serbs is obscene.'

'Did you go to Karlovac when you were in Zagreb?' Mara asked.

'Unfortunately, yes,' Petar said, with a snort of disgust. 'I felt it my filial duty to visit the old family home, more for Mama's sake than Papa's. But I wish I hadn't gone. I certainly won't be going back. Ever!'

'Not even to see Mama?' Mara was surprised.

'Not even for her!' Petar declared firmly.

'Why?' Mara asked.

'Better you don't know,' Petar said.

But Mara persisted.

'I want to know.'

'It was Papa's boasting that settled it for me, if you must know. That and the fact that Mama sat and listened to it all without batting an eyelid, as if he had been talking about the price of corn. I have never been more sickened in my life.'

'Tell me about it,' Mara said.

'Must I?'

'I want to know.'

Petar stared at her unhappily.

'Papa has some kind of political responsibility for part of Bosnia; not exactly a governorship, but he has to go there often. He was blowing about it and going on about how the Ustashi parade before him everywhere he goes.' Petar hesitated, but he continued at Mara's urging. 'It seems that the Ustashi like to show off to visitors when they've been on a raid,' he said, groping for words. 'They present their commander with proof of all the Serbs they've killed – buckets full of eyes.'

'Eyes?' Mara's white face went paler still. Petar did not spare her.

'Butchering defenceless men, women and children is not enough for them. They gouge out the eyes afterwards and present them as trophies. Our father seems to think that it's a most amusing little custom.'

Mara bowed her head. 'I'm sorry I asked,' she said, her voice faint.

'Now you know why I wish I was back on the Eastern Front,' Petar said.

'And why I respect the Partisans,' Bleyer added. 'We gave them a good hiding last winter, but they fought well – more like an army than our propaganda gives them credit for. They're well disciplined and well led. I became quite friendly with two of their leaders last spring.'

Mara could not contain her surprise.

'You became friendly with Partisans. How?'

'It was after our Operation Weiss had run out of steam,' Bleyer explained. 'We thought we had their army encircled, but they fought their way out, across the Neretva River and up into the barren lands of the interior. We were as happy as they were to call an unofficial truce. They sent over delegates to negotiate an exchange of prisoners.'

'I have never heard of this,' Mara said.

'Not many people have,' Bleyer told her, with a smile. 'So don't go blabbing about it. It's privileged information. Some of our people found it most embarrassing.'

Mara blinked at Bleyer, astonished at his candour, yet liking him for it.

'Why should it be embarrassing?' she asked, amusing both Bleyer and her brother with her naivety.

'Our Nazi masters in Berlin were apoplectic,' the German said, grinning. 'They haven't got round to admitting that the Partisans have got an army, so they were furious when they heard that we were acknowledging the fact by treating them as an honourable enemy and doing deals with them under a white flag. Mind you, it didn't win the Partisans much applause in Moscow either. According to all reports, Stalin and his crew were enraged at the idea of a Marxist army swopping prisoners with anybody. Hitler and Stalin are two of a kind, of course. Neither of them subscribe to the military convention of taking prisoners. They much prefer to avoid the necessity of housing and feeding opponents of a different political colour. Better to shoot them.'

Mara looked around the restaurant anxiously.

'Isn't it dangerous to talk like that. The Gestapo. . .?'

Bleyer laughed.

'I don't give a damn. If there was a squad of them at this table, I would tell them the same as I'm telling you. It's only the plain truth.'

'You said you became friendly with two Partisan leaders,' Mara said, encouraged by Bleyer's openness. 'How did you manage this?'

'I more or less lived with them for the best part of a month – in Zagreb. I won't pretend I didn't have an ulterior motive. I was after every scrap of information they could give me. But they knew that. We treated it as a game. We had some great discussions – once they realised that we had no intention of harming them and that we wanted to negotiate in good faith. I think they suspected trickery and were agreeably surprised by how well we treated them.'

'And did an exchange of prisoners ever take place?' Mara asked.

'Oh, yes,' Bleyer said. 'Only a handful each way, I admit. But both sides honoured the bargain.' He laughed softly. 'And the cunning blighters put one over on us. They told us that one of the Communists they wanted us to hand over – a woman whose importance was an absolute mystery to us – was the girl friend of one of their top officers. That wasn't quite the truth. We have since found out that she was the wife of the Partisan leader, Tito. If we had known that, we might not have been in such a hurry to let her go.'

Mara smiled.

'So, your two Partisan friends pulled the wool over your eyes?'

Bleyer smiled back.

'They did not lie to me. They simply withheld part of the truth. I do not grudge them their little success. They were good fellows. One was a soldier, a senior com-

mander in their army, and he conducted himself at all
times as a soldier should. The other was a political
commissar; cultured, clever, a man of great intelligence
and silver-tongued with it – a far cry from the uncouth
louts that Dr Goebbels talks about. And he argued the
case for the Partisans well – with great dignity, without
fear, and with no self-pity for the desperate suffering that
they have been enduring just to survive. He asked only
one thing: that we Germans recognise that the Partisan
army is a legitimate army conducting a national war of
liberation and that we treat it as such and respect the
civilised conventions of war in our struggles with it.'

'And will the German Army honour these conventions?' Mara inquired, with just a trace of waspishness.

'Oh, it would if it was left to the Army,' Bleyer said,
and made an eloquent shrug of his shoulders. 'Alas, the
Army takes its orders from Berlin. And Berlin has no
more intention of respecting the Partisans' wishes for a
conventional war than they showed for the truce.'

'You broke the truce?' Mara asked, and again both
Bleyer and Petar seemed to find her naivety amusing.

'My dear,' Bleyer said. 'The truce suited both sides at
the time. It afforded a breathing space. But neither side
had any intention of observing it indefinitely. It was
simply a matter of who recovered his breath first. It
happened to be us.'

Mara was bemused. The ways of men were beyond
her comprehension.

On the way back to the hostel, Petar sat in the back of the
car beside his sister and made a joke of the chauffeur
status he had conferred upon Bleyer. 'Back to the palace,
driver,' he commanded regally.

'Yes, Your Excellency,' Bleyer replied with suitable
servility. But not even their jesting lifted the mood of
despondency that had settled on Mara.

'Did you mean what you said about wanting to go

back to the Russian Front?' she asked Petar, disturbed by what she saw as a suicidal wish on her brother's part.

'I meant it, all right,' he said. 'The issues there are clear-cut. Here, they are a mess. I don't want to fight people who were once my friends.'

'What if you are ordered to fight?'

'Then I'll do it. I'm a soldier.'

'But it doesn't make sense, Petar.'

'Does war ever make sense?' he said, with a sad little smile. 'Unfortunately, war is the only profession I have. And I'll have no complaints if the only reward it ever brings me is a shallow grave on a cold mountain.'

'You mustn't talk like that, Petar.'

'Why not, Mara? The thought of dying doesn't worry me. Dying is an occupational risk.'

'But what you die *for* is surely important.'

'You mean an ideal?' He laughed. 'Communism, National Socialism? Croatian independence? Serbian nationalism? Roman Catholicism? Capitalism? There's a bit of all these isms in me . . . in most of us, if we admit it. But don't ask me to sort out how much of one or how much of the other. I would become a nervous wreck if I tried. Soldiering is all I know and all I care about and, if I'm going to be damned for it, I'll be damned for it.'

'But it's a matter of conscience,' Mara argued.

Petar smiled.

'Bless you, Mara, you've got enough for both of us. If it ever comes to the stage where I suffer a crisis of conscience, I can always follow the example of Marko Kraljevic.'

Bleyer, who had been unashamedly listening to their conversation as he drove along, chipped in from the front seat: 'Who in the name of creation is Marko Kraljevic, Petar?'

'Keep your eyes on the road, Chauffeur,' Petar advised him breezily. 'Didn't the *Abwehr* teach you anything about Serbian history at training school?'

Bleyer laughed. 'Myth and legend, most of it,' he replied. 'And the names went in one ear and out the other. What was Marko Kraljevic's claim to fame?'

It was Mara who supplied the answer.

'He was a famous Serbian soldier who had a crisis of conscience,' she said. 'He found himself on the wrong side when the Turks came face to face with the Serbian army of Voerod Mircea.'

'How did he manage that?' Bleyer asked, over his shoulder.

'He was in the service of the Turks, a vassal who'd sworn an oath of allegiance to his Turkish overlord. He didn't want to fight against the Christian army, but his oath of honour obliged him to.'

'So how did he get out of it?'

'He didn't,' Petar explained. 'He fought for the Turks and was killed in battle.'

'I see,' said Bleyer. 'Problem solved.'

'No, you don't see,' said Mara. 'The point was that, on the eve of the battle, Marko Kraljevic prayed for victory for the Christians, even if it meant he lost his own life.'

'Ah, now I see!' Bleyer exclaimed. 'In this war, the Muslims are on our side, which gives you, Petar, the same kind of problem that old Marko had. The only snag is that the Partisans don't have any religion, unless you count Communism. They're certainly not Christians. So you don't need to have any qualms about fighting them. They're the ones who have abandoned God.'

'They would argue that God has abandoned Jugoslavia,' Petar commented ruefully.

'They could be right,' Bleyer said, with feeling. 'The more I see of it, the more convinced I become that all the people here are crazy. That includes you, Petar, old friend, and it certainly includes me!' He grinned round at Mara. 'It doesn't include you, my dear. You may not know it, but you're the first sane person I've met since I got here. As well as being the most beautiful.'

'Listen to him!' Petar scoffed. He nudged his sister. 'Watch him, Mara. These *Abwehr* types are not to be trusted.'

'She could trust me with her life,' Bleyer protested, pretending outrage. 'I was about to suggest that she have lunch with me tomorrow. Just the two of us. The poor girl must be fed up with all your doom and gloom, Petar. She needs a break. What do you say, Mara?'

'I'm sorry, I'm on duty all day tomorrow,' Mara murmured.

'She's also engaged to be married,' Petar informed Bleyer, who was crestfallen.

'Who's the lucky fellow?' he asked.

'Someone she met at university,' Petar said, before Mara could answer. 'Quiet, unassuming, good-looking, intelligent. You don't have a chance.'

'I'd like to meet him,' Bleyer said. 'He sounds just like me.'

'Forget it, Wolf,' Petar advised him. 'Mara hasn't seen him since the war started. We have no idea where he is.'

'Maybe I could find him for you,' Bleyer suggested. 'I'm pretty good at tracking people down. It's part of my job.' He brought the car to a halt. They were outside Mara's hostel.

'Why should you want to help?' Mara asked Bleyer.

He swung round in his seat to face her.

'Because Petar is my friend,' he said. 'Because you, too, are my friend, I hope. And because, if there is one thing I should like above all others, it would be to do something that would chase away that sad look in your eyes, to make you smile. No one as beautiful as you should be so sad.'

Mara blushed in the darkness, confused by the feelings that ran through her. She had wanted to resent Wolf Bleyer but, in spite of herself, she found herself liking him more and more as the evening wore on. She

422

wanted to respond to his candour, to return trust with trust. He was clearly attracted by her and – if she were truthful – she by him. But it was disloyal to Jamie even to make that admission. It required effort on her part to get through the formality of goodnights, and it was with relief she reached the privacy of her room.

In bed, sleep eluded her. So, too, did the image of Jamie which she tried to conjure to her mind as she sought sleep. Always, before, Jamie's had been the face she summoned as she gave herself to sleep, and his had been the presence that filled her dreams and stayed with her until morning. But tonight the longed for image would not come. The love-filled dreams that made the night her friend refused to be beckoned.

She cried herself to sleep, calling his name into her pillow.

Jamie had the sensation of falling through space, sinking through black swirling mists, weightless, clawing out with his hands but powerless to arrest his drifting descent. Then the mists became a river, the colour of tar, and he was trying to swim. But his strokes were feeble and the sinking sensation recurred. Now, he was drowning: pulled down into the black depths. Above him, he could see light, and he thrust for it, lungs bursting. He shot through the surface of water that now foamed all around him. The light was not the light of day but explosions of pyrotechnical brilliance that flashed red and yellow and orange and threw dancing rainbows of colour across the dark waters of the river. Jamie threw himself towards the black shape that was the river's edge. It was beyond him. He fell on his hands and knees and found he was in shallow water. Where the river swirled around him, its dark tones took on a crimson hue – as if it were running with blood. Still the flash and thunder of bursting light filled the air above him: great spears of leaping red that streaked from darkness into darkness, and bright star-bursts of blinding white that erupted and hung like balls of bursting flame.

Jamie could not breathe and, kneeling in the water, clutched both hands to his chest. The water that poured from him was icy but the liquid oozing stickily between his fingers was warm, and he recognised it as his blood, welling from within him. He cried out.

The cry was heard by the bearded man who was bent over a cot at the far end of the room. It was heard, too, by Stefan, who had arrived in the doorway at that moment. The two men converged on the bed where Jamie lay.

'How is he, doctor?' Stefan asked.

'Very weak and still fevered,' he replied. 'We have done all we can.'

Stefan looked down at Jamie. His restless heaving had stopped but he was sweating profusely. Droplets of perspiration beaded his forehead and face and trickled down his neck. His hair was damp and sticking to his scalp.

'If you want to help your friend, you could bathe his face and head,' the doctor said. 'I'll get some water and a cloth.' He brought water and watched Stefan gently sponge Jamie's forehead.

'He seemed to be having a nightmare when I came in,' Stefan said.

'The fever,' the doctor said. 'Probably reliving the horrors he has been through. I am told that he would have died on the Sutjeska River but for you.'

'We had to fight our way across the river at night to break through the German line. They spotted us when we were crossing. Jamie was leading the attack when he was hit. I found him after we had knocked out the two machine-guns that nearly did for us. He was lying half in and half out of the water.'

'He could have drowned, I suppose.'

'The river was very low. No more than knee-high in places. We waded across.'

'It would be a pity if he dies now, after all this time,' the doctor said. 'His wound had almost completely healed when the infection set in. They say you carried him on your back from the Sutjeska.'

'Only for two days. Then we made a stretcher. It was either that or leave him.'

'You left the other wounded,' the doctor said. 'My brother was one of them. He didn't make it across the Sutjeska.'

'We were trapped,' Stefan said. 'We were surrounded by Germans. The only people who got out were those who could fight their way out.'

'I'm not accusing you, young man.' the doctor said. 'I know how bad it was. We lost five thousand men on the march from the Tara into Bosnia. I was with the Supreme Staff brigades and got out with them. You must have been with the wounded when the army split up. It must have been hard for you in the end . . . when you had to leave them.'

'We had no choice,' Stefan said, his face bleak. 'We did the best we could. We carried them all the way from Montenegro, with the Germans on our tails every inch of the way until they had us completely ringed.'

He stopped in the act of bathing Jamie's face, remembering the misery of the Partisan retreat that had brought him all the way from the highlands of Montenegro into Bosnia, to the relative peace of Mount Vlasic. Only a few months earlier, the retreat – equally bloody – had been in the opposite direction, from Bosnia and Hercegovina towards the wastes of the Sandzak and the mountains of Montenegro. Before that, there had been the calamitous defeat at Uzice, when the Partisans were driven out of Serbia into the Sandzak and beyond. It was a crazy war: back and forward, back and forward, with each string of minor Partisan victories followed by massive enemy offensives that drained the Partisan strength and reclaimed all the liberated territory.

The doctor left Stefan to continue his ministrations to Jamie. He checked each of the other patients crowded into what had been a schoolroom and was now his hospital. Most of them were asleep, and the doctor, taking one of the two storm lanterns that lit the crowded ward, whispered goodnight to Stefan and left.

'Don't die now,' Stefan murmured to Jamie, who lay unhearing. Stefan rested the damp cloth on his friend's brow and recoiled, startled, when Jamie suddenly sat up and screamed: 'No! No! No!' The dish of water was knocked from Stefan's hand. He ignored it and gently pushed Jamie back on the pillow, talking quietly to him and urging him to relax.

Jamie's eyes opened wide, as if sprung. He stared up at Stefan without seeming to see him. His eyes seemed to be focused through and beyond Stefan into distant space. Then his lips were working and he was talking in a low, unintelligible babble. In his delirium came two distinct phrases, delivered with near vehemence: 'I won't murder to eat!' and 'Give them my food.' Then, he convulsed, his mouth snapping open and shut as if electrical shocks were hitting him in waves.

In his nightmare, Jamie was hearing shots. They were ringing out in the still morning air. He was trying to close his ears to the sounds as they struck at his mind like the blows of a whip. The shots came from a gully lower on the mountain, close enough for each report to be heard distinctly, but far enough away for the weeping pleas of the victims to be muffled.

Jamie could not move. He was tethered, wrists and legs, to the men either side of him. All told, nine men were roped to each other, leg to leg and wrist to wrist; all were face down on the ground, just far enough apart to restrain movement of leg or arm. Four Partisans stood over them, rifles ready to use as clubs. Some of the men on the ground bled from head gashes, inflicted by rifle butts. Jamie had a trickle of blood from his temple. He

426

had been one of the most vociferous in his refusal to obey the Partisan officer's orders. The officer had felled him with a blow from his pistol.

The nine men on the ground had been the loudest in the almost general refusal to kill the Italian prisoners. They had not been cowed by the commander's threat to shoot any man who persisted in protesting his decision. The commander had finally ordered in a trusted squad to seize the noisiest of the protestors, as an assertion of his authority. The protest had crumbled.

A commissar delivered a short speech to the sullen men. The commissar was an eloquent man, noted for his bravery in battle. The sullen Partisans listened to him. The decision that the Italian prisoners must die – all three hundred of them – was as much an agony for him and the senior officers as it was for any man present. But it had to be done. There was no food to feed them and they could not be set at liberty. They knew the Partisan strength, their location and intended route. It would be suicide to let them go.

The Italians, most of whom had shared the hardships of Partisan life for months, sensed without being told that they were the cause of the general commotion. Their sudden fear and restlessness was akin to that of sheep who sense they have been marked for slaughter. They anxiously sought out Partisans who had become friends: men for whom they had cooked and carried and laundered. They could not believe their eyes when these same friends pointed rifles at them and shouted harshly at them, driving them down the hillside from the bivouac lines to the narrow gully that had been chosen as the place of execution. Their pleas for mercy and compassion went unheard, albeit many of their executioners wept openly as they performed their grisly task.

The shots echoed in Jamie's fevered brain like the lashes of a whip, each with its portion of agony, the pain no less real because it came to him in the flashing images of delirium. When the shooting ended, the Partisan commander returned to where the nine mutineers lay trussed on the ground. It had been in his mind to have all nine shot, in the interests of discipline. But, after watching the slaughter of the Italians, not even he had the stomach for more killings. He ordered the men to be released and, as a punishment, they were assigned to the heavy porterage previously undertaken by the prisoners: carriage of the dismantled components of the few howitzers that had not been abandoned on the trail. Carrying these loads over rough mountain tracks – in addition to personal equipment – was a murderous task and, in the days that followed, Jamie and his companions agreed that shooting might have been the preferable fate.

Stefan, continuing to bathe the sweat from Jamie's face, breathed a sigh of relief at a sign of calming in his friend. His restless heaving and turning subsided and his breathing became easier, although the sweat still poured from him. He seemed to be sleeping peacefully and Stefan was contemplating leaving him when he suddenly opened his eyes.

'Stefan?'

'It's me, old friend. Good to have you back.'

'Where am I?'

Stefan told him.

Jamie shook his head, bewildered.

'I'm confused,' he said.

'You were delirious. The fever. But you look more like your old self now.'

Jamie suddenly became fretful. 'Where are my clothes . . . my photo of Mara?'

His clothes were folded in a neat pile under the bed. Beside them was a small cardboard box containing the contents of his pockets. Stefan retrieved the box and fished from it a dog-eared and rather faded snapshot of Mara. He handed it to Jamie.

'Is this what you want?'

Jamie clutched it and let his breath out in a sigh as he subsided back on the pillow. 'Thank heaven!' he murmured. He frowned up at Stefan. 'I was trying to remember her face. For the life of me, I couldn't. Can you believe that?'

'It's been a long time,' Stefan said. 'I admire you. You've never looked at another girl.'

'I've been tempted,' Jamie confessed. 'That girl soldier in Uzice. The blonde, remember? She had a little garret room all to herself and she offered to share with me. I made an excuse . . . said I couldn't.'

'You never told me about that.'

'She was lonely, and a bit scared. She was only nineteen.'

'I rather fancied her myself,' Stefan said.

Jamie gave a bewildered little shake of his head.

'I can't even remember her name.'

'Her name was Lidija and she came from Slovenia,' Stefan said.

'I wonder what became of her?'

'Didn't you hear?' There was an inflection of surprise in Stefan's voice, and a sadness. 'The Cetniks caught her, up near Nova Varos. They shot her.'

A look of pain clouded Jamie's eyes. 'I didn't know,' he murmured.

'They say she died bravely,' Stefan said. 'At least they gave her the dignity of a soldier's death. The Cetniks boast that they don't waste bullets on our women. They usually hang them.'

Jamie had drifted off to sleep when, finally, Stefan left him. The photo of Mara was still clutched in Jamie's hand. He had fallen asleep, staring at it in rapt concentration, the rest of the world excluded.

Stefan left the makeshift hospital to find it almost as bright outside as it had been inside. A full moon was bathing the Vlasic Planina in silver light. The moon had been his friend on the previous night, allowing him to make good time on the return leg of a journey that had taken him away from Supreme Headquarters for a week and involved a tour of nearly five hundred kilometres.

Tito, personally, had asked him to make the fact-finding tour into western Croatia and the Lika, to assess morale and fighting strength, and Stefan set out in a mood of excitement heightened by news of Italy's surrender to the Allies. Throughout his journey, he was exhilarated by the enthusiasm he found for the Partisan cause and by the size of the areas under Partisan control.

The only rude shock came at his last stopover on the way back to Mount Vlasic. It was at Otocac, the town chosen by the Croatian Communist Party, ousted from Zagreb, for their base and administrative headquarters. The town lay at the northern end of the mountainous coastal region known as the Lika – an area renowned for the ferocity of its warrior inhabitants, who had a long tradition of piracy. Thirty kilometres from the sea, Otocac was sufficiently far from the key road and rail routes to have been largely ignored by the invaders. The Partisans had freed much of the surrounding countryside during the summer, aided in no small measure by the rebellious Licani and fugitive Serbian villagers who had fled from Ustashi depredations in Bosnia and inland Croatia. Indeed, so successful had the summer campaign been that the Ustashi thought twice about venturing anywhere in the Lika. They preferred the safety of the fortified coastal towns, which had become more and more isolated as the summer wore on. Otocac, therefore, had been considered reasonably safe when, in September, Stefan made it the last stop of his arduous tour. Yet it was there that three hundred Ustashi attacked out of the blue on his first night there, achieving complete surprise. They were driven off, but not before inflicting heavy casualties on the Partisans and civil population.

The incident provided the only adverse note in the otherwise glowing report which Stefan intended to present to Tito. It was in the early evening, twelve hours after leaving Otocac, that he arrived at Supreme Headquarters on the wooded slopes of Mount Vlasic, bursting to tell Tito about his travels. That eagerness did not last. His first disappointment was the discovery that Tito was absent from HQ. It was a chance encounter with his brother, Marko, however, that banished his haste to announce himself to the Supreme Commander.

Meeting Marko at HQ came as totally unexpected. Two months had passed since Stefan last saw him and, on that occasion, Marko had been setting out with the battalion to which he was attached as second in command. They had been ordered north, along the Una River. Stefan's happy surprise at seeing his brother again quickly turned to shock when Marko told him what had brought him back from active duty with his battalion.

Marko cheerfully revealed that he had been summoned back to Headquarters to answer a charge of 'promiscuous behaviour' and the accompanying accusation that he was unfit to hold officer rank. Stefan's dismay and anger in no way dented his brother's confidence that the inquiry he had to face would be a formality, and last only a few minutes while the tribunal established the facts. As far as he was concerned, the charges were a joke. The regrettable thing was that they had to be answered, nevertheless, because his principal accuser was the battalion's political commissar.

Stefan did not share his brother's unbounded confidence. He was acutely aware that, whatever the rights or wrongs of the case, the fact that it had arisen at all was an almighty embarrassment to him as the newest member of the Party's Central Committee. No member of that exalted body could afford even the whiff of scandal. Marko seemed to have no appreciation of the responsibilities which went with Stefan's new position, nor how important they were to him.

His elevation to the Central Committee had come as a surprise, but it was a source of great pride to Stefan, the more so because his sponsors were the idealistic Djordje and no less a personage than the General Secretary of the Party and Supreme Commander of the Army, Josip Broz Tito. Djordje had been left behind in Montenegro, earlier in the year, when the Partisan Army was driven from the Tara mountains of Durmitor, but not before he had recommended Stefan to both Tito and the Party. It was on Mount Vlasic, in July, that Tito sent for Stefan and told him that he had been coopted to the Central Committee.

'From now on, you'll be working closely with me,' he promised, and Stefan became a member of his inner circle from that day, acting as a sounding board for Tito's ideas and helping him draft tracts and pronouncements for the Party and the Army. A new gleam of commitment shone in Stefan's eyes. All who worked with Tito were exposed to his mercurial changes of mood but were also touched by the charismatic leader's certainty that destiny had selected him for great purposes – and Stefan was touched by it more than any. He felt as if divine forces were somehow directing his own life, like the chosen of God, and he was filled with a holy righteousness to be worthy of the role allotted to him. In particular, he wanted to prove worthy of the trust Tito had placed in him. He did not care that jealous elders disparaged his vigour and enthusiasm and talked about him as the 'court favourite' and *Stari's* 'blue-eyed boy'. What mattered to him was that Tito, the man he believed to hold Jugoslavia's destiny, should never be given cause to regret his choice of disciple.

As a result, it was a sickening blow that Marko dealt to Stefan's pride when, within an hour of his return to Mount Vlasic, he revealed his involvement in a scandal.

Marko's folly – whether proven or unproven – was going to hurt Stefan more than it could ever hurt Marko. It was Stefan who had persuaded the Party to invite Marko into membership as, equally, he had persuaded Marko that Party membership was the key to advancement in the Partisan Army. These facts would surely be remembered, when as a result of Marko's stupidity, the tongues started wagging and the fingers started pointing. It would not be at the ex-royalist officer and womaniser that the venom would be directed, but at his brother, who was guiltless of any deviation. And the worst could happen. Tito himself might be compelled to review his close association with a disciple who had become tainted in the Party's eyes.

Stefan had arrived at Mount Vlasic in a state of jubilant eagerness to see Tito. Within an hour, he was dreading the prospect and preoccupied with the repercussions which he was convinced would follow Marko's indiscretion. These, however, had fled from his mind on discovering that Jamie lay close to death in a village nearby. He had ridden down to the schoolhouse hospital like a man demented, afraid that he might be too late and ashamed that his own trifling worries had taken precedence over any thought for his dearest friend.

It was at a more leisurely pace and in a happier frame of mind that he made the return journey through the Headquarters defence line by moonlight. The sheer beauty of the silver landscape relaxed him – and one fear had been removed. Jamie was not going to die. He looked on it as a good omen. It would be next day, at the earliest, before his face-to-face with Tito; and, in the fresh light of tomorrow, today's problems would not look nearly so bad.

The horse lines were in a clearing below the HQ encampment, and Stefan chatted with the guards there before hoisting his saddle on his shoulder and climbing the tree-clad slope to the bivouac area. It was there that a staff orderly found him, with the message that Tito wanted to see him immediately.

'Where is he?' Stefan asked.

'The Command Post,' he was told.

'It's after midnight,' Stefan said. 'He's keeping late hours tonight.'

'Not by choice,' the orderly assured him, in an aggrieved tone. 'He said he wasn't going to turn in before you showed up – and the same went for me! I was beginning to think you had cleared out. Somebody said you had taken off down the mountain like a bat out of hell.'

'Something urgent came up. Sorry if I kept you from your sleep,' Stefan apologised. He walked up the hill to the Command Post with an air of foreboding.

2

The Man Called Tito

Stefan had no doubt in his mind that the urgency of Tito's summons was connected to the fact that Marko faced possible disgrace. Headquarters had probably been buzzing with the scandal for days and, no doubt, some of the old guard had taken advantage of his absence to poison Tito's mind against him. It was just a pity that, in the past, Tito had singled him out so openly for praise and made such a show of treating him like a favourite nephew. He had seemed to enjoy antagonising older Party activists by comparing Stefan's diligence and zeal with their bureaucratic plodding. Well, the old guard were going to have a field day now, thanks to Marko's stupid skirt-chasing. Stefan wondered how many of them had postponed going to bed in order to witness Tito's displeasure with his 'blue-eyed boy'.

In the event, none had. To Stefan's astonishment and relief, he found Tito in sole occupancy of the Command Post. Even Zdenka had gone. By the light of a paraffin lamp, the Supreme Commander was sitting at the roughly hewn table that served as a desk, poring over a mass of papers and maps. There was not a hint of animosity in his greeting to Stefan, which was cordial without being effusive.

'I was looking for you earlier,' Tito said. 'Zdenka said you had gone down to the hospital.'

Trust Zdenka to know everything, Stefan thought. He allowed himself a private smile. Zdenka was probably coming back into her own again. She was very subdued after Tito's wife, Herta, had turned up at Headquarters out of the blue, having been unexpectedly released from German custody. Unfortunately, Tito had recently moved his wife up north to a safer area.

'I was visiting a comrade,' Stefan said.

'Ah, yes. The Tiger of Bioce. How is he?'

'Very weak, and fevered. But he came to while I was with him. The doctor is confident he'll pull through.'

'I'm glad,' Tito said. 'I'm very glad.' And there was no doubting he meant it. One of the things Stefan liked about Tito was his passionate concern for the wounded and the sick. It was a concern that he had instilled in the entire Partisan movement. He looked up at Stefan with a flicker of uncertainty in his eyes. 'Do you think it would cheer your friend up if I were to look in and see him?'

'I'm sure it would,' Stefan said, with an enthusiasm that brought a smile to Tito's handsome face.

'Then I shall make a point of it,' Tito promised. He moved quickly to other business. 'Now, tell me, Stefan. How did you find our comrades in the north?'

The question took Stefan by surprise.

'You . . . you want my report?'

'Why do you think I've waited up half the night?' Tito's tone was impatient. 'I don't want chapter and verse right now, just a quick résumé. I've heard things that worry me, and I want to know if your impressions confirm them.'

Stefan gave a quick summary of his travels and the encouragement he drew from them, but there was little reaction from Tito. He cut short Stefan's account of the Ustashi raid on Otocac.

'You can deal with that fully when you get round to writing a full report,' he said. 'Tell me, when you were in Otocac did you encounter any criticism of the Croatian Party leadership? I want you to speak freely.'

'There was talk about their wives.'

'Any wife in particular?'

'Comrade Hebrang's mostly,' Stefan murmured,

diffidently. He was acutely aware that this was minefield territory. Next to Tito, Andrija Hebrang was probably the most powerful man in the Party. He was undisputed boss of the Party in Croatia.

Tito smiled: a disarming smile.

'Olga Hebrang,' he said, 'is young – a lot younger than Andrija – and she is a very attractive woman. Attractive women are often the target of malicious tongues. What do they say about her?'

'It may be malice,' Stefan said, thoughtfully, 'but it is the way she dresses that has caused the talk – always dolled up like a Paris model, while most of our girls don't have a change of clothes. They have to make do with poorly made uniforms that fit where they touch.'

Tito smiled again.

'A lot of them look none the worse for that. Do you know how Olga managed to acquire her magnificent wardrobe?'

'That's what hurts,' Stefan said. 'I was told that when our soldiers captured Otocac, Comrade Hebrang placed all the shops out of bounds for twenty-four hours before annexing the properties. This was so that Madame Hebrang and one or two of the other wives could help themselves to all the dresses and clothes they fancied.'

'Others have told me this,' Tito said, which was no surprise to Stefan. There was very little went on that did not come to Tito's ears. He stored the information, seldom showing the extent of his knowledge and rarely revealing his thoughts on the more contentious items. He could be impulsive at times – reckless, even – but usually he thought hard and long before disclosing his hand. 'And what about criticism of Comrade Hebrang himself?' he asked. 'Did people talk to you, make complaints?'

Stefan shrugged. People had talked all right – but he had heard people talk the same way about Tito.

'Some people resent his flashiness,' he said. 'You

437

know, nothing but the best is good enough for Hebrang – the best food, the grandest house, the finest clothes, the biggest car. . . . His aristocratic ways don't go down well with the rank and file. What is the point of having a revolution, they ask, if our Party leaders are just going to ape our class enemies?'

'Is that your opinion, too, Stefan?'

'There must be some privileges available to our leaders,' Stefan said carefully, conscious of the intent way Tito was watching his face. He went on, 'But I do object to privileges being flaunted.'

Tito gave no sign of agreeing or disagreeing with the observation. He changed tack.

'I am told that Comrade Hebrang places too much emphasis on Croatia and the Croats in his approach to the national struggle. Was that your impression, Stefan? That he neglects the Serbian and Montenegrin and Slovenian and other elements as second class, or at least incidental to Croatian interests?'

Stefan smiled.

'Comrade Hebrang does give the impression that the sun, moon and stars revolve around Croatia and that what's good for Croatia is good for the world. He distrusts us Serbs, he distrusts Russia, he distrusts anyone who isn't a Croat. It seems to be a failing of all Croats. . . . ' Stefan stopped and wished he could have bitten his tongue off – but Tito was regarding him more with amusement than reproach.

'I am a Croat,' he reminded Stefan softly.

Stefan tried hastily to make amends.

'You are the exception, Comrade Secretary. If you will allow me to say so, you submerge your Croatianism. . . . ' Stefan was floundering and he knew it. 'What I mean is that you bend over backwards to understand the Montenegrin point of view, the Serbian point of view . . . you *think* Jugoslav.'

Stefan's embarrassment amused Tito.

'Thank you for the vote of confidence,' the General Secretary said. 'It is reassuring to know that I may have a wider vision of things than Comrade Hebrang. Did you know that he opposed your admission to the Central Committee when it was proposed? Not because he knew very much about you, but because you are a Serb. He wanted a Croat for the job. Indeed, if he got his way, the Central Committee would be made up entirely of Croats. And he seems to think that, because I am a Croat, I should feel the same way.'

'I spoke without thinking,' Stefan admitted. 'It was a stupid remark to make. I'm sorry I made it, Comrade Secretary. I am against sectionalism in the Party and I know you are above it.'

'I think I can forgive one thoughtless generality,' Tito said, beaming. 'And there was a grain of truth in it. I didn't always *think* Jugoslav. There was a time when it was the Party line to oppose the unification of all our peoples under one flag and describe the creation of a single state as artificial – a parcelled-up product of the Treaty of Versailles. This war has changed all that kind of thinking. It has shown us that our strength lies in the union of all our peoples. We do not just seek freedom for the Serbs or the Croats or the Montenegrins but for all the south Slavs – and we alone speak for all the south Slavs. We Communists! Our struggle is the struggle of all our peoples and for the freedom of all our peoples, whether they are Christian or Muslim, Serb or Croat, Catholic or Jew.'

It was a long speech for Tito, who was not usually so loquacious. He sat back and rubbed his eyes, as if the effort had tired him. Stefan interpreted it as a signal to go but, before he could move, Tito – still massaging his eyes – spoke to him.

'Is there a matter you wish to discuss with me, Stefan?' When a reply was not immediately forthcoming, he added, 'I am told that your brother is in a bit of trouble.'

439

Stefan flushed. 'You know about it?'

'It was drawn to my attention. The charges against him are serious. Have you spoken to your brother?'

'Yes. According to him the charges are laughable. He doesn't seem to be unduly worried.'

'The matter will still be investigated. You appreciate that you must not interfere? And that I would not, even if you asked me to?'

'I have no intention of interfering. Nor of involving you, Comrade Secretary.'

'Yet you must be worried.'

'Marko isn't worried about it, and there's no reason I should be if it's just the storm in a teacup he says it is. He says that the woman who has accused him is a pathological liar and that it will take the inquiry only five minutes to realise that and dismiss the case.'

'The woman you talk about is not just any woman. She is the regimental commissar. What makes your brother so sure he can get off?'

Stefan hesitated. To tell the truth would be venturing on to delicate ground. He knew he was regarded as old-fashioned and puritanical in his attitude to sexual relationships, and this inhibited complete candour with Tito; he strongly disapproved of the General Secretary's liaison with Zdenka.

'I don't share my brother's casual attitude to adultery,' he said carefully. 'It's no crime in his eyes.'

Tito frowned.

'Would you stone adulterers, Stefan?'

'It's been said that I have a bourgeois morality,' Stefan replied, evading a direct answer. 'That isn't true. I abide by the Party's rulings on the kind of relationships that are permissible or not permissible. Not bourgeois concepts of marriage, overlaid with religious mores, but stability and commitment in relations between the sexes.'

'Are you lecturing me, Stefan?' Tito asked, with a

trace of annoyance. 'No one is questioning your moral integrity. We all know that you are as pure as the driven snow. But it is your brother who has been accused of playing fast and loose with other men's wives, not you.'

'All I have been trying to say, Comrade Secretary, is that Marko thinks it's all harmless fun. I don't. He says that if adultery is a crime – and he admits freely to it – then half the Central Committee would be put on trial.' Stefan was conscious of the colour flushing his face. He had not meant to put things quite so baldly but, there, he had said what was on his mind. Now he waited for Tito's anger. But the General Secretary's face remained impassive: a mask that betrayed no emotion or any sign that he had taken Stefan's words personally.

'So you do not approve of your brother's amorous attachments, Stefan?' Tito spoke solemnly, in a detached manner, as if thinking aloud.

'No, I don't. He has been a Party member for less than a year and second in command of a fighting battalion for only a month or two, but he doesn't seem to realise that moral obligations go with both functions. He thinks the job ends by being brave in battle. I've tried to tell him that the Party demands more than that. He has to show moral leadership as well as military leadership. What was good enough in the Royal Army isn't good enough in the Partisan Army.'

Tito nodded gravely.

'Perhaps it is just as well for him then that you will not be one of his judges.'

'I certainly wouldn't go easy on him just because we happen to be brothers,' Stefan confirmed with feeling. 'I just hope that this sorry affair brings him to his senses. He has not only let the Party down and let the Army down . . . he has let me down. And that's what hurts more than anything.'

'You feel he has betrayed you?'

'In many respects, yes.'

441

'Hmmm. What if he had betrayed our cause?'

Stefan's mouth tightened.

'If he had done that, I, personally would have demanded the privilege of shooting him, brother or no brother!'

Tito blinked at him.

'I believe you would,' he murmured. He shuffled a hand through the papers in front of him and sighed. 'So much to do. So much to remember.'

'I'll bid you good night, Comrade Secretary.'

'No. There was something else.' Again, Stefan waited. Tito rummaged through the papers until he found what he was looking for. 'This will interest you,' he said. 'I have had a long report from Montenegro, from our old friend, Comrade Djordje. . . . And there's news of another friend. It seems the Cetniks didn't get him, after all.'

Stefan's eyes were popping in amazement.

'Mannion! The American . . . he's alive?' It did not seem possible. They had long since given Mannion up for dead – ever since that winter day, almost a year ago, when he did not return from a raid on a Cetnik village that had gone disastrously wrong. The Partisan attackers had found themselves outnumbered and been compelled to scatter and extricate themselves in penny numbers from a mountain valley teeming with enemy. Mannion had last been seen leading an heroic charge on a machine-gun post that blocked one of the few exits.

'The American is very much alive,' Tito informed Stefan. 'I don't know how or why. Comrade Djordje gives no details. But it's clear from what he says that the American has been serving with one of the Montenegrin brigades for some time. Djordje wants to send him on a special mission.' Stefan's joy that his and Jamie's old friend was still alive was tempered by the final piece of information.

'If it's a suicide mission, Brad will have volunteered

for it,' he said gloomily. 'After he got out of Uzice, he seemed to have a death wish. He hogged all the most dangerous jobs. We were sure he was doing his damnedest to get himself killed, but he led a charmed life . . . until . . . it must have been January –'

'Djordje mentions his fearlessness,' Tito interrupted. 'He also reminds me of the American's tactlessness. You may remember the occasion yourself, Stefan – in Zagreb, when you escaped from prison? Do you remember? Your friend suggested that the Jugoslav Communist Party was probably the next best thing to the American Democratic Party.' Tito smiled. 'He meant is as a compliment but not all of us who were there saw it as such.'

'Not many of us regard Roosevelt as a convinced revolutionary,' Stefan commented, with a broad smile. 'What kind of mission has Comrade Djordje dreamed up for my friend from Lepoglava?'

'Would you believe a diplomatic one?' Tito asked, with a smile as broad as Stefan's.

Stefan stared at him incredulously.

'The American is like a brother to me, a dear friend and a comrade. But he is not even a member of the Party. . . .'

'That's what makes Djordje's choice so inspired. It is an act of genius.'

'You – you approve?'

'Of course I do!' Tito exclaimed. 'The Americans have treated us shabbily. Who better to point out to them the error of their ways than one of their own, this Mannion? He is not a Party member, so they have no reason to believe that he has a political axe to grind. He can tell them a few home truth about the Cetniks. They'll maybe believe him more readily than any of us.'

'But how will he do this?'

'The Italians are finished in Montenegro and, with the Allies taking over their homeland, Djordje has

443

established direct contact with the British in the south. He wants to slip someone over to Italy with the express purpose of contacting the Americans and convincing them that it's *us* they must support if they get it into their heads to send an expeditionary force across the Adriatic – not Mihailovic.'

'Do we need their support?' Even before the words were out of his mouth, Stefan realised that it was the wrong thing to say.

Tito glowered at him.

'All we get from Moscow is advice. We shall die with their fine words ringing in our ears. We need guns, ammunition – far more than the British are able to give us! America gives us nothing! She does not even recognise that we exist! Can you credit that, Stefan? The richest country in the world! A country that claims to be the champion of anti-colonialism and one that is free from any embroilment with the royal houses of Europe – and yet she does not even recognise us in our struggle!' Tito paused for breath and gesticulated angrily with his hand. 'It has taken the British two years to acknowledge that ours is the only true anti-Fascist force in Jugoslavia and that Mihailovic will be content to sit forever on Durmitor and watch us bleed. Two months ago, the Americans had the opportunity to follow Churchill's lead and show that they were with us in the struggle – but what do they do? They insult us by sending a military mission to that impostor, Draza, on his mountaintop!'

'Does Djordje know about this American mission?' Stefan ventured, cautious of the anger that gripped Tito.

'Of course he knows,' Tito snapped. 'And he knows that Draza will have been poisoning the minds of the Americans against us ever since they arrived. That is why he is so keen to let them hear our side of the story. Not by going cap in hand to them, but by giving them someone like this Mannion and letting him tell the truth.

444

Even if their officials do not choose to listen, their news reporters and their war correspondents certainly will. The world will hear about us!'

'The Americans did not lift a finger to help Mannion before, when the dictatorship sent him to prison for shooting one of their agents *in self-defence*. They said he was a gangster, which wasn't true. Perhaps they will discredit him.' Stefan offered this pessimistic view diffidently.

Tito dismissed it.

'America was not fighting the Nazis at the time and Russia was not her ally. Your American friend was imprisoned by real gangsters, the gangsters who tried to sell our country to Hitler . . . and he has been fighting his country's enemies for two years with great bravery. He will be welcomed as a hero.'

When, finally, Stefan had gone, Tito remained seated at his desk, pencilling the text of a signal for encoding and immediate transmission to HQ, Montenegro. It authorised Djordje to proceed with the plan to send Mannion to Italy. There were one or two provisos. The mission was to remain 'unofficial', inasmuch as Mannion would not have any kind of diplomatic status. The object of his mission was military, and Mannion was to present himself as an officer of the National Army of Liberation, anxious to compare notes with his American counterparts on targeting military installations for possible land/air operations in the future. In general, he would seek to improve communications and liaison between the American land, sea and air forces at present in Italy, their British allies, and the Partisan armies. It would do no harm if Mannion were to give the impression that the Americans were lagging behind the British in supporting the liberation struggle. He was not to feel inhibited in revealing to the Americans his own view of the Partisan/Cetnik strife as he had experienced it at first hand. Tito had no doubt that any such account might well reveal Partisan errors and shortcomings, but these would be heavily outweighed by revelations of the Cetniks' open collaboration with the Fascists, their terror tactics and their supine attitude to prosecution of the *real* war.

His message to Djordje despatched, Tito sat for a time, alone, contemplating the words he would use to inform his war council on the morrow of Mannion's mission. There would be no need to give Djordje all the credit for his inspired idea, for his would not be the ultimate responsibility. No, it was not the originator of an idea who mattered. It never was. The honour belonged to the person who recognised the idea's worth, distilled it, refined it and ordered its execution.

In the twenty-three-month period since Djordje instituted it in Uzice, the Office of Headquarters Security had not quite died of neglect. But it had lain moribund and ineffective during and after the retreat from Serbia as a result of the frequent movements and precarious existence of Supreme Headquarters itself and the drafting to more immediate concerns of Djordje, its founder, and his protégé, Stefan Markovic.

Its staff had shrunk to next to nothing and the office had never functioned in the manner intended, but it had continued in one shape or another, thanks to the dogged persistence of one man who had a vested interest in its survival. It provided an occupational refuge for Chief Commissar Gubec; the exigencies of war made the work undemanding, and it gave him what he saw as a useful power-base for the future.

By the autumn of 1943, with the threat of extinction temporarily removed from Headquarters, the infant department – conceived by Djordje and nursed by Gubec – had begun to grow. It rejoiced in a new name, *Odeljenje Zastite Naroda*, or OZNA; the Department for Security of the People. This extended the scope and nature of its activities and, even at this early stage of its development, it was beginning to show characteristics of the monster into which it would develop. The acronym OZNA concealed what some would come to call in simpler terms: the secret police. Among the duties of its head, Chief Commissar Gubec, was a task that he did not find disagreeable: that of investigating cases of Party in-discipline and disaffection. He carried out the function with no less a holy zeal than any Grand Inquisitor who relished the smell of burning flesh.

As convener of the tribunal assigned to investigate the allegations against the ex-royalist officer, Marko Markovic, Gubec's only regret was that, on the face of it, the charges did not warrant the death sentence – not that he was above stretching a point if that end could be achieved. An edict from the supreme Staff demanding exemplary punishment for Partisan soldiers found guilty of looting had encouraged Gubec to order the immediate execution of two unfortunates who had confessed to helping themselves to a jug of milk in a peasant's kitchen.

Marko's trial – for that is what it was – was held in a former stable in the same village that housed the schoolhouse hospital. The first testimony heard was that of the regimental commissar. She was brought before the trestle table at which Gubec sat, flanked by two Partisan officers whose presence was almost ornamental. Gubec had already briefed them that he would ask the questions. He held before him a written statement from the first witness, whom he treated with some deference.

'You are twenty-eight years old, comrade, and have been an active member of the Party for eight years?' he asked her.

'Yes, Comrade Commissar.'

'You have been many times commended for your work, is that not so?' Gubec went on, without waiting for an answer, 'And your bravery under fire has been an inspiration to your comrades?'

'I have only done my duty, Comrade Commissar,' the witness replied modestly. She was a dark vivacious beauty, on the plump side, and pretty when she dropped her severity and smiled, as she did now, nervously.

'You are a married woman?' Gubec inquired.

'Yes, Commissar. My husband is serving with the First Proletarian Brigade.'

'And you are First Commissar of the Second Sandzak Regiment?'

'Yes, Commissar.'

'You have complained against the officer, Markovic. Is it the case that, almost from the moment he was appointed to your regiment, he forced his attentions on you?'

'Yes, Commissar. He kept finding excuses to get me away from the others – on my own. He . . . he made advances. . . .'

'Which you rejected, of course?'

'Yes, Commissar.'

'You did not think to complain to the battalion commander?'

'I did not think to make a fuss.' The witness dabbed a tear from her eye. 'And I had my position to think of. I did not want the men talking about me and perhaps laughing at me behind my back.'

'Why should they laugh at you?'

The witness bowed her dark head. Then she looked around her uncertainly.

'I don't know,' she blurted out. 'Because I was one of only a handful of women amongst many men. I had to be as strong as the men.'

Gubec frowned. 'But you weren't quite strong enough for *him*, were you, comrade? In the end, he overpowered you, did he not? He forced his sex upon you – he raped you!'

'No!' The girl screamed the word. In a broken voice, she continued, 'He may have tried, but he did not

448

succeed. He humiliated me but he did not rape me.'

Gubec consulted his notes with an air of disappointment. He frowned at the witness.

'The battalion commander was wakened by your scream. He found you lying naked near the door of Markovic's tent, injured. As a result of the consequent interview with the commander, you lodged a serious complaint about Markovic. Are you now trying to protect him? Should he not now be facing far more serious charges than those that we have in front of us?'

'No!' the girl insisted, almost hysterically. 'He did not violate me . . . I swear it! I would not let him lay a finger on me. He wanted me to sleep with him but I would not have it. I wanted only to escape. When I ran from his tent, I fell over one of the ropes. That's how I hurt myself.'

One of the officers beside Gubec tapped on his shoulder and whispered something in his ear. Gubec frowned at him and returned his attention to the witness.

'My colleague wishes to know how you came to be naked in the officers' tent,' he said.

The girl avoided the eyes of the tribunal as she sought to frame her answer.

'He . . . he lured me to his tent . . . a message. He sent one of his men. There was no reason – only that Officer Markovic wanted to see me urgently . . . an emergency . I – I was undressed. I just grabbed a blanket to cover me and ran to see what he wanted. . . . It was foolish, I know, but I did not stop to think.'

The officer who had whispered to Gubec was now regarding the rafters of the stable with an expression of wonder, as if he had suddenly heard the strain of distant violins.

Gubec cleared his throat.

'We know this must embarrass you to speak of it, but tell us of his assault. He tore the blanket from your body and seized you?'

The girl stared at Gubec, confused.

'I can't remember,' she stammered. 'He took me in his arms. I was shocked, taken by surprise. . . . The blanket must have fallen. . . . It's all so jumbled in my mind. I can't remember clearly.'

There was something grotesque about Gubec's sympathy. 'We are upsetting you with these questions,' he growled, in what was meant as a kindly manner. 'The man behaved like a monster and it must be very painful to you to talk about your ordeal. But you were not his only victim. Is this not so?'

'There were other women, yes,' the witness confirmed.

'How many?'

'Three . . . four. . . . There may have been more.'

'Tell us about them,' Gubec prompted. 'They were ordinary soldiers, serving under Markovic, were they not?' One of the officers beside Gubec suppressed a giggle at the Chief Commissar's choice of words. Gubec glared at him. 'Were these women married?' he asked the witness.

'Two have husbands,' came the reply. 'The other was a child of eighteen.'

'A virgin probably,' said Gubec sagely. 'You have no doubt that Markovic had sexual relations with these three?'

'None at all. All three have admitted it.'

For the second time, the officer on Gubec's right whispered in his ear. Again, Gubec frowned at the interruption.

'Did these women consent to sexual acts with Markovic?' he asked.

The woman standing before the table frowned.

'They did not resist,' she said.

'Because they were afraid of Markovic?'

'Because they did not know any better,' the witness replied. 'They are soldiers. When an officer tells you to do something, you do it.'

'So, Markovic used his rank to obtain a steady string of bed partners. He treated the battalion's complement of women soldiers as a sultan treats his harem. No doubt it was his intention to work his way through all of you before he was finished – a gross abuse of his position.'

The witness appeared to goggle with awe at the suggestion. She did not reply. Gubec dismissed her and called to an orderly to fetch the officer, Markovic. On the way in, Marko came face to face with the departing commissar.

'Happy now?' he inquired, with a look of sad reproach. She glared at him and marched past him, blushing furiously.

Standing before the seated tribunal, Marko smiled nonchalantly at Gubec.

'Well, gentlemen, shall we get this nonsense over quickly?'

Gubec was on his feet instantly.

'Watch your insolent tongue, sir,' he warned Marko, with cold fury. 'Or it will go all the worse for you.'

Marko smiled genially.

'It's going to be like that, is it?'

'Silence!' Gubec rapped. 'This is a court of the people and we'll have none of your royalist arrogance here. You will show proper respect and speak only when you are invited to do so.'

He started the questioning by asking about Marko's 'bourgeois' background and his service in the Royal Army, dwelling at length on the fact that while Marko's brother was in prison, he was in the service of the dictatorship and living it up in Belgrade. Gubec had done his homework.

'You fought with the Cetniks in Serbia?' he went on icily. 'Against whom were you fighting during this interesting period? Against the Fascists or the Partisans?'

'We fought the Germans,' Marko replied just as icily, his anger mounting.

'But you changed sides,' Gubec goaded him. 'You became a Partisan. Why did you not run to the Fascists, like so many of your Cetnik comrades?'

'Because the thought never crossed my mind,' Marko answered fiercely. 'As for my Cetnik comrades, most of them died fighting Germans.'

'You are a new member of the Party,' Gubec continued, unruffled. 'This was a remarkable step to take for an officer in the Royal Army. Do you believe in revolution?'

'We are fighting a war, not a revolution,' Marko replied. 'I was asked to become a member of the Party and I accepted.'

'Oh, you *accepted*?' Gubec frowned. 'How gracious of you! We should be honoured. No doubt you thought that an officer of your standing and experience could set a shining example to our humble proletarian soldiers?'

'I'm not ashamed of my record in the field,' Marko growled. 'It's as good as any man's.'

'Oh, we've been hearing about all the night actions you've fought,' Gubec said, nodding his head. 'There's hardly a woman in your regiment that you haven't straddled. Is that what you see as an officer's obligations, comrade? To go through your regiment like a ram through a flock of ewes?'

Marko took a step forward, eyes blazing. 'I don't see it as an officer's obligation to take that crap from you or anyone else!' he challenged, his voice rising. 'Who the hell are you that you think you can sit there and – ' He got no further. At a signal from Gubec, two of his henchmen guarding the door leapt on Marko and pinioned his arms. Gubec ordered a chair to be brought and the proceedings were suspended while Marko was roped into it, sitting.

'This is a nonsense,' he protested, as thus bound, he was made to face the table.

'You have stretched the toleration of this tribunal to

dangerous limits,' Gubec warned him. 'If you offend again, you will be dealt with summarily.' He went on to recount the episode which ended with the naked commissar sprawling at the door of Marko's tent. 'Do you deny any of this?' he concluded.

Marko stared at him with disbelief. 'It is a fabrication,' he declared. 'A malicious distortion of the truth.'

'What is the truth?' Gubec asked sarcastically. 'Enlighten our poor peasant minds.'

'To start with,' Marko said, 'I did not entice that lying bitch to my tent. She came uninvited. Produce this soldier who took this message to her. You will find it difficult, because he does not exist! He is a figment of that woman's imagination.'

Gubec's eyes narrowed. 'You would have us believe that the woman came to your tent of her own free will?'

'I certainly did not ask her,' Marko stated firmly. 'I was sound asleep. The first thing I knew was this hand groping at me. I woke with a fright and found this creature had crawled under my blanket. She was crawling all over *me*! I didn't even know who it was.'

'But you knew it was a woman?'

'That wasn't difficult. She was stark naked and panting like a bitch on heat!'

Gubec scoffed. 'You would have us believe that this woman – a first commissar and a married woman who takes pride in her fidelity to her husband as she takes pride in her fidelity to the Party – was seeking to seduce *you*?'

'She certainly hadn't come to discuss Marxist theory!' Marko replied with feeling.

'And how did you respond?' Gubec inquired.

'I threw her out of the tent,' Marko stated flatly. 'I told her to go and try another tent. I wanted my sleep.'

A stunned silence greeted the statement. Gubec found his voice.

'You . . . you rejected her?'

'She had been pestering me for days, asking me to go here with her, asking me to go there with her. Oh, I knew what she wanted, all right. But I didn't want any part of her. I could get all the consolation I needed elsewhere, without her and her non-stop yapping on Party dogma. . . . ' Marko stopped.

Gubec reacted to his remark about Party dogma by wincing as if he had been stung. A thunderous frown darkened his face.

'Enough!' he snapped. 'Your effrontery astonishes me, Officer Markovic. Might I remind you that you are the one facing charges. It does your cause no good to malign a respected official of the Party. She is the one who complained to your battalion commander, not the other way round.'

'She had to!' Marko retorted. 'She had to say something! It was her who was lying stark naked on the ground, screaming her leg was broken, when the commander came out to see what the din was. She started blaming me to save her own neck.'

'Save her neck?'

The look that Marko directed at Gubec left the latter in no doubt what he thought about the speed of Gubec's mental processes.

'Her husband is reputed to be a very violent and jealous man,' Marko said, in tones that he might have used to a particularly obtuse child. 'If he had got to hear that his beloved wife was going around army camps at night offering her body to this, that and the next fellow, the likelihood is that he would beat the life out of her.'

Gubec gave no sign of acknowledging the logic in the explanation. He backtracked to something Marko had said earlier.

'You said,' he began 'that you could get all the consolation you needed elsewhere. Are we to take it, Officer Markovic, that any number of women were available to you?'

'That is exactly what I meant,' Marko said.

'And you did avail yourself of them?' Gubec went on.

'I'm human,' Marko admitted. 'With human appetites. And I'm a soldier, not a monk. I'm not bound by any vow of celibacy.'

'A soldier at the front does not often have the opportunities to indulge his carnal appetites,' Gubec said blandly. 'But, of course, you did not have that problem. You had, in the unit you commanded, an ample supply of female soldiers who were only too eager to creep below your blanket?'

'I can't deny it,' Marko said. 'For some reason that I can't explain, women have always found me attractive. I've never had any difficulty in bedding a woman who really took my fancy.'

'Particularly,' Gubec said, and his voice took on an icy timbre, 'when the woman you fancy is your subordinate in rank and all you have to do is order her to your bed? You could make life very unpleasant for any who dared to refuse.'

Marko bridled.

'I have never needed to use that kind of persuasion. If a woman has gone to bed with me, it has been because that is what she wanted to do.'

Gubec glared at him with unconcealed hate.

'Your conceit is odious,' he thundered. 'We have been informed that you have had sexual relations with a least three women, probably four, who were under your command. Two, at least, were the wives of other men, and a third was a virgin of eighteen. Do you admit this?'

'I don't remember the virgin,' Marko said, with a rueful smile. 'As for the others, it is possible that some were married. It's not a thing that's usually discussed. But if they were, they knew what they were doing.'

'You have condemned yourself out of your own mouth,' Gubec roared. He signalled to the two guards. 'Take him outside. We shall have him brought back when it has been decided what to do with him.'

The deliberations of the tribunal took longer than Gubec would have wished, mainly because one of the Partisan officers believed that Marko had been truthful. The same officer was frankly envious of Marko's success with women and curious to know the secret of it. It took Gubec some time to convince the officer that Marko had been too candid for his own good, that he had been almost boastful of his promiscuity. And that was what he had been charged with – promiscuity. All else was academic. Gubec also hinted to the officer that if he had any desire to emulate Markovic's tally of female conquests, it might only be a matter of time before he, too, was standing before a disciplinary tribunal. Thereafter, both officers found themselves agreeing with everything that Gubec said. Both had decided that the Chief Commissar was a dangerous man to cross.

Marko was brought back to the stable to hear the verdict. Gubec did not beat about the bush.

'The behaviour to which you have confessed is a disgrace,' he lectured Marko. 'It makes it patently clear that you are unfit to hold the rank of officer in the Army of Liberation and that you are equally unfit to be a member of the Communist Party. You bring discredit to both. Your expulsion from the Party is ordered herewith and will become fully effective upon ratification by the Party Executive. You are also ordered to be stripped of the entitlement to hold the rank of officer in any branch of the Army of Liberation. It is the recommendation of this tribunal that you serve a period of indefinite duration in penal labour, attached to a works battalion. You will remain under close custody until the transfer is effected.'

Marko was unable to believe his ears and was making his protest known while Gubec was still delivering the pronouncement. He was still protesting when Gubec ordered him to be taken away, with the advice that he should be chained and gagged if he did not shut up.

When it was over and the officers who made up the tribunal had departed with some haste, Gubec collected his papers and smoked a cigarette, enjoying the satisfaction of having discharged his duties to the Party. When he strolled outside the stable, it was to find that the regimental commissar from the Sandzak Brigade was still waiting outside, alone. She fluttered about nervously at the sight of him.

'What are you doing here?' he asked her.

'I was waiting to ask your permission to go, Chief Commissar,' she replied.

'Are you staying in the village tonight?'

'Only if I can find a place to stay,' she said. 'Otherwise, I shall have to walk up the mountain to Headquarters, although I don't have to report back for service there until noon tomorrow. I was told I had to make myself available to you until then.'

Gubec smiled at her words. They put ideas in his head.

'Perhaps we can find accommodation for you,' he said thoughtfully. 'I have a house at the far end of the village. It is really much too large for just me. Perhaps I can use the time at our disposal to offer you some advice. As a Party activist within the Army, it disturbs me that your conduct may not have been without error. It is clear to me that you need friends in the Party, friends who carry some weight.'

'I would consider your advice invaluable, Chief Commissar,' she said. 'I know I have been silly.'

'And you should be punished for it,' Gubec declared. 'Although there are ways that you can make amends.'

'I'll do anything, anything,' she pleaded.

'Yes, my dear, I believe you would,' he murmured, his eyes on the bulge of her breasts where they thrust against her tunic.

She intercepted his gaze.

'Anything,' she repeated. 'Anything you wanted.'

'I'll show you my house,' Gubec said. 'Come there – as soon as it gets dark.'

The hotel to which Mannion was taken was a handsome grey stone edifice that looked out towards the Adriatic. From the balcony of his room, he had an uninterrupted view across Brindisi harbour to the sea beyond. Three motor torpedo boats flying the white ensign were moored side by side near the port entrance. One of them was the craft that had picked up Mannion and two downed RAF fliers at a rendezvous location, fifty kilometres off the Montenegrin coast. The transfer from the tuna-fishing caique in which the three men had spent two uncomfortable days, being constantly seasick, came as a blessed relief. The airmen had been with the Partisans for three months and had provided Djordje's British contacts in Italy with an added incentive for the pick-up operation involving Mannion.

The transfer from the caique coincided with a change in the weather. The northeaster which had made life so unpleasant for the fishing boat's three passengers had blown itself out and the two-hundred-kilometre dash to Italy in the MTB was exhilarating, in contrast to the misery of what had gone before. Across a glassy calm sea and through a night of drifting haze, the trim navy craft arrowed towards her destination with the speed and grace of an aquatic gazelle. She glided into port just as the rising sun was beginning to streak the misty eastern horizon with reddish light.

A fifteen-hundredweight truck with RAF markings was waiting on the jetty to whisk away Mannion's aircrew friends, and there was time only for a quick goodbye before they disappeared out of his life forever. The truck was still pulling away when a British Army officer appeared on the jetty and hailed the MTB's young commander.

'You got a Joey for me?' he inquired.

Mannion was the 'Joey' in question, it transpired. The term was not derogatory. In Special Operations parlance, the word was used to preserve the anonymity of all clandestine passengers going to or from all occupied territories.

'Major Blair, Special Forces,' he introduced himself, extending a hand. '*Dobar dan*,' he added, with an air of triumph, before the more hesitant inquiry, 'Do . . . you . . . speak . . . English?'

'*Dobro jutro*,' Mannion replied, inclining his head and smiling.

'Dob-raw yoot-raw?' Blair mimicked in a fair imitation of Mannion, his expression puzzled.

'It means good morning, Major,' Mannion explained with a grin. 'At sunup, it seems a mite more appropriate than good day.'

Blair stared at Mannion, taking in his riding breeches, Italian leather jacket, the service cap with its five-pointed red star. None of it seemed to go with the effortless English delivered with an unmistakable American accent.

'You're American!' he exclaimed.

'Once upon a time, Major. Once upon a time. Right now, I'm not sure what the hell I am or what the hell I'm doing here – but I'm pleased to meet you, for all that.'

The hotel above the harbour was the temporary abode of a mixed bag of Special Forces officers already in the process of moving out to new headquarters in Bari, further north. Blair conducted Mannion to a room vacated only the day before by a brigadier. It had its own bathroom *en suite* and, compared with what Mannion had become used to in Jugoslavia, it was the height of luxury.

'Best room in the house,' Blair assured Mannion. 'Bit noisy at night if the Luftwaffe come calling,' he added apologetically, with a nod towards the ships in the harbour below. 'Comes from living a bit close to the target area.'

He left Mannion to settle in and enjoy a tepid but nevertheless welcome bath, with the promise that a man-sized breakfast would be on the table downstairs in half an hour. Mannion, who, only the previous day, had been convinced he would never again be able to look a plate of food in the eye, discovered that he was ravenous when he rejoined Blair – and a huge platter of ham, sausage, eggs and tomato was set in front of him. Blair chatted away companionably while Mannion ate. The British officer had been apprehensive at the prospect of having to entertain the promised visitor from Jugoslavia and, indeed, had been prepared to treat him with wary suspicion. His relief at discovering an American 'cousin', however – instead of a stiff-necked revolutionary who spoke no English – prompted him to drop all restraint. Mannion fascinated him.

'You've come at an awkward time,' he volunteered freely to Mannion. 'Between us moving shop to Bari and getting ready to push the button on an army support stunt further up the coast, the brass have got rather a lot on their minds at the moment.'

Mannion, who had not the haziest notion of the function of Blair or of Special Forces, could only apologise for his timing and try to make polite conversation. He idly asked Blair what he meant by army support stunt.

'In this case,' Blair said, 'we're giving the Seventy-Eighth Div. some backup up near Termoli. We're landing a commando strike force behind the line from the sea, so that we can deliver a good kick up Gerry's backside while the Seventy-Eighth are bloodying his nose. Our boys are sailing from Manfredonia today.'

'I get the picture,' said Mannion, although the place names meant nothing to him. What was crystal-clear to him was that the straightforward war being fought on mainland Italy was vastly different in character to the war he had left behind in Jugoslavia.

'I gather,' said Blair, 'that you're here to talk about the coordination of land-sea-air ops on the other side of the water.'

'Something like that,' Mannion said.

'You'll find our people are all for it,' Blair said. 'I can't speak for the Yanks. They're thin on the ground on this side of Italy – but that's only because they've been based on Algiers and concentrating more on the Western Med. Things'll maybe be different, now that they've taken Naples.'

'Naples has fallen?'

'Yesterday,' Blair confirmed. Mannion was cheered by the news. German communiqués had been boasting that the Anglo-American armies that had landed south of Naples would be thrown back into the sea. 'The Armistice with Italy is official now, too,' Blair went on. 'Eisenhower and Badoglio signed the papers in Malta on Wednesday.'

'It's an important part of my coming here that I get the chance to speak to American officers,' Mannion said.

'That's understandable,' Blair said. 'They're your own people.'

'My own people . . .' Mannion echoed, with a pensive sadness. 'Who are my own people? Am I American?' He smiled at Blair, who was regarding him with a puzzled frown, and answered his own question. 'I suppose I am. There's a part of me that's as American as blueberry pie and the Hudson River. I was raised there. But there's an awful lot of me that's Jugoslav – maybe the only piece of me that has ever mattered a goddamn in the crazy mess I've made of my life.'

His introspective musing intrigued Blair more than it enlightened him. The British officer sensed mysteries and depths in the man opposite him. They lay hidden somewhere beyond his deep-set knowing eyes: eyes that hinted of suffering and weariness and things that were better not seen.

461

'Has it . . . has it been bad over there?' Blair asked softly.

'Bad enough,' Mannion replied, his mind not fully with Blair but ballooning away on a flight of its own. *Who am I?* he asked himself. *How much of me is alive and how much of me is dead, buried forever beneath a mountain in Serbia? How much of me is the American child I was, and how much of me is the suffering man I've become? Why is it that so much of me wants only to die, and yet part of me wants to live?*

'A penny for those dark thoughts,' Blair said, smiling at him. 'Is there something you would particularly like to do while you're in Brindisi?'

'What is there to do in Brindisi?' Mannion countered.

'Look at the sea, drink wine,' Blair said, laughing.

Mannion grinned at him.

'Well I've done the first thing I'd set my heart on. I've scrubbed myself clean in a bath. Maybe the second thing ought to be to get good and drunk – but not until I've done what I came here to do. You got some kind of programme lined up for me?'

'A list that'll make you dizzy,' Blair said. 'But this is Sunday, and you don't start making the rounds until tomorrow morning, nine o'clock sharp.'

'Then today,' said Mannion, 'maybe we could look at the sea, and later maybe we could drink some of that wine you talked about.'

In the next three weeks, Mannion did not have much time for looking at the sea but he drank a lot of wine and did a lot of talking. Blair was a companionable host, escorting him here and there and taking it on himself to see that, in addition to the official discussions, Mannion was entertained. The most notable social occasion – as far as Mannion was concerned – was a trip to Bari, where he was guest of the two commando groups operating with the British Eighth Army. Nos. 3 and 40 (Royal Marine) Commandos had been returned to Bari for rest after taking the port of Termoli from the sea and distinguishing themselves in the massive German counterattack which had followed. These elite and seasoned warriors welcomed Mannion as a brother and bombarded him with questions about the Partisan war, in which they had an intense curiosity.

At the airfield at Foggia, Mannion met his first Americans. They were fliers with a squadron of P-38 fighters, and had flown in soon after the field was captured by the Eighth Army. They had been giving tactical support to the American ground troops in the west and the British in the east. Their commander was particularly interested in the activities of German fighter and bomber squadrons based on Mostar, only 270 kilometres away in Jugoslavia.

'Can your Partisan amigos on the ground over there give us any hard intelligence on that Kraut field?' he asked Mannion. 'You would be doing us a favour. We can handle the Krauts who come flying at us from the north, but the ones coming at us from the sea have been catching us on the hop. They come in low across the water, so's they're under our radar. Then they hit Bari, Brindisi, even this field here at Foggia, before our guys can get airborne. We're sure it's Mostar they're working out of.'

Mannion promised to see what he could do. Thanks to Blair's HQ, he was in daily radio contact with Djordje's HQ in Montenegro, and Djordje was in touch by radio with other Partisan groups and Tito's HQ: so Mannion was hopeful that something could be arranged. Next day, he received word from Djordje that a Partisan team, equipped with a radio, would keep Mostar under twenty-four-hour observation and that a steady stream of intelligence would be relayed to Italy. The Luftwaffe at Mostar had been giving the Partisans problems, too. Bombers from the base had attacked the Partisan forces which had taken the coastal city of Split, and they were driven out after a brief occupation.

It was at Foggia, a few days later, that a small party from American Staff HQ on the east coast of Italy landed to have talks with the American-speaking Partisan officer who had arrived so mysteriously from Montenegro. The meeting with Mannion took place in an upper room of a handsome villa only a few miles from Foggia airfield. Before leaving Mannion to his discussions, Blair introduced the American team. The leader was a civilian political officer attached to the State Department, a slightly stooped, bespectacled man in his mid-fifties. His name was James C. Herbertson. Accompanying him were two officers in army uniform: a Major Adrian Costello, from G-2 Staff, Fifth Army, and a Major Ed Wylie, from OSS.

As he shook hands with Herbertson, Mannion was aware of a stirring of recognition, but it was not until all four were seated around a long oak table that he placed the civilian. Almost a decade had passed since he last saw him. Herbertson had put on a fair bit of weight since that last meeting and his hair had receded, but there was no mistaking the man. He had been a consular official at the US Embassy in Belgrade all that time ago – and Mannion had walked out on him, refusing to accept the expulsion order which Herbertson had presented to him.

Herbertson, becoming aware of the way Mannion was staring at him intently, returned his gaze.

'Don't I know you from somewhere?' he asked.

'Belgrade . . . the Embassy.' Even as Mannion spoke, Herbertson was remembering and, from the look that came into his eyes, there was no pleasure in the memory.

'Your name should have rung a bell,' Herbertson admitted with a tired little smile. 'When did they let you out of jail?'

'They didn't,' Mannion said, unsmiling. 'Me and a couple of friends decided to leave.' He was aware of the goggling attention of the two officers sitting on either side of Herbertson. Their eyes were bright with interest all of a sudden.

'You escaped?' Herbertson said, and made a face that seemed to indicate he was impressed. 'It figures, I suppose. That maybe accounts for you being a big man with the Partisans. Most of their leaders did time. You must be high in the Party now to rate them sending you out to parley for them.'

'I'm not in the Party,' Mannion replied. 'Not that I haven't been asked. But old habits die hard. I was brought up to vote Democrat and maybe I still would . . . if I ever got the chance.'

'You're trying to say you're not a Communist?' Herbertson scoffed.

'I'm not trying to say anything, mister. I'm telling you. In any case, I didn't come here to talk politics.'

'Just why are you here?' Herbertson asked.

Mannion tightened his lips, betraying his anger.

'To talk about killing Germans,' he replied. 'We've been doing it for two years and getting no goddamn thanks for it from you, the Russians, or anybody else. I think it's time the State Department got round to making some kind of sign that the Partisans exist . . . that we're fighting in the same goddamned war!'

'We know what's going on in Jugoslavia,' the officer called Wylie put in. 'We sent in a mission nearly six months ago.'

Mannion turned on him.

'To the Cetniks! To Mihailovic! I can just imagine the crap they've been feeding you!'

'I've got facts and figures,' Wylie said, remaining unruffled. He glanced at Herbertson. 'With your permission, sir, maybe I could talk about specifics with this officer before we go too deep into anything else. I got here hard intelligence that I'd like to have confirmed or denied or commented on one way or another before we come to any conclusions.'

Herbertson waved a hand carelessly. 'Suit yourself, Ed,' he said. 'You're assuming Mannion here will give you straight answers. I wouldn't make that assumption.'

'If I know the answers, he'll get them,' Mannion said sharply. To Wylie, he said, 'Just what do you want to know?'

Wylie frowned.

'You were in Montenegro, where there's been a lot of fighting between Cetniks and Partisans, right? I got details of Partisan atrocities that'll make your hair curl.'

'Not mine, Major,' Mannion replied calmly. 'I've seen them! I've seen a lot that I can't and won't even try to defend . . . things I can't even begin to understand. But you're wrong if you think that just one side is to blame. You've got families fighting families over there. You got feuds that are political, feuds that are religious, feuds that have been going on for so long that they don't even make sense any more and probably didn't make sense in the first place. But what you got to realise is that the war has confused all these issues and doesn't even matter a bean in some of them. You got guys there who hate Nazis but will cut each other's throats because a hundred years ago the great-grandfather of one guy had an argument with the great-grandfather of another guy –'

'I'm talking about specific atrocities against Cetnik communities,' Wylie interrupted. 'Cetnik communities that Mihailovic has been trying to enlist on our side.'

Mannion glowered at him.

'Major, I fought with the Cetniks in Serbia until the fall of 'forty-one. I married a Cetnik woman. I was all for what Mihailovic was trying to do then. But he's the one who stirred up the hatreds that have been pulling his country apart. He started it in Serbia and, when Serbia got too hot for him, he started all over again in Montenegro.'

'Our information is that the Communists started it in Montenegro.'

'They started the war there,' Mannion said. 'They rebelled against the Italians. And I admit they did some terrible things there when they didn't get things all their own way. You don't need to tell me. "The Pitmen" is what the Cetniks called them – because they went crazy with their executions, shooting anybody they thought had collaborated with the Italians. They buried a lot of innocent with the guilty in the pits they dug for them. But a lot of that was the result of local vendettas and clan feuding. It had no sanction from the top and there was hell to pay for it afterwards. Most of the people responsible were weeded out and punished.'

Wylie was consulting a notebook. He looked up from it.

'Have you heard of the village of Ozrinici?' he asked Mannion.

Mannion smiled.

'I should have. I helped to burn it down.'

Wylie was taken aback.

'You admit massacring innocent civilians and burning down their homes?'

'Hey, wait a minute,' Mannion protested. 'Let's get things straight. What happened at Ozrinici did happen on orders from the top, and after the people in the village had been warned.'

'Would you care to elaborate on that?' Wylie asked.

'Sure. I'm not saying it was right, but I understand why it was done. You heard of what the Italians called the *milizia voluntaria anticommunista*?'

'No,' Wylie confessed. 'Perhaps you will tell us.'

'They're a volunteer militia organised by the Cetniks with the help of the Italians – the guys we were supposed to be fighting. It was a deal that we in the Partisans didn't appreciate. You see, the Italians said they would burn down any villages that helped the Partisans but would look after any villages that played ball with them. If the villages cooperated in setting up a system of road watches to report Partisan movements, then the Italians would give the Cetniks guns and ammunition. The

467

result of this was that a lot of villages went over to the Italian or Cetnik side, to stop being burned out of their homes. We had to do something about it. We warned the villages that siding with the Italians wouldn't save their homes – because we would burn them down.'

'And you did?' Wylie prompted.

'They didn't believe we meant it. They were getting free guns from the Italians and they didn't have to scratch for bullets the way we did. Maybe they reckoned that fighting us and keeping sweet with the Italians was the easy option. Ozrinici changed that. We warned them umpteen times we were going to do it – and, in the end, we did. And just to put the record straight, Major, the civilian population didn't stay around to be massacred. They got out as soon as they knew we meant business.'

Wylie snapped his notebook shut and remained silent.

'Have you changed your mind about listing specifics, Major?' Mannion asked him. 'Or is it my turn? Would you like to hear about Cetnik atrocities? Their appetite for executions is, I can assure you, quite prodigal. Any Partisan who falls into their hands is shot on the spot – unless, of course, the Partisan is a woman. They don't waste bullets on women, they prefer to hang them. In public. They like to exhibit corpses, as opposed to disposing of them in pits. Partisan justice may be harsh at times, Major, but it has much to commend it compared with Cetnik justice. We do not encourage loyalty with the lash. Nor do we repay religious intolerance with the slaughter of children. That's why more and more Cetniks are coming over to the Partisan side. By the hundred! By God, we may have our faults, but the people know that it's their freedom we're fighting for. The Partisans are Communist-inspired, but it's not Communism they're fighting for! They're fighting for Jugoslavia!'

Mannion's passionate little speech was received with embarrassed silence. It was Herbertson who finally broke it.

'Just what do you expect of us?' he asked Mannion.

'Recognition would do for a start,' Mannion replied sharply. 'The British know the score. Mihailovic is not conning them any more. It's us they're supplying now – guns, ammo, food, boots. . . . And now they got bases in Italy, they're going to send us tanks, even.'

'Seems like you're getting along without us just fine,' Herbertson said.

Mannion could have hit him. Wylie and Costello threw sidelong looks at Herbertson as if detecting an unpleasant odour from that direction. It was Costello who spoke.

'Let's not go slamming any doors,' the G-2 officer said. 'I don't give a goddamn whose political toes get stood on, but I don't think we can afford not to get involved with the Partisans. From what I hear, they sure took some of the heat off us earlier in the year.'

Herbertson scowled at him. 'Perhaps you'll elucidate for my simple political mind, Major Costello.'

'It don't take much elucidatin',' Costello replied. 'The simple fact is that before we hit Sicily, we went to a lot of trouble to make the Nazis think we'd hit the Balkans. Hitler moved a lot of divisions outa France and Norway and the Low Countries to beef up his strength in Jugoslavia and Greece. And this guy Tito kept 'em pretty busy, from all accounts.' He looked to Mannion for confirmation.

'We've been on the receiving end of two big offensives since January,' Mannion said. 'They threw six German divisions and seven Italian divisions at us in the first. Our army in Bosnia was encircled at the Neretva River in March. It was lucky to get out.'

'How *did* it get out?' Wylie questioned.

'Across the river and by fighting its way through the weakest part of the enemy ring,' Mannion said.

Wylie raised his eyebrows. 'Through the Italians?'

'No, Major,' Mannion said with a smile. 'Through the Cetniks. Twelve thousand of them.'

Wylie shrugged and inclined his head, in the manner of one acknowledging defeat. He smiled.

'Point taken. And if it's any consolation to you, I'd like you to know that I'm on your side. I go along with Costello. I say the sooner we do something to let you know we're in your corner, the better.'

Herbertson regarded Wylie and Costello with a glazed smile.

'I'd like to remind you gentlemen that all we came here to do was talk. We came out of curiosity, and because the British asked us to. Uncle Sam's foreign policy isn't going to be decided in this room. Washington tells us what to do.' He directed his gaze at Mannion. 'I would just like to know exactly what your status is, Mr Mannion, and why precisely you have been sent here? Are you here as Tito's official representative?'

'No,' Mannion replied, 'I'm not Tito's representative, although I'm told he approved of the Montenegrin War Council's decision to send me to Italy. Why was I sent? I think because there's a lot of anger in Montenegro at the way America and the Americans are ignoring the Partisans – especially when it is the Partisans who are bearing the entire brunt of the fighting. It was a slap in the face when you sent a mission to Mihailovic – who isn't interested in fighting Germans – and you did not send a mission to the Partisans. At a time when the British were realising that backing Mihailovic was a mistake, America went and made the same one – in spades!'

'So the Communists don't send one of their own to do their talking for them, they send the next best thing, an American sympathiser?' There was no mistaking the sneer in Herbertson's voice.

Mannion controlled his anger.

'Maybe they thought that what had to be said would come better from an American,' he said.

'And what did they *tell* you to say?' Herbertson goaded him.

'They said, tell the Americans the truth, comrade. For God's sake, tell them over there the truth about what's been happening in this country of ours!'

Herbertson was silent, thoughtful. Then he shrugged.

'So you're just a mouthpiece for them? Strictly unofficial. Your mission could come under the heading of agitprop?'

Again, Mannion was filled with the urge to hit Herbertson, to wipe the smug, unconcerned look from his face.

'I've given you what I believe to be the unofficial reasons behind my mission,' he said. 'The official reasons are military. We're fighting a war, and in a war it helps if there's a little teamwork between the guys who are supposed to be on the same side . . . a little coordination of effort. You guys – and that means you and the British – have planes and warships and a lot of the things that we don't have. But we know the situation on the ground. We know where the enemy's strong and where he can be hurt. And that's what I'm here to talk about – ways of hurting him.'

'Oh yeah, sure. Big deal!' Herbertson's tone was sarcastic. 'You tell us what you want, we pick up the tab.'

Wylie saw Mannion bunch his fists and half-rise from his seat. He threw him a cautionary frown.

'Let's be sensible about this, Herbertson,' he began, but got no further. The ring of a telephone bell interrupted, causing all four men to look around to locate the source of the clamorous sound. It was Wylie who found the instrument, concealed from view behind a curtain, sitting on the broad ledge of a window. Wylie picked up the receiver while the others, their eyes on him, listened to the monologue that followed.

'Yeah. Major Wylie here. . . . Yeah. . . . Yeah, he's here. We're in conference right now. D'you want me to put. . . ?' There was a long pause, then: 'OK. . . .

Sure.... Yeah, I'll tell him.' Another long pause. 'OK.... You bet I will.... Yeah, definitely.... Yeah.... It'll be a pleasure.... Sure.... Goodbye.' He returned the receiver to its cradle and came towards the table. He looked at Mannion.

'It was for you,' he said. 'A Major Warren out at the Air Force base. I offered to put you on but he said no, so long as I could pass on a message. He hopes you can be his guest tonight, if you're free. They're having a party out at the base....'

'Major Warren?' Mannion had to search his memory. 'Oh yeah, Major Warren. He's the fighter pilot guy.'

'And a very happy fighter pilot guy,' Wylie added. 'He landed only half an hour ago. Seems they got a tip from the Partisan guys you got watching some airfield ... Mostar? Anyway, they got this tip during the night that the Krauts were warming up for something big and planning a dawn takeoff. Warren and his guys were in the air before it was light and sitting there in the sky over the Jugoslav coast when they spotted three big formations of Stukas underneath them. He said they'd never had a turkey shoot like it. His P-38s shot them goddamned Stukas clean outa the sky. They scored more kills in twenty minutes than they've had in a month.'

Mannion allowed himself a quiet smile of satisfaction. Herbertson was staring at Wylie with a face like a frozen cod. Wylie grinned at the State Department man.

'Looks like our Air Force boys and the Partisans talk the same language,' he said. 'You were talking about picking up the tab.... Seems like the Krauts picked it up this time!'

Herbertson had nothing to say. Nor did he have much to contribute to the discussions that followed. It came as no surprise to the others when he announced that more urgent matters were waiting his attention in Naples and that he intended to fly back that day. He had no objection to Wylie and Costello staying on in Foggia for as long as they liked. Wylie cornered him before he left.

'We can work something out with the Partisans,' he told the State Department man. 'You ain't gonna make things difficult, are you? Politically?'

'I'll make my report,' Herbertson said. 'Any reservations I have will go into that.' He smiled weakly at Wylie. 'These reservations are strictly political. They should not be any impediment to military cooperation with the Partisans. After all, goddamnit, if we can get along with Stalin, we can at least try to get along with this guy Tito.'

That evening, Wylie had no qualms about gate-crashing the party that was in full swing in the Mess the American P-38 pilots shared with their RAF colleagues. Getting Mannion on his own was difficult – he was the toast of the American squadron and everybody wanted to talk to him – but Wylie finally succeeded.

'When are you going back to Jugoslavia?' he asked.

'No idea,' Mannion told him, 'I don't know when I'm going back and I don't know how. It's up to the British Navy, I guess. Why do you want to know?'

'Because I'm going with you,' Wylie said.

Mannion stared at him in surprise.

'You're not drunk? You mean that?'

'I'm stone-cold sober. I want to be the one that tells this Tito that the Yanks are coming.'

Mannion was ecstatic. The Jugoslav in him was overjoyed. And the American in him awoke with new national pride. In one simple sentence, Wylie had somehow restored to him a new sense of identity and an optimism for the future that had long been dead.

'We got to drink to this,' he told Wylie. His sudden leaping joy was an overreaction, he knew. It was the sum of many things: the alcohol he had consumed, the spectacular success of the P-38s above the coast near Split, the feeling of having won a moral victory over Herbertson, and now this thoughtful American major's crazy eagerness to go to Jugoslavia. It was as if a summit had been reached after a climb that had often seemed pointless and without end. Now, suddenly, the way was downhill.

Mannion found drinks and raised his glass to Wylie's. 'Here's to you, Major Wylie,' he toasted. 'Here's to all crazy Americans.'

'Confusion to our enemies,' Wylie replied. A few moments later, he was confiding to Mannion that the idea of going to Jugoslavia by sea did not appeal to him. He had spent most of the past six weeks on a ship, the USS *Ancon*. It had been his home before and after the landings at Salerno, and he had come to the conclusion that he did not like ships and he did not like the sea. Air travel was quicker and it was more comfortable.

'Have you ever done any parachute jumping?' he asked Mannion conversationally.

3

Spring, 1944

The cell was clean: a scrubbed stone floor and cream-painted brick interior that was hosed down regularly. The bed board, with straw mattress, was suspended by two chains from eyebolts in the brick wall. A small barred window, above head level, admitted a shaft of bright spring sunlight. The cell's lone occupant, Marko Markovic, looked a shadow of the handsome man who – a little more than six months before – had stood before Chief Commissar Gubec and been told that he was unfit to hold officer rank in the Partisan Army. But he had no complaint about his treatment at the hands of the Germans. Indeed, he had put on a little weight during the two weeks he had been in German custody.

It was a sorry figure, emaciated and in rags, who emerged from the forests near Banja Luka and surrendered himself to an astonished soldier on guard duty at German Army HQ in the town. Marko expected to be shot – the Germans were not noted for extending hospitality to Partisan deserters – but he was treated with military correctness, even kindness. There was much questioning – and then he was whisked north to Zagreb, to this cell in the military barracks where he was now incarcerated.

There was more questioning – lots of it – by officers who came and went at all hours of the day and night, but he was given new clothes and was fed regularly. He began to feel human again. The spartan cell was a considerable improvement on the draughty forest lean-to that had been his only shelter for most of the Bosnian winter, as a Partisan labourer.

In Jajce, where the Supreme Staff was quartered until January, he had spent the bitter winter days carrying stone and timber for building workers. When the German winter offensive drove the Partisans out of Jajce, the labour squads – and Marko with them – were moved west into Bosnia to carry out construction and maintenance work on the airfield which the Partisans had built at Bosnanski Petrovac. Conditions there were grim. It was into this airfield that the Allies flew their transports from Italy to unload thousands of guns and supplies for Tito – and the Germans knew of its location and function only too well. Scarcely a day passed without a bombing raid.

Then Marko was moved to the highland town of Drvar, not far from Petrovac, where the Partisans had established their new Headquarters. Throughout the whole of this time, Marko kept body and soul alive on hatred: hatred for the sanctimonious Gubec, who had stripped him of his officer rank and committed him to the slavery of a labour battalion; hatred for the system that had allowed such an injustice in return for the countless times he had risked his life in battle for that system's survival; hatred for the ideology that had sucked in his own brother and swallowed him whole; hatred, too, for his own brother for his stupidity in believing (and almost persuading him) that Communism could save mankind. When Marko ran short of things to hate in his brooding unhappiness, he had only to look round at the men with whom he shared the rigours of penal servitude. Not all were there as punishment, as he was. Many were volunteers who had offered their brawn and muscle to the cause and gloried in the digging of a field latrine as if they were building the New Jerusalem.

Marko endured until he could endure no longer. In the labour battalion, they were not guarded as prisoners, but enjoyed a limited freedom within the camp. Marko walked away from it one dark night, and daylight found him miles away, alone in a wilderness of forest and mountain. He wandered for days, lost and hungry, in the forests of the Vrbas valley, before reaching Banja Luka and throwing himself on the mercy of the German Army. If, instead of locking him up, the Germans shot him on the spot, such was his misery that he would not have been displeased with the fate.

But they did not shoot the scarecrow who had wandered in out of the forest. They fed him and clothed him and brought him to Zagreb. It was scarcely kindness, but now, two weeks later, it was so much more than Marko had expected that he came close to weeping with gratitude to his captors when each new day dawned and they gave no sign that any bore him ill will. The twelfth day in Zagreb brought a break from the routine he had come to expect.

Marko was brought fried bacon and bread for breakfast. It was the first time that anything cooked had been offered in the morning. Then the morning passed without any interrogation; the first time it had happened. Just after midday, he *was* taken to the interrogation room on the first floor. It was occupied by only one officer, no stenographer. Marko recognised the *Abwehr* captain who had already questioned him on several occasions: a blond handsome man called Bleyer.

Bleyer was sitting at a small square table, smoking a cigarette. He invited Marko to take the vacant chair opposite him and offered a cigarette, which Marko accepted.

'I have been checking up on you,' Bleyer said, without preamble. 'You had an excellent record at the academy in Belgrade. I am sad that so much talent has been wasted in the wrong cause.'

'Not so sad as I, Herr Hauptsturmfuehrer. Look where it has landed me.'

'That is exactly what I have been considering,' said Bleyer, with a smile. 'But it's never too late. A good soldier is a good soldier – and this is something that the German Army has always recognised. It respects a good enemy. And it has always been willing to forget old grudges and offer a home to a respected enemy who is ready to do the same. It is ready to offer you such a home.'

Marko blinked at him.

'You want me to join the German Army? Is that what you are offering me?'

'I am offering you back your honour . . . a chance to win back your self-respect, with service in a military organisation that is second to none. I am offering you the opportunity to be a soldier gain, among real soldiers. You have told me that you hate the Communists, that they degraded you and robbed you of your honour as a soldier. I am offering you the chance of taking revenge. It's what you want, isn't it?'

'I've scarcely thought about anything else,' Marko admitted, with feeling. 'I can never forgive what they did to me. I've wanted to ram their stupid Marxist slogans back down their lying throats!' He threw a questioning look at Bleyer. 'But I never expected. . . .'

'That we much maligned Germans would be so accommodating,' Bleyer finished for him. 'My dear fellow, you have simply learned the hard way what we have been saying about the Communists for years. You would have no qualms at seeing them eliminated from the face of the earth?'

'None,' Marko said fiercely.

'Not even if this brother of yours, whom you told us about, was eliminated with them?'

Marko's face darkened.

'He is no brother of mine any more. He was the one who handed me the poisoned apple of Communism. I swallowed it whole – not because I believed his talk, but because he was my brother. Now he's one of their big shots, but he did not lift a finger to help me when they took away my soldier's pride and made me dig latrines and do the bidding of illiterate peasants. They made me a pariah, and that was how my brother treated me – as a pariah. He cast me off as if I were dead – dead and forgotten. And that's what he is to me now – dead and forgotten. I have no brother!'

Bleyer listened to Marko's bitter words, nodding sympathetically.

'I am told he was a writer, an intellectual?'

'Oh, yes. You don't have to tell me. I've had it thrown at me all my life how clever he was, what a great mind he has. But where did it get him? A long term in jail – that's what he got! And not a care about the disgrace it brought on the rest of the family! God knows, it made life difficult for me in the Army. Everywhere I went, his disgrace followed me around . . . made me suspect.'

'It still does,' Bleyer said. 'It is the only thing that now stands between you and your freedom. Between you and the opportunity I am offering you to redeem your honour in the service of Germany against our enemies. There are some who doubt your ability to give unswerving loyalty to the Reich because you fought for the Communists, because your brother is still fighting for the Communists and is known to be close to Tito, their top man. You will have to convince these colleagues of mine that you can be trusted, that you are ready to give to the Reich that unswerving loyalty they demand.'

Marko stared at him, bewildered.

'Send me into battle with your soldiers,' he appealed. 'Give me the chance to die doing the only thing I know how to do – fighting. Let my death be the proof of my words.'

Bleyer smiled.

'Oh, the chance to die might come your way soon enough,' he said, 'but a less dramatic demonstration of good faith would go a long way to convincing my colleagues that we can count on you.'

'What do they want me to do?'

'You have been cooperative,' Bleyer said, 'without telling us a great deal that we don't know about the Partisans. But there's still a great deal more that you can tell us – meticulous detail, which will help us finish them once and for all. I want you to give me that information. And more, I want you to take an active part in helping to plan the destruction of their Supreme Headquarters and everyone connected to it. That includes your brother, Stefan Markovic. Tito's the man we want, but we have no intention of sparing any of his followers.'

'I'll give you every scrap of information you want,' Marko declared. 'And I'll not only help you make your plans to attack these bastards at Drvar, I'll lead you there. I'll take you right into the vipers' nest and help you to finish them off.'

Bleyer stood up. He was well pleased. He had not misjudged the hatred he had sensed in this angry Serb since his first meeting with him.

'Good,' he said to Marko. 'I shall arrange for you to be given more comfortable quarters, although for the time being you will be restricted to these barracks. If there's anything you need, all you will have to do is ask the duty officer. His office is downstairs, next to the main door.'

Bleyer called in a sergeant and, in front of Marko, instructed him that the prisoner he had brought from the cells was henceforth to be accorded the same respect and privileges enjoyed by *Kroatische* officers on the staff.

'And see if the quartermaster can fit out our guest with a decent uniform,' Bleyer added.

The sergeant stared at him in bewilderment.

'A *Kroatische* uniform, sir?' he asked, wide-eyed.

'No, sergeant, a Wehrmacht uniform, with one of those armbands to show that he is Serbian and proud of it.' He turned to Marko. 'You will be given the rank of Untersturmfuehrer and dress as one of us but, for administrative purposes, you will appear on our strength as having been attached from Serbian Volunteer Corps Headquarters in Belgrade. For your own good, it would be best not to advertise where we did get you.'

Marko could only nod dumbly. He was still trying to come to terms with the breathtaking realisation that the Germans were not only giving him his freedom but the chance to make amends for his folly in fighting for the Partisans. It had been a madness – a madness that saw him turn, in spite of all his instincts, against those thousands of Cetniks who had been right all along in opposing and striving to extinguish the red menace of Communism. He wanted to embrace Bleyer, whose generosity and magnanimity had opened his eyes to the truth. He wanted to express the gratitude that coursed in him like a leaping tide. But before he could open his mouth, Bleyer was speaking to him again.

'I shall come back this afternoon. We have a lot of talking to do. Then, in the evening, I'll get you out of this place for a while. I thought we might have dinner together – with a mutual friend.'

Marko stared at him blankly.

'We have a mutual friend?'

Bleyer grinned.

'Sturmbannfuehrer Petar Richtman. He's celebrating a promotion. With luck, we'll be seeing quite a lot of him in the next few weeks.'

'Petar! Petar Richtman?' Marko's voice shook with an absurd joy. 'Who was at the academy with me?'

'The same,' Bleyer confirmed. 'I haven't told him about you. It'll be our little surprise for him, eh?'

Surprise, indeed! The thought of seeing Petar again was enough to fill Marko's cup of happiness. The last time he saw him, Petar had been on his way to Austria before the war, buoyed with the notion of training at a mountain warfare school with German Army officers. Petar had always had a profound admiration for the

German Army, and it was no surprise that he had become part of it. And he had done well if he had become a major. There was comfort to Marko in the knowledge that, after all that had happened, he and Petar – the best friend he had ever had – would be on the same side. He had a lot more in common with Petar than any of the Partisan officers he had served with – even those who, like himself, had been former Royal Army men. Come to think of it, he had more in common with Petar than he had ever had with his brother, Stefan. Stefan was no soldier, he was a book-learned politician – a radical and a revolutionary of the kind that caused wars by creating wider divisions in mankind than already existed. Well, damn Stefan. He and his kind had sewn the seeds of their own destruction, and they could damned well reap the consequences.

The Staff Colonel, in whose car Bleyer was riding, was unhappy about the consequences of a Partisan deserter being given refuge in the German Army. 'I just don't trust the fellows, any of them,' he told Bleyer. 'Damn it, the man is a traitor to his own people – a turncoat! And we give him the privileges of a German officer!'

'We in the Abwehr have always had a little latitude in whom we employ, Herr Oberst,' Bleyer said soothingly, 'and as this Serb, Markovic, will be working exclusively for the Abwehr and constantly under our supervision, I can assure you there's nothing to worry about. The best way we can hide him from Tito's spies is by giving him a uniform. He becomes just another man in uniform. In civilian clothes, he would have attracted attention floating in and out of Headquarters. This way, he remains anonymous.'

'The idea of him floating in and out of Headquarters makes me nervous on its own. It is really necessary?' The Colonel was far from mollified.

'He's the biggest fish we've ever caught,' Bleyer said.

'From an Intelligence point of view, that is. The Partisans lost a good officer when they dismissed Markovic and put him to work digging ditches. They may have stripped him of his rank but they didn't stop him thinking with a military brain and taking in everything he saw and storing it up in his mind. He was just another worker with a shovel to them, but he was assessing every job they did with the critical eye of a professional soldier – whether it was the siting of an anti-tank gun or defensive positions round their airfield. He noted the units deployed round Drvar and Petrovac and he has given us assessments of their fighting strengths and worth that are of far more value to us than the stuff we get from informers who aren't so expert.'

The Colonel sniffed.

'I suppose, if he helps us to get Tito, it will all be worthwhile.'

'Markovic has drawn us a map, with the exact location of the cave where Tito lives and works. He actually carried the timber which the carpenters used to line part of the interior. Tito uses a shed outside the cave as his office. When he's in the cave, there are always five men with machine-pistols guarding the entrance. The cave is about four kilometres outside Drvar and is heavily defended by the best troops the Partisans have.'

'This Markovic does appear to be a positive mine of information,' the Colonel said appreciatively. 'Does he know the times when Tito goes to the toilet?'

'As a matter of fact, he does,' Bleyer replied, his eyes twinkling. 'At least, he told us that Tito likes to shave at the same time every morning and that he is most meticulous about it. He is almost obsessive about being clean-shaven before beginning the day's work. He is quite fastidious about his appearance.'

'It would be rather interesting if we could take him alive,' the Colonel said, almost wistfully. 'I'd like to meet this fastidious troglodyte who has given us so much trouble.' He made a little snorting noise, dismissing the idea as too fanciful. 'It's unlikely, of course. Operation *Rösselsprung* is not being designed with the aim of taking prisoners. It'll be a bloody affair, mark my words.'

Bleyer murmured his agreement.

'Yes, Herr Oberst. I am afraid it will be a bloody affair. These things usually are.'

The Colonel turned a little sideways in his seat, so that Bleyer could get the full benefit of the stern warning in the senior officer's grey-blue eyes. He tapped Bleyer's tunic front with a finger, to give emphasis to his words.

'This Markovic of yours must not be given access to the details of *Rösselsprung*,' he said, 'no matter how much you trust him. Especially, he must be kept in the dark about the surprise packet we have in store for Tito. Absolute secrecy is essential.'

'He will only be told what he has to know, Herr Oberst . . . and that does not include a thing about the special strike force. As far as Markovic is concerned, we are planning another offensive, much the same as Operation *Weiss* or Operation *Schwarz*.'

The Colonel sat back in his seat and folded his arms. 'The less we say about these operations the better,' he commented. 'I don't need to tell you that both were conspicuous failures. Tito got away.'

But Tito won't get away this time, Bleyer thought. This time would be different, because *Rösselsprung* would have an element that all five previous offensives had lacked. Tito's headquarters would be encircled, as before, but this time the fox would not be given the chance to run from his lair. This time the lair was the number one target, and it would be attacked in the first hour of the offensive. Tito would not know what had hit him. There would be paratroops running all over his headquarters before he had time to rub the sleep from his eyes, descending from the sky in their hundreds.

Yes, *Rösselsprung* would be different. And it was well

named: Knight's Move. The objective was to capture the enemy's king.

A convoy of trucks, laden with men, was crossing the bridge over the Pliva River and being directed down into the lower part of the town of Jajce as Petar Richtman approached from the other direction. He told his driver to pull over into a side street; there was no point in heading into the steady stream of vehicles. Out of the traffic flow, Petar stepped nimbly from the scout car.

'No need to hang around,' he told the driver. 'I'll find my own way back.' On foot, he made his way up towards the bridge, dodging the lumbering vehicles. He saw Mara, waiting near the bridge, before she saw him.

Mara was not watching the troop convoy trundling over the bridge. Her attention was on a lone shepherd sitting at the side of the road. Knife in hand, he was idly gouging little chips of wood from the staff that he held across his knees. It seemed to be a crook that he was fashioning. The man wore the turban and *kalpak* of the Bosnian hillman – no oddity in Jajce – but there was something odd about him in Mara's eyes. The face did not go with the hillman's garb and there was something disturbingly familiar about it – although when and where Mara had seen the face, she just could not recall.

She turned at Petar's cheerful greeting and immediately put the shepherd out of her mind. Petar enveloped her in a hug and kissed her on the nose.

'How's my little sister?' he asked her. 'You must have got my message all right.'

'It was waiting for me yesterday, when we arrived. There are twelve of us – girls, that is – crowded into a little house near the Palas Hotel. But we'll be going under canvas when the convoy with our equipment gets here. How did you know we were coming to Jajce?'

Petar smiled. 'I make it my business to know where all our field hospitals are. You never know when you're going to need one in a hurry.'

'I thought you were in Zagreb.'

'I was – and I've got lots to tell you. Let's take a walk. How much time do you have?'

'All the time in the world,' Mara declared happily. 'We've nothing to do until our stuff gets here.'

Petar took her arm in his and they walked up through the high end of the town towards the ruined castle: home, and place of execution by the Turks, of Bosnia's last king. It was a sombre place, grassed over within the crumbling walls and dotted with cypress trees – but with a magnificent view of the town and the high forested hills from the battlements on that fine May morning.

On the way up, Petar told Mara of meeting Marko in Zagreb and of his defection from the Partisans.

'The Partisans treated him terribly,' he said. 'He's changed – eaten up with hate for them. He says he wishes now that he had got the chance to go to Austria like me, before the war started. It would have saved him a lot of grief.'

'What did happen to him?' Mara asked.

'He was with a cavalry regiment on the Romanian border when the war started. They didn't obey the surrender order . . . or some of them didn't. They formed a Cetnik group in the hills near Cacak.'

'I thought you said he was with the Partisans.'

'The group he was with were wiped out and he got mixed up with the Partisans in the retreat from Serbia. He met up with Stefan again – and he blames Stefan now for just about everything that has happened to him.'

'Why Stefan, Petar?' Mara said. 'I don't understand.'

'I'm not sure I do,' Petar admitted ruefully. 'Marko said that in Montenegro, it was Cetniks they were fighting, when he had been expecting to fight Italians; and it was Stefan who convinced him that the Cetniks were being paid bounty money by the Italians for slaughtering Partisans. He said it was terrible – Jugoslav fighting Jugoslav and nobody really knowing why it was happening.'

'I had no idea it was like that.' It seemed to Mara, daily witness to the suffering caused by war and by the human debris disgorged by it, that there was no end to the senseless nature and futility of the conflicts tearing her country apart. Right and wrong had long since become confused and undistinguishable; she had seen too many maimed young bodies. She longed only for an end to the wounding and killing.

Petar told her more about Marko and how he had come to hate the Partisans. She found it hard to associate this obsessively hating Marko with the happy-go-lucky young man she had known in Belgrade. Petar told her, too, about Stefan, and how the charismatic young writer whom she had worshipped like a god was now a member of the Communist hierarchy and said to be Tito's right-hand man. Petar made no mention of Jamie, and Mara assumed at first that this was because he knew nothing. They had reached the castle on the hill before she sensed that her brother was holding back all he had learned from Marko; that he was saving for last something that he was reluctant to tell her. Mara became so sure of this that she shrank from voicing her suspicion; she was afraid that there was only one thing Petar would shy away from telling her: that Jamie was dead. They had reached the battlements when she could contain her mounting fears no more.

'What about Jamie, Petar?' she cried, facing her brother. 'What about Jamie? It's not Stefan I want to hear about, it's Jamie – and Stefan must know what has happened to him!'

Petar avoided her eyes, looking away over the rooftops of Jajce as if, in doing to, he would find the inspiration he was seeking.

'I . . . I was going to tell you about Jamie,' he said, only adding to her suspense.

'Is he dead? Tell me he's not dead,' she sobbed. He blinked at her, not having realised that the answer to that one agonised question could end her turmoil.

'Jamie's alive,' he said, and caught her as she collapsed against him, weeping and sobbing her relief.

'Oh, thank God, thank God, thank God. Oh, Petar, why didn't you tell me? Why did you keep me waiting all this time when you knew?'

'Because he's a Partisan. He's at Drvar, no more than sixty-odd kilometres from where we're standing right now. Marko saw him a couple of times. He says Jamie was the only one who showed him any kindness. He tried to get Marko released from the labour squads to help him with officer training. That's what Jamie is doing, apparently – training young cadets to be Partisan officers. He was badly wounded about a year ago, and that's the job he was given when he got over it.'

Mara could scarcely take it all in. Petar had not said a word about Jamie and then, all of a sudden, he was bombarding her with news about him. She was soaring with happiness.

'Oh, thank you, thank you for telling me,' she bubbled excitedly, putting her arms round her brother. 'Don't you realise how much it means to me just to know this . . . just to know Jamie's all right?'

'Is he all right, Mara?' Petar's sober tone and grave expression sent a chill through her.

'What do you mean?' she asked, her voice shaking.

He stared at her with bleak eyes.

'Don't you know why you've been brought here? Why I've been brought here? Why that town down there is filling up with guns and men by the hour?'

Her saucerlike eyes widened with fear.

'The Partisans? You're going to attack?'

'There's no way out for them this time, Mara. Tito's next birthday is going to be his last. He thinks he's safe up in Drvar, with twelve thousand men protecting him, but twice that number wouldn't be any help to him now. We've closed the ring. He's surrounded. North, south, east and west. You mustn't build up any hopes that you'll see Jamie again. We don't underestimate them. We know they'll fight like demons, and I'll be surprised if they give in when they find out they're trapped. They'll fight to the last man.'

Petar's words were to haunt Mara for the rest of that day and through most of the night. *When they find out they're trapped, they'll fight to the last man.* Petar had given her a cup of hope and dashed it from her lips just as she had tasted its sweetness. It was agonising to know that Jamie was so near – and yet for all that she was able to do about it, he could have been on the moon. She slept little that night. The thought kept recurring that, somehow, she could devise a way of crossing the sixty kilometres that separated her from Jamie and warning him of the impending attack that would surely take his life. Even if there was nothing that could be done about it and the attack still came, the agony of being apart would be over. Then, side by side, they could welcome death with the sure certainty that the next world would be better than the planet of sorrow from which they escaped.

The cold light of morning scattered Mara's tortured dreaming and gave perspective to her thoughts of running with warnings for the Partisan lines. She realised that her hopes of getting anywhere near Drvar were fantasies; she could put them out of her mind.

There was still nothing for the nurses to do, in the absence of the transport bringing up the tents and equipment of their field hospital. Sleeping six to a room in the small house near the Palas, they felt a need to escape the crush and claustrophobia of their quarters. Without any enthusiasm, Mara allowed herself to be persuaded to join three of the sorority in a walk round the streets of Jajce. One of the girls wanted to shop for *tasici* – the hand-carved wooden mugs that seemed to be the main local cottage industry – and Mara tagged along.

The girls were about to go into a tiny shop to inspect its display of handmade souvenirs, when Mara saw the shepherd again: the man from the day before. He was striding down the street towards the bridge.

'I'll catch you up later,' she called to her companions, and, without waiting for a reply, set off after the shepherd. She followed him to the bridge, where he squatted in the same place that he had occupied the previous day. He gave a friendly wave to two Ustashi guards stationed at the near end of the empty bridge. They stared at him indifferently. They did not return the greeting.

Mara saw the knife appear in the man's hand. He began to whittle aimlessly at his shepherd's staff. Mara approached him. He met her curiosity without any sign of fear, returning her frank study of his face with an insolent smile. Mara gave no sign of the sudden throbbing excitement that gripped her.

'Good morning, Djuro Djakovic,' she said softly. 'I didn't recognise you in that get-up yesterday – but I do now, when I see you close up.' The smile vanished and the stark fear that replaced the insolent gleam in the shepherd's eyes was enough to tell Mara that she had not been mistaken.

'Who are you? What do you want?' As he spoke, the man glanced sideways towards the bridge and the Ustashi guards. His alarm was palpable, although he was doing his best not to show it. But Mara had no intention of attracting the attention of the Ustashi.

'Don't you remember me, Djuro?' she asked, still keeping her voice low. 'You always sat behind me at Russian lectures. Fourth row from the front. At the University. You kept asking me to go dancing with you, but I never would. I already had a boy friend. He was in prison.'

The man's eyes widened. He was placing the face – but the German nurse's uniform did not make sense in conjunction with the face he was remembering.

'I don't know you. My name is not Djuro. It is Jussuf –'

'You are no more Bosnian than you're a shepherd,' Mara interrupted sharply. 'Where are your sheep, Djuro? Would you know a sheep if you saw one?'

'What do you want of me?'

'Your help, if you are what I think you are. I won't give you away.' She nodded towards the staff on his knees. 'It has just dawned on me what you were doing yesterday. Those notches on your stick . . . is it one for every truckload of Germans that crosses the Pliva?'

'You have a vivid imagination, Fräulein,' he said, but he was almost rigid with fear. Mara wasn't going to let go. She wasn't going to let him run off, as she had allowed the professor in Belgrade to run off, pleading mistaken identity. Alerted by a shift in the frightened man's gaze, she turned to see what had taken his attention. Two German officers – in SS field uniform – were strolling towards them. One of them greeted her with a smile.

'Do you need any assistance with this rascal, Fräulein?' he asked, with a polite little inclination of the head.

'Thank you, no,' she said, smiling back. 'I am just curious to know how they carve these crooks. He's a little shy, I think.'

'Show the lady your handiwork, you rogue,' the officer admonished the shepherd, in German. The man stared blankly back. Turning to Mara, he said something in his own tongue.

'What does he say?' the officer asked Mara. 'Do you understand him?'

Mara gave a little laugh.

'It pays to know the language, Herr Obersturmfuehrer. He says that an audience makes him all thumbs.'

'Tell him that if he doesn't oblige you, we'll hang him up by his thumbs,' the officer said.

Mara met his laughing gaze reproachfully.

'Such a cruel thought does not go with such a kind face,' she murmured. 'Would you really allow me to make such a threat to a poor peasant?'

The young officer blushed in confusion. 'I said it only in jest,' he apologised. 'I am sure that you are perfectly capable of charming anything you want from the rascal.' He clicked his heels together and inclined his head in a respectful bow. 'Forgive the intrusion, Fräulein.'

His companion repeated the salutation, and they continued their leisurely stroll across the bridge. Mara returned her attention to the 'shepherd', whose relief was written all over his face.

'Well, Djuro? Do you still feel threatened by me? Or has your memory improved?' He remained obstinately silent. 'I can still call them back,' she prompted him. 'I have a name, and I want to hear you say it.'

'Mara Richtman.' He uttered the words so faintly that they were almost inaudible.

Mara smiled.

'At last,' she sighed. 'We're getting somewhere. Now I'll give you another name. A Scottish name. Jamie Kyle. He was at the university, too. Do you know him?'

'I might.'

'He's with the Partisans – at Drvar, with Tito. I want to get a message to him. Is it possible?'

He blinked at her in fearful disbelief.

'You seem to know a lot.'

'Can you get a message to Jamie Kyle?'

'Perhaps. I don't know.' He got to his feet without taking his eyes off her. 'We can't talk here. It's too dangerous.'

'Where *can* we talk?'

'Walk up the hill, towards the castle. I'll follow you.'

She considered this. 'Very well. But no tricks. I'm trusting you. It's a matter of life or death.'

'For both of us,' he said earnestly, and then he allowed himself a brief smile. 'Their uniform suits you. I would

492

still like to take you dancing.' She would have replied but he got in first. 'I know, you already have a boy friend. He has a new name now. They call him the Tiger of Bioce.'

The classroom was a small patch of hillside above the tiny village of Sipoljani. A blanket had been spread on the ground and, neatly laid out on it were the component parts of a Bren gun. Jamie squatted on one edge of the blanket and, around him, a dozen cadets were clustered in a horseshoe. Jamie had a scarf wound round his eyes and knotted behind his head, effectively blindfolding him. Standing just behind Jamie was a British officer, holding his wristwatch in his hand. Captain Teddy Cameron wore a pom-pom balmoral which sported the red hackle of the Black Watch. He had parachuted on to a hill near Mkronjic Grad some months before, when Tito's headquarters were in Jajce. The Partisans had taken an instant liking to him not because he had a lively and likeable personality – which he had – but because they believed his red hackle had a political significance. He did nothing to disillusion the mistake and, indeed, would entertain any who cared to listen with outrageous stories of how the Black Watch came to be known as Stalin's Own. Some of his fellow Britons did not appreciate these tall stories, which were always different, but the Partisans – who took them with a pinch of salt, anyway – loved them and thought the world of their teller.

'Right,' he called out to Jamie. 'Begin at the count of three. One, two, three. . . .'

Jamie, who had never had any formal weapons training but had become an expert in three years of handling many varieties, began assembling the Bren. He worked with a sure touch, identifying each component with his fingertips. He slipped the last piece home, dropped flat on his belly, pulling the Bren to his shoulder in the firing position, and clipped in the magazine.

'Ready to fire,' he announced.

'Award that man the VD and Scar,' Cameron proclaimed. 'Time taken was one minute and eight seconds.'

Jamie jumped to his feet and whipped off the blindfold. He translated Cameron's announcement of the time for the benefit of the cadets.

'*Jedan minut i osam,*' he said, to a murmur of approval. 'That is your time to beat, comrades. But you pass the test if you can do it in one minute and a half.' He selected one of the cadets. 'You first. Strip the gun down, without the blindfold and then we'll see how long it takes you to put it together again with your eyes covered. And remember, this is not a game. War is fought at night as well as during the day, and if your gun jams in the dark, your knowledge of your weapon could save your life.'

The cadet was dismantling the gun with easy familiarity when the exercise was interrupted by a shout from below, near the river. Two men were standing there, having walked from the village along the bank of the Unac. Jamie recognised one of them as Stefan.

'Will you take over?' he asked Cameron.

'Leave them to me,' the Scot replied. 'These laddies are mustard. I'll just stand here and look intelligent and let them get on with it.'

Jamie wondered what Stefan wanted with him. He saw little of his friend these days. It was not choice on Stefan's part, he knew, nor aloofness because he was now one of the top echelon; it was due to Stefan's workload. Their paths crossed with growing infrequency. There was a rumour that Tito planned to make all the members of the Central Committee lieutenant-generals, as a prelude to his own election to marshal. For some reason, this amused Jamie. He was able to take a detached view of the jockeying for power that went on around Supreme Headquarters. The Partisans made a great show of scorning status and titles, and yet they all wanted to be the Duke of Plaza Toro.

494

Reaching Stefan and his companion, the first thing to strike Jamie was the look of intense worry on his friend's face. High responsibility, it seemed, did not agree with him. His companion, on the other hand, was a flamboyant figure: a Bosnian hillman, in *kapala* and turban. Stefan was the first to speak.

'Do you remember Djuro? From our University days?'

'Mine were cut short, unfortunately,' Jamie said, with a wry smile. He looked closely at the hillman, and stuck out a hand. 'I'm sorry. You look like a person that wouldn't easily be forgotten, but I can't quite place you.'

Djuro Djakovic grinned, shaking Jamie's hand.

'Maybe, when I get back in uniform, you may remember my face. Your girl friend didn't have your difficulty. She spotted me in Jajce . . . nearly gave me a heart attack.'

Jamie stared at him as if he had been struck by a thunderbolt.

'My girl friend . . . Mara? In Jajce!' His voice rising almost to a shout, he asked, 'When was this?'

'Four, nearer five days ago.'

Jamie was shaken to the core.

'Djuro's an Intelligence officer – one of the best we've got,' Stefan explained. 'He has been keeping an eye on the German buildup for the offensive they're planning. He was spying for us in Jajce when Mara spotted him and spoke to him.'

Jamie was having difficulty absorbing what he heard. The news that, one, Mara was alive and had not become a victim of war filled him with such overwhelming relief that nothing else seemed to matter. The news that, two, she was in Jajce – only seventy kilometres away – was almost too much to take in at the same time.

'She's a German Army nurse, Jamie,' Stefan was saying. 'Or, at least, she was in the uniform of one.'

Jamie rounded on him.

'What are you saying? That she's one of them?'

'I didn't say that,' Stefan said soothingly. 'It's possible she was conscripted. There's no way of telling. Heaven knows, we've had plenty of Croat conscripts coming over to our side as soon as they've had the chance. Pavelic has been so desperate that he has been conscripting Christian boys into Muslim regiments. We don't know if Mara was forced into uniform or is using it as a cover. All we really know is that she thinks you are in Drvar training Partisan officers, and she's scared stiff you'll get killed when the Germans attack.'

'She asked me to give you a message,' Djakovic said. 'She says she loves you with all her heart and that she always will. She lives only for the day when she can give herself to you as your wife. Nothing but that matters to her. She was most anxious that I deliver her words to you personally.'

Djakovic spoke solemnly, conveying the impression of humble gratitude at being Mara's chosen instrument. Jamie clasped his hand warmly.

'Thank you, my friend,' he murmured, unashamedly moved.

Djakovic inclined his head, in a bow that was almost apologetic.

'Now comrades, if you will excuse me,' he said, 'I shall get back to Drvar and some sleep. I've been on my feet for three days and nights. With so many Germans about, it was a lot trickier getting back from Jajce than usual.' With that he turned and walked back along the river-bank towards the village.

Jamie watched the retreating figure, appreciating that Djakovic had wasted little time in seeking him out, at the end of a journey of considerable danger.

'Mara gave him quite a hard time,' Stefan said, behind him. 'He really thought she was going to blow the whistle on him.'

Jamie turned.

'But she didn't.'

'No, but he had some bad moments when a couple of SS officers butted in on their chat. Apparently Mara saw them off in good style.'

'There are some things I don't understand,' Jamie said. 'How did she know where I was? How did she know I was training Partisan officers? I mean, nobody pays much attention to me. You're the big shot.'

Stefan smiled.

'You weren't the only one who got a message from Mara, Jamie. There was one for me, too.'

Jamie stared at him in surprise.

'What kind of message?'

'A rather naive one – but then Mara always was a little naive. She wanted me to use my influence with Stari – with Tito – to get out of Drvar before the Germans attack. Otherwise, we'll all be killed.'

'Have you told Tito about this?'

'Of course. All of it: Mara sending you her love – everything. Djuro's an Intelligence officer, not a message boy for you or me. The entire war staff had to be told everything.'

'Did they?' Jamie said diffidently. 'And what did Tito say?'

'He laughed. He thought the whole thing was priceless. He said that any warning from a woman in love had to be taken seriously. But, in this case, it would not be necessary to evacuate the whole of Supreme Headquarters. All we had to do to make this starry-eyed young lady happy was evacuate one man – the Tiger of Bioce.'

'Very amusing,' Jamie said, without any sign that he found it so. 'No doubt, this was greeted with hearty guffaws all round.'

Stefan frowned.

'I can assure you that it was the subject of very earnest debate. We had to make up our minds whether Mara's warning was genuine, or some kind of German trick.'

'Mara would die before she would allow herself to be part of a German trick,' Jamie protested heatedly.

'She could have been used,' Stefan pointed out reasonably. 'However, the general consensus was that Mara was genuinely trying to warn us. She wasn't to know that *we know* and have known for some time that the Germans are about to hit us with another offensive.'

'What we don't know is when,' Jamie said.

'That's exactly the point that suggests Mara was a hundred per cent genuine!' Stefan exclaimed with an air of satisfaction. 'Something she said to Djuro. He asked her if she knew when the attack was coming, but she couldn't give him a date. All she knew was that she had heard a German officer say the new offensive was going to finish Tito for good, and that his next birthday would be the last he'd ever see.'

'It's a way of speaking. What German officer would know when Tito's birthday is? It could be next December, for all he knew.'

'Only it isn't, Jamie. It's the twenty-fifth of May. And that's the day after tomorrow.'

Jamie frowned.

'Just my luck. It rather knocks my plans on the head.'

'What plans?'

Jamie grinned at him.

'I was hoping that you and Djuro might help me fix up a trip into Jajce to see Mara.'

There was an air of expectation in the operations conference room at German Army HQ in Zagreb as the thirty or more summoned officers took their seats and awaited the arrival of the commander of XV Mountain Corps. He strode into the room at one minute to ten, took his place on the dais in front of a huge wall map and opened the briefing at precisely ten o'clock.

'Gentlemen,' he began, 'this meeting is timed to end at 1100 hours to allow you to return to your commands today. I shall therefore waste no time. It is my intention only to underline the importance of securing all objectives in the execution of Operation *Rösselsprung* and acquaint you further with the broad plan. From tomorrow, I shall make my headquarters in the town of Bihac – and I hope that by nightfall on the day after tomorrow I shall be able to announce the elimination of Tito, his headquarters, the British, American and Russian military missions which he shelters, his radio communications, his airfield at Petrovac and the greater part of the twelve-thousand-strong bandit force known to be grouped in the Drvar-Petrovac area.'

Wolf Bleyer, sitting in the front row below the General, stifled a yawn. There was little of the finer detail of *Rösselsprung* that he did not already know, and he found these glorified pep talks boring. He was impatient for the operation to begin and not a little nervous about the part he would have to play in it. The General was now outlining the role of the Prinz Eugen Division, as the 7th SS Mountain Division was known.

' . . . with an assault battalion of Panzergrenadiers will advance on a broad front between the Sana and Unac Rivers . . . '

Bleyer was wondering what it would be like landing on a Bosnian hillside in a glider. It was going to be an entirely new experience. He tried to dismiss stories he had heard of gliders smashing up like matchwood when they hit the ground.

The General droned on.

' . . . one-oh-five Reconnaissance Battalion will overcome resistance at Livanskopolje. The battalion, with the armour of an SS tank company in support, will thrust towards Drvar and destroy any of the enemy seeking to escape southwards . . . '

Forty-eight hours from now, I could be dead, Bleyer was thinking. And for what? Some godforsaken Bosnian hill which, if it has a name, nobody would be able to pronounce anyway. Maybe it would be better to die in a field, where someone might have the decency to bury me. *Polje* was the Jugoslav name for a field. They stuck it on the end of every other village and hamlet. High-field, low-field, green-field, broad-field, Petar's-field, Radovan's-field. Maybe they would call his patch on earth Bleyer*polje*. Ah, now the General was getting to the nitty-gritty: the poor beggars who were going to have to land right on top of Tito's headquarters. Skorzeny's boys. The good old SS *Fallschirmjaeger*. The death-or-glory brigade. Bleyer returned his attention to the General, wondering if he would mention that the glory boys were taking Wolf Bleyer along for the ride.

' . . . the transports will have to fly low and in tight formation,' the General was saying, 'because the drop zone presents many difficulties. Our *Fallschirmjaeger* will have no altitude to play with: a drop time of no more than twenty seconds between deplaning and hitting the ground.'

Sooner them than me, thought Bleyer. That's scarcely time for the parachute to open. Maybe it will be safer in a glider. Ah, this is it!

' . . . the gliderborne group will take off from Zagreb one hour before zero hour. It will include Number One Company of the Brandenberg Regiment, all but one platoon of Number Four Company, the Benesch Detachment, the Luftwaffe Liaison Units and six Abwehr personnel, whose job will be to secure all codebooks, documents and files found at the enemy headquarters.'

When the General had finally completed his address, he was followed by several specialist officers, who briefed the assembly on such things as signals and communications and the movement of rations and supplies. It was two minutes before eleven when the General got up again to conclude the proceedings.

'Officers of the Reich,' he addressed the gathering,

'the bandit Tito has over two hundred thousand men under arms throughout Jugoslavia. This force is like a serpent, receiving its orders, its cunning, its inspiration, from its head and brain. The time has come when, with one brave blow, we will strike off the serpent's head and kill the beast. What is left will wither and rot. May God grant you a speedy victory.'

The General left the gathering on the stroke of eleven. Bleyer glanced at his watch to verify the time. If *Rösselsprung* was carried through with the same precision timing, it would be a cakewalk. No, not a cakewalk – a miracle.

4

Knight's Move: The Fateful Hours

0500 hours, 25 May 1944

Mara woke with a start. It was not yet light. The five other nurses sharing the tent were stirring, too – wakened by the noise. Getting up, Mara padded on her bare feet to the door and undid the flap. She peered outside. The tented village of the field hospital had been set up on flat land between the river and the road to Mrkonjic Grad. The road was packed with army trucks moving nose to tail along the road. The trucks were filled with helmeted soldiers, shoulder to shoulder. The men were grim-faced and silent as each truck was waved past a team of checkers at the starting line. The air was thick with exhaust fumes and the racket of throbbing engines.

'So it's starting?' A nurse whose name was Greta had joined Mara. 'Good luck, boys,' she called out and, at the sight of two pyjama-clad nurses standing in the gloom among the tents, a chorus of shouts and wolf whistles came back. More nurses emerged from the tents to wave at the never-ending line of passing trucks. A spectacular variety of night attire was on view, but a senior nurse's order – more a suggestion than a command – to cover themselves was shouted down.

'Let the poor devils see our legs,' a buxom blonde encouraged loudly. 'There won't be anything to cheer them up where they're going.'

'The old haybag's legs aren't worth showing,' an anonymous voice commented.

'Seeing them go off like this always makes me go all

cold inside,' the nurse called Greta confided to Mara. 'It usually means that we'll be going like a meat factory before night.' Unable to watch, she turned away from the congregation and walked through the lines to look out across the river. Mara followed her. The girl was sobbing quietly, and Mara knew why. She put an arm round Greta's shoulder.

'Does this bring it back, Greta?' she asked quietly.

The girl nodded, unable to find her voice right away.

'That was how I last saw my Walther – riding off like that in a truck to fight. He was not meant to be a soldier . . . he was so gentle, so loving.' She shed tears, remembering. Then she found her voice again. 'My Walther was the very first casualty they brought back – only four hours after I waved him goodbye. I had scrubbed the table on which they laid him. I didn't recognise him when. . . . He died without ever knowing that it was me holding his hand.'

'Don't hurt yourself like this, Greta,' Mara murmured. 'Don't torture yourself.'

The girl called Greta straightened herself and sniffed. She took a deep breath.

'You're right, Mara. I must stop snivelling. I must pull myself together. It's foolish of me to carry on like this. I'm not the only woman who has lost her man.' She glanced at Mara. 'What makes you so strong, Mara? Is it because you avoid men?' She stilled Mara's reply. 'No, don't deny it. I've seen you. Is it because there *is* a man somewhere, someone special?'

Mara's eyes misted.

'I won't deny there is a man. And yes, Greta, he's special. Very, very special.'

'I knew it. You must be glad he's not in this, going out into those hills.'

'He's not so very far away,' Mara said, and bit her lip to stop her own emotions from taking control.

'Then he is here, somewhere?'

'Where I am, he is . . . and where he is, I am. That's what I meant. We are never far from each other.'

'I think I know what you mean,' Greta said, and fell silent. Across the river, an armoured train went slowly past where the track ran parallel with the stream. Guns were mounted on its sandbagged flatcars. SS troopers were crowded on others. The train was headed west, towards Drvar.

Mara remembered Petar's confidence that the battle would be decisive. From the north and south and east and west, the German ring of steel that encompassed the hills round Drvar would be drawn tighter – and just the sight of so many men and guns on the move iced her heart with fear for Jamie. The knowledge that her own brother would play a part in his destruction added another terrible dimension to her fears. Somewhere out there in the night that was lightening into morning, Petar, too, would be on the move.

0515 hours

Petar had been on the move for fifteen minutes, but from a starting line well to the west of Jajce, near Mrkonjic Grad. At a cautious speed, in order not to get too far ahead of the assault group of which he was part, his *Schwimmwagen* had travelled five kilometres and was approaching a T-junction in the narrow road.

'Do we keep straight on, sir?' the driver asked.

'No, turn left. The track goes right up over the hills. There's a village on the other side, about another five or six kilometres after we get to the top.'

'Are there bandits up there, sir?'

'That's what we've got to find out,' Petar said curtly.

'We're not going up there to picnic,' the third occupant of the *Schwimmwagen* advised the driver. 'Just you keep your eyes on the road. And watch out for mines.'

'In this light?' the driver complained. 'Maybe you should walk in front.'

Turning off at the junction, the *Schwimmwagen* was soon labouring up a steep gradient into the dark shape of the desolate hills. Behind them, streaks of pinkish light were rimming the hills to the east. The worst of the slope behind them, Petar ordered a halt.

'Time to report,' he said. He turned to the second crewman, who doubled as radio man and machine-gunner. 'Tell Green Leader that Junction One is undefended and that we made the turn-off. He can close up as fast as he likes. We'll push on to RV Two.'

As the radio man got to work, Petar scanned the track ahead. They were high up, and the way led through narrow defiles, which made ambushes easy and played havoc with radio communication.

'Green Leader closing up fast,' the radio man reported.

'Let's get going,' Petar said. So far, so good – he was thinking – but there's a long way to go.

0535 hours

It promised to be a beautiful day. The dawn had come in a blaze of pink light as Jamie shaved in the cottage yard. He had long since learned to use the white-handled cutthroat razor without the luxury of mirror or soap, and had completed the task and was vigorously sluicing himself down from a bucket of icy water when he became aware of the brilliantly hued sky to the east. He had risen early because today was the day he had promised his section – Cameron had dubbed them 'the Kyle and Cameron Highlanders' – a twenty-five-kilometre route-march with full pack and weapons. It was going to be sticky work when the sun came up, but Jamie was looking forward to it.

As much fresh air and exercise as you can get, was the

505

medical advice offered when he recovered from his infected wound. It was laughable at the time because there were few members of the Partisan Army who did not get a surfeit of both – but it had worked for Jamie. He had never felt fitter and stronger than on that bright May morning, and he attributed it to the active open-air life that had been his lot for so long.

He was going into the cottage to rouse Cameron and remind him that their routemarch was scheduled for a seven a.m. start, when he heard the first drone of aircraft. Then he saw them: lots of them, black shapes in wide formations across the sky to the north, like skeins of geese.

There was no need to rouse Cameron. He came running from the cottage, clad only in his underpants. The roar of aeroengines was enough to wake all but the heaviest of sleepers. The flights of Junkers 87s came from the direction of Petrovac, straight to Sipoljani, where they wheeled to begin their bombing dives, although it was the silver ribbon of the Unac and its horseshoe curve round the town of Drvar – not the village – that provided a guide to their target.

'Stukas!' shouted Cameron unnecessarily, adding 'It's Drvar they're after!' Both facts were patently obvious to Jamie, who could only watch in impotent horror as aircraft after aircraft hurtled towards the hidden bowl in the hills, where Drvar lay. They disappeared below the closest ridge, to reappear in upward flight as they screamed away, their bombs released.

Smoke erupted and drifted upwards in clouds from the rim of the hidden bowl, as if the lip concealed a volcano that had sprung to life. The thunder of explosions echoed dully in quick succession as Jamie and Cameron watched.

'A good job we moved the mission out of the town when we did,' Cameron commented, his first thoughts for the compatriots who had landed with him in Jugoslavia. Less than forty-eight hours before, both the British and American missions had moved out from Drvar to Bastasi, where Tito's cave was located. The Russian Military Mission had elected to stay where it was, refusing to be panicked by talk of an imminent German offensive. It was possible they were already regretting the decision.

'This is the start of it,' Jamie said. 'First the Stukas, then the ground attack. We're wasting time, standing here.' He disappeared into the cottage and emerged, seconds later, buttoning up his battledress blouse. Slung over one arm was a German Schmeisser and the webbing belt to which his holstered Luger was attached.

'Where are you going?' Cameron wanted to know. 'If this is the attack we've been waiting for, there won't be any routemarch, surely?'

Jamie squinted at him, buckling on his belt. 'We've been training the best men we've got to be officers. Today could be the day we see how they measure up as soldiers. This army doesn't carry any passengers.'

Cameron goggled at him.

'But half of them are just kids.'

'If they can shoot, they're old enough. What about you? You're just on loan to us – and unofficial loan at that. Maybe you'd better report to Bastasi.'

'Like hell I will!' Cameron flamed. 'If the Kyle and Cameron Highlanders are going into action, I'm going too! And I don't give a monkey's what the brass think about it!'

Jamie shrugged. 'It's your funeral,' he said.

'It could be,' Cameron agreed, with a grin. 'And I don't want to be late for it! Just give me a sec to put on the old breeks and grab my rusty – I mean trusty – claymore.'

The Stukas were still appearing in what seemed a neverending stream and screaming down to attack

Drvar and its immediate surroundings. When the bombardment started, Stefan had been asleep in the basement of the building that housed the radio and communications nerve centre of Supreme Headquarters. He had spent half the night working on signals to and from the new Partisan Liaison Centre that had been established in the Italian port of Bari and, instead of returning to the Bastasi encampment, he had bedded down on a mattress in a cellar recess.

He had a rude awakening. The building was shaking to the foundations as he raced for the stairs and made his way up three flights to the signals room. The night officer was still on duty, and mildly panicking at the prospect of a direct hit and the loss of so much sophisticated radio equipment. Recent hit-and-run air raids had convinced him that it should be moved out of the town; most of the Supreme Headquarters staff had already been evacuated. Now, it seemed – with bombs dropping all around – that he and the irreplaceable radios were doomed.

Stefan calmed him and ordered him to get out signals placing all units on general alert. Some perimeter posts had already flashed in, reporting visible enemy movements on roads in their sectors.

'Has the Supreme Commander been told?' Stefan sought to know.

'We haven't had time,' the officer complained. 'I was going to do it myself when the bombs started dropping.'

'I'll buzz the Commander,' Stefan told him. 'You get on to Escort Battalion Command Post and order an instant stand-to. If it turns out to be a false alarm, I'll take responsibility.' Stefan was taking no chances. He had, however, no doubt in his mind that the dawn raid, by what sounded like all the airworthy Stukas in Croatia, was the prelude to the big attack that had been expected for weeks.

It was a clearly frightened Zdenka who answered his call to Tito. Stefan peremptorily ordered her off the line

508

and told her he wanted Tito personally. There was a brief silence before Stefan heard Tito's calm voice. His words were temporarily drowned by the thunder of bombs bursting within a few hundred metres of where Stefan was standing.

'They seem to be concentrating on the town,' he heard Tito say. 'You had better get out here as quickly as you can.'

Stefan reported what he had done, and was happy to hear the Supreme Commander endorse his decisions. Like Stefan, Tito was in no doubt that the long-awaited German offensive was finally under way.

'Is there anything else you want me to do before I leave here?' Stefan asked. There was. Now would be a good time to test the efficacy of the new links established with Bari and find out how long it took to scramble RAF fighters from their Italian bases. In the past, during raids on the Partisan airfield at Petrovac, scrambling fighter support from four hundred kilometres away had proved futile because the raiders were back at their home bases before the fighters were halfway to Jugoslavia. But this time was different. It looked as if the Stukas intended to pound away for some considerable time.

Stefan got a signal off to Bari. Leaving the Communications Centre, he ventured out in the street. He was immediately tempted to return whence he had come and take refuge in the cellar. Stukas were still diving down, apparently selecting their targets in accordance with what took the pilot's fancy. A pall of smoke hung over the town. Bracing himself, Stefan took to his heels and ran.

0550 hours

The Henschel tug aircraft and their gliders were ready for takeoff out on the airfield at Zagreb. Inside a large hangar, more than three hundred men were drawn up in lines, ready to march out and board the gliders. A senior

SS paratroop officer addressed them. He was apologising to the *Fallschirmjaeger* for the necessity of bringing them to the assembly point, not in their own distinctive battle gear but dressed as ordinary infantrymen. The reason was security. For the same reason, they had been told nothing of the coming operation or their vital part in it until only a few hours ago. It was not his intention, now, to make a long speech or burden them with platitudes about glory. He knew they would fight courageously and well. Not all of the glider force had the good fortune to be *Fallschirmjaeger*, so he invited those who were to demonstrate their spirit and pride to the others by singing the paratroops' battle anthem.

Wolf Bleyer, who took pride in his detachment and tended to stand back from the drum-beating and flag-waving rituals of military life, found that he was deeply moved as the *Fallschirmjaeger* among the assembled warriors launched into their rousing marching song and a deep melodious sound filled the hangar. Bleyer was standing in a group slightly segregated from the main body. This was *Draufgänger* Group, which was to be accommodated in seven gliders and included the Intelligence and Luftwaffe signals personnel as well as fifty strike troops.

Bleyer attributed his emotional response to the jangled state of his nerves. As the day for *Rösselsprung* had neared, his stomach had churned at thought of the unknown hazards which lay ahead for him. He was no stranger to battle but he had grown used to fighting his war at a safe distance from the front and never, in his wildest dreams, had he imagined that the day would come when he would be pitchforked into the heat of battle by making an aerial descent into the enemy's stronghold.

He realised it was probably a disadvantage to have been involved in *Rösselsprung* from its inception. The paratroops around him had not, until late the previous night, known a thing about what they were being thrown into – and maybe that was the better way. They would be fighting for their lives before the realities had had time to sink in. Bleyer knew every minute detail of the plan – and the knowledge was a burden. So much could go wrong.

He knew that the para and glider forces were on a hiding to nothing. Once they were on the ground at Drvar, they would be completely isolated; surrounded by the enemy, even although they captured all their objectives. And they had no hope of getting out if the conventional ground forces, battling through the mountains from as far as eighty and a hundred kilometres away, did not drive to the centre of the ring in the short time allotted to them.

From reveille at 0300, Bleyer had never stopped looking at his wristwatch and mentally ticking off the *Rösselsprung* schedule, wondering if things were going on time. Had the far-flung spearheads of XV Mountain Corps got off to a flying start? At Knin in the south and Bihac in the north? At Banja Luka and Jajce? In the foothills west of the Sana River?

And so it had gone on. First light, and were the Stukas and the Messerschmitts in the air above Drvar as the timetable demanded? Had Battle Group William – the force on which the paras would depend for relief – met any opposition yet, or were they racing unimpeded towards Drvar from the southeast?

Bleyer glanced at his watch again, as the SS officer-in-charge gave the order to march out and board gliders. It was 0555.

As they tramped across the field, Bleyer caught the eye of his Abwehr recruit, Marko Markovic, and gave him an encouraging smile. The Serb looked dazed – and it was no wonder. He had only been told the evening before that he was going on a trip. The nature of the trip had not been revealed until an hour ago. He was going to

Drvar and he would act as guide for the *Draufgänger* Group leader, an SS Divisional Intelligence officer from Staff HQ, Bosnia. This same rather overbearing officer had vetoed the issue of weapons to Marko, which had not gone down too well with the Serb – although he had not complained, accepting that he was still on probation.

Bleyer watched Marko file away to board a glider, some distance from the DFS 230 to which he himself was directed. A few moments later he was sitting, strapped in, with the rest of his party, like so many sardines. The glider jerked as the tug plane took the weight and surged forward. A knot tightened in the pit of Bleyer's stomach, and a feeling that was half exhilaration and half dread seemed to well up. He glanced at his watch. It was two minutes past six.

0652 hours

The Junkers 52 transports were flying so close that their wingtips were nearly touching. They had taken off from their base, just inside the Hungarian border, while the glider force was still on the ground at Zagreb. The aircraft carried the first wave of strike troops from the crack SS Paratroop Battalion 500, including their dashing young commander, *Obersturmfuehrer* Rybka. They were now approaching the drop zone.

Astern of the transports, the glider force from Zagreb was strung out across the sky. As he prepared to jump with his men, Rybka tried to shut from his mind the frustration he felt at an enforced change to his assault plan, forty-eight hours before he was due to put it into effect. A shortage of Junkers 52 transports had meant abandoning his intention to land all his men in a single drop. Rybka was far from happy at having to revise his plan and split his force – but there had been no alternative. The transports would now drop three hundred men in the first run and then make the short trip to Banja Luka – a hundred kilometres away – to pick up a second wave of two hundred paratroops. It was going to take three hours to collect and drop the two hundred men from Banja Luka, and Rybka did not like this time gap one little bit. The absence during the first three hours of battle of so much firepower might mean the difference between success and failure.

There was no time to worry about that now, however. The *Absetzer* in charge of despatching the aircraft's human cargo sounded the klaxon signal and shouted the order: 'Make ready!' It was the only spoken word of command. The door in the port side of the transport was already open, and the drill from here on was silent and so well rehearsed that it had become automatic. The *Fallschirmjaeger* clipped their static lines to the fore-and-aft metal cable and, sliding their hooks along this line, they shuffled in close towards the open door. Through the open door, the rocky terrain below seemed to be desperately close as it hurtled by, but there was no faltering as the exit was reached and each man plunged through. As the men deplaned, they extended their arms, birdlike, to meet the rushing air. Whisked away in the slipstream, there was the crack as the static line whipped open the pack and was left trailing. The ground seemed to leap up at the paratroops. There was scarcely time to absorb the shock of the flowering chute before they were swinging their feet to make the thudding impact with the stony earth. Only twenty seconds had passed between exit and touchdown.

Rybka rallied his men, who were shedding their parachutes as they rolled on the hard-baked ground. There was a rush to retrieve the canisters that held their precious weapons and, as yet, no murderous stream of gunfire to impede this operation. Section leaders were shouting and organising orderly grouping from the chaos of running men. Still, there was no fire from the enemy, who seemed to have been taken totally by surprise. The drop also appeared to have achieved one hundred per cent accuracy – slap against the town's edge. Drvar lay open before Rybka and his three hundred SS warriors.

A pall of smoke and rising dust hung over the town, evidence of the devastation wreaked by the Stukas and Messerschmitts still circling and watching above. Grouped and armed, the paratroops moved into the deserted streets: forty men to seek out and destroy the headquarters of the British Military Mission; fifty men to destroy the Russian Mission; and fifty to wipe out the American Mission. Now men were spilling from gliders to augment the invasion, as paratroops advanced deeper into the town.

There was a blaze of riflefire, followed by a flurry of bursts from machine-pistols. Then from the hillside, where Tito's cave was known to be, came the racket of multiple firing: machine-guns, rifles, grenades.

The battle had been joined.

0702 hours

Marko Markovic was no coward, but he had never felt so scared in his life. It had not been idle bravado when, seeking to prove his hatred of Tito and the Partisans, he had demanded the privilege of leading a vengeance mission into Drvar – but, at no time had he imagined that his return to Drvar would be from the sky.

He had never before flown in an aeroplane, although he had always believed that he would enjoy the adventure of powered flight. Flying in a DFS 230 glider was something else again. Strapped into his seat in the windowless interior of the tiny machine, he felt a fine film of perspiration wet his brow long before the craft became airborne.

His apprehension grew as the bumping takeoff began and the glider whisked into silent flight. It did not diminish during the fifty-five minutes of aerial passage to Drvar. Nor was there any solace for him in the taut faces of his fellow passengers. Like him, perhaps, their thoughts were on the hazards of journey's end and the competence of the two pilots – sitting in tandem in the nose – to bring their machine safely to rest on a boulder-strewn mountainside.

Had he been able to see anything, his terror of glider flight might have been reduced; but only the pilots had the luxury of seeing the sweep of earth and heaven through which they passed. Marko's seat was in the tail, furthest from the door under the wing. It had been impressed on him that, as soon as they were on the ground, a speedy exit was essential. Glider troops were at their most vulnerable at the moment of touchdown. Survival depended on the alacrity with which weapons could be brought into use. The fact that he had no weapon no longer dismayed Marko. Feeling solid earth under his feet was his sole ambition.

As the minutes ticked towards seven o'clock, tension in the glider was high. 0700 was zero hour, and even the overbearing SS officer to whom Marko had been allotted as guide was betraying his nerviness. He kept glancing at his watch at five-second intervals. It was he who shouted in alarm as the glider suddenly bucked unexpectedly and then yawed. Fear ran like a current through the strapped-in passengers as the machine failed to recover to even flight. Now, it was diving almost vertically and the pilots were fighting to regain control.

The steepness of the descent was terrifying but, at last, the pilots seemed to triumph in the battle. The nose began to lift. Marko was letting out his breath in a long pent-up sigh of relief when the moment of impact came. For ten or fifteen seconds, Marko was aware of the glider sliding and slithering, then his world turned upside down and everything was spinning as the craft disintegrated around him and he was hurled into blackness.

Overhead, the Henschels and their tows maintained a steady course towards the open bowl of Drvar and the rocky valley beyond. Pilots who had watched the diving descent of a single glider fifteen kilometres short could only shake their heads grimly. They were too pre-occupied with the task of guiding their own craft to the target opening below them.

Unaware that his Abwehr recruit lay amid the scattered wreckage of a DFS 230, Wolf Bleyer was trying to ignore the churnings of his insides as his own craft parted company from its tow. He was reminding himself of the excellent reputation of German pilots for achieving spot landings. They were the world's best. Thousands of hours of training went into making them masters of their art. And it *was* an art: handling two tons of unpowered machine with such skill that they could bring it soaring from the heavens to land on a pinhead.

Unlike Marko, Bleyer had not been appalled by the flimsiness and slim shape of his form of transport. Rather, he had marvelled, on his first close-up view of the glider, at the sheer economy of its features: the narrow wing, with its span of 22 metres almost exactly double the tiny craft's nose-to-tail length. It was a thing of beauty.

It was also a thing of extreme fragility – as Bleyer discovered when it bumped to a halt on the rocky hillside edging Drvar. One wingtip touched a large boulder and the entire wing ripped off, taking with it part of the fuselage. Bleyer unstrapped himself and leapt out through the resultant hole.

Automatically, he threw himself flat. But it was not his glider that was the target of the intense firing that echoed across the valley. Most of the fire was from higher ground, towards Bastasi, and was directed murderously at the gliders carrying *Panther* Group: the company-strength strike force allotted the task of storming Tito's cave dwelling.

Bleyer did not know it then but the *Panther* gliders had navigated almost to the door of the cave, at the head of the rocky defile which was the only access. The defile itself was dotted with fortified gun positions and dug-outs, sited to ward off any landward approach and – thanks to Stefan's stand-to order at dawn – these positions had been manned and ready by the Escort Battalion for more than an hour. As a result, the gliders of *Panther* Group had come under withering crossfire as they landed, and the strike troops had debarked to a hail of death coming at them from all directions. Those who had managed to get out of the gliders and reach cover were pinned down within sight of the cave they had codenamed *Citadel*.

Bleyer's immediate concern, however, was his own objective: the radio and communications heart of the Partisan headquarters. And this was located in the town of Drvar. Within minutes of landing, he was jog-trotting behind the fifty SS troopers, who had been detailed to locate and storm the Partisan nerve centre. Bleyer was surprised at the empty streets. Only German uniforms were to be seen and, ahead, Rybka's paratroops moved to their objectives almost without opposition. Here and there lay the body of a paratroop – evidence that some resistance had been met and that the order not to stop for wounded had been obeyed.

No resistance was encountered by Bleyer's group until they were in sight of their objective. The lead section came under riflefire from a three-storey block, causing two casualties and helping to confirm that the building, its roof festooned with antennae, was the one they were looking for. As the leading SS troopers raked the windows of the building with automatic fire, the following sections were quickly deployed and continued to advance. A door was demolished by a grenade and a dozen attackers were inside in the twinkling of an eye. More followed.

The interior was a warren of passages and rooms, and the Partisans defended every inch of the labyrinth with the desperation of men and women who realised that escape was impossible. Room by room and floor by floor, they fought and died.

Nearby, access to the telephone exchange proved more difficult. It was quickly encompassed, but the heavy doors were barricaded and had to await the arrival of engineers with explosive charges to blast a way through. The attackers charged through the dense smoke and dust raised by the blasts, but it required twenty minutes of desperate hand-to-hand fighting to overcome the forty defenders, many of them women. None survived.

Bleyer, who had been no more than a spectator, lost no time in leading his team of Abwehr specialists through the smoke-filled premises, collecting such books and documents as could be found. These were collected in sacks, although a hasty perusal disappointed Bleyer. There seemed to be little of outstanding intelligence value in the haul.

The Group Commander ordered the captured buildings to be cleared, and engineers went in with charges to reduce the radio and telephone centres to rubble. One object had been achieved: Tito's link with the outside world and other Partisan groups throughout Jugoslavia had been severed.

The Group's next task was to reinforce the paratroopers attacking the British Military Mission, but that was aborted on a signal from Command HQ. Both the British and American missions had flown the coop, and only the attack on the Russian Mission had proved fruitful. Most of Drvar was now firmly in German hands.

Obersturmfuehrer Rybka had established his Command Post in a downed glider at the opposite end of town from Bleyer's *Draufgänger* Group. Fresh orders were not long in coming from the CP for this group, who were exhilarated by their success. Bleyer and his Abwehr personnel were to return immediately to the CP; the SS strike troops were to secure the roads, leading into Drvar, and establish strongpoints on the high ground at their end of the town.

Although it was not yet eight o'clock, the sun was already hot, promising scorching conditions for the rest of the day. Rybka, crouched in the shade of a glider wing, was running sweat as he relayed orders by field radio. In spite of the speed with which his paratroops had taken the town, he was far from happy. All his concern centred on *Panther* Group and the terse reports emanating from the *Citadel* attackers. One attempt to storm the cave entrance had ended disastrously. The charging glider troops had been systematically cut down by lethal crossfire, and the slope below the cave was littered with German dead. The remnants of *Panther* Group were hemmed into a small semicircle, with their backs to the River Unac, and desperately needing relief.

It was clear to Rybka that every man he could spare would now have to be concentrated on a drive to assist *Panther* Group and a renewed attack on the cave. Anger gripped him anew at the circumstances which had compelled him to leave two hundred of his meagre force in Banja Luka. Never had he needed them as he needed them now – but the second drop was still two hours away. Too long to wait. He would have to attack without them.

0805 hours

The recently established Partisan Liaison Headquarters in Bari, Italy, had been buzzing since the dawn signal from Drvar that Supreme Headquarters in Bosnia was under intensive aerial attack. A second signal, soon after seven a.m., had reported that enemy paratroops were landing on the town. A third had barely got beyond the call signs when Drvar suddenly went off the air.

Brad Mannion had been roused from his bed after the first signal, and he had been in the Operations Room ever since. The signal from Drvar had made it clear that the dawn raid was on a scale never seen before and that air support from Italy was urgently requested. It was anticipated that the RAF and USAAF might be reluctant to send such support – in view of blanks drawn in the past, following similar requests – but the sender indicated that the unprecedented severity of the attack suggested a major enemy offensive and no shortage of targets for any Allied fighters and bombers that could be spared.

Mannion had been a member of the liaison team since its inception, largely as a result of the contacts made on his first trip to Italy and because of his bilingual advantages. He had made three trips to and from Jugoslavia with OSS officers before being made second in command of the Bari HQ. He was, however, effectively the man in charge, because the commander – a trusted Communist who spoke no English – was a total stranger to that kind of responsibility and would have been lost without Mannion's guidance. His first reaction to the emergency, on that May morning, had been to summon Mannion and unload the burden of handling the situation on to his shoulders. It was hard work from the outset.

The Allies had reacted quickly and positively in the past to requests for air support where good intelligence allowed them to anticipate German aerial activity. They had become decidedly reluctant, however, to scramble fighters to combat raids already in progress. Too many responses had proved a waste of time and fuel. In consequence, Mannion's first attempts to summon help from the British and American air commands met with polite apologies. Fighter sweeps over Rome the previous day had resulted in the shooting down of eight Focke-Wulf One-Nineties, and resources were strained by plans for further sweeps that day.

Mannion did not give up trying. His opposite number at RAF, Foggia, had stalled for time when informed that paratroops and gliders were attacking Drvar. He promised to relay this information higher up, because such a development obviously made a difference. He would buzz Mannion back, one way or the other, as soon as he had spoken to Operational Control.

It was ten past eight when the RAF man came back on the line.

'We're in business,' he told Mannion. 'We can have a squadron in the air in an hour, without knocking too big a hole in today's ops programme. It's going to leave us pretty thin on the ground, but anything we can get in the air, we'll get in the air. That's a promise.'

Mannion thanked him and hung up. Staring at the huge wall map of Jugoslavia and the Adriatic, he felt strange pangs of guilt at the remote part he was now playing in the war. From the safety of Bari, his contribution was now indirect. Five times the Germans had launched major offensives in an effort to end Jugoslav resistance, and five times he had been in the thick of it. Now, it looked as if offensive number six was under way and he was stuck, helpless, hundreds of miles from the action: a go-between who could only wait and wonder what the hell was going on over there. It didn't seem right somehow.

He resolved there and then to get out of his present job, by hook or by crook. Since Lela's death, the only satisfaction he had gained from life had been with a gun in his hand. And the sooner he was back in the business of killing, the happier he would be. His personal score was a long way from being settled yet.

0830 hours

Marko became aware of the sun burning his face. He had no idea where he was or what had happened to him. He could feel no pain – and he tried to move, to escape that burning glare in his eyes. Excruciating pain shot up from his legs. He howled out in agony. He let his head loll back, almost fainting. He could not feel his legs as such – only as a sea of pain. The pain did not go away.

Minutes - it could have been hours – passed before he tried to move again. This time, he managed to turn on to a shoulder and avert his face from the sun's torture. It was a moment or two before he could see from his blinking eyes. But what he saw made no immediate sense to his shocked brain. Pieces of glider were scattered wherever he looked. So, too, were the men who had been inside: sprawled grotesquely here and there along the arid, rock-strewn desert of hillside. The rag-doll corpses were awful to see – but there was life there, too. Marko could hear two, perhaps three, who lived. Something or some things living were making those pitiful sounds: whimpering cries and wailing drawn-out screams.

Marko made no further attempts to move his legs. It seemed he only had to think about it for the shooting pains to intensify. Flies came to add to his torture. They droned about his nose and eyes and mouth, and he had not the strength to brush them away. The dryness of his throat and mouth was yet another dimension of the general torment. His thirst was unendurable.

He lay, partly on his side, between waking and fainting, oblivious to the passage of time, powerless to arrest his suffering. He was lying thus, when the sharp report of a rifle close at hand startled him from his enveloping misery. He stared with shock at the figure of a man standing only five metres distant. The man raised the rifle in his hand from the head of the rag-doll corpse into which he had fired from point-blank range. Marko then became aware of a second man, near to the first. The men conversed.

'Put that howling bastard out of his misery,' one said, in Serbo-Croat.

522

'There's no hurry,' said the other. 'He'll be a long time dead.' But he vanished from Marko's line of vision and, moments later, a second shot rang out. Marko heard footsteps and suddenly found himself propelled flat on to his back by a rifle barrel thrust against his shoulder. One of the men stood above him.

'This one's alive,' he said. The face came lower to stare into Marko's. 'By God, I know this whore's son.'

Marko felt his helmet jerked from his head. The voice came again, shrill with excitement.

'Look, Sloban, you know him! This is the lazy sod they sent us in Jajce, when we were laying those tank traps, remember? The royal officer, whose backside you threatened to kick when he moaned at you about the loads you were making him carry.'

The second man came and looked.

'By God, you're right! It's the same cocky devil. But what's he. . .?' He stared round-eyed at Marko. 'The bastard must have been a spy!'

'Shoot him, Sloban,' the other encouraged.

The Partisan called Sloban poked his rifle in to Marko's face in teasing fashion, prodding the tip of the barrel between his open lips. Marko closed his eyes, beyond caring. He waited for the explosion that would end his misery. It did not come.

'Maybe we should keep him alive,' the man called Sloban said.

'They would have sent medics up here, not us, if that's what they wanted,' his companion said. 'Shoot him and get it over with.'

Still Sloban hesitated.

'The ordinary soldiers they shoot straight off. Not spies. Spies they question first. Then they shoot them.'

'Shoot him. He's half-dead anyway. What use is he?'

'I don't know – but I think we should take him back.'

'How? He's not going to be able to walk. Look at that leg. The bone's sticking through his trousers.'

'We'll drag him,' Sloban said. 'Come on, damn you. You take an arm. I'll take the other,' Grumbling, Sloban's companion did as he was told.

Marko almost passed out as his wrists were seized. He screamed as the two Partisans began to drag him, his legs banging on the hard ground. He had never felt such pain. The men ignored his screams, which did not last too long. They had gone less than thirty paces when Marko passed out.

0927 hours

The Kyle and Cameron Highlanders had been on the march for a little over an hour. They constituted less than a platoon of the company of cadets and instructors who had assembled at Sipoljani and had been marched off towards the sound of battle. The Officer School Commander, a grizzly-haired veteran of the Spanish Civil War, marched at their head. Like Jamie, he had pointed out to Cameron that his participation was not obligatory, but Cameron had not been deterred. 'I'm going with my laddies,' he had insisted resolutely.

The Commander's eyes had popped at the sight of Cameron's armaments. In addition to his service revolver, he had a Turkish sword slung on his back. Cameron had purchased it in a curio shop in Jajce and referred to it as his claymore.

'Shouldn't that thing be hanging on a wall in some museum?' the Commander had inquired, with a trace of sarcasm.

'I'll have you know it's the finest steel,' Cameron had replied in an aggrieved voice. 'And I havena brought it along to sharpen my pencils.' When Jamie had translated, the Commander raised his eyebrows expressively and said no more. It was plain that he thought Cameron, who had served in Africa, had spent too long in the sun.

The morning sun was as fierce as the desert sun that

had scorched down on Cameron, as the cadet force marched towards Bastasi. For a time, they followed the Unac. Then they routed their approach to arrive from the southwest on the high ground flanking the valley that climbed from Drvar to Bastasi. Their arrival was timely.

Obersturmfuehrer Rybka had regrouped his force and was slowly but surely working his way up the valley to Tito's cave HQ. The SS paratroopers were advancing in the face of sustained machine-gun and mortarfire from the prepared positions of the Partisan Escort Battalion. Although outgunned, the Germans were making headway, one small group providing covering fire for another small group and then reversing roles so that they leapfrogged from one cluster of rocks to the next. They were sustaining casualties but they were advancing relentlessly. In particular, they were achieving most success with a flanking drive over high ground that threatened to get round the side of the Partisan defences.

It was this manoeuvre that the arriving cadet force met almost head-on. Instinct, more than certainty of what was happening beyond the valley ridge, prompted the Officer School Commander to deploy his hundred rifles to the best advantage. He quickly designated Jamie to lead his 'highlanders' at the double, along behind the high ridge in the direction of Drvar – to form the right flank. His own group followed to form the centre, leaving the third group on the left. Then he signalled a cautious advance over the lip of the valley.

The first German knowledge of their presence came with a sustained volley of firing from above and behind their flanking force. Looking up from the rocks behind which they crouched, they found themselves exposed and their existence threatened from a new and un-expected quarter. Their reaction was swift and desperate. In some cases, the distance between the surprised paratroops and the encroaching cadets was only a few metres – and it was not the paratroop instinct to turn and run. To run was to surrender what little chance they had, so they faced the threat head-on, overcoming the disadvantage of ground inferiority by the ferocity with which they rushed the intervening slope.

Lesser troops than the disciplined officer trainees might have buckled before the sheer audacity of the German response, but only here and there along their narrow line was it breached. The gaps occurred where bursting grenades took out or stunned cadets on the ridge and allowed rushing paratroops to spill over on to the valley top, where fierce hand-to-hand fighting ensued. Jamie, Luger in hand, found himself attacked from behind by a maniacal trooper who had dropped his machine-pistol and was swinging at him with a trenching spade. His reflexive shot stopped the man in his tracks. Similar close-quarter tussles were taking place wherever the cadet line had been penetrated, but were as short-lived as they were brutal. Only a handful of Germans survived the desperate rush to break through on to the ridge, and those who did were so heavily outnumbered that they had no chance to consolidate their gain. They were shot and clubbed down, although not without heavy cost to the youthful Partisan company.

Jamie found Cameron cradling a seventeen-year-old who was vomiting blood from his mouth and nostrils. The boy died as he arrived. Cameron lowered him gently on to the ground and turned away before Jamie could speak. He went briskly off along the line, roaring angry encouragement to the sweat-soaked cadets.

'Watch your front, laddies! Don't waste your bullets! Select your target, take aim and fire.' It is doubtful if his words were understood, but the strutting presence of the rumbustious figure seemed to have a tonic effect on the young warriors, who grinned their approval and wormed forward to resume the battle from better firing positions.

Now the only Germans immediately in front of the ridge were dead or dying. Below, the advance up the valley towards the cave had faltered. The hillside was strewn with German dead, and mortar bombs continued to rain down from the Escort Battalion positions. So deadly had been the combination of mortarfire and the flanking attack from the cadets that the most forward German troops were in acute danger of being cut off from the largely intact rear units. It was a danger that must have been all too apparent to the German commander. A red flare went soaring out across the valley: a recall signal.

The forward paratroops, showing the same discipline and courage as in advance, began the equally difficult exercise of retreat, moving and firing, moving and firing, despite no let-up in the raking machine-gun and rifle fire from the Partisan lines; jockeying their way back down the valley, across ground which they had won at great cost.

The cadet line Commander, aware of a fresh Partisan battalion climbing the hill at his rear to join the battle and seeing the paratroops falling back towards Drvar, signalled his own company over the ridge into the valley in pursuit. Jamie and his thirty rifles were nearest to the withdrawing enemy and they flooded down the hillside in a rush. Cameron, revolver in one hand and waving his Turkish sword aloft in the other, led the frenzied charge. He was the first to fall as the German rear guard halted their now speedy flight and turned in orderly fashion to take up defensive positions across the valley. The victory-scenting Partisans ran into a wall of fire. The charge faltered but resumed when the enemy was seen to be falling back again. The German rearguard gave two hundred metres before repeating their defensive posture and stopping the Partisans with controlled bursts of automatic fire that scythed great gaps in their ranks.

Jamie, screaming at his section to abandon the

527

senseless rush and take cover, was overtaken by the Training School Commander, who seemed drunk with euphoria. 'See how well they died!' he exulted. 'I am proud of them! We turned the battle and won it!'

'It's not won yet,' Jamie said curtly. 'With your permission, I'll give the order to fall back and re-assemble. We can take the wounded as we go.'

'Fall back?'

'Let them take over,' Jamie said, nodding in the direction of the newly arrived Partisans who had streamed over the hill behind the cadets and were cautiously advancing through the halted cadet line. The newcomers were prudently making use of the gorse and boulders to screen their progress from the Germans, who were no longer firing and seemed intent on retiring to the valley's lower end, on the edge of Drvar.

'It's a pity to lose our initiative,' the veteran soldier said.

'We've lost half our training school,' Jamie ground out. 'We should save the other half for this afternoon.' There was no concealing the implied criticism in the remark. Nor in the follow-up Jamie added: 'This isn't the Russian Front.'

It was an intended jibe at the Training School Commander. As a military theoretician, he was always lauding the Russian formula for successful aggressive warfare: wave after wave of frontal infantry assault, ad infinitum, until the enemy just folded under sheer weight of numbers. It was not a method that commended itself to Jamie – nor to many infantrymen. The Commander regarded Jamie uncertainly.

'Our warrior babes have earned a rest,' he said. 'Give the order to fall back.' He was not sure how to take this half-Serb, half-Scots Partisan. He could be a sarcastic devil at the best of times, and the Commander never knew whether to put up with it or jump on him. He tended to be deferential to Jamie – and had been ever since he heard that Tito had visited him personally in hospital, when he was wounded. Why? What was so special about this half-foreigner? He had a pal on the Central Committee, too. Maybe it meant nothing, but the Training School Commander believed in keeping his nose clean as far as the Party was concerned. And if that meant staying sweet with one of his best weaponry instructors, it was a small price to pay.

Climbing back up the valley, Jamie came upon four cadets clustered round the body of Cameron. He was still alive, but only just. He managed the semblance of a smile for Jamie.

'They're . . . brave . . . laddies,' he croaked. 'Bonnie fechters. . . . Look after them . . . Jamie.' A spasm gripped him and his jaw sagged. He jerked out the words: 'Och Jamie, I think I'm going. . . .' And he died.

1035 hours

Petar Richtman watched through his binoculars as riflemen of the Reconnaissance Battalion fanned out on the hillside below him. They were now about a thousand metres from the crossroads occupied by the Partisans, and advancing confidently. The crossroads itself was shrouded in smoke, and fresh plumes erupted as the German howitzers continued to saturate the area with bursting shells. One attempt to dislodge the Partisans, by driving at them along the road with light armour, had already failed, and a trail of wrecked vehicles testified to the accuracy and efficiency of the Partisan gunners, who were extremely well dug in around the junction approaches. It was because of this failure that a company of riflemen, with a mortar platoon, had been sent out on the flank to make a downhill assault on the Partisan positions.

The delay was infuriating. The *Rösselsprung* timetable required that the column – with its SS tank reinforcement – reach Drvar not later than four o'clock in the afternoon. And already two precious hours had been lost. At the present rate of progress, they would be lucky to reach Drvar the following day – perhaps too late to relieve the paratroops isolated in the town.

Petar waited until he saw the mortar platoon deploy and bring their weapons into action before he left the hilltop. It was time to get back to the *Schwimmwagen* and be ready to move out. He should have been miles ahead of the column, instead of stuck at its top. On this east slope of the hill, German vehicles were nose to tail on the road as far as Petar could see – stretching out of sight beyond a point where the road looped round the brow of stark barren hilside.

He was almost at the road when he heard the roar of low-flying aircraft. They were overhead in an instant, seeming to materialise from nowhere: sleek hurtling shadows with blazing cannons. Petar got a glimpse of pale blue underwings and slim fuselage with RAF roundels. The fighters, three in all, made two runs each in swift succession, before soaring away westwards. They made one lucky hit: an ammunition truck that exploded spectacularly and sent a pillar of smoke three hundred metres high. The explosion wrecked the two trucks on either side of the ammo wagon, but the damage and loss of life were small in relation to the massive blast.

Five other vehicles were set on fire and had to be pushed off the road, while medics tended a score of seriously wounded men. Ambulances, at the rear of the column, had to be detached to take the injured back to Jajce. They were given an armed escort – because it was that kind of war. The Red Cross emblem offered scant protection from attack.

The delay, caused by the stubborn defence of the crossroads and compounded by the strafing, frustrated no one more than Petar. The need for speed of movement had been the most consistently laboured topic in every

530

tactical planning discussion, and he was acutely conscious of the minutes slipping irretrievably away. In Russia, more than once, he had experienced being cut off and isolated ahead of a relieving force. He knew what it was like to be hemmed in, short of food, short of water, short of medical supplies, and counting a shrinking quantity of ammunition.

It was just before eleven when a green flare, fluttering skywards, signalled that the crossroads ahead was now in German hands. The *Schwimmwagen* led out towards the junction and was soon negotiating round the wrecked armoured gun cars destroyed by the Partisans. Nearing the crossroads, two riflemen came loping towards it, waving it to stop. Ordering the driver to halt, Petar leapt out and bustled towards the two soldiers. The men were breathless.

'It's impassable up there, sir,' one of them blurted out. 'Mines all over the place. It's a deathtrap. If you've got a field phone, maybe you could call up some engineers. It would be suicide trying to get through before it's cleared.'

Petar fumed. This was all they needed! They'd be lucky to reach Drvar inside a week!

1112 hours

Jamie made a tour of the new cadet positions. The Officer School company had lost nineteen dead and seventeen wounded, which was bad enough but not nearly as bad as Jamie had feared after the charge down the hill. A semblance of cohesion had been imposed on the Partisan forces defending Tito's cave HQ thanks to the initiative of the Escort Battalion Commander in employing teams of runners, who had covered miles of countryside during the morning and provided him with a steadily sharpening picture of the general situation.

There was no doubt that Drvar was the centre of a

German attempt at large-scale encirclement and, although the Germans had advanced quickly in places, they were far from getting things their own way. They were putting a lot of pressure on Petrovac and the airfield, and making some progress in the wooded hills to the north, but they were being held in the west and southwest and being slowed down in the east. The critical situation was here in Bastasi, where time had to be bought for the extrication of Tito, the Supreme Staff and the three Allied HQ missions. And the likelihood of them going anywhere was remote while the SS paratroops blocked their only exit.

The Escort Battalion Commander knew that the paratroops would not sit around on the edge of Drvar, waiting for something to happen. They would attack again towards the cave HQ. So he saw, as his first priority, the deployment of such forces as he had, in defence of the Supreme Commander's cave. He set about this task as soon as the German attack in mid-morning had failed. It would be time to think about offensive action when the next German attack had been blunted. By then, he hoped, reinforcements would have arrived from the First Partisan Brigade in the hills round Resanovci. The indications were that they would be able to spare five hundred men from their own front.

The officer cadets were assigned to defensive positions on the slope down which they had made their brave but expensive charge. With an enthusiasm at which Jamie could only marvel, they hacked hide-holes out of the dust-dry earth, cut gorse-bush screens, pushed and carried rocks; constructing minor fortifications in preparation for the attack they knew was coming. They raised a cheer when a flight of RAF Spitfires winged low overhead, but this glimpse of aerial support was brief. The hunter fighters streaked off to the north, towards Petrovac, in search of prey.

Obersturmfuehrer Rybka, who had gathered the bulk

of his strike battalion in a shaded gully protected by a huge tusky monolith of rock, also saw the Spitfires, and their appearance worried him. The second wave of paratroops was now overdue. The lumbering transports would be easy game for the marauding fighters, and Rybka hoped that the brief passage of the Spitfires did not mean that the Junkers 52s from Banja Luka had already been intercepted. A more hopeful interpretation of it was that the coast radar had tracked the Spitfires' inward flight from the sea and had warned Banja Luka to hold the transports on the ground.

Rybka tried to dismiss the gloomier prospect by moving among his men with smiling encouragement. It required summoning optimism which he did not altogether feel. Ammunition was low and he exhorted his men to use their bullets sparingly and well when it was time to move out. He had words of cheer for the wounded, too – those, that is, who had not been carried down to the field hospital that had been established in a large villa on the outskirts of Drvar. They would not be abandoned, Rybka promised them. He forebore to add the reservation: if any of us get out of this.

The sudden drone of approaching aircraft engines sent Rybka racing back to the high end of the gully. His heart lifted as the sky immediately overhead was blotted out by the thirty-metre span of thundering shadow that was a Junkers 52. The roar of its three radial engines throbbed in his ears as it cascaded dark falling shapes, from which, suddenly, trailed the billowing flowers of parachutes.

The second wave had arrived.

Rybka's joy was short-lived. To his horror, he realised that his reinforcements were dropping in no-man's-land: a hilly stretch of the lower valley exposed to the Partisan guns. The enemy lost no time in sweeping this open hillside with a torrent of machine-gun fire. Then, from higher in the valley, Partisan mortars began to rain shrapnel and blast bombs across the landing area, inflicting fearful casualties. The carnage highlighted the appalling cost in human life that had to be paid when the paratrooper is robbed of his chief weapon: surprise.

Rybka's second-wave troops were dying as they hit the ground and before they could reach their canisters and get their weapons. But for every man who died, two survived the withering fire and, arming themselves and welding themselves into cohesive defensive groups, fought back. Although several of these groups found themselves pinned down and temporarily rendered immobile, most managed to withdraw with commendable coolness and discipline and reach the security of Rybka's line.

There, respite was brief. Time only for a quick cigarette; a quick exchange of greetings, perhaps, with a comrade among the first arrivals; and then they were re-forming sections, making a final ammunition check and getting ready to move out. The sun was at its zenith and Knight's Move had still to accomplish its purpose: the capture of the enemy king still lurking in his cave.

Rybka moved among his men with last-minute instructions and firing them with purpose.

'You, soldier, would you recognise the bandit Tito?'

'Yes, sir. I was given his photo.' They had all been given a photograph of Tito.

'How does he dress?'

'Plain uniform, sir. No rank badges or insignia.'

'Good. There'll be an Iron Cross for the man who gets him. And a case of cognac from me.'

'The cognac will do, sir. Never mind about the Iron Cross.'

Gusts of laughter.

There is no laughter when they begin to move out. Rybka, the handsome young Commander, despatches sections out to right and left to fight their way up the flanks and win the high ground. The main body will advance up the valley, employing the same fire and movement tactics of earlier in the day. Rybka has no intention of sitting in the rear and waiting for results. He will lead from the front.

High on a hill looking down towards Drvar, an observer in a Partisan OP is watching the German positions through binoculars. He sees movement. His heliograph winks to another position. Orders are shouted down to other positions. The Partisans wait.

'Be ready fo fire,' Jamie shouts to his cadets. 'They're coming!'

Moments later, the battle begins again. Relentlessly, the Germans advance, firing and moving, firing and moving. On they come through the rain of bursting mortar bombs and drifting smoke.

As the smoke clears from one bomb blast, two paras are seen to be dragging a comrade towards cover at great risk to themselves. It is unusual, because they have been ignoring their wounded and leaving them where they fall.

On the floor of the valley, Obersturmfuehrer Rybka, only semi-conscious, is trying to protest as a paratrooper stuffs a field dressing into a gaping wound in the commanding officer's chest. 'Leave me,' he orders his benefactor. 'Leave me. The attack must continue.'

The paratrooper has done as much as he can. He props Rybka against a rock and leaves him there. The soldier's section is fifty metres ahead, having reached the cover of a bank overhung with gorse. The paratrooper judges the moment and, leaving his own cover, sprints to join his comrades. When the section makes its next dash forward, he is with them.

The attack has not faltered.

1220 hours

The atmosphere in Tito's spartan cave headquarters

535

was electric. Stefan was to remember it for the rest of his life. He could cheerfully have strangled Zdenka. The Supreme Commander's personal secretary was, as usual, on – if not over – the verge of hysteria. The situation was quite bad enough without her running round like a demented hen, screaming: 'They'll kill us! They'll kill us all! We're all going to die!'

Tito seemed able to ignore her ranting tongue as if he were deaf to it. He also seemed to be unaware of how much she was getting on the nerves of the other Central Committee members present; they would all gladly have wrung her neck. It was a continuing puzzle to Stefan how a man of Tito's sensitivities could remain blind to Zdenka's capacity for unpleasantness and the animosities she stirred up. Even more puzzling now, however, was his behaviour in this, the gravest crisis of his entire leadership. Since early morning – when German gunners had got close enough to the cave mouth to spatter it with bullets from their MG42 – Tito had retired into a state of frozen immobility, as if all nerve and courage had deserted him.

One by one, members of his Supreme Staff had tried to draw him from the paralysis of mind that gripped him. Rankovic – who had once endured Gestapo torture and knew what fate they might all expect if taken alive – urged Tito to leave the cave at once. But Tito shook his head. He would not leave. Kardelj, the Moscow-trained Slovenian, had no more success than Rankovic with a reasoned and calmer approach.

'I am not putting a foot out there,' Tito told him, stubbornly refusing to budge.

Streten Zujovic, the fiery Serb who had been a teenage soldier in the 1914 war, did not mince words with his leader.

'You must show yourself to your soldiers,' he raged. 'You can't skulk in here while they are dying out there.'

This brought immediate reproach from others in the

entourage, but Zujovic was unrepentant. With a shrug of his shoulders, he left the task of persuasion to others. He walked towards the door.

'It sounds worse than ever out there. I'm going out,' he said. He caught Stefan's eye, in passing. 'Anyone else?'

'I'll come,' Stefan said.

Outside, the noise of battle was intense. Bullets were ricocheting from rocks above their head and the lower valley was hung with smoke, drifting, hanging, as if the ground had been bedded with red-hot ash. Tito's jeep was parked nearby and Stefan and his companion crouched behind it to peer across its bonnet as, five hundred metres away, half a dozen SS paratroopers burst from behind a bank of scrub and immediately disappeared behind fountaining clouds of smoke and earth as a shower of mortar shells dropped like a blanket in front of them.

Zujovic was still burning from his failure to goad Tito into action.

'The man is a craven coward,' he roared, beating a fist on the jeep. The words were not spoken at Stefan. The older man was just letting off steam, venting his anger and disgust. He noticed the way Stefan was looking at him. 'I'm sorry,' he growled. 'I'm no good at hiding my feelings. I have to say what I think. It took me all my time to stop myself shaking him out of that chair.'

Stefan crouched down beside him, ignoring the battle. 'I don't think it's cowardice,' he said.

'Then what the hell is it?' Zujovic demanded.

'He's frightened – but not for himself. I know what's going through his head.'

'Nothing, I would say,' Zujovic bellowed. 'His mind's a blank. He's terrified!'

'But not for himself,' Stefan persisted. 'It's the way he thinks now. He sees it as his destiny to save Jugoslavia . . . to save it from the Germans and to save it for

537

Communism. He thinks that if he dies now, everything will be lost. . . .'

'None of us are indispensable,' Zujovic snapped.

'He is, don't you see? He's utterly convinced of it.' Stefan was shouting, to make himself heard above the din. 'He's risked too much and for too long for it to end here. That's what's stupefying him . . . that's what he can't bear.'

Later, Stefan was to remember his defence of Tito, while the battle of Bastasi hung in the balance, and wonder if he had manufactured excuses for a man he had come to consider great. Was it an exaggerated sense of fairness that made him want to make allowances for the man who saw himself as his country's salvation? It would nag at him that the truth lay somewhere in a grey area between Zujovic's opinion and his own; and that the key, perhaps, lay in Tito's vanity. As he was emerging as a national leader who could walk and talk on equal terms with the Stalins and the Churchills of the world, so had the sense of his own importance grown and so, too, had his conviction that he alone could wear the mantle of national saviour. And the more he became aware of the status that was his and could still be his, the greater and more acute became his concern for his personal safety. This concern was to become even more acute as the war continued. He had started out with burning ambitions and modest dreams but, gradually, with fateful steps along the road, the dreams had burgeoned beyond all imaginings and, more, had suddenly become attainable realities. He did not want to let them go. He wanted to seize them when they were so close to his grasp; to finish the work he had begun.

During one dreadful day, it seemed that he was to be denied the final glory. It was almost more than he could take. Thursday, 25 May 1944, was the day Josip Broz Tito came face to face with his own mortality.

The battle outside the cave where he vacillated raged

on through the afternoon. Relentlessly, the SS paratroops pushed to within sight of their goal: the cave at the head of the defile in the high part of the valley. To their rear, their comrades guarding the approaches to Drvar looked in vain for the battle group from the east that should have arrived at 1600 hours. But it was from the southwest not the east that fresh troops arrived, and it was not to the relief of the battling paratroops that they came. They came flooding over the southwest rim of the valley, five hundred in number and eager to get to grips with the enemy. The First Partisan Brigade had kept its promise of aid to the beleaguered Supreme Staff. The fresh battalion streamed through the positions occupied by Jamie and his cadets, carrying the fight to the Germans below.

As in the morning, the sudden counterattack from the flank stopped the German advance in its tracks. Shrill whistle blasts recalled the weary paratroops as they tried to regroup and face this new threat. But there was no containing the newcomers, who spilled down the hillside like a tide and were soon grappling with their enemy in a confusion of man-to-man combat. The battle reached a peak of ferocity as dividing lines between the opposing forces became hopelessly obfuscated, and the Germans tried to fight their way out of pockets left by the sudden surge of screaming Partisans which had all but engulfed them.

With rifle, bayonet and Sten gun, the Partisans stormed over the MG42 positions which the paratroops had fought so hard to win in order to cover their leapfrogging rushes. Still the Germans did not lose their discipline. As Very lights arced skywards to signal general withdrawal, they contrived to fall back in tight little sections, one covering for the other in a manner that sought to plug the huge gaps in their line and restore its cohesion.

As they withdrew, the Partisans who had held them at

bay now took the initiative. Emerging from their defensive positions, they swarmed after the retreating paratroops, mopping up groups who had been cut off from the main body and had no way back.

High on the north-facing hillside, Jamie and his cadets were on the move, keeping to the high ground. They immediately encountered one of the three-section probes that Rybka had despatched deep beyond the Partisan flank. A running fight developed as the cadets sought to block the paratroops' escape route to Drvar. This they finally succeeded in doing by harrying the Germans into occupying a cluster of farm buildings about a kilometre from the town. The cadets quickly surrounded the German refuge.

When darkness fell, the besieged paratroops were still holding out and giving every indication that they intended to fight to the last man. Not far away, the battle had reached the streets of Drvar. Flashes lit up the night and crimson tracers streaked out in burning rods from German machine-guns as the paratroops' Acting Commander sought to bring the remnants of his force within a single perimeter.

2200 hours

If Tito's nerve had failed him earlier in the day, there was no sign of it as he took a last look round the cave that had been his home for several months.

'It has been a long day,' he said to Stefan. He was the essence of calmness. Not that he had exhibited anything other than calm throughout the day. But his calm was different now from the paralysed inertia that had seemed to affect him. 'Did you pass on my orders?' he asked Stefan.

'Yes. Drvar will be abandoned . . . although the Field Commander says it may take some time.'

'I said immediately.' There was an edge to Tito's voice.

'I think he's anxious that you get well clear before he disengages,' Stefan said. 'It's not just him. The men feel the same way. All I heard on the way up here, was: "Has the Old Man got away?" That's all they're concerned about – your safety.'

'And you, Stefan? Is that what you feel? That my life is so important?'

'Yes, I do,' Stefan said, meeting Tito's troubled stare. 'Those Germans attacking the cave today had copies of your photograph. You were the big prize. You were why they were ready to sacrifice a thousand men. They know your worth. They know that without the magic of your name our armies would melt away. Oh, Kardelj or Rankovic or somebody else would try to rally them . . . but it wouldn't be the same. The legend would be no more. The myth would be finished – exposed as a myth. They want to shout from the rooftops that Tito, the indestructible, has been destroyed.'

'But Tito lives,' Tito said softly.

'And Tito must go on living,' Stefan said, choosing his words carefully. 'Even if it's in some other hole in the ground and you only poke your head out every second month. Because as long as you are alive, the legend lives. And the legend grows. It's not Tito the man that the Germans want to destroy but the *idea* you have come to represent. The longer that Tito the man lives, the stronger Tito the *idea* grows – and the more indestructible it becomes.'

Tito took a deep intake of breath, as if gathering himself.

'I know this, Stefan,' he murmured, his voice almost inaudible. 'It's a daunting thing to accept. But I think I have known it for some time.'

He became businesslike.

'Are you coming with us?'

'No, I'll follow with the battalion they sent up from First Brigade. The news from their sector has all been

541

good. They're holding the Germans without too much difficulty and have stopped any hope they had of a link-up with the north. Our salient is sixty kilometres wide and in no danger for the time being. Have our friends from the Allied missions already gone?'

'Minutes before you arrived,' Tito said. 'It's time I joined them.'

He led the way out, through a door that led on to a timber walkway that skirted that side of the cave complex. Half a dozen Partisan guards, armed with Schmeissers, were stationed along its length. One stood over a metre-wide gap in the walkway, where boards had been prised up to create the opening. A rope dangled into the darkness below.

Stefan peered into the hole.

'Are you going to climb down there?' he asked Tito, incredulously.

'It's too far to jump,' Tito answered, his teeth showing white in a grin. He added, with devilment, 'Zdenka will catch me if I fall.'

'Please take great care, Comrade General,' the Partisan guard cautioned him. 'We cannot afford to lose *you*.'

'Am I so precious?' Tito asked, with a laugh, taking hold of the rope.

'We can lose a brigade and another will rise in its place,' the man said, with an anxiety that was palpable. 'We could never find another General Tito. There will never be another like you.'

Tito's silence, and his delay in putting his weight on the rope, told Stefan that the simple soldier's words had pierced clean through the Supreme Commander's emotional armour. It was no wonder that he believed he was some kind of divine instrument when ordinary soldiers like this man on the walkway were so ready to proclaim his uniqueness. Tito found his voice at last.

'It's good fellows like you who are our country's

strength,' he said. 'And mine.' With that, he swung on to the rope and climbed down with an agility that would not have shamed a man twenty years his junior.

Shadowy shapes, waiting below, reached out arms to ensure the safe completion of his descent. From the darkness came a shout to pull up the rope.

'What's down there?' Stefan asked the guard.

'A streambed. It leads off the mountain.'

'I don't hear any water running. Has it dried up?'

The man laughed. 'It floods only when there are big rains. In this weather it makes a handy back door, eh? Not a bad thing to have when unwelcome visitors come beating at the front door.'

'So, the Comrade Commander could have left by this way at any time after the Germans attacked this morning?'

'Of course! If he had wanted to.'

'I wonder why he didn't?' Stefan said.

'Because he didn't want to leave us to die,' the man said, as if Stefan was a simpleton. 'It's obvious. He thought we were all for it – every last man of us. I thought so myself. He stayed to die with us – and that took a kind of courage I don't have. He waited to see how the battle would go before worrying about his own neck. I salute him for it.'

Stefan returned through the cave to the front opening. Here, the door had been shot from its hinges. And over there, Tito's abandoned jeep stood where it had in the morning, shot full of holes and likely to be of little use to the Germans, except as a trophy. The noise of continuing battle echoed up the valley from Drvar. Stefan suddenly felt exhausted but he resisted the temptation to bed down somewhere and have forty winks. Sleep could wait. He started walking towards the town.

2350 hours

Wolf Bleyer was thinking it was a hell of a place to die. A

Bosnian cemetery! The mausoleum in which he had taken refuge was in a poor state of repair. Bleyer had almost broken his neck on the loose and broken steps leading down into its interior. Putting his weight on a cracked slab which had wobbled dangerously, he had quickly transferred his footing to the next – also loose – and pitched headlong into the decrepit vault. He wondered if the bloody nose that resulted counted as a battle wound. He thought it ironic that, having spent most of the afternoon under fire, he should sustain his only injury falling headfirst into a grave.

He had taken no part in the assault on the cave, but he had made himself more than useful to the SS paratroops by helping to retrieve the wounded and carrying them back to the field hospital. That chore now seemed to have been a waste of time. When the fighting reached the streets of Drvar, the hospital had had to be abandoned before all the casualties were evacuated. Bleyer had been just another infantryman ever since. Armed with a dead paratrooper's machine-pistol, he had been coopted – for his own safety – to a young SS officer's section, and the group had staged a fighting retreat through the town.

Runners from Battalion Command had directed them to Drvar Cemetery, as an attempt was made to rally the scattered German force – or what was left of it. The cemetery was an ideal location; the rectangle of hillside was contained by a stout stone wall and it was not too big to stretch the defensive capabilities of two hundred well-trained men.

By the time Bleyer's group had reached the cemetery, organisation for its defence was well under way, with officers directing the siting of machine-gun posts to cover approach to the wall, and secondary lines being established to deal with any breach of the perimeter. One officer was overseeing the distribution of ammunition to groups freshly arrived within the wall.

Bleyer collected his ration and made a casual inquiry about the likely duration of stocks.

'It depends on how many times the bandits hit us before morning,' the officer told him. 'With any luck we'll still have something left at daylight. Three-seven-three Division shouldn't be far away.'

'They should have been here eight hours ago,' Bleyer commented. 'They must have run into trouble.'

'They weren't the only ones,' the officer said with feeling.

Bleyer ate the last of his ration pack in the mausoleum and smoked a cigarette. He was stubbing it out with his heel when all hell broke loose. Grabbing his Schmeisser, he crawled up the steps of his foetid-smelling bunker to peer outside. He kept his head well down. Mortar shells were exploding all over the cemetery. Offering up a silent prayer, Bleyer scurried to the wall and joined some paratroopers crouching behind it.

'Look to your front!' an officer bellowed from twenty metres away. 'Here they come!' With a shrug of resignation, Bleyer clambered up the wall, wedging his Schmeisser on the stone top. He could see nothing but streams of tracer zipping out from the wall. Then there was a puff overhead as a flare burst and the hillside was bathed in bright pink light. Charging through this unnatural incandescence came a screaming horde. Bleyer pointed his weapon and fired. The horde came on.

0100 hours, Friday 26 May

The handsome moustachioed Commander of the 1st Battalion, First Partisan Brigade, had established his Command Post in the offices of a cellulose factory. He was flattered that a member of the Central Committee had elected to stay behind in Drvar and attach himself temporarily to Battalion Headquarters. Stefan had endeared himself to the veteran officer – a Serb from Kraljevo – by saying, 'Don't let me get in the way. Throw me out on my ear if things get hectic.'

The Battalion Commander had laughed off any such likelihood. He had invited Stefan to share a snatched supper with him and sit in on the forming of a fresh plan to attack the cemetery, where the remnants of the German paratroop force were surrounded. The first assault, at midnight, had been driven back.

'We've got to knock a hole in that wall and get our men inside,' he confided to Stefan.

They were listening to a young officer expound on the possibility of loading one of the factory hand-trolleys with explosive and running it downhill at the cemetery wall, when there was a commotion outside the office. They all went out to investigate the disturbance. An officer was shouting at a rather elderly Partisan soldier.

'What's the meaning of this racket?' the Battalion Commander demanded.

'It's this man, Comrade Commander,' the officer complained. 'I gave him an order and he's refusing to carry it out.'

The soldier immediately began to protest, but the Battalion Commander silenced him.

'Don't you know the punishment for disobedience?' he asked the man angrily. 'Do as you are told at once, or I'll have you put against a wall.'

'But, Comrade Excellency . . . you do not realise. We were ordered to bring this man to Headquarters in Drvar.'

'What man?' thundered the Battalion Commander.

'The prisoner. The man we – '

'We have no time for prisoners,' the Battalion Commander interrupted. 'Take him away and shoot him.'

'That's what I told him,' the officer said. 'He refuses to do it. His own unit officer apparently ordered him and another fellow to carry this prisoner here on a stretcher.'

'What unit is this?' the Battalion Commander wanted to know.

It was the unhappy Partisan who answered.

'Number Three Labour Company, Comrade Excellency. The man is a spy. We have carried the devil the best part of thirty kilometres, from where we were working in the hills above Srnetica. We would have shot him when we found him if we had known this was going to happen.'

'Where is this spy?' Stefan asked.

The Partisan pointed.

'Over there, at the gate. With my comrade.'

The little party all trooped over to the gate, led by the Battalion Commander, who called for a light. The officer who had been involved in the altercation unclipped a battery lamp from his belt and shone it in the face of the man lying on the stretcher. The elderly Partisan felt that a commentary was necessary.

'He has the dress of a German officer, but he is no German. He's a Cetnik, and was put to work with our detail when we were in Jajce. I would have recognised him anywhere. His name is – '

'Marko Markovic,' Stefan supplied. He stared down at his brother, his mouth contorting with rage. Marko was conscious, but more dead than alive. Beads of sweat stood out on his blackened face and his eyes were open. A blanket had been thrown over his lower limbs, but from it rose the unmistakable stench of gangrene. The Battalion Commander took a step back from the stretcher, wrinkling his nose.

Stefan did not step back. He found the sight of his own brother in a German uniform more offensive that the smell from his mangled legs. Every member of the little group was staring at Stefan, wondering how he knew the name of the half-dead wretch on the stretcher. Mouths opened in surprise as the Central Committee officer wrestled his revolver from the canvas holster on his hip.

Before any could move, Stefan took a step forward and, levelling the gun at the forehead of the wounded man, he fired a single shot. Then he turned on his heel and walked stiffly back towards the Command Post.

At the doorway, the Battalion Commander overtook him.

'You solved that little problem, comrade,' he said cheerfully. 'Thanks. I wonder if the fellow was a spy.'

'He was a traitor,' Stefan ground out.

'Well, you certainly didn't beat about the bush. What made you so sure?'

Stefan stared at him, with agony in his eyes. His reply exploded from him as a shout of anguish.

'He was my brother!'

0115 hours

Jamie waited for the noise of the grenade blast to stop ringing in his ears before rising from behind the stone wall and making a run at the kitchen doorway. The door had fallen inwards but the lower hinge still hung by a sliver. The door collapsed flat under his feet as he ran over it into the farmhouse kitchen. He fired as he ran, spraying bullets high and low as an insurance against the possibility that any defenders still lived in the dark, smoke-filled interior. None did. An SS paratrooper, slumped against the window, tumbled to the floor – dislodged by Jamie's raking burst – but he was already dead.

Jamie was joined by the cadet who had tossed the grenade, then by others. They made their way cautiously through the other rooms of the farmhouse and then methodically explored the outhouses. They found only corpses, and marvelled that so few men had been able to resist them so fiercely for so long. Jamie ordered a collection of the enemy weapons that were still serviceable. He was puzzled at the ease with which the final

attack on the farm buildings had been pressed home –
and now the answer stared him in the face. The
ammunition boxes that they found were empty.

The German paratroopers had run out of bullets
before they had run out of courage.

0600 hours

Wolf Bleyer could scarcely keep his eyes open. He had
never known such fatigue. He was slumped against a
gravestone, his Schmeisser resting on his thighs. He had
rested in that position for over an hour, waiting for the
signal from the wall that the Partisans were coming
again. But the signal had not come. Through red-
rimmed eyes, he had watched the dawn break. With the
dawn had come visible evidence of the unforgiving
ferocity of the night's battle.

One hundred metres away was the corner of the
cemetery where the Partisans had breached the wall and
come swarming through. At the time, Bleyer had
thought it was the end, but the Acting Commander had
prepared for just such an eventuality by holding a 'fire
brigade' reserve in readiness to respond to a break-
through. The Partisans had held their bridgehead for
more than an hour before the paratroops, fighting with
the fury of desperation, had driven them back beyond
the wall. Now, that area was strewn with the dead:
appalling witness to the night's carnage.

The quiet of the brightening morning was eerie. Still
the paratroops, watching from the perimeter wall,
scanned the corpse-strewn hillside beyond – but nothing
moved. It was if man and nature lay exhausted and
stunned by the frightfulness of what had taken place. No
bird sang, and there was not even a sign of the carrions of
the air; it was as if even they, too, had fled in awe at the
magnitude of the waiting feast.

Suddenly the silence was shattered by the chatter of a

distant machine-gun. Bleyer was startled alert. It was a German gun, there was no mistaking the signature. But that meant little. The Partisans had German guns in plenty. Again the rattle came, from beyond the silent town. The paratroops in the cemetery stirred. Weapons were checked, magazines clipped into place. Men grey with fatigue braced themselves to be ready to kill again, or die.

A new noise came – motor engines. A distant hum at first and then a definite, recognisable rhythm of sound. A cheer rose from the wall as the first vehicle came into sight – a *Schwimmwagen*. It was followed by others.

Bleyer found himself among a small group of paratroopers who ran out to meet the vanguard of the relieving column. An officer leapt out of the first *Schwimmwagen*. It was Petar Richtman.

'Petar!' Bleyer's shout stopped him in his tracks. Petar stared in disbelief at the dishevelled figure in front of him.

'Wolf!' They hugged each other, grinning with delight.

'You're late,' Bleyer accused with a smile.

'We were unavoidably delayed,' Petar said. He nodded towards the paratroop lines. 'Is that a cemetery?'

'Take a good look round, Petar,' Bleyer invited him, waving an arm at the hillside. 'The whole of Bosnia's a goddamned graveyard.'

0700 hours

Stefan marched blindly, like an automaton. The going was rough, over open and arid hillside that seemed to throw up the heat of the sun. It was going to be a hot day, even hotter than yesterday – and that was saying something. Heat and fatigue did not seem to trouble the men of the First Partisan Brigade's 1st Battalion. They had marched all day through yesterday's heat and they had fought all night, but here they were, maintaining a blistering pace as if they had risen fresh from their beds. Stefan kept up with them, without consciously dwelling on the effort demanded of his tired legs. His mind was occupied on a plane far removed from the demands of his body. He was now trying to understand the rage that had seized him in so consuming a manner that he had, without hesitation, pulled out his revolver and blown out his brother's brains. Now, he felt misery and contrition. What had happened to the idealistic young writer he once had been: the advocate of reason and compassion and tolerance, the champion of freedom and justice?

Was what he had done justice? Or revenge? Revenge for what? Was it shame or pride or revulsion that had made him pull the trigger? No answer that came to Stefan offered a consolation to the raging in his mind.

Elsewhere in the marching column – which numbered perhaps two thousand – Jamie strode along with his cadets. Fatigue showed on their faces, but pride, too. They had come through their first battle with their numbers thinned but with their bravery acknowledged on all sides: a bravery that would be confirmed by the war diaries and battle reports of an elite enemy, the SS Paratroop Battalion 500 of German Special Forces Command.

On the march from Drvar, Jamie was depressed. It was as if he had come this way before. It was the Moraca and Uzice and Durmitor and the Sutjeska all over again. March and fight, march and fight – from one side of Jugoslavia to the other, and then back again, for ever and ever and ever, without end. How much more could the human spirit take without wanting to lie down quietly somewhere and give up?

Jamie's blood froze at the sound of aircraft engines. There was no protection here on these barren hills. Hand raised to shade his eyes from the morning sun, he saw the black shapes and knew what was coming.

'Scatter!' he shouted to his cadets. 'Stukas!'

Out of the sun, the Stukas came, wheeling into their screaming dives, to blast the scorched land with thundering death. It was another day in war, and the dying was about to begin again.

5

The Turning Tide

Stefan was pouring sweat beneath his British-made battledress blouse, which was buttoned to the neck. Walking ahead of him – with the British Mission chief, Brigadier Maclean – was Tito, who looked even more uncomfortable in the blazing heat of the August morning. The Supreme Commander, resplendent in a uniform of gold and sky-blue – a gift from Stalin – was clearly suffering. The tunic seemed too tight at the neck, making the flesh bulge over the collar; and the redness of Tito's face suggested that the price of indulging such finery was slow asphyxiation.

At least – Stefan thought – there was no mistaking which of us is the Marshal and which is the Lieutenant-General. He had found wry amusement in the fact that, earlier in the day, when they paid a call on General Alexander's COS, a British colonel had mistaken Stefan for Tito's bodyguard, because his lieutenant-general's uniform was identical to that of a private soldier in the British Army. The Colonel had been astounded to learn that the young Serb from the Jugoslav Army of National Liberation outranked him.

As they were shown on to the terrace of the Villa Rivalta – a palace of a residence that had become shabby through wartime neglect – Tito and the British Brigadier paused to stare at the magnificent view of Naples and its bay. Dominating the panorama was the smoking chimney of Mount Vesuvius. The blue waters of the bay were crowded with military transports and warships of every shape and size. An armada had gathered for the invasion of southern France and was ready to sail. As Tito gazed at this display of Allied might, a portly figure in a white suit came bustling along the terrace to greet his visitors.

'Marshal Tito!' boomed a deep melodious voice and, advancing with hand outstretched, the Prime Minister of Great Britain seized Tito's hand and clasped the Marshal to him with an embracing arm. Tito seemed to be taken by surprise at his host's enthusiasm and emotional warmth. Tears shone in Winston Churchill's eyes as he declared: 'You are the first person from enslaved Europe I have met. I welcome you in the name of the free peoples of the world.'

Tito waited while this was translated. Whatever he had expected from a man whom he regarded as an arch-imperialist and champion of capitalism, it was not this emotion-charged greeting. That Churchill was plainly moved at meeting him was all too evident, and yet Tito – cautious as ever – seemed not quite ready to believe the other was sincere. His response was formal, reserved, as if suspicions lurked.

Churchill appeared not to notice, sliding easily into the mantle of considerate host.

'Perhaps you would like to see General Wilson's war room,' he suggested affably. The party moved inside the villa. Stefan and the two soldiers who *were* Tito's official bodyguards made to follow, and it was only after intervention by Brigadier Maclean that Tito was persuaded that the bodyguards could be safely left on the terrace.

In the war room, Churchill drew attention to the huge wall maps of the European war fronts and gave a succinct discourse on the strategic objectives of the Allied armies in Normandy. He talked of the pressure being exerted on Hitler by the armies in Italy and the Russian armies advancing from the east, and he illustrated how the German position was constantly being weakened by Hitler's stubborn insistence on keeping valuable divisions in the occupied countries, from Norway to the Balkans.

Then he drew Tito's attention to the Istrian peninsula – Italian territory to which Jugoslavia laid claim – and sounded Tito out on the cooperation of the Partisans if the Allies were to make a landing on the peninsula.

'I would certainly be in favour of an operation against Istria,' Tito said. 'And, most certainly, would our forces join in. Although the Germans have been hitting us hard recently and our losses have been severe, we can raise considerable strength in Croatia and Slovenia.'

'It would help your cause greatly,' Churchill said, 'if we had access to a port on the Jugoslav coast further south, where we could land the war materials you need. In the past two months, we have lifted two thousand tons of supplies to you by air – but we could get that amount alone in the hold of a single ship. We could increase the quantities dramatically if we could supply you by sea.'

Tito accepted this was so, but refrained from answering Churchill's question directly. His sidestepping of the issue amused Stefan. Tito had often declared that the Partisans would resist any large-scale landing of British troops on the Jugoslav coast, because it would almost certainly prelude a return of King Peter to Jugoslav soil and provide a rallying point for Mihailovic and the Cetniks.

When the British Prime Minister and the Marshal of Jugoslavia went into private session, which extended through lunch, Stefan found himself excluded from the discussions. It was afternoon before he was reunited with Tito and able to ask him about his impressions of Churchill. One thing was quickly evident. The British statesman had made a far greater impact on the Jugoslav leader than Stefan had suspected. Tito had thawed considerably in his attitude.

'Did you see the tears in his eyes when he greeted me?'

Tito asked, glowing with pride. 'I was so moved, I didn't know what to say.'

'Your talks with him went well, Comrade Marshal?'

'Oh, he's a wily old bird – so knowledgeable. . . . But I think I handled him well. He wanted to know if there was any chance of a reconciliation between us and Mihailovic.'

'And what did you say?'

'No chance at all. I told him that if it hadn't been for the help that Draza is getting from the Germans and the Bulgarian Fascists, he would have faded from sight long ago.'

'He wouldn't have liked that. The British have a soft spot for Mihailovic,' Stefan said.

'Oh, I think he accepted it. He says that the British have no wish to interfere with our internal affairs. All Churchill is interested in is defeating Hitler.'

'So they won't try to force the King on us?'

'He did bring up the question of the King and that Britain had a feeling of obligation to him. But I told him flatly that it was up to the people of Jugoslavia to decide if they wanted a king and that they would make that decision when the war was over – not before!'

'And did he accept that?'

'I think so – although he asked me if it was my intention to impose Communism on Jugoslavia. Naturally, I told him that I had no intention of doing any such thing.'

'Naturally?' Stefan's eyebrows shot up. 'But we must–'

'We must be cautious,' Tito interrupted, with a smile. 'Churchill wanted me to make a public statement, making it known that I had no intention of imposing Communism on our people – which, of course, I refused to do. I pointed out that if I did make any such announcement at this time, the world would think that he had twisted my arm and forced me to make it.'

'But surely we must consolidate the power we have won,' Stefan said. 'We have political power now. AVNOJ represents all parties and shades of opinion in the country, not just Communism – and we control AVNOJ. We only need to keep that control to make all of Jugoslavia Communist.'

'Do you think I don't know this?' Tito snapped impatiently. 'But Serbia is our weakness. The Germans crushed us in Serbia, and the British know this. And the British know that Serbia is where support for the King is strongest. We must change all that. We've got to renew the battle in Serbia, show our strength there . . . even if it means weakening our armies in Croatia and Slovenia, where the Party is strong. Otherwise, Churchill and Roosevelt will try to divide Jugoslavia after the war. They will let us keep the west for Communism, but they will put Peter back on the throne in Serbia.'

'Did Churchill say this to you?' Stefan asked.

Tito smiled grimly.

'Not in so many words. But he hinted. He backed down a bit when I told him that I took the gravest possible exception to any suggestion that the Partisan movement was divorced from the Serbian people and their aspirations. Now we've got to show that these were not just empty words on my part. And you will play your part, Stefan.'

'Me, Comrade Marshal? In what way?'

'You will go to Serbia at the earliest possible moment,' Tito said. 'Your job will be to rally Serbs to the Partisan cause, organise the cadres and the battalions which must be ready to join with the brigades we send from Bosnia. And help will not only come from Bosnia, Stefan. The Red Army is not that far away now. Sooner or later, they will break through from the east and sweep across Romania in an unstoppable tide. When that happens, we must be ready to greet them with a Partisan army that's strong enough to march on Belgrade.'

'Will you be returning to Vis, Comrade Marshal?' Stefan asked. Vis was the Adriatic island – thirty kilometres long by thirteen kilometres wide – which British Special Forces had occupied and where Tito had established his Supreme Headquarters after his escape from Drvar.

'In due course,' Tito replied, with an enigmatic smile. 'But first, I must humour the British. I shall meet and talk with Dr Subasic – whom our British friends regard as the Prime Minister of Jugoslavia – and I shall resist their attempts to contrive a meeting between myself and King Peter. Then, when the British are not looking, I intend to consult friends whose backing we shall need if we are going to achieve our political ambitions in Serbia.'

Stefan's puzzlement amused Tito.

'I am going to Moscow,' the Marshal revealed. 'But keep that to yourself. The British, if they were to find out, would think that I was hatching secret deals with Marshal Stalin behind their backs.'

'Which of course, you wouldn't dream of doing,' Stefan said, with a smile.

Tito frowned.

'I am going at Marshal Stalin's invitation,' he said stiffly. 'And we shall be discussing matters of mutual interest.' Then his eyes twinkled. 'I think that our comrade in the Kremlin is scared stiff I do or say something to antagonise Churchill. I want to put his mind at rest – and ask him for a hundred tanks!'

The DC-3 made a bumpy landing and taxied to the side of the field, where a group of Partisans waited. Before the big Wasp engines had feathered to a stop, Mannion had dropped from the cargo door. He was closely followed by Major Blair, the British SF officer from Bari.

A shout greeted Mannion from the waiting group, and he recognised the familiar figure of Djordje striding towards him. Moments later, he was welcomed back to Montenegrin soil by the Communist leader in typically exuberant fashion.

'What have you brought us from the fleshpots in Italy?' Djordje wanted to know.

Mannion grinned at him.

'Two cartons of decent American tobacco for that foul pipe of yours, for a start,' he said. 'But there's a couple of tons of medical supplies, too. The pilot presents his compliments and asks if you'll unload it in a hurry. He doesn't want to hang around.'

Partisan unloaders were already swarming about the cargo door as Mannion spoke, and Djordje's assurance that his men would waste no time was unnecessary. The group were joined by a third passenger from the Dakota: a lean forty-year-old with a shock of blond hair showing from below his service cap. He wore the sheened khaki trouser-and-shirt issue of an American officer, but it was devoid of rank badges. Twin shoulder flashes, however, bore the acronym UNRRA.

'This is Mr Nilsen of the United Nations Relief and Rehabilitation Administration,' Mannion introduced the newcomer. 'He wants to talk to you and the Montenegrin leadership about shipping in food supplies. Mr Nilsen is Swedish.'

The Swede was greeted politely but with a noticeable lack of warmth. It was not until a little later, when he had the chance to talk to the Montenegrin alone, that Mannion commented on Djordje's apparent coolness towards the Swedish official.

'Don't you like Swedes?' he asked casually. 'I got the impression you weren't too pleased to see the guy.'

'We should have been warned he was coming,' Djordje said. 'I have nothing against Swedes. But this relief organisation of his is trouble. We have had strict instructions from Supreme Headquarters to have nothing to do with UNRRA.'

'Why, for God's sake?' Mannion was perplexed. 'All they want to do is distribute food and medicine where it's needed most. Children have been dying of starvation in Montenegro. You must know this.'

Djordje nodded, grim-faced.

'I know it. The Supreme Staff knows it. And God knows, we could use the food – but that's not the problem. It's the Americans in charge of UNRRA who are at fault. They are insisting on landing with the food and distributing it themselves – in the Cetnik villages as well as our villages. We will never allow this. Never!'

'They only want to make sure that the food goes to the most in need,' Mannion said.

'And we are going to make sure that we and we alone are the judges of who needs what. The Cetniks have tried to starve us out. Now it is their turn to suffer. If they are hungry, let them go to their German friends with their bowls in their hands. Didn't you tell the Americans how things were over here, comrade?'

'Until I was hoarse,' Mannion replied, with a smile. 'The military know the score, all right. It's the State Department people who keep pussyfooting. They haven't been obstructive, but they have this crazy idea that they've got to be seen to be even-handed in the help they give to the Partisans and the Cetniks. They want to play ball with us and keep sweet with Mihailovic at the same time.'

'But Mihailovic wouldn't exist if the Germans didn't allow him to exist!' Djordje protested.

'You try telling that to the State Department,' Mannion said. 'And they'll tell you what they keep telling me – that if Mihailovic is as bad as we paint him, how come he and his Cetniks are able to smuggle American bomber crews clear across Jugoslavia and over to Italy? They're scared stiff that if they do anything to offend Mihailovic, he'll start turning these shot-down fliers over to the Germans.'

560

Djordje did not blame Mannion for what he saw as lamentable blindness on the part of the American Government. And he left Mannion in no doubt that the UNRRA official, Nilsen, was going to be on the receiving end of some hard talking before he returned to Italy. Mannion felt a pang of sympathy for the Swede, whom he had met only the previous day and found to be a rather dour and pedantic individual.

The war had gone badly for the Montenegrin Partisans during the summer, mainly because the guerrilla army had been as reluctant as ever to abandon their wounded, and this had proved a severe handicap to mobility. Djordje talked about it as he filled his pipe with the tobacco that Mannion had brought from Italy.

'The Nazis have got wise to us,' he was telling Mannion when Blair arrived. They were sitting on crates at the side of the primitive airfield, and Djordje waved his pipe in invitation to the British officer to join them. 'This is excellent tobacco,' he commented, puffing away. 'Better than the shoe leather I've had to make do with lately.'

'What do you mean that the Nazis have got wise to you?' Mannion asked.

'They've twigged the fact that we'll go to great lengths to prevent our wounded falling into their clutches and being slaughtered out of hand, so they've changed their tactics. They've been going for the wounded like wolves after a lamb, and they've drawn us into running battles we would otherwise have avoided. Our losses have been catastrophic.'

As a result, the Partisans had been deprived of the initiative throughout the summer. They had been unable to slacken the German hold on the coastal areas and had failed to cause much interruption to the communication routes between German forces in Albania and northern Jugoslavia. Instead of taking the war to the enemy, the Partisans had been forced on to the

561

defensive and confined to pockets where the mobility of their forces was severely encumbered by the large numbers of wounded who had to travel with them.

The Montenegrin Partisans' problem with their wounded was not news to Mannion and Blair. Indeed, it was a plan to alleviate it that had brought them to Montenegro. Djordje had been warned of their arrival in advance, but even he was staggered by the ambitious nature of what was envisaged: the airlift in a single day of as many seriously wounded as the Partisans could bring to the airfield at Bajovo Polje.

'I have been pleading with Supreme Headquarters for weeks to do something to help us . . . but this is magnificent!' he declared. 'More than I dreamed possible.'

'From what I hear, you have Marshal Tito to thank,' Blair told him. 'He made a bit of a stink in high places – and we've been told to pull out all the stops. The order came from the very top.'

Djordje frowned and eyed Blair suspiciously.

'Are there any strings attached?'

'None that you would object to, I hope,' Blair said. 'It'll be an international effort on our side – British and American personnel – and the air boys want to put in their own people to handle ground-air communications and any maintenance that's needed to keep their kites in the air. They'll fly their people in, a day or two before Big Lift Day, and pull them out when it's all over. We'd also like to put in a ground force – no more than a company – as airfield defence. They would be pulled out, too, at the end of the operation. What are the chances of the Germans mounting a ground attack on the field?'

'Fifty-fifty at the best of times,' Djordje said thoughtfully. 'If they get wind of what's happening, it's a near certainty they'll do their damnedest to stop it.'

'Then you'll go along with it?'

'That's up to our Command . . . I'm only part of it,'

Djordje said gravely, and saw Blair's face cloud. 'But I promise to shoot anyone who opposes it,' he added impishly, his white teeth gleaming in an ear-to-ear grin.

'There is another condition,' Blair said, and smiled as Djordje's grin vanished.

'What condition?' the Montenegrin growled, all suspicion.

'The release of one of your officers to serve with the British Special Forces.' Blair eyed Mannion with eyebrows raised. 'Have you mentioned it?'

'Not yet,' Mannion confessed. Djordje was regarding him questioningly.

'You?' the Montenegrin said. 'You are the officer?'

'I'm sick of being stuck behind a desk in Bari,' Mannion said defensively. 'I wasn't cut out for it. Major Blair's guys are going to be raiding in the Dalmatian islands – blowing bridges . . . that kind of thing. They're short of guys who speak Serbo-Croat and English.'

'The Commander at Partisan HQ in Bari says that he doesn't have the authority to make a decision,' Blair put in. 'He said it was up to Comrade General Djordje in Montenegro. He said if it was OK with you, it was OK with him.'

Djordje seemed less than happy with the idea.

'Let me think about it,' he said. After a moment of thoughtfulness, he asked: 'How long do we have to bring our wounded here, to Bajovo Polje?'

'Less than a week,' Blair said. 'Unless there are snags. The air boys have pencilled in August twenty-second for the Big Lift. That's next Tuesday.'

'I'll let you know before then,' Djordje promised.

Jamie had not gone north into the Lika after the flight from Drvar, as many of the surviving Partisan units had. At the time, the crazy notion had filled his mind that going north was taking him further and further away from Jajce – where Mara was – and, in the confusion of

563

the retreat from Drvar, he had contrived to remain in Bosnia. This, in itself, was not difficult – because, in those first days after the order to disperse had been given, the prime concern was: survive now, organise later. The rule had obtained from the morning when the German Stukas caught the Partisans on open hillside, only a few kilometres from Drvar. They had wreaked a terrible revenge for the near destruction of SS Paratroop Battalion 500. The Partisan officer cadets had been split up amongst small units when the main force was ordered to scatter, and Jamie was given charge of a handful of Bosnian hill men whose officer had been killed.

Recalling that summer later, Jamie would describe it as his eighty days in the wilderness and contend that, far from being the leader, he was the one who was led – because his hill men had taken him deep into their home terrain: that merciless burning desert of shimmering rock known as the Karst. Without those sturdy and self-reliant Muslim highlanders – Jamie came to acknowledge – he would not have survived. It was one of the most inhospitable regions on the face of the earth, but it had one redeeming feature: its alien wastes deterred even the German Army from straying far from the few roads that passed through it.

It was mid-June before Jamie and his Bosnians re-established contact with other units in the Partisan chain, and the month was almost over before they were participating in forays that brought them down out of the burning hills. In mid-August, on the day that Mannion and Blair landed in Montenegro, Jamie was setting off on one such raid with his Bosnians.

Their operational base in the hills near Livno had received a signal from Area Command, near the town of Split, that intelligence reports from the interior had noted an increase in enemy troop movements towards Mostar from the north. Jamie's unit was detailed for a mine-laying raid on the main Zagreb-Mostar highway.

Jamie targeted a stretch of roadway through wooded hills, where the road descended into the Vrbas valley from the village of Gornji Vakuf, and noted, with a rueful smile, that the chosen location was just over thirty kilometres south of Jajce. And Mara?

He wondered what madness had prompted him to think that, by going into the Karst with his Bosnians, he was somehow staying closer to Mara. As long as this bloody impossible war continued, she would always be just beyond reach. There was no crossing of the chasm that separated them, and there would not be one until the guns had fallen silent and the killing had ceased.

The sun was low in the west when Jamie and his six men left their base on the long trek to the Mostar-Jajce highway. It would take them two days to reach their destination, resting during the heat of the day and travelling in daylight hours if the terrain was sufficiently remote to do so safely. Only on the latter stage of their journey would there be woodlands to provide cover. All seven men carried backpacks weighing thirty kilos and more. Only a tenth of that weight comprised personal rations and equipment. The bulk was explosives.

There was an hour of daylight left on the second day when, from a wooded crag, they sighted the road below. While the Bosnians set up camp, Jamie reconnoitred the road from several vantage points, scanning the visible stretches through powerful binoculars which had once been the prized possession of a German SS major, now deceased. Nothing moved on the road. The light had nearly gone when Jamie rejoined the hill men, his course of action decided.

The road skirted the west bank of the Vrbas River, and Jamie had selected, for his sabotage plan, a stretch of five kilometres between two small streams which cascaded down the hillside above the west bank and flowed under the road to join the river. Small bridges carried the road over these streams. It was Jamie's intention to place time charges under the road at these two extremities and mine the northern approach of the most southerly bridge.

Thirty minutes after dark, Jamie led his team down the hill to the south bridge. There was little more than a culvert under the road, and here they set to work, laying the charges in the stonework. The detonating device, with its acid delay-fuse, would be attached later in the night. Mining the approach to the crossing was hard work. The baked surface of the road would have resisted the bite of a pneumatic drill, and it was necessary to prise stones out of the road to hollow recesses into which the ten-kilo canisters of explosive could be laid. Gravel and small stones then had to be collected and scattered over the road to conceal the freshness of the excavations.

It was long after midnight when Jamie and the hill men began the five-kilometre hike to the second stream, although it was downhill all the way and the distance along the flinty road was quickly covered. Again, the team set to work under the roadway.

They were back at their hilltop camp by three-thirty a.m. and, deciding that there was little danger of it being seen, Jamie allowed one of the Bosnians to light a fire and boil up coffee in the quaintly shaped kettle which was an essential part of his equipment. They breakfasted on the inevitable rice; Jamie had become heartily sick of it, but more than once it had stood between him and starvation. Then they rested. Jamie had decided they would stay in the neighbourhood only long enough to ascertain that the fused charges went off. There was no point in hanging around to see if traffic happened along; it could be two or three days before any did. The object of the exercise was to cause maximum inconvenience to any German convoys moving to Mostar, at a suitably inconvenient place on the road. With luck, a bottleneck would be created, providing the kind of situation that the Partisans were adept at exploiting: a stranded column which could be attacked from the hills.

Although the Bosnians were Communists, they had not abandoned their Islamic religion, and Jamie was in the habit of finding something else to do when they made their morning obeisances to Mecca. This morning, a little before eight, he made his way to the craggy observation point from which he had previously studied the road. If the detonating fuses worked on time, the first explosion was due about eight-thirty and the second at about nine-fifteen.

He had no sooner reached his crag than he heard the rattling approach of a vehicle. It was coming uphill, from the direction of the railhead village of Bugojno. Jamie saw it when he focused his binoculars on the little hump that marked the road's passage over the stream at the north end of the five-kilometre stretch. It was a German military half-track – a *Panzerwerfer* 42, the Germans called it, and a particularly vicious weapon it was when used against advancing foot soldiers at short range. On its armoured tail was the ten-tube launcher that fired 15 cm rockets. A machine-gun was mounted above the driver's turret.

At first, Jamie thought the half-track was unaccompanied, but following it up the road came a *Schwimmwagen*. The scouting amphibian was, in turn, followed by several heavy trucks and half a dozen low-slung field ambulances with red crosses emblazoned on their canvas sides. There were nineteen vehicles in the convoy, and all passed safely over the mined hump and laboured on up the valley. Jamie's strongest reaction was surprise at seeing any German traffic at all on this part of the road so early in the day. The Germans, as a rule, kept off the roads at night. But if this convoy had started out from Banja Luka – the usual staging point for Mostar – it must have set off three hours before daylight.

Even if it had started off from Jajce – a possible explanation – it must have set out in darkness.

There was little time for speculation. The six Bosnians, alerted by the sound of the convoy, came crawling up behind Jamie as an explosion echoed along the valley. A spiral of oily smoke rising above the trees pinpointed the location, but it was hidden from Jamie's viewpoint. The cause was easily guessed, however. The *Panzerwerfer* had hit one of the mines in the roadway as it approached the southerly culvert.

'Do we attack?' one of the Bosnians asked Jamie. The tail end of the convoy had come to a stop almost directly below them, and soldiers were spilling from the trucks to take up defensive positions in the brush above the road.

'Seven of us?' Jamie said. 'No, comrade. They must have two hundred men down there.' He nodded towards the high hills to the east. 'Our comrades in the hills over there will have heard that bang and will be along to investigate. We've caught their fish for them, but it's up to them how they fry it.'

The Bosnians were plainly relieved. They were the bravest fighters, who would have defied any odds, but they preferred to wage war with guile rather than reckless bravado. They approved of Jamie's prudence.

It was at precisely eight thirty-two that a second thundering explosion occurred. Stone and earth spewed upward in a great fountain from the northern extremity of the five-kilometre stretch of road. The visible hump where the road crossed the hill stream had disappeared. Now, there was a jagged chasm where it had been. Jamie and the Bosnians watched as a squad of soldiers were despatched along the road to investigate the explosion. They walked in file, cautiously – their machine-pistols cradled close to their bodies, ready for use.

Jamie moved his position to get a view of the front portion of the stopped convoy. The smoking wreck of the *Panzerwerfer* 42 was lying on its side, well ahead of the

Schwimmwagen. In its vicinity, a squad of German sappers with mine-detection gear were carefully searching the road. Scanning the far hills, Jamie wondered if the Partisan observers – who, he knew, kept the road under daily surveillance – were alert to what had happened. When he set the charges, he had not envisaged that a German convoy would chance along the road quite so early in the day. The chances now were that, if the sappers cleared the mines on the road, they would find the explosives in the second culvert and defuse that, too. The convoy could be on its way to Mostar within the hour.

Jamie summoned up his Bosnians to tell them that he had changed his mind about attacking the stopped column – but he wanted no recklessness, he said, as he told them precisely what he wanted them to do. As they had applauded his prudence before, they now nodded approval of what he intended. They quickly dispersed to do his bidding.

While he waited for the hill men to get into position, Jamie continued to survey the stranded column through his binoculars. Below, the initial fear of an ambush seemed to have vanished, and troops and drivers were stretching their legs beside their vehicles as if any danger had passed. There even seemed to be some relaxation among those deployed into defensive groups along the roadside, although here and there officers could be seen and heard exhorting vigilance. From one truck, a group of nurses had descended and were sitting on a grassy bank on the river side of the road.

Idly scanning them, Jamie felt his heart miss a beat when, amongst the flaxen-haired girls, the head and shoulders of a nurse with raven-black hair came sharply into focus. The magnified image brought Mara as close to him as if she had been sitting only a few metres away. There was no doubt that it was her. His hands shook as he tried to adjust the focus and confirm the fact: it *was*

569

Mara. His own beloved Mara. Jamie's surprise was total. Often in his mind, since that day in Sipoljani when he learned of Mara's presence in Jajce, he had toyed with wild fancies of contriving to meet her or catch sight of her – without ever convincing himself that such notions were any more than foolish daydreams.

Now his reaction was shock. She had been far from his mind, and seeing her was so unexpected that it almost paralysed him. He wanted to go running down the hill to her and take her in his arms, regardless of the consequences, but he remained frozen in impotent horror at the full implications of the situation. Only a minute before, he had been considering ways of ensuring that the convoy, which had strayed – fortuitously perhaps – into a trap of his making, would be destroyed. Jamie shuddered with fear as realisation seared his mind. Was this to be the supreme irony, after all the years of suffering and separation, that he should unwittingly put into jeopardy the one person whom he cherished more than life?

The thought crossed his mind that, even now, he could avert the worst possible scenario unfolding: he could recall his Bosnians and let the stranded convoy take its chances. But he knew it was already too late. There was no way of recalling them.

Confirmation of the fact came almost in the same instant, with the crack of a single rifleshot from the hillside two hundred metres away. There was a scurry near the second culvert, where the German sappers were working. They all suddenly sought cover, leaving, in the middle of the road, the body of the officer who had been supervising their mine-lifting operations.

A second shot rang out; this time, as far away to Jamie's left as the first had been to his right. A German officer walking along the roadside fell and pitched on his face. The Bosnians were carrying out Jamie's orders to the letter: selecting single targets, preferably officers, and conducting indiscriminate sniper-fire on the column below.

There was no answering fire from the soldiers on the road, for the perfectly good reason that they had no idea where the shots were coming from and they could see no target on the hillside above them. His glasses still trained on Mara and the nurses, Jamie saw a soldier run towards them and, with shouts and waving of arms, direct them to take cover below the grassy bank on which they had been sitting.

More shots echoed from the hillside as the Bosnians, well spaced out along the craggy tops in good positions, carefully selected individual targets and fired with expert accuracy. Two German gunners, manning weapons mounted on the cabs of trucks, started to spray the hillside with bullets – but they were firing from guesswork. Each, in turn, paid for his audacity when the unseen snipers picked them off. A stationary armoured car began to blast the slope with cannon and machine-gun to cover a probing sortie up through the trees. This culminated in a sudden blaze of automatic fire, some four hundred metres to Jamie's left, but whether or not it resulted in the demise of one of the snipers could not be seen. The men on the hill were recalled by whistle-blasts from below when the second culvert blew up with a noise that boomed and echoed around the valley.

Jamie had warned the Bosnians to take the second explosion as a signal for ending their sniping efforts and retiring to an arranged rendezvous, where he would meet them. He would confirm the disengagement order by firing three rapid shots from his pistol. Now that moment had come, he felt a strange reluctance. The knowledge that Mara was so close was an agony to him, filling him with impulses that were suicidal in their folly. He had to force himself to put them from his mind and face the fact that there was no way of reaching her or spiriting her miraculously out of the enemy conclave. He had to abandon her where she was, and take himself away. He had no other choice.

And yet he hesitated. A madness to do something gripped him – and it was not to be denied. Scrambling to his feet, he cupped his hands about his mouth and shouted her name at the hilltops.

'MA – RA! MA – RA!'

The sound echoed around the heights and went out across the valley. Jamie raised his pistol and fired three shots in quick succession. For a full minute, he stood there against the skyline, in full view from the road below, wild and defiant. There was a volley of fire from a line of Panzergrenadiers crouched behind the low armoured wall of a troop-carrier. But, when they looked again, the shouting apparition which had momentarily surprised them had disappeared from the hilltop.

All along the road, those who had seen the appearance of the lone man and heard his shout, took the phenomenon to be typical defiance by a crazy Bosnian native: a war cry or insult hurled by an enemy. Only one person had reacted oddly. As the shout had echoed down the valley, one of the nurses sheltering behind a grassy bank had leapt to her feet and stared, open-mouthed, at the distant figure. A soldier nearby, witnessing her folly and fearing for her, grabbed her and hauled her to the ground as the Panzergrenadiers opened fire. Shielding her, he breathed a sigh of relief when the Partisan ducked down and disappeared from sight.

'You could have got yourself killed,' he reproached Mara, wondering why the girl had tears in her eyes. 'I'm sorry, did I hurt you, tumbling you like that?'

'No,' Mara murmured.

'They missed him,' said the soldier, commenting on the Panzergrenadiers' aim. For a moment, he thought she was going to faint. She wobbled and said something which the soldier could not make out. Her 'Thank God' was almost inaudible and came out in an exploding sigh, born of relief. She was still coming to terms with *knowing* that it had been Jamie up there on that hill. What madness had made him show himself and shout her name like that? The answer, of course, was the same kind of madness that had gripped her. She had been on the point of shouting Jamie's name at the top of her voice when the soldier leapt on her and knocked the breath from her body.

In five days, the population of Bajovo Polje had grown dramatically. In the immediate vicinity of the primitive airfield, more than a thousand Partisan wounded were camped in the open. With them had congregated the sixty or more medics, nurses and doctors who had been caring for them, plus the several hundred Partisans who had portered the casualties for many kilometres over difficult mountain trails to the rendezvous and several hundred more men of the wounded's defence cordon.

They had arrived at Bajovo Polje in plodding files, like bands of pilgrims trekking to Lourdes in expectation of miracles. In their case, however, miracle cures were not expected. Salvation would come from the heavens – in the shape of flight after flight of DC-3 transports.

On Sunday, August the twentieth, support teams for the airlift operation had flown in from Italy and installed their equipment around the field, and a ring of steel had been set up to frustrate any German intrusion. Attracting less attention than these arrivals, however, a small delegation of high-ranking Communists reached Djordje's HQ armed with special powers by the Central Committee. They had no interest in the planned airlift and assured the Montenegrin leadership that they wished only to go about their business inconspicuously and without help or interference. Their business was winkling out traitors, informers and spies, and they had the authority to carry out this work unimpeded. They made this very clear to Djordje. They had been entrusted with guardianship of the faith, and *no one* – regardless of Party status, past service or senior rank – had immunity from their powers of exacting retribution. They were officers of OZNA.

They arrived on August the eighteenth, with their baggage and radio equipment loaded on mules and with their own escort unit. Djordje arranged for them to be quartered in a village some kilometres from the airfield, and promptly forgot about them. He had other things to think about. There was the added distraction of an unexpected problem, the very next day. Nilsen, the man from UNRRA, failed to return from a trip to an outlying village. The Partisan officer who had been escorting him was also missing.

No light was thrown on the mystery until the afternoon of the twentieth, when one of the OZNA officers rode up to the airfield with an escort of six. One of the escort was leading a horse, across which were draped the bodies of Nilsen and the missing Partisan.

'Are these your men?' the OZNA officer asked Djordje.

'One of them is,' Djordje replied. 'Where did you find them? What happened to them?'

The man smiled at Djordje.

'It seems they ran into a Cetnik ambush,' he said, and described the place where the bodies had been found.

Djordje stared at him in disbelief, liking neither the man's apparent pleasure at his gruesome discovery nor his story. The chances of Cetnik raiders operating where Partisan support was a hundred per cent was as unlikely as hell freezing over. Either the OZNA man had got the location wrong or he was lying in his teeth. The ambush story looked stranger still when one of Djordje's guards drew his attention to the dead men's injuries. Both men had been shot in the back of the head and – the wounds indicated – from very close range.

'You and I had better have a talk,' Djordje told the

OZNA officer. Alone with him in his Command Post, he did not beat about the bush. 'Now I want the truth, Comrade. . .?'

'Zarko,' the other provided, unruffled by Djordje's no-nonsense manner. He became almost conspiratorial. 'I can be frank with you, Comrade General. What I told you outside is the official version of what happened – the one that you will allow to be circulated.'

'Is that so?' Djordje replied, his anger rising. 'And what is the unofficial version? Do you know who these dead men are?'

Zarko smiled.

'Of course. They are traitors, both of them. The name of the American is Mannion. The other is not known to us, but he was obviously in league with the American because he tried to support Mannion's ridiculous story that he was working for some relief organisation.' Djordje was staring at Zarko aghast, unable to believe his ears.

'You – questioned them? And then you shot them? Is that what you are telling me?'

'In the strictest confidence, Comrade General,' Zarko replied blandly. 'We do not want the traitor Mannion's associates to be put on guard by learning that he has paid for his crimes against the Party. Better to let them think that he died in a Cetnik ambush. One of them is very high up in the Party – a member of the Central Committee.'

Djordje could scarcely contain his anger and his shock, but he retained a semblance of calm. He had to know more. He encouraged the talkative Zarko.

'Anyone I know?' he asked icily. 'As you know, I am a member of the Central Committee, and I was unaware that I shared that honour with traitors. I had better be on my guard.'

'These things are not easy to prove,' Zarko said, 'but you must know the man we suspect . . . . Stefan Markovic. Have you met him?'

'I recommended him for the Central Committee,' Djordje declared, with a note of angry challenge in his voice.

Zarko did not seem to notice it.

'Then your help will be invaluable,' he said eagerly. 'You can tell us things about him that will help us to nail him.'

'I'll see you in hell first!' Djordje roared in his face. 'Guard!' he shouted.

A guard came in through the door at a run.

'Arrest this man,' Djordje ordered him.

Zarko started to reach for the revolver at his belt, but Djordje felled him with a blow of his fist. The guard disarmed the AZNO officer as he lay on the floor. The fallen Zarko stared up groggily at Djordje, uncomprehending and angry.

'You're making a great mistake, Comrade General,' he growled. 'You will regret this.'

'Not so much as you,' Djordje growled back. 'And the mistakes that you've made are going to take some beating! Unfortunately, it's going to be the entire movement that will have to pay for your blundering incompetence and stupidity. Shooting you is not going to pacify anybody but, by God, it'll do to be going on with!'

'You're crazy!' Zarko howled.

'Crazy?' echoed Djordje. 'You imbeciles don't even know what it is you've done! That's no dead traitor you've got out there!' he roared. 'And no American! You and your idiots have shot a neutral! A Swede! Who was what he said he was – a relief organisation worker! A man who was under our protection. And the officer who was with him was one of the bravest men in this Command – and no traitor! I have a mind to hand you over to his family, so they can cut you up and throw you to the crows!'

Djordje was working alone in his Command Post when

576

Mannion was shown in. He sat at a table, writing by the light from two candles which had been waxed into the necks of old wine bottles. He looked up as Mannion entered.

'Did you think I had forgotten my promise?' he asked with a smile.

'I was beginning to think you had,' Mannion admitted. 'It'll be a big day tomorrow. I was just about to turn in when I got your message.'

'Your friend Major Blair thinks very highly of you. He has presented a very strong case in favour of you being allowed to serve with the British. They want to give you a temporary commission in their Army, with the rank of captain. When I spoke to him yesterday, I told him that we rated you a lot more highly than that and that we couldn't afford to lose men of your calibre. Besides – ' Djordje waved a hand airily – 'it is all so ... so irregular.'

'He hinted that you weren't keen, Comrade General.' Mannion smiled resignedly. 'He bet me a bottle of Scotch whisky that you would veto the idea.'

'Yesterday, he would have won his bet,' Djordje said.

'Yesterday?' Mannion brightened. 'Does that mean that you're going to let me go?' When Djordje said nothing, he added, 'I'll go off my head if I've got to stay in that office in Bari. The move would only be temporary. . . .'

'No, comrade,' Djordje said, with a gravity that surprised Mannion. 'The move will be final, permanent.' He handed Mannion a sheet of paper. 'This is your full and final discharge from the Army of National Liberation.' Mannion bent nearer the candles to read the neatly typed document, when Djordje's words registered.

'Did you say *full and final discharge*?'

'Read it,' Djordje instructed.

Mannion did so, with growing astonishment. It was a

577

testimonial. It recorded the gratitude of the JANL (Montenegro Command) and AVNOJ – the Anti-Fascist Council for the Liberation of Jugoslavia – to the American volunteer, Bradislav Mannion, for his loyalty and fortitude in the struggle against the Fascist invaders of Jugoslavia, 1941–1944. It listed, with names, places and dates, instances of Mannion's conspicuous bravery in battle, and confirmed that he had been honourably discharged and exempted from further service on this day, Monday, 21 August 1944.

The document had been signed by the JANL's military commanders in Montenegro, by two members of the civil government, AVNOJ, and by Djordje, on behalf of the Central Committee of the Communist Party.

'I don't understand,' Mannion said, staring at Djordje.

'It is the least I can do for your protection,' Djordje said. 'You have enemies among us that you know nothing about. I myself knew nothing of their existence until yesterday.' He told Mannion of Nilsen's murder at the hands of the OZNA officers, adding that he had placed them in close custody and had their escort troop disarmed.

Mannion was flabbergasted.

'They killed Nilsen, believing it was me? But why?'

'Partly because of their own incredible stupidity,' Djordje said. 'They were looking for an American and, clearly, they had very little to go on. They picked on that poor Swede for no other reason than that he *looked* American. Then they tried to beat him into confessing that his name was Mannion and that he was a spy. The more he protested that his name was Nilsen and that he worked for UNRRA, the more he convinced them that he was lying. So, they shot him – *and* the man we had looking after him!'

'But why should they be looking for me?' Mannion

asked, bewildered. 'Why should they think that I was a spy?'

'Not just you, comrade,' Djordje said bitterly. 'They suspect anyone who had as much as a passing acquaintance with your old friend Marko Markovic. At the top of their list – and the man they're really after – is Marko's brother, Stefan. Which is the most ridiculous thing I've ever heard. They're after your other friend from Belgrade, too – the one you call Jamie.'

'But it's a nonsense!' Mannion exploded. 'I've never heard of anything so crazy!'

'You don't have to tell me,' Djordje agreed angrily. 'But these murdering idiots weren't playing games. And don't think they don't have power. They do. So much, that it frightens me. If they don't have their wings clipped now, nobody will be safe from them.'

'Why are they picking on Marko's friends?'

'That takes a bit of believing, too,' Djordje said. 'All I know about it is what I've been able to get from the fools who came here looking for you. They say that Marko deserted to the Germans and told them all about our Supreme Headquarters set-up in Drvar.'

'I don't believe it!' Mannion protested.

'Neither did I, at first – and I didn't know the man as well as you. But I know his brother. And the idea of any brother of Stefan's going over to the Germans was inconceivable to me. But it seems he did betray us.'

'You believe it?'

'*Stefan* must have believed it. Stefan killed him. Stefan shot his own brother.'

Mannion stared at Djordje in horror.

'Stefan shot Marko?'

'When the Germans attacked Drvar in May. Or so those OZNA bravos say. Apparently Marko had been sent to a punishment battalion for some crime or other, but he deserted. Then he was taken prisoner at Drvar, wearing a German uniform. They say that nobody got the chance to question him . . . that Stefan just pulled out a gun and shot him dead. Now they're saying that Stefan shot Marko in order to save himself – that he did it to stop Marko talking and incriminating him.'

Mannion was silent. It was too much to take in. He had liked Marko, shared many a tight spot with him. He could not conceive of him turning traitor. He was numbed by what Djordje had told him.

'Now you know why I no longer have any hesitation in supporting your wish to fight with the British,' Djordje said. 'And why the severance must be final. I cannot guarantee your safety from these OZNA maniacs if you remain as one of us. They have a nasty habit of killing their suspects and considering the matter of guilt or innocence posthumously. You will be safer with the British.'

'What will you do with Nilsen's killers?' Mannion asked.

'They will be executed for their crime,' Djordje said flatly. 'That may help to lay the dust that's going to rise when news of his death gets out.'

'What about you, Comrade General?' Mannion stared at Djordje with troubled eyes. 'Where will that leave you? If OZNA's part of the party apparatus, won't you be bringing trouble on yourself if you shoot these guys?'

'I think there is every likelihood of that,' Djordje replied with a smile. 'But leave me to worry about that. I am prepared to fight within the Party for the kind of party I believe it should be. You may not know it, but Marshal Tito once introduced me at a rally of the faithful as the Conscience of the Party in Jugoslavia. It will be a sad day for all of us if the time ever comes when the Party is no longer willing to listen to its Conscience.'

Smiling, and suddenly feeling a great affection for Djordje, Mannion thrust out his hand.

'Will you shake my hand, Comrade General?' he

asked. 'It has been a privilege to have served under you
. . . to have known you. I'm grateful to have had that
honour.'

Djordje took the proffered hand and pulled Mannion
to him in a comradely hug. He kissed the American on
both cheeks.

'Good fortune, my friend,' he declared. 'I shall never
forget you. And I shall never forget the service you have
given to Jugoslavia. Now go. And tell your friend Blair
that he owes you a bottle of whisky.'

At the doorway, Mannion paused.

'I have only one regret,' he said, 'and I want you to
know it, Comrade General. From all I hear, Marshal
Tito seems a pretty good guy . . . but I've always thought
it's a pity that it wasn't you running the show.'

He did not wait for Djordje's reaction – which,
typically, was one of amusement, tinged with pleasure at
the compliment.

With the first light of the morning came the first of the
great armada of USAAF and RAF DC-3 transports which
were to stream to Bajovo Polje throughout the hours of
daylight and airlift more than a thousand Partisan
wounded to the safety of hospitals in Italy. With the
aircraft came the Allied nurses and doctors who had
volunteered to minister in flight to the wounded.

Not all were to survive the hazardous mission. Seven
aircraft were destined not to make it back to base. The
hazards increasing as the day wore on. As anticipated,
German reaction was swift and a fierce ground attack
was launched towards Bajovo Polje. By noon, the
airfield was within range of the German guns, with the
result that the transports had to run a gauntlet of fire as
they landed and took off. By evening, although the
attack was still being held, the situation was critical. But
still the aircraft continued. Blair and Mannion were
slotted for the last aircraft – but only if there was room.
The wounded took precedence.

In the event, there was room to spare. The red disc of the sun was slipping below the horizon when the penultimate DC-3 took off across the field and lifted away, leaving only half a dozen casualties to be evacuated. These wounded were hoisted through the door of the last aircraft into the waiting hands of the in-flight medical team. They were followed by a doctor, several nurses and the aircrew of a transport which had crash-landed on the field earlier in the day, with its landing gear shot away. The wrecked aircraft still sat at the edge of the field – a reminder to all of the risks run by the mercy fliers in their unarmed air ambulances.

It was nearly dark when Mannion boarded the DC-3. It was lumbering into its takeoff run as the door was closed after him. His last view of Bajovo Polje, through a fuselage port, was of crimson tracer shells cutting fiery trails through the evening dusk as the aircraft powered into flight and banked away to the west.

6

Cold Wind from the East

As the summer of 1944 faded and another winter loomed, the struggle within Jugoslavia was delicately balanced. But a new and hitherto unseen element was about to make its presence felt in a decisive manner. Ahead of the winter, the Red Army arrived like a gale from the east.

A decade had passed since that other summer in Belgrade when the lives of Jamie, Stefan, Mannion, Petar and Marko first touched and intermingled. Ten turbulent years had passed, tossing them this way and that in the whirlpool confusion of events which had caught them in its swirling currents. None had been able to exert much control over the direction of their lives or the shape of their relationships with each other. Their fates had been governed less by their desires and hopes than by the fickle chance that their destinies might collide like corks trapped in the boiling surge of a millrace.

They were well scattered at the decade's end, flung far and wide by the whirlpool's whim to cast them where it swirled: Jamie to the inhospitable Karst of Bosnia-Hercegovina; Mannion to Italy; Mara, with her field hospital, to the high-plateau oasis that was the town of Mostar; Petar, with his German battalion to Belgrade; Marko to an unmarked grave in Drvar; and Stefan to Serbia.

Only one of the six had made a conscious decision at the outset to try to influence the course of events. In his commitment to revolution and Communism, Stefan

Markovic had sought in his way, however small, to make his imprint on history. It was perhaps ironic, therefore, that Stefan – the one most committed to change and pursuit of the power to change – was the one most changed by changing fortune.

Belgrade was where it had begun for Stefan, and it was on his return to Belgrade that he found his faith wavering. Corrosive doubts were already at work by then, tormenting him with the very real fear that his vision of the promised land was illusory, and had been all along. It took the sweetness from the taste of victory.

Stefan had flown from Italy to a secret airfield in Serbia, charged with the certainty that the defeat of Germany was only a matter of time. And, if he had nursed any fears that Partisan support in Serbia had been extinguished, these vanished within days of his return to that staunchly royalist territory. The Partisan armies in Serbia might have been decimated in 1941–42, but the ashes of the fires they lit had not been stamped out. Now, they only needed fanning into fresh flame. In every town, village and hamlet across the mountainous land, the cells and cadres had been organising in expectation of a fresh call to rise against the invader. And to them, like a runner bearing a fiery cross, Stefan brought that call.

Everywhere that Stefan went, it was the same: volunteers flocked to join the Partisan cause. Cetniks, disillusioned by their own leaders and encouraged by the news that King Peter now recognised Tito as a patriotic leader, came over in their thousands to answer Stefan's rallying call.

Not all the Cetnik bands were ready to throw in their lot with the Partisans, however, and only the Germans drew satisfaction when fresh fighting flared up between Serb and Serb. But the tide had turned against the once predominant Cetniks, and events were now moving at a breathless pace in a manner that did nothing to strengthen their hand.

News of what was happening beyond the borders of Serbia came mainly via radios tuned to the BBC in London. On the day after Mannion had flown out from Montenegro with the Partisan wounded, Germany's ally Romania deserted Hitler. King Michael dismissed the puppet dictator Antonescu and sued for peace with the Western Allies. The German response was prompt. They bombed Bucharest and sent troops against the city. The attacks were repelled by the Romanian Royal Guard. Three days after Antonescu's fall, the new Romanian Government declared war on Germany.

On the very next day, Bulgaria announced that it was getting out of the war, too, and started disarming German troops stationed in the country. In the meantime, Russian troops moved into Romania and were soon occupying the oilfields of Ploesti. It took them only another day to cover the fifty-five kilometres south to Bucharest, where huge crowds greeted them as liberators.

On September the fifth, Russia declared war on Bulgaria. In less than six hours, Bulgaria was seeking an armistice. On September the eighth, Bulgaria declared war on Germany. Two days earlier, the Russian army that had swept unopposed across Romania had reached the Danube. On the other bank, Jugoslavia lay before them, but the Russians awaited Tito's invitation to cross. It was not long in coming.

It was in the days that followed that Stefan first began to have misgivings about the cause he had embraced. He was unhappy when Radio Free Jugoslavia announced that Tito had landed in Serbia, having flown in from his headquarters in Vis, and had been welcomed by cheering crowds. In was an outright lie, aimed at convincing the British and Americans that Serbia was as wholeheartedly behind Tito as the rest of Jugoslavia. And – in Stefan's view – it was an unnecessary lie. In fact, Tito had not set foot on Serbian soil. He had flown to Russia via Romania, to confer secretly with Stalin.

Confusion reigned, meantime, along Jugoslavia's frontiers with Romania and Bulgaria. The Russians crossed the Danube, to be welcomed by bands of Cetniks, who readily linked forces with them to drive on Pancevo and Belgrade. Further south, where Stefan was, Partisans were engaged in furious battles with Cetniks – and had to force a way through them in order to join hands with the Russian troops who had crossed into Jugoslavia from Turnu-Severin in Romania. Still further south, Partisans were happily cooperating with the hated Bulgars, whom the Russians had persuaded to throw two armies into the fray. In the Sumadija, Cetniks had joined with the Germans to fight the growing Partisan forces.

In every liberated town and village, the Partisans – with their highly organised political echelons – were ready to take over as the civil authority, while the disorganised Cetniks were not. They did so in the name of AVNOJ, the all-party Council of National Liberation, but made sure that all the AVNOJ councils and committees which they set up – had enough Communists aboard to outvote all the other representatives. Although no Communist was more dedicated to the cause than Stefan, even he had reservations about some of the heavy-handed tactics used to ensure Communist domination. He had a grudging respect for the democratic parties who had opposed the prewar dictatorship as resolutely as the Communists but had eschewed revolution or violence as a means of removing it. Now, it disturbed him when these same idealistic democrats were brushed aside where they sought a share of political power. Stefan was particularly disturbed when patriotic democrats who had fought Fascism from the outset were accused of being collaborators or self-seeking nationalists, and executed out of hand. Their only crime, as far as Stefan could see, was to demand a bigger say in government in the wake of a victory they had helped to win.

The immediate prize was Belgrade – and it fell to Russian and Partisan forces on October the twentieth, within six weeks of the Russians entering Jugoslavia. It should have been a momentous occasion for Stefan as he rode up King Milan Street in a commandeered car, a red flag with the five-pointed Partisan star fluttering bravely from a stick lashed to the door-pillar, but the devastation of the city sickened him, and it dismayed him that the capital owed its liberation to the Russians. Only six weeks had passed since Stefan welcomed the Russians with open arms, ready to love them. Here, at last, were the saviours of mankind; the apostles of revolutionary socialism; the godlike sons of the great god Stalin himself. Stefan had overflowed with goodwill as he greeted the Red Army with tears of joy and an open heart. Six weeks later, he was beginning to hate them, and he rode into Belgrade with the sombre look of a sadly disillusioned man.

At first, Stefan had blamed himself for his disappointment in the Russians. He told himself that he had expected too much of them; that their soldiers could not all be perfect ambassadors and shining examples of the world's prime Communist state. But the more he saw of them and the more he made allowances, the more appalled he became.

They showed no overt friendliness, treating all Jugoslavs, if not with hostility, with a contemptuous disdain. Their ordinary soldiers displayed an animal-like ferocity, which no doubt was an admirable trait in battle, but which alarmed and disgusted the hospitable Serbs who opened their doors to them. They treated the native population not as hosts, but as a conquered people: vassals without rights.

It shocked the Serbs to find that most of the Russian soldiers were primitive illiterates with no conception of where in the world they were. They had never heard of Jugoslavia, and it meant nothing to them when told that

that was where they were. They could have been told they were in Timbuctoo or Greenland for all the relevance it had.

Wearing a Partisan uniform and boasting the rank of lieutenant-general did not save Stefan from indignity at the hands of the soldiery, but it gave him a shock introduction to their bullying rudeness and acquisitive habits. Paying a courtesy call to one of their units, he was jostled and pushed by Russians who accused him of spying on them. He was rescued from their hands by an officer, eventually, but not before he had been relieved of his wristwatch and the cigarettes in his pocket. The officer was uninterested in his complaints about the theft of his personal possessions, and more or less accused Stefan of deliberately encouraging the outrage by flaunting such a prize as a gold watch on his wrist.

Stefan's misfortune was little compared with what others suffered at the hands of the Russian comrades. Wherever he went, Stefan was bombarded with complaints from outraged Serbs about wives and daughters being raped; homes ransacked and looted; beatings, robberies, murder. In an effort to end these depredations, Stefan sought an interview with the Russian commander, General Korneyev. He was given short shrift from this coarse and obnoxious man, who laughed contemptuously in his face and told him that the Jugoslavs should get down on their knees and thank their liberators instead of wasting his time by moaning about the behaviour of his troops. His men had fought halfway across Europe and, if they indulged themselves by taking a woman or filling their bellies by slaughtering some farmer's pigs, it was only their entitlement. Stefan emerged from the interview white-faced with shock and fury. A colleague who had accompanied Stefan – a former schoolmaster – commented: 'As an ambassador for Russia and Communism, that Korneyev does for the ideology of international socialism what the Vandals did for third-century civilisation.'

The liberation of Belgrade and the arrival there, a week later, of Tito did nothing to curb Russian excesses. Another Central Committee member – angered by sneering Russian comments on the fighting capabilities of the Partisans – saw fit to confront Korneyev in a snarling match. It came close to causing an international incident, and the official concerned – a cultured man – was later to earn the personal odium of Stalin, to whom it was duly reported.

In November, anti-Russian feeling in Belgrade reached a peak after a particularly gruesome incident in the outlying district of Cukarica. Soviet soldiers seized a pretty twenty-five-year-old woman and raped her in turn. When they had had their fun, they wantonly killed her by slashing her open from neck to belly with a bayonet. There was a public outcry that such a girl – she was a model of respectability and worked as a chemist – should be so abused and mutilated. But the Russians made no move to punish the culprits.

Stefan felt obliged to attend the young woman's funeral as a way of displaying publicly his own anger and disapproval. To his surprise, he was not alone. A crowd of several thousand turned the funeral into a demonstration of public anger. In spite of the numbers, Stefan's presence did not go unnoticed. Next day, he received a visit from Chief Commissar Gubec of OZNA.

'This is just a friendly call,' he advised Stefan. 'I hope you can spare a few minutes of your time.' Considering the hour – it was six-thirty in the morning and not yet light – Stefan was surprised, to say the least. And he had never liked Gubec. Since first encountering him in Uzice in 1941, there had been a mutual antipathy between them and very little contact.

Stefan had been shaving when Gubec knocked at the door. He invited the commissar into the shabby little hotel room which had been his personal quarters since the return to Belgrade, not troubling to conceal his irritation.

'I'll shave while you tell me what it is you want,' he said to Gubec. 'I don't have much time. A car's coming to take me out to the Srem Front this morning.'

Gubec parked himself on the end of the unmade bed and looked around with distaste.

'Is this place the best you can do for yourself, Comrade General?' he inquired sniffily. 'I should have thought that one of the Central Committee could do a little better.'

'It's quite adequate for my needs,' Stefan replied. He despised those Party officials who sought out luxurious accommodation as a right of rank. 'Why do you want to see me, Chief Commissar?'

'There has been talk, Comrade General.'

'Talk?'

'About you, Comrade General. And many rumours.'

Stefan put down his razor and stared at him.

'Why should anyone bother to talk about me? What kind of rumours?'

'That you have Trotskyite leanings.' Gubec treated Stefan to an oily smile. 'My agents hear many things.'

'Well, forget them,' Stefan said sharply. 'They're nonsense. You should know better than to pay attention to idle gossip – especially if it concerns anyone on the Central Committee.'

'Ah, that's just it, Comrade General. I cannot ignore what I hear – especially if accusations are made against the leaders of our movement. Are you trying to suggest that the Central Committee are above suspicion . . .? That they are incapable of error?'

'The man isn't born who is incapable of error,' Stefan snapped. 'That includes you, Comrade Gubec. And you're making a grave error if you think I can afford to waste my time discussing backstairs trivialities.'

'The betrayal of our Supreme Headquarters in Drvar

can scarcely be called a triviality,' Gubec said icily. 'It is a pity, is it not, that the traitor responsible did not live long enough to be questioned about his treachery?'

Stefan coloured.

'Just what the hell are you implying?' he asked angrily.

'I'm not implying anything,' Gubec said, his eyes narrowing. 'But let me ask you a question, Comrade General. Why was the Drvar traitor disposed of so hastily? Was it because the person who killed him believed that he deserved to die? Or was it because that person feared who he might betray if he lived?'

'You bastard!' Stefan cried, and grabbed Gubec by the jacket front. Gubec tried to shy away from Stefan's raised hand, which still clutched his open razor – but Stefan made no move to strike. He let Gubec go and turned away, his face twisted with anger. 'You'd better go,' he snarled at the Commissar, 'or by God, I may kill you, like I killed my brother!'

Gubec remained sitting on the bed, staring at Stefan and saying nothing. Stefan rounded on him.

'I don't know what the hell it is you're trying to accuse me of, Gubec, but you'd better come right out in the open and say it to my face or, by heaven, I'll drag you up to Marshal Tito himself and demand that you're thrown out of the Party.'

'That won't be necessary,' Gubec growled, standing up. 'The Marshal knows you are under suspicion.' Stefan blanched at the revelation but Gubec seemed not to notice. With a shrug of his shoulders, the Commissar added: 'Oh, Marshal Tito regards you highly and believes you incapable of error but we of OZNA have to be vigilant at all times. It disturbs me greatly, Comrade General, that while so many questions about the treachery of your brother remain unanswered, your conduct should again draw you to the attention of my agents.'

591

'Just what the hell are you talking about?' Stefan demanded.

Gubec frowned.

'Taking part in a demonstration against our Russian comrades was not the most prudent of activities for a member of the Central Committee. It betrays an incredible insensitivity to the aims and interest of the Party.'

'I attended a funeral,' said Stefan, keeping his anger under control.

Gubec stood up.

'The next one could be your own,' he warned, eyes glittering.

'And what the hell is that supposed to mean?' Stefan flared. 'Are you threatening me?'

Gubec shrugged placidly.

'Why should I threaten you? I came here as a friend . . . and because I respect Marshal Tito, who takes a protective attitude towards you. It would be regrettable if something unfortunate were to happen to you that was, well, outwith my control.'

'Just what are you trying to say?'

'That you have enemies, Comrade General. And mistakes can be made. . . .' Again he shrugged, and made a gesture with his hands, suggesting helplessness. 'Marshal Tito himself has signed the order that has been given to all my men, that all enemies of the Party are to be shot on the spot. You must know about it. The decision was made by the Central Committee.'

'That order referred to traitors – those who were known to be supporters of the renegades Nedic and Ljotic.' Stefan was incensed that Gubec insinuated he might be classed with collaborators.

Gubec smiled.

'But that's the point, Comrade General. Yesterday, you took part in an anti-Russian demonstration that was undoubtedly organised by Nedic's troublemakers. We let things go because the numbers surprised us. But if that kind of thing happens again, the bullets will fly. It would be unfortunate if someone like yourself should be among the casualties.'

'You're talking nonsense,' Stefan protested. 'That crowd yesterday was not organised. These were just ordinary people – people who were outraged at the way that girl was butchered and nothing done about it.'

Gubec frowned.

'I do not propose to argue about it, Comrade General. I have delivered my warning.' He moved towards the door. Stefan followed him.

'Not so fast, Comrade Commissar. Let me give you a warning. I've heard a lot in the past few weeks about your OZNA goons, and I haven't liked much of what I've heard. It's high time the Central Committee clipped their wings – and I intend to put the matter to them at the first opportunity I have.'

Gubec seemed in no way discomfited.

'You may find that I have more friends on the Central Committee than you, Comrade General,' he sneered. In icy tones, he added: 'And I would thank you not to refer to my agents as goons.'

'That's what they are,' Stefan flamed. 'Trigger-happy goons.'

Anger showed on Gubec's face.

'Not quite so trigger-happy as your Montenegrin friend Djordje,' he snarled. 'Both you and he will answer to me one day.'

Stefan met his blustering threat with a grin.

'Now you're talking like the old Comrade Gubec we used to know,' he taunted him. 'Now the truth is coming out. We clipped your wings in Uzice, didn't we? And that's what this is all about. You've never forgiven us.'

There was no concealment of the hate in Gubec's face now, but he tried to keep a semblance of composure.

'I won't pretend that I admire either of you,' he

mumbled. 'You intellectuals are all the same. You think you're a cut above the rest of us. But you're right about one thing. I don't forgive . . . and I don't forget! I'll get you all in the end – because you'll keep on giving me more and more rope to hang you with.'

'Now you're talking,' Stefan egged him on. 'Spill it all, Gubec. Show me you're still the same repulsive moron I used to know.'

The OZNA chief needed little egging on. He faced Stefan, livid with rage.

'Tito won't always be there to protect you,' he blustered. 'Neither you nor your Montenegrin friend. Nor your other friends – the American and the other foreigner, with the English name. I have dossiers on all of you. Every one of you who had anything to do with that traitor brother of yours. I'll get you all!'

'You're crazy!' Stefan roared at him, appalled that somehow Gubec was bringing Jamie and Mannion into his vindictive scheming. The man clearly had to be stopped. But, in the meantime, Stefan had had enough of him. He pushed him out of the door. 'Get out of my sight,' he ordered him. 'Go and take a swim in the Sava!'

Gubec departed, still howling threats.

It did not occur to Stefan to seek other than 'democratic processes' as a means of having Gubec removed from office and the activities of OZNA curtailed. Consequently, he wrote a paper for discussion by the Central Committee, which he entitled: 'OZNA – Excesses and Accountability to the Party.'

It was a reasoned and moderate document, which praised OZNA's contribution to the war effort – an abundant flow of high-value military intelligence. It called into question, however, OZNA's wide powers to weed out and deal summarily with class enemies, factionalists, traitors, war criminals, revisionists, etc. It gave to the officers of OZNA the right to be principal accuser and also that of judge, jury and executioner. As the penalty allotted in most cases was death, there was no redress available for offenders whose guilt was in doubt or who were subsequently found to be innocent. This, Stefan argued, was an indefensible practice, which offended against all the laws of natural justice and made it easy for great injustices to occur.

Stefan warned that, if the powers and apparatus of OZNA were allowed to develop unchecked, they would automatically become an inbuilt part of the postwar Communist government which the Party hoped to establish in Jugoslavia after Germany's defeat. If this happened, OZNA could become a secret police force with the capacity to terrorise ordinary people to a far greater extent than the secret police of the prewar dictatorship. The object of Communist revolution, he argued, was to free the people from injustice, not to impose a regime that perpetuated the injustices of the past.

In his discussion paper, he did not name Gubec and advocate his dismissal per se – but he did advocate the break-up of the OZNA organisation into smaller and separate units, which would be controlled by watchdog committees to guard against any units retaining power. All would be accountable for their actions, and a legal apparatus would be installed overall to ensure that offenders against the Party or the Communist state-to-be were given the right to a fair trial before competent judges or people's juries. A right to appeal against conviction would also be incorporated in the system.

Stefan was proud of his document – because so much of it embodied what he saw as the tenets of the freedom that only revolution could bring. These ideas, he believed, also lay at the heart of his countrymen's struggle and sacrifice during the long years of war. It came as a profound shock to him, therefore, when the Central Committee dismissed his document with scorn and condemnation, as if it were a pronouncement of blasphemy. The few in favour of OZNA's reconstruction were intimidated by those who argued vehemently that, without OZNA's protective zeal, the Party would be infiltrated by self-seekers and traitors, and the Party's class enemies would have a free hand to establish the old order. The paper was condemned as a 'charter for Cetniks and royalist plotters'.

Even Tito, although he was not condemnatory of the document's author or forceful in his criticism, opined that it was 'perhaps premature'. He conceded that a good deal of noble idealism had gone into the paper, but there was some naivety, too. OZNA had proved to be an intelligence-gathering machine whose value to the military command was incalculable, and he thought that the present was the wrong time to start tinkering with its apparatus.

Stefan was plunged into gloom by his defeat. The blindness of his colleagues, and their seeming lust to avenge themselves on those Jugoslavs whom they deemed anti-Communist, saddened rather than angered him. It stirred in him even deeper fears that a Communist Jugoslavia might not prove to be the Utopia of his vision. The thought was heartbreaking. He tried to tell himself that it was not the principles of international socialism that were imperfect; the imperfections were in man.

Winter came to Belgrade and its greyness was no bleaker than the chill gloom that held Stefan in its grip. There was no let-up in the war but, on the Srem Front, the Germans continued to beat off attack after attack by the Partisans, inflicting appalling losses. Morale fell and tempers rose at Supreme Headquarters when a single German battalion destroyed an entire Partisan division that had been thrown against it. Stefan questioned the tactics – and was immediately accused on all sides of maligning the fighting qualities of the Partisan soldiers, which, of course, he had not. He deplored their waste but felt their readiness to die was being exploited by commanders who had been angered by Russian comments that the Partisans could not fight a frontal war.

Stefan was further dismayed by the behaviour of his fellow members of the Central Committee. As the banners and slogans of Communism adorned Belgrade in growing profusion, the fiercer became the jockeying by the Party leaders to appropriate the most palatial dwellings for themselves, their families and their relations. Stefan stood aloof from the undignified scramble to acquire the finest villas in Dedinje, a suburb which, traditionally, housed Belgrade's richest and most well-to-do citizens. A new order was taking over and – it seemed to Stefan – it intended to acquire, as a right, the dwellings and life style of the regime it had displaced.

Not all of liberated Jugoslavia submitted meekly to Communist rule. In the south, throughout Macedonia and Kosovo, the Muslim population – mainly those of Albanian extraction – resisted the programmes of 're-education' and conscription to the Partisan armies, and rose in rebellion. The first conflict flared up in December, 1944, and – unknown to the outside world – it was to drag on for three months before it was finally suppressed in ruthless fashion by a Partisan army.

In January 1945, Stefan – although he had sought a job with the party's official newspaper, *Borba*, where he could exercise his talents as a writer – was appointed to a post with the oversight of army recruitment and conscription. It was important enough work, but he felt a little slighted at his exclusion from the agitprop division, where he might have made a positive contribution to the dissemination of ideas. It was as if his recent differences with other members of the leadership had earned him a step sideways, with the design of keeping him quiet.

Even his choice of modest quarters had earned him criticism from his peers, who interpreted it as a deliberate attempt to remain aloof from them. More to keep the peace with them than through any desire to move to more comfortable surroundings, he gave in to pressure and took up residence in a well-appointed city apartment, from which a prominent banker and his family had been evicted. It was luxurious, compared with the drab little hotel where he had roomed; and it was serviced by a caretaking staff on the ground floor. Unless he gave orders to the contrary, a hot meal was waiting for him in the kitchen oven on his return in the evenings, and all the heaters had been lit to provide a welcoming warmth. It niggled at Stefan's conscience that, despite a chronic shortage of fuel, his own quarters were like a hothouse, but he was human enough to enjoy the comfort and made no move to effect economies.

On one particular bitter January evening, he had eaten and settled down to listen to Radio Moscow when there was a knock at the apartment door. He sighed in irritation. The newsreader had just announced an important communiqué from the Polish Front and was about to give details.

Stefan opened the door, and gawped in surprise at his unexpected visitor. The bulky greatcoat and Russian military cap did not altogether conceal the fact that his caller was a woman, and an exceptionally pretty one at that. Saucerlike eyes stared up at him from a pert gamine face with a questioning wonder.

'Comrade General Markovic?'

'Yes?'

'I am *Starshiy Leytenant* Karpov. I have something for you. May I come in?'

Stefan stood aside to let her enter, and then led her through to the sitting room. The voice from Radio Moscow droned on sonorously.

'An important announcement,' Stefan murmured

apologetically. 'Perhaps you will want to hear it, too?'

'Of course, please,' the girl assented. 'I am sorry if I am disturbing you.'

They both listened attentively as the Moscow broadcaster gave news of three bridgeheads which the Red Army had established by forcing the River Vistula to the north and south of Warsaw. It was expected that the Polish capital would fall to Zhukov's forces within the next seventy-two hours. The news excited Stefan's caller.

'All Poland will rejoice,' she said happily.

Stefan frowned at her.

'Perhaps,' he commented bitterly, 'the people of Warsaw may think that Zhukov has left things a little late. He has been sitting on the Vistula for four months now, and he did not lift a hand when the Poles were crying out for his help.' Stefan was not the only Jugoslav Communist to have been anguished by the Russian failure to assist the Polish patriots who had risen against the Germans in Warsaw. Even the most ardent Russophiles had been shocked by the Red Army's cynical inertia, a few miles distant, while the SS starved the insurgents into surrender and razed Warsaw to the ground in a calculated act of vengeance.

'General Zhukov would have saved the people of Warsaw if he could,' Stefan's pretty young visitor defended spiritedly. 'But he was too far ahead of his supplies. Do you think he did not suffer torments of frustration to be so near and yet so powerless to help?'

The girl seemed so hurt by Stefan's comment criticising her compatriots that he felt impelled to relent.

'Perhaps it is wrong to judge these things from so far away,' he admitted with a smile. 'I'm sorry if I have offended you.'

The frown left her face in an instant and her answering smile was warm and gracious.

'This war,' she said, with a little shake of her head. 'So much is difficult to understand.'

Stefan switched off the radio.

'We'll let the war take care of itself,' he said. 'You said you had something for me?'

Again, she flashed the dazzling smile. 'I come with an apology,' she said, 'and with a token of friendship between our peoples.' She treated him to a round-eyed gaze. 'May I take off this heavy coat?'

Stefan helped her off with her coat and she took off the ungainly cap to reveal short bobbed hair, enhancing her comeliness at a stroke.

'It's very warm in here,' she murmured and, without Stefan's leave, undid the buttons of her heavy tunic and threw it over a chair. Her undershirt was collarless – a floppy shapeless garment, unbuttoned at the low neck and inadequately covering the pale skin of her thrusting, unsupported bosom. Its immodesty did not seem to trouble her half so much as it troubled Stefan. He was unsure where to look.

'May I offer you some wine?' he asked politely, trying to cover his embarrassment.

'Thank you,' she said. 'We must toast the friendship of our peoples, but please – ' She broke off and crossed to the couch on which Stefan had draped her coat. 'From this,' she said, producing a bottle of vodka from a cavernous pocket. 'If you have two glasses. . .? I insist.'

Stefan fetched two glasses and watched her pour, enchanted by her prettiness and open friendliness. He wasn't quite sure what to expect next. She handed him an overflowing glass and then scurried to the greatcoat. From another pocket, she extracted a small package, which she presented to Stefan with a beaming smile.

'I bring you this small gift with fraternal wishes,' she said. 'It comes as a token of continued friendship between the Soviet people and the glorious freedom fighters of Jugoslavia. We apologise for the loss you unfortunately suffered, and it is our hope that any past misunderstandings may be forgotten.'

She urged Stefan to open the package and watched, smiling, as he tore away the wrappings. Removing the lid from the rectangular box he uncovered, he found himself staring at a magnificent gold wristwatch with a matching gilt band. It was the finest-looking watch he had ever seen.

'I . . . I don't know what to say,' he murmured, tears glistening in his eyes. He was deeply moved. The despair that had gripped him for weeks melted away in the rush of warm emotion that filled him, making him wonder why he had ever come to doubt the Russians. At a time when disillusion with his own comrades was at a peak and he was convinced that the culture gap between the Jugoslavs and their Russian allies was rapidly becoming an unbridgeable chasm, the Soviets had extended an olive branch. It was – as the attractive Lieutenant Karpov said – a small token of friendship, a compensation for the loss of his own watch; but it was so thoughtful and so unexpected that Stefan was quite overwhelmed. At a time when acts of reconciliation were as rare as cherry blossoms in winter, the deed shone with bright new hope for the future.

'I shall treasure this,' Stefan said, stammering out his thanks. 'When my watch was stolen, I didn't make a song about it, and none of your people seemed the least concerned. I was obviously mistaken. . . .'

Lieutenant Karpov frowned.

'You have my assurance, comrade, that when it was realised that you had been robbed and insulted by criminal elements amongst our soldiers, there was the most rigorous inquiry. The men responsible were found and severely punished. Unfortunately the stolen property was not recovered. We regret this deeply. We realise that the watch which was stolen from you was probably of great sentimental value – '

'Not half so great as the sentimental value I shall attach to its replacement,' Stefan interrupted her. He smiled ruefully. 'To tell the truth, I stole the watch which your soldiers took – from the body of an Italian officer whose unit we ambushed.'

'There is a difference between robbing a dead enemy and robbing a comrade-in-arms who is very much alive,' she excused him.

'Perhaps,' he conceded. 'I must admit that I was much more upset by the unfriendly treatment I got than by my loss. That really knocked me sideways. It was like the end of the world. It shattered all my notions of the Soviet Union.'

She blinked her huge eyes at him, puzzled.

'But every army has its riff-raff – rough types who would steal the gold from your teeth or the boots from your feet. Surely you wouldn't judge our people by one or two ignorant savages in uniform. It's a joke with us that General Korneyev emptied half the jails between here and the Urals to fill his army.'

'Unfortunately, they didn't stop at stealing watches,' Stefan told her grimly. 'Some of the things that have happened are unforgivable.'

Her pretty face clouded and she turned her head away, downcast, as if he had accused her personally.

'I know there have been outrages,' she admitted bitterly. Then she turned to face him, her saucerlike eyes wide with agonised appeal. 'But please, please, Comrade General, you *must* forgive. You must find it in your heart to be forbearing.'

'Forbearing!' Stefan's anger flared. 'There is a limit to forbearance when innocent women are raped by gangs of Russian soldiers and then butchered like cattle!'

She winced at his words, as if each was a slap in the face. Lights of anger danced in her eyes.

'Do you think we condone these outrages?' she cried.

'You do nothing to stop them,' he retorted.

'That's not true.' Flushed with anger, she faced him. 'Can't you understand how difficult it is for us? Our generals are proud men, and it shames them when their soldiers misbehave and cause trouble with the Jugoslav people. But they resent it when your officers howl at them for vengeance and demand this and demand that. They don't need to be told.'

'But they do nothing,' Stefan protested. 'That's what makes people like me so angry and disillusioned.'

'So much so,' Lieutenant Karpov snorted, 'that you take to the streets with a mob that chants anti-Russian slogans! And you a member of the Jugoslav Party's Central Committee!'

Stefan blinked.

'You know I was at that funeral in Cukarica, do you?'

'We know everything about you, Comrade General. In Moscow, yours is a respected name. No one in the Jugoslav Party is better known for his dedication to Communism. We might not be so concerned at this anger of yours, this disillusion, if we did not see you as a future leader of Jugoslavia.'

Her calm statement astonished Stefan.

'That's very flattering,' he said. 'You must also know that my dedication to Communism is equalled only by my dedication to justice. If my presence at the funeral of an atrocity victim was seen as a protest, it was a protest at a singular absence of justice in your Army's reaction to a crime that outraged all of Belgrade.'

'The criminals were dealt with, Comrade General.'

'Were they? You've kept remarkably quiet about it.'

'Do you think we take pride in such things?' she cried. 'Do you think we want to shout our shame to the world? We executed seven soldiers – all of them brave patriots who fought through the snows of two winters and across a continent. . . .'

'I did not know about this,' Stefan said quietly. 'Even if you had told us in confidence, it would have made a difference.'

'You thought we didn't care – although apologies were made?'

603

'We doubted the sincerity of the apologies.'

'Do you still doubt them?' she asked. 'Do you doubt me?'

Stefan smiled.

'On the contrary. You'll probably never know just how much you've done to restore my faith in the mother country of Communism. I want to thank you for that. I haven't been thinking straight lately. I keep getting worked up over the least little thing.'

'Maybe you should relax more often,' she said seriously. 'Get drunk. Or take your frustrations out on one of those pretty girls who work at your secretariat. Do you never bring any of them up here?'

Stefan laughed.

'You said you knew all about me,' he accused. 'If you did, you'd know that I live like a monk and I hardly ever drink.'

She threw her hands in the air expressively. 'No wonder you are so tense!' She exclaimed. Impishly, she added: 'Does it make you uncomfortable to be in the same room with a woman? I saw how you looked at me when I took my jacket off, Comrade General. Like a little boy going hot under the collar wondering why his sister sticks out in places where he doesn't.'

Stefan blushed. Her assertion, embarrassingly, was too near the truth to be denied.

'That was cruel of me to say such a thing,' she murmured, with a coy little smile. 'If you were to beat me for it and throw me out into the night, it would be no more than I deserved. For a moment I forgot that I was a mere lieutenant and you were a general.'

'I'm the one who forgot myself,' he excused her. 'I didn't mean to stare at you.' He smiled shyly at her. 'The more we talk, the harder it becomes for me to ignore that I am a man and you are a woman ... and a very beautiful woman.'

She bowed her head modestly at the compliment.

'It has been an honour to meet you Comrade General.' She crossed to the chair where her jacket lay, and quickly put it on. He helped her into her greatcoat, trying to conceal his sudden chagrin that she intended to leave. She stirred long-subdued desires in him. When she had gone, he felt bereft and angry with himself for making no move to detain her. He had sensed that it would only take a word; that she had felt as powerful an attraction for him as he had felt for her. Now, the chance had gone, and it dismayed him to think that he might never see her again.

Restlessly, he prowled round the apartment. He switched on the radio. Radio Moscow was still going on at length about the imminent capture of Warsaw. Stefan switched it off. He tried to read, but couldn't concentrate. He went into the bathroom and lit the gas boiler above the tub. When it heated, he ran a bath and sank into the warm water, trying to shut all thought from his mind.

He was no sooner immersed than a loud knocking at the front door echoed through the apartment. Cursing, he got out, wrapped a towel round his middle and padded in his bare feet along the narrow corridor, leaving a trail of wet footprints.

He opened the door a fraction, ready to vent his anger at whoever had disturbed him. Then he saw her: standing there in her greatcoat, which still bore flakes of snow.

'My truck back to Zemun left without me,' she said. 'Can I use your telephone?'

'I was having a bath,' he explained.

'So I can see,' she said, staring, and gave a little giggle. He grinned at her.

'Come in.'

He showed her where the telephone was.

'Will they send you transport?' he asked her.

'I don't know. It's blowing a blizzard outside. You finish your bath. I'll ring headquarters.'

He padded across the room but stopped at the doorway.

'By the way, you left your bottle of vodka.'

She smiled.

'I meant to. It's yours. Off you go now, before you catch cold.'

Still he hesitated.

'What if they can't send a truck?'

Her smile dazzled.

'Then I'll join you in the bath. Don't lock the door.'

He hurried across the corridor, not sure if she had been joking or not. He ran more hot water into the tub and climbed in. He soaped his shoulders and arms, scarcely aware that he was doing it. His body was on flame with desire for her and his arousal was like an anguish. Yet the rattle of the doorknob turning startled him. Then she was standing there. She had discarded her greatcoat and her jacket.

She threw off her boots and stockings. With a wiggle of her body, she eased her thick army skirt over her bare feet and stepped out of it. Her thick unglamorous bloomers quickly followed. Only the loose undershirt remained. She pulled it high over her head. Stefan held his breath at the beauty of her: the wisping black triangle of pubic hair, so dark against the pale skin of her belly and flowing thighs. Her breasts sprang free from the tugging folds of the undershirt as she pulled it clear of her head. She smiled at him shyly, letting him feast his eyes on her nakedness.

'Aren't you going to help me in?' she asked.

He stood up, catching the perceptible widening of her eyes as she glimpsed the unashamed splendour of his rampant manhood. She came to his outstretched arms, stepping gingerly into the bath and then allowing her body to lean against his as he took her weight. Gently lowering herself on to him, she gave a little shudder of delight at the meeting of their flesh. Their tongues met in

606

a lingering kiss. Feet apart and firmly placed, he took her full weight effortlessly in hands spread below her buttocks, while she clung to his neck, moving her thighs up the outside of his and thrusting her body towards him and gasping as he achieved penetration. With her cradled thus, Stefan rocked her and thrust with growing eagerness until, both spent, they tumbled in an ungainly sprawl in the cooling water.

They sorted themselves out, laughing and spitting soapy water. Then he carried her to his bed.

For a full week, Stefan believed that *Starshiy Leytenant* Katya Karpov was the best thing that had ever happened to him. Women had attracted him in the past, but none had measured up quite so fully as Katya to his demanding expectations. Stefan had dallied briefly with women who exerted strong physical attraction for him – but invariably they had fallen a long way short of his intellectual expectations. Love affairs which might have blossomed had foundered on his discovery that physical beauty was not accompanied by any profundity of mind or a hunger for socialist revolution that matched his own. Katya, however, delighted him on all counts. She had a stunning natural beauty that wakened in him a ferocity of desire such as he had never known, and she had the appetite and sexual repertoire to satisfy the most demanding lover. She was also a child of revolution who had been educated so well and so widely in Marxist theories that she could argue their intricacies with a style and wit that delighted Stefan. This made a change from some of the female adherents of Marxism that Stefan had known. Too often in the past – while he had approved and admired the polemical skills of such women and been enthralled by their depth of mind and witty talk – he had been repelled by their looks. They tended to have the sexual allure of a sack of potatoes.

Katya was different. It seemed that all her passions

had been made to complement Stefan's. On the day after their first meeting, she sought – and obtained with surprising ease – permission from her unit commander to 'live out'. She moved into Stefan's apartment the following night, to Stefan's great joy. His entire outlook was transformed overnight. His old enthusiasm for the Party returned and, with it, a new optimism for the future.

His euphoria lasted for one short week. It began to die one night as he lay in bed with Katya, in the after-bliss of lovemaking; in a moment when it seemed that no cloud darkened his heaven. The conversation started innocuously.

'Will you do something for me, my sweet?' Katya asked, snuggling against his body.

'Anything, my love. You know you only need to name it.'

'This meeting that you have tomorrow, with Tito and the other leaders. . . .'

'Yes?' Stefan raised himself on an elbow. He was puzzled that Tito or anyone else should come into Katya's bedroom talk. 'What about the meeting?'

'When you come home at night, will you tell me everything that is said?'

Stefan's puzzlement grew.

'Why, my love? What possible interest can it be to you?'

'I want to know what goes on,' she said.

'Well, you'll just have to want, my pretty one. It's a secret session,' he said, stroking her forehead. 'I could be drummed out of the Party for talking about what goes on in secret session.'

'You can tell me,' she urged.

'Sorry, my sweet. There's no concession made for wives or sweethearts. Secret session means exactly what it says – secret. We can't tell anyone.'

'But I must know, Stefan.'

'But why?'

'Because I've been given my orders,' she said.

Her anxiety disturbed him.

'Who gave you orders, Katya?'

'Who do you think? My boss, of course – *Polkovnik* Gornev.'

'Why the devil should your colonel want to know what goes on at secret sessions of the Jugoslav Party?' Stefan demanded, shocked.

'Because *it's his job*, Stefan,' she said, her voice rising. Her anxiety was now acute.

A terrible chill descended on Stefan's heart.

'His job! I thought his job was Transport Supply . . . yours, too!'

'That's what we're told to say, don't you understand?'

'No, I don't understand,' Stefan snapped angrily. He pulled away from her, sitting upright in the bed; his mind working overtime. The ugly truth dawned slowly. He did not want to believe it.

'You're with their Intelligence Service.' It was a statement, not a question, and Stefan made it in a voice that was no more than a whisper.

'I was going to tell you,' she said, a defensive edge to her voice. 'I thought you would have guessed before now. It doesn't need to make any difference to us, Stefan . . . to the way we feel about each other.' Stefan did not seem to hear.

'You've used me,' he said, staring into the darkness, numbed. 'Right from the very start, you've used me. I believed everything you said – all that about friendship between our peoples . . . the gold watch. . . . It was all a trap, and you were the honey, Katya. By God, what a fool you must think I am.' He felt sick, more pained to the soul than angered by the betrayal.

'I love you, Stefan,' she cried out.

'You played the whore, Katya,' he said bitterly. 'You played it to perfection. And, by heaven, I fell for it. The

609

really galling thing is not my own stupidity – it's knowing that you were under orders all along. That's what hurts the most.'

He got out of bed and dressed, switching on the light only when he could not find a sock. He could not bear to look at her.

'What are you doing?' she asked, weeping.

'I'm going out,' he said. 'And when I come back in the morning, I expect to find you gone.'

'No,' she cried, and got out of the bed to plead with him. As he struggled to get into his clothes, she followed him around, naked, begging him not to leave her. It needed iron will on his part to ignore her protestations of love and not to be beguiled by her body and her tears.

When he tried to leave, she clung to him, beseeching him not to leave her. He flung her roughly from him – and that was how he left her: lying naked on the floor, her body racked with her sobbing.

He walked the streets all night, not caring where his steps took him. Dawn found him huddled in his coat, staring at the Sava from below the Kalemegdan. The morning was well on when he retraced his steps to the apartment. It had been tidied and the bed had been neatly made up. There was no sign of Katya, nor her belongings.

Desolate, Stefan sat down on the edge of the bed and wept.

7

The Closing Ring

They had withdrawn ten kilometres during the night, but there was no rest at the end of it. Petar chose the site for his Battalion Command Post and, detailing men to evacuate an earthwork defence to give it some protection, he went off to supervise the Battalion's digging-in operation and make sure that every section commander was conversant with his orders. As he made his rounds, Petar could only marvel anew at the stoic heroism of his German soldiers. They had fought all winter with uncomplaining fortitude and, since the Partisans had made their breakthrough on the Srem Front on April the twelfth, they had been magnificent in retreat, conceding ground day after day to the Partisan Army but exacting a terrible price in human life from the enemy for every metre of earth.

It was already clear to Petar that the war was lost. Russian guns were bombarding Berlin and the Allied armies from the west were spreading all over Germany. Here in Jugoslavia, Army Group 'E' – a force of four hundred thousand men – was still largely intact as it tried to funnel back towards the 175-kilometre-long border with Austria, but it was beset with supply problems and being pushed back on every front by the Partisans.

No one knew better than Petar how critical these supply problems were. His battalion – nominally a battle reconnaissance group with sixty vehicles – had been compelled to destroy forty-two of their own personnel carriers and scout cars because there was no fuel to tank them. Even worse than the shortage of fuel was the shortage of ammunition. That, more than any other factor, was the reason the Germans were now fighting a losing battle. The front-line units were not being overrun because they had lost the will to fight but because, with their bullets exhausted, they had been reduced to defending with bayonets and bare hands.

Here in the rolling lowland plain, it was a different war from what had gone before. The irony of it was not lost on Petar, or his men. The pattern, when it was their job to attack the Partisans, had been a thankless one: seeking to dislodge a determined enemy from mountain fastnesses. Now, when it was their turn to defend, there were no craggy heights to make the task easier – nothing but undulating grassland, turned softer and greener than usual by an exceptionally wet spring.

The soft April rain brought one blessing. It eased the task of digging foxholes. The soft earth surrendered speedily to the practised burrowing of trenching tools.

'Dig deep,' Petar advised his men, as he inspected the perimeter, thinning it here and there by ordering men back to form second and third lines of defence. 'Make every bullet count,' he exhorted. He knew that the men had heard it all before. He had made the same exhortations every day for a week, but the men did not resent the repetition of advice that was no longer necessary. They would have been more concerned if their young commander had not chosen to show his face. His tour of the foxholes – with the same-as-yesterday admonitions and same-as-usual jokey comments – showed that he still cared, and that was reassuring.

Petar's Command Post was little different from the other foxholes: just a little roomier, to accommodate more bodies, such as his radio man and runner and a dogsbody junior officer. In Petar's absence, the latter had been talking on the field telephone to Division HQ.

'Anything fresh?' Petar asked him.

The young officer shook his head.

'Same as before, sir. They're doing their best to get some ammo up to us, but they can't promise anything. Everybody's yelling for it. The roads are chock-a-block with trucks that have run out of petrol, and only horse wagons are getting through. Orders are to hold where we are for at least twenty-four hours.'

Petar spoke to Division himself, but not even his warning that, without more ammunition, the Battalion might be quickly overrun brought any promise of comfort.

'Do the best you can,' he was told. He was advised tht a Panzergrenadier battalion was still holding the enemy, five kilometres to his front, and – for the moment – was shielding him from immediate attack. 'Werner and his Panzergrenadiers may give you the day's breathing space you need, *Sturmbannfuehrer* Richtman,' an unemotional voice informed Petar. 'Let's hope so. The longer they can keep the Reds at bay, the more time we shall have to do something about your supplies.'

The hope proved optimistic. Before daylight came, the Panzergrenadiers began streaming back through Petar's battalion lines. It was not an undisciplined retreat, but dejection and frustration were written on the faces of the tired troops.

Their commander – a tall reedy man called Werner – stopped off at Petar's Command Post, seeking ammunition for his men. He was not surprised when Petar told him he had none to spare.

'Then we shall just have to keep going back until we get some,' he said resignedly. Like his men, Werner was on foot. He was deeply unhappy at having made a decision which – he said – had been the only option open to him. He had not left the line undefended. He had left behind one company, stretched out across a perimeter where previously three had been – after distributing to them all that remained of the battalion's ammunition.

And that had been precious little. They had all but exhausted their supply in repelling an attack by the Reds just after midnight.

Werner had done his manpower and firepower sums and concluded that a hundred men with all the ammunition available would provide a more effective defence than three hundred with the same stock thinly spread. It made no sense at all to him to sacrifice the lives of three hundred men, so he had ordered the withdrawal of two companies and left one to face the enemy – a decision that had extracted its own degree of pain. Not a single man in the Panzergrenadier Battalion had had any doubt that Werner was purchasing two hundred lives by assigning a hundred comrades to almost certain death – and the anguish weighed heavily on those Panzergrenadiers who had been ordered to withdraw. This anguish was made all the keener by the fact that – as so frequently occurs amid the brutality and inhumanity of war – those elected to die had been able to accept their portion with a cheerful equanimity.

The April dawn came with a blush of pink suffusing the grey overcast to the east. With it came the crash and thunder of battle from across the gently undulating plain. Flashes lit the eastern horizon, which soon became obfuscated by a curtain of ascending smoke rising like a line of distant poplar trees to shimmer grey in the distance. The mirage of poplars seemed to creep perceptibly closer.

With the arrival of daylight, Petar made a second tour of his lines. He had had a good mental picture of the terrain when he deployed the Battalion during darkness, but it was still reassuring to confirm that the features were as he had imagined them. He took no credit for choosing the location, having been directed to it by the Divisional Commander. It had natural aids to defence, which were some compensation for the absence of high ground. A river swollen by spring floods protected the

Battalion's right flank. On its left, stretching for several kilometres to the north, were reedy flats of swampy ground dotted with tiny pools of standing water. The Battalion occupied a slightly elevated grassy plateau a kilometre wide, which stood like a causeway between the swampy flats to the north and, to the south, equally boggy ground that stretched to the river's bank. The Partisans had been advancing on a broad front across the open plain, but it was obvious that here they would have to funnel across the narrow stretch occupied by Petar's Battalion or make a wider detour to the north.

Surveying the ground that he had been ordered to hold for twenty-four hours, Petar had no doubts about what the Partisans would do. Their tactics in this new frontal war had become wholly predictable. It seemed not to matter to them whether they flung their massed infantry attacks at the weakest or strongest point of the enemy line: the pattern never varied – to attack and keep attacking until a breach was opened and the tide could flood through.

Somewhere south of the river, artillery was booming away as Petar returned to his Command Post, but the racket of the fierce fire-fight to the east had died down.

His junior dogsbody was waiting for him with not unexpected news.

'Division have lost all contact with Werner's rearguard, sir. They want us to keep an eye open for any of them coming this way. I've passed the word.'

Petar shook his head sadly.

'If the Reds hit them with their big battalions, I don't think we'll be seeing any more of Werner's men. He left those poor devils out on a limb. It would have made more sense to pull them back here instead of leaving them in the middle of nowhere. If the river bridge up there had still been standing, I could have understood it – but it's been down for days.'

'I suppose he was only buying us a little time, sir,' the

younger man suggested, almost apologetically. 'And he had orders to hold where he was.'

Petar smiled.

'You're right, of course. And we have similar orders. I shouldn't criticise Werner for the decision he made. Who knows? If any of us are still alive when the sun goes down tonight, I might be faced with exactly the same kind of dilemma.'

'We'll hold the Reds, sir,' the young officer said stoutly.

'Of course we will,' Petar agreed.

Half an hour later, they heard the approach of the Partisan army almost in the same instant that it came in sight. The sound they heard was a distant droning rumble, like the buzzing of tens of millions of bees – but it came from human voices, thousands of them, raised in deep throated hymnlike chanting.

They appeared first like ants on the horizon – tiny figures, who seemed to bob in a way that made a rippling movement across the great swarm. They came on like a great creeping carpet, a bristling black mass whose surface stirred endlessly as if fanned by the breath of a gentle breeze. Across its front, the human wave was four kilometres wide and seemed no less deep, from what Petar could see of the body. The chanting grew louder as the van neared the German positions. The Partisans were advancing in loose order and the flanks began to edge in towards the centre as it was realised that boggy terrain lay ahead to left and right. The great horde had no scouts or reconnaissance groups ahead to probe for lurking enemy or natural obstacles. It simply came on, ready to collide head-on with whatever it encountered.

The sight of the recklessly advancing enemy sent a strange thrill through Petar. It was not fear. He had long been reconciled to the imminence of his own death and had expected it on successive days, ever since the Partisans broke through at Srem. He had counted every day since as borrowed. No, fear was not the cause of the fluttering sensation of thrill. It was a kind of pride at the sight of this chanting Jugoslav horde. Circumstances, not Petar Richtman, had dictated that they were his enemy. Perhaps, if he had felt as strongly about political issues as Mara or Stefan Markovic, he could have chosen a different path: a path that might have made him one of that Jugoslav horde instead of its enemy. But he did not regret, even now, that he had chosen to soldier with the German Army. The Army had been his home and his life and had provided him with as fine a fellowship as any man could hope for. The German soldier was still the finest in the world, and never had that been more evident than in recent weeks, with defeat staring him in the face. There would be no dishonour in dying in such company. And, Petar thought, as he watched the oncoming Partisans, there will be no dishonour in sharing paradise with as brave a band as you. Maybe the blood we both shall shed will make this land the happier place we'd like it to be.

'Pass the order to hold fire. Front positions will wait for my signal.' Petar gave the command to the junior officer at his side in flat, unemotional tones. It was quickly relayed from hole to hole, before being drowned by the shouts of the Partisans, who were now only five hundred metres distant and advancing shoulder to shoulder in a dense mass.

'Do you know what it is they're shouting, sir?' the young officer asked.

Petar smiled.

'Death to the Invader. Victory to the People.'

'Some of the men call them the Antichrist,' the young man commented.

'They call us worse than that,' Petar replied with a grin. 'Are you a Christian, Hecht?'

'Lutheran, sir.'

'Do you hate the Antichrist?'

617

'No, sir. Christ taught us to love our enemies.'

Petar stared at the young man in surprise.

'You love the Reds?'

'I don't hate them, sir. It's the crazy way they come at us – as if they want to die. I can hate cowards, but not brave men.'

Petar had unsheathed his automatic.

'It's a soldier's job to kill brave men,' he said.

The young officer gave a nervous little smile.

'I know that, sir. I've learned to kill. But it's not the enemy I hate when I'm doing it, it's myself.'

'Get ready,' Petar murmured softly. Through the hole cut in turfs built up in front of him, he could see that the Partisans were no more than one hundred and fifty metres from the Battalion perimeter. Still he waited. He counted slowly to ten. Then he raised his pistol and fired a shot in the air. Almost instantly, a torrent of fire erupted from the grassy mounds that marked the German perimeter, causing terrible carnage in the advancing khaki throng. The Partisans fell like wheat before a reaper. A hundred died in the winking of an eye as the machine-guns on the wings of the German line raked the massed ranks. Soldiers manning the foxholes stood up in their cunningly concealed dugouts to send burst after burst of automatic fire into the Partisans, who, far from faltering, were still surging forward in a frenzied charge, trampling their fallen comrades underfoot.

Last into action on the German side were the two-man *Panzerfaust* teams, who leapt from their foxholes in order to bring their fearsome antitank weapons to bear. Six unleashed their rockets almost simultaneously, with whooshing roars. The missiles tore huge holes in the descending human tide, as if an invisible locomotive had carved a bloody path to its heart.

The Partisan charge faltered and stopped only thirty metres from the German perimeter – but only momentarily. Weapons blazing, the tide came on again. A piercing whistle-blast shrieked above the din as Petar's second in command emerged from his foxhole and signalled the front line to fall back. Those with heavy weapons picked them up and ran as fast as their legs would carry them. Those with machine-pistols showed less haste, firing as they retired. Some, slow to leave their foxholes, were overrun by the charging mass of Partisans and were shot or bayoneted as the tide flowed over them. Now the Partisans were on the kilometre-wide causeway that separated the two stretches of boggy morass. Indeed, their right flank, denied space on the firm ground by the sheer number of their own comrades, were splashing about in the swamp to the north, to little effect. The battleground was the centre. Here, the Partisans maintained their momentum, encouraged by their success. It was short-lived.

Having disposed of one line of enemy that had suddenly appeared out of holes in the ground before them, some in the Partisan ranks might have felt that the battle was won. If so, many died with this happy illusion, because the phenomenon repeated itself almost at once. Only fifty metres beyond the captured German line lay the second, and it was now that the hundred men positioned along its length rose from their turf-disguised trenches to direct their firepower at the jubilant Partisan infantry. The effect was no less deadly than before. The German gunners could not miss, and they shredded swatches through the oncoming host like clippers through a fleece. The charge was stopped in its tracks and, this time, the front Partisans fell back before the hail of death, colliding with the forward surge from the rear.

With screams and shouts, their officers drove them on yet again over the fallen bodies of their comrades. And forward, again, they came to die in their hundreds. Such was their weight of numbers that it was only a matter of time before they engulfed the second German line. As before, those German soldiers who were not caught up in the merciless tangle of hand-to-hand fighting withdrew as best they could to the waiting third line.

Petar, at its centre, gave the signal for his third company to make their first contribution to the battle – which they did with the eagerness of relief, for watching and waiting had torn at their nerves and their discipline.

For a third time, they stopped the advancing human wall – but only momentarily. Again it came, as the defenders counted the last of their ammunition and grimly hoped that death would come quickly at the last.

Petar loaded his last four bullets into the magazine of his pistol and clipped it home. The young officer, Hecht, was watching him and managed a weak smile.

'I've got five,' he said.

'Make them count, Hecht,' Petar told them. 'Sell your life dearly. You're a good soldier. One of the best.'

'Thank you, sir.' He glanced up. 'Here they come.'

Petar peered over the top of the dugout. The Partisans, shoulder to shoulder, were fifty metres away, running straight at him like men possessed. He could see their wide-open eyes, bright in distorted faces. He felt a terrible sadness. It was tinged with an anger at the Partisan military leaders who had drilled these brave young men in the wasteful folly of massed infantry attack, straight from the Red Army's military manual. It offended the professional soldier in Petar in its total disregard for the value of human life.

Bracing himself, he fired four times at the onrushing khaki figures. He was climbing out of the dugout to meet them when he felt a blinding pain in his head. A body collided with him and he was thrown aside. His face hit soft earth and the world went black.

When he came to, he was aware of one side of his face giving pain, but he had no other hurt. He staggered to his feet. It was strangely quiet. He blinked his eyes and there, lying half in and half out of the trench was young Hecht, eyes staring at the heavens. He had been bayoneted and his hands, in death, were still clutching at the wound.

Petar was still staring dazedly at the corpse of the young officer when he was struck a savage blow from behind by a rifle butt. It hit him between the shoulder blades and sent him flying. He looked up to find a wild-eyed Partisan soldier standing over him. Another Partisan came into view. The pair seized Petar and dragged him unceremoniously towards a group of Partisan officers, who were having a heated discussion over a map stretched on the ground. One of them looked round.

'What have you got there?' he asked.

'This one's an officer, Comrade Potpukovnic.'

'Take him over there. To the Kaplar. He knows what to do.'

Petar was prodded to his feet and made to walk. He was taken towards another group. Seven German prisoners were sitting on the ground, with their hands behind their heads: two officers, a junior NCO, and four soldiers. All had wounds of one kind or another but only one – a lieutenant – was badly hurt. He was having great difficulty keeping his hands behind his head and was saturated in blood from waist to knee on one side. Four Partisans stood with rifles pointed at the men. A corporal, using a German helmet as a receptacle, was relieving the prisoners of their personal possessions.

Petar was made to hand over his wristwatch and the contents of his pockets and told to sit with the others. He spoke up for the wounded lieutenant.

'The man is badly hurt,' he complained to the corporal. 'Let him lower his hands.' To Petar's surprise, the corporal indicated they could all lower their hands. He seemed to find Petar's request amusing and said something to the guards, which Petar did not catch. They all laughed.

621

Brusquely, the corporal ordered the noncommissioned German soldiers to their feet. They were marched away by the four guards. Petar watched in horror as the corporal unslung his rifle from his shoulder and, without ado, pointed at the wounded lieutenant's face and fired. Then he shot the other officer between the eyes. Petar watched dumbly as the rifle was swung round to poke him on the bridge of the nose. The corporal pulled the trigger a third time.

The sound of the report echoed across the battlefield. Petar's death brought the number of German dead to 322, out of 327. More than three thousand Partisans died to win that sorry strip of earth between the boggy flats and the flooding river. The battle had lasted two hours and, at its end, the heavens wept as dark clouds rolled across the April sky and heavy rain fell to give new life to the bloody land.

Rain was a luxury that came too seldom to that part of Bosnia-Hercegovina, where – it seemed to Mara – she had been forever. In fact, only nine months had passed since she was given that tantalising glimpse of Jamie, and scarcely an hour of any day had passed without her remembering it and being torn by conflicting emotions that raged between black despair and soaring hope. One moment, her heart would be as bleak as the wintry winds that roared through Mostar from the Karst and, in the next, it would be joyful with wild optimism that the day must be near when they would find each other again.

The coming of spring brought a new intensity to the yearning love that four years of war had failed to extinguish. Often, since her sighting of Jamie, she had wrestled with the idea of deserting from the hospital unit and trying to reach the Partisan lines, but opportunities were few and far between and the chances against success so great that she had chosen to stick things out. After seeing Jamie vanish from sight on a hill above the

Vrbas River, the stranded German convoy had been attacked by Partisans descending from the hills beyond the river. Mara had spent two dangerous days and nights under fire as a result, but the guerrillas had not tried to cross the river and the convoy had eventually managed to get moving again and reach Mostar.

The days and nights of winter had seemed endless to Mara, but the coming of the spring brought a renewal of all her hopes and longings. It brought real hope, too, that the bitter war was surely nearing its end. Defeat was in the air all around her. It was etched in the faces of the casualties brought in from the battlefields and in the grim expressions of the German soldiers who patrolled the streets of Mostar.

The officers she met fretted about their families in the bombed and fallen cities of Germany. Her nursing colleagues – most of whom were Austrian – listened in fear to the radio bulletins, which told of the Russian advance into their homeland. The news they were dreading came on a suitably ill-omened Friday the thirteenth, as the nurses ate dinner on an April evening. Many wept openly as they heard the sombre announcement that Vienna had fallen to the Russians.

Mara, who had secretly rejoiced at every reported Allied success, found herself strangely affected by the distress brought to the German camp as one reverse followed hard on the heels of another. She longed for the downfall of Hitler, and yet she could not extend hate to those Germans with whom she had worked and lived for so long. There was the odd Nazi admirer, but most betrayed not the least enthusiasm for Hitler or Nazism. Mara had long ceased to see them as personal enemies. She would have lost her sanity if she had. It was impossible to withhold liking and sympathy from men and women whose hopes and aspirations were not much different from her own. The concern of the soldier casualties she nursed centred on their wives and children and sweethearts, and they longed for the day when they could go back to their homes and their work on farms and in offices and shops and factories. Mara knew she should feel enmity to Germans for the rape of her country and the death they had brought to Jugoslavia, but there was no room for hate in a heart that was wrenched daily by the suffering of war's victims. She consoled and ministered to the young blue-eyed Berliner who talked to her of his happy times as a saxophonist in a travelling dance band, his tales made the more poignant by the fact that he now only had stumps for arms. She could not hate such men. No more could she hold back compassion for the blinded eighteen-year-old from Hamburg to whom she read a relative's letter revealing that his mother and three sisters had died in an air raid.

The only Germans who stirred fear and dislike in Mara were the SS, who flaunted their Nazi allegiance in ways that often offended their compatriots as much as the native Jugoslavs. But there were none in Mostar. Mara had not seen an SS trooper since leaving Jajce.

Mara felt constantly confused by her feelings, inasmuch as she could confide in no one the true nature of her loyalties and hopes. Concealing this had been easy at first, when she had *felt* alien to all around her; but the passage of time had imposed a bigger and bigger strain, particularly in her relationships with the other nurses. As she got to know them and was drawn into friendships, she felt almost guilty at times for the reserve she had to maintain. At times, when her closest friend, Greta, unburdened her soul to her, Mara longed to reciprocate. But she never dared.

For Mara, the Army Nursing Corps had become both her refuge and her prison. She longed to escape its confinement, but it was the only place she felt safe. The coming of spring brought with it an excited certainty that the doors of her prison would soon be open and that she would be able to emerge from behind its protective walls. But what lay beyond? What kind of world? Was Jamie there? Mara's heart soared with hope, like a lark in the warm April sunshine, but it fluttered, too, with nameless fears of what she might find beyond the beckoning horizon.

When the news was broken to the staff of the Mobile Field Hospital that the entire unit and its patients were to be evacuated from Mostar, it was greeted almost with jubilation. The atmosphere was akin to that at a boarding school breaking up for the summer holidays. Some of the off-duty nurses celebrated by going on a shopping spree in Mostar. Mara and her friend Greta elected to do what they had been promising themselves all winter. They went for a swim in the River Neretva.

Even in the depth of winter, the river's blue-green waters had exerted a fascination on them, but they had been content to look and admire until the weather became warmer. Now, with their departure imminent, both women decided to take advantage of a glorious day.

The water was icy but exhilarating, and the current languid enough to make it an easy swim across to the far bank: a distance of less than thirty metres. A flat low shelf of rock on one side and a slightly higher spur on the other provided an ideal natural crossing place, with the spur making a splendid diving platform. Greta, who had won diving trophies as a junior, displayed her prowess by climbing up repeatedly to make graceful plunges into the river below. Mara, having accustomed herself to the chill of the water, preferred to swim around in mid-stream, paddling around on her back and applauding Greta's efforts.

Later, the girls climbed up the rock above the diving shelf to dry their glowing bodies and bask in the warm sun. They had been swimming almost in the shadow of the beautifully curved single span of the centuries-old Turkish bridge from which the town derived its name. The bridge was manned by German soldiers, who had been joined by others to observe the spectacle of two shapely females disporting themselves in the river. The soldiers cheered and clapped as Greta and Mara climbed to their rocky sunspot.

'Your diving exhibition seems to have attracted an appreciative audience,' Mara observed.

Greta laughed.

'Don't you believe it. If they're appreciating anything, it's the sight of more female flesh than they see on the streets.' Greta grinned. 'Maybe the word got around that the only virgin in Mostar was swimming in the Neretva. They'd come from near and far to see that.'

Mara blushed.

'There are times, Greta, when you can be very coarse.'

'I was just teasing. I just don't know how you've managed to hold out.'

'You know why.'

'Oh, yes, Mara. This great love of your life that you're so coy about. Don't you wish you'd given yourself to him when you had the chance – that is, if you ever had the chance.'

'Sometimes I do regret it,' Mara admitted, and smiled. 'But sometimes I don't. A joy postponed is a joy in store.'

Greta regarded her friend doubtfully.

'I'm glad you can look at it that way.' She shrugged, and towelled her blonde hair vigorously. 'I've always grabbed for the things I wanted, afraid that the second chance never comes. I'm not sorry now. The war is lost. What's going to become of us all, Mara? What's going to become of us?'

'I don't know,' Mara said.

'Aren't you frightened?'

'I'm trying not to be. I want the war to finish. But not knowing how or when or where we'll be is what makes me go all shivery when I think about it.'

'In some ways, I'll be sorry to leave Mostar,' Greta

said. 'I know a lot of the girls hate it but it's so different from any other place I've been . . . so Turkish.'

Mara smiled.

'I know what you mean.' From where they sat, the view was idyllic, quaint. The high arched bridge, with its stone towers at each end, framed a short stretch of green river on which shimmered reflections of stone-coloured bank and leafing trees. Beyond could be glimpsed the red-pantiled rooftops of the town, statuesque cypresses and the white needle shapes of two or three of Mostar's two dozen minarets. Beyond the town itself rose the bald barren hills of the Karst, light stony grey in the sunlight, and a shield for the fields and vineyards of the river valley. 'It's so tranquil,' Mara said. 'It makes you think twice about leaving it, because heaven knows what we'll find when we do.'

Uncertainty on that score was not unduly prolonged. Two days later, the hospital unit – with its wounded in ambulances – pulled out of Mostar and set off on the road to the north. Ahead, a heavily armed German force had already fanned out in a protective formation and, on the following day, the last of the German units in the south streamed through and out of Mostar, abandoning the town to the Partisans. A slow exodus began as the commander of the German 97th Corps, whose head-quarters had been in Mostar, regrouped the divisions under his direction to form a spiky, elongated oval. Before, his forces had been severely overstretched, but now they contracted and linked so that the Corps became a mobile entity.

On a course parallel to the Adriatic coastline, the great hedgehog moved north. At the centre travelled the most vulnerable units – the wounded, with their hospital staffs attendant, and the service auxiliaries – and at the outside, the fighting troops. Between the Corps and the bulk of Army Group 'E', which was retiring towards the Austrian border, were many miles of Partisan-held territory. Partisan armies also stood between the beleaguered German Corps and the sea, and were harrying its flanks and rear.

After four days of movement, the great moving pocket came to a standstill, unable to force a way through the Partisan army in its path. Simultaneously, pressure on the left flank of the cordon became so intense that its collapse seemed imminent. The flow of wounded towards the field hospitals at the core increased until it became clear that they would be unable to cope unless it slackened. Mara and Greta were worked off their feet. By the light of hurricane lamps in hastily erected canvas theatres, they toiled well into the night. From the hills all around came the boom and rattle of constant gunfire.

At three in the morning, their theatre officer ordered the nurses to take a breather before they collapsed on their feet. A kitchen orderly had tried to keep coffee in constant supply and he regarded the nurses quizzically as he ladled steaming brown liquid into their mugs.

'Have you heard the news?' he asked. 'There's a rumour going around that Hitler is dead.'

'Who cares about rumours?' Greta snapped at him. 'And who cares about Hitler? What's going to happen to us?'

'We're finished, too,' the orderly said gloomily. 'I heard an officer saying that our position is hopeless and that the General is talking of surrendering to the Reds. God help us all if he does.'

At the field headquarters of Comrade General Drapsin, commander of the 4th Partisan Army, the heady excitement of victory was in the air. This was due in part to confirmation that a request for a truce parley had been received from the large German force that had tried to fight north from Mostar but was now hopelessly encircled. It was significant that the truce plea had come in the sector where the Germans were fighting with the greatest determination. The enemy division – identified as the 41st Infantry and, according to intercepted German intelligence signals, 'unreliable' as a result of its composition from 'military criminals and convicted deserters' – had fought with far greater resolution than any other elements of the trapped Corps. It had, however, sustained casualties at an unacceptable level – convincing the German Corps commander that his break-out attempt was doomed.

Comrade General Drapsin had reason to be pleased at the measure and speed of his army's success. He had sought only to hold and contain the German Corps and, indeed he had ordered the bulk of his forces in the south to bypass the enemy and augment the divisions driving towards the Istrian peninsula and Trieste. The Supreme Command in Belgrade had lately become obsessed with the need to reach Trieste – so long a bone of contention between Slavs and Italians – before it was captured by the Allies. So the fate of the German 97th Corps was almost incidental – although its total eclipse was an unexpected bonus. There was, however, no equivocation in Comrade General Drapsin's reply to the 97th Corps commander's request for a parley. He gave the German General twenty-four hours to surrender his entire force or be wiped out.

While depending heavily for military intelligence on the strong OZNA presence that accompanied his headquarters staff, Comrade General Drapsin tended not to interfere with the politically oriented activities of that organisation. He considered himself first and foremost a soldier – and it suited him to concentrate on his military duties and leave OZNA to take care of the political niceties that concerned his army. He knew they received secret orders direct from Belgrade but he displayed no curiosity in their content, believing that the less he knew, the less he had to worry about. He was not unduly disturbed when, in early April, the 4th Army ranks were

629

suddenly swollen by an influx of OZNA agents from Belgrade, ostensibly for clandestine operations. He ordered his brigade and divisional commanders to render the OZNA officers every assistance, including that of manpower for forays into enemy-held Istria.

If Drapsin felt any astonishment when he heard that, on such forays, no attempt was made by the raiding parties to destroy enemy supply dumps or disrupt communications, he betrayed none. When told that all these raiders seemed content to do was to daub buildings with Communist Party slogans, he exhibited no surprise, giving the impression that if Belgrade believed in the psychological value of plastering graffiti all over Istria, it was not up to him to question such activities. This soft-target approach certainly enhanced the chances of the Partisan raiders returning to their own lines without a single casualty.

The paintbrush raids drew a different reaction from the British and American special forces who, in the previous months, had greatly increased the range and scope of cooperation with the 4th Partisan Army. The promised invasion of Istria had never materialised – largely because of the diversion of men and landing craft from Italy to other theatres of war – but the Allies had launched dozens of attacks throughout the Dalmatian islands and had inserted enemy-spotting patrols in Istria and the German-held littoral to feed information to the Partisans. The British and Americans began to suspect that the daubing in Istria was not designed to taunt the Germans, nor inspire the local inhabitants, but calculated to give the peninsula's eventual liberators the false impression that the region was solidly pro-Communist.

Comrade General Drapsin would later laugh at assertions of such deviousness. He would also bridle with injured innocence at the suggestion that he had anything to do with a sudden deterioration of relations between the 4th Partisan Army and the Allied operational groups who were serving alongside it. He would insist that he had not sanctioned, nor had any knowledge of, Partisan activity – which led to considerable acrimony. Nor did he seek to attribute blame for the ill feeling to OZNA, for to have done so would have been to admit the nature of this shadowy beast and its considerable power. The Western Allies may have known of its intelligence-gathering function, but it is likely that they suspected that the monster had as many arms as the hydra had heads. And it was sharp enough in claw to instil uncharacteristic caution in army commanders – or, in Comrade General Drapsin's case, a convenient blindness to its activities.

It was Jamie Kyle's good fortune that, although his name had been on a secret list of Party enemies compiled by Gubec and circulated to a chosen few henchmen, he had escaped the attention of OZNA's growing army of agents for nearly a year. This was partly due to a mistake by the only agent to have taken any trouble to locate him. He reported, belatedly – and incorrectly – that this suspect had perished soon after the fall of Drvar. His information came from the former commander of the Officer Training School at Sipoljani and three cadets, who were quite convinced that Jamie had not survived.

That was Jamie's good fortune. It was his misfortune that, in his anxiety to establish the identity of Mara's hospital unit and determine its fate after the ambush on the road to Mostar, he unwittingly reawakened OZNA's interest in him – by coincidence, at precisely the same time that OZNA was stirring up trouble for the British and American personnel who were fighting alongside Drapsin's 4th Partisan Army.

OZNA, during that last April of the war, embarked without subtlety on a cynical campaign to prevent Allied soldiers from taking part in the liberation of Istria. That right was to be reserved exclusively for the soldiers of Communism. It was Jamie's bad luck that, at the time, he and his Bosnians were acting in concert with a British patrol.

Jamie had taken no part in the fighting against the German 97th Corps. When the break-out started, he had been more than a hundred kilometres from Mostar, in the coastal plain near the ancient Dalmatian city of Zadar. The British Navy and an Allied commando group had been using the port as a supply base for some time, but it was to the newly established airfield, thirty kilometres inland at Prkos, that Jamie and his six Bosnian hill men had been ordered, to join forces with a British spotter patrol being flown in from Italy.

The British squad numbered fourteen men: a captain, a sergeant and twelve other ranks. Every one was a specialist in long-range penetration of enemy lines and all but two were veterans of the Western Desert war. Their destination was Istria, where they would relieve a group who had been behind the German lines since early March, pinpointing targets for the Balkan Air Force. A first attempt to relieve the men in Istria by sea had failed, when the craft carrying the relieving patrol hit a mine. There had been no survivors. Now, a decision had been taken to insert the British patrol by an overland route. The British had asked the Jugoslav 4th Army to ensure that the unit enjoyed a safe passage through Partisan territory, and Jamie and his Bosnians were assigned to accompany them.

It was a joy to Jamie to become involved with English-speaking soldiers. They, in turn, were astonished and pleased to find themselves with a Partisan officer who spoke their language with the unmistakable burr of a Scot. The British soldiers struck up an immediate rapport with the Bosnians. This developed into a friendly rivalry when the luxury of motorised travel was left behind at the Croatian coastal town of Senj and the group set out on foot through the bald, arid hills and rocky gorges beyond. The British soldiers seemed intent on proving that they were every bit as tough as the Bosnians, whose stamina they admired. No winners or losers were declared in the competition, but the hill men, who set the pace, were still fresh and grinning broadly at the end of the day, whilst the smiles of their sweating rivals were a trifle forced.

All went well until they made their first contact with local Partisans in a rocky treeless wilderness, not far along the coast from the port which the Italians called Fiume and the Jugoslavs Rijeka, each word meaning river. A friendly herder they encountered led them to a round-roofed stone hut tucked away in a high limestone hollow, and suggested they make camp there. He was a shrewd old fellow, and guessed they were heading into Istria. He said they would need local help to guide them round the German garrison posts of Rijeka. True to his word, he returned before dark with a dozen Partisans, who gave no indication of the treachery in store.

Jamie's first intimation of trouble was when he was awakened during the night to find the hollow filled with Partisans – more than fifty of them – who had disarmed the British patrol and herded them into a tight little huddle surrounded by a circle of pointing rifles. Outraged, he forced his way through the milling Partisans to confront a dapperly uniformed officer who seemed to have a lot to say for himself.

'What's happening? These men are our friends,' he protested.

'They are under arrest,' the officer said. 'They are to be returned to wherever it is they came from. Perhaps you can make this imbecile understand this.' The imbecile he referred to was the British captain, who was utterly bewildered at being unceremoniously wakened and manhandled before the Partisan spokesman. Ashen-faced, he now appealed to Jamie to demand an explanation for the rude treatment of himself and his men.

'You had better call your men off at once,' Jamie told the Partisan officer. 'These British soldiers are our allies and have a job to do in Istria. It's my mission to see that they get there, and I intend to do so.'

'Your orders are cancelled. I cancel them. So just stay out of this, or I'll have you arrested, too.' The dapper little man, whose black moustache gave him a passing resemblance to Hitler, drew himself to his full height and stared imperiously at Jamie.

'And who are you to have authority to cancel my orders?' Jamie demanded, bristling with anger.

'I am Brigade-Commissar Radonic of the Fourth Army OZNA Commissariat, and you will do what you are told,' the other snapped.

'I'm damned if I will!' Jamie raged, his temper lost. He took a step closer to the OZNA officer, to emphasise his defiance. The move was interpreted as the first towards a physical assault on the Brigade-Commissar, and a burly figure at his side threw himself at Jamie to ward it off. Jamie went down in a heap, helped by a clubbing blow from the rifle which his attacker wielded like a stave. The sight of their leader being knocked to the ground was enough to bring Jamie's puzzled Bosnians crashing to the rescue. Using their rifles to push bodies out of the way, they charged to his defence, reaching him and standing over him, their weapons pointing threateningly at the Brigade-Commissar and his ring of riflemen.

No one dared move, knowing a single shot would detonate the charged atmosphere and trigger a bloody battle which could only end with six dead hill men. The Bosnians left no doubt in the minds of any present, however, that a lot more lives than theirs would be extinguished at the slightest sign of a rash act.

It was Jamie who defused the situation. Struggling to his feet, he suggested to the Brigade-Commissar that some quiet talking was preferable to confrontation.

Perhaps, if weapons were lowered on both sides, the conflict in orders could be discussed reasonably. The Brigade-Commissar agreed. In the orders which he had received from 4th Army HQ there was a caution to avoid the spilling of blood. He did not add – although it was apparent in his conciliatory manner – that the blood-spilling he most wanted to avoid was his own.

The British Captain was drawn into the subsequent discussion, with Jamie acting as his interpreter. It went on for two hours, often descending into heated argument between the OZNA officer and Jamie, with the British Captain trying to act as peacemaker. He, at any rate, was the one most anxious to arrive at compromise, conscious that he and his men were the aliens on Jugoslav soil and that the Partisans had to be deferred to as hosts, however prickly.

Brigade-Commissar Radonic did not know the meaning of the word compromise and was insistent that his orders superseded Jamie's, and must be carried out to the letter. All Allied personnel operating in or near Istria were to be arrested and returned under escort to the southern naval base at Zadar. He would not budge on that point.

In the end, on Radonic's assurance that the British patrol could keep their weapons and that no harm would befall them if they complied with his orders, the British Captain prevailed on Jamie to accept the OZNA officer's demands. The British officer was not prepared to cause an international incident. So Jamie backed down and conceded victory to Radonic. He was regretting it by morning – and so were his Bosnians. Resigned to returning south with the British patrol and lulled by Radonic's seeming amiability, Jamie and his men were taken off guard as they breakfasted in the open. They were seized and disarmed by Radonic's men and told that they were being arrested for their rebellious behaviour during the night. They were not to be trusted to escort the British back to Zadar. That task was now being allotted to two dozen of Radonic's own men.

So it was that when the British patrol was marched out from the hollow encampment, the party starting south comprised forty-five men. The British carried their weapons, but they did not conceal their chagrin at the sight of Jamie and his hill men marching in file, roped one to another like members of a chain gang.

The news that the German 97th Corps had laid down its arms and surrendered to the 4th Partisan Army was of sufficient import for a meeting of the Central Committee to be interrupted and Marshal Tito informed of the development. It put him in a good humour, which still prevailed long after the meeting had ended and he was closeted alone with Stefan in a room above the former Belgrade restaurant where the Central Committee had its headquarters. The Marshal's good humour had, by then, been further bolstered by confirmation that Hitler was dead and the Red Army had taken Berlin.

'What's the matter with you, Stefan?' Tito asked. 'There's so much to be joyful about and yet you go about as if you carried the weight of the world on your shoulders.'

'That's how I feel, most of the time,' Stefan admitted with an attempt at a smile. 'I wake up tired in the morning, as if I was a hundred years old.'

'And you a young man of just thirty.' Tito was jocularly reproachful.

'I won't see thirty again,' Stefan said. 'Was there something particular you wanted to see me about?'

'I worry about you,' Tito said disarmingly. 'I see so little of you these days. I miss our little chats. I have to rely on others to hear how you are getting on, and it bothers me when people say that you're not your old self.'

'I'm all right,' Stefan said.

'Are you?' Tito asked softly. 'Have you got over the business with that Russian girl? You haven't taken it too much to heart?'

Stefan had not got over it. He had done all the right things. He had confessed to the Party that he had been taken in by a pretty face and that the Russian Intelligence Service had made an attempt to subvert him. But he had not got over it. He still yearned for the arms of the temptress who had deceived him.

'It was a hard lesson,' he said to Tito.

'You did a courageous thing, Stefan,' Tito said. 'Not every man would have stood up as you did and tell that he had been made to look a fool.'

'It didn't do much good, did it?' Stefan commented bitterly. 'It hasn't stopped the Russians playing their little games.'

Tito laughed softly.

'Oh, they apologised profusely . . . said the usual things about one of their officers being overambitious and exceeding orders, and it would never happen again. They recalled your lady love fast enough. We won't see her in Belgrade again.'

Even that hurt Stefan: the thought of Katya being punished. He remembered her protests that her love was genuine, that she had not feigned that. Was there even a remote possibility that she had been telling the truth – that, although she had set out to deceive him, she had fallen as hard for him as he for her? The possibility haunted Stefan.

Tito changed the subject.

'How is your work going?' Almost as an afterthought, he added: 'I hear that you have not been altogether happy.'

Stefan looked up sharply, realising that this was why Tito had sent for him. This was what the chat was leading up to! He decided to be frank.

'I would have been happier if I'd been given a job on agitprop. I'm a writer and I could make a contribution there. At Conscription and Recruitment, I feel I'm just another bureaucrat. I have no particular talent for it.'

Tito frowned.

'That's no excuse for not putting your heart into the work. I have been told that you were less than enthusiastic about raising the Austrian battalions, and that you have been outspoken in your criticism of the whole business.'

'Because I'm not a conjuror,' Stefan said, with unconcealed anger. 'I can't produce Austrians out of a hat. I can't make bricks without straw. The whole idea was ill-conceived.'

'I was party to that idea,' Tito said icily. 'And it has a purpose, you know.'

'I know the purpose,' Stefan said, needled by Tito's tone. 'But, forgive me, with the best will in the world, I can't see any wisdom in wanting to annex part of Austria. We're going to have our work cut out consolidating the territory to which we have a legal right, without trying to grab land that doesn't belong to us. Let's finish this war before we do something that's likely to start another.'

'When this war's over, there's going to be some hard bargaining over national boundaries. We're going to need something to bargain with.' Tito's good humour had worn thin.

Stefan was undaunted.

'I'm sure you're right,' he conceded, 'but do we have to stop being honest? I was given the job of recruiting four Free Austria battalions for the Partisan Army, and I did – but I take no pride in it. They're bogus. It was a cosmetic exercise from start to finish. I had to comb the jails and the lunatic asylums to find genuine Austrians. Believe me, a lot of imagination was needed to give the few hundred recruits we got even the remotest Austrian connection. As for their fighting value, I hope I never have to depend on them.'

'Their fighting value is neither here nor there,' Tito argued, plainly annoyed. 'It's their progaganda value that counts. They will provide us with a legitimate reason to carry the war into Austria.'

'Legitimate?' Stefan echoed, incredulously. He saw the quick flash of anger in Tito's eyes and realised he had gone too far.

Tito got to his feet, his stare cold.

'You disappoint me, Stefan. I had such high hopes for you . . . but you disappoint me.'

Stefan pushed back his chair and stood, resisting the temptation to tell the most powerful man in Jugoslavia that the disappointment was mutual.

'Would you prefer it that I never spoke my mind?' he asked. 'Should I confine myself to saying only the things that I think it will please you to hear?'

Tito's unsmiling expression did not change.

'There's such a thing as being too outspoken,' he said. 'Don't make the mistake of thinking that because I have always been a patient listener in the past, you have some kind of *carte blanche* to tell me or the Party what is best for it.'

'I've always thought that the Party cherished honesty – demanded it. That's what upsets me with this charade of the Austrian battalions. It's dishonest.'

Stefan's earnestness brought a glimmer of a smile to Tito's face.

'Now you're confusing honesty with political stratagem. Of course, the Party expects honesty from its members, from all of us! But honesty is not something we extend to the Party's enemies, any more than they extend it to us. If you can't understand that, you are very naive.' Tito's good humour returned, now that he seemed to have satisfied himself that Stefan's wilfulness had naivety at its source. There was innocence at the heart of naivety. The Marshal became more avuncularly hearty and bade Stefan goodnight, advising him to be more cheerful; to stop worrying as if he were the nation's conscience.

Stefan was little comforted. He had always believed that those things that he most deeply desired in his own life would be valueless if they could not be achieved virtuously. It was a creed he had thought embodied in the ideals of Communist revolution, to which he had given his life. He wanted Communism to win with virtue, not lies and chicanery and deceit. What use was freedom without truth?

8

Retribution

Mannion sat in the jeep, drinking hot sweet tea from an enamel mug and enjoying the sunshine. On the first seven days of May, it had rained on and off every day, but the eighth brought warm sunshine and Mannion was luxuriating in it. The day was to be remembered as Victory in Europe Day, but the benign weather was the sole cause of Mannion's sense of wellbeing. The historic significance of events taking place far to the north in Germany had not quite permeated to Klagenfurt, a pleasant town in the southern border region of Austria known as Carinthia. Certainly, since the sudden surrender of the German forces in Italy more than a week ago, there had been a buoyant it's-all-over exuberance in the air – but it was tempered by a nasty suspicion that not everyone had got the message.

Two small pockets of German troops had demonstrated ignorance of the ceasefire on the hectic drive up from Italy – with the result that the journey was punctuated by two fierce battles of merciful brevity. Mannion had no clear idea why he and Major Blair had been sent racing into Austria with a front-running reconnaissance regiment of the British Eighth Army's 78th Division, but he had enjoyed the experience. It was as if these battle-hardened veterans had been given the signal to get to Berlin in a week. They were positively charged up with pride and excitement at crossing the border into the Reich: their goal for so long. The Regiment's starting line was in Egypt's desert, and the trail of battle was a long one, which only a few of the beginners survived, through Libya, Tunisia, Sicily and up through the mountains of Italy.

It had surprised Mannion how quickly he felt at home with the British after leaving Montenegro the previous August. He had spent most of the time with small Commando raiding groups, striking at targets in the German-held islands of the Adriatic south of Istria, and revelling in the easy-going camaraderie that existed between officers and men in the close-knit units of a piratical elite.

The Allied armies had made their final break-through in Northern Italy, and Mannion was relaxing at an R and R camp when an emergency call came from Blair, saying that he was needed for special duties of an unspecified nature.

Blair, it transpired, because of his previous dealings with the Partisans, had been ordered by Alexander's HQ to get himself into Austria ahead of the Jugoslav 4th Army, which had ignored British, American and Russian advice to halt at the border.

'It seems that some diplomacy with your Partisan comrades is going to be needed,' Blair told Mannion, 'and I'm going to need you to do the parleying for me. Tito seems hellbent on causing trouble that nobody wants.'

So it was that Blair and Mannion, with the back-up of a Royal Corps of Signals radio unit, were tagged on the end of a hard-driving recce squadron of the 78th Division and became part of the helter-skelter race to Klagenfurt. In the main square, under the curious gaze of the Austrian citizens, Mannion parked the jeep while Blair went off with the signals team to report Klagenfurt's occupation to HQ in Italy. The crew of an armoured car nearby brewed up on arrival and hospitably invited Mannion to share their huge kettle of tea, a gesture which delighted him. He had, since his attachment to the British, developed a strong partiality for their treacly brown tea, laced with sugar and condensed milk.

It surprised Mannion that he should feel glad to be alive, that he could enjoy so great a contentment and serenity from the simple pleasure of feeling the sun's rays on his skin. It forced him to realise that he no longer had the desire to give up even the simplest pleasures of life. It was good to feel the kiss of the sun and to think that tomorrow, and the next day and the day after that, it would still be there to bathe him with its benevolent warmth.

This, in turn, forced him to think of all the tomorrows that lay before him: tomorrows when the machines of war were silent and the nations of the world were no longer locked in a struggle to destroy each other. It made Mannion wonder what he would do with the life he had not wanted.

'Enjoying a snooze in the sun, Brad?'

The words startled Mannion. He stared into Blair's smiling face and realised he must have dozed off. The empty enamel mug was still crooked round a finger, although he did not remember finishing the tea it had contained.

'I could sleep for a week,' Mannion said, betraying nothing of his thoughts.

'The Signal boys have set up shop in a park. I've told HQ we're in Klagenfurt, and they have told me to stand by for orders. The stuff's coming in now, yards and yards of it. By the time we get along there, they'll have some of it unscrambled. We can leave the jeep here.'

There certainly seemed no danger in leaving the jeep. The square was lined with armoured cars of the Reconnaissance Regiment, and gunners wearing the yellow-on-black battleaxe emblem of the 78th Division were detaching a battery of howitzers from their tow-trucks and deploying them in a line below the elms of the square, to display a formidable array of power. In the park, a short walk away, a mixed light AA and machine-gun company were setting up camp. Blair and Mannion made their way through these new arrivals to the Signals team, who advertised their presence with metal masts and antennae.

In a trailer at the rear of the radio truck, a telegraphist was sitting typing the text of decoded signals. He handed Blair a pile of flimsies. Several bore the legend 'SACMED TO RED DRAGON'; others were labelled 'JISMED TO RED DRAGON'. The first were direct orders to Blair from Supreme Allied Headquarters. The second were updated intelligence reports from Caserta, relating to Jugoslavia. Blair and Mannion retired to a secluded park seat to read the signals. Blair read them first, passing a sheet to Mannion as soon as he had finished with it. Neither man spoke. At the end, Blair waited impatiently for Mannion to finish reading the final sheet.

'Now you know what it's all about, Brad,' the British Major said. 'We're sitting on a bloody gunpowder keg.'

Mannion stared at Blair with a dazed look.

'It's unbelievable!' he cried. 'The Eighth Army will fight the Partisans?'

'Not just the Eighth Army,' Blair pointed out. 'The Americans, too. You saw what it said. Clark's getting five divisions ready to move.'

'It's crazy,' Mannion said.

'It's Tito who's crazy,' Blair said. 'He seems to be determined to grab all the territory he can get away with before there's time for peace talks – and he means to hang on to what he gets. He's already got all Italian Istria and he's eyeball to eyeball with the New Zealanders in Trieste, saying it's his. And now he wants a piece of Austria. . . .'

'Unless we stop him,' Mannion said.

'Somebody's got to stop him. With due respect to your Partisan friends, Brad, what they're doing in Istria is inexcusable. When an enemy surrenders, he's entitled to some protection under the Geneva Convention.'

'Geneva Rules have never counted for much in Jugoslavia,' Mannion observed.

'That still doesn't excuse the massacres in Istria. Didn't you read the report on Pola?'

Mannion confessed that he had. Intelligence from the former Italian naval base had revealed the wholesale murder of German army and naval officers who had surrendered to the Partisans. They had been rounded up and lined up on the sea breakwater, and then machine-gunned. Others had been bound and, with iron bars tied to their feet, cast into the sea.

Blair stared unhappily at Mannion.

'I've got to ask you this, Brad,' he said. 'You've still got friends on the Partisan side. How are you going to feel if it comes to a showdown with them.'

'Sick,' Mannion replied. 'In a word – sick!'

'That's how every Eighth Army man I've spoken to feels about it, too. Not one of them wants it. They admire the Partisans. None of us want a scrap.'

'So what do we do?' Mannion asked.

'We talk to them,' Blair said. 'We show them that we mean business, but we talk until we're hoarse.'

The talking was not long delayed. An SOS for Blair's services was received almost immediately from a squadron commander of the 6th Armoured Division whose tanks were deployed on the southeast edge of Klagenfurt. Partisan scout cars had been sighted coming towards the town.

When Blair and Mannion arrived at the tank positions, it was to find a conference already in progress between British and Partisan officers. The discussions had made little headway because of language difficulties. The British officers were only too pleased to hand over negotiations to the newcomers. They were plainly put out by the hostile manner of the Partisans.

That hostility did not diminish when Mannion translated Partisan intentions to Blair. They made no bones about their determination to occupy Klagenfurt and all of Carinthia.

On Blair's behalf, Mannion told them, 'We do not wish to fall out with our Jugoslav friends, but we must ask you to withdraw your forces to the border. At the Yalta Conference of the big powers, it was agreed that the occupation of Austria would be left to the forces of Britain, the United States and the Soviet Union, and it is the intention of the Allied armies to stand by that agreement, to ensure that any dispute over prewar boundaries is settled at the peace table. As Klagenfurt and a large part of Carinthia has already been peacefully occupied by an Allied army and all civil functions are passing to military control, there is no need for the presence of Jugoslav forces. Indeed, such a presence will only complicate the transfer of power from the defeated German Army and put undue strain on the resources of the occupied territory.'

The Partisan spokesman's immediate response was that, since Free Jugoslavia had not been represented at the Yalta Conference, his soldiers had no obligation to be ruled by its decisions. Blair contested this. The Partisans *had* been represented at Yalta, and they had not opposed the agreement on Austria. Blair also reminded the Partisan spokesman that Marshal Stalin had endorsed the agreement. Was it the Partisans' intentions to embarrass Soviet Russia with actions that would not receive Stalin's support?

The Partisan response was curt. The Partisan Army would carry out its orders until such time as Marshal Tito instructed them otherwise.

On strict orders not to restrain the Partisans, the British soldiers made no move to stop Tito's troops from marching into Klagenfurt, where they found that every public building had been taken over by the Eighth

Army, and tanks and armoured cars had been strategically placed on every thoroughfare. They promptly withdrew, to fan across the surrounding countryside and install their troops in every hamlet and village where the Union Jack was not already flying. A stalemate rapidly developed, with both sides making it clear that they had no intention of backing down.

While telegrams flew between London, Belgrade, Washington and Moscow, relations between the twin occupying forces in Carinthia deteriorated. By night, the Partisans sent out men to stick up posters on buildings and trees and barn doors and gates. These bills proclaimed Jugoslav occupation and rule and issued regulations for the civil population. By day, the British sent out parties to tear these notices down. In villages where the British had stationed only a token force, the Partisans would pour in a battalion or more of soldiers to parade provocatively around the British post, to taunt and jeer the few men guarding it. Where the British stationed an armoured car outside a town hall, the Partisans would confront it with two of their own and a company of slogan-shouting soldiers demanding the British vehicle's removal. The men of the Eighth Army met every provocation with a discipline and calm that showed remarkable restraint. In a couple of isolated cases, Partisan commanders deployed troops and guns in a manner that indicated a readiness to fight if their orders to withdraw were not obeyed. In both cases, the beleaguered British commander ordered his men into battle positions, where they turned their guns on the encroaching Partisans in a way that left no doubt that fire would be met with fire. On each occasion, the Partisans backed down and slunk away.

Elsewhere, the confrontations were less dramatic, and frequently ludicrous. A Partisan show of strength, with a military band, would be countered by a turnout of immaculately uniformed British guardsmen, marching, as only they can, to the pipes and drums of a Highland regiment. In these displays, in which spit and polish and parade-ground skills were the telling factor, the superior bull-shine training of the Eighth Army made them easy victors. Webbing blancoed, weapons shining, howitzer barrels gleaming, tanks and armoured cars burnished and spotless, they made the JANL formations look scruffy and poorly drilled in comparison. So much so that the Partisans soon lost their eagerness for that kind of competition.

Blair and Mannion, in the meantime, covered miles of Carinthian roadway in their jeep, answering calls to defuse situations which would have needed little to start a shooting war.

Disputes constantly blew up over the congregation, just south of Klagenfurt, of some thirty thousand refugees from Slovenia. Most of those in the great field encampment, men, women and children, were civilians, but the number included several thousand Slovenes and a thousand or more Cetniks who had tried to keep the Partisans out of Slovenia. With the Partisans driving on the Slovenian capital of Ljubljana, the pro-German State Parliament had made a belated attempt to escape Tito's wrath by declaring Slovenia independent of the rest of Jugoslavia and inviting King Peter to be their head of state. Tito had replied by launching a hundred thousand Partisans against Ljubljana and driving the non-Communist population and tiny defence army into the hills and forests of the Austrian borderland.

There, the fleeing Slovenes had encountered British troops and surrendered. Laying down their arms, the Slovenes had been allowed to camp near Klagenfurt, where their future became a matter of heated dispute between the British and the JANL units who came storming into the area. The Partisans demanded the immediate return to Jugoslavia of all the refugees.

Blair and Mannion took part in the first negotiations,

which rapidly reached impasse. And it was Mannion, rather than Blair, who was most adamant that the British must not permit the repatriation of the refugees. Blair quizzed Mannion on what he saw as a hardening of attitude towards his old comrades in the JANL.

'I don't understand you, Brad,' he confided. 'You heard the catalogue of crimes which the Slovenes have committed against anyone with Partisan sympathies. Why shouldn't we let the Partisans weed out the murderers and collaborators and try them as war criminals? They've promised to give them fair trials and to let the innocent go.'

'Do you believe that?' Mannion asked him.

'Why shouldn't I? There's got to be some trust between us. Besides, it's a Jugoslav problem. The Slovenes are Jugoslav. The people they slaughtered were Jugoslav. So it's only right that the whole thing's sorted out by the Jugoslavs.'

'You forget, Major, that I've had a taste of Jugoslav justice – the old kind and the new. The old was bad enough; it landed me in the penitentiary at Lepoglava. I got a hint of the new in Montenegro, and it sure as hell didn't impress me as being an improvement.'

Blair raised his eyebrows.

'You mean what happened to the Swede from UNRRA?'

'I wouldn't be here with you now but for that Swede. He got what was coming to me, if I'd hung around. But maybe you go along with a system of justice that shoots a guy first and then holds the trial to find out, (a), was the guy guilty and (b), was it the right guy?'

Blair laughed.

'Point taken, Brad. But what do we do about it? Do we go to war with the Partisans over the Slovenes or do we hand over some of them to get shot, as they probably deserve?'

'The Partisans don't want a few,' Mannion pointed

out. 'They want the lot. And I've heard what they're saying amongst themselves – the kind of talk I never heard when Comrade General Djordje was running things. He'd have come down on it like a ton of bricks.'

'What kind of talk?' Blair asked sharply. 'You never mentioned it before.'

'You never asked,' Mannion said. 'I hear a lot. These guys look at my fancy British officer's uniform and forget I know the lingo. And I didn't much like the sound of what they were going to do to the women in that Slovenian camp. Not the sort of thing you would like to happen to your sister or your girl friend.'

Blair stared at him, round-eyed.

'They'll have to reckon with us first,' he said fiercely. He meant it, but it turned out to be an empty declaration. As a result of a bitter row the following day, both Partisans and Slovenes blamed Mannion and Blair for a total breakdown in communications. The Slovenes elected two priests to negotiate directly with the JANL representatives, effectively eliminating the third party.

To Blair's astonishment, the two sides seemed to reach some sort of accord, because a JANL negotiator sought British agreement for the removal of twelve hundred Slovenes. It was an arrangement with which the Slovenes were quite happy. They believed themselves to be a pioneer shipment of the entire group, who would be placed in camps in the south, with a view to resettlement in Italy. The twelve hundred entrained at the railway station at Maria Elend for the return to Jugoslavia, and Blair was happy that a solution had been found that pleased both the Slovenes and the Partisans. He was undisturbed by a report of an unfortunate accident at the railway station, which had resulted in the death of a Slovenian priest. It was not until much later that he learned that the priest had been beaten to death by the Partisan escorts.

Later still, a gaunt-eyed scarecrow of a man, his

clothes in tatters, arrived at the Slovenian camp near Klagenfurt and sought out the leaders. He was raving and incoherent but, in lucid spells, he begged the Slovenes not to be fooled by promises of resettlement in Italy or any other promises made by the Partisans. Although no one could remember the man, he claimed that he had been one of the volunteers of the pioneer shipment, and that he was the only one left alive.

In his rambling, crazy way, he tried to tell all who would listen what had happened to him. But his tale was beyond belief. He had obviously undergone some terrible experience that had unhinged his brain. No one took his story seriously. No one except Mannion.

Mannion questioned the man with great patience and sympathy, conforting him like a baby when he was reduced to whimpering and tears. He was an uneducated man, not very articulate, but he painted the same picture over and over with a consistency and detail that convinced Mannion of its terrible truth.

He remembered the train journey from Maria Elend. Why? Because he was hungry. He remembered the camp to which they were taken. Why? Because there was no food. None at all? Just scraps and leftovers that everybody fought for. But he never seemed to get any. What else did he remember about the camp? The women screaming. At night, they came for the women. They used to try to hide, but it was useless. There was no place for them to hide.

What did they do to the women? The man would look at Mannion slyly. He would avoid a direct answer. *You know*, he would say. *You tell me*, Mannion would say. The man would still try to evade. *You know*, he would repeat —*what men usually do to women*. It was their screams he could remember, and their weeping.

There was one woman in particular he remembered. Not a young woman. And not a very pretty woman. She cried a lot and kept asking him to give her his jacket. In the end, he gave her his jacket.

651

Why did she want his jacket? Because she was ashamed to be the way she was. What way did she mean? Without anything to cover her breasts. It shamed her to be like that. He had been sorry for her.

The man remembered being marched through the forest. What forest? He didn't know. Kojevce? It could have been Kojevce. Why were you taken to Kojevce? The man's eyes would widen, terror filling his mind. He would shake, as if he had the palsy. To be killed, he would answer – and break down.

Mannion would coax him back to coherence and get him to tell what had happened in the forest of Kojevce. The story never varied. They killed the officers and the priests first, smashing their heads in with heavy clubs. But this became too hard work and was taking too long. The Titoists set up a machine-gun and began shooting the prisoners in batches of twenty.

He could not account for his own escape. He remembered being lined up with nineteen others and waiting his turn. He had closed his eyes and prayed. He had heard the machine-gun fire and then – nothing. Maybe he had fainted. He had wakened in total darkness, thinking he was dead. Then he had discovered that he was roped by the wrist to a corpse. But he had no wounds. Not a scratch. Maybe it was because he had been right at the end of the line or because he had fainted. He had freed himself and blundered around in the dark, stumbling over corpses everywhere. It had been a nightmare without end. He could not remember how many days and nights he had spent in the forest or how he had made his way to Klagenfurt. Only one thought had filled his mind: he had to get back to Klagenfurt to warn the others.

But the Slovenes at Klagenfurt did not believe his story. They did not want to believe it. They were going to Italy, they were sure, where they would be given the chance to build new lives, albeit in exile. Mannion tried to warn them that they were taking too much on trust. But they would not listen. Blair, alarmed by Mannion's credence of the fugitive madman, urged the British authorities to seek assurances from the Tito Government in Belgrade about the future of the refugee Slovenes, but the British Government was loath to intervene, especially as a diplomatic offensive to reduce tension in the area was paying off. Britain and America had made it clear that they were ready to go to war with the JANL if Tito did not pull his army out of Austria, and Tito had appealed to Moscow for the Red Army's help in a shooting war. Stalin had turned him down flat, telling him that if he did choose to provoke war with Britain and the US, Jugoslavia would be fighting alone. Tito was now having second thoughts.

On the day Blair was told that there would be no British interference with the repatriation of the Slovenes, he found Mannion in the bar of the Klagenfurt hotel they had made their headquarters, and broke the news to him.

'That's the bad news,' Blair said. 'The good news is that Tito is pulling his troops out of Austria, which means that you and I are pulling out, too. Not that we've done a fat lot of good.'

'Where do we go from here?' Mannion asked.

'Trieste.' Blair smiled. 'Trieste is still a problem.'

'What about the Slovenes?'

'They're Tito's problem now, not ours. They're going back to Jugoslavia.'

'God help them.'

'We certainly can't,' said Blair. He frowned. 'I honestly don't think it'll be so bad for them as you think. Good Lord, there are nearly thirty thousand of them. Tito wouldn't dare kill off that number of people. He's got the respect of the whole world now, he won't throw it all down the drain by carrying on like Attila the Hun. It's the twentieth century, not the Middle Ages. There would be a worldwide outcry.'

'If the world gives a goddamn,' Mannion said sourly. 'And if the world ever gets to know.'

'You can't kill off thirty thousand people and keep it a secret,' Blair said.

'Hitler seems to have done it pretty well. There was a guy on the radio last night talking about what they found in those concentration camps in Germany . . . . Gas ovens, for God's sake! They don't know how many millions of Jews he burned in them.'

'The Nazis were capable of anything,' Blair said. 'Hitler should have been nipped in the bud. He should have been stopped long before he got to power.'

'Who's going to stop Tito?' Mannion asked.

'Tito's no Hitler.'

'They both started off much the same. Hitler was a little Austrian boy, who made it to corporal in the German Army during the First World War. Tito was a private in the Austrian Army. I don't know if he made it to corporal before he deserted. But he's a marshal of Jugoslavia now and he's got a lot more muscle than King Peter. It's going to need a big man to knock him off his perch.'

'I won't argue with that,' Blair said. 'At least he's promised free elections. Maybe the Communists won't get things all their own way, now that the shooting's stopped.'

'That's what worries me,' Mannion said. 'Has the shooting stopped? Mihailovic and his Cetniks haven't surrendered yet. Is it because they know what's going to happen to them if they do – the same as happened to that first bunch of Slovenes? The same as is going to happen to all these other Slovenes – and anybody else who gets in the way of Communism.'

'You've still got these Slovenes on your mind, Brad?' Blair gave a helpless little shake of the head. 'Maybe you're putting too much into what that crazy man said. Maybe he exaggerated it. Maybe he imagined it all.'

'Maybe he did,' Mannion said, with a shrug. 'But whatever it was that made him crazy is making me crazy, too. I don't think he imagined it. Because I keep seeing the pictures he painted. I keep hearing the screams of raped women. I keep seeing that great dark forest that stinks to the heavens with the smell of death . . . .'

Mannion downed his drink and stared sombrely at Blair. 'Major, with your permission, I think I'll get drunk.'

Blair laughed.

'Captain Mannion,' he declared, 'that's the most sensible thing you've said today. May I join you? I want to get drunk, too.'

They set about the process systematically, matching each other glass for glass, until the problems of the world receded. Some hours later, it only needed one to make an utterance – no matter how trivial the subject or mundane the observation – for the other to greet it with helpless laughter. The fate of the Slovenian refugees was forgotten; and what became of them was of little consequence to a Europe still dazed by the advent of peace.

Radio Free Jugoslavia made no comment on the successful repatriation of the Slovenes from Klagenfurt or on their permanent settlement in the forests of Kojevce. The only persons taking any interest in the protracted slaughter were residents of the region, drawn to the scene by the sound of gunfire and the harmonious chanting of hundreds of voices. The singing came from the Slovene prisoners as they were marched to the place of their death, knowing what was in store for them. They sang a requiem for the dead.

The few peasants who came to witness showed no surprise at the mass executions, agreeing that it was no less a fate than traitors and collaborators deserved. They did, however, express concern that many of the prisoners wore good and serviceable clothes, while they were clad in rags. It seemed a great waste.

The executioners agreed with the sentiment. It was a waste. So, they compelled the remaining prisoners to strip to their underwear as they waited their turn for death. The spectators were allowed to help themselves and took away as many garments as they could carry. The death squads tied what remained in bundles and carried them off, for sale or barter later.

Three weeks had passed since 97th Corps had surrendered to the soldiers of the 4th Partisan Army, and for Mara and the unfortunates made prisoner with her, each passing day had been one of mounting misery. The complement of women in the shielded core of the German force numbered well over a hundred. In addition to the Nursing Corps personnel, the female ranks had been swelled by Signals staff, radar operators, catering workers and clerks from Mostar HQ. No concessions were made by their captors to the so-called weaker sex, although all were noncombatants. The Partisans themselves made little distinction between the sexes – many women serving as front-line infantry – so they were perhaps only showing consistency in treating women prisoners with equal harshness to the men.

In the first hours of surrender, the nurses' main concern had been for the wounded in their care. They had been shocked when they were forced to abandon their charges at gunpoint, fearing that the Partisans would not give the wounded adequate care. They did not associate the sound of distant shooting with the manner in which the Partisans solved the problem. The nurses had, by then, been marched three kilometres away and herded together with the other female prisoners to become part of a marching column of two thousand captives.

They were told they were being marched to a camp. It

was a myth they would soon get used to hearing, because no camps for prisoners existed – and, indeed, the Partisans had no plans for establishing any. They were marched deep into Bosnia, without – it seemed – any pattern to their route, and their guards maintained a blistering pace. There was a steady stream of casualties. Straggling was not allowed. If a prisoner became lame or ill and did not rejoin the column with the encouragement of kicks and blows from rifle butts, he was shot on the spot and the body left at the roadside.

It was on the eighth day that the first women died. One, weak with dysentery, dropped in the roadway, and a companion fell out to aid her. Screaming for compassion from the guards for the fallen woman, the samaritan's reward was a bullet between the eyes. Her murderer then despatched the sick woman.

The column slept at night in the open on the bare ground. The prisoners were fed once a day, in the evenings, but the food was almost uneatable and insufficient, causing outbreaks of dysentery and other stomach disorders.

It soon became evident that the route was not entirely without direction or plan, despite its meandering course. It was designed to pass through as many villages and small towns as possible, so that the local inhabitants could turn out in force to abuse and humiliate the vanquished Germans. The Partisan guards made no attempt to interfere as the prisoners were jeered and stoned and beaten, and often forced to surrender boots and clothes and such valuables as had not already been stolen. Many were reduced to marching in shirts and underpants and ragged socks, with nothing else to protect them from the elements by day or night. The German soldiers did their best to guard the female contingent from these attacks – but they were powerless to prevent the partisan guards from sexual abuse of the women captives. These became more frequent as the days passed.

It was at night that the Partisan guards came looking for sport with the defenceless women prisoners, roaming among them like cattlemen viewing livestock at a market, making their choice and hauling their selected victims beyond the perimeter of the camp for a few moments of frenzied violation.

Mara came to dread these nocturnal inspections, knowing that sooner or later one of the young Partisans would fix lusting eyes on her and command her to accompany him to the hillside. She and Greta would huddle in fear each evening, expecting the worst and then almost fainting with relief when they were passed over. For no apparent reason, it was never the prettiest women who were singled out for rape. The favourites were the bigger buxom Fräuleins: those who in the past had been relegated to wallflower status at dances and parties. This was so marked that it seemed the youthful guards had inhibitions about assaulting the most attractive women.

Then the night came when a Partisan – a fresh-faced boy of eighteen – seemed unable to make up his mind between Mara and Greta. His hand was reaching out for Mara when Greta pushed in front of her and smiled invitingly at the youth.

'I'll show you a good time, big boy,' she promised the shy soldier. To Mara she murmured. 'Save it for a rainy day, Mara.' With a twisted smile she added, 'My privilege. Age before beauty.'

She was gone less than an hour. Mara wept, trying to thank her, when she returned. Greta seemed to have survived the ordeal with good humour.

'Forget it, Mara,' she said. 'That kid could have damaged you, he was so eager. It's difficult for a woman doing it for the first time, and that youg ram could have turned nasty if you'd panicked. I pretended I wanted it as much as he did.'

'Did he hurt you, Greta?'

'No. He was rough, but the only thing hurt is my self-respect. Look, Mara, don't take on. Worse things can happen than getting poked until your teeth rattle.'

'He was going to take me, Greta. If you hadn't – '

Greta did not let her finish. She put an arm round Mara's shoulder.

'I couldn't let him take you, Mara. Not until . . . not until . . . . What I'm trying to say is, I had to let you see that it isn't the end of the world if one of those pigs gets his hands on you. It's dirty and degrading, but it's not the end of the world. You'll live. But don't fight the sons of bitches. Don't struggle - that's when they get mad and start hitting and punching.'

The next evening, the same young Partisan returned. Greta prepared to go with him, but it was Mara he wanted. Greta stood between them.

'Take me,' she insisted and, in sign language, tried to make the soldier understand that Mara would be no good to him. He did not understand. He wanted Mara. Greta tried to tell him in German that it was Mara's menstruating time. He still did not understand.

Greta finally pulled up Mara's skirt, frightening and shaming Mara with her unexpected action, and pointed at the bloodstained front of Mara's knickers. The stains were a week old but they were enough to frighten off her would-be violator. With a grimace of disgust, he turned away. Then, seizing Greta by the wrist, he dragged her off towards the hillside.

A nurse who had witnessed the episode commented to Mara, 'That trick always works once, dearie, but most of them are getting wise to it. You mightn't be so lucky next time.'

Mara sat down on the ground, sick with disgust. Although bone-tired from another day's exhausting march of thirty kilometres, she could not sleep. Greta did not return until the early hours of the morning. She could scarcely drag one leg after the other, yet she still tried to disguise her pain and discomfort with humour.

'I feel like a doormat that a regiment's wiped its feet on,' she confessed to Mara. 'We had an audience tonight.'

'An audience? Oh Greta, no!' Mara's chagrin was all the greater for knowing that Greta had sacrificed herself a second time to save her.

'That young buck was banging the backside off me when some of his pals came along and wanted to get in on the act. There were half a dozen of them, no more than kids.'

Mara cradled Greta's head in her arms, trying to console her with words that sounded pitifully in-adequate.

'I don't think I could take another night like tonight,' Greta told her, sobbing now and not trying to hide her misery. 'I'm filthy from them, Mara. I'm like raw liver down below. I lost count of the times they did it. They couldn't wait for one to finish and another get started. They were off and on me like rabbits, pushing at each other, with two waiting as stiff as rolling pins for every one that ran out of steam. I couldn't take it again. I couldn't.'

Mara held Greta's trembling body close, stroking her hair.

'I won't let them take you,' she said. 'You shouldn't have protected me, Greta. They can do what they like with me. I won't let them take you again.' Greta fell alseep in her arms. Above, the sky was ablaze with stars. Mara prayed silently, head raised to the canopy of night. Where under its limitless spread was Jamie? She had saved herself for him and him alone, and had lived only for the day when she could surrender with joy to his embrace. But was that now to be for nothing? Already, she felt degraded, deprived of the normal civilised trappings of bodily function and hygiene, so that her body smelled and disgusted her. And now it was only a matter of time before some lusting soldier violated and defiled her womanhood. Would it be tomorrow, or the next day? She shuddered – and prayed for courage to face the ultimate humiliation.

Wolf Bleyer had never met Petar's and Mara's parents, so when he did finally encounter them during the second week in May 1945, the Richtmans were strangers to him. They were to remain strangers to him, because the encounter was brief and conversation between them did not reach the point where the connection was uncovered.

As far as Bleyer was concerend, the Richtmans were just two more Croatian refugees seeking to find a way into Austria and hoping to avoid capture by Tito's army. Their gleaming black limousine, packed with such possessions as could be crammed into it, had run out of fuel. Richtman stopped Bleyer's car, which was not difficult on a road crowded with humanity. The entire Croat nation was on the move north, migrating to avoid retribution for their joyful union with the Nazi cause four years earlier.

Richtman imperiously demanded fuel from Bleyer for the stranded limousine. Alternatively, Bleyer could hand over his own transport so that Richtman and his wife could be driven into Austria. Bleyer's customary politeness deserted him. He informed Richtman in no uncertain manner that the only fuel he had was in the tank of his vehicle – and that was likely to give out in the next few kilometres. If Richtman wanted to get to Austria, he would have to do what everybody else was doing: walk!

His answer did not please Richtman. Did the German officer not know that he was talking to an important minister of the Croatian Government, whose safe journey to Austria was a matter of national importance and had been given the highest priority by the German military commander? Bleyer did not know. Nor did he care. He had a war to fight – and that was what he intended to get on with.

Bleyer ordered his driver to drive on. And he did so, furiously hooting his horn and forcing a passage through the milling throng. Richtman stood, shouting after the slow-moving car. But his threats were lost on Bleyer who was beginning to despair of ever reaching the border town of Bleiburg, where he had been ordered as temporary commander of a *Croatische* volunteer battalion. The makeshift battalion – a hotchpotch of survivors from other units found in Zagreb – had already been thrown into the battle near the small market town on the Austrian border. Bleyer had remained in Zagreb, destroying secret papers.

He was one of the last Germans to leave the city, which was abandoned without a fight. The Partisans entered an empty and relatively undamaged Croatian capital, from which most of the population had fled in a great migratory scramble towards Austria. The drive westward from Srem had cost Tito's army dearly, however. In the month-long offensive, thirty-six thousand Partisans had died.

Germany's surrender came on the day that Zagreb fell to the Partisans and, on that day, all military movement by the Germans and their allies should have ceased. The order was ignored by the Croatian and German units shielding the mass migration to Austria. The way to Bleiburg was barred by the 51st Partisan Division, and the Croats fought their way through, aided by the way the Partisans launched their soldiers against them in suicidal waves. The Partisan division was decimated, but it had delayed the Croatian exodus long enough for massive reinforcements to arrive. The delay allowed for other developments, which were to seal the Croat nation's fate. Ahead of them, their route into Austria was being effectively blocked.

One great natural barrier stood in the way of the Croat advance into the Austrian province of Styria, to the east of Bleiburg. This was the River Drava, which rises in the Austrian Tyrol and flows east, then south-east, for seven hundred kilometres to join the Danube. It runs east through Carinthia, above Bleiburg, and crosses into Slovenia a little further on. In Jugoslavia, it flows almost parallel with the Austrian border before dipping southeast into Croatia to become the Jugoslav-Hungarian border. The Croat migration intended to cross this great tributary of the Danube and move north into Styria, but a shock awaited them when they reached the river. The north bank was occupied. The Croats found themselves staring across the river at the guns and armour of a Bulgarian division that had no intention of letting them cross.

The Bulgars were part of the Russian General Tolbhukin's Ukrainian Front armies, which had pushed the Germans out of Hungary and driven west into Austria. With the river crossing barred to them, the Croats still hoped to get into Austria by remaining south of the river and passing through the narrow gap of Austrian territory between the Drava and Bleiburg. Another nasty surprise was in store for them. Blocking this route were freshly arrived units of the British Eighth Army, astride the frontier. The British had streamed eastward from Klagenfurt, south of the Drava, and, indeed, had made contact with the Bulgarian troops on May the thirteenth – two days previously.

Wolf Bleyer had left Zagreb on May the seventh. On the ninth he had encountered the Richtmans. On the next day, he had finally located his *Croatische* Volunteers. For the next four days and nights, he was never out of action as his makeshift battalion beat off attack after attack from Partisans. On the fourth night, a Croat paratroop battalion took over protection of that part of the flank to allow Bleyer and his men some rest.

Little rest was forthcoming, because the weary volunteers were rushed up to probe ahead of the units, which were now wheeling west below the Drava to avoid the Bulgars on the river's north bank.

It was Bleyer's men who discovered a squadron of British tanks blocking the way into Austria. A Croat delegation hurriedly came forward to parley with the British. They told the Eighth Army officers that they wished to surrender to them and would lay down their arms if allowed to pass over the border. The British commander was polite, almost apologetic. His orders were explicit. No one was to be allowed to cross the border from Jugoslavia. If the Croats wished to surrender, they had to do so on Jugoslav soil, to the Partisan Army.

The Croats protested that, if they did so, they would be tortured and butchered by the Partisans, who had sworn vengeance on them. The British officer dismissed their fears. Marshal Tito's Government in Belgrade had assured the British Government that the Geneva Convention would be rigorously observed by the Partisan armies.

'You have one hour to consider what you wish to do,' the British officer told the Croats. 'At the end of that time, if you have not disarmed your forces, I will be obliged to assist our Partisan allies to enforce your surrender.'

Ashen-faced, the Croat leaders withdrew, to discover that in their absence an ultimatum had been received from the Partisans, who now had them boxed in. The square was complete. To the west, ahead of them, the British blocked the way into Austria. To the north, was the Drava, with the Bulgars on the far bank. On their south flank and behind them, the Partisans were massed in strength and awaiting the signal to attack. There had been no equivocation about the Partisan ultimatum.

'Indicate your surrender before 1600 hours or you will be wiped out,' the JANL commander threatened. The Croats received the message at quarter to four in the afternoon. They had fifteen minutes to comply.

Ringed within the Croat fighting units – a force of

perhaps fifty thousand men – were the people they protected: a locustlike swarm of civilian refugees, spread over field and hillside and numbering more than four hundred thousand men, women and children. Their leaders looked across this great congregation of terrified and homeless humanity and knew they could protect them no longer. The order was passed to the fighting perimeter: cease fire and display white flags.

The decision to surrender did not meet with unanimous approval in the Croatian ranks. Here and there, along the perimeter facing the JANL, officers in charge of some units rejected the order to display white flags, electing to try fighting a way through the Partisan lines, rather than be taken alive. A series of short sharp one-sided fights resulted, with the Partisan ring remaining intact. The isolated groups who sought to break out were wiped out to a man.

Nor was the surrender decision welcomed by some of the civilian refugees. Many had given enthusiastic support to the Nazi-style regime of Pavelic's Croatian Government, and they were convinced that torture and death was all that awaited them at the hands of the Partisans. Hundreds were not prepared to endure that fate, and pitiful scenes were enacted as weeping fathers shot their wives and children and ended their own misery with the final bullet. Some, who had no weapons, begged those who had to perform the executions for them.

Wolf Bleyer assembled his battalion and gave the men the option of fighting a way out under his leadership or laying down their arms. Only a handful indicated by raising their arms that they were prepared to fight on. He accepted the will of the vast majority, to surrender.

'Let's do it like soldiers, then,' he exhorted. 'With discipline. With dignity. And with our heads held high.'

He formed the battalion in marching order and stood at their head. Then, with a soldier beside him carrying a white flag, he gave the order to march. They marched away from the Austrian border, down the road through the encamped mass of frightened refugees who enveloped the landscape. It was a six-kilometre march to the grassy meadow, where other uniformed units were already heaping their weapons in mounds under the watchful eyes of a red-bannered array of Partisans. The latter had sited machine-guns all along one edge of the field and had them pointed at the growing congregation of disarmed Croatian troops.

As Bleyer and his men neared the meadow, a dishevelled figure leapt out in the roadway in front of the German officer, pleading with him to give him his revolver, so that he could save his wife and himself from Tito's butchers. With a start, Bleyer recognised the pompous official who had flagged him down less than a week before. Richtman was in a sorry state; his black jacket and striped trousers mud-stained and incongruous in that place and at that time. Bleyer ignored him, keeping his eyes steadily to the front and never losing his stride. He was aware of the man badgering the soldiers marching behind when his appeal to Bleyer failed. The soldiers, grim-faced and erect as their commander, filed past as resolutely as Bleyer had; Richtman was brushed aside.

It was not, however, the last time that Bleyer was to catch sight of Richtman. The third occasion came two days later. By then, the Partisans were herding their Croatian prisoners – nearly half a million of them – along steep tracks that led across the Pohorje Mountains. At regular intervals, Partisan soldiers would nip off the tail end of the huge procession, directing as many as a thousand to leave the track and venture higher into the more remote gorges of the rolling green uplands. Sudden bursts of pistol, rifle and machine-gun fire would erupt and echo across the hilltops, filling the main body of trekking prisoners with dread.

It was on the afternoon of the second day that Bleyer found himself at the extreme tail of the trekking horde. At the start, there had been a straggling column of seventy thousand or more strung out in a six-kilometre-long trail behind him. Now there was no one behind him but a couple of dozen Partisan guards. Suddenly the column ahead stopped – or so it seemed at first. In fact, the Partisans had stopped only the rear portion of prisoners – a group of perhaps seven hundred, which included thirty women with children at their heels.

On the hillside below, Bleyer could see houses to the north – a little hamlet that was white and peaceful in the bright May sunlight. But it was to the south, that he and the other prisoners were pushed and shoved, along a stony path that entered a small rocky valley floored with lush grass and ablaze with wild flowers.

Bleyer found himself vying for room on the narrow path with a man and a woman. It was Richtman, still wearing the black jacket and striped trousers that were torn and muddied. He was holding on to a woman in a tattered frock of flowery design, whom Bleyer took to be his wife. If Richtman recognised the man who had refused him fuel for his car and a gun to end his misery, he gave no sign.

'They're going to kill us,' Richtman said to Bleyer.

'I'd worked that out,' Bleyer replied. He threw the woman an encouraging smile. 'Are you afraid?'

'I am resigned,' the woman said. There seemed to be a wetness of tears in her eyes and her lip trembled involuntarily, but she was composed. 'I will not be sorry to die.'

They were halted at the end of the little valley. Then, singly, they were made to mount a sharp incline and walk out along a broad rocky platform, which ended abruptly over a ravine. When a dozen prisoners were on the platform, they were ordered to stand at the edge of the ravine. Partisans with Sten guns waited for them.

Then the shooting began. The force of the bullets hitting their backs pitched the bodies of the prisoners into the ravine.

Five batches of twelve had been executed when the Richtmans, followed by Bleyer, were ordered up on to the platform. They stood facing the drop. The edge of the rock was greasy with blood. Richtman held his wife's right hand in his. She reached out her left to hold Bleyer's hand in a trembling grip. From somewhere in the waiting throng behind them, a frightened child was wailing pitifully.

'Long live Croa – ' Richtman's sudden defiant shout was cut off as the Sten guns blasted. They were the last sounds Wolf Bleyer heard before his bullet-riddled body tumbled into the ravine, where it sprawled grotesquely on the growing mound of dead.

Away to the east, the long winding procession of prisoners heard the sixth sudden rattle of gunfire in the space of ten minutes. They knew its meaning and wondered how long it would be before their turn would come to face the execution squads. Some were not kept in dread too long. By evening on the third day of the trek away from Bleiburg, the long column had shrunk considerably. Behind, its path through the green hills of Pohorje was well marked by a trail of blood, and more than a hundred thousand corpses lay along the way.

For the Croats, the marching and the dying was destined to continue for most of the summer. Across Jugoslavia to the Danube and then south into Macedonia, the trek was to continue, and a hundred thousand more corpses would mark the dwindling column's progress. The world knew nothing of the genocidal punishment inflicted on the Croat people for their nationalistic fervour and their support of the terror politics of Ante Pavelic. It was a sad reflection on the heroic struggle of the Partisans, however, that in the hour of a momentous victory they should tarnish it forever with deeds of everlasting shame. Frightful atrocities committed in the heat of battle may be understood if not condoned. When genocide and the murder of men, women and children is carried out as a deliberate act of governmental policy, its architects forfeit all right to honour and forgiveness.

The great irony in the near extinction of the Croats was that the chief architect of the policy was a Croat – Josip Broz Tito. But his excesses proved no impediment to subsequent worldwide veneration. Nor did the other villain in the piece suffer undue hardship for his crimes. Ante Pavelic did not share the sufferings of his people. While they were being butchered, he was en route to Argentina and a comfortable survival to ripe old age.

The Death March was not exclusive to the migrant Croats alone. When the German armies in Italy surrendered to Alexander, a week before the general capitulation of the German forces in Europe, it left Army Group 'E' without a protected right flank and an escape route into Austria. As a consequence, the survivors of a German force which at one time had numbered four hundred thousand surrendered to the Partisans. Many of the officer prisoners were shot out of hand, but the surviving soldiers were assembled by the thousand and made to march across the length and breadth of Jugoslavia. Abused and humiliated wherever they went, the prisoners died by the hundred.

Stefan Markovic was one of only a few Communist Government ministers to express reservations over official policy to parade the defeated German Army in this inhumane and degrading manner. He did not express these reservations in public, but in private, when he had the ear of other members of the Central Committee. He dared even to raise the matter with Tito. The Marshal heard him out patiently.

'Still the conscience of the Party, Stefan?' Tito's smile was broad. 'What is it about you that makes you worry for the health of our enemies?'

'I don't give a damn for the Germans,' Stefan replied. 'They've done nothing to earn my sympathy. It's the image of the Party that I'm concerned about. What we're doing is barbarous. Do we want the world to think that anything Hitler could do, we can do, too? Do we gain anything by stooping to Nazi levels of savagery?'

'You exaggerate everything, Stefan,' Tito chided amicably. 'What else can we do with all those prisoners but keep them on the move? We have no camps for them. They are no worse off than thousands of our own people whose homes have been destroyed and who are desperately short of food and clothes and medicine and all the other things we want to give them. Our duty is to our own people first, not to those who oppressed them and caused their suffering.'

'I'm not saying we should mollycoddle them,' Stefan persisted. 'But making a public spectacle of a beaten enemy's misery makes me ashamed. You know, as I know, what it was like to be persecuted. So it disturbs me now when I see ourselves as the persecutors. It makes me feel that, after all, we are no better than the people we despised. I fought them with all my heart and soul because I believed that, if our positions were reversed, we could show the world that our ways were better; that we were fitter than they to govern and make the rules; that we could make life better for all our people without beatings and terror and persecution.'

Tito regarded Stefan with a sadness that was almost a reproach.

'Stefan, Stefan. Do you think that the things I want and have struggled all my life for are any different from the things you want? Do you think that I don't want an end to all the killing and suffering? I do. I long for it with all my heart. But I can't be weak or show the Party to be weak. I have to be strong. I have to harden my heart to make sure that the evils of the past never come back to threaten everything that we've won. We cannot afford to be distracted by undue worry about German prisoners. Their welfare comes second to the welfare of our own people, and if they've come in for some rough treatment, they've brought it on themselves. After what they did at Kraljevo and Kragujevac, we would have been justified in shooting every German we laid our hands on.'

'Maybe that would have been more merciful, Comrade Marshal,' Stefan suggested unhappily. 'If I were in their shoes, I think I would have preferred a quick death.'

'Only because you're blessed with more compassion than any ten other men I know,' Tito said with a smile. 'But don't think you have a monopoly of it. I have been exercising my mind on what we do with all these able-bodied Germans. They laid waste out cities and our farms, so it would be justice if they were put to work restoring what they have destroyed. It's only fair that they earn their keep.'

The sentiment was one with which Stefan could fully agree, and he felt happier for having raised the subject with Tito. In the meantime, the prisoner marches continued – and would do so throughout the summer, without any sign of end – although Stefan was repeatedly assured that plans to utilise the prisoners as a labour force were well advanced.

In late May, an old friend returned to Belgrade. Comrade Djordje arrived from Montenegro, by way of Italy and Trieste – where, briefly, he had taken part in diplomatic talks with the British and Americans over the future of the city. Stefan was overjoyed to see him, not just because of genuine friendship but because, in Djordje, he had a Central Committee colleague whose ideological thinking and aims were closely in tune with his own.

Djordje's return to Belgrade was not without trauma. He was distressed to find that the prewar Communist cells which he had organised and held together in the days of the Regency dictatorship had not survived the German occupation and the ferreting work of the Gestapo. Djordje had left a core of three hundred activists behind in Belgrade – mostly men and women whom he had recruited personally – and all had died. Most had perished before firing squads at the Gestapo killing ground of Jajinici.

Stefan's reunion with Djordje was sufficiently joyful an occasion, however, for both men to abandon for once their customary frugality. They celebrated with a sumptuous dinner at a restaurant reserved for high Party functionaries and inbibed more wine in an evening than they normally consumed in a month. It was in the course of this feast that Djordje told Stefan of OZNA's interest in Mannion, and the American's dramatic departure from Montenegro. But that was not the end of his news of Mannion. Djordje joyfully recounted how, in Trieste – only two days previously – he had encountered Mannion again, looking every inch a British officer. Djordje had been tickled pink to discover that the Partisan whose transfer to the British he had sanctioned, was representing the British point of view to *him*.

'Just think of it, Stefan. Here is a man who shot a Regency agent in mistake for a Pavelic hood, who was jailed with Communists and who told Tito his Party was the next best thing to Roosevelt's Democrats; a man who fought with the Cetniks and then against the Cetniks with us; who bargained with the Americans and the British *on our behalf*. . . . And he is now negotiating for the British and *trying to persuade us to get out of Trieste*! And he's not British and he's not Jugoslav – he's an American!'

Mannion's involvement with so many contradictory bodies of opinion delighted Djordje mightily. It represented a tangle which only a Montenegrin, with an appreciation of Montenegrin-style political complications, could savour with great gusto.

'But what about the other one?' Djordje wanted to

know. What became of the third member of the gang of desperadoes who went over the wall at Lepoglava?

It shamed Stefan that he did not know what had happened to Jamie Kyle. He confessed to Djordje that he had not seen Jamie since the paratroop attack on Drvar. And Stefan did not like to be reminded of Drvar, with its awful memories of the rage and hate with which he had killed his own brother.

Fresher memories loomed unbidden in Stefan's mind; memories of the consequence of Marko's death. The sneering face of Gubec and the OZNA chief's threats. He had named Mannion as a target of his hate. And only by the grace of God had Mannion escaped Gubec's goons – because, according to Djordje, they had shot the wrong man by mistake.

That still left Jamie. Had Gubec sent his men after Jamie, too? The thought made Stefan's blood run cold. Maybe Jamie was already dead. Dear, brave Jamie, who had gone through so much for him. Where was he? What had become of him? Stefan knew he had to get the answers to these questions – but another question hammered at his mind. Was it too late?

9

Deliverance

The prison cell was no more than a grotto, a cavity built into the massive outer wall of the ancient castle. The wall was on the seaward side of the craggy stronghold, looking across blue water to the barren shape of the island of Krk. Jamie had noted that fact before they locked him in the cell, which had no window. The only light admitted came through the tiny grille in the heavy door, which opened on to the wide castle yard.

The castle was occupied by a small detachment of Partisan soldiers – not one of them under the age of fifty – and two OZNA officers. Jamie suspected that the grey-haired soldiers had been relegated to guard duties to release younger men for front-line service. They were a tough old bunch, for all that, and watchful as hawks, giving the impression that they took their work very seriously and itched to use their rifles. They did get regular target practice – as Jamie learned very quickly – from the executions that took place regularly in the yard beyond his cell. The victims came from the steady stream of suspected 'Party enemies' brought almost daily to the castle for interrogation and judgement by the OZNA officers. These prisoners never stayed overnight, which meant that Jamie's cell was the only one ever occupied.

Jamie suspected that if the treacherous Brigade Commissar Radonic had not chosen to stay in Istria, he – Jamie – would not be alive. But Radonic had not returned south with the Partisans escorting the British patrol from Istria; and the OZNA officers to whom

Jamie had been delivered were easier to awe than Radonic. They had been bewildered by Jamie and his Bosnians, and Jamie had had little difficulty in persuading them to free the hill men.

'Keep me, if you like,' he had told his new captors, 'but they have done nothing wrong. They did not know if the Istrian Partisans were genuine or not, and thought when the Istrians turned their weapons on the British that we had fallen into a German trap. What would you have done in your shoes if people who said they were friends suddenly turned their guns on you?'

Jamie created enough uncertainty in the OZNA officers' minds for them to order the Bosnians back to their parent brigade in the south. Jamie might have talked his way to his own freedom, too, if one of the OZNA officers had not decided to seek information about him from his Bosnian brigade headquarters. The reply he got from his OZNA counterpart in Bosnia had made him both suspicious and cautious. It was a glowing testimonial to Jamie's military record with the Partisans, but it had one puzzling postscript. On three separate occasions, Jamie had sought out military intelligence officers in Bosnia and asked them if they could identify and locate a unit of German Army nurses known to have been in Jajce. The officers concerned had thought his interest odd but had taken no action, other than to record it in Jamie's dossier.

Jamie's custodians at the castle near Senj had decided to hold him until such time as some higher authority gave them specific orders. They did not want to take precipitate action against an officer who had an awesome reputation and had won the accolade 'Tiger of Bioce', and was known to be the close friend of a Central Committee member.

At least once a day, Jamie was led across the yard to a bare little office, which at one time might have housed a janitor or some such castle functionary. Here, he was interrogated by the two officers. The interrogations took on a monotonous regularity.

'Are you a member of the Communist Party?'

'No.'

'Why?'

'I am a soldier.'

'Many soldiers are members of the Party. Why not you?'

'Membership is not compulsory. Is it a crime not to be a Party member?'

'It is a crime to be an enemy of the Party.'

'Is that what you think I am?'

'Can you prove that you are not?'

'What do I have to do? I spent six years in Lepoglava prison because I would not betray the Party. I have spent the last four years killing the Party's enemies. What more must I do?'

'You can explain your unusual interest in enemy units. Why should you be so anxious to find the location of German Army nurses? When Supreme Headquarters was in Drvar, were you passing secrets to the Germans in Jajce?'

'I have never passed secrets to the Germans.'

'Why then did you want to find those enemy nurses?'

'Because one of them was my fiancée. She was risking her life passing information to us. You should know this. Her contact was one of your OZNA officers, who was working undercover in Jajce.'

'Can you prove this?'

'Ask Marshal Tito. He'll confirm it. Ask anyone on the Supreme Staff who was at Drvar. They all knew about it.'

Whenever Jamie mentioned Tito or the Supreme Staff or his friend, Comrade General Markovic, it always had the same effect on his interrogators. They began to flutter nervously, riddled with self-doubts. There was, however, one other question that came up, which Jamie was unable to answer until the fourth interrogation. Try as he might, he could not remember the name of the intelligence officer who had brought him Mara's message from Jajce. Then, one night, it came to him.

Next day, he was able to tell his interrogators that the agent's name was Djuro Djakovic. The information was greeted like gold by the OZNA officers. They obviously knew of him. But they did not tell Jamie what they intended to do with the information. In fact, Jamie had been in their custody for more than a week before the officers did anything at all. It took them that long to come to the conclusion that if any decision was going to be made regarding the fate of their well-connected prisoner, then it would be made by someone in the system who had the muscle to take care of himself if a mistake was made. The two men thought nothing of handing out a dozen death sentences, seven days a week, but in the case of Jamie Kyle, they suspected they were playing with dynamite.

Consequently they did two things. They wrote a long report for OZNA Headquarters in Belgrade, which was faintly critical of Brigade Commissar Radonic for saddling them with the problem; and they despatched a shorter missive to 4th Army Headquarters to Djuro Djakovic, inviting him to take responsibility for a case with which he seemed to be a lot more familiar than they.

In the meantime, Jamie was treated well and the daily interrogations – which more and more took the form of friendly conversations – continued. If anything worried the OZNA officers, it was the growing anger and impatience of their prisoner at his detention. Unknown to all of them, the matter of Jamie's arrest had come to the attention of others who were not directly concerned. The LRDG Captain who had been prevented from entering Istria by Radonic's intervention reached British HQ in Zadar and made a strongly worded protest about the incident. In it, he expressed great concern for the Partisan officer who had accompanied his patrol. The officer was a British subject, a man of exceptional courage and character who had behaved correctly despite great provocation – and he had been rewarded by being placed under arrest. The Captain urged the British military authorities to do their utmost to intervene, through the channels open to them, on the Partisan officer's behalf.

Of the several initiatives taken to resolve the problem of the lone prisoner, one produced a response during Jamie's fourth week of captivity. At just after midday, his cell door was opened and two of the veteran guards ordered him out. He was marched to the interrogation room where, to his surprise, he found three OZNA officers waiting for him. He was mystified when the third greeted him with a smile.

'So, we meet again, comrade,' he said. Jamie stared at the man, who wore a brand new uniform but was hatless, his hair slicked down. Recognition came slowly; the eyes and the nose were the clues. The last time Jamie had seen the man, he had been wearing the turban and *kalpak* of the Bosnian hillman. His name – the one Jamie had had difficulty remembering – was Djuro Djakovic.

Djakovic got up from behind the table at which he had been sitting, and came round to shake Jamie's hand and clasp him in a comradely embrace. 'It is good to see you,' he said, and added: 'In spite of the circumstances.'

'I scarcely recognised you from the last time,' Jamie apologised. He was encouraged by the open friendliness of the other man. Their past acquaintanceship had been slight, to say the least.

'My comrades here tell me that you fell foul of Brigade Commissar Radonic up in Istria,' Djakovic grinned.

'You know what happened?'

'I know Radonic. He would stir up trouble in an empty room.' Djakovic shrugged. 'He was only carrying out orders from Belgrade. . . . Although there was a very

678

clear instruction to be firm but tactful with the British. Radonic has about as much tact as a rabid dog. The sensible thing would have been to explain the situation to you. All we can do now is apologise to you.'

Relief surged through Jamie.

'You are letting me go?'

Djakovic smiled.

'You're a free man. As soon as you're ready, we'll go.'

'We?'

'We have unfinished business. I have already told our comrades here of the debt that we owe to the beautiful Mara and how she warned us of the attack on Drvar. But for her, I could have ended up in an SS torture chamber. I want to find her and thank her.' He grinned. 'Unless I'm wrong, you're the one she'd really be happy to see. So, if you don't mind me playing Cupid. . . ?'

Jamie thought his heart would burst within his breast. He could have hugged this big friendly man, whom he scarcely knew. The anger and resentment which had built up within him during the long days of incarceration fell away in an instant. He even felt benevolent to the two OZNA officers who, in their bumbling way, had brought to him this unlikeliest of angels. It was like a miracle.

Within the hour, Jamie was seated beside Djakovic in his recently acquired Willys jeep, with its red flag and Partisan star fluttering bravely from a staff. Djakovic wore no insignia to indicate rank, so it came as a surprise to Jamie to learn that his companion was now a lieutenant-general in the JANL and Chief of Military Intelligence for the 4th Partisan Army. He was scornful of the new breed of OZNA officers – including Jamie's recent custodians – who were proliferating everywhere. They were not fighting men, drawn from the Army and with records of *real* intelligence work in the field, but opportunists who would gut their own grandmothers to get advancement in the Party.

'Did you see how they bowed and scraped to me?' he

asked Jamie. 'Enough to make me sick. Right now, they'll be sitting clapping their hands and telling each other how clever they are because they've offloaded you on to me. You may not know it, comrade, but you were a problem to them. Whatever they did with you, they knew it would be the wrong thing – so they did nothing. They would have let you rot there forever if I hadn't come along and taken all responsibility. That's all they were waiting for – and now they'll be happy as pigs in shit. They can go back to frightening the hell out of scared little shopkeepers that some neighbour has accused of selling vegetables to the Ustashi.'

Jamie could not have cared less about the OZNA officers. Now that his initial euphoria had gone, he was contemplating the magnitude of the task in hand. He had been swept along by the joy of being free once again – but now reality returned. How and where were they to begin the search for Mara?

Djakovic smiled when Jamie expressed his concern.

'They didn't make me a chief of intelligence for nothing,' he said. 'Even though I say it myself, I'm good at the job. And I've done my homework. Before I left Headquarters, I did some detective work on the divisions the Germans had around Jajce, with particular attention to identified field hospitals. There were four that we know of. Three went north after the shambles at Drvar, and the fourth was sent south to Mostar. I have a hunch that that was where Mara went, because a lot of nurses were seen in Mostar – '

'I *know* Mara went to Mostar,' Jamie interrupted, almost exploding with excitement. He told Djakovic of the stranded German convoy and catching sight of Mara.

Djakovic was pleased to have his hunch confirmed.

'That simplifies everything,' he said. 'That means she was caught up in the mess of their retreat from Mostar. The whole of their 97th Corps surrendered to us. I could give you its entire order of battle.'

'Then Mara must be a prisoner?' The realisation brought a sudden dread to Jamie. For the past two years, neither side in the conflict had troubled much about taking prisoners. But surely, now that victory had been won. . . ? 'What happened to this Corps that surrendered?'

'There were thousands of prisoners,' Djakovic said, but Jamie sensed an unease in the other man.

'Where are they? What happened to them?' Urgency made Jamie shrill.

'They were kept on the move,' Djakovic said, almost defensively. 'Belgrade ordered it. We don't have any prisoner camps. God, she could be anywhere in Bosnia!'

His tone alarmed Jamie.

'Is there something you're not telling me?'

Djakovic threw an angry glare at Jamie, ignoring his question.

'Damnit, I want to find her as much as you do,' he said. 'I'm not doing this just for you.'

'Why are you doing it?' Jamie roared.

'I don't know,' Djakovic shouted back at him. 'Yes I do, damnit! It was when you were in prison. She didn't look twice at me, but I worshipped her. I would have done anything for her. Anything! I still would! I've never wanted anyone else. . . . '

Djakovic was so distracted that he suddenly had to correct the wheel of the jeep to avoid a precipitous drop beyond the road's verge. They were climbing away from Senj on a very bad road that twisted and turned and required a concentration that Djakovic had momentarily lost. He sagged over the wheel, breathing hard.

Jamie was shaken, as much by the other man's revelation as by the narrow escape from the precipice.

'I don't know what to say,' he confessed. 'You want Mara for yourself?'

Djakovic laughed bitterly.

'I don't stand a chance,' he said. 'I never have. It's

ridiculous, isn't it? Feeling this way after all these years. I thought it would pass. There have been other girls, but she was the perfect one. The one I couldn't have. I've never forgotten her. And I've never wanted anyone quite so much as I wanted her.' He smiled lopsidedly at Jamie. 'I didn't mean to tell you this. I was upset at the thought that maybe something bad had happened to her.'

'Why should you think that?'

'Things I've heard about the prisoners we took. About them being marched until they dropped. I was told they were dying like flies.' Djakovic saw Jamie's eyes widen with fear. 'You'd better be ready to face the fact that maybe we're too late. Maybe she's dead. If she is, I promise you that I shall personally crucify the bastards responsible.'

Jamie was shaking like a leaf. In the space of minutes, his spirits had soared to the mountaintops and tumbled to the depths. He stared at Djakovic.

'Let's go,' he said. 'All we're doing here is wasting time.'

Djakovic gunned the jeep at the gradient. They drove on, and no words passed between them.

The savage Karst had taken a terrible toll of the marching prisoners. The heat and the marching had been punishing enough, but the Partisan guards had devised a diabolical additional torture for their charges. They had rationed water – of which they had a plentiful supply – to one cupful per prisoner per day.

Greta had suffered much more than Mara because of this deprivation. Weakened and debilitated by dysentery, dehydration had undermined the little strength she had left and, without Mara half-carrying her along the road, she would have given up and perished.

On the day after Greta had endured multiple rape, the entire guard force of the prisoners had been changed. A new detachment of Partisan soldiers had taken over at a village along the way and the old had driven off in three trucks. The two remaining heavy trucks now drove ahead and behind the straggling procession for the long march across the Karst.

The women prisoners prayed and hoped that the fresh contingent of guards would not resort to the nightly combing of their number for playthings, as their predecessors had done. Their hopes were soon dispelled. At the first evening stop, they discovered that the fresh guards were precisely that – fresh. Their eagerness to avail themselves of the women was disheartening, to say the least.

Greta was almost prostrate with dysentery, and Mara, resigned, made no struggle when a swarthy young soldier seized her by the wrist and led her off towards the stony hillside. Mara was as shocked as he was when a stocky figure suddenly barred their way.

'I will take that woman,' the man ordered Mara's abductor. 'Go and find yourself another.' He was obviously senior to the young soldier, who let Mara go as if he had been electrocuted.

'Yes, Comrade *Kaplar*,' the young soldier replied, and took himself off in a hurry. Mara stared with fear at the other man. He was one of the ugliest she had ever seen. He had no left eye, just a twisted socket. And he was old. How old, she could not guess. His hair was cropped to a wiry grey stubble. He looked anything between fifty and sixty, but he could have been over seventy, judging by the worn lines of his leathery face. He stared at her with his good eye.

'You will do,' he said approvingly. 'From now on, you will be my woman. You will not go with any other of these scum. Do you understand what I am saying?'

'Yes,' Mara murmured fearfully.

'Good,' he said. 'Follow me.' At his feet was a shoulderpack, against which a rifle was propped. A plaid blanket lay across the top of the pack. He picked up the blanket, threw it across one shoulder, and then, carrying the pack and rifle, he strode off resolutely up the hill.

Mara followed. The sun had not yet set and it was still hot. The hillside was steep and she was bone-tired and thirsty. She struggled to keep pace with the man in front. He kept going until they were out of sight of the encampment and its sounds were faint on the evening air. In a rocky little bowl, the *Kaplar* sat down and ordered her to do the same. She was gasping for breath from the effort of climbing. He threw her a water bottle.

'Drink,' he ordered. She did so, greedily. Then, spilling some water on her hands, she bathed her head and neck. The water bottle was snatched from her hand.

'I told you to have a drink, not a bath,' the *Kaplar* complained. She looked at him fearfully. 'Stand up,' he ordered. 'Let me see you.'

She stood, staring at him helplessly. He glared at her impatiently.

'I want to see you. Those rags . . . take them off.'

She began to undress, hesitatingly. He told her to be quick. She shed all but the soiled and stained knickers which were such a shame to her. She tried not to look at the man. His fierce command made her jump, startled. Self-consciously, she did as he had bidden her. She took off the knickers and stood, cowering.

'Stand up straight. I want to see you! Don't cover yourself with your hands!'

She stood erect, her eyes directed upward. A tear burned down her cheek as she held her hands away from her body and displayed her womanhood. He came towards her then, pawing her and kissing her breasts. Then his slobbering lips were on hers, which were caked and dry and sore. His breath had a stale oniony smell.

There was momentary relief as he threw the blanket on the hard rock. He threw himself on her, fumbling desperately with the belt of his trousers. She gritted her teeth in the expectation of violation but, although she could feel him wet against her thighs, none came. He clung to her, grunting in frustration at his spent softness. His mind was afire with lust but his flesh was not equal to its demands.

The *Kaplar's* impotence was obviously not a new thing to him, or so it seemed from his subsequent behaviour. He was almost apologetic to Mara for failing to rape her and joked good-humouredly about times when his virility was a byword among the women of his village. He had not been the same since he was wounded in the stomach at the Neretva.

His first failure did not deter him forcing himself on Mara at every successive halt made by the slowly moving column and, although she felt foul and degraded by his pawing at her body and gloating one-eyed voyeurism, she had the small consolation that her maidenhood remained intact. And, such was the proprietorial guardianship of his sex toy by the *Kaplar*, she remained unmolested by the other guards. None dared look twice at the prisoner, whom the fearsome-looking veteran had singled out as his own.

In some ways, the *Kaplar* was extraordinarily kind to his chosen. Extraordinarily, that is, amid the Partisans' lack of charity or compassion for their prisoners. The *Kaplar*, however, brought Mara little titbits of food, and every evening topped up the water bottle – which was a gift to her. He even brought her a tiny piece of soap, which was a treasure beyond price.

Mara shared what she could, especially with Greta. Mara's friend grew steadily weaker and more dependent on her.

Through arid hills, they came at last to a river, where they were given permission to bathe and clean their filthy rags as best they could. But the next day was a particularly arduous one because, perversely, the Partisans made them march along the railway track, rather than on the road on the opposite bank of the river.

Greta kept falling and, finally, she went down and stayed down. Mara's pleadings as she tried to get her back to her feet were of no avail. Greta was unconscious. Mara scarcely had the strength to raise her, let alone carry her. The other prisoners passed them by, hissing at Mara to leave her friend, that she was obviously finished. But Mara would not desert the girl who had protected her.

The tail end of the column moved past, leaving Mara crouched over Greta on the railway track. The stumbling footsteps grew fainter. Mara looked up into the barrel of the rifle which a Partisan guard was thrusting at her face. He ordered Mara to leave her friend and catch up with the column.

'No,' she screamed. 'I'm not leaving her!' She begged the soldier to help get Greta to her feet. She would walk, if only she could get her to her feet.

The soldier repeated his order to move. Still Mara refused. The soldier tried to move her away with his rifle, so that he could get a clear aim at Greta. Mara flung herself protectively over the immobile body, shielding Greta, clinging to her. She heard the clicking sound of the rifle bolt as the soldier cocked a round into the breech. Mara closed her eyes tight shut and waited to die.

A little more than thirty-six hours after Jamie and Djakovic left the castle fort near Senj, a motorcyclist arrived from 4th Army HQ with sealed orders for the senior of the two OZNA officers in residence. Although it was well after midnight, the pair were not in bed. They had thoughts in that direction, however. Since nine, they had been drinking wine with two women specially brought out from the small town for their entertainment; and their little party had reached the stage where the women's laughter had become raucous from drink and blouses had become unbuttoned in the general jollity.

The arrival of the despatch rider had thrown a

momentary damper on the proceedings. The senior of the officers was sufficiently distracted to take a glance at the delivered missives, especially one that bore the stamped imprint of OZNA Headquarters in Belgrade. There were four sheets of paper in the yellow manila envelope. He read the typed message on the first, and then, with growing alarm, the other three. Returning to his companions, he rudely told the two women to go and powder their noses. Alone with his companion, he blurted out the bad news from Belgrade, waving the letter in his face.

'It's from Chief Commissar Gubec,' he wailed. 'He wants the prisoner to be sent immediately to Belgrade for interrogation. It seems he's wanted in connection with the activities of the traitor Marko Markovic and the betrayal of the Supreme Headquarters in Drvar.'

'What prisoner?' the other officer asked drunkenly. 'We don't have any prisoners.'

'We did until yesterday, you fool! We let him go – with Djakovic!'

The other officer stared at him in horror.

'What are we going to do? Where did Djakovic take him? Do we put out a general alert?'

'For Djakovic, too! Are you crazy? No. We've got to get Djakovic to hand the traitor back to us. You'll have to go. One of us has to stay here.'

'Why me?' the junior of the two bleated.

'Because it was your idea to bring Djakovic in the first place.'

'It was just as much your idea. And you're the one who's supposed to be in charge.'

'I'm still in charge. That's why I'm telling you to go and find Djakovic. You'll need to take an escort. You'd better get into Senj right away. Second Brigade has plenty of transport. They'll give you a couple of cars and half a dozen men. I'll authorise it.'

'Where will I find Djakovic? They were going to look

for that girl. They could be hundreds of kilometres away. They could be in Bosnia.'

'Well, go to Bosnia! I don't care what you do. Just find them – and bring that traitor back here! Get moving. Now!'

The junior officer scuttled for the door. The senior man read the missive for a second time. It pained him to do so. The message from Gubec ended with the Chief Commissar's warmest congratulations for unearthing an enemy of the Party, who had clearly taken great pains to cover his tracks. An earlier search for him had been called off in the belief that he was dead. Gubec hinted that the traitor's arrest would not go unrewarded and that the officers concerned could look forward to positions of greater responsibility in the organisation. The officer imagined with some dread what kind of reward he could expect if he were blamed for such a catastrophe. It did not bear thinking about.

The Slovenian Party leaders had put out the red carpet for Comrade General Stefan Markovic, Minister for Conscription and Recruitment. They had laid on a huge Fiat limousine to transport him around Ljubljana and perform a number of ministerial duties, the most important of which was to review one of the Free Austria battalions of the Partisan Army, formed to buttress Tito's expansionist ambitions. They were a sorry-looking bunch, and Stefan was aware of his hypocrisy as he addressed the assembled ranks with the verve of Caesar exhorting the Tenth Legion. The square in which the parade was held was thronged with a crowd liberally sprinkled with well-trained Party fanatics. They carried banners portraying Tito and Stalin, and it behoved Stefan to answer their well-rehearsed chanting of slogans with the ritual responses of an archbishop of Communism. He did so, burning with inner shame. He longed to proclaim what he now held to be the truth: that the Utopia they had been promised was a myth; that unless the regime which had brought them victory changed its direction and style, the *new* Jugoslavia they were hailing would be more oppressive than the old. Because its apostles had abandoned the truth; and, without truth, there could be no freedom, no justice.

This heresy had converted Stefan when he was agonising over the fate of his friend Jamie Kyle, and it had coincided with Djordje's return to Belgrade. Djordje had been shocked by the fact that within a week of Tito's own return to Belgrade, the Marshal had set about restoring the royal palaces for his own occupation – while Partisans were still dying by the thousand, only a few kilometres away at Srem. He was no less shocked than Stefan by the hierarchy's mad scramble to possess all the finest villas in Dedinje and stock them with art treasures sequestered from private homes as 'property of the state'. Nor did Djordje see the joke when the Central Committee was jestingly spoken of as 'the Court'. He also had grave misgivings about the well-organised adulation of Tito – which the Marshal himself encouraged – as the Saviour of Jugoslavia.

'Are we trying to convince the people that he can walk on water?' he asked Stefan one day.

All of this reawakened Stefan to much that was happening around him, and it had disturbed him deeply, convincing him that somewhere the Revolution had made a wrong turning. They were heading down the wrong road. The second Jugoslavia, of which he had dreamed and for which he had struggled, was going to be no better than the first, created less than three decades before in the aftermath of another war. The thought appalled him because it was an admission of heresy. His gods were Communism and the Party – and to even *think* that either was a false god was heretical. He forced such thoughts out of his mind, clutching at the consoling thought that the ideology he had embraced was pure, that what was wrong was the manner in which men, including Tito and his Moscow-trained lieutenants, interpreted it. Somehow, he had to turn them away from the path they were already on, towards a third Jugoslavia, where truth and liberty and justice for all men truly prevailed.

These were sentiments which – Stefan knew – he could not shout from the rooftops. That kind of madness would gain nothing. If he were to achieve anything, he had to retain the power to influence others, and that could only be done by consolidating his position within the Party and Government and winning doubters over with patient and reasonable argument. It would be like walking a tightrope; he would still have to make the obeisances expected of a Party priest, but it was the only way he could reach his new goal. He did not realise it, because he believed his whole life had been one of political expression, but in deciding on his course, he was, for the first time in his life, practising politics.

It was in this frame of mind that the fate of the closest friend he had ever had haunted him, like a constant reproach. Always, Stefan had put the Party first, ahead of friends, family, health, life itself. Now it seemed that he had not always got his priorities right, particularly where his friends were concerned. He had leaned on friends when he had needed them, but he had usually been absent when they might have needed him. He saw now that he had failed his brother. That weighed heavily on his conscience. As for Jamie. . . . He had simply left Jamie behind, unmindful of whether he lived or died, while he forged blindly on in pursuit of his own holy grail: a grail that, once grasped, turned to dust at the touch.

With the fear that he had left it too late, he had tried to trace Jamie and find out what had happened to him. The first results of his inquiries had not been encouraging. It was believed, although no one could confirm it, that

Jamie had perished in the fighting after the fall of Drvar in 1944. But one response had yielded a ray of hope, despite an element of uncertainty in it. This had suggested that the Tiger of Bioce had been active with a Bosnian brigade, six months after the fall of Drvar. It filled Stefan with a longing to do some inquiring in the west of the country for himself. The opportunity arrived almost immediately, in the wake of the German surrender. Tito urged his ministers to get out across the land to proclaim the gospel of the New Jugoslavia to the people – and Stefan had leapt at the chance to get out of Belgrade. He had delivered speeches at two well-orchestrated public demonstrations in Zagreb before moving on to the Slovene city of Ljubljana.

In the evening, after the march past of the Free Austria battalion, he was the chief guest at a 4th Army victory banquet, where he made another speech. When the formal part of the celebration was over, he found himself in the company of a divisional commander, an old comrade from the days of the first rising against the Italians in Montenegro. They found a quiet corner and talked about old times.

'We weren't sure what to make of you student revolutionaries from Belgrade,' the veteran reminded Stefan, 'but you proved yourself when the bullets started flying.'

'Do you remember my friend from Belgrade, Jamie Kyle?' Stefan asked him. 'I've been trying to find him, but nobody seems to know what happened to him after we were chased out of Drvar in 'forty-four.'

The General shook his head. But his eyes lit up when Stefan jogged his memory by adding that, after the fighting in the Moraca valley, they'd nicknamed Jamie the Tiger of Bioce.

The General beamed. Of course he remembered the Comrade Minister's friend. How could he forget such a warrior! He frowned suddenly, as another cloud of memory crossed his mind.

'Isn't he the fellow who's got the British in Zadar kicking up such a fuss? I was in Zadar a week ago and the British were making an awful din about us kicking their patrols out of Istria. Wasn't our Tiger half British?'

'Jamie's father was Scottish. His mother was a Serb. But he was a Partisan, like you and me. He wasn't in the British Army.'

'But that's the point. They were going on about this Partisan officer who, they claimed, was British. He and a squad from one of our Bosnian brigades had been sent up north with one of their spotter patrols. I don't know what happened – it had nothing to do with me – but it seems we arrested this Partisan officer and his men . . . and the British have got it in their heads that we're going to shoot the lot for something that wasn't their fault. Maybe it's something you should look into, particularly if it's our tiger who's at the centre of it!'

'It's got to be him!' Stefan declared fiercely, hope and alarm filling him in equal measure. 'I'll look into it all right,' he promised vehemently. 'Who would know about this affair?'

'There's damned little OZNA doesn't know about,' the General said, with more than a little cynicism. 'They ought to be able to help.'

Stefan's sharp doubting look made the veteran smile.

'I would prefer to keep OZNA out of it,' Stefan said firmly.

The General shrugged.

'Suit yourself. But if there's anything I can do to help, you only need to say it. I don't know what your programme is but, if it was my friend and I was a Government minister, I'd head straight for Zadar and find out what the hell was going on.'

'Then that's what I'll do,' Stefan said. 'This victory tour I'm on is supposed to take in the full circuit – Croatia, Slovenia, Dalmatia, Montenegro – but there's no planned itinerary. Zadar's as good a place as any to make my next stop.'

'How will you get there? Has Tito loaned you the royal train that he's having refurbished? Or do you have your car?'

Stefan cocked an eye at the mention of Tito. Here, perhaps, was a revolutionary after his own heart.

'Tito has decided that the royal train isn't plush enough for him. He's having a new one specially made.' Stefan confided this in a low voice. 'As for me,' he went on, 'getting to Zadar could be a problem. I've been depending on the local Party committees to take me from one place to another, but I doubt if our Slovene comrades could get me to Zadar by tomorrow night.'

'Let me take care of that,' the General said. 'Half the men in my division are sitting around on their backsides with nothing to do. I think we can rise to a car that's suitable for a minister of state and an escort.' He grinned. 'You won't mind if the car was once the property of the Chief of Gestapo for Slovenia?'

'If it's got four wheels and goes, it'll do,' said Stefan, delighted for once to take advantage of the privileges of rank and power.

The General was as good as his word and, next morning, feeling uncomfortably like a royal prince, Stefan was on his way out of Ljubljana, ensconced in the roomy rear of a big dun-coloured Mercedes. The front was occupied by the two soldiers who would share the driving duties. Two pairs of motorcyclists rode ahead of the Mercedes, and two more cyclists brought up the rear.

Stefan had been housed in a fine house on a pleasant square, named after the Slovene poet and philosopher whose statue graced its centre. The square, with its blossoming trees, was deserted at this early hour and, as the procession of cycles and car moved off, Stefan felt a pang of guilt at the haste of his goodbyes and thanks to his Slovene hosts. He would have liked to have seen more of their city. To a Serb like himself, Ljubljana was almost foreign – although the name, which means 'well-loved', had always enchanted him.

The sun was a ball of red, low above the marshlands away to the east, as the Mercedes and its escorts picked up speed on the Rijeka road. As he watched the first of the 240 kilometres to Zadar slip away, Stefan smiled wryly at his thoughts. There would be some eyebrows raised in Belgrade if it got back there that the conscientious Minister for Recruitment and Conscription – always such a paragon about showing a good example to the less privileged – was riding in state like royalty and putting personal business ahead of Party duties.

It surprised him that he did not care. The Party had come first for too long. And today, preaching platitudes to an organised slogan-shouting audience, came a poor second to the finest comrade he had ever known.

It seemed to Jamie that the search for the marching column of German prisoners could go on forever, without them ever getting any closer to it. He and Djakovic had sought information about its location at every town and village along a route that had taken them out of the Lika to Otocac and south, via Perusic, Gospic and Medak to Ricice, where they had backtracked and detoured to Udbina before they discovered that they had been misinformed. With mounting frustration, they had retraced their track to Ricice and, ten kilometres further on, they picked up their first solid clue to the column's whereabouts. At the village of Gracac, they encountered a Partisan company which had been marching guard on several thousand 97th Corps prisoners until four days before, when another company had taken over.

Djakovic asked the questions and Jamie's heart lifted when the Partisans' commander confirmed that, yes, there were women amongst the prisoners: nurses, telegraphists, army auxiliaries. Jamie and Djakovic exchanged pained glances when the Partisan officer volunteered diffidently, 'With respect to the Comrade General, I hope he is not looking for sport with these women. They have been rather well used.'

'What the hell do you mean?' Djakovic flared. 'Have they been mistreated?'

The officer floundered, realising that he should have kept his mouth shut.

'They are Germans,' he said, as if it explained his first comment. 'They are no better than whores.'

Jamie resisted the urge to smash a fist into the man's face.

The Partisan company had been relieved about fifty kilometres along the Knin-Bihac road. The road from Gracac joined this highway only twenty kilometres to the west, but Jamie reasoned with Djakovic that, if the north-moving column had got a four-day start on them their best chance of cutting it off was by driving over the Karst through Bruvno to the same highway. It would save a detour of fifty kilometres.

This was familiar territory to Jamie – the home country of his Bosnian hill men – and a high fever of excitement gripped him when, at Bruvno, a group of locals revealed that they knew all about the column's progress, although it had not come within thirty kilometres of their village. The prisoners had indeed been moving north along the Knin-Bihac highway, which lay on the other side of the barren hills to the east of the village. After the column had reached the Una River, the Partisan guards had made the prisoners march on the railway track instead of the road, and this fact had amused the Bosnians. By their reckoning, the procession – at the slow rate it was moving – would not be far from the village of Doljane. It depended on whether or not they had stayed on the railway track, in order to keep close to the river and its water supply, or had returned to the road. The road and the railway parted company at Doljane. The railway followed the Una through a gorge to the little town of Kulen Vakuf; while the road took a right-angled turn west through the hills, away from the river.

'How far to this place Doljane?' Djakovic asked Jamie when they were on the road again.

'A couple of hours at the most,' Jamie said. 'And we've got a good four hours of daylight left. We'll find them.' He looked sideways at Djakovic as the Willys jeep bucketed over a massive pothole in the road. 'That's if we don't break an axle. I have to warn you that from here to the highway, the road is probably the worst in Europe.' He grinned. 'And the highway, when we get to it, is not much better!'

Behind them, their passing left the helpful group of Bosnians with something to talk about for the rest of the afternoon. The same group were astonished when a truck laboured up the road from Gracac and an OZNA officer alighted to ask if a general and a Partisan officer had passed that way in a Willys jeep. The OZNA officer had become quite excited when told that they had, and that the pair were looking for a column of German prisoners.

The prisoner column had not taken the road through Doljane. It had stayed on the railway track. But Doljane was not far away when, just after five p.m., the great straggle halted on the Una's bank to camp for the night. The village – big enough for its inhabitants to think of it as a town – was only half an hour's brisk walk away, on the far side of the railway bridge over the river. The prisoners, seeing the sprawling habitation across the river, knew what would be in store for them the following morning. They would be paraded in their misery through the streets, to face the sticks and stones of the jeering residents. The halt, short of the village, would ensure that word could be spread among the locals to organise an appropriate reception.

Mara's spirits had never been lower. She would have welcomed death on the railway track when Greta collapsed, at the end of her strength. That Mara had survived was not her own doing. As she had lain over Greta and waited for a bullet to end her life, eyes closed, she had not expected to be suddenly seized by strong hands and lifted into the air and then carried away from her stricken friend, across broad shoulders. She had been carried twenty metres or more along the track when she heard the rifle shot which killed Greta.

Her unwanted saviour had overtaken the other plodding prisoners before he put her down and silenced her weeping protests with two fierce slaps across the face. It was the one-eyed *Kaplar* who had rescued her; and he had raged at her for her folly, ordering her to march and keep marching, or he would whip her every step of the way.

She had marched, hating him and glancing back every so often at the pathetic bundle by the track until Greta's body could be seen no more. Her zombielike despair irritated the *Kaplar* when he came for her in the evening and she was apathetic to his frenzied fumbling. She had at no time demonstrated any enthusiasm for his abuse of her body, but this new lifelessness infuriated him. She had even forfeited the sympathy of the other nurses who were previously friendly to her, she alienated them by her apparent excess of self-pity. She began to despise them for the way they made the best of the constant rape of their bodies, cooperating eagerly with their violators and using their wiles and sensuality to obtain favours from them. Never had Mara felt more alone and lost.

When the column camped near Doljane, she sat listlessly with her head on her knees, waiting for the usual pattern of evenings to unfold. She knew that the *Kaplar* would come looking for her as soon as he had fed. He did, bearing with him, in a can, a morsel of tinned tuna and a spoonful of boiled rice which he had saved from his rations. He watched while she wolfed the offering with her fingers, past shame at her eagerness.

'Come,' he said, when she had finished. Head bowed in resignation, she followed him up through the Partisans' camp. The eyes of the soldiers followed her. There was envy of the *Kaplar* in some of the frank stares. The rags did not conceal Mara's girlish shape nor did the unkempt hair lessen her sad-eyed beauty. She was skinny, perhaps, though pretty enough for the soldiers to look twice and wonder at the *Kaplar's* luck; but none challenged it.

He led Mara past the rail bridge and along the rocky riverbank. A tributary joined the Una, a few hundred metres on. It was the Unac, which flowed down from the hills around Drvar to meet the larger stream. The *Kaplar* sat down on a rise that overlooked the confluence and invited her to sit by him.

'Let me go down to the river and wash myself,' she said. She was grimy with dust from the march and wanted to wash, but she was playing for time: putting off the moment when she would have to endure his groping hands and slobbering embrace.

He raised no objection. He took a cigarette from a tin and lit it.

'Watch the bank. It is steep,' he warned.

Djakovic drove the jeep through Doljane without stopping. Half a kilometre beyond the village, he swung the vehicle off the road on to a stony shelf above the river.

'There they are!' he exclaimed. Jamie's heart was going like a trip-hammer. He had seen the curls of smoke coming from cooking fires on the far side of the river, and had come to the same conclusion. On the opposite bank, beyond a rail bridge, hundreds of men were sprawled on the stony hillside for almost as far as he could see. Many were half-naked, their brown torsoes dark above bleached shorts and against the white kerchiefs which many wore at their throats.

'I want you to say here,' Djakovic told Jamie. 'If Mara is over there, I'll bring her back to you.' He silenced Jamie's protest. 'Please, comrade! It's better if I handle this. I have the authority.'

Djakovic did not add that there was no telling what they would find on the other side of the river – and that he did not trust Jamie to behave rationally if what they found was grim. Jamie, aware of the almost unbearable tension that held him in its grip and the explosive volatility of his feelings, allowed the OZNA General's will to prevail.

'I'll wait,' he promised Djakovic. 'I've waited five long years. Ten years, really. I'll hold myself back for another thirty minutes. But that's all. If you're not back with her in half an hour, I'm coming after you.'

He watched as Djakovic loped down to the railway track and walked along it to the bridge. Stringing his binoculars round his neck, Jamie left the jeep and walked down as far as the railway track. He saw Djakovic stop to talk to some men on the bridge and then walk on. There were four of them – all Partisan officers. They approached Jamie and asked him if he had seen two of their company's trucks in the village. Jamie said he had not noticed.

'They went ahead to pick up supplies,' one of the men said. 'They should have got back from Kulen Vakuf by now.'

'Are you in charge of the German prisoners?' Jamie asked. 'General Djakovic and I are looking for a nurse who might be among them.'

'So the Comrade General told us.' The officer laughed. 'We told him to help himself if he could find her but not to blame us if she's got a fanny like a farm gate. Our men have been rattling the backsides off them.' He grinned. 'The fortunes of war: first come, first served.'

The grin faded, shrivelled by the look on Jamie's face, and the man turned nervously away. 'We'll have our fun at the village,' he said, with less gusto, and with a nod to his companions went on towards the road. Jamie watched them go. He was shaking with anger and revulsion. At that moment, he was ready to commit murder. He let it pass, controlling the passions stirred by images of what Mara might have suffered. He had to let it make no difference to his own feelings for her. There was no saying what obscene horror had been forced on her – but *she* was the one who had been wronged and tortured and had her innocence defiled. Her agony was *his* agony now and it would be up to him to help her to recover from its shame, with tenderness and understanding and loving care. He had to forget his own needs and his own hurts – because hers would be so much greater. *How she must need him now!*

His impatience boiled as the minutes ticked by and Djakovic did not return. Unslinging his binoculars, he scanned the bridge and beyond for a sign of the OZNA General; but he could not see him because the spars of the bridge obstructed much of his view. A glimpse of movement, far away to his left, made him swing the glasses round. He focused on the figure of a soldier. In close-up, the man's face came clearly into view: an ugly face, like a dried walnut, with a crimson dent where one eye should have been. He saw the lips open and heard the shout that followed. Jamie scanned lower and saw the girl clambering up rocks from the river's brink. He saw the dark head, damp and glistening like a raven's wing; the ragged shirt and skirt; the brown limbs. Tears filled his eyes as he focused on the half-face in profile – and he knew his searching was over.

He ran down to the river's bank, shouting her name at the top of his voice.

'Mara! Mara! Mara!'

She stopped and turned to look across the river, uncertain, bewildered. Then she *knew*.

'Jamie!' The cry was ecstatic, a hymn of thanksgiving

encapsulated in a word. She came running and slipping along the bank, working lower. Then she fell and slithered down smooth rock to splash into the stream. Jamie threw off glasses and gunbelt and boots, and plunged into the river, making for her with thrashing strokes. They met in midstream. His arms enfolded her and the soft body was vibrant and vital against his: clinging, entwining, straining. They sank below the surface, to rise again embracing and spluttering, their streaming tears joining and mingling with the water cascading from their faces.

They were literally in danger of drowning in their happiness; Jamie realised it and pulled Mara towards the bridge. They worked along a stringer beam that skirted the timber pillars until they were able to gain footing on the rocky bank and clamber to safety. On dry land, they clung to each other again, incapable of words, so great was the fullness in their hearts. It was Jamie who was first to recover coherent speech. Voice shaking and tears running down his cheeks, he made a promise.

'Mara, Mara. Thank God, I've found you. I'm never going to let you go again . . . never, never, never. I'm never going to let you out of my sight . . . never, as long as I live.'

She clung to him, saying his name over and over again, not quite able to comprehend the miracle that she was in his arms. They were oblivious of Djakovic's arrival on the bank above them until he spoke.

'Have you no word of thanks for the one who never stood a chance with you, Mara?' he asked. 'I brought him to you.' Both Mara and Jamie looked at him, startled. Before either could speak, they were startled anew by a shout from across the river. The *Kaplar* was beside himself with rage and demanding the return of his German whore. Jamie blanched at his words, but it was Djakovic who acted.

Pulling his automatic from its holster on his thigh, he

fired several shots in quick succession. The bullets whined off the rock on which the *Kaplar* was standing, making him dance and shout in panic. One bullet carved a bloody path across the calf of his leg. He fell awkwardly and began to slide forward on bald, sloping rock. As he tried desperately to gain a hold with his fingers, but failed, his slipping descent accelerated and he went plunging into the river, arms and legs flailing. He was carried downstream as the current took him in its sluggish flow. He was an indifferent swimmer and his screams were now for help.

'Let the pig drown,' Djakovic growled.

'Unfortunately, he won't,' Jamie observed. 'He's too full of wind. Listen to his screeching! He'll wash up somewhere.' This forecast proved true; they saw the *Kaplar* grounded on a rocky outcrop that glistened black below the river's surface. He was still there, bellowing like a stranded sea-lion as Jamie lifted Mara up in his arms and carried her up to the jeep.

They decided to head back towards the coast. Jamie felt an obligation to report back to Brigade HQ and request to be officially discharged from service with the Partisans. He did not know what he would do if it was refused, because he had no intention of getting separated from Mara again – but he did not rule out desertion. There had never been anything 'official' about his attachment to the Bosnian Brigade after the debacle at Drvar. It had just happened. Jamie saw no reason why his disjunction should not be just as casual.

It worried Jamie that heading for Jasenica – where his brigade had been based, latterly – would be taking Djakovic out of his way. He was conscious of an enormous debt of gratitude to the OZNA General. Djakovic laughed at Jamie's fears that 4th Army HQ would be concerned about his absence.

'They're used to me disappearing for days at a time,'

he said. 'One of the good things about running an intelligence network and dealing in secrets is that you can behave as mysteriously as you like and no one ever asks any questions. If anyone ever does, you don't have to tell them the truth.'

'We can never repay what you've done for us, Djuro,' Mara told him.

'I'll be repaid if you two just live happily ever after,' he said. 'I shall feel noble, just thinking about it. Of course, if you ever get tired of this man, Mara. . . . '

She laughed, for the first time in months.

'I know,' she said, 'you'll be waiting.' She squeezed Jamie's hand as she spoke. The three of them were crowded in the front of the jeep.

'You'll forget I exist,' Djakovic prophesied. 'Just like in Belgrade all those years ago. I would have walked on hot coals to get a smile from you but I might just as well have been invisible. All you could think about was this reprobate here, languishing behind bars at Lepoglava. He seems to spend a lot of time in jug. Did you know that's where I found him? Why does he keep getting himself locked up?'

'Because he's very precious,' Mara said. And again she gave Jamie's hand a squeeze. 'Aren't you, Jamie?'

He laughed and pulled her close.

'I'm the luckiest man alive,' he said.

Djakovic sighed.

'And I think that the sooner the pair of you get married, the better!'

Darkness had fallen soon after they left Doljane. They had encountered nothing on the road. But, as they neared the turn-off which would take them over the high Karst to Bruvno, the jeep's headlights illuminated a military truck sitting near the crossroads. The bonnet was up and there were soldiers standing about. One of the uniformed figures made a belated attempt to wave down the jeep. He had to skip smartly out of the way as

Djakovic made a sharp left turn and carried on up the hill road. He stopped the jeep a hundred metres from the corner.

'Did you see who that was?' he asked Jamie. 'The one I nearly ran down?'

Jamie had not had a good look at the man and said so. 'Should I know him?' he asked.

'He was your jailer until a couple of days ago. One of the officers from Senj.' Djakovic delivered the information with a puzzled air.

'What in the devil's name is he doing here in the middle of nowhere?' Jamie asked uneasily.

'That's what I was wondering,' Djakovic said.

'He can't have been following us . . . can he?'

'If he has been, I want to know why,' Djakovic declared. 'Stay here, both of you. I want to get to the bottom of this.' He got out and walked back to the crossroads.

Jamie's uneasiness affected Mara. She became anxious, fearing that her rescuers had stirred up trouble for themselves by snatching her from the prisoner column.

'Will they send me back?' she asked Jamie fearfully.

'No,' he assured her. 'You have my promise on that.' Jamie took the pistol from his belt and checked that it was loaded. He did not return it to its holster.

Djakovic was gone for nearly fifteen minutes. Jamie, alert and tense, put his pistol away when he was sure that it was Djakovic coming up the road, and that he was alone.

'We've got trouble,' the OZNA General said, without preamble. 'That idiot down there wants to take you back to Senj,' he told Jamie. 'And he's got a bunch of trigger-happy goons to make sure he does. Anything I say isn't going to make any difference to him because he's got orders from Chief Commissar Gubec in Belgrade – and he's a damned sight more frightened of Gubec than he is of me. It puts me in an awkward spot.'

'If he thinks I'm going back with him, he's crazy,' Jamie said fiercely. 'Let's just get the hell out of here.'

'No. Right now, he thinks I've come back here so that I can collect the jeep without putting you on your guard. He's expecting me to back down the road and give you to him on a plate.' Djakovic talked quickly over Jamie's attempted interruption. 'Let me finish, comrade. There's a limit to how far I can stick my neck out for you, and I think we're just about there. So do exactly as I tell you and don't ask questions. Get yourself behind that wheel, and when I say go, light out of here as fast as you can. From here on, you and Mara will be on your own. And I'm banking on it that the pair of you will make it clear out of the country – because, believe me, if Gubec wants your blood, you're not going to be safe anywhere. I know that son of a bitch.' Again he had to stop Jamie's interruption. He went on, 'Make for Zadar, comrade. The British Navy has ships there. They won't turn you away. Just tell them you're one of their agents – anything, so long as they take you to Italy.'

'What about you?' Jamie finally managed to get in.

'I'll look after me,' Djakovic answered quickly, glancing back at the crossroads. 'And the good comrades from Senj! They won't be going anywhere in a hurry. Not in that truck of theirs, anyway. They've burned the guts out of the engine. Now go!'

Jamie throttled the engine.

'Go!' Djakociv urged. The jeep surged forward. The OZNA General waited until the tail lights had disappeared round the first series of hairpin bends, and then he strode back to the crossroads. There, the OZNA officer from Senj was jumping about in a state of great agitation. With a show of fury, Djakovic silenced him.

'It was your fault!' he shouted at the bewildered man. 'He must have recognised you when you jumped out in front of us. My friend Gubec will eat you for breakfast when I tell him of your incompetence.'

705

Through the open porthole, Jamie could see the white pencil-like spire of Zadar's Serbian church. It rose defiantly amid the rubble of buildings destroyed by bombs. Jamie turned at a fluttering of the door curtain, and his heart lifted at the sight of Mara, framed in the entrance of the tiny cabin. She wore a white polo-necked sweater, which reached almost to her knees. Below it, the wide legs of a pair of Royal Navy tropical issue white shorts were just visible. Her brown legs were bare and her feet were enveloped in plimsolls at least three sizes too large. They flapped as she waddled into the cabin doing a Charlie Chaplin walk. She pirouetted for Jamie's benefit.

'Well, how do I look?'

'Like a cuddly doll. What was the doctor's verdict?'

'He said that if he got the chance to examine more bodies like mine, he would sign on for another ten years in the Navy.'

'Seriously, Mara, what did he say?'

'Seriously, I'm undernourished and need fattening up. It seems that I haven't been eating the right foods, and not enough of anything. I had a shower, with a special delousing shampoo, and a scrub from top to toe with special soap. He's given me ointment to rub on one or two little sores. And he says that if I watch my diet and get some vitamins inside me, there's nothing to stop me having twenty children and living to be a hundred.'

'Do you want twenty children?'

'Only if they all look like you,' she said with an impish smile, and slipped into his arms. They were kissing longingly and oblivious to the world when a sound intruded. A male throat was being cleared noisily. They turned to find the British destroyer's captain standing in the room.

'I knocked on the curtain,' he said with a grin. 'Am I interrupting? I'm afraid your plans for a honeymoon cruise are off.'

They stared at him in dismay.

'Too many people getting in on the act,' the Captain said. 'The operation of getting you to Italy has been taken out of the Navy's hands. But you must have friends in high places. Everything is being laid on to take you out by air.'

'We have no friends in high places,' Jamie said, puzzled.

'You have at least one,' the Captain replied. 'He's on the quay right now, waiting to come aboard. I've sent a boat over to collect him. I must say it seems rather odd to me that if the Jugoslavs are after your blood, Tito should send one of his government ministers down here to give you a royal send-off.'

'I don't understand,' Jamie said.

The mystery was not explained until they all went out on deck in time to see Stefan Markovic piped aboard.

Stefan had reached Zadar twenty-four hours ahead of Jamie and Mara, and did not waste the time. He received an enthusiastic welcome from the local Party and used their anxiety to please him to institute a wide-ranging inquiry for clues to Jamie's fate. Simultaneously, he sought out the British military liaison officers who had protested to the Jugoslav authorities about the treatment of the patrol Jamie and his Bosnians escorted to Istria.

It did not take long for Stefan's efforts to bear fruit. The six Bosnian hill men who had been with Jamie had returned to Jasenica on their release. There, they had reported to the Brigade Commander, who was enraged to learn that one of his best officers – and the one he had personally nominated for the Istrian foray – was being detained by OZNA, near Senj. He had sent a strongly worded protest to 4th Army, but it had not, so far, been acknowledged. In the Brigade Commander, however, Stefan found a ready ally, and it was through him that he learned of Jamie's imprisonment in the old fortress near Senj.

Stefan was on the point of heading for Senj when the British contacted him with surprising news. The Partisan officer for whom he had been looking had turned up at British Naval HQ in the early hours of the morning, with a girl in tow. They had asked for asylum and a quick passage out of Jugoslavia. There was no problem as far as the man was concerned – his British nationality was being verified – but the girl had no papers of identification. (The British officer did not tell Stefan at this stage that the girl claimed Jugoslav nationality and admitted serving as a German Army nurse, which made for tricky political complications.) The man, Stefan was told, had offered to resolve the girl's nationality difficulty by marrying her on the spot and giving her the right to British protection. This was a solution, the spokesman said, which the British authorities viewed with some sympathy, and they hoped the marriage could take place in Zadar.

Stefan established that, at that moment, Jamie and Mara were being cared for on a British destroyer in the harbour and were probably resting. The girl, in particular, seemed to have had a pretty bad time and could scarcely stand up. Stefan left them to rest. He was euphoric at the turn of events and determined to make his own contribution to the happiness which, he reckoned, was Jamie's due. He recognised that Jamie and his beloved Mara might be denied that happiness in the New Jugoslavia – especially while brutes like Gubec still had the power of life or death over those whom they deemed to be enemies of the state – but he could send them on their way with memories of the true Jugoslavia: the Jugoslavia that might have been and was yet to come.

Consequently, Stefan spent a busy night, some of it in the radio room of British Headquarters – where he found that the undemonstrative British could be surprisingly romantic and sentimental when the right nerves were touched. Now, as he stepped on to the deck of the British destroyer, he was well pleased with his efforts.

Jamie came to greet him, and there were tears in Stefan's eyes as he clasped his old friend to him. The same eyes were misty when it was Mara's turn to be embraced. Memories flooded Stefan's mind of those days, so long ago, in Belgrade, when he and Jamie and Mara had made such a happy threesome. So much had happened since that last summer of innocence and carefree happiness.

In the destroyer's wardroom, to which Stefan and the welcoming party adjourned, the Captain made a short speech in honour of Tito's Minister for Recruitment and Conscription. Glass in hand, Stefan replied.

'Captain, friends, I am honoured to be your guest, but I have not come here today simply to give and receive expressions of cordiality between our countries. The question of a long-lasting alliance has been very much on my mind, and it is this alliance that I invite you all to celebrate today. In some respects, it is an alliance between our nations but, more essentially, it is an alliance between two people: a man and a woman, to whose love and fidelity I can personally testify. They have come a long and testing road and suffered many hardships, but their love for each other has never weakened. It has shone like a beacon in the darkness through the bad times, and it is as bright today as in its beginning. Today, my friends Jamie and Mara are to be married. The arrangements were at a very tentative stage only yesterday, but I am happy to say that – as a result of my unsought interference and an unprecedented degree of Allied cooperation, string-pulling and conspiracy, to put it mildly – everything has been arranged for the wedding to take place today. All that is needed now is the consent of the happy couple.'

Stefan turned to Jamie and Mara amid a burst of applause from the destroyer's officers, who were all broadly grinning. Some raised their glasses and toasted: 'The bride and groom.'

'Of course it's what we want,' Jamie assured Stefan, getting over his bewilderment. 'But what's it all about?'

'The ceremony's fixed for three o'clock. A civil judge, and all perfectly legal. Then I've got to get you to the airfield at Prkos for six o'clock. You'll be in Italy by eight.'

Jamie looked at his watch.

'It's half-past two now!'

'I know,' said Stefan. He grinned. 'Time you got moving.'

The next few hours passed in a daze for Jamie and Mara. The marriage ceremony was over in five minutes, with Stefan and the destroyer's Captain as witnesses. The officiating justice's wife attended Mara, for whom a neat white dress and fetching straw hat were found. Then, there was the thirty-kilometre dash to Prkos airfield in Stefan's Mercedes, with its outflanking escort of motor-cyclists.

To Jamie's astonishment, they were met at the airfield by a guard of honour from the Bosnian Brigade, and a band whose musical shortcomings were made up for by the exuberance of their playing. Also on hand was the Brigade Commander, who presented Jamie with a written testimonial of his bravery and service with the JANL. Stefan was called upon to make another speech.

When the time came to bid farewell, Stefan was beyond speech. His heart was bursting with joy for Jamie and Mara, but it was overlaid with a terrible sadness at seeing them go – and the words he had wanted to say lay trapped and unarticulated in the emotion that held him.

The aircraft which carried Jamie and Mara to Italy was a Dakota. They were its only passengers, sitting in little canvas seats behind the pilot's cabin. Its big hold was scattered with grains of rice – spillage from the cargo the sturdy American transport had delivered on behalf of UNRRA.

The surprises of the day were not yet over. They landed at an airfield near Treviso and were feeling just a little lost and bewildered, when a familiar figure came rushing towards them, arms outstretched. Brad Mannion had received unexpected orders only that morning to meet two visitors from Jugoslavia and escort them to a hotel in Venice, where they were to be accommodated temporarily. He had not been told who these visitors were or why he, personally, had been assigned the task. All that Blair had been able to tell him was that the order came from higher up as the result of a special request made by the Jugoslav Minister of Recruitment and Conscription and relayed by British Military HQ in Zadar.

Mannion was overjoyed to meet Jamie and Mara again, and questioned them nonstop on the drive into Venice. It was not until all three had arrived at the unpretentious little hotel overlooking the Grand Canal that he made a momentous discovery. He found that only two rooms had been allotted for himself, Jamie and Mara.

'Looks like we'll have to share,' he said to Jamie.

Jamie grinned.

'What makes you think I want to share with you? This is Venice, not Lepoglava.'

Mannion was shocked.

'You're not thinking of bunking in with Mara? You, Jamie, the guy who was always so proper?'

'Mara has told me she doesn't mind,' Jamie told him. 'Besides, she's my wife. If you'd given me a chance, I would have told you. We got married at three o'clock this afternoon.'

The supper that followed was a celebration, with Mannion ordering the best wine in the house and

711

sending out for flowers to present to the happily blushing bride. Later, he slipped quietly off to his room, saying that he needed an early night and hinting that others should follow his example.

Jamie and Mara need little prompting to take the hint. Alone in their room, Jamie held Mara in his arms as they stood looking out at the canal. The moon lit a glittering track across its waters.

Jamie kissed his wife.

'Well, Mara, the end of a perfect day?'

She snuggled up to him.

'It's not the end of anything, Jamie. Not for us. It's the beginning.'

Epilogue

It was some time after the birth of a second son to Jamie and Mara Kyle that the letter arrived. Mysteriously, the envelope bore Egyptian stamps and was datemarked Cairo. They knew no one in Cairo.

The letter itself was written on sheets that might have been torn from a school exercise book. They were dog-eared and stained, and had been folded and unfolded so many times that it was difficult, in places, to decipher the minute scrawl. The letter read:

Dearest Jamie and Mara,

I do not know if you will ever receive this letter, because the person to whom I have entrusted it is in the greatest danger, merely by having it in his possession. He runs a great risk in order to satisfy my need to communicate with you, but he is leaving the country soon and he has promised to post the letter as soon as he reaches a place where the secret police cannot intercept it. I am grateful to him for this service to me, although he dismisses it as a trifle in return for kindness that I was able to show to him. He insists that but for me, he would have died. Perhaps he would have done, although all I did was show him a little human mercy in a place where that commodity is not in evidence.

If you are wondering why you have not heard from me for a long time, it is because I have been incommunicado for a long time. How long, I don't know – because, here, I have lost all track of the days and months and years. I know that if it's hot, it must be summer, and if it's cold, it must be winter. But that apart, time is without meaning.

The last letter I received from you in Scotland was in 1948, at the time of our troubles with Moscow. Was that two, three

713

years ago? I told you, I've lost all track of time. You may have written later, but the secret police were intercepting my mail from 1947 onwards – yes, as early as that – and latterly they weren't bothering to pass my letters on after they'd read them and made copies for their files.

You probably read in your British newspapers about me being removed from office for the crime of 'revisionism'. At the time, of course, I was a minister without portfolio. The reason why I had no portfolio, in the first place, was because Tito did not trust me with a ministry. He ceased to trust me before the end of 1945; to begin with because I dared to criticise his kingly taste for luxury, and later, because I spoke up too loud and too long on the need to democratise our regime.

I upset him, too, because I urged him to initiate some sort of reconciliation with Mihailovic and the Cetniks. I often wonder to what extent Mihailovic really did cooperate with the Germans during the war. How much was collaboration and how much was mud, thrown by our agitprop machine at a hated rival? Draza certainly hated us Communists and sent his battalions agains us, but was he the traitor we claimed? After the war was over, it was a surprise to find that the Germans had put a price on his head. They offered a bigger reward for Tito, but perhaps this was because Tito was the bigger threat.

Anyway, Tito decreed that there could be no forgiveness for Draza and his Cetniks. Maybe he was right – but the longer he fought on against us and the more hopeless his position became, the more I admired his guts, and it made me long for an honourable end to the conflict. We tricked him in the end. We lured him out of the Bosnian mountains by leading him to believe that all of Serbia was ready to rise up and aid him. He tried to make the break for Serbia, with the five or six thousand followers he had left, and he walked right into the trap. We surrounded his little army and wiped it out. Mihailovic and a few hundred Cetniks were taken alive – not that any of them lived to tell the tale. They were all tried and executed within twenty-four hours of capture. The haste with which Draza was despatched was unfortunate. History demanded that we should have put his side of the story on record. That, of course, is blasphemy coming from a Communist. I didn't know then but I know now that the Party believes in rewriting history so that the people and events making history can be painted red.

Truth is not important, if it does not serve the interests of international socialism. Neither, for that matter, are people.

I wonder what history will make of Tito. He gave the people of Jugoslavia a revolution – by leading them in a complete circle. You came to us, Jamie, when Alexander ruled as dictator, and he kept us revolutionaries at bay with tough old birds like Luk and the political police. Now, we have an absolute monarch called Josip Broz Tito, who has taken over all the royal palaces and estates (and a great lot more) and who has more power than the old king ever dreamed of. He has yachts, villas, hunting lodges, aeroplanes, liveried servants, and when he needs the cash to indulge in any new luxury or extravagance, he just dips his fingers in the national till. It doesn't matter that the economy is in ruins, thanks mainly to compulsory collectivisation of the land and the nationalisation of any market activity that makes money.

And how does this great bureaucratic machine of state function and its monstrous head remain in control? By fear. By oppression. By courtesy of the secret police, who intrude into every level of life and stifle every dissent at birth. Gubec and his secret army of thousands have more power and are twice as ruthless as old Luk and his goons. Government buildings are bugged, so that people in responsible positions can be checked for the slightest indiscretion. The humblest in the land can be whisked off to prison for 're-education' for no greater crime than an innocent remark. The revolution has to protect itself, as all revolutions must, by constant vigilance against challenge from any quarter. The revolution gave Tito power, so Tito protects the revolution. Tito gives the revolution power, so the revolution protects Tito. Tito is the revolution and Tito is the state. The state is all-powerful. Tito is the power.

I am a traitor. The state says I am a traitor. The state compels me to wear round my neck a placard, on which is printed the word, 'TRAITOR'. That is one of the more tolerable indignities which are now part of my life. I am punched, kicked and beaten frequently to remind me that I have offended against the state. I have had my head thrust into a bucket of human excrement because I was not responding quickly enough to the processes of political re-education. I have since learned to mouth, with apparent sincerity, declarations of penitence. I confess to the sins which my tormentors demand I confess. But the words of my mouth do not reflect the beliefs I hold in my heart. They have not, so far, been able to make me believe my own lies. They can bruise my body and my mind but they cannot have my soul.

The regime, too, has a way with words. My crime was 'revisionism'. My punishment by the state is 'an indefinite period of socially beneficial work'. Socially beneficial work! Do you know what form it takes? For twelve or more hours a day, I labour, breaking stone in a quarry, here in the stink-hole island of Goli Otok – an island of the damned, if ever there was one.

The great irony is that nearly all the prisoners here are Stalinists: men who wanted Stalin and his Soviets to control Jugoslavia. Most of them despise me, because no one supported the break with Russia more vigorously than I did. I feel only pity for them, because, no matter what their crimes were, they do not deserve what is happening to them now. It is no consolation to them that if they had dissented in Stalin's Russia, they would have been shot. They and I have Tito to thank for escaping a death sentence. Tito was prepared to sentence us to political death – a living death, as he once described disgrace and exclusion from the Party – but he would not sanction liquidation for those of us who had supped with him in his wartime caves and followed him across so many mountains and rivers. He does not want our blood on his conscience. Not because he does not believe our 'crimes' merit death – he does – but because he would have to acknowledge publicly that he signed our death warrants. No one would believe that those like myself, who have enjoyed high office and Tito's friendship, could be liquidated without his authority. It suits him politically, therefore, to consign us to political perdition and express his profound regret at the error of so many friends. He has not decreed that we are to be kept alive indefinitely, but if we die while under correction and re-education, the blame will not directly be his.

It is a strange facet of Tito's character that I do not recall him ever ordering death as a punishment or act of revenge. Such things were often discussed, but he would turn his face

716

away from them, like Pontius Pilate. This aloofness always seemed to declare: 'What has to be done must be done – but let it be done by those of you who have a stomach for it.' He never sentenced anyone to death, but he never raised a finger to halt the orgies of killing at the end of the war. Hundreds of thousands have died, but Tito was not responsible. The slaughter was done by others. When they looked to Tito in expectation of a signal of restraint, he looked the other way.

Now, he rules in a splendour that would befit an emperor of Persia, and his loyal subjects hail him as a god: the author of all such bounty as they enjoy but – in their sightless eyes – none of their miseries. Oh, Jamie, the people expect power to live in a palace and direct their lives. I thought it would be so different. I never really understood power, because I never sought it in a personal sense, other than to do good and proclaim freedom and justice for all. But power and the protection of that power is all that Tito understands. And he knows – as the Communist Party has always known – that freedom and justice for all can only be given in direct proportion to the amount of power that authority is prepared to surrender. Too much liberty invites opposition to authority: it invites reform and change and reasoned discussion. It questions dogmatic beliefs and unfair practices. It opposes autocratic assumption and demands a slackening of fetters. It seeks wider freedoms. But, most dangerous of all, it demands that power be diluted and spread more thinly. It abhors the pyramid of power and would eventually cause its demolition – so it's no surprise that those on top of the pyramid resist any liberty that threatens their place in the sun.

There is one ray of hope for Jugoslavia. Tito's power will die with him. Unlike the Kardjordjevic dynasty, Tito's line will not follow him to the throne. There is no heir apparent, and Tito will make sure that none exists. To have an heir apparent of any stature, while he lives, would mean living with an ever present threat to his throne. And that would not do. Better to leave a vacuum, where his uniqueness is mourned. The majesty of an oak is unquestioned, when the other trees of the forest have been cut down to enhance its prominence.

I live in hope that a new leader may emerge for our people. Today, he may still be a boy at school, attentive to the Marxist doctrine being crammed into his head; a boy innocent of the spilled blood that has washed our land and given it a legacy of so much hatred and fratricidal conflict. His vision will be of a land where old hatreds lie buried and old crimes are not perpetuated, a land where truth and justice and liberty prevail. His dreams will be revolutionary dreams, but he will aspire to power in order to give back power to the people. There will be no more secret police. Reason and humanity will rule, without fear and without favour.

That day must come. It must. It must. It must.

If I live, that hope lives. And there are countless thousands like me, whose hopes are no less. They are not new hopes and my ideas are not new ideas. They are born in the blood.

Do not sorrow for me in my present straits, dear friends. Take heart from the knowledge that I am not defeated. I think of you often and rejoice that we shared so much that was good. My greatest comfort is knowledge of your happiness and the freedom that is yours.

Pass on my affectionate greetings to Brad. I know you keep in touch. I am sorry that he had difficulty settling down again in New York. But after all that happened to him, it was scarcely surprising. So much had changed when he got back. I was delighted to hear about his move to Texas and his work in the oilfields. He seems to have found something that suits his adventurous nature.

Au revoir, good comrades. With much love,

Your devoted friend,
Stefan.